T. Csernis & Julia Bland

THE SILVER CLAW
A NUMEN CHRONICLES INTERLUDE STORY

ORIGINAL EDITION

For more information on the world, this series, other books, or to contact the author, head to: https://www.numenverse.com/

Cover designed by Tate Csernis
Cover drawn by Simon Zhong
Cover edited by Julia Bland

ISBN – Paperback: 978-1-917270-19-9
ISBN – Hardcover: 978-1-917270-20-5
ISBN – E-Book: 978-1-917270-21-2

THE NUMEN CHRONICLES is a collaborative work written by

Tate Csernis (T. Csernis) and Julia Bland (Julia B.)

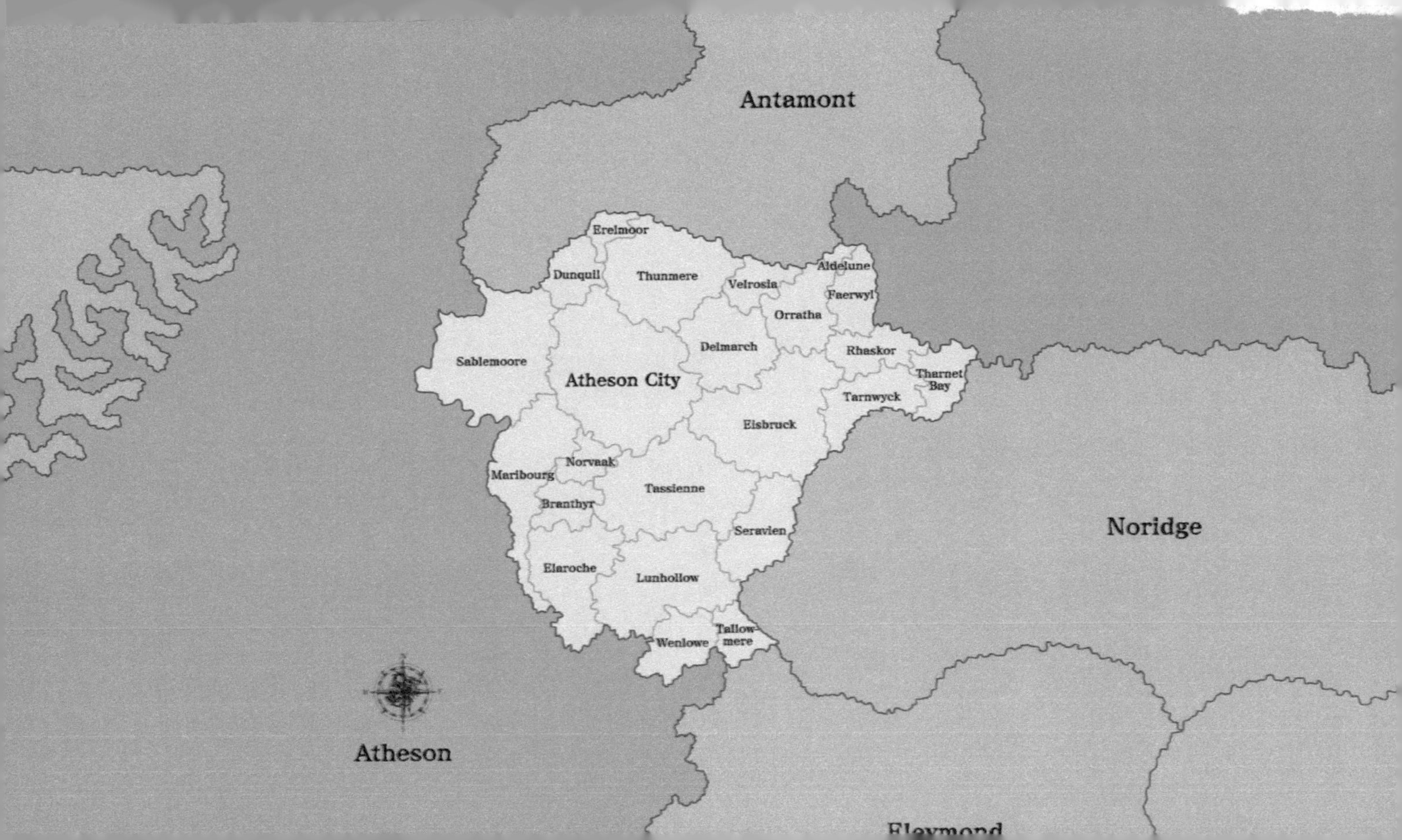

Antamont
Noridge
Fleymond
Atheson
Sablemoore
Erelmoor
Dunquil
Thunmere
Velrosia
Aldelune
Faerwyl
Orratha
Delmarch
Rhaskor
Tharnet Bay
Tarnwyck
Atheson City
Eisbruck
Norvaak
Maribourg
Tassienne
Branthyr
Seravien
Elaroche
Lunhollow
Wenlowe
Tallow-mere

Ethos [ee-thos] - The energy within someone that can be used to create or manipulate other energies

Dor-Sanguis [door-san-goo-wis] - Translates roughly to Pain *[Portuguese]* and blood *[Latin]* (aka, Romania)

Nefastus [neh-fas-tus] – Translates to Unlawful *[Latin]* (aka, the Americas)

Eltaria [el-tar-ia] – Zalith's homeworld

Numen [noo-men] - God-like beings that chose to show themselves to the world rather than remain anonymous

Aegis [ee-gis] - The Dragon Gods, children of Letholdus

DeiganLupus [day-gan-loo-pus] - Translates roughly to 'refused to turn to the wolf' *[Icelantic, Latin]* (aka, UK)

Lumendatt [loo-men-dat] – Numen crystals containing the power to create life

Obcasus [ob-cass-us] – Knives capable of putting Numen in a frozen statis

✝

Proselytus [pros-elly-tus] – A heart-like organ which creates ethos inside a body

✝

Scion [skee-on] – ethos-crafted children of the Numen

✝

Infățișare [in-fuh-tsee-SHAH-reh] – vampires able to shift into animal forms

✝

The Seven Realms:

Aegisguard [ee-gis-guard] - The world
(aka, Earth)
Mareaeternum [Mar-ay-ter-num] Translates to eternal tide *[Latin]*
Glaciaqua [Glass-ee-aqua]
Letholdus [Lee-fold-us]
Tengetso [Ten-get-so]
Celitrianas [Sel-it-ree-a-nas]
Yilmana [Yeel-mana]

The Months and Currency

Months

January – Primis
February – Cordus
March – Tertium
April – Aprilis
May – Quintus
June – Iunius
July – Quintilis
August – Tria
September – Novem
October – Decem
November – Undecim
December – Clausula

Currency

Copper – Equivalent of $0.01
Bronze – Equivalent of $0.20
Silver – Equivalent of $2
Gold – Equivalent of $10
Coronam – Equivalent of $100
Cidaris – Equivalent of $1 million

CONTENTS

CONTENT HEADS-UP

This book contains **frequent and graphic sexual content**, much of it tied to one very unlucky (or lucky, depending on your perspective) character going through a **full-blown supernatural heat**. That means things get…intense. Often. In detail. Sometimes aggressively on a couch that'll end up needing replacing.

If you're not into explicit scenes or the consequences of magical biology wreaking havoc on self-control, this might not be your sorta thing.

If you *are* into that? Welcome. You're in the right place at the exact right time.

SO…HOW FREQUENT ARE WE TALKING?

If you want that bigger heads-up, you can expect to find the *"is that even physically possible?"* moments in the following chapters, usually marked by an increase in tension, biting, growling, the occasional smirk that says *you're not leaving this room upright*, and someone inevitably forgetting how shirts work (or tearing them off with fangs, same difference).

If steamy scenes aren't your thing, feel free to use this as your "skip-it guide" so you can dodge the heat without losing the plot. No judgement. Your comfort > fictional hormones.

Chapters:

1, 4, 12, 23, 28, 29, 37, 43, 45, 46, 52, 55, 56, 59, 61

And in equally graphic fashion, it *almost* happens (but gets tragically or tantalizingly interrupted) in these chapters—some stop just short, others linger on every sinful thought, and some even have no act but still have enough explicit detail to make you blush *and* bite your lip.

Chapters:

2, 5, 16, 17, 25, 51, 58

Now that you've been properly warned, enjoy the heat, the fangs, and the chaos.
May your pages curl and your demons behave (or not).

Understanding Alucard's Accent

Alucard's dialogue in this edition of the story has an accent. He doesn't pronounce Hs, THs and some Rs. Below are some examples to help you understand his dialogue:

You'll see words like 'ead (head), 'ere (here), and 'owever (however), missing the H.

THs are often ZHs, such as zhat (that), zhis (this), zhe (the), and zhere (there). In other cases, you'll see ozzer (other).

Ws become Vs, such as vhat (what), vhere (where), and vhy (why).

Some Ds become Zs, such as Zamien (Damien), zon't (don't), and Zetlaff (Detlaff).

Fs also become Vs, such as vollow (follow), vriend (friend), and vor (for).

And some Rs become Vs, such as vest (rest), Veiner (Reiner), and Remont (Vemont).

Understanding POV Date and Location

How you'll see a new POV change laid out:

| Alucard—*Tuesday, Tertium 28th, 960(TG)* |
| *Vharakaal, Eshkunda, Anaket, Thaleus Village* |

What the hell does this layout mean?

| Name of whose POV it is—*Day, Month, Year(Period)* |
| *Continent, Country, Province, The Place in the Province* |

The date is shown only when a chapter or POV begins on a new day

The continent is displayed only when the narrative shifts either to a different country in the current continent or to an entirely new continent

Chapter One

— ⸲ ✝ ⸳ —

Irresistible Pull

| **Zalith—*Tuesday, Tertium 28th, 960(TG)*** |
| ***Aestrael, Uzlia Isles, Usrul, Castle Reiner*** |

The afternoon grew later, and Zalith tapped his pen against his desk, staring down at the paperwork spread across its surface. He was supposed to be working out what supplies to send to the Yrudyen Elves now that he'd started setting up the promised supply lines, but he couldn't focus. All he could think about was Alucard. Even from his office on the other side of the castle, he could feel his fiancé's pull, he could smell the pheromones, and he couldn't ignore the desperation to fuck him.

He tried, though. In an attempt to grasp his concentration, he moved the supply logs aside and began reading the rosters that Idina had sent him, showing where she'd assigned each new demon among his growing army. She mentioned that Tyrus suggested promoting his best-performing Beta, Nymeris, to Alpha and giving her charge over Sirrus' pack—it was a good choice, so he signed off on it.

But even that wasn't enough.

He pushed it all aside and instead read the list of prisoners locked away in Dargamoore Prison. He needed to supply the elves with three sacrifices before Aprilis; the worse their crimes were, the better. The Yrudyen offered the most disgraced, most atrocious beings to Khila, and that was exactly what the list showed him. Murderers, traitors, rapists, robbers, arsonists, kidnappers, and conmen.

If it were an option, he'd just pick three murderers to get it over with, but according to the information that Castellan had sent, Khila preferred variation. He stopped tapping his pen and circled three names before summoning an izuret.

"Take this to Tamara in Dor-Sanguis; tell her to send these three over to Idina as soon as possible, and then tell Idina to let me know when she receives them."

With a nod, the izuret took the paper and disappeared.

Zalith then tried to turn his attention back to the supply logs.

But that *pull*…he just couldn't resist it anymore.

He pushed to his feet, barely aware of leaving his office as instinct took over. The scent was too much, it was too thick, intoxicating, and impossible to ignore. It called to him, a silent demand threading through his veins, winding around his thoughts like a noose. He prowled through the castle corridors, following the lure with unerring precision; every inhale made his blood burn hotter and his restraint fray thinner. He was a predator on the hunt, drawn by something he couldn't resist even if he wanted to.

By the time he reached Alucard's workshop, he didn't hesitate. He took the steps up to the vampire's office two at a time, and when he got to it, he shoved the door open without knocking.

Alucard was already looking at him.

His fiancé sat behind his desk, his pale fingers curled lightly against the wood, and when their eyes met, Alucard's lips parted just slightly. A quiet invitation. There was relief in his expression, a soft, unmistakable eagerness, like he'd been waiting for Zalith to arrive, like he knew exactly why the demon had come.

And he wanted the same thing.

Zalith moved nearer to the desk, his body thrumming with anticipation. Alucard stood as he approached, meeting him halfway, and Zalith wasted no time. He slid his hands around the vampire's waist, pulling him in, pressing him close. His fiancé's lips adorned the faintest smile before Zalith captured them in a kiss.

Alucard melted against him.

The kiss started slow and deep, a taste, a tease, a moment stretched between them, held in tension. But Zalith was already burning, and so was Alucard. The heat simmering between them snapped, giving way to something messier, something urgent. Zalith's fingers tightened at Alucard's waist, pulling him against his body as their mouths moved together, desperate, *devouring*.

Alucard exhaled a low, eager sound against the demon's lips, and that was it.

Zalith lost the last of his patience.

He tore at the vampire's blazer first and let it slide to the floor. Alucard was just as eager, his fingers slipping beneath the demon's shirt, pushing it up, dragging his claws over heated skin. The clothes between them disappeared—shirts discarded, belts unbuckled, fingers tangling in fabric until nothing remained. By the time Zalith pushed him against the desk, Alucard was breathless, his pupils blown wide, his chest rising and falling with desperation.

Zalith slowly dragged his palms down the vampire's bare back before gripping his hips and turning him around. Alucard braced his hands against the desk, arching slightly as the demon pressed in behind him, his breath ghosting over the back of his neck.

"Relax," Zalith murmured, his voice thick with desire. He reached for the small bottle of lube he'd carried instinctively—he didn't know when he'd grabbed it, only that his body had known he'd need it. He uncorked it, poured the slick liquid over his fingers, and massaged it into Alucard's ass, working it in with gradual, careful strokes.

Alucard shuddered beneath his touch, his knuckles tightening against the desk.

The demon's own breath caught as he slicked himself next, the sensation sending another pulse of heat through him. He was already too hard, aching, his body screaming for the only thing that would sate it.

With one hand firm on Alucard's hip, he eased forward, pressing the tip of his dick against the vampire's hole, feeling the heat of him, the way he tensed… and then Alucard welcomed him in.

A groan escaped from Zalith's throat as his shaft sank inside, his breath shuddering at the sheer, intoxicating tightness enveloping him. Every inch, every slow, agonizing stretch was heaven and torment at once, Alucard gripping around him like a vice, hot and perfect and made just for him.

Alucard arched beneath him, a tremor running through his body as his fingers dug into the wood. His moan was thick with relief, his breath sharp as he took all of Zalith, his body yielding, opening in a way that sent a vicious pulse of satisfaction through the demon's veins.

Zalith felt everything—the way Alucard's body clenched around him, the way he submitted so easily, his muscles taut with anticipation but his posture speaking of nothing but acceptance, trust, and desire.

The sensation was overwhelming, twisting through Zalith's body like fire, scorching through every last thread of his control.

And he hadn't even begun to move.

Zalith exhaled shakily, his fingers flexing against Alucard's hips as he drew back, slow at first, feeling every unbearable inch as he pulled nearly out before easing forward again. The initial movement was controlled, his instinctual need warring with the part of him that still wanted to devour this, to feel Alucard tremble under him.

But the heat.

The scent.

It was everywhere, consuming, pressing into every fibre of his being until his mind was drenched in it, and the slow, teasing pace he'd intended was no longer enough.

His jaw clenched, and a low growl came from deep in his chest as the thought took hold—no, as the *purpose* took hold. The reason his body had driven him here in the first place was just so that he could please Alucard. He was here to *breed him.*

The instinct crashed over him in a tidal wave, impossible to resist. His hand raced up Alucard's body and to his throat—Zalith gripped it *tight*, a possessive snarl leaving him. His hips snapped forward harder, faster, the sound of their bodies meeting filling the air as he plunged himself deeper, filling the vampire, taking him, claiming him the way every primal instinct inside him demanded.

Alucard whined, high and breathless, his claws cutting into the desk. The sound sent fire through Zalith's veins, making his pulse hammer, his own moan spilling from his lips unbidden. The growing heat, the enveloping tightness, and the perfect way Alucard took every thrust—it was too much, it was *too good.*

The demon buried himself deeper, pressing inside until there was nowhere left to go, until he was fully sheathed, the base of his dick flush against Alucard's skin. His tip nudged against the deepest part of the vampire, a hot, pulsing wall that quivered in response. He could feel the tight clutch of Alucard's body around him, every inch squeezed in burning warmth, but at the very end, there was a flutter, a soft resistance, like his fiancé's body had wrapped around him completely and refused to let him go.

And it hit.

Pleasure, blinding and sharp, coiled so intensely that it felt like a new plane of euphoria, a sensation so primal and right that it stole his breath. *This.* This was what his body wanted. To be buried to the hilt, locked inside his mate, thrusting with nothing held back, nothing restrained.

Zalith growled against the nape of Alucard's neck, his grip firmer as he thrusted again, each push hitting harder, sending them both spiralling. The more he drove himself in, the more his body demanded, his rhythm turning almost frenzied, his breath harsh, his moans tangled with Alucard's as pleasure built like a storm ready to break.

And Zalith knew as his claws scraped over Alucard's skin and his body desperately and ruthlessly thrust into him that he wasn't stopping until he'd filled him completely.

Until his mate was bred.

It didn't matter if it wasn't possible because right now, his body swore that it was. Every nerve, every instinct, every primal thread of his being screamed that once he achieved his goal, once his cum spilled deep inside Alucard, his mate would take it and accept it, his body responding exactly as nature intended.

The thought drove him wild.

His mind conjured the image unbidden—Alucard's body changing, adapting, growing, incubating his offspring, carrying the proof of his claim, and the sheer idea of it sent a feral hunger surging through him. It was madness, but it felt real.

It felt right.

And Zalith was past the point of questioning it.

He thrusted harder, driven by nothing but instinct and desire, his rhythm turning relentless. His fingers slid down from the vampire's throat and dug into his hips, holding him in place as he slammed into him, the pleasure spiralling out of control, scorching through his veins like fire. He should have been focused on Alucard's pleasure, on drawing it out, prolonging it, but that wasn't enough anymore. Not now. Not when his body was urging him to take, claim, and breed.

Alucard suddenly tensed beneath him, his body clenching so taut around his dick that Zalith nearly lost it right then and there. A strangled moan tore from the vampire's throat as he came, his muscles tightening, trembling, pulling Zalith deeper, locking him in as he spilt against the desk beneath them. The sound of it, the feel of it—it undid Zalith.

Fuck, *he loved it.*

The way Alucard's body reacted, responded, *surrendered.* The way his heat coaxed him further, how it made everything slicker and hotter and pushed Zalith closer to the edge until there was no stopping it.

His thrusts turned erratic, aggressive, each one harder than the last until he was burying himself entirely with every push, hitting so deep that both he and Alucard cried out with every movement.

And that final plunge—

Pleasure crashed over him, too strong, too sharp, too fucking much. His muscles locked, his entire body tightening as he came, oozing inside Alucard, fulfilling the demand that his instincts had been screaming for all along. A deep moan broke free from the demon's throat, and he bit down on Alucard's shoulder, his fangs pressing in just enough to stifle the sound, enough to keep himself grounded as his body shook with the force of it.

He'd done it.

The feeling consumed him, a satisfaction so intense that it felt undeniable and absolute. His instincts sang with victory, his entire body shuddering with the pleasure of having completed his purpose.

And yet…reality slammed into him just as hard.

Zalith frowned, his grip on Alucard's waist loosening slightly as a whisper of confusion cut through the haze. His body believed that he had bred his mate, that he had achieved the goal that his instincts had set. But that was impossible.

Alucard was a man.

Zalith knew this. He'd always known this. But as his gaze flicked down, he watched the slow, languid rise and fall of Alucard's back, feeling the residual heat and tightness still pulsing around him. His fangs lingered against Alucard's shoulder, his breath still uneven, still sharp, still drunk on whatever his mate's body was doing to him.

His frown deepened, uncertainty creeping in. Something about this wasn't right. Alucard's heat—it was doing something to him. Something he didn't understand. He tried to make sense of it again; it had to be because Alucard was Numen-blooded…and maybe it had something to do with *him*, too. He was an incubus, after all; his natural purpose was to breed more demons.

Zalith's breath was still unsteady as he eased his grip on Alucard, his body thrumming with the aftershocks of his orgasm. But as he started to pull out, he felt it—

the *resistance*. Alucard's body clenched around him, a subtle, involuntary squeeze, as if trying to keep him there, to hold him inside just a little longer. Zalith couldn't hold back a pleased groan; the pheromones still lingered in the air, thick and heady, intoxicating, curling around his senses like a vice. His incubus instincts flared, recognizing the pull for what it was—Alucard wasn't done. His heat was still calling to him, still wanting more.

"*Fuck*," the demon hummed, torn between indulging the need clawing at his skin and knowing he shouldn't. He could feel his own body reacting, ready to give him more, to take him again, to fuck him until the heat was completely satisfied—

No.

Zalith swallowed hard, his jaw tightening as he forced himself to stay still. He had already taken so much; he'd already pushed Alucard's body to its limits. If he kept going, he risked draining him too much, taking too much of his energy.

With a sharp breath, he pressed a hand against Alucard's back, steadying him as he carefully withdrew, ignoring the way Alucard's body tried to hold onto him, ignoring the way his own instincts screamed at him to stay.

Alucard let out a soft, breathy whine, shifting slightly against the desk, his fingers relaxing from where they'd been dug into the wood.

Zalith ran his hands over his fiancé's back, a silent attempt to soothe him, even as his own chest ached with the need to stay buried inside. Instead, he took a step back, exhaling slowly to calm himself. "I know, baby," he murmured, his voice still thick with desire, with lingering desperation. "But you need to rest."

Alucard didn't protest; he didn't even move for a long moment, still coming down from the high of it all.

Zalith reached for a cloth, his hands still slightly unsteady, and began to clean them both, his touch gentle, almost reverent as he wiped away the mess. His instincts still buzzed with satisfaction, and he chose to focus on *that*.

He handed Alucard his trousers, and once the vampire slipped back into them, he slumped down into his seat with a huff and a content smile.

"How do you feel?" Zalith asked curiously, leaning against the desk.

Alucard exhaled deeply and tilted his head back, closing his eyes. "Veally fucking good," he purred.

The demon smirked, a feeling of victory and deep relief enthralling him. "Do you think you can hold out until later?" he asked seductively, his voice carrying a promise.

"Maybe," he mumbled, sitting up straight, his gaze meeting Zalith's. "Can *you*?"

"I'll try," he said with an amused scoff, pulling his trousers back on.

Alucard exhaled again, and then his eyes scanned the papers on his desk. "Did you vigure out zhe elv stuff?"

He nodded, getting dressed. "I sent an izuret to handle the prisoner delivery. I was going over the supply logs before I came to see you—before I came *in you*," he added, his smirk widening.

Despite the war Zalith knew was still raging inside him, Alucard flushed, his pale skin betraying a hint of colour as he glanced away. "I've been trying to pick new brood nurses," he mumbled. "Bevore zhat, I vas vriting down a vew tiny details in my memory journal—noving 'uge, zhough."

"Have you made a decision about the vampires?"

"Vell, Lăcrămioara is a good candidate; she's vone of my older vampires, so she 'as zhe experience needed. But I zon't veally know who to pick vor zhe second vone. I vas considering Cerboaica, but she's vone of my last Paladins, so I zon't know if I can spare 'er or not."

"Can you make new Paladins?" he suggested.

"Maybe," he said with a sigh. "I could Dignivy some of zhe older Ad'erents."

"Is that a difficult process?" Zalith asked curiously.

"No. I just give zhem zhe new title and make sure zhat everyvone else knows."

"Sounds simple enough."

"Is just picking zhem zhat's zhe 'ard part."

"Well, if I can do anything to help, let me know."

Alucard smiled up at him. "Vank you." He looked down at his papers again. "I vill likely 'ave to go to Aveson soon to investigate zhis Silver Claw business, but I'll let you know vhen—I assume you vant to come vith me."

Zalith nodded. "I do." He leaned closer and kissed his lips. "I'd better get back to work. Let me know how things go."

"Okay. I love you."

"I love you, too," he said contently. He then headed for the door, but the further away he got from his fiancé, the more intense the pull became. He wanted to turn back, to give in, to take and to give and to indulge, but he wouldn't. Alucard had work to do, and more importantly, he needed to rest. So the demon continued down the stairs, trying his best to focus on the day's tasks.

Chapter Two

— ⚔ ✝ ⚔ —

The Werewolf and The Hybrid

| Alucard |

| *Uzlia Isles, Usrul, Castle Reiner* |

Lăcrămioara and Cerboaica. Alucard had decided that they'd be the new brood nurses he required to begin increasing his coven numbers. As for replacing Cerboaica, he thought that Vulpea and Bogdănel were ready. All that was left to do was Dignify them and alert the rest of his vampires.

As he tidied his desk, putting all the gathered information on the Silver Claw back into its folder, he sent a message to each Coven Master, as well as those he planned to assign new roles to, ordering them to head to the fort. Then, he left his office and headed down into his workshop. He wanted to go to Zalith and tell him that he was heading to Fort Rudă de Sânge, but he knew that if he went up to his mate's office, his desires would take over. Of course, he wanted to; the lingering desperation for sex hadn't stopped enthralling him since it began. It *urged* him to go to the demon and get what he needed. But if he gave in too often, he'd become exhausted, even despite the increased vitality that his heat gave him.

With a deep exhale, he moved through the quiet halls of the castle, heading for the front door. He wasn't as skilled with telepathy as Zalith; if the demon reached out first, the thread of connection was easy to grasp—it was steady and familiar, like catching a hand in the dark. But initiating it himself was harder. Messier. It meant opening his mind without knowing exactly what to reach for. Their imprints allowed for telepathic contact so long as they were within a mile of each other—he knew that, and he knew Zalith wasn't anywhere near that far away. But logic didn't always silence his old fears, and that kind of vulnerability still made his skin crawl. So he didn't try. He'd just have to try and resist the temptations.

He changed course, making his way to Zalith's office. He climbed the stairs, and the closer he got to his mate, the greater the urge became. But he did his very best to focus.

He knocked and pushed the door open, and Zalith took his eyes off his work and smiled at him.

"Back for more already?" the demon asked with a smirk.

Alucard smiled amusedly. "Not zhis time," he said, staying by the door. "I 'ave to go to Vort Rudă de Sânge; I decided on Lăcrămioara and Cerboaica."

"Do you want me to come?"

He *did*, but Zalith had his own work to do, and the fort was as safe as Uzlia. "I'll be okay," he assured him. "Zhe vort is safe."

"I know but..." he paused and hesitated. "Okay," he replied, his smile slowly returning—clearly, he was trying to get over his paranoia-fuelled protective instincts. "Just be careful, please—and... can you take someone with you?"

The vampire nodded. "I *vould* say Zhomas, but I'm going to a vampire vort villed vith vampires, most of whom still 'aven't accepted zhe idea zhat ve're vorking vith verevolves."

"That's true." Zalith looked like he was pondering. "What about Danford? He's a hybrid. I know he's a little bit of an idiot, but maybe having him there *with* Greymore would make them less resistant to the idea of working with werewolves."

Alucard thought about it. "Maybe. Is Zhomas even available?"

"He's been watching over Anburidge and the connected islands, but I'm sure he can put one of his Betas in charge for a few hours."

"Okay. I vill go and see 'im and pick up Zanvord."

Zalith's smile grew. "Do I get a kiss goodbye?"

Alucard felt a little flustered. He wanted to kiss him... and his body wanted him to kiss him, too. So he moved closer, dismissing the urges, and when he reached Zalith's desk, he leaned in and kissed his lips. "I'll be back soon," he told him.

The demon brushed his cheek with his fingers. "Okay. I love you."

"I love you, too," he said... but he didn't pull away. He *couldn't*.

Zalith stared into his eyes, and then he kissed the vampire again.

Alucard felt the anticipation surge through him, gnawing away at his willpower. And the longer he gazed into his mate's dark, seductive eyes, the harder it became to resist. He let himself kiss the demon once more... and he let Zalith kiss him back.

His mate's lips were warm and inviting, too easy to sink into, and Alucard found himself giving in without thought. The slow press of their mouths turned deeper, hungrier, their breaths mingling as the heat between them thickened.

He knew he should stop.

But he didn't.

Not when Zalith's fingers curled around the back of his neck, drawing him in with a possessive sort of tenderness, not when his body leaned forward on its own, pressing closer, feeding off the low hum of desire curling between them.

He shouldn't have let it go on.

But then Zalith's hand drifted lower.

Alucard inhaled a sharp breath as Zalith's palm slid over his crotch, rubbing slow circles, his touch firm enough to send a spiralling pulse of pleasure through him.

And just like that, his body betrayed him.

Fire flared inside him, the response so fast and immediate that it made him ache. His hips twitched, falling into the touch, chasing the friction before he could stop himself; his pulse pounded as arousal rose quickly and intensely, his body desperate to let Zalith keep going, to let his mate take him again.

But he couldn't. He *shouldn't*.

He was already worn from before. If they kept going so soon, he'd drain himself dry—he'd end up too exhausted to even function. But his body told him that it didn't matter, insisting that he give in and sate his desires.

No.

Not now.

Later.

He gritted his teeth, forcing himself to pull back, even as his instincts screamed at him to stay. His movements were stiff and reluctant; he grabbed Zalith's wrist, gently but firmly pulling his hand away.

Their eyes met.

Zalith's gaze was dark… and *questioning*.

Alucard exhaled shakily. "Ve can't." His voice was strained, hoarse with unspent need. "Not yet." His dick still throbbed from Zalith's touch, and he knew that the demon could feel the press of it through his trousers before he stepped back.

Zalith studied him for a moment, and then, slowly, he smirked. "You're hard already."

The vampire pouted and turned away, ignoring the way his skin burned with frustration. Sometimes, he hated how easily Zalith unravelled him; it flustered him, and it made him feel meek…but he wasn't going to lie and say that he didn't enjoy that. "I know," he mumbled, still fighting the desperation. "But I 'ave to go to zhe vort."

His mate chuckled as he reached out, his fingers stroking Alucard's waist before he could step too far away. "You say that like you're not still hard," he murmured amusedly. He didn't press or pull him back, but the warmth of his palm lingered just above the curve of Alucard's hip, his touch taunting, tempting.

Alucard's willpower frayed at the edges. He could still feel the heat pulsing through him, pooling in his gut, his body demanding he just give in. It would be so easy to turn back, to let Zalith touch him and fix this ache.

But he had to go.

His fangs pressed into his lower lip as he smirked, tilting his head just enough to meet Zalith's eyes. "Not now," he murmured, his voice softer, breathier than he meant it to be. His fingers curled lightly around Zalith's wrist, prying him away again with a slow, lingering reluctance. Then, in a lower, more flirtatious tone, he added, "But later? You better be veady."

Zalith's eyes glinted with satisfaction. "Darling," he purred, leaning in just enough so that Alucard could feel his breath against his lips, "I'm always ready."

The vampire huffed, his resolve hanging by a thread, but before he could be tempted further, he turned away, muttering something in Dor-Sanguian about having to leave before he did something stupid.

His mate only laughed, watching him go.

The vampire left his office and headed downstairs. His body protested, of course, but he did his best to ignore it.

He made his way to the entrance hall, where he grabbed his coat, cape, and gloves. The moment he stepped outside, he dematerialized into vermillion smoke and raced up into the air. He landed in Anburidge, where he spotted Greymore sitting on his porch with a cigarette clamped between his teeth, a glass of whiskey in one hand, and a piece of oddly shaped carved wood in the other.

But Alucard didn't immediately approach. The strange fatigue that had struck him the last two times he'd travelled in his smoke form returned. Maybe it had something to do with him being in heat; perhaps his body was focusing the majority of its energy on his need to have sex.

With a quiet sigh, he shrugged it off and walked to Greymore's house.

"Oh, hey buddy," Greymore said as Alucard walked up onto the porch. "How's it going?" He put the wood down next to a few other pieces.

Was he building something?

"Is going okay," the vampire replied. "Vhat about you?"

"Eh, the usual. I went over to Akavine the other day, took a look around. The forest isn't bad, but it's not like Eltaria…or Nefastus—or Ordvell, for that matter. We can make it work, though."

"Vell, zhe village on Ordvell should be veady soon, so you can move over zhere."

"Looking forward to it," he said with a nod.

"Are you making someving?" he then asked, nodding at the wood.

Greymore stubbed his cigarette out in the ashtray on the table beside him. "Oh, yeah. I thought I'd make a crib for Danny's kid…or kids," he said with a chuckle. "Gives me something to do when I'm not working. Helps me relax."

Alucard nodded and said, "I need to ask you a vavour."

"Shoot," the werewolf said and sipped from his drink.

"I 'ave to 'ead to my vort and talk to a vew vampires. I need to take some backup in case someving 'appens."

"Say no more," Greymore said and downed his drink before standing up. "Let's go."

"I need to pick up Zanvord, too. Zaliv vinks zhe vampires might be more open to accepting zhat ve vork vith verevolves if zhe vampire-verevolf 'ybrid is zhere."

"I think he's with that teacher lady right now."

"Zhat's vine. 'E can veturn to 'is lessons vonce ve get back."

"All right. Lead the way," Greymore said with a nod.

Alucard turned around and headed down off the porch. He faced Greymore, holding out his hand, and when the werewolf gripped his wrist, he dematerialized them both into vermillion smoke and flew over to Eimwood.

He landed and rematerialized outside the house he'd dedicated to Danford's training—the last thing he wanted was him training in his own home and accidentally hurting Freja.

Ignoring the exhaustion, he led the way inside, where he found Păzitoarea and Danford in the lounge mid-combat. But when they noticed him and Greymore, they stopped, lowered their hands, and turned to face them.

"My Lord," Păzitoarea said with a small bow.

"Uh…hi," Danford said nervously.

"I'm 'eading to Vort Rudă de Sânge; you're coming vith us," he said to Danford, and then he looked at Păzitoarea. "Lăcrămioara and Cerboaica are going to become brood nurses, and Vulpea and Bogdănel are being Dignivied to Paladins."

"I'll spread the word to the vampires working in Uzlia," she offered.

Alucard nodded. "Let's go."

Danford grabbed his coat from the couch and followed Alucard and Greymore out of the house. "Um…what are we doing at the fort?" he asked unsurely.

"Telling my vampires vhat I just told Păzitoarea."

"Oh."

"My vampires also need to get used to zhe vact zhat ve're vorking vith verevolves," he added, leading them to an alley. "'Aving an 'ybrid zhere vith a verevolf should 'elp."

He looked much more nervous now, but Danford nodded. "O-okay."

"What do we do if these vampires ain't so happy with me being in their fort?" Greymore asked.

"Zhey von't attack. Zhe last ving any of zhem vould do is 'urt vone of my vriends, verevolf or not."

"What about me?" Danford asked quietly. "I-I just…well, some of the vampires still kinda look at me a certain way."

"You'll be vine," he mumbled.

Once hidden in the shadows of the alley, Alucard exhaled a slow sigh and held out his arms. Greymore clasped one wrist. Danford took the other.

"W-wait a sec," Danford said anxiously. "I've heard that this whole vampire travel thing makes people feel sick. What if—"

Alucard rolled his eyes and dematerialized with them, vanishing into the afternoon, his mind set on finishing this mission as quickly as possible… because the sooner it was over, the sooner he could go home and finally surrender to what his body craved.

Chapter Three

Tasks

| **Alucard** |
| *Ascuns, Fort Rudă de Sânge* |

When Alucard landed in the fort docks with Greymore and Danford, he ignored the fatigue, already shifting his focus to the task ahead.

Until the unmistakable sound of retching made his head snap to the side. Danford gagged, doubled over, and vomited into the water.

Alucard sighed, rolling his eyes.

Greymore let out a low chortle, amused. "Well, that's one way to mark our arrival," he quipped, crossing his arms as Danford groaned.

"S-sorry—I'm sorry," Danford stammered, one hand clamped over his mouth, his face pale.

Alucard shook his head, already turning towards the fort entrance. "Let's go."

Danford scurried after them as they headed inside.

The vampire guard at the doors straightened as Alucard approached, inclining his head. "My Lord." But the moment his gaze flicked past him to Greymore and Danford, his expression tightened, his lips pressing into a thin line before a scowl briefly surfaced. "Welcome…to the fort," he said, his voice clipped and forced, as if the words tasted bitter on his tongue.

"Uh…thank you," Danford said.

A quiet hiss escaped the guard, his fangs barely flashing, but he made no move to act on his obvious disdain.

Alucard strode past the guard, Greymore and Danford flanking him closely. The fort's halls were dimly lit, the air thick with tension as he led them to the meeting hall.

The moment Alucard pushed the doors open and stepped inside, the vampires gathered around the table stiffened. Some hissed quietly under their breath, others scowled outright, their gazes flashing with thinly veiled contempt. But as expected, they rose to their feet and bowed respectfully, even if a few pairs of eyes lingered warily on Greymore and Danford.

"My Lord," they all called in unison.

"Sit," he said.

They returned to their seats.

Alucard stood at the head of the table with the werewolf and the hybrid beside him. "Lăcrămioara, Cerboaica," he started, his eyes shifting between the two of them. "You vill be zhe new brood nurses."

The pair glanced at each other, looking excited, *glad*.

"Vulpea and Bogdănel, you are being Dignivied to Paladin."

They looked just as excited, too—surprised, but excited.

"We won't let you down, My Lord," Bogdănel said humbly.

"When do we begin, My Lord?" Lăcrămioara asked.

"Immediately," he answered. "Ve need Day Valkers, so I vant each of you to vound up enough 'umans to strengthen your covens to at least a 'undred vampires." He looked at Eyra. "I vant *you* to take a vew 'umans vrom Aveson City; zhat vay, zhe people may be more likely to accept and support your presence because zheir vriends and or vamily are now a part of zhe coven. Eizer zhat or zhey vill vear you turning zhem, too."

Eyra nodded. "Understood, My Lord."

"Not too many, zhough."

She nodded again.

"'As zhere been any new invormation gazzered on zhe Silver Claw?"

"I received a message from one of my Acolytes just before we were called to this meeting. The Silver Claw…My Lord—" she paused, looking hesitant, "—he has killed a lot of stray vampires. It seems that up until now, he has only been hired to kill vampires who aren't part of a coven."

"So, he's getting brave," Greymore commented.

Some of the vampires hissed.

Alucard sighed deeply. "Zhis is Greymore," he said, gesturing to him. "And as some of you know, zhis is Zanvord," he said, gesturing to him, too. "I know zhat verevolves 'ave been our enemy vor centuries, but zhese volves are not vrom Aegisguard, and zhey do not share zhe same 'ate as zhis vorld's verevolves do vor us. I know zhis makes a lot of you uncomvortable, but zhese volves are our allies. Vill be 'ard, *da*, but I need you to try and accept zhis."

A lot of unsure whispers circled the table.

"I need you all to pass zhis news on to your covens, as vell as Lăcrămioara, Cerboaica, Vulpea, and Bogdănel's Dignivications."

Every Coven Master nodded in response and called, "Yes, My Lord."

"Lăcrămioara, you'll go vith Eyra and prepare to teach Vledgelings in Aveson."

"Yes, My Lord," she said with a small smile.

"And Cerboaica, I vant you to start in Boszorkány vith Vane."

She bowed her head and said, "Of course, My Lord."

"Bogdănel, 'ead to Boszorkány, too. 'Elp gazzer vhirty-vive 'umans and keep zhem secure in zhe Sanctum. I vill come and turn zhem vhen I can."

He bowed his head and said, "Yes, My Lord."

"Is zhere anyving else to veport?" Alucard then asked.

Everyone looked around the table, but no one said anything.

"Vight. Send me a veport vonce you've gazzered 'umans."

"Yes, My Lord," they replied.

Alucard then said to Greymore and Danford, "Let's go."

They left the room as the vampires began departing, transforming into bats and smoke and leaving through the small windows.

"Who's the Silver Claw?" Greymore asked curiously.

"A provessional vampire 'unter. 'E's been killing covenless vampires—Straybloods, ve call zhem—and 'e's been 'ired by zhe people of Aveson to kill my coven."

"Oh, shit," he replied. "So, you're hunting him, right? You need help?"

"Maybe, I zon't know. If I do, I'll let you know. But zhere *is* someving I vill need you vor, zhough," he said, leading the way back to the docks. "Vreja 'as veached out to zhe verevolf packs of Dor-Sanguis. I'll be meeting vith zhem on zhe vhirty-virst of zhis month to see if zhey vill join and vork vith us. I vink 'aving you zhere vill 'elp assure zhem zhat Uzlia is safe."

"Yeah, all right. Just let me know when it's time to leave."

"Do, uh…do you need me?" Danford asked.

"Maybe," Alucard mumbled, leaving the fort and stepping out onto the docks. "Vill probably ease zhem into zhe idea of vorking closely vith vampires." He held out his arms again. "I'll let you both know."

They gripped his wrists, and then Alucard dematerialized, taking them with him.

| **Zalith** |

| *Aestrael, Uzlia Isles, Usrul, Castle Reiner* |

Idina's message arrived via izuret. Zalith stopped daydreaming; despite Alucard no longer being in the castle, his scent remained, and it was enough to continue stealing his focus, enough to drive him close to mad.

The izuret told him that Idina had received the three prisoners.

He nodded and said, "Thank you." He paused and recalled which of his demons were in the city, one who could travel between this world and the Astral Plane—he didn't want to trek through the woods on horseback, not this time. "Tell Basilan to collect them from her and meet me outside the Yrudberg Woods in ten minutes." He opened his desk drawer filled with small treasures. "Take *one*."

With an excited grin, the izuret floated down and perched itself on the edge of the drawer. It pondered for a moment, its huge eyes darting between each trinket. It finally settled with a small gold ring with an encrusted sapphire. Then, it saluted and disappeared into smoke.

Zalith got up, took one copy of the supply list he'd been working on, and headed downstairs. After grabbing his coat, he stepped outside, adorned his demon form, and took off.

Moments later, he landed outside the Yrudberg Woods. There was no sign of Basilian yet, so he leaned against a tree and exhaled deeply. Something moved in the corner of his eye, and when he turned his head, he set his eyes on a small fox-like creature—well, it looked *exactly* like a fox, save for the fuzzy tendrils snaking backwards from the sides of its face. It stared at him with wide yellow eyes, but it returned to the woods after grabbing a large stick from the grass just past the tree line.

The demon smiled lightly, watching it scurry back into the shadows. He'd never seen a single creature in these woods since arriving in Uzlia, and he was glad to see that the animals of the forest were comfortable enough to begin revealing themselves. Evidently, it wasn't just the people of Eimwood benefitting from Cecil's removal.

"Sir," came Basilan's voice.

Zalith shifted his gaze to the approaching man, who tugged three men ensnared in rope behind him.

Basilan's ashen-gold eyes glowed faintly beneath a dark brow, their gaze sharp with satisfaction yet laced with respect. His fingertips twitched around the ropes, the subtle movement betraying the urge to tear apart the trembling figures trailing him. "This is them," he said smoothly, giving the ropes a sharp tug. The humans stumbled forward, their sack-covered heads jerking frantically as muffled whimpers filled the air.

The demon nodded. "Let's go," he said, and as he stepped into the space between this world and the Astral Plane, Basilan followed, dragging the humans with him.

He led Basilan through the forest, along the mountain paths, and into the Yrudyen Woods. Not too far from the Yrudyen village, he stepped out, and once Basilan emerged, Zalith continued. He could feel the eyes of the guards on him, but they knew that he was no threat—and some of their hushed voices sounded excited, likely because of the three humans; they *were* for the elves' ritual, after all.

"It's very beautiful here, sir," Basilan said.

It was. The forest seemed to breathe easier, its vibrance returning now that Eimwood was recovering—perhaps a direct result of no longer having its waters tainted by a troll and a man-sized insect rotting in the river. Soft pulses of golden light flickered between the trees, glowing insects drifting lazily through the dusk. Near the roots of an ancient oak, a pair of tiny-winged rabbits nibbled at the grass, their delicate wings fluttering with each twitch of their ears. Everything felt alive again, thriving in a way it hadn't before, and it made Zalith smile discreetly. Alucard would love to see this.

"Lord Silas," came a familiar, graceful voice.

He halted and turned his head, watching as Tianel emerged from behind a willow tree. Her lavender eyes locked onto him as she approached, her silvery hair floating in a non-existent breeze.

"It's good to see you again," she said, smiling.

"And you," he replied. "I've come to deliver the promised humans as well as a list of supplies that I'll be sending over. I've brought it for the queen to take a look at in case she wants to add anything."

With a nod, Tianel turned around and began leading the way. "Follow."

Zalith trailed behind her, and Basilan shadowed him.

As they approached the entrance to the Yrudyen settlement, the familiar sight unfolded before Zalith. The dense forest gradually yielded to a carefully kept path, where the trees stood in perfect symmetry, their roots cradling many more clusters of wildflowers and moss than he'd seen just a week ago. At the path's end stood the archway woven with twisting vines, shimmering blossoms, and hand-crafted charms of feathers, fur, and string. From beyond the entrance, the distant strains of flute music whistled through the air, accompanied by the steady pulse of rhythmic drumming, the sounds as much a part of this place as the whispering leaves.

"Woah," Basilan's quiet voice broke through the peace.

"Queen Syllia Caiyarus of Yrudberg is with her collection inside the Sacred Tree," Tianel said, stepping into the village.

As he moved through the archway, Zalith's demon form appeared, as did Basilan's. He folded his wings against his back and continued following Tianel to the colossal oak, inside, and past the queen's throne. There was a door three yards from the shadowed entrance, and Tianel knocked.

A few moments later, a man opened it—armoured, scowling cautiously. A guard.

"Lord Silas is here to deliver his promises to Queen Syllia Caiyarus of Yrudberg," Tianel told the man.

With a grunt, the guard nodded and let them pass.

Tianel led them into the chamber, and as soon as he stepped inside, Zalith's gaze was met with a sparkling spectacle of wealth and history.

The low glow of enchanted lanterns cast flickering light across heaps of gold, silver, and a rose-gold metal that he hadn't seen before—well…it looked like the giant rod on the castle's tallest tower. Maybe that was what it was.

Jewels—sapphires, emeralds, and opals—it all spilt from ornate chests, their brilliance nearly outshone by the delicate golden circlets and intricately wrought tiaras resting atop them. Stacks of aged coins and crisp, modern banknotes sat in tidy piles, a quiet testament to wealth that stretched across centuries.

Beyond the treasures, ancient statues of forgotten deities and long-dead rulers stood watch, their stone eyes hollow. Some bore intricate carvings, others were inlaid with gemstones, their artistry untouched by time.

The air carried the faint scent of aged parchment and polished wood, mingling with something earthy, like the breath of the ancient tree itself. And sitting on a jewel-encrusted stool by a pile of gleaming crystals was Syllia. Her silken-white hair glowed under the lanternlight, reflecting the sparkles of gems, and when she turned, she set her platinum eyes on Zalith.

"Well, well," she said with a sultry tone, leaning forward, ensuring that her cleavage was more than visible. "Are you here to take me up on my offer?"

He laughed a little, shaking his head. "Unfortunately not. I'm here on business."

She pouted and said, "Such a pity. Where's that *really* good friend of yours?"

"Away on business elsewhere," he said, maintaining a pleasant smile.

Syllia giggled, sitting up straight. "I see you've brought me my sacrifices."

Zalith glanced back at the three men…but he noticed Basilan's captivated stare. He scowled, and when Basilan's eyes shot to him, the man looked away. With a sigh, Zalith then shifted his focus back to Syllia. "I've also put together a list of supplies that I plan to send to the village. I'd like you to look it over and add anything if need be." He took the list from his pocket and unfolded it. "May I?"

"You may," she granted, a seductive smile on her lips.

He moved towards her and handed her the paper.

"Hmm…" she pondered, reading it. "Oh, how wonderful—puffpeaches, one of my *favourites*." She then gasped. "Emberfruits? Celestine melons? You are spoiling me, Lord Silas."

Zalith chuckled and said, "I made sure to give you the best." He hoped that giving her the more exotic fruits traded with Sinéad would please her—these fruits, after all, came from elven land.

"I think that everything here is acceptable," the queen then said; she rolled up the paper and slowly slid it between her breasts. "When will it be delivered?"

"I'll send Basilan here with a shipment tomorrow," he answered. "It's a lot to bring over the mountains, so we'll dock a ship down on the shore not far from here, and then he and several others will bring it to you in wagons."

"Wonderful," she beamed. "Will you be coming along with the delivery?"

He hesitated. He didn't want to…but he didn't want to upset her, either. "If that is what you'd like, yes," he agreed.

"Of course I'd like that," she purred.

Zalith smiled, hiding his discomfort. "Okay," he said with a nod. "I'll see you in a day or two."

"Make sure you arrive before the ceremony begins," she warned him.

"Rest assured, we'll be here in time," he said firmly.

Syllia's smile became a smirk. "Then for now, it is farewell."

The demon bowed his head a little. "Have a wonderful evening." He then turned around and waited for Basilan to hand the ropes and prisoners to the guard. Once he was done, he followed Taniel out of the tree.

"Should I get started on the shipment once we get back to Eimwood?" Basilan asked.

"Yes," Zalith replied. "But first, I need you to go to Greymore and ask him for four or five wolves who can come and help protect this place."

"Yes, sir," Basilan replied.

"Let's move," he then said, stepping into the space between this world and the Astral Plane. Now that his task was over, he just wanted to head home and wait for his fiancé to return.

Chapter Four

— ⸱ ✝ ⸱ —

Surrender

| **Alucard** |
| *Uzlia Isles, Usrul, Castle Reiner* |

Once he dropped off Danford and Greymore, Alucard headed home. Desperation began consuming him, outweighing any tiredness he felt when he rematerialized. He walked into the castle, took off his cape, coat, gloves, and shoes, and when he stepped into the lounge, he set his eyes on Zalith.

His mate was waiting on the couch, relaxing, but his eyes told a different story. The second their gazes met, an excited smile spread across the demon's lips, sending a pulse of heat surging through Alucard's body. He tensed slightly, a sharp, instinctive response to the anticipation winding tight in his chest.

Zalith was waiting to give him what he needed, waiting to take what he desired.

And Alucard was more than willing to let him.

"Hey, baby," the demon purred, holding out a hand, an invitation and a promise.

Alucard didn't hesitate. He crossed the room in an instant, climbing onto Zalith's lap, straddling him without an ounce of restraint. The demon's hands found him immediately, sliding to either side of his waist, thumbs pressing into the firm lines of his body. The touch sent a shiver of pleasure up Alucard's spine; Zalith pulled him in, their bodies pressed together.

He'd waited long enough.

After just one kiss to Zalith's lips, the vampire breathed, "Fuck me."

Zalith's smirk sharpened the second the words left Alucard's mouth. His hands tightened on the vampire's waist, his fingers digging in just enough to tease. "You don't have to ask me twice," he murmured, his voice a low, hungry drawl, thick with anticipation. He flipped them in an instant, pinning Alucard on the couch beneath him, his breath hot against the vampire's throat. "I was planning on it the second you walked through that door."

Alucard desperately crashed into the kiss, his lips parting the moment Zalith pulled him in. Their breaths mingled, sharp and ragged, the anticipation between them enthralling as hands grasped, pulled, and claimed.

His fingers fumbled for Zalith's belt, his urgency turning his movements clumsy and rushed. The clink of metal, the slide of leather—not fast enough. His body ached, his pulse pounding in his throat, every fibre of him screaming for more, for *Zalith*.

The demon growled against his lips, the sound deep, primal. "In a hurry, are we?" he teased, his voice thick with amusement.

Alucard barely heard him. The belt was gone, forgotten, the leather slipping free from his fingers as he eased his hand into Zalith's trousers. The moment his fingers wrapped around the demon's growing arousal, Zalith let out a low, quiet groan; the sound sent a fresh wave of heat crashing through the vampire, tightening the desperation already wound too tight within him.

He needed more.

He wanted to feel that thick, pulsing length inside him, stretching him open, filling him completely. He craved the fleeting sting, that delicious ache when Zalith pushed in deep, the overwhelming sensation of being claimed, possessed, undone. And more than anything, he wanted to feel the moment Zalith lost control. To feel his mate throb in him, filling him with warmth, with cum, with everything he was. The thought alone made Alucard's breath tremble, his body craving, *yearning*, starved for Zalith.

Zalith captured his lips again, harder this time, his kiss deep, consuming, relentless. Alucard melted into it, moaning softly against his mate's mouth as fingers tangled in his shirt, pulling and tugging, eager to rid him of the fabric.

The vampire barely registered his own hands working just as feverishly, undoing buttons, pushing at Zalith's trousers, eager to feel nothing but skin against skin. A sharp tear of cloth, a buckle hitting the floor, the brushed heat of bare flesh—it was all a blur, a haze of longing, a frantic race towards the inevitable.

Alucard kept tending to Zalith's shaft, taking the lube from him when he offered it, and he eagerly smothered his mate's dick with the viscous liquid.

Then, without warning, Zalith seized him firmly and flipped him onto his hands and knees, and then he took a towel that he'd obviously set by and spread it beneath Alucard.

Alucard didn't have a chance to brace himself before he felt it—Zalith's thick, aching length pressing against him, the heat of it sending a shuddering pulse of anticipation through the vampire's body.

And then came the long-awaited bliss.

Zalith eased inside, pushing past resistance, sinking deep into the tightness of his ass, stretching him in a way that sent pure, electric pleasure surging through him. It made him whine, long and breathless, his fingers gripping the cushions as his body welcomed the intrusion, and he craved more of it. The feeling was perfect—overwhelming, consuming, everything he'd been waiting for.

The demon's breath was hot against the back of his neck, his grip demanding and unwavering as he buried himself to the hilt. And Alucard could feel it all, every pulse, every dizzying sensation sending him deeper into pleasure's grasp. He didn't want it to stop.

A deep groan escaped Zalith's throat as Alucard clenched around him, his body gripping him firmly and desperately—Alucard wanted to feel every inch, every vein.

The demon tightened his grip on his hips, his fingers digging in just enough to bruise. "Fuck," he rasped, his voice thick with lust and praise. He shifted his hips slightly, dragging his dick halfway out before pushing back in, hard and deep. "The way you squeeze me." He groaned again, pushing Alucard down onto his stomach, possessively trapping the vampire beneath him. "Your body knows who it belongs to."

His words sent a violent shudder down Alucard's spine, his breath catching as another helpless moan spilt from his lips. He could barely think; his body was a mess of sensation, heat, and hunger, craving nothing but this.

But Zalith wasn't interested in teasing him—not tonight.

Without warning, he thrusted *hard*, plunging into Alucard, aggressive, assertive, so deep that it knocked the breath right out of him. The vampire shivered, his body instinctively urging him to crawl forward, seeking even a moment to process the intensity, but Zalith growled, keeping him exactly where he wanted him. The sudden force sent a shock of pleasure tearing through Alucard, and before he could even recover, Zalith did it again.

And again.

And again.

And again.

Fast, rough, relentless—

Alucard cried out, his hands desperately fisting the cushion beneath him as Zalith drove into him with an eager, primal need. Each thrust sent pleasure spiralling higher, deeper, dragging him closer to madness.

Zalith groaned against the back of Alucard's neck. "You take me so *well*," he snarled, his voice heavy with satisfaction and admiration. "Let me breed you."

Alucard whined a struggled, *"Yes"*, submitting, his back arching into every punishing thrust, his body demanding more, more, *more*. Zalith's words ignited something in him, stirring the desire to accept his mate's demand, to fulfil the duty that his body insisted was attainable. His heat raged through him, impossible to ignore, every nerve alight with the devouring need to be filled, to be claimed.

He didn't care how hard Zalith fucked him.

He wanted it *hard*—harder than he'd ever had it.

He wanted to feel this aggression etched into his body for hours after—the lingering ache in his muscles, the dull throb of overuse, the bruising sting that would remind him of every deep, merciless thrust. He wanted to feel the stretch every time he moved, the way his body would ache in the best way, a constant, unshakable reminder that Zalith had taken him completely and thoroughly until there was nothing left of him but pleasure and exhaustion.

Zalith must have sensed it, he must have felt how badly Alucard needed it, because his grip constricted, his pace quickened, and his thrusts grew even more brutal, his breath coming in rough, heated pants against Alucard's ear. "You love this, don't you?" he murmured, voice dark and taunting and sinful. "Being fucked like this. Being *ruined* like this."

Alucard whined, succumbing to the intensity. "Yes," he moaned in response, pressing his forehead against the cushion. "Zon't...let me 'eal," he cried, struggling to speak through his ragged breaths. "I...vant...to veel zhis...vor *hours* avter." And then Zalith pushed in harder, making him wail and whimper as sheer delight raged through his trembling, aching limbs—he didn't know how many times he'd came, but it was definitely more than once.

The demon responded with an amused but deeply satisfied groan before he purred contently and pressed a soft kiss to the side of Alucard's neck. "You're such a perfect little thing for me," he murmured, his tone a mix of pride and indulgence. "So eager— so fucking *desperate* to be wrecked."

Alucard shuddered, his fingers clenching into the cushion, almost ripping it with his claws as his body tightened around Zalith's dick in response.

Zalith laughed, a low, taunting sound as he slowed, rolling his hips forward in a slow, teasing grind; he obviously knew that Alucard was beyond overstimulated, but even gradual thrusts made the vampire cry out—he still craved more all the same.

The demon bit at Alucard's ear, relishing the way he trembled beneath him with a pleased hum. "God, I fucking *love* the way I fill you." He growled and moaned. "I love how you cling to me...like you don't want me to stop." He thrust in hard, dragging another helpless moan from Alucard's lips.

"I...zon't," he whined, pushing his ass back towards Zalith when the demon pulled away. "Keep going."

He laughed again before licking the side of Alucard's neck. "Yes, darling."

Zalith thrust his dick in abruptly, making the vampire whine again, collapsing back into his submissive position, letting the demon take control. "I won't stop again, even if you beg." He murmured and then moaned, his fingers digging into Alucard's hips possessively as he set a brutal pace again. "Not until I've given you exactly what you want."

The demon didn't slow—he couldn't; Alucard could feel his struggle. His thrusts were relentless, driving into him with a punishing desperation, his fingers pressing into his hips hard enough to brand his touch into his skin.

Alucard winced, his body trembling, nerves hyperstimulated, muscles aching from too much pleasure. His limbs were exhausted, his skin flushed, every inch of him so thoroughly used that it was almost too much.

Almost.

But he still didn't want it to stop.

His fingers clenched around Zalith's wrists, gripping onto him for stability because if he let go, he wasn't sure he'd be able to hold himself together.

Zalith let out a high-pitched whine, his rhythm faltering for just a second before he thrust in deep, shuddering violently. "Fuck—do that again," he panted, voice thick with pleasure. "You feel so good when you do that."

Alucard's walls clenched around the demon's length again, a helpless, obeying response to the rapture tearing through him.

And that was all it took.

Zalith slammed to his hilt, burying his dick completely, his entire body tensing as he came with a sharp, ragged groan. Alucard could feel it—the way Zalith trembled against him, the way his grip tightened, the way every muscle in his body locked up as pleasure ripped through him.

"Fuck, Alucard—" the demon moaned, his voice breathy, almost weary as his dick throbbed rapidly, his hot cum pouring into the vampire. "You're gonna kill me one day." His hips twitched, gently thrusting forward a final few times, pushing his cum deeper into Alucard's body.

The vampire let out a euphoric hum, feeling the warmth of his mate's load trickle further.

And then Zalith slumped, pressing against Alucard's damp back—but it wasn't wet with sweat; demons didn't sweat. So what was it?

Moments later, Zalith slowly eased his dick out of him; Alucard shivered, his breath deepening as his aching body protested the loss of the demon's hard length. His muscles clenched involuntarily, sensitive and stretched beyond their limit, and he could still feel the thick weight of his mate's cum inside him, hot and heavy.

The absence left him burning, throbbing, every movement sending a lingering, delicious sting deep into his core. His hole felt tender, used, utterly wrecked, a constant reminder of how thoroughly Zalith had taken him, how deep and relentless. Even as his mate's warmth began to trickle out of him, slick and slow, the dull throb remained, an aftershock of everything his body had endured. His muscles quivered, but beneath the soreness was satisfaction, deep, euphoric, and addictive.

He'd wanted this.

And he could still feel every moment of it.

Zalith dragged his tongue up Alucard's damp back, and a pleased groan escaped his deep breaths before he licked him again.

"Vhat…is zhat?" the vampire breathed.

His mate groaned again; another lick, a quiet suck, and a soft kiss. "Pheromones," he replied before *another* lick.

"Vhy is zhis 'appening now?"

"Because you're in heat," he murmured and stroked his tongue all the way down to Alucard's waist. "It isn't noticeable to you when you're not in heat," he continued and rested his body against the vampire's back once more. "I can still taste it on you, but it's a lot more intense when you're in heat—and it's an aphrodisiac." He groaned into his ear, grinding his dick against his tender ass. "It's making me want to fuck you again already." And then he licked his neck. "Mmm," he hummed.

Alucard tensed beneath him. His body wanted it—of course it did. But he was exhausted, and he was savouring the soreness, the feeling of complete domination.

"How do you feel?" his mate asked softly.

He groaned pleasurably. "Vavaged," he murmured. "In zhe most amazing vay."

Zalith let out a low, satisfied laugh, rich with seduction. "Good." He pressed a lingering kiss to Alucard's shoulder, his lips warm against sensitive skin. "Do you think you can sit up?"

Alucard huffed a breath, his body still heavy with exhaustion, sore in all the best ways. "Maybe," he mumbled, though he wasn't entirely convinced.

His mate moved first, sitting up, and then he hooked an arm around Alucard's waist, pulling him upright, guiding him onto his knees.

The moment Alucard shifted, he felt it—a trickle of warmth sliding down the inside of his thigh, thick and still hot, a reminder of how thoroughly Zalith had flooded him. A shiver ran through him, the sensation sending a lazy spark of leftover pleasure curling through his spent body.

Zalith chuckled behind him, and there was no mistaking the smirk on his face. "You came so much," he purred, his voice like silk, teasing but appreciative. His hand trailed possessively around Alucard's waist before sliding down to grasp his softening dick, his grip firm but indulgent.

Alucard exhaled shakily, his body melting against Zalith's, too spent, too thoroughly ruined to do anything but let his mate savour him. His gaze drifted downward, and when he saw the mess coating his stomach and thighs—evidence of just how many times he'd came—heat curled low in his stomach, but this time, it wasn't from arousal, it was from embarrassment. Had it been twice? Three times? It could have been more. It *felt* like more. His entire body ached with it, pulsed with it, the lingering pleasure still buzzing faintly beneath the exhaustion.

And Zalith had felt all of it. He'd *seen* all of it.

Zalith leaned into his ear, stroking his dick until it hardened again. "Good boy," he whispered.

His words sent an intense wave of arousal through Alucard. Whatever Zalith was about to do to him, he wanted it.

The demon pulled the damp towel away, barely sparing it a glance before scrunching it up and tossing it towards the laundry basket. It missed, landing somewhere on the floor—but neither of them cared.

His focus was solely on Alucard.

He turned the vampire to face him, claiming his lips in a slow kiss, a tease, a promise, a lingering taste of what was coming next. Then, without hesitation, Zalith pushed him onto his back, settling between his legs with a hunger that sent anticipation curling hot inside Alucard.

Zalith's tongue was on him in an instant, tracing over the cum on his stomach and thighs with a sinful, delighted groan. He licked up every drop, his pace unhurried, relishing him like he was something decadent, something meant to be devoured.

And then, just as Alucard's body shuddered under the attention, Zalith took his dick into his mouth.

Alucard inhaled a sharp breath, his body too overstimulated, too sore, too used—but he couldn't stop himself. Zalith's mouth was hot and wet and perfect, his tongue swirling over his tip with that devastating skill. The vampire's sensitive, stretched hole throbbed; every shift, every small movement sent a deep, aching pulse through him, a lingering reminder of how aggressively he'd been fucked.

And yet his body still wanted more.

It was too much. It wasn't enough. Both at the same time.

Alucard whimpered, his fingers twitching weakly against the cushions, the strength to grab at Zalith's hair just out of reach. His thighs quivered, his muscles barely able to hold tension, but the pleasure…it was unbearable.

Zalith's pace wasn't slow, it wasn't teasing. He sucked him down deep, eager, like he had no intention of letting up, no interest in dragging this out. The delightful sounds of wet heat, of his mate's satisfied groans only drove Alucard higher, faster, too fast—

He couldn't hold back.

His body seized, his back arching weakly, and then he climaxed *hard*, gasping out a broken moan as waves of blinding pleasure crashed over him. The orgasm ripped through his exhausted frame, making his spent, trembling muscles lock up helplessly.

Zalith groaned in delight, low and pleased, his grip tightening around Alucard's hips as he swallowed every drop, dragging his tongue over him like he couldn't get enough.

Alucard shuddered, helpless in Zalith's grasp.

And still, as he felt his mate's tongue lazily swirl around his tip one last time, as Zalith finally pulled back, licking his lips with pure satisfaction, the vampire's dazed, ruined body still twitched with need.

Because even now…he wanted more.

"Zaliv…" he whined weakly, his voice barely a whisper.

The demon purred again, dragging his tongue up Alucard's body, and then he leaned into his ear. "Don't try to talk, baby," he murmured. "Let it take you."

He gave in, closing his eyes, sinking into it. The exhaustion was taking over, but he let it. Even though his body was begging for it, he couldn't take any more. He needed to rest, and when he felt Zalith place a blanket over him, he surrendered completely.

He'd had enough for now.

Chapter Five

Full

| Alucard |
| *Uzlia Isles, Usrul, Castle Reiner* |

How long had he been asleep? When Alucard opened his eyes to the sound of Zalith's voice, he saw the dark, star-filled sky outside the windows, and the light of the moons shone in through the glass.

"Hey," Zalith said, sitting beside him and helping him rest his head in his lap.

Alucard smiled up at him. Of course, the first thing his mind focused on was the growing desire for another round of sex—but the second was the deep, aching throb settling in his body, reminding him exactly why he was so tired in the first place.

The soreness was *everywhere*, a low, pleasant ache that pulsed in his lower back, his thighs, and most noticeably, between his legs. His body still felt loose, stretched, a faint, lingering heat clinging to him where Zalith's length had been buried inside him for so long. Even now, he could feel the remnants of his mate's orgasm—warm, slick cum, shifting slightly with every tiny movement.

A slow, content hum left the vampire's lips as he melted further into Zalith's lap, eyes fluttering shut for a moment as he let himself feel it—*really* feel it.

He loved it.

The aftermath, the way his body still held the memory of Zalith's touch, the faint shiver of overstimulation still buzzing beneath the exhaustion. Even the subtle soreness made him want more.

Zalith must have noticed. The demon's fingers slid into his hair, massaging gently, but there was amusement in his touch. "You're smiling," he murmured, his voice deep and full of satisfaction.

Alucard opened his eyes, looking up at him through his lashes. "Mm-hmm." His voice was still laced with sleep, thick with contentment.

The demon grinned. His other hand slid lower, teasing over Alucard's waist, his fingertips barely grazing his sore, well-used skin. "How do you feel?" he asked, a purr creeping into his voice.

A slow shudder worked its way through Alucard as his body reacted to the lightest touch. He smirked, shifting slightly; the movement sent a fresh wave of warmth trickling lower, and he exhaled a shaky breath. But he couldn't take it again—he couldn't let Zalith devour him. "'Ow long vas I asleep?" he asked, trying to change the subject.

Zalith fiddled with his hair, laughing softly. "A few hours."

"A vew?" He glanced at the windows again. "Vhat's zhe time?"

"Half past eleven."

He frowned. "Zhat's so late."

The demon shrugged. "I wanted to let you rest. You've had a long day," he said with a smirk, stroking the tip of his index finger down the side of Alucard's face.

Alucard smiled at the teasing sensation, but he fought to keep it from arousing him. "Did you 'ave dinner?"

He shook his head. "I waited for you."

His smile grew. "Vank you."

"You're welcome, baby. Do you want to eat now?"

He *was* hungry… for *blood*, but food actually sounded good. So, he nodded.

"*Right now*?" Zalith asked, his smirk returning. "Or do you want me to stretch your tight little hole again first?"

Flustered—and maybe a little embarrassed—Alucard pouted and looked away, sure that his face had gone red. But his body tensed, and his ass ached. Despite the pleasing soreness, though, everything pleaded for more.

Zalith laughed amusedly, still caressing the side of his face. "Sorry, I couldn't help myself."

Alucard exhaled deeply and looked up at him again—*he* couldn't help it either. "At least take me to dinner virst," he said with a smirk of his own.

The demon smiled. "Deal."

With a tired huff, Alucard sat up—and he immediately felt it.

The shift sent a deep, lingering ache rippling through his lower body, a slow, pulsing throb that settled heavily in his hips, thighs, and deep inside him. His body protested the movement, sore and well-used, his leg muscles weak and unsteady after how thoroughly Zalith had claimed him

The pressure of sitting fully upright only made the sensation more obvious—his hole was still loose and stretched, a faint burn of overuse tingling at the edges, reminding him of just how deep and relentless Zalith had been. Even now, there was a soft slickness between his legs, a fresh trickle of cum that made his breath catch involuntarily.

He swallowed, gripping Zalith's thigh for balance, his fingers tightening as he tried to ignore the way his body clenched around nothing, a reflexive reminder that he was still adjusting to the emptiness.

Zalith saw it—of course he did. The demon's smirk was unmistakable, his gaze dipping lower, drinking in the way Alucard shifted, the way he tensed slightly before forcing himself to relax. "Careful, darling," he murmured, his tone rich with amusement. "Don't overdo it."

Alucard shot him a look, but there was no real bite behind it. The soreness wasn't unpleasant, it was addictive, intoxicating, a lingering reminder that Zalith had ruined him.

And he wasn't in any hurry to recover.

He slowly pulled his clothes on, and then he took Zalith's hand. When he stood up, though, his body immediately reminded him of earlier. A slow, deep pull settled in his lower half, a tight, lingering strain that made his breath stutter as his muscles adjusted to the weight of standing. His legs threatened to buckle for a fraction of a second, a faint tremor running through them, and he had to grip Zalith's hand tighter than he meant to.

The shift in position sent a warm, wet sensation sliding lower, the unmistakable evidence of his mate's climax still inside him. He exhaled sharply, his body reflexively clenching again, unsure whether it was to hold onto the feeling or to recover from it.

A faint burn lingered at his core, not painful, just ever-present, ensuring he didn't forget how deeply Zalith had stretched him open. Every slight adjustment sent an aftershock of sensation through him, his movements slower than usual, not from injury, but from the sheer thoroughness of his mate's attention.

The demon squeezed his hand, steadying him, his dark eyes glinting with something smug, something wicked. "Need a moment?" he teased.

Alucard gave him a half-hearted glare, but it was ruined by the way his fingers tightened involuntarily around Zalith's grip, his body still adjusting, still remembering. "…Shut up," he muttered, shifting his weight carefully, pretending he wasn't enjoying the feeling just a little too much.

Zalith chuckled, and then he began slowly leading Alucard through the castle.

The first step was the worst. The moment Alucard's legs moved, a deep ache pulsed between them, the unmistakable throb of being mercilessly fucked. His insides felt well-used, gaped beyond what should be possible, every motion sending a dull, lingering soreness rippling through him. It wasn't pain—it was the kind of ache that made his breath stammer, the kind that carried heat, memory, and something far more sinful.

Each step forced more of Zalith's cum to trickle lower, slicking the inside of his thighs, an undeniable, filthy reminder of just how deep the demon had been. The sensation made him tense, his muscles clenching, fluttering around nothing, desperate for a fullness that was suddenly gone.

His stride was stilted, hesitant, and he knew Zalith was watching.

The demon's grin grew, his grip on Alucard's hand just firm enough to keep him steady but teasing enough to remind him that he was observing every reaction. "Still feeling me?" he murmured, his voice smug.

Alucard huffed, glaring ahead, but he couldn't hide the way his hips stuttered mid-step, his body still adjusting to the absence of the thick strain that he had surrendered to.

He should have been embarrassed, but this time, he wasn't.

The sting, the wetness, the slow, deep pull that made his body crave something it had just been given—it was intoxicating. Even as he walked, even as exhaustion settled deep in his limbs, he couldn't help but relish the soreness, savour the reminder.

And Zalith could see it all.

"You're quiet," the demon mused, his thumb brushing over the back of Alucard's hand. "Enjoying yourself?"

Alucard pouted, but the way his fingers tightened in Zalith's grip betrayed him. "Maybe," he mumbled.

Zalith only laughed, leading him further into the castle, and Alucard hated how much he wanted to be ruined all over again.

But the vampire was curious, and he wasn't afraid to ask, "'Ow come you 'aven't fucked me like zhat bevore?"

The demon chuckled again, taking him into the dining room. "Because before, it would have probably put you in a coma," he said with a smirk. "You've got more energy while you're in heat—enough that I don't have to hold back as much."

Alucard nodded in understanding. He sat down—and he regretted it right away.

The moment he sank into the seat, a deep, lingering pressure flared between his legs. His already tender muscles slowly adjusted, and the weight of sitting forced a slow, obscene twinge deeper inside him.

He couldn't stifle a pleased but tired groan.

He could still feel everything—the ghost of Zalith's dick, the way his body had been held open for so long, the dull, stretched sensation refusing to fade. Even worse, the shift in position pressed his thighs together, soaking them further with his mate's cum, still leaking from him in slow, lazy drips.

Alucard's fingers gripped the armrest firmer, his thighs twitching, but it only made the feeling worse, deeper, more maddening.

Zalith watched him adjust and react in ways he couldn't hide. Alucard knew that look, knew the wicked amusement gleaming in those dark eyes.

"Comfortable?" his mate drawled, clearly far too pleased with himself.

Alucard glared in warning, but his attempt at composure was already ruined by the way his body refused to cooperate—by the way he shivered faintly, settling deeper into the chair even as his body protested. "Stop," he muttered, heat curling up his spine.

Zalith grinned at him.

He wasn't going to let this go, was he?

The staff door then opened, and two cooks walked in with their dinner. They silently placed two plates on the table, bowed humbly, and left.

Alucard looked down at his food—steak, potatoes, and other vegetables.

Zalith poured him a glass of wine.

"Vank you," he said and took a sip.

"How was your day?" his mate asked as he cut his steak.

Alucard shrugged, but the simple movement sent a fresh, unwelcome awareness through him. The warmth between his legs had only spread, the sticky heat trapped against his skin, soaking deeper into the fabric of his trousers. It wasn't just a faint trickle anymore—it was noticeable, thick, and every shift of his hips only pressed the dampness further into him.

He swallowed hard, forcing himself to sit still, to act normal, but how could he when every second reminded him of what Zalith had left inside him? His hole still felt open, a constant, aching throb, and now, with the way he was sitting, his thighs pressed together just enough to make the leaking worse.

"Vine," he muttered, willing his voice to sound even.

Zalith hummed, slicing into his steak, as if he wasn't sitting beside him, fully aware of the mess pooling between Alucard's legs.

He knew.

Of course he knew.

The demon's eyes flicked to him, just briefly, just enough for Alucard to catch the glint of amusement beneath his lashes. "Are you sure?" he asked, taking a bite, chewing leisurely, as if this wasn't absolute torture.

Alucard stiffened, fighting the urge to shift, to do anything that might make the dampness more obvious. "I said I'm vine," he repeated, sharper this time.

Zalith's lips curled, far too entertained. "...Good," he murmured, cutting another piece of steak like he didn't just make the air between them ten times heavier.

The vampire ate one of his potatoes, trying to focus on his food. "I Dignivied zhe vampires I told you about, and I 'ave each coven capturing 'umans vor me to turn."

That was when his mate's smirk faded, and he donned a concerned frown. "That's a lot of vampires, Alucard—that's a lot of your *blood*."

"I know, but I need Day Valkers. Zhey can't stop zhis Silver Claw if zhey can't be avound during zhe day." He could *still* feel cum oozing from his ass. How much had Zalith came? It felt as if he'd fucked and came in him at least four or five times—perhaps more.

Thinking about it wasn't helping.

"Well, when you do it, can I come with you? I want to be there so that you can have my blood to make up for what you lose," Zalith offered.

He wasn't going to say no. "Okay," he said, glancing at him. "'Ow vas your day?"

"Well, I went to see Syllia. I gave her three prisoners for her ritual, and she seemed happy with the supply list that I showed her, so I'm going to join the demons I'm sending tomorrow to drop everything off."

Alucard frowned. "Vhy do you need to go?"

"Syllia asked me to be there. I wanted to say no, but I don't want to upset her."

The vampire pouted. He knew that Syllia was no threat, but he couldn't help but feel aggravated. That woman wanted *his* mate, and he wanted to be there to protect and claim him, but he knew that would only make things tense—it might even ruin the alliance that Zalith was in the process of completing.

He sighed deeply, his chest rising, his body tightening ever so slightly—and *of course*, the movement made his body clench instinctively, a slow, involuntary flutter that sent a fresh pulse of warmth trickling lower. His breath caught for just a second, his thighs pressing together as the wetness pooled further, seeping into the fabric beneath him.

Fuck.

It wasn't just the wet heat that made his muscles tense—it was the awareness of it, the way his body still felt open, too used to hold anything in.

A slow, unwanted shiver crept up his spine, his grip on the table flexing subtly as his pulse thudded in his ears. He shifted just a fraction, but it only made it worse—the damp fabric clung to his skin, and another faint pulse of liquid warmth followed.

Zalith chuckled.

Alucard didn't have to look at him to know that his mate had noticed everything.

"Something wrong?" the demon teased.

Alucard's fingers tightened against the table's edge.

He was going to kill him.

"Stop," he grumbled and ate some of his steak.

After another quiet laugh, Zalith said, "We have the city celebration on the thirtieth. We don't have to be there the entire time, but we should make an appearance."

Alucard nodded. "Do ve 'ave to make a speech?"

"No, but I'll say *something*. That's what good City Lords do, right?" he said with a smirk. "Something about how we'll take care of them and their city—we should mention that we've formed an alliance with the Yrudyen Elves, too. That'll make them feel a lot safer. I'm hoping to do something about the Orrivain Elves before the celebration; I'm going to ask Syllia for more information on them tomorrow."

"Vhat about Desmond? Did you deal vith 'im?"

"I didn't have him killed because the city would suspect that it was us after his little tantrum outside Cecil's home, but I did have him thrown in one of the holding cells at the sheriff's station for a few days."

"'E's probably not zhe only vone who vinks like zhat."

"That's my worry. I know how quickly ideology like that can spread. I've got people keeping watch for others, though. I won't let it spread."

"And Desmond?"

"I'll have someone try to educate him, but if he doesn't want to accept the way Eimwood is changing, we'll look into sending him somewhere else."

Alucard shrugged and said, "Or ve turn 'im into a non-'uman. 'E'll 'ave no choice but to accept vings zhen."

"We *could*, but that might scare the people into thinking that anyone who disagrees with us will be turned into one of us," the demon said and sipped from his wine.

He wasn't wrong. "Vell, I guess zhe best ve can do is vatch 'im."

"For now."

"Mm-hmm," he responded. He then tried to think of something else to say, but he couldn't focus anymore—he'd been hanging on by a thread, and now he was losing his grip.

The simmering, ever-present hum beneath his exhaustion was stirring. What had once been a simple reminder of what Zalith had done to him was now an unbearable tease, a slow, insidious kindling of something deeper, something desperate. He fidgeted slightly, testing it, and felt another slow trickle of cum slide lower, soaking further into the fabric clinging to his thighs.

Alucard could feel the demon's eyes flick to him; he could feel the amusement rolling off him in waves, but Zalith didn't say anything.

That made it worse.

His focus continued to fray, his thoughts growing hazy, heavy, sinking into the way his body throbbed. His hole still felt loose, it still ached faintly from earlier, and the more he sat there, the more he became painfully aware of how empty he was.

It wasn't fair.

His mate had ravaged him, completely and thoroughly, and now his body was selling him out to his instincts, to *Zalith*, craving more, craving to be filled again. His thighs pressed together, but it didn't help. If anything, it only made it worse; the soaked fabric rubbed against his skin, the wet heat pressing exactly where he didn't need it. He exhaled slowly, trying to steady himself, but his focus was unravelling with every passing second.

He needed Zalith.

And judging by the way the demon had been watching him this whole time, Zalith already knew.

"Fuck me again," the vampire demanded, but it was more like a helpless plea.

Zalith smirked. "I thought you'd never ask."

And his mate didn't hesitate.

Strong hands gripped Alucard's wrist, pulling him up from the table, guiding him away from the dim glow of the dining room. Zalith took him through the corridors, his pace unhurried, but his grip firm—*possessive*. Alucard's breath was already shallow, his pulse already racing, the anticipation curling tight in his gut as they disappeared into the shadows.

And when the bedroom door closed behind them, when Zalith's lips crashed against his own, when rough, eager hands tore away his clothing piece by piece—

He knew that he was about to be ruined all over again.

Chapter Six

The Yrudyen Treaty

| Zalith—Wednesday, Tertium 29th, 960(TG) |
| Uzlia Isles, Usrul, Castle Reiner |

Birdsong, sunlight…and Alucard's captivating scent. Zalith pressed his lips against the sleeping vampire's neck and inhaled softly—that was all it took for his body to tense, for desire to enthral him. He wanted to wake him up, he wanted to claim him despite how many times he'd let himself get carried away last night. He shouldn't, though. Not only did he not want to disturb his fiancé's sleep or exhaust him, but he also had to get up and get down to the docks. He had work to do.

He lingered for a moment, inhaling the scent, letting his body react. But when he was teetering on the edge of his control, he forced himself away from Alucard and to the end of the bed. Silently, he got up and headed into the bathroom. He showered quickly, brushed his teeth and combed his hair, and then he got dressed. Before he left the room, he kissed Alucard's forehead, resisting the urge to act on his desires.

Zalith made his way downstairs and to the entrance hall—

"Sir," came Edwin's voice.

As he slipped his shoes on, Zalith looked at the butler. "What?"

"Sabazios has left three raccoons on the porch."

He grimaced. "Raccoons?"

"Yes, sir."

The demon sighed deeply. "Just get rid of them." He grabbed his coat.

"We have tried, sir, but he refuses to let anybody near them."

With another deep sigh, Zalith shook his head. "Wait until Alucard wakes up and tell him. If he doesn't get up before I get home, I'll deal with it."

The butler nodded. "Your briefcase is here, sir," he then said—he went into the waiting room and came back out with Zalith's black leather briefcase. He handed it to him and said, "Have a good day, sir."

"Thanks," he muttered, pulling his coat on before he took the case.

Then, Edwin walked off.

"Raccoons," Zalith grumbled under his breath before he huffed and rolled his eyes—he didn't want to think about a pile of dead rodents right now. He left the castle, adorned his demon form, and then he took off, racing towards the Eimwood docks.

When he reached them and landed, his wings and horns swiftly crumbling away, he set his eyes on Basilan, who was working with five of Greymore's wolves and three demons to load crates and materials onto a trade ship. "Progress report?" he asked, walking to them.

"Oh, sir," Basilan said, turning to face him while the others continued working. "We're almost ready to go; we're just loading the last of the food."

Zalith nodded and watched each of the werewolves. Persis, Abner, Wiley, Letha, and Adelia; they were good picks, some of Greymore's best guards—or Etas, as they were called in Aegisguard, and Letha was their commander... or Epsilon; everyone was still getting used to the way things worked here, Zalith included—and they weren't bad fighters, either. "You all know why you're here, yes?" he called.

"We do, sir," Letha replied, and the others nodded. "We won't let you down."

With a half nod, Zalith made his way up onto the ship. The first thing he did was scan over the crates, stacks of materials, and wagons, making sure that everything was there, and then he went up onto the quarterdeck, where the captain was waiting. "How long is it going to take to get around to the Yrudyen Village?"

"About thirty minutes, give or take. This ship is low enough to fit under the Yrudberg-Usrul Bridge, which shaves down on time massively," the captain explained. "The tides are looking pretty calm between the shore and the Aestrael Curve, too."

"Good," the demon said, and then he headed back down the steps.

When he got into the cabin, Zalith sat at the table and took the papers from his briefcase. He read over the treaty he'd written, ensuring that it included everything he and Syllia had agreed to. Every time the Orrivain Elves were mentioned, though, he was reminded of how important it was to get as much information about them as possible. The city celebration was tomorrow, and he'd rather deal with them before that happened because if *he* were an enemy of the city and the elves who had allied with it, he'd use the noise and commotion of the celebration to attack, especially since the festivities were bound to stretch into the night.

The ship started moving, and Zalith glanced at his pocket watch. They'd be there just past 8:30 a.m.—maybe he'd be home in time to be at Alucard's side when he woke; he knew that his fiancé preferred it that way, and so did he.

A knock came at the door.

"What?" he called, leaning back in his seat.

The door opened, and Letha stepped in. "Is it okay if I ask you a few questions about the assignment, sir?"

He didn't have anything better to do, so he nodded.

"Basilan was a little vague—well, he didn't know much."

"Did he tell you that you'd be guarding the Yrudyen Village?"

"He did, sir. But we're not exactly sure what we're guarding them from," Letha said.

"Another clan of elves," he replied. "The Orrivain. All we know at the moment is that they prefer to attack at night. When we reach the Yrudyen, though, we'll know more. The Yrudyen Queen requested werewolves; it doesn't feel like a matter of preference or belief, so I believe that the Orrivain may be susceptible to werewolves."

She nodded. "Understood, sir. What about hunting? Are we allowed to find food in those forests?"

"Another thing to ask when we get there."

Letha tilted her head in understanding.

"Anything else?"

She replied, "We've come up with alternating shifts, and I wanted to get your approval—changes can be made, of course—and in light of the Orrivain attacking at night, I'm going to alter things now."

"Tell me," Zalith said.

"I'll be on the night shift with Persis and Abner—we're the best night spotters. Wiley and Adelia will be on the day shift. I'm very flexible, too, so if we need to up our defences at any point during the day, I can join them."

"What about sleep?" the demon questioned. "If you don't get enough of it, you'll get sloppy."

"I've trained extensively for years, sir. I assure you that I can focus just as well as any other wolf with half the amount of rest."

Zalith didn't doubt her, and she wasn't lying either; her pulse was steady, and her mind was clear. "All right," he responded. "And time to hunt?"

"Wiley is our best hunter. When he hunts, I'll take over his shift."

The demon nodded. "Protecting this village is a very large part of this treaty. If you ever need backup—even for the smallest thing—you ask for it. Understood?"

"Of course, sir."

"You're allowed to use the izurets to contact me or Greymore." He took a piece of paper from his briefcase and held it out to her. "This is what you say when you want to summon one. You tell it what you want it to say and to whom, and it will deliver your message promptly."

Letha took the piece of paper. "Thank you, sir."

"Go," he then said dismissively.

Obediently, Letha turned around and left, closing the door behind her.

With a quiet sigh, Zalith looked back down at the treaty papers. He couldn't stop wondering: were the Orrivain the only other elves out there? The Yrudyen mountains stretched endlessly, and the surrounding forests were vast, dense enough to swallow entire cities. Then there was the Aestrael Curve, that jagged crescent of unmapped peaks shielding Uzlia from Avalmoor's brutal seas, harsh winds…and prying eyes. A natural wall. A perfect place to disappear.

He hadn't forgotten about the Aestrael Shards, either, dozens of floating islands hovering over the sea that separated the Curve from the rest of Uzlia.

Alucard had scoured these isles thoroughly before settling on Uzlia, long before Nefastus fell. But even his meticulous searches had limits. Elves could be elusive. Some could mask their auras. Others could suppress scent, even silence their own heartbeat. If Alucard hadn't found the Orrivain…it meant they were strong.

The question was, though, *how* strong?

He tapped his fingers on the desk, listening to the calming waves outside clashing with the quiet chatter of the crew and werewolves. As the thought of elves and the treaty faded from his mind, all he could focus on was Alucard. But it wasn't the alluring scent or desperate need to have sex with him. He missed him. He wanted to hold him, he wanted to listen to his heartbeat, and he wanted to feel his skin against his own. Maybe he *should* have woken him up…maybe he should have invited him along.

However, he was sure that his vampire knew as well as he did that Syllia's flirting would upset him. The last thing they needed was for her to say something that Alucard simply couldn't ignore—and Zalith wouldn't blame him. The Yrudyen Queen had waltzed past one too many boundaries already. But Zalith had the strength to put up with it. He was used to that sort of attention, after all, even from women.

Thinking about Alucard made his thoughts shift to his fiancé's predicaments. The Silver Claw? A professional vampire hunter. He knew that Alucard could handle himself, but Zalith couldn't help but worry, especially since his fiancé would soon be giving up so much of his blood to create new Fledgelings. Alucard had agreed to let him go with him, though, so he'd do everything in his power to protect him and ensure that he was comfortable and healthy.

With a deep exhale, he leaned back in his seat again and watched the sunrise through the round window, preparing himself for another session of flirting, smiling, and cleavage being shoved in his face. The sky was a wash of molten gold and soft amber, streaked with the lingering remains of night, its deep indigos and violets retreating behind the growing light. The first rays of sunlight glinted off the water's surface, scattering like fractured glass, illuminating the mist that still clung to the waves.

The steady chug of the steamship's engine rumbled beneath him; outside, the hiss of steam mixed with the distant cries of gulls, their sharp calls cutting through the crisp morning air. The smell of salt and damp iron clung to everything, the scent of the open sea mingling with the faint traces of coal smoke curling from the ship's stack.

From somewhere on the deck, footsteps rang against the planks, accompanied by the occasional low murmur of crewmen conversing in hushed voices, their words carried away by the sea breeze. The faint scent of strong coffee drifted from below deck, mixing with the lingering remnants of last night's oil and the damp musk of old wood.

Coffee sounded good right now… but he'd have breakfast with Alucard when he got home. His fingers tapped idly against the armrest of his chair, his thoughts still focused on both his vampire and the treaty. This was peaceful, different from the chaos of the city, from the ever-present tension of command, from the weight of expectation. He just wished that his fiancé was sitting beside him. He'd give anything to hear his voice… even for just a moment. But when he focused and tried to speak into Alucard's mind, there was only silence. He was still asleep.

Zalith smiled softly. His vampire slept so much; it was adorable.

The ship then started slowing.

Zalith glanced over his shoulder, looking out the small window on the door. The island loomed in the distance, its golden cliffs and dense forests taking shape in the morning light. Soon, he would disembark, and Syllia was sure to throw a flurry of seductive words and flirty smiles his way.

With a quiet sigh, he rolled his eyes and slipped his papers back into his briefcase; he snapped it shut and pushed to his feet. The air outside was cooler now, tinged with the briny scent of the sea. As he stepped out of the cabin, the ship creaked beneath him, slowing as it neared an old wooden dock.

Five elves stood waiting on the platform, bows in hand, their postures rigid. His gaze flicked over them, but he barely needed to search. He could feel her eyes on him. Tianel. She was already watching, assessing. And a moment later, she lowered her goggles and signalled to the others. They hesitated, but at her silent command, their hands relaxed on their weapons, tension easing just slightly.

"We're about to dock now," the captain called over the hum of the engine.

Zalith strode to the edge of the ship, his fingers resting against the railing as the vessel glided nearer to the platform, the waves lapping against the hull in rhythmic, muted slaps. The dock was worn, warped by time and neglect, its wooden beams groaning under the shifting weight of the tide.

As the crew descended, ropes in hand, they moved swiftly, securing the ship to the moorings. The platform creaked under the pressure, old planks straining as they settled, not reassuring, but at least it held.

Zalith exhaled, rolling his shoulders. It was time to move.

"We'll start unloading everything, sir," Basilan called, and then he shouted to everyone else, "Let's get those wagons down!"

The demon walked over to Taniel. "Is Queen Syllia ready to receive us?"

Taniel nodded. "Her Radiance is waiting for you in her jewel room."

"They'll bring the supplies," he said, glancing back at Basilan and the werewolves. "I'll meet with her now."

"Of course," she said and then turned to the other elves. "Stay here and help them with the supplies."

The five of them nodded and headed to the ship.

"This way," Taniel said, walking into the woods.

Zalith followed, the damp earth giving slightly under him. The forest was dense and alive, a world of twisting roots and sprawling canopies that filtered the golden morning light into slanted beams. Through the gaps in the trees, he saw the village, woven seamlessly into the forest. From this distance, he heard the far murmur of voices, the rhythmic drumming of something ceremonial, and the wind weaving through the treetops like a whispered song.

The path shifted, the forest floor becoming smoother, lined with worn stone and intricate wooden carvings tucked into the roots of ancient trees. His demon form took shape as he stepped into the village; Taniel led him to the massive oak, past the throne, and into the room filled with treasures.

Syllia was sitting in front of a mirror, brushing her hair and admiring the diamond pendant that Zalith and Alucard had given her. And then her eyes moved, landing on Zalith in the mirror.

"Silas," she said pleasantly, turning to face him. "That will be all, Taniel."

With a nod, Taniel left.

Syllia stood up and gracefully strode towards him. "I was beginning to think that you'd forgotten about me."

Zalith smiled and said, "Of course not. I was merely working hard to write out the alliance details." He gestured to one of the tables crafted from roots. "May I?"

She nodded.

He placed his briefcase on the table and opened it. "I've also sent five very capable werewolves to guard your village; they're down at the dock unloading your supplies."

Syllia glided closer. "So, that gives us some time alone," she said seductively.

Zalith did his best not to roll his eyes and turned to face her. "I was hoping you'd tell me more about the Orrivain Elves," he said, trying to change the subject.

She gazed at him for a moment, as if she was pondering, and then she returned to her seat and leaned back, spreading her legs. "What do you want to know?"

"Everything. We all need to be prepared for them."

"Hmm..." she murmured. "Well, you know that they dwell on the mountain peaks. During the day, they retreat into caverns to wait out the sunlight. They use vargr to guard their settlement and the border of their territory, which is exactly where the ice meets the grass. They use ethos to keep their land under snow."

"And when this treaty is signed, how soon will they hear of it?"

"The Orrivain have messengers in the forests—birds mostly. They will likely hear of it by the end of the week."

With a quiet sigh, Zalith took the treaty papers out of the case, and then he walked over to Syllia. "You'll need to read over this and tell me if everything is as it should be. If it is, we'll both sign three copies—one for you, one for me, and one for the city."

She took the papers from him, brushing his hand with her fingers and smiling at him. "The Orrivain are smart," she continued, glancing down at the papers. "Not only have they manipulated the people of Eimwood into thinking that *we* have carried out every one of their sieges, murders, etcetera, but they have also blamed murders and livestock mutilations on animals. See, their most powerful can hide their tracks *extraordinarily* well—their auras, too. Of course, they can't change their appearance, so if you were to see one, you'd know. But no type of sensory ethos can detect them." She smiled at him again. "It's a good thing you demons have such keen sight, isn't it?"

Great. Undetectable enemies were annoying as fuck, but Zalith had eyes just about everywhere. His people were prepared, and so was he.

Syllia went on, "In Eimwood, the Orrivain are just stories, elves who supposedly died out when our kind were kicked out of the city and forced to retreat to the land of our ancestors." She looked up at Zalith. "Their leader, Moonwarden Calitharion, is a very bitter man," she said, reading the treaty. "And he is *very* old. His family built the very foundations of Eimwood; he was alive when Khila and Aresphis were of this world."

Zalith exhaled deeply and nodded.

"You know of them?" she asked, flipping to the next page.

"I do. Your God and the serpent."

Syllia giggled. "You know about our history?"

"I studied what I could find."

"Well, here is something that the history books won't tell you." She looked up at him again. "When humans began emigrating here, the elf clans were hostile and reluctant to share their land. But Khila saw merit in the humans. He allowed them a plot of land, where they built the old farm on the outskirts of the forest. Moonwarden Calitharion didn't agree with Khila's vision, and it isn't fact—more of a superstition—but many elves believe that Moonwarden Calitharion conspired with Aresphis to destroy Khila, and *that* is why he and his clan hide up in the mountains—*shame*, and the humiliation of defeat." She stopped reading. "Of course, we *all* resent the humans for taking Eimwood, but if one were to look at it from the outside of all of this, they'd see that a lot of the elves *left* Eimwood of their own accord, and in their absence, the humans moved in—in fact, Khila invited them in when Aresphis began slaughtering them, and that's another reason why many believe that the Orrivain sided with him."

Zalith frowned skeptically. "Forgive me, but you and your people don't seem very fond of humans, either."

"I never said that we were," the queen giggled. "Cecil allowed us to pillage—in fact, he welcomed it."

That was something Zalith didn't know. "Welcomed it?"

"He kept his rich friends rich and the poor people poor; he scared those who didn't follow him into relying on him, using us as their common enemy. We benefitted from it, of course, but we lost people. *Your* arrangement removes the risk of losing my people, and yours." She held out a hand. "I assume you have a pen?"

Zalith took his pen from his pocket and handed it to her.

"Do you have a plan?" she asked, signing the treaty.

"For?"

"The Orrivain." She handed him the papers and the pen back.

"I do," he lied and signed the papers, too. He may not have one yet, but now that he had some more information, he could come up with something. "Do you have the exact location of their settlement?" he asked as he took out the other two copies and signed them before giving them to her.

"Starborne Ridge," she replied, signing them before leaning back in her seat again. "You'll be crossing into dangerous territory, though. There are a lot of wild things out there." She handed one copy back to Zalith.

"What kind of wild things?" he asked.

"Vargrs, gremlins, sprites, pixies…" she listed, pondering. "Arieto graze out there sometimes, and we've seen some oxaldia, which aren't particularly dangerous, but wolves hunt them."

Zalith nodded, retaining it all. He didn't know where exactly Starborne Ridge was, though. "Do you happen to have a map of the forests and mountains? Something we can use to find the Orrivain."

Syllia hesitated. "Any map we possess wouldn't only show you to the Orrivain."

"You have my word that it will only be used to find them. I'll be the only person who lays eyes on it, and once the problem is solved, I'll return it," he said firmly.

She tapped her fingers on the vanity beside her, a long silence falling between them. "What about your *really* good friend, Ezra?"

"He has his own business to tend to, but on the occasion that I need his help with this matter, you can trust him with the map, too. All either of us wants is to protect the entirety of Uzlia. If we can make a deal with the Orrivain, then—"

Syllia laughed, cutting him off. "Oh, you won't get very far proposing a deal, Silas of Eimwood. Those elves want nothing to do with anyone; all they want to do is remove every human from the isles and anyone who associates with them."

"Still, I'll try," he said. "I'd rather offer them a chance before wiping them out."

"Then all I can do is wish you luck." She got up and headed over to a crate beside a stack of gold. She reached inside and pulled out a large piece of rolled-up parchment. "This is the map of our forest, the mountains, and the woods beyond our territory. It will show you the way to Starborne Ridge, and it will help you avoid treacherous areas." As she sat down, she handed him the parchment.

Zalith took it from her. "Thank you."

And then she smirked at him. "You're not leaving already, are you?"

"I have to make preparations for the Orrivain issue," he said with a smile. "The sooner I find and deal with them, the better—for everyone's sake."

She stared at him briefly before turning and looking into her mirror. "Do you ever rest, Silas?" she asked curiously.

"Not while there's work to be done," he replied with a small laugh.

Syllia giggled and said, "Well, once the Orrivain are dealt with, I hope that you'll spare me some of your free time."

He didn't want to agree because he knew exactly what she wanted from him, but if he said no, would she attempt to back out of the alliance? "We'll see," he said with a half smirk. "Basilan will be here momentarily with the supplies," he then said—he could hear the wagons approaching. "He'll stay here with the werewolves until everything is unpacked, and he'll take a new supply request list from you."

"Wonderful," she said contently. "So, I'll see you soon."

Zalith nodded. "In the meantime, if you need anything, you can contact me through any of the werewolves or through your own means."

"Thank you," the queen replied.

He tucked the treaty papers back into his briefcase, closed it, and held it in his free hand, still holding the rolled-up map. "I'll keep you updated, too."

She smirked at him in the mirror. "Good luck with Starborne Ridge."

Zalith headed for the door, dreading that Syllia might call him back before he could leave, but to his relief, she didn't. He let out a quiet sigh of relief and made his way over to the arriving wagons.

"Everything's here, sir—well, mostly. The rest is coming," Basilan said, gesturing towards the path that the last of the wagons were on.

"Stay here until everything is unloaded, and then take down a list of what they want next," he ordered.

"Of course, sir. Should I bring the list to you?"

"Send an izuret with it."

"Understood."

Zalith then flapped his wings once, propelling himself into the sky. The treaty was signed, and he'd gathered some helpful information on the Orrivain Elves. Now, all he wanted was to get home and spend some time with his fiancé.

Chapter Seven

Map

| **Alucard** |
| *Uzlia Isles, Usrul, Castle Reiner* |

When Alucard woke, he groaned quietly; his head ached, and his body felt sore. He wasn't surprised, though. He'd asked Zalith not to take the ache away this time—he didn't regret that part; what he *did* regret was letting himself get so carried away. Even the increased energy that being in heat gave him was gone, and he didn't know how long it would take for him to recover.

He rolled onto his back and stared up at the ceiling. Something shifted in the corner of his eye, and when he looked over there, he saw an izuret sitting on the couch and kicking its feet with a tiny cup of what smelled like tea in its hands.

How long had it been there?

"Vhat?" he grumbled.

The izuret put the cup onto the table beside the couch, jumped up, and floated over. When it landed on Alucard's nightstand, it told him that Freja had received confirmation from the Veylin Pack, Grimholt Pack, Cinderfell Pack, and Othros Pack that they were willing to meet on the specified date in his DeiganLupus estate.

"Good. Tell 'er to get zhem zhere vor noon—but go to Vasmus virst; she vill need 'im to get 'er zhere; only 'e knows zhe vay."

With a nod, the izuret disappeared.

Alucard sighed and dragged his hand over his face. He glanced around the room, but Zalith was nowhere to be seen—he was probably still with the Yrudyen Elves.

The thought of Syllia made him snarl. She was definitely flirting with his fiancé right now. Thinking about it wasn't going to help at all, though. So he got up and headed into the bathroom. After brushing his teeth, he lazily climbed into the shower; although the falling water did help, it didn't take away the pain in his head.

Maybe blood would help. He had to wait for Zalith to get home for that.

He wouldn't have to wait long, though. When he climbed out of the shower, he heard footsteps coming up the stairs. After wrapping a towel around his waist, he stood in the doorway and watched Zalith step into the bedroom.

"Oh, hey," the demon said with a smirk.

Alucard smiled, and of course, his body immediately pleaded that he give in to desire, but his eyes flicked from Zalith's face to the large piece of rolled-up parchment in his left hand. "Vhat's zhat?"

"A map of Yrudberg," he said as he placed it on the bed. "It should help us find the Orrivain settlement," he added as he walked towards him.

The vampire's smile grew when Zalith reached him and gripped his waist, pulling him closer. "And vhen are ve doing zhat?"

He shrugged. "Well, if we don't have anything planned for today, I thought we might as well get it out of the way. Once we know where they are and what their numbers and defences are, we can make plans."

Alucard nodded. "Okay."

"First, though…" his mate drawled, easing one hand into his towel.

The moment Zalith's fingers brushed over his crotch, Alucard tensed up, but the pain in his head throbbed. He groaned with a grimace, leaning forward and resting his head on the demon's shoulder. "I zon't vink I should," he murmured—the words felt like glass leaving his mouth.

"Are you okay?" Zalith asked worriedly.

"I 'ave a 'eadache," he grumbled.

"Do you want blood?"

"If zhat's okay."

"Of course it's okay," his mate said, caressing his hair, and once Alucard lifted his head, the demon kissed his lips a single time before tilting his head to the side and pulling his shirt collar away.

Alucard nuzzled into the curve of Zalith's neck, inhaling deeply, letting his mate's scent enthral him, feed his need, and fuel the growing hunger. It was exhilarating. Bergamot's crisp brightness, sandalwood's deep warmth, and the clean, earthy trace of white sage—a captivating blend, something uniquely Zalith, something only his.

For a moment, he simply breathed him in, relishing the tension beneath his skin and the anticipation thrumming between them… until he finally bit. His fangs sank in slowly, carefully piercing Zalith's skin. His mate flinched—just slightly—but then exhaled a low, quiet moan, his hands smoothing down Alucard's back, welcoming the bite, pressing closer.

And *the blood.*

It rushed over Alucard's tongue, thick, rich, impossibly warm. He groaned softly, his lashes fluttering as he swallowed the first slow mouthful, letting it slide down his throat, sinking into his body like liquid fire. The taste—it was always intoxicating. Dark honey and slow-burning spice, edged with something potent, something ancient, something he still didn't have words for years after first tasting it; there was a depth to it, a power humming beneath the surface, the taste of pure energy demanding to be claimed. Perhaps being in heat made the taste more intense—his senses were alight, after all, and it was quickly devouring him, sinking into his limbs, racing through his veins as his body absorbed it almost immediately, loosening every tension, soothing every ache.

Relief.

Blissful, overwhelming relief.

He let himself drink deeper, savouring every drop, each swallow drawing a low, satisfied hum from his throat. It was heady, rich, wholly consuming. And he didn't want to stop.

But he had to. He wasn't going to let the enthralling taste control him.

After another gulp—no…just one more…and half another—he pulled his fangs free and licked them and his lips, a satisfied hum upon his exhale. "You taste so good," he murmured and dragged his tongue over the puncture wounds, which healed just enough to stop the bleeding.

Zalith laughed softly as he pulled Alucard's body against his and leaned his back against the wall. "Your venom *feels* so good," he replied, stroking Alucard's hair.

With a curious smile, Alucard asked, "Vhat does veel like?"

"Hmm…" he pondered, gazing into the vampire's eyes, rolling his shoulders as if trying to shake off the lingering effect of his bite. He then tilted his head, smirking at Alucard as he considered his answer. "It's…." He paused, closing his eyes with a pleased groan. "It's fucking overwhelming, is what it is."

Alucard pressed his forehead against Zalith's.

But his mate wasn't finished. "It's like fire spreading through my veins, but instead of burning me, it consumes me. It doesn't just settle in my body—it sinks deeper." His voice dropped, a rough edge creeping in. "Like it's touching every inch of my existence." His fingers flexed slightly against Alucard's waist. "And it doesn't just feel good, Alucard. It feels…unnatural, like something I shouldn't be able to feel, but I do; it's like I could drown in it if I let myself. And there's something about *you*, too."

He frowned slightly, intrigued. "Vhat about me?"

"I don't know. I've experienced both a vampire's bite and a demon's, but neither of them are quite like yours—everything is amplified, and I feel hyperaware of every single nerve in my body just before the euphoria takes over." He chuckled softly, but there was something almost dangerous behind it. "It's addictive."

For some reason, that flustered Alucard. He knew that Zalith enjoyed his bite, that he relished the way he fed only from him, but hearing him describe it so intricately— so *reverently*—made something in him stir, twist, and fold in on itself.

Shyness. That was what it was. Unexpected, strange. Maybe because he wasn't used to being praised like this. Not in a way that felt genuine, not in a way that wasn't meant to shape him, control him, mould him into something for someone else's pleasure. Zalith wasn't just tolerating it. He wasn't just indulging him. He wanted it. He enjoyed it. And Alucard wasn't sure what to do with that.

"Veally?" he asked, his voice unintentionally hushed.

His fiancé nodded, gazing into his eyes as he dragged his thumb along Alucard's bottom lip. "I don't just feel it, I *crave* it. Every inch of me wants more, even after it's gone. It makes me want to lose myself in you completely."

Alucard smiled away the fluster. "I veel like zhat vhen I drvink your blood."

Zalith smirked at him. "You can have as much as you want."

"Mm, zon't tempt me," he teased, stroking his fingers over the wound, making Zalith tilt his head back and groan quietly in delight. "But ve 'ave vork to do, no?"

The demon huffed before setting his eyes back on him. "Yeah."

"I'll get dressed, and zhen ve can—"

"I want to watch you," Zalith interjected, smirking again.

The fluster returned…but Alucard didn't want to say no. Not this time. "You can vatch," he murmured.

"Lead the way, vampire," his mate said lowly.

Alucard took hold of the demon's hand and went back into the bathroom. He pulled the towel from around his waist, dried off the rest of his damp body, and grabbed another towel to dry his hair. Feeling Zalith's eyes on him made him nervous, but he didn't cave; he pulled his clothes on, and then he combed his hair.

"Is zhe plan just to vind vhere zhe Orrivain Elves are 'oled up?" he asked as he put the comb down.

"For now, yeah," the demon said with a nod. "I don't know how many of them there are, so I don't want to risk there being hundreds of them and it's just us."

"Zhat's true." He tucked his hair behind his ears. "Did you eat breakfast?"

"Not yet. I'll grab something in the city, though; I need to drop off Eimwood's copy of the Yrudyen treaty."

Alucard then followed Zalith out of the bathroom and over to their bed. He watched as the demon unrolled the parchment, revealing the map of Yrudberg. The forests and mountains were *very* detailed; dangers and risks were marked—specific animal territories, old traps, paths that were intentionally there to get intruders lost. It was typical elf terrain.

"Syllia said that the Orrivain are on the Starborne Ridge. They use vargrs to guard their territory borders and settlement, and the forest is apparently home to gremlins and pixies…and sprites," Zalith explained, dragging his fingers over the forest.

"Vell, ve can't vly over zhe mountain because zhere are likely vards up zhere to keep zhe skyvish vrom bovering zhe settlement, and ve can't vly too close, eizer, because zhey vill see us." The vampire placed his finger over the beginning of a path and dragged it along. "If ve vollow zhis path and take a levt at zhe vork, ve can vollow zhis trail up zhe mountain. Zhis looks like zhe Orrivain's actual path, zhough—elves usually cveate a lot of decoy paths to vhrow people off."

"How do you know it's the actual path?"

"Because zhis path 'as zhe most turn-avound enchantments. All of zhese curves," he said, pointing to several curves on the path that turned into the trees and didn't show a way out. "Zhey're enchanted trails zhat vill make you valk avound in endless circles until you die of exhaustion or starvation, vhichever 'appens virst."

Zalith looked hesitant.

"If ve got caught in vone—not zhat ve vill since ve know vhere zhey are—I know 'ow to break zhem."

The demon chuckled. "You've been caught in one?"

He was admittedly embarrassed about it, but he said, "Yes."

With an intrigued smile, Zalith asked, "When? And how?"

"Vhen I vas in Yilmana a long time ago. I vas 'unting somevone vor Zamien, and I chased zhem into elv territory. Zidn't take me long to vealize zhat I vas valking in circles. Anyvay, you can break zhe loop by severing zhe path vith dark ethos. I vigured my blood vas dark since my vather vas a Numen, so I spread zhat across zhe path."

"How did you work that out?"

He shrugged. "Vell, I tried vlying up virst, but all I saw vas endless vorest. I knew enough about elv ethos to know zhat certain kinds can be disrupted, and looping traps is vone of zhem."

"Well, at least we'll be safe from those," Zalith said with a small laugh.

"As vor vargrs, zhey're susceptible to vire, so zhey shouldn't be a problem, eizer. Zhey're 'ard to detect, zhough. Zheir aura is old, maybe cveated by a Numen ve zon't know about."

The demon looked cautious. "What about gremlins and pixies?"

"Iron and salt vor gremlins. Iron vorks vor pixies, too, but zhey vhrive on veaction, so ignoring zhem vill send zhem avay," Alucard explained.

Zalith nodded and asked, "Sprites?"

"Depends on vhat kind zhey are; sprites are tied to zhe elements. Iron vorks on zhem, zhough."

"So basically we just take a lot of iron with us?" he laughed.

"Basically," the vampire agreed.

"All right. I'm sure we have some iron in the weapons room."

Alucard looked the map over one last time. "Ve can vind a vantage point up 'ere," he said, pointing to a cliff above the ridge. "Vrom zhere, ve can see vhat ve're dealing vith."

Zalith asked, "Are you ready to go in a few minutes?"

"I'm veady vhen you are."

The demon rolled up the map. "I wish this thing was smaller," he muttered.

"At least ve zon't 'ave to lug zhe ving avound; you can just put in zhe vault and take out vhen ve need."

His mate created a small rift and eased the map into his vault. "Now we just have to hope that this forest isn't full of anti-ethos wards."

Alucard smiled and took his hand. "Zhere von't be. Zhe elves vould be avvected by zhem, too." He began leading the way downstairs.

"So, just endless paths and creatures of the woods?"

"Mm-hmm."

With an amused scoff, Zalith sarcastically said, "I look forward to it."

When they got to the entrance hall, Edwin walked in wearing a pair of cleaning gloves.

"Sir," the butler said.

Both Alucard and Zalith turned to look at him as they pulled their shoes on.

"I have managed to remove the raccoons, but Sabazios attempted to fight a porcupine while I was doing so. He has several pines in his muzzle, sir."

Zalith sighed and said, "Get a vet over here."

After a bow, the butler left.

"Is just vhat Sabazios does," Alucard said, shrugging. It wasn't the first time the hellhound had challenged a small but deadly creature. "'E vill be okay." He pulled his redingote on.

"Will he attack your chickens?" the demon asked, concerned.

He shook his head. "'E knows not to 'arm zhem."

"Good," Zalith said as he took the vampire's hand and led the way outside.

It was time to head into elf territory.

Chapter Eight

— ⸯ ✝ ⸰ —

Conduit

| Alucard |
| *Uzlia Isles, Yrudberg, Yrudyen Woods* |

After dropping the Yrudyen treaty off at the Eimwood City Hall, Alucard raced towards the Yrudyen Woods with Zalith. He flew as close to the mountain as he could get without risking being spotted, and he landed in a dense grove, rematerializing.

The forest was different here.

Darker. Quieter.

The golden beams of light that had once filtered through the canopy were gone, swallowed by twisting, gnarled branches that clawed at the sky, their bark ashen and cracked, long withered yet stubbornly alive. The air was thick, but not with the scent of fresh moss or wildflowers; it carried a stagnant, damp, almost metallic odour, like rain-soaked stone and distant decay.

There were no hidden birds singing in the shadows, no rustling of small creatures darting through the brush…only suffocating silence. Even the wind barely moved, like it had been caught in the grip of whatever lingered here. The undergrowth was sparse, replaced by patches of slimy, dark earth, and knotted roots protruding like ribs.

Alucard inhaled deeply, his senses stretching outward, searching for any sign of life.

But there was nothing, not as far as he could tell. No familiar hum of elves or wildlife, no rhythmic pulse of nature that should have been there. Just an unnatural stillness, as if the entire forest were holding its breath.

He didn't like it.

And neither did the shadows that coiled at the edges of his vision, stretching just a little longer than they should have, shifting without a breeze to move them.

"I hate it here already," Zalith muttered.

"Zhere are a lot of vards and spells all over zhe place; vill mess with our senses."

The demon took hold of his hand. "We'll move slowly," he said cautiously.

Alucard nodded and followed Zalith's lead, leaving the grove and heading deeper into the woods. The path they found was narrow, barely more than a winding strip of squelching mud cutting through the undergrowth. Darkness stretched long beneath the twisted canopy, branches knitting together overhead, blocking out what little light had managed to slip through.

The turn-around enchantments laid deep within these woods were meant to confuse and lead intruders in circles, but as Alucard followed closely beside him, Zalith traced each misdirection and false clearing, and now, they weaved through the true path, carefully sidestepping the illusionary trails that might lead them astray.

A slow breeze then stirred, whispering through the trees.

They both stopped.

Alucard tightened his grip around Zalith's wrist, his instincts telling him that they weren't alone anymore.

Something moved ahead. Not the sluggish sway of branches in the wind or the distant flutter of a creature disturbed from its perch. A shape shifted through the trees just beyond their reach, its form weaving between the trunks.

They moved slowly and cautiously as they pressed deeper into the woods. The stillness had settled thick around them, the air heavy with a threat unseen, a threat watching.

Alucard narrowed his eyes, scanning the darkness. For a moment, there was nothing—just trees and silence—but then he saw it. Massive, looming, half-hidden behind the mangled trunks. At first, it looked like a fallen tree, its massive body draped in thick moss, its form blending seamlessly into the forest… until he saw the subtle rise and fall of breath, the way its bark-like scales shifted, the faint glow of runes carved into its hide, shimmering in slow, steady intervals like a heartbeat.

A Mossback Warden.

"Zaliv—" he said cautiously, his voice barely a whisper. "Ve can't get too close. Is vesting, but if ve disturb, zhe elves vill likely 'ear zhe vight."

"It's in the way of the path we need to take," his mate murmured back. "And we can't turn around or go another way."

Alucard clenched his jaw. He knew that. He also knew the dangers of stepping off the mapped route. They'd memorized the enchanted traps woven into these woods; if they strayed too far from the designated path, there was no guarantee that they'd be able to correct their course.

He exhaled, eyeing the massive creature again. It hadn't moved—yet. "Ve go past very slowly," he instructed, recalling his first encounter with such a creature. "No sudden movements or loud sounds, and ve should 'ide our auras."

Zalith smirked slightly as he gave a slow nod. "I love it when you boss me around."

Alucard pouted.

The demon chuckled quietly. "Lead the way, vampire."

With a nod, Alucard tightened his grip on Zalith's hand and moved forward, keeping his eyes focused on the beast. He slowed his breaths and hid his aura, and Zalith did the same. Even the slightest sound could wake that thing up.

The closer they got to the sleeping Warden, the slower Alucard moved, cautiously scanning the ground at their feet and the branches clawing down from the canopy. And when they were mere feet away from the creature, Alucard carefully stepped over a fallen branch. His boot met the ground again, and as he lifted his other foot, Zalith mirrored his moves, following him one step at a time.

To Alucard's relief, the beast didn't wake, though he didn't pick the pace back up yet. He kept leading the way along the path, glancing back over his shoulder. Only when the Warden's sleeping form had faded into the mist did the vampire return to their walking pace.

"What was that thing?" Zalith whispered.

"A Mossback Varden. Zhey 'unt in zhese vorests—mostly physical astrals."

"Would it have eaten us?"

"Zemons aren't zheir usual prey, so no—probably vould 'ave just killed us and launched our bodies off into the vorest vor volves or vhatever to vind."

"What a waste," the demon chuckled.

Alucard scoffed amusedly. "So you'd vather be eaten whole by a giant snake— *alive*?"

"Rather that than eaten alive by wild dogs or something."

"Zhe Varden vould kill us bevore zhat 'appens."

"But what if it didn't? What if it thought it would be funny to throw us out there somewhere and be eaten by wolves?"

"I zon't vink zhey vink like zhat."

"You never know."

With a deep exhale, Alucard looked at his mate for a moment. "Ve zon't 'ave to vorry about any of zhat 'ap—"

Zalith abruptly grabbed his arm and pulled him down, making him crouch.

"Vhat?" Alucard whispered, frantically scanning the gloom around them.

The demon slowly lifted his free hand and pointed to their left.

Alucard frowned, staring, his sight sharpening. At first, he saw nothing…just the dark sprawl of roots and the warped silhouettes of trees. Movement quickly snatched his focus, though.

A shadow slipped between the trunks, low to the ground, its massive shoulders rolling beneath ragged fur. It was hound-like but far from any natural beast. Its broad, hunched frame was coated in thick, coarse fur; in patches, it was ripped away, exposing raw, scarred flesh that stretched over sinewy muscle. The creature's hyena-like maw was scarred and cracked, its teeth jagged, some broken, others far too long, curling past its lips in uneven protrusions. And its eyes were glowing violet pools, shifting and searching aimlessly.

The hound sniffed sharply at the air, head tilting in a way that seemed wrong, too quick, too aware, its movements jerky and fractured as though stitched together from the remnants of something that should not be alive.

Alucard frowned at the rattle of metal. His gaze snapped lower, spotting a thick, rusted chain looped around the beast's throat, its taut length stretching from the creature's neck to a tree behind it. The bark at the base was worn away and clawed deep—the hound had clearly fought against its restraint over and over again.

The fact that it was chained meant that someone had put it here, and Alucard was certain he knew who.

Zalith exhaled quietly beside him. "Is that a vargr?" he murmured.

Alucard's eyes flickered between the creature and the unnatural glow of its gaze. He hadn't seen one in a very long time, but it was unmistakeable—a rare, ancient wolfkin that belonged to the old world, the world that existed before Year Zero. They'd guard places where no human was allowed to step, but they grew sparser with every passing century.

"Yes," he replied, watching the beast as it attempted to break free from the chain.

"We're at the border of the Orrivain's territory," his mate said. "I can see the snow."

The vampire looked in the same direction as Zalith, spotting the gradual freeze of the grass, which stretched further away, thickening into snow.

But then the beast sniffed the air again, suddenly jerking its head in their direction.

Zalith's fingers tightened around Alucard's arm, and Alucard tensed.

However, it hadn't seen them yet.

"Zhey're dangerous in zhe shadows, and zhey're not stupid, so zhey know to avoid zhe light and vire. If ve stick to zhose small gaps, ve should be able to pass zhe border unseen," he said, nodding at the very small cracks in the tree canopy allowing tiny streaks of sunlight to creep through. "But do *not* take your eyes off zhat border."

The demon nodded. "All right, let's go."

Zalith led the way this time. Alucard followed behind him, staying low to the ground; he kept his eyes on the vargr while his mate's gaze remained ahead. The hound still hadn't spotted them, though. It sniffed and scurried around, trying to break its chain every few moments before giving up and sitting, hanging its head defeatedly. Alucard felt sorry for it—of course he did; no animal should be chained and forced into guarding something. But despite the vargr's clear desire to escape, it was cursed to howl and bark when it laid eyes on any intruder.

Once they reached the border, Alucard took his eyes off the hound. The forest stretched on, still dark and gloomy; the blanket of snow that covered the ground hadn't fallen naturally because there were no gaps in the trees to allow such thick ice. It was created with ethos, and Alucard wondered…—

"Vait," he snapped quietly, pulling Zalith back before he could step on the snow.

"What is it?" the demon asked worriedly.

Alucard eyed the snow for a moment. He couldn't detect an aura or ethos emanating from it, nor did he spot runes on the surrounding trees. "Can I 'ave zhe map, please?"

With a nod, Zalith silently took the map from his vault and unrolled it, holding one end while Alucard held the other. "What are you looking for?"

He didn't reply. The vampire's eyes scanned the map of their area. There weren't any traps or obstacles beyond the border—any marked ones, at least—but there *was* a conduit. Two hundred yards from their position was a beacon that would set off if anything other than vargr and Orrivain Elves stepped foot on the snow.

"Zhis," he said, pointing to it on the map. "Ve can't step on zhe snow until I turn zhis conduit off."

"Why?"

"Zhe snow is vone big alarm—zhis kind of ving vocuses on aura and ethos etcetera, so if ve step on, even vith our auras masked, zhe snow vill alert zhe Orrivain zhat somevone is in zheir territory."

"How do we turn it off?"

"*I* vill," he said firmly. "Zhis snow von't pay attention to vildlife, so I'll use vone of my animal vorms."

Zalith looked hesitant, tightening his grip on Alucard's hand. "Isn't there another way? Can't we target it from here?"

"If ve use ethos attacks, zhat vill alert zhe vargr."

With a deep exhale, Zalith adorned a reluctant, conflicted frown. "Can't you fly us from here?"

Alucard shook his head. "Ve can't visk being seen." He then placed his free hand on the side of Zalith's neck. "I'll be okay, I promise. Vill only take me a vew minutes and I'll be vight back."

His mate didn't look at all convinced, but he knew as well as Alucard did that they didn't really have another option. "Okay," he mumbled sadly. "Just please be careful. If you see any danger at all, come back."

He nodded. "I vill."

Zalith slowly loosened his grip and kissed his lips.

Alucard smiled before he dematerialized and morphed into his fox form. He didn't waste a second, either. He crossed the border, stepping onto the snow; it felt strangely warm at his paws, but that was because of the conduit. It would fall cold again soon enough, and he wasn't looking forward to it at all.

He focused on the task, though. As he moved through the ice, he scanned the area, and when he spotted the conduit—a stone statue of a vargr—he crept closer, eyeing every detail and rune carved into the rock. He circled it, searching for the gem that powered it. When he located the deep blue sapphire, though, his attention was stolen by a low, hostile snarl.

Alucard froze. Slowly, he leaned to the side until he could see around the statue. Standing in the shadow of one of the trees stood a growling, mangled hound—another vargr. It stared at him, its purple eyes filled with both confusion and anger. It was trying to figure him out…trying to decide whether he was a threat or not. And if he touched the conduit, the vargr would definitely trigger.

Cautiously, he backed off, and then he scurried away like an ordinary fox would. Instead of fleeing completely, though, he darted behind a tree; he listened to the gradual footfall of the hound as it sniffed around, and when he heard it moving away, he peered around the tree and watched it leave, disappearing into the gloom.

He swiftly returned to the conduit. With his small paw, he reached into the statue's centre and pulled the sapphire out. The snow immediately went cold, and he heard the snarl of a hound. This time, though, he wouldn't run—he couldn't. He needed the Orrivain to believe that it was just a mere fox that had disabled their conduit. So when the vargr returned, he rolled onto his back and started tossing the gem up into the air, playing around with it—the Orrivain would see him through the hound's eyes, and they'd only send an elf or two to fix it.

The vargr snarled and darted forward, and Alucard dropped the gem and sprang into the forest, leaving the hound to guard the sapphire.

He quickly reached Zalith and returned to his normal self. "Ve von't 'ave long until an elv or two come to vix zhe conduit. Ve should move now."

"Are you okay?" the demon asked quietly.

"I'm okay," he assured him, taking his hand.

With a nod, Zalith moved with him, crossing the border onto the snow. Things were only going to get harder the closer they got to the Orrivain settlement, though. There'd be more vargrs, other beasts, and scouts. But Alucard would do his best to ensure that they reached the vantage point without having to battle anything or anyone. He wanted this to go as smoothly as possible.

Chapter Nine

— ⟨ † ⟩ —

Starborne Ridge

| **Zalith** |

| *Uzlia Isles, Yrudberg, Orrivain Territory* |

Vargrs were patrolling the mountain path, their hulking forms moving rigidly. The creatures were everywhere, chained to trees, lashed to boulders, even shackled to one another.

From behind the frozen, moss-covered boulder where he and Alucard crouched, Zalith scanned the ground ahead, his grip tightening around his fiancé's hand. There was no clear way forward, no route that didn't pass too close to things. He focused, watching; their movements were too precise, and their steps were too identical for it to be instinct. This wasn't the chaotic, unpredictable nature of a wild beast on patrol. These creatures were programmed, ensnared by something deeper than chains.

Step, pause. Step, pause.

Zalith exhaled slowly, thinking, hypothesizing. Every stride was measured to the inch, repeating over and over and over, an eerie, methodical rhythm that never altered. They had to be under some sort of spell—a curse, perhaps. A force stronger than their own will.

Could he use that to get past them?

He spoke into Alucard's mind, *"Can we disrupt whatever's making them move around like drones? It looks like they're under a spell."*

Alucard frowned, his eyes quickly shifting from vargr to vargr. *"Ve can, but ve need to vigure out vhat kind of spell zhis is virst. If ve use zhe vrong kind of counter ethos, ve could end up alerting zhe Orrivain zhat ve're 'ere."*

"What are the options?"

"Could be an obedience curse or a loyalty vune."

Zalith sharpened his focus on one hound. *"I don't see any runes."*

"Neizer do I."

He eyed another vargr, but there were no runes in sight. "*So, a spell?*"

"*Seems zhat vay.*"

"*So how do we disrupt their obedience curse? The same way we'd disrupt one if it were on a person?*"

Alucard shook his head. "*Animals are very divverent to people. In zhis case, ve'd be better off vinding someving to overpower zhe curse.*" He paused, looking around. "*All animals 'ave zheir instincts, some of vhich are stronger zhan ozzers. Vargrs aren't much divverent to verevolves.*" He nodded towards one of the vargrs. "*Can you get into zhat vone's 'ead?*"

"*Probably,*" he said with a nod.

"*Make 'im attack vone of zhe ozzers. To zhe vest, vill look like a rivalry or vight over vank. Zhe vest of zhem vill likely leave zheir posts to vatch or at least become distracted enough vor us to move past zhem.*"

Zalith smirked a little—he loved how perceptive Alucard was… and thinking about it quickly stole the focus he'd managed to fix onto the task instead of the vampire's intoxicating scent. He exhaled deeply and did his best to concentrate, though. There'd be time for him to indulge his desires later. "*All right. That one?*" he asked, gesturing to one of the vargrs near the beginning of the path.

Alucard replied, "*Mm-hmm.*"

The demon locked his gaze on his chosen target. While he watched the beast patrol thirty steps to the left and thirty to the right, he eased his way into its head, and inside, he found a strange mess of instinct and struggle. The beast was trying to resist what had been done to it, and Zalith could use that. He grasped onto it, breaking past the curse and its commands, and then he told the vargr to attack the beast a few yards away because it was about to do the same.

And that was all it took.

With a savage snarl, the vargr abandoned its post and clashed with the beast that Zalith had suggested was about to do the same thing. And just as Alucard predicted, moments after the fight started, other vargr began leaving their posts to watch the fight, howling and snarling, cheering on their packmates.

Alucard grasped his hand, a firm, urgent pull that sent them both moving. Zalith followed without hesitation, his gaze flickering back to the battle, but the vargrs remained locked in their violent frenzy. Not one of them noticed.

Together, Zalith and his fiancé weaved through the skeletal trees, slipping between twisted trunks and frost-laden branches, their breath ghosting in the cold air. The snow beneath their boots was deep and uneven, crunching softly with each step—until it suddenly wasn't. The ground shifted, ice giving way to slick, uneven rock, patches of frost clinging to the surface where the cold had hardened the stone; the wind was sharper, whistling through the narrowing mountain pass, and it carried the smell of residual ethos, smoke, and cooking herbs.

The settlement couldn't be far.

Zalith exhaled slowly, keeping his movements measured and precise. They stayed low, pressed close to the jagged wall of the mountain, the rough rock biting his skin as he braced himself, navigating the treacherous incline without a sound.

They were past the trees now, and with every step upward, the forest below faded into the mist, swallowed by distance and shadow. A thick fog coiled around them, rising from the frozen rock like breath from a sleeping beast; overhead, a light flurry drifted from the grey sky, delicate flakes swirling aimlessly before landing on their coats.

Zalith lifted his gaze. Beyond the haze, he caught glimpses of skyfish gliding in slow patterns, their elongated forms barely visible through the clouds. And just faintly, he noticed the shimmer of a protective ward. Alucard had been right about that—of course he had.

The demon might have lingered on it longer, but he felt Alucard shiver. He felt it through his hand first, and then he saw it in the slight tremor of the vampire's shoulders. His fiancé's grip tightened, his fingers squeezing Zalith's just slightly, and when the demon turned to glance at him, he wasn't surprised to see a scowl—not one of anger or deep focus but that subtle, unmistakable frown that Alucard made when he was cold and utterly miserable.

Zalith exhaled softly and reached into his vault with his free hand, pulling out a pair of gloves and a scarf. "Here," he whispered, holding the gloves out to him, and when Alucard took them, he put the scarf around the vampire's neck.

Alucard smiled. "Vank you."

He smiled, too, and once Alucard put the gloves on—struggling a little to ease his claws through the fingertip slits—they continued up the path. As they moved, he recalled the map, and he was certain that they must be nearing the ridge that overlooked the Orrivain settlement. The smell of smoke and herbs was getting stronger, and through the whistling wind, he could hear voices.

"*We're close,*" he said into Alucard's mind.

The vampire slowed, lifting his gaze to the looming mountain wall.

Zalith knew exactly what he was looking for. "Here," he murmured, pointing to a series of jagged, protruding rocks that jutted out just enough to serve as footholds.

Without hesitation, Alucard let go of his hand and began the ascent.

The demon followed, his fingers gripping the frozen stone, testing each hold before pulling himself up. It had been a long time since he'd climbed without wings, without shortcuts and ethos. But muscle memory was a stubborn thing, and the movement came easily, his strength and agility sharpening every step.

In place, the rock was slippery, ice clinging to the crevices, forcing him to adjust his grip quickly, but he held on, climbing up and to the right, weaving along the jagged incline, carefully manoeuvring past sections where the rock was too sheer to hold weight. Zalith spotted a ridge ahead, a narrow outcrop of stone that overlooked the path below. It had to be the vantage point that they were searching for.

"Is 'ere," Alucard told him quietly, adjusting his path towards it.

With a nod, Zalith followed him to the ledge.

After a few final, calculated movements, they reached it, lowering themselves onto the ridge's uneven surface. The wind was much stronger, whistling through the crags and crashing against their faces, and Alucard shivered much more violently.

Zalith crouched low and pulled Alucard closer, hugging him tightly in an attempt to warm him. "Are you okay?" he whispered.

The vampire nodded and exhaled shakily. Then, he very slowly led the way to the edge of the ridge.

Zalith mirrored him, and once they reached the fringe, his sharp eyes searched the world beneath him—and there it was.

The Orrivain settlement was much larger than the Yrudyen Village. While the Yrudyen Elves had woven their homes into the living forest, hidden beneath the canopy's embrace, the Orrivain had carved their kingdom into the mountain itself. The settlement stretched across a vast plateau, its buildings constructed from dark stone and carved timber, their slanted roofs layered with thick blankets of snow and ice. Smoke spewed from several chimneys, the scent of burning wood and charred meat drifting faintly in the air.

Beyond the village's perimeter, tall wooden stakes jutted from the ground, forming a crude but effective barrier. Alongside them, steel cages stood half-buried in the snow, some empty, some holding skeletal remains that had long since frozen over. Vargrs stalked the outskirts, patrolling the entrance and watchpoints. Some paced in tight, unnatural patterns, their fur thick and matted from the cold, while others sat chained to heavy stone posts, their glowing violet eyes scanning the settlement for threats.

Zalith's gaze flicked to the centre of the village, where the largest structure loomed over the rest. It was easily twice the size of the other buildings, a long hall with carved pillars and thick support beams reinforced with steel. The wooden doors were adorned with intricate glyphs, glowing faintly beneath a thin layer of frost. It was regal, fortified, and unmistakably the seat of power. That had to be where Moonwarden Calitharion was.

A few fires burned throughout the village, some contained within stone hearths, others left open to crackle against the cold, surrounded by elves cloaked in thick furs. They spoke in hushed voices, the occasional clang of metal or shift of leather breaking the otherwise quiet tension that hung over the settlement.

The demon watched carefully, his eyes sweeping over every patrol, every watchful elf, and every possible opening. There were families—women, children, elderly. But there were also soldiers. A lot of the grey-skinned elves were armoured and carrying weapons, and there wasn't just one blacksmith workshop…he spotted at least three. It looked almost as if they were preparing for war, and Zalith didn't need to wonder who it was with. Had they already caught word of Syllia's alliance with Eimwood?

"Zhere's a lot of zhem," Alucard whispered.

"Mm-hmm," he replied, counting as many as he could see. "Easily more than three times the number of Yrudyen Elves."

"I vink is alveady safe to assume zhat zhey're not intervested in an alliance. Zhey're getting veady to vight."

"We're going to need to send Syllia more help," he muttered, pondering. "When's the meeting with those other werewolf packs?"

"Zhe vhirty-virst at noon. Zhe Veylin, Grim'olt, Cindervell, and Ovros packs are coming."

Zalith nodded and asked, "Do you think they'll agree to move to Eimwood?"

"Maybe. Zhis whole…Alpha of Alphas Prime ving isn't zhe norm 'ere in Aegisguard, but Vreja's pack 'as taken vell to zhe idea, so I'm sure zhat zhese ozzer packs vill eventually settle, too."

"I don't think these elves are going to wait two days to make their move," he said with a sigh, watching one of the blacksmiths hand out swords. "The fact that they're out here working through the day makes it obvious that they're determined." He huffed and observed as two elves attached a chained collar to a vargr. "Can we spare some demons or vampires?" he asked but then frowned. "Well, not vampires. You're still in the middle of creating more."

Alucard pondered with a quiet, "Hmm…" as his eyes scanned the village, too. "Maybe Zhomas can spare some more verevolves just vor a vew days."

"I'll ask him. We should also try and increase the security around Eimwood. I don't want to risk these elves deciding to attack the people first—or at the same time."

"Syllia told you about zhese elves, no?"

"Yeah."

"Did she say anyving zhat might 'elp us determine who zhey'd attack virst?"

Zalith exhaled deeply, thinking. "I feel like they might come for the city first. Syllia said that Calitharion—this clan's leader—built the foundations of Eimwood with his family. She also told me that he was around when Khila and Aresphis were, and after Khila gave the humans a little bit of land, Calitharion conspired with Aresphis to kill Khila because he and the Orrivain didn't support Khila's decision to welcome the humans," he explained slowly. "The Yrudyen weren't exactly fond of the idea, either, so

I think it's entirely possible that the Orrivain might try to remove the humans and take Eimwood back before trying to convince the Yrudyen to join them."

Alucard nodded, tapping his chin. "So, ve send a vew veinvorcements to Syllia, and ve up zhe devences avound Eimvood as much as ve can. I'll try to speed along my vampire number problems and see if I can spare some of my stronger vones to come and 'elp out 'ere." He looked at Zalith. "I can 'ead to Aveson avter ve're done 'ere and get started. Zhe sooner, zhe better."

"Are you going to start turning people?"

"I zon't know. If I do, I'll tell you. Vor now, zhough, I vink you should stay and make avvangements. Ve'll get more done if ve vork on both vings at vonce."

Zalith didn't want to agree. He didn't want to part, especially since they'd be an ocean away. But Alucard was right. There was no room for paranoia right now. The sooner Alucard got on top of his vampire conundrum, and the sooner *he* figured out how to deal with the Orrivain if they attacked, the sooner they'd deal with two very pressing matters—matters that couldn't be postponed.

With a quiet sigh, he nodded and said, "Okay." He looked back down at the settlement. "I need to count as many of them as I can first, though."

"You count zhe armoured vones and I'll count zhe vones vithout. Zhen, ve can count zhe vargr."

"All right," he agreed, and then he started counting.

The worry clawed at the back of his mind, though. What if something happened to Alucard over there? He wouldn't be there to help him, and he wouldn't be able to get there immediately, either. Although he knew that his fiancé could handle himself, he couldn't help but need just a little bit more assurance.

He stopped counting for half a second, glancing at the vampire. "Can you take someone with you again, please?"

Keeping his eyes on the settlement below, Alucard half nodded. "Is probably a good idea to take a verevolf anyvay."

"To help ease into the fact that we're all working together?" he asked with a chuckle.

"Vell, zhat, yes—but zhere is speculation zhat zhe Silver Claw is a verevolf."

Zalith felt a little sick. "A werewolf?"

"Is only an assumption. Eizer vay, I'll be okay," Alucard replied, trying to assure him. "I'll take Zhomas…and maybe Zanvord."

The demon exhaled deeply, trying to fight off the paranoia, but it was hard because he couldn't help but think about what happened to Alucard with Ada. He knew what werewolf venom did to vampires…and to his fiancé. However, Alucard wasn't broken and distracted this time, was he? No. Zalith was just worrying too much. So he did his best to shove aside the uncertainty and said, "Okay." And then he counted the last of the armoured elves. "There are sixty-one armoured ones."

"I counted tventy-nine unarmed elves, but zhere could be more in zhe 'ouses. Zhere are also vivteen vargrs."

"We'll say there's a hundred just to be safe. I'll make preparations as soon as we get back to the castle."

The vampire looked over Zalith's shoulder. "Ve'll probably 'ave to distract zhose vargrs again on zhe vay down, and deal vith zhe conduit. I just 'ope zhat zhere von't be elves at eizer obstacle."

"We'll deal with them," he said firmly, watching the elves.

Alucard's gaze landed on him. "Vhat are you vinking?" he asked.

With a quiet huff, he shook his head. "I'd honestly still rather try to make an alliance. These elves *were* here long before us and the humans."

"Vell, ve managed to bargain vith zhe Yrudyen. Surely zhere is someving zhat zhese elves vant, too."

"Maybe," he murmured, pondering. He wondered… or maybe he *hoped* that some of the Orrivain felt differently than their leader. Syllia said that Calitharion was very bitter and old, and old men were notorious for clinging to the past. What if there were elves among the clan who didn't share his desire to kill the humans and take Eimwood? What if some of them were like the Yrudyen? He had to take that possibility into account, but he wouldn't prioritize it over the lives of the people of Eimwood and the Yrudyen. "If they attack, I think that we should try to detain them rather than kill them."

Alucard frowned. "Vhy?"

"Some of them might be like the Yrudyen. It's entirely possible that they're just following orders."

"Zhat's true," his fiancé murmured. "Ve should send vord to zhe people guarding zhe borders."

"I'll do it as soon as we get back. Come on," he said, moving away from the ledge.

He was glad that Alucard agreed—but then again, why would he *disagree*? Sure, his vampire was creative and devious, but he wasn't stupid, nor was he so heartless that he'd kill an entire race just because some of them were their enemy. That was what Zalith hoped, though… because *he* didn't want to wipe out an entire race either—not if they were innocent or capable of change.

And he sorely hoped that they were.

Chapter Ten

— ⸴ † ⸵ —

Lysandra

| **Alucard** |
| ***Rhenovaalis, Atheson, Atheson City*** |

By the time Alucard arrived in Atheson with Greymore and Danford, midnight was near. The Rhenovaalisean continent was five hours ahead of Uzlia, and though the time shift barely registered, he welcomed the veil of night. No harsh sun glaring against his skin, no burning daylight forcing him into discomfort. Just darkness—cool, quiet, and undisturbed.

Though beneath the odd fatigue that had been hitting him after travelling recently, he couldn't help but notice he'd taken a little longer than he thought to get to his destination. After Damien removed those runes, he'd been able to fly *much* faster… faster than he just had. Was it because his body was focusing on giving him more energy to sate his needs?

He was overthinking it.

With a quiet sigh, he relaxed. The stillness settled around him, bringing him repose he hadn't realized he needed; Uzlia was always loud, always buzzing with life, its pulse a constant thing beneath his feet. But here, there was no sea of voices, no endless movement pressing in on all sides. Just peace.

However, he knew what lay beneath the thin veneer of quiet.

Alucard's gaze shifted left; he watched as Danford doubled over, retching violently behind a berry-laden bush. Greymore barked out a laugh, thoroughly amused, and the vampire exhaled sharply, rolling his eyes before turning his attention forward.

The city loomed in the distance, its silhouette rising against the night sky like a slumbering giant. Tall, spired rooftops pierced the darkness, their pointed edges dusted with the last remnants of winter's touch. The air carried a lingering crispness, the kind that clung stubbornly at the tail end of Tertium, neither fully winter nor truly spring.

"Let's go," he mumbled, walking towards the dirt road. Before heading up to greet the coven, he wanted to assess the state of the city.

Alucard led the way to the gates, and when he stepped inside, the remnants of demon attacks became evident immediately. Gas lamps lined the main avenues, their golden glow flickering unsteadily, some dimmed, cracked, or snuffed out entirely. Soot-blackened glass distorted the light, casting warped shadows over uneven cobblestones, some split, others freshly patched where deep gashes marred the road.

Here and there, thin wisps of smoke curled from the chimneys of townhouses and bakeries, their warmth a stark contrast to the burned-out husks of buildings left ravaged in the last wave of attacks. The scent of coal and wet stone still clung to the air, but beneath it lingered the bitter tang of charred wood and sulphur.

The streets were mostly empty, but not abandoned. A lone carriage rattled over the stones, its lantern swaying with each uneven jolt, wheels rolling over a road still scarred by claw marks and shattered glass. Further down, a pair of men in woollen coats exchanged murmured words beneath an iron streetlamp, their breath rising in faint silver plumes, though their gazes flicked warily to the alleyways, where shadows stretched too deep and too still.

Somewhere, a church bell tolled the hour, its deep chime echoing against the silent facades of narrow brick buildings, some of which bore fresh reinforcement, new barricades where walls had been breached.

Alucard pulled his coat closer around himself. The air was stagnant; Atheson City was far from peacefully silent. The place was wounded and unsettled, like it was an injured creature huddled up in a corner, dreading that a predator might find and finish it off.

"Your vampires do this?" Greymore asked curiously.

"No," he grumbled, turning right at a bend. "Liliv's zemons 'ave been vaiding zhis city and zhe surrounding towns on a vegular basis. Zhat's 'alv zhe veason vhy ve're 'ere. Zhe 'umans aren't veally avraid of my vampires anymore and 'ave started 'unting zhem."

"That Silver Claw guy, right?"

He nodded.

"Silver Claw?" Danford asked.

Alucard had admittedly forgotten that Danford was with them. "A 'ired provessional vampire 'unter."

"Oh…is he here?"

"Ve zon't know. Ve're looking into 'im."

"You found anything yet?" Greymore asked.

"Not yet," Alucard murmured, but then he halted, his breath stilling as something sharp sliced through the cold air.

Blood.

But not just any blood.

It was vampire blood.

Faint, nearly lost beneath the dampness of the city, but unmistakable—a scent that stood out against the smoke, the filth, and the lingering remnants of demon destruction.

He veered left, his boots barely making a sound against the uneven cobblestones; the city had been eerily quiet, but as he followed the scent, faint voices rose ahead, growing clearer with every step. Laughter, sneering taunts, and cruel amusement were woven into the wind.

And then he entered the square.

The space was small but open, its perimeter lined with buildings that loomed like witnesses of a trial. A single oil lantern flickered atop a post, casting a weak, amber hue against the weathered wood of the gallows. The execution platform stood at the centre, elevated just enough to make a spectacle of its victim.

And there, hanging from the rope, ensnared in a grotesque display of cruelty, was a vampire. She was barely alive. Her body was wrapped in silver barbed wire, its jagged coils cutting deep into her exposed skin, the metal burning her flesh, veins blackened where the poison had seeped in. Thick, hemlock-infused rope bound her wrists and ankles, ensuring that even if she escaped the wire, the paralytic toxin would keep her weak and defenceless. Pinned against her collarbone, her ribs, and her arms were crucifixes, each one held in place by silver nails driven straight through her skin.

She screamed a ragged, broken sound, her body jerking as another handful of holy water splashed across her raw wounds by one of the men who stood at the base of the gallows, grinning amusedly as the scent of burned flesh thickened the air.

"Sing for us, monster," one of them sneered, tossing another splash of holy water at her feet.

"You should be grateful," another chuckled, leaning lazily against a wooden post. "We're giving you time to repent before the sun does the rest."

Alucard's jaw tightened, and his hands curled into fists.

Danford muttered something indiscernible.

And Greymore mumbled, "We saw shit like this all the time during the war." He looked at Alucard. "What do we do?"

Eyra could wait. Alucard wasn't going to leave this vampire whether she was part of a coven or not—and he assumed she wasn't because no one had reported her missing. "I need you two to get zhose people avay vrom 'er so I can get 'er down."

"What about all the silver and stuff?" Greymore asked.

"I'll be vine."

"How should we get them away?" Danford chimed in.

"Vigure zhat out," Alucard muttered.

Greymore patted Alucard's shoulder. "Don't worry, man. I got this. I'll meet you back here." He then strolled out into the square and approached the sneering men.

Alucard glanced at an alley between two boarded-up buildings, and then he looked at Danford, who was still lingering beside him. He wanted to tell him to go with Greymore, but he didn't want to risk those humans realizing that he was a vampire. So he shifted his attention to Greymore and watched him stop in front of the spectators.

"You guys been down on West Street?" Greymore asked.

West Street? Alucard deadpanned.

"Nah. What's down there?" one of them replied.

Alucard exhaled quietly in relief.

"One of this bitch's buddies," Greymore replied, nodding up at the hanging vampire.

They all turned their attention to him.

"Another one?"

"Fucking undead scum."

Greymore gestured to the street behind him. "You wanna go get him? We can string him up right here."

The men snickered and pulled out weapons.

"Let's go," one of them said and marched across the square.

Alucard waited, eyeing them all as they left; their laughter faded into the distance, swallowed by the empty streets, leaving only the ragged, uneven breaths of the vampire hanging thirty feet away.

He left the cover of the shadows and ascended the gallows in silence. The woman was slumped in her bindings, her head tilted forward. Her breath was weak, a sound more reflex than will.

"Zon't move," he murmured, trying to figure out where to start.

Her eyelids fluttered, sluggish, unfocused. Her reply was indiscernible.

Alucard stepped closer, the scent of burning flesh heavy in the air, but he barely registered it. His focus was on the barbed wire that coiled around her arms and torso, biting into her skin like jagged teeth. The moment his gloved fingers curled around the metal, though, pain ripped through his hand, the silver searing into his palm like fire, even through the fabric. His breath hissed through his teeth, but he didn't stop. With a sharp yank, he began pulling the wire loose, each tug sending new jolts of agony up his arm. The barbs sliced deep, dragging against his skin, but it didn't matter. She needed to be freed.

He unwound the wire coil by coil, ignoring the stinging heat racing through his blood, the way the silver fought him, the way it resisted. His fingers worked steadily, pulling, unravelling, tossing the cruel bindings to the ground. By the time the last strand fell, his hands were trembling; he took his torn gloves off to see his bloody, raw skin. But he'd heal soon enough.

Alucard took no time to breathe or recover. He reached for the hemlock-laced ropes, their fibres soaked through with the paralytic toxin. They were no bother to him, and he pulled them away easily. The silver nails were next, though, gleaming brightly in the dim light. He didn't hesitate—he couldn't afford to waste time.

With one swift movement, he gripped the first nail and tore it free.

The woman let out a strangled, broken sob.

He kept going. One by one, he removed them all, each pull sharper than the last, leaving behind torn skin and slow-healing wounds, and when the final restraint fell, the woman sagged forward, too weak to stand. Alucard caught her before she collapsed, easing her down onto her knees. But there was no time to sit there. He dematerialized with her and swiftly flew into the alley, and Danford hurried to join him.

Once he rematerialized, Alucard leaned the woman's back against the wall. "You're safe now," he told her.

She was still weak, but she managed to lift her head and look up at him. A frown flickered across her pale, bloody face. "L-Lord…Alucard?"

He nodded.

"Y-you…you came," she breathed, sounding relieved. "I-I prayed—"

"Stop talking," he interjected. "Zon't vaste your strength. Vonce my vriend gets back, I'll take you to zhe Coven Sanctum, and zhen—"

"N-not…the coven," she refused, shaking her head. "I-I…I have…my wife."

He was convinced that she was likely covenless since he didn't recognize her, but what she just said proved it. That didn't bother him, though. She was still a vampire, and he knew that coven life wasn't right for everyone. "Vhere is she?" he asked.

"B-B…Brack…Brackenford…Lane," she answered with a struggled grunt.

"Is she vampire?"

She looked hesitant to answer.

And he was certain he knew why. "Zoesn't matter vhether she is a vampire or a verevolf or vhatever. She could be in danger."

Her eyes widened, and she grunted, "She's…human…M-My Lord." She sounded ashamed—wary, maybe.

"Zhat's vine," he assured her despite his hate for them, a feeling that grew stronger the longer he spent here. "Vhat's zhe address? I vill send 'im to get 'er," he said, nodding at Danford.

The wolf-vampire looked a little flustered. "Uh…yeah, I'll go get her."

With a deep, shaky exhale, the woman closed her eyes. "It's…five…one-seven," she started and took another long breath. "Brackenford Lane—i-if…if you go back…into the square, go down the street between…between the bookstore…and the café. T-turn left—t-the first left, and then…second right. It's there," she explained slowly, some of her words drawn-out and slurred.

She needed to be healed *fast*.

"Go," Alucard told Danford. "Vhen you 'ave 'er..." he paused and looked at the woman. "Vhat's your name?"

"Ly…sandra Velmont, My Lord. And my wife…she's Rosaline."

Alucard looked at Danford again. "Go. Tell 'er vhat 'appened and who sent you. Vonce you 'ave 'er somevhere safe zhat is *not* 'er 'ome, send me an izuret."

With a nod, the wolf-vampire left the alley.

Then, Alucard summoned an izuret, and when it appeared, he told it, "Go to Zhomas, but zon't approach 'im until 'e is alone. Tell 'im zhat I've taken zhis voman up to my coven, and Zanvord 'as gone to collect 'er vife. Tell 'im I vill come back vor zhe vhree of zhem soon, and tell 'im to vait somevhere safe."

The izuret saluted and disappeared.

"N-not…the coven," Lysandra pleaded.

"Vhy not?" he questioned. "Your vife vill be safe vith zhem—"

"I-I…I left…for a reason, My Lord."

"Zhe Aveson Coven?"

"Y-yes."

He frowned confusedly. If she *had* been a member of the Atheson Coven, she must have joined and left between his most recent visits. But that didn't matter right now. "No veason vor leaving is so important zhat you'd vather stay down 'ere and visk not only your own life but your vife's, too," he said firmly. "Vhatever issue you 'ave vith zhe coven, ve vill deal vith. Understood?"

Lysandra looked hesitant again, but she nodded. "Okay."

Alucard gently grasped her wrist, and then he dematerialized them both into vermillion smoke. He raced up into the sky and set his sights on the Atheson Coven Sanctum—a looming estate of dark stone and towering gables, its silhouette cutting sharply against the mist-laden hills beyond the city. Even from this distance, gas lamps flickered against the stained-glass windows, casting muted colours across the sprawling courtyard.

He shot forward, the wind carrying him in a surge of cold vapour. The Sanctum loomed closer, its darkened spires piercing the night, windows glowing dimly behind wrought iron balconies. He swept over the high stone walls, past the withered rose gardens, and then sped down to the courtyard.

The moment his boots touched the cobblestones, his form reassembled, smoke curling back into solid shape, his coat snapping against his legs, and his cape settling behind him. Lysandra, limp at his side, let out a weak, shuddering breath.

As he helped her walk, he strode towards the entrance, his steps echoing against the frost-dusted stone. The doors creaked open before he reached them, as if the building itself anticipated his arrival. Inside, the entrance hall stretched wide, its vaulted ceiling lost in shadow. A black chandelier hung overhead, its many wax-drenched candles casting flickering light against the polished marble floors.

Several vampires lingered near the staircase, their hushed conversations cutting off the instant Alucard stepped inside. One by one, they turned to him and dipped into bows, their movements fluid, respectful.

Alucard barely acknowledged them—they weren't his focus right now. He pivoted right, his pace quick and measured, leading through a long corridor lined with towering bookshelves and gilded torches. At the end, he pushed into the lounge. The fire burned low in the hearth, its embers casting a subdued glow over the dark leather furniture and grand piano tucked into the corner. Heavy velvet curtains shrouded the windows, sealing the room in warmth and gloom.

He took Lysandra to the couch, lowering her onto the cushioned surface. "Vait 'ere," he told her.

She leaned back with a hushed wince, nodding in response.

Alucard turned to the decanter stand—

"My Lord," Eyra said, looking startled. "Sorry, I didn't know you were coming." Her eyes then drifted over his shoulder. "M-My Lord…*she* has been Severed."

He frowned. "Severed?" Lysandra said that she *left*. But of course she'd say that…if Eyra threatened her, and he was quite certain that was the case—he had recently come to learn too well what kind of person Eyra was.

Eyra replied, "She married a human, My Lord."

Alucard rolled his eyes. "Ve do *not* punish vampires and 'umans vor 'aving consensual, vespectvul velationships vith each ozzer," he said sternly, his irritated gaze shifting from her to the vampires lined along the hall behind her.

Eyra looked confused. "But…she married a *human*."

Now really wasn't the time, but the last thing he needed was discord among his covens. He continued on his way to the decanter stand as he said, "You all know zhe vules." He took a glass. "And I'm sure zhat Lysandra is avare of zhem, too." Once he reached the couch, he used his claw to cut his wrist and let the blood pour into the glass. "You only begin serious velationships vith 'umans if you intend to turn zhem at some point." He handed Lysandra the glass of blood and asked her, "Vere you planning on turning Vosaline?"

She desperately drank the blood, and after a relieved hum, she sank into the couch a little more. "I was, My Lord," she said, already sounding much better.

"A lie!" Eyra insisted. "When I asked her that question myself, she told me that she didn't want to take that human's mortal life away!"

"*Yet,*" Lysandra snipped, tilting her head back. "She wanted me to turn Rosaline *immediately*."

Alucard dragged his hand over his face and sighed. "Vings are bad enough 'ere vithout you vighting amongst yourselves. Zhere are very clear vules vor just about any situation, including zhis." He looked at Lysandra. "'Ow long ago did you marry Vosaline?"

"Three weeks," she answered, opening her eyes to look at him.

He shifted his sights to the coven. "Ve give 'umans a year to get zheir avvairs in order." And then his frown landed on Eyra again. "Vhat made you vink zhat avter vhree veeks you could Sever 'er?"

Eyra didn't reply. Embarrassment clung to her face, and her pale cheeks reddened as the coven whispered behind her.

Alucard had far too much to do for his covens right now. Eyra was evidently proving herself to be a bad leader, but he didn't have anyone lined up to replace her—yet. "Eyra, you are starting to make me question my choice to make you Coven Master. 'Ow can I trust you to take care of a coven if you can't even envorce zhe vules properly?"

Now she was nervous. "I-I'm sorry, My Lord," she said with a stiff shake of her head. "I acted out of fear. The humans of this city are a huge threat—"

"I zon't need you to tell me zhat." He held up his index finger. "Vone more fuck up and I vill veplace you."

She nodded obediently. "Yes, My Lord. I won't disappoint you again."

He glanced back down at Lysandra. "Vonce you are 'ealed, you can't go back to zhe city—is not safe vor you. I can velocate you and your vife to a divverent city."

"Which city?"

"Vhichever 'as space. If you 'ave preverences, I'll see vhat I can do," he said firmly, and then he turned his attention to the izuret that had just arrived. "Vhat?" he asked it.

The creature told him that Danford had gotten Rosaline to safety—a small hotel at the end of Ferndale Road in the Oakley Quarter.

"I vill be back very soon. Make sure you know zhe number of 'umans you 'ave captured, and gazzer any invormation you've collected on zhe Silver Claw zhat you 'aven't alveady shared with me," he instructed the coven.

Eyra nodded and said, "Right away, My Lord."

Alucard then dematerialized into vermillion smoke and raced out through one of the windows. His work here was only just beginning.

Chapter Eleven

—⸲ ✝ ⸱—

Thirty-Seven Humans

| **Alucard** |

| *Atheson, Atheson Coven Sanctum* |

Once he collected Greymore, Danford, and Rosaline, Alucard summoned the coven to the Noctuary, the hall at the heart of the Sanctum. The high, arched ceilings disappeared into blackened stone, their surfaces etched with shimmering sigils first carved centuries ago. This Sanctum was one of his oldest properties.

At the back of the room, elevated slightly above the gathered vampires, was the stage, where Alucard settled onto a long, velvet-upholstered couch, its dark fabric absorbing the dim light of the candelabras mounted along the walls. From there, he could oversee the room, observe every face, and notice every subtle reaction.

To his right, Greymore sprawled lazily in a high-backed chair, and beside him, Danford sat stiff-backed, his hands clasped tightly together in his lap. His gaze flitted around the room, uneasy, like a lone animal stepping into unfamiliar territory.

Some of the vampires stared openly at the two werewolves, expressions ranging from wary to outright disdainful. One, seated near the front, arched a brow before turning to whisper something to the vampire beside her.

Alucard exhaled slowly, his fingers drumming against the arm of the couch. He had expected this reaction—of course he had. It was going to take time and a lot of exposure to ease his vampires into this new alliance. But that wasn't why he'd gathered them.

He tried focusing, but he was suffocating under a growing storm of frustration. As he fidgeted a little, he attempted to relax, though it got worse with every passing moment. And he was almost certain of the reason. Next to the aggravation were nagging, consuming thoughts of Zalith. His body was urging him to seek out his mate and sate his hunger—now really wasn't the time, though.

His desires were going to have to wait.

"'Ow many 'umans 'ave you gazzered?" he called.

The room fell into immediate silence.

Eyra stepped forward. "Thirty-seven, My Lord."

Alucard nodded slowly, quickly counting every vampire in the room. There were thirty-two of them—thirty-five if he included Lăcrămioara, Lysandra, and her soon-to-be-turned wife. Turning thirty-seven humans wouldn't take too much of his blood—not enough to need Zalith with him—and since Lăcrămioara was here, he thought he might as well make a start.

"Avter zhis meeting is over, bring all of zhe 'umans 'ere. I vill start turning zhem."

Eyra nodded and said, "Yes, My Lord."

His eyes then swept the crowd again. "'As zhere been ozzer news on zhe Silver Claw?" he asked. "Anyving I 'aven't yet been told?"

"His last job was apparently in Athene, My Lord," Knight Salvorn called. "Before that, he was reported in Scelerisque."

"'Ow many vampires 'as 'e killed?"

"Unknown, My Lord," he replied. "But our investigation suggests that he killed all sixteen Strayblood vampires in Scelerisque and five in Athene, as well as two Severeds." He glanced at Knight Lenore and Adherent Evaphene.

"Is zhere any vord on vhere 'e might be moving next?"

"Here, My Lord," Knight Lenore answered. "We haven't caught word of him being hired anywhere else."

Alucard sighed quietly. "I vant every Knight and Ad'erent patrolling zhe city borders and taking note of any new people entering. I'm going to compel 'umans in zhe city to keep a vecord, too." He set his eyes on Acolyte Alson, a young but determined man who'd recently graduated from the need for a mentor. "Vone of zhe 'umans vill deliver a list every day, and vill be *your* job to vead both lists to ensure zhey match."

Alson's face lit up.

"You are Dignivied to Scribe," he said firmly.

With a content smile, Alson nodded and said, "Yes, My Lord."

"What about the demons?" Eyra asked. "What if they come back?"

He thought about it for a moment. There weren't a lot of people to spare right now, but he had to make this a priority. "I vill send some of my own zemons over 'ere to 'elp, and Vulpea, too. If and vhen zhe 'ostile zemons come back, kill zhem."

The coven nodded and replied obediently.

Alucard then glanced at Greymore and quietly asked, "Do you 'ave any volves you can spare?"

Greymore nodded. "Yeah, I can recommend a few."

"*Multumesc*," he said. Then, he shifted his sights back to his coven. "Some verevolves vill also be coming to 'elp."

A concoction of wary, confused, and hostile murmurs echoed around the hall.

"I know zhat verevolves 'ave been our enemies vor a long time, but zhose of you who lived in Dor-Sanguis knew zhat I vas vorking on an alliance zhat spread vurther zhan Tobias' pack. Zhe verevolves vorking vith us are our allies. Is time to get used to zhat vact. But if any of you vink zhat you're veally going to struggle, I'll veassign you."

The room went quiet for a moment.

But then someone raised their hand.

Alucard stared at him.

"Uh…sorry, My Lord, but…I think we're all just a little worried about the fact that their venom kills us. What if one of them accidentally bites someone?" Fledgeling Casran asked.

"Are any of your volves stupid enough to slip on someving and dig zheir teeth into vone of my vampires?" Alucard asked Greymore.

Greymore scoffed amusedly. "Not that I know of."

"No vone is going to get bit," Alucard said firmly. "Are zhere any ozzer questions?"

Alson raised his hand and asked, "What do you want me to do if I notice a difference between our list and the humans' list?"

"Contact me. I zon't vant anyvone to investigate until I'm 'ere."

He nodded, lowering his hand.

"Anyving else?"

Nobody raised a hand.

"Okay," Alucard said, slouching back on the couch a little. "Eyra, Lăcrămioara, take a vew Acolytes; go and get zhe 'umans and bring zhem all 'ere. Zhe vest of you, get to vork," he instructed.

The vampires began leaving the hall, murmuring to each other.

Alucard looked to his right. "You're lucky zhey took zhat vell. I vas 'alv expecting zhem to be a whole lot more suspicious of you," he said to Greymore and shot a very brief glance at Danford, who still looked out of place.

Greymore chuckled as he leaned forward, resting his arms on his knees. "I kinda was, too. But I guess they're not entirely new to the idea if they were working with wolves before—not as closely, though, right?"

"To be 'onest, my vampires 'ardly ever saw Tobias' pack. Zhey knew *of* zhe collaboration, zhough, and none vaised concerns."

"Maybe having Danny Boy here helped, huh?" he said with a grin, patting Danford's shoulder.

Danford laughed awkwardly. "Maybe." But his eyes shifted to the right.

Alucard followed the wolf-vampire's gaze, and his sight landed on one of the Fledgelings. "Vhat?" he questioned.

The Fledgeling stood a few feet from the stage, small and pale, her wavy blonde hair half-tucked behind her ears. She gripped a broom awkwardly, her posture uncertain, as if she weren't sure whether she should be sweeping or shrinking into the shadows. The hem of her dark dress barely brushed the floor, her shoes scuffed from hesitance rather than wear. "Um…sorry, My Lord," she said nervously.

He frowned, recalling the girl's name. "Is Odette, no?"

She nodded, a smile tugging at her lips. "Y-yes, My Lord—or Odi."

"Vhat do you vant?" he asked.

"Well…" she answered, her crimson eyes flicking towards Danford for a moment. "I was just…curious."

"About?"

"Um…him." She pointed at the wolf-vampire. "I heard that he's a hybrid."

Alucard slowly tapped his fingers on the armrest. "'E is."

Odette fidgeted with the broom handle. "Acolyte Marius said that…you were shot, My Lord, and the bullet went through you and into him—that's how he became a hybrid."

"Zhat's 'ow 'appened," he confirmed calmly, but his frustration was returning, urging him to wrap things up and get home to Zalith.

"Does that mean that you could make others like him?" she asked, intrigued.

"Probably," he replied, and then he looked at Danford. "Do you vant a little pack of volf-vampires, Zanvord?" he asked flatly, hiding his sarcasm to see how he reacted.

Danford's eyes widened a little. "My own pack?" he asked and glanced at Greymore.

Greymore grimaced at him.

"Per'aps someday," Alucard mumbled, setting his eyes back on Odette.

"Yeah, maybe," Greymore echoed.

"Can I join?" Odette asked eagerly.

Alucard laughed a little, sitting up straight. "Zoesn't vork zhat vay. Vampires can't become someving else."

"Oh…well, I just wanted to help," she said, lowering her head.

"Sorry," Danford quietly said to her.

"Who put you on cleaning duty?" Alucard then questioned.

"Um…Madame Lăcrămioara."

"Vhy?"

"Because I'm a problem student, My Lord," she answered honestly.

"Vhy are you problem student?"

She didn't hesitate. "I attacked Acolyte Isabeau during feeding training. I'm learning slower than the others to control my hunger."

He nodded slowly. "Zon't give up," he encouraged her. "Sometimes, zhe slower learners acquire sharper 'unting skills because zhey learned to understand viner details about zheir prey."

Odette's face lit up. "Really?"

"*Da.*"

She smiled, hope filling her eyes.

"Go now," Alucard told her as he watched Eyra and Lăcrămioara lead the panicking captured humans into the hall with a group of Acolytes.

With a nod, she turned around and hurried out of one of the doors.

"Here they are, My Lord," Eyra said as she stopped by the stage, leaving Lăcrămioara and the Acolytes to group the humans up.

Alucard watched the group fumble around, blindfolded, their arms and ankles bound with rope. Their annoying, muffled grunts and cries made him scowl, and as he eyed each one, he calculated exactly how much of his blood he'd need to draw. Three or four small glasses would do.

He then glanced at Greymore. "Vould you vather not be 'ere vor zhis? I'm sure zhat vatching a bunch of 'umans turn into vampires isn't exactly 'ow you planned to spend zhe vest of your day."

Greymore shrugged. "I don't mind, man."

Alucard nodded and then set his sights on Lăcrămioara. He held up four fingers, and the woman quickly went over to one of the cabinets, took out four small drinking glasses, and then returned, handing them to him.

He sat up, putting three of the glasses aside. After rolling up his left sleeve a little, he used his claw to cut his wrist; he watched his blood quickly fill the first glass, and once it was full, he handed it to Lăcrămioara. When he filled the second, he gave it to Eyra, the third to one of the Acolytes, and the last to another.

And then the four vampires got to work.

Lăcrămioara started. One of the other Acolytes removed the human's blindfold and gag, revealing wide, unfocused eyes and lips trembling from parted, ragged breaths. The Acolyte gripped the man's jaw and forced his mouth open, and Lăcrămioara tilted the glass against his lips, letting the thick, dark liquid coat his tongue, making him swallow.

The change began immediately.

A sharp, suffocated gasp escaped the human, as if his body had realized it had taken in something that shouldn't belong. The man convulsed, his muscles seizing as the blood raced through him, making his breaths broken and uneven.

Alucard could hear his heart racing—the man's pulse spiked…and then it faltered.

A single, violent shudder wracked the human's body. His veins blackened beneath his skin, creeping from his throat outward like dark tendrils burrowing through flesh. He jerked against his bindings, spine arching, eyes rolling back. His breath caught before coming in wet, unsteady gasps as though he were drowning.

Alucard narrowed his gaze. He'd seen this many times before—the body's resistance, the desperate clawing at mortality, at something slipping away. But his blood was already within the human, warping his flesh, stripping away his humanity thread by thread. There was nothing his body could do but yield.

And then the man's heartbeat faltered before coming to a halt. For a long moment, his body hung in eerie stillness, the ropes holding it upright as though the only thing keeping it from collapse.

In the corner of his eye, Alucard saw Danford lean forward—

The man suddenly inhaled sharply, and Danford exclaimed quietly in surprise.

However, the man's inhale wasn't a breath. It was a dragged-in, unnatural sound, as if his body needed a moment to remember how to function without a beating heart.

Slowly, the blackened veins receded… and the man's eyes snapped open.

He wasn't human anymore.

The Acolyte who helped turn him gripped his jaw, forcing him to meet Alucard's gaze.

Alucard watched the recognition slowly seep into the new Fledgeling's crimson eyes, the moment where confusion melted into something deeper, something irreversible. And then he shifted his sights back to Lăcrămioara. "Continue."

He watched as one by one, the humans went through the same process, their humanity burning away as his blood raged through their frail bodies.

But he was starting to feel the weight of his blood loss. It wasn't *that* which had him conflicted, though. He knew that Zalith was going to be upset with him for making the decision to turn humans without him being there, but he'd understand, too, right? He had to do this. He wasn't going to risk the coven.

One of the humans suddenly cried out.

Alucard's attention snapped to her. He watched as the woman's body seized, her limbs pulling taut against her bindings, her veins bulging, pulsing too fast, too hard. She let out another horrible scream, one that warped mid-sound, turning wet and broken, as if her own throat was dissolving mid-shriek.

And then something else started—not transformation but the other, rarer result that came when a human consumed Alucard's blood.

Her skin darkened, blistering from the inside out, the blood within her veins boiling, thickening, turning black. It spread across her body like ink dropped into water, curling through her flesh in uneven waves. Her cheeks caved inward, flesh sagging like overheated wax before it began to slide from her bones; her eyes liquefied, dripping from their sockets in thick, viscous trails, her lips slipping away to reveal teeth that no longer had anything to hold them in place. She tried to scream again, but her jaw was already gone, the skin of her neck collapsing, sloughing off in heavy chunks that hit the floor with a sickening splatter.

The other humans writhed on the ground, their own transformations continuing, some convulsing violently, others whimpering as their bones reshaped and their bodies accepted the change.

But not her.

Her ribcage collapsed inward, the entire weight of her torso sinking into itself, her arms splitting at the elbows, bones pushing through liquefied skin before they, too, dissolved. Her body was eating itself, consuming every last part that tried and failed to hold onto the borrowed blood. And by the time her spine buckled, curling into the thickened pool of what remained, there was nothing left but the last sluggish trails of melting viscera.

A moment of silence followed, broken only by the wet sound of the last of her collapsing remains oozing across the marble floor.

The vampires leading the ritual exchanged glances, tense and uneasy.

"What the fuck?" Greymore grimaced.

"Did she just... *melt*?" Danford asked with a revolted frown—he looked like he might throw up... again.

"Vejection," Alucard muttered.

Danford's frown shifted to him. "Why did she reject it?"

"'Er body vas alveady vailing bevore zhe change. Zidn't 'ave zhe strength to vithstand vhat vas vequired." He glanced towards the dark, congealed remains. "Most who turn need only enough blood to sever zheir mortality, to veplace vhat vas 'uman vith someving stronger. But very vew vequire more zhan vhat is standard. If zhey zon't veceive zhat, zheir body breaks down instead of adapting. Zhe blood vights to vemake zhem, but zhere isn't enough of to sustain zhe process." He gestured at the mess on the floor. "Zhis is vhat 'appens vhen zhe body vails to keep up."

A few of the younger vampires shifted uneasily.

Alucard straightened. "Next time, you'll be more carevul vhen selecting who is vorth turning." His tone wasn't cruel, but it was absolute. Turning was not a gift—it was a threshold few were meant to cross. And those who weren't paid for it.

"F-failing how?" the wolf-vampire asked.

"Assuming zhat none of you noticed physical signs," Alucard muttered, glaring at each of the vampires he'd sent to collect the humans, "vas probably cancer."

Greymore grunted. "I guess vampire blood can't heal everything."

"Sometimes," he mumbled, eyeing the surviving Fledgelings. "Take zhem all to zhe Dvelling Space," he instructed. "Begin training zhem as soon as zhey're all lucid." He set his eyes on the Acolyte who'd fed the melted woman. "You, clean zhis shit up."

"Y-yes, My Lord," he said and hurried into one of the closets.

Eyra, Lăcrămioara, and the Acolytes began pulling the Fledgelings to their feet, and once they were all standing—albeit stumbling and staggering—they slowly led them out of the hall and deeper into the Sanctum.

Now, Alucard wanted to go home.

He turned his head, looking at Greymore and Danford. "Are you veady to 'ead back?"

They both nodded.

Alucard stood up and led them down from the stage, passing the Acolyte as he frantically scrubbed the floor. He rolled his eyes, ignoring the foul smell, and left the Coven Sanctum. The moment they were outside, he gripped Danford and Greymore's wrists, and then he dematerialized them all into vermillion smoke, racing back towards Uzlia.

For now, his job here was done, but he knew he'd be back very soon. The Silver Claw was on his way, and Alucard was going to do whatever was necessary to ensure that the Atheson Coven was kept safe.

Chapter Twelve

— ⋖ † ⋗ —

Moments Like These

| Zalith |
| *Aestrael, Uzlia Isles, Usrul, Castle Reiner* |

As 8 p.m. neared, Zalith leaned back in his seat, tapping his fingers on his desk. Alucard had been gone since noon, but it felt like a century. He was worried about his fiancé, and he also longed to hold him—those feelings combined made it hard for him to concentrate on his work.

He kept trying, though, looking down at the information he'd gathered on the Orrivain, as well as what Syllia had told him. It was likely that Calitharion would want different things than Syllia, so in order to come up with a treaty that he could confidently offer the elves, he'd need to talk to one and find out what their leader desired.

But how was he going to talk to one of them? Would they even talk to him?

With a deep sigh, he leaned back in his seat again. Perhaps he'd have to capture one. Sure, kidnapping someone and then trying to have a civilized conversation with them probably wasn't the best way to go about things, but the only other option was to send a message to Calitharion himself—a message that might go ignored or cause the elf leader to move up whatever plans he might have for the Yrudyen and Eimwood.

He tapped his fingers on his desk. Maybe he could send a message to one of the elves instead. However, that could have the same effect.

Another sigh escaped him. He sipped from his bourbon—when he heard the castle front door open and close, though, a heavy sense of relief *and* desire washed over him. His heart beat a little faster, and his instincts urged him to get up and rush downstairs. He didn't want to let his desperation rule him, though—not entirely. So he waited, focusing on Alucard's aura, feeling him getting closer as he walked through the halls.

The moment his fiancé pushed the door open and stepped into his office, Zalith smiled and stood up.

"Hey," the demon said, walking to him.

Alucard smiled and said, "Hi."

Zalith wrapped his arms around him and hugged him tightly. "How did things go?"

"Zhey vent okay," he said.

The demon stepped back, but as he admired Alucard's face, he noticed the fatigue in his eyes, and in the hints of sunlight that flowed in through the windows, he didn't fail to see that his fiancé's skin was a tad paler than usual. "Are you okay?" he asked worriedly.

Alucard nodded.

That didn't settle his concern, though. He tucked the loose strands of Alucard's hair behind his ears. "Are you sure? You look exhausted, baby."

He shrugged lightly, and as he donned a conflicted frown, he looked away for a moment. "Zon't get mad at me," he murmured.

Zalith tensed a little. What was he about to tell him?

"Vings in Aveson are vorse zhan I vhought. Ve vound a vampire 'anging in zhe city square. Zhe 'umans aren't avraid at all, and I'm vorried about zhe coven. I know I said zhat I'd vait to bring you vith me, but I 'ad to make some new vampires vight zhere and zhen—only vhirty-seven, zhough; I zidn't make a vull 'undred."

With a heavy sigh, Zalith straightened Alucard's shirt collar. He was annoyed—what if something happened? What if someone took advantage of Alucard's vulnerability?—but he understood. His fiancé was just trying to protect his people, and he knew more than anyone what that felt like. So he wasn't angry. He wasn't going to scold him as if he were a child.

He pulled him into another hug. "I'm not mad at you," he murmured…and he couldn't help but quietly inhale his scent. "I just worry about you all the time."

Alucard nuzzled his neck. "I know, but you zon't 'ave to. I can 'andle myselv."

Zalith chuckled and said, "Even so, I still worry." He kissed Alucard's cheek, and then he gazed at his face again. "How did making new vampires go?"

"Vent vell. Vone of zhe 'umans vejected zhe blood, zhough, so zhere's a 'uge mess in zhe Sanctum Noctuary."

He frowned curiously. "Rejected?"

"Zhe blood zidn't take. 'Appens sometimes vhen zhe 'uman is terminally sick or someving, and zhey eizer zon't get zhe extra blood needed to 'eal zhem, or zhe sickness vas just too severe," the vampire explained.

"Huh…" he responded, intrigued. "I'm over six hundred years old and I'm still learning new things about vampires—but I *am* engaged to their creator, so I shouldn't be surprised." He smirked and kissed his fiancé's lips.

Alucard smiled amusedly. "Soon, you'll know all zhe intricate details."

Zalith stroked his hands down the vampire's body and gripped his waist. He then slowly guided him back towards his desk, the desire and instincts quickly taking over.

But when they started kissing, each more frantic than the last, he let himself hesitate. Before he could give in entirely, he needed to make sure that Alucard was truly okay.

After one more kiss, he stopped and gazed into the vampire's eyes—eyes filled with anticipation. "You need blood first."

His fiancé huffed lightly. "Okay."

The demon kissed his lips a few more times, and then he gently gripped a fistful of Alucard's hair and guided his face to his neck.

Alucard didn't waste time. He sank his fangs into Zalith's neck; the demon groaned delightedly in response, and the vampire hummed in satisfaction, gulping down his blood. With every passing second, Alucard's venom spread further through his body, enthralling him in a desperate, pleasing high. He did his best to hold on, though, to wait until Alucard was finished.

The instant Alucard's fangs withdrew from his neck, Zalith felt the sting of loss—but only for a moment. Heat replaced it. Desire. The urgent need to have him. He grabbed him, spun him around, and bent him over the desk, his pulse hammering with anticipation.

Alucard didn't resist. His hands braced against the wood, his breath uneven, his body already yielding. Zalith's blood was still on his lips, his pupils wide and dazed.

Zalith worked quickly, one hand seizing the lube while the other ripped Alucard's belt open, dragging his trousers down. His fingers spread over the vampire's ass, kneading into soft flesh before massaging the slick liquid between his cheeks, pressing inside just enough to feel him clench in response.

Perfect. Always perfect.

His own belt came undone next, his trousers falling in a careless heap around his ankles, the weight of his own need making his hands shake as he slicked his length. He didn't waste time. He pressed the tip against Alucard's ass and pushed in, feeling the tight heat stretch around him, taking him in inch by inch.

A pleased moan escaped his lips the moment he buried himself inside, the sheer relief of it crashing over him like fire.

And Alucard—Alucard whimpered delightedly, his fingers gripping the desk, his back arching instinctively to take more.

Zalith set a rhythm, slow, deep thrusts that sent pleasure rolling through him, each push making Alucard tense and tremble beneath him. The sound of their bodies meeting and the faint creak of the desk beneath them only heightened the intoxicating pull inside Zalith's blood.

He shouldn't have been thinking about it.

But he was.

There it was again.

The whispering desire to breed him.

It shouldn't have mattered. It wasn't possible.

But his instincts didn't care. The need to claim—to spill into him and ensure every drop stayed buried—burned hot in the back of his mind. He tightened his grip on Alucard's hips and drove into him harder, deeper, pulling him back against his dick with each thrust, like he could push the release deeper into his body and make it *take*.

His fiancé wasn't ready to cum yet.

And Zalith wasn't about to let him.

Instead, he kept Alucard teetering on the edge, keeping him right there—enough friction to drive him wild, enough pressure to make him whimper and squirm, but not enough to let him climax.

But him?

He was close.

And the moment was coming fast.

The pressure built too quickly, too deep, too strong. Zalith growled, his fingers tightening bruisingly around Alucard's hips, dragging him harder against his thrusts, chasing that final moment.

And then pleasure slammed through him like a shockwave, his whole body tensing as he buried himself to the hilt, his cum spilling deep inside Alucard's trembling body. He let out a low, shaking moan, his breath ragged, his muscles locking as wave after wave of relief and satisfaction rolled over him.

Alucard was *his*.

The thought lingered, intense and possessive in the haze of his pleasure, his hands lingering on Alucard's waist, his grip instinctively firm, like he wanted to keep him there—keep him full.

But he wasn't done.

Still catching his breath, Zalith eased back, sliding out of his fiancé with one last slow drag that left Alucard shuddering.

Before the vampire could protest, Zalith turned him, gripping his thighs, lifting him slightly onto the edge of the desk. Alucard's breath caught in confusion, but it turned into a moan when Zalith dropped to his knees.

His mouth found him instantly. Hot and irresistibly sweet. The moment his lips wrapped around Alucard's dick, the taste sent a deep, satisfied hum through him. He savoured it, teasing him with slow strokes of his tongue, tracing every inch as if he hadn't already committed him to memory.

Alucard's hand shot into his hair, fingers curling, gripping, yet he was too wrecked to say anything, too overwhelmed to do more than gasp, whimper, and let himself go.

And Zalith wanted him to.

The demon pressed in deeper, taking him into his throat, swallowing him in with greed and determination.

It didn't take long.

Alucard tensed, his moan breaking into something desperate as he climaxed, his cum spilling into Zalith's mouth.

Zalith swallowed every drop. The taste was exquisite—dark and rich, familiar in the way that only his mate's essence could be. Contentment curled in Zalith's chest as he pulled back, licking the last traces from his lips before kissing his way up Alucard's stomach, past his ribs, over his sternum, up the curve of his throat. And by the time he reached his lips, Alucard was barely holding himself up.

The demon pulled him into a hug. He felt the way his vampire melted against him, how his breath still came in uneven, delicate shudders. His own heartbeat slowed, the lingering haze of climax gradually ebbing into something softer, something calmer. He exhaled against Alucard's hair, tightening his grip slightly, his lips brushing against the side of his head in a quiet, wordless affection.

For a moment, they just stayed like that, letting it settle, letting it linger, and letting the quiet hold them.

"I love you, Zaliv," Alucard murmured, his voice soft and drowsy.

A slow, pleased smile tugged at Zalith's lips. Those were the words he loved most from Alucard, the ones that settled deep in his chest, warm and absolute. "I love you too, darling," he whispered, pressing a gentle kiss to Alucard's temple.

The demon then kicked his trousers from around his ankles and helped Alucard free of his; he guided him over to the couch, where they fell and rested, the vampire laying his head on Zalith's shoulder.

For a while, they lay in silence, no sound but the fading birdsong and distant ocean outside. Zalith enjoyed moments like these, moments that made him feel far from all the troubles of his life—*their* lives. Moments where it was just him and the man he loved. Right now, nothing else mattered.

He kissed Alucard's head again, stroking his arm, smiling as the vampire hummed contently and nuzzled his neck.

"'Ow vas vork?" his fiancé asked quietly.

Zalith shrugged. "The usual. I'm going to try and talk to an Orrivain Elf. I want to see if they all feel the same way as their leader."

"Vhen?"

"Tomorrow. Maybe after we're done showing our faces at the city celebration."

"I'll come vith you," Alucard offered.

"Are you sure? Will your vampires be okay?"

"Mm-hmm. I sent Vulpea to 'elp zhem, and some of my zemons—Zhomas spared some of 'is volves, too. Zhe coven vill contact me if anyving 'appens."

"Okay. Have you decided when you'll be turning all those other humans?" he asked.

"Not yet. Probably vonce all of my covens 'ave zhe exact number I asked vor."

"Well, let me know. I'm still coming with you."

The vampire nodded lightly. "Zhat's okay." He exhaled deeply, shuffling around and making himself comfortable. "Zon't vorget zhat ve're meeting zhe ozzer Dor-Sanguian verevolf packs zhe day avter tomorrow."

Zalith chuckled a little. "Do you think it'll go well?"

"I 'ope so. But vith zhe virus and Liliv's zemons sveeping zhe vorld, I can't imagine zhey'd say no to all zhis extra security."

He let out a deep sigh and started fiddling with Alucard's hair. "Do you think Lilith will give up?" he asked, but he was quite sure he knew the answer.

"I zon't know. Vrom vhat I vemember of 'er, she vas alvays very adamant and determined…but zhat vas only ever to prove 'erselv to Luciver, so I zon't know."

"We just have to wait it out, I suppose," he said, but he didn't let the despondency take hold. He wanted to remain in this perfect moment.

"Ve'll vigure vings out, zon't vorry. Ve're alveady making good progress," his fiancé assured him, and then he kissed his neck. "Zon't vink about 'er vight now. She'll never vind us 'ere."

He was still struggling to settle into that idea despite the existence of the Aestrael Curve, *and* despite knowing how many wards and barriers and spells had been put around Uzlia. "Yeah," he replied, resting the side of his head against Alucard's…but he could feel himself slipping—the paranoia that he'd managed to fight off the past few days was trying to break through. He wasn't about to let it. "Alucard," he said, smirking as he focused on his fiancé's intoxicating scent.

"Zaliv," he replied.

"Can I fuck you again?"

Alucard laughed a little. "I vas beginning to vorry zhat you'd never ask."

Zalith's smirk grew. He was going to make the most of this—now, later, tomorrow, this week, and the rest of Alucard's heat cycle. He wasn't going to waste a moment.

Chapter Thirteen

— ⸱ † ⸱ —

The City Celebration

| Alucard—Thursday, Tertium 30th, 960(TG) |
| Uzlia Isles, Yrudberg, Eimwood City |

The air was thick with the sound of revelry.

As Alucard and Zalith rode through Eimwood's stone-arched gates, the streets of Oklens unfolded before them in a spectacle of celebration. Banners of deep crimson and gold draped between lampposts, their silken edges fluttering in the crisp afternoon breeze. Garlands of laurel and ivy coiled around iron balconies, and ribbons in every shade imaginable cascaded down from windows, catching in the wind like the tails of kites.

Main Street was lined with wooden stalls and carriages, their vendors shouting over the din, offering steaming roasted meat, sugared almonds, spiced cider, and rich honeyed whiskey poured from glass decanters into gleaming tumblers, and the scent of freshly baked bread, charred meats, and mulled wine wrapped around them.

Musicians had taken their places on hastily erected wooden platforms, their fiddles and banjos setting the rhythm of the celebration, while further down, a brass band struck up a triumphant march, its horns and drums booming over the cobblestone streets.

And the people filled every space in sight.

Men wearing pressed waistcoats and polished boots leaned against posts, laughing and clinking their glasses. Women in layered skirts of satin and lace gathered in clusters, their hats adorned with ribbons and feathers, their fans fluttering as they whispered and cast glances at Alucard and Zalith.

Children wove through the throng, their laughter ringing out as they chased one another with handmade paper masks, some shaped like bats, others like wolves, an homage to their new Lords.

From a balcony, a woman in an emerald silk dress raised a glass, her voice clear above the crowd, "To our new Lords—may their reign be long and their rule be just!"

A cheer erupted, voices rising in unison as tankards and glasses were lifted.

Alucard's gaze swept the crowd, taking in the beaming faces, the enthusiasm, the fevered energy pulsing through the city like a beating heart. It wasn't a bad welcome. He flicked a glance towards Zalith, who was smirking faintly, his dark eyes gleaming as he took in the celebration like a man savouring the finest of wines; he tilted his head slightly at Alucard, his smirk deepening.

The vampire smiled at him, but in the corner of his eye, he spotted a familiar scowling face—wavy black hair, jealousy-filled eyes.

Desmond.

"Look who decided to show 'is vace," Alucard muttered, taking his eyes off the man.

Zalith glanced over there and scoffed under his breath. "I'll get someone to keep an eye on him. The last thing we need is him causing shit."

Alucard nodded and flicked the reins, guiding his horse forward alongside his fiancé as they moved deeper into the heart of the city.

The crowd thickened around them, people pushing closer, eager to catch a glimpse of their new Lords. Some reached out, fingers grazing the hems of their coats as they passed, murmuring blessings, congratulations—some even daring hushed reverence.

Main Street unfolded ahead, its wide avenue flanked by towering brick storefronts adorned with banners and velvet drapery. Lanterns hung from iron hooks, their glass panels etched with intricate designs, waiting for nightfall to set them aglow.

Ahead, where the street met the river, a wide stage loomed, built against the grand stone bridge that arched over the waterway. A temporary platform of polished oak, draped in deep red fabric embroidered with the city's sigil, had been raised in their honour. Gold-accented chairs lined the back of the stage, meant for local dignitaries, but for now, they remained unoccupied.

As they approached, two attendants in navy tailcoats stepped forward, each reaching to take the reins of their horses.

Alucard swung a leg over the side, dismounting, his boots landing on the cobblestone with a muted thud, and he held his cane at his side—if the elves *did* show up, he was prepared. Beside him, Zalith dismounted too, his coat ruffling slightly as he adjusted his stance, exuding the same effortless confidence he always did.

A low murmur rippled through the gathered citizens as they ascended the steps to the stage. Some clapped, others cheered, voices lifting in excitement as the swarming mass of people gathered at the base.

The street was packed shoulder to shoulder, a sea of colour and movement. Some perched on crates, barrels, and even the ledges of storefront windows to get a better view. A few waved handkerchiefs or small flags, while others whispered eagerly, anticipation thick in the air.

Zalith's fingers brushed against Alucard's wrist—a small, almost absent gesture, but enough to make it clear that he was enjoying this. And then the demon stepped forward, stopping at the edge of the stage, his gaze sweeping over the crowd. The noise slowly tapered off, voices dying down, replaced by the sound of the river lapping against the bridge's stone foundation.

A hush settled over them, a collective inhale.

"People of Eimwood," Zalith called—his voice rang out over the square, smooth, assured, carrying the weight of authority without the stiffness of formality. "Ezra and I stand before you today, honoured to take on the responsibility of leading this city. Eimwood has suffered—its people have endured—but those days are over."

A murmur of agreement travelled through the crowd, some nodding, others watching him intently.

"We are here to rebuild, to restore Eimwood to what it once was, and make it stronger. Safer. No more unchecked threats. No more destruction. No more fear. No more corruption. We will ensure that no enemy sets foot within these walls again."

Applause broke out, a few cheers rising above it.

Zalith let it swell for a moment before he lifted a hand, easily regaining their attention. "And to that end, we have secured an alliance with the Yrudyen Elves."

That got a stronger reaction—some surprised gasps, hushed whispers weaving through the crowd.

Zalith continued, "That means no more kidnappings, no more raids, no more pillaging. The hostility is over. The borders are secure. The trade roads and railways will reopen without fear of ambush. Eimwood will no longer be caught in old blood feuds."

The relief was visible, people clapping wildly, excited chatter darting from person to person.

"But we aren't stopping there," the demon said. "We will attempt an alliance with the Orrivain Elves as well."

A heavier silence fell. This time, Zalith's words were met with uncertainty and hesitation. The Orrivain were an unknown enemy to many of them—more isolated, more unpredictable.

"I know what you're thinking," Zalith said understandingly. "But we will not walk into negotiations blindly. We do this for both the sake of Eimwood and the elves—for stability, for safety, for the future of these islands."

A few scattered cheers, cautious but hopeful.

The demon glanced at Alucard briefly before turning back to the crowd. "Make no mistake—our loyalty is to this city and its people. Eimwood is our priority. That is why demons and werewolves have been joining our ranks—not as a threat, but as a means of securing Eimwood and, in turn, all of Uzlia." He paused for a moment before continuing, "They are here to strengthen us, to stand beside us. The city's protection will be unmatched, and under our rule, Eimwood will be a place where no citizen has to fear for their life again."

Cheers erupted, louder this time, voices rising in approval.

Zalith let the sound settle before offering the crowd a sly, knowing smirk. "But let's not spend the entire day talking politics, shall we?" His voice took on a lighter edge. "There's a celebration happening, after all—and far too much fine whiskey waiting to be poured. Enjoy the party, drink, dance, and revel in the fact that Eimwood is safe." With that, he stepped back, lifting a hand in a final parting gesture.

The cheers rose again, stronger than before, the crowd finally breaking into a full-fledged celebration.

Alucard exhaled quietly beside him.

Zalith, still smirking, leaned in just enough to murmur, "I think they like us."

The vampire smiled at him. "I vink so, too."

"Come on. We should enjoy the party for a little," Zalith said, taking his hand.

Alucard followed him down off the stage, and the energy of the celebration swallowed them whole. People gathered close, patting Zalith's back, bowing slightly to Alucard, offering firm handshakes and clinking glasses. The tension of speeches and politics faded beneath the hum of music, the scent of spiced cider, and the weight of warm bodies pressing in with eager conversation.

Zalith, ever the effortless charmer, steered them through the crowd with an easy confidence, accepting a drink from a passing server and nudging a second into Alucard's hand. Alucard took it, the cool glass settling against his fingers, and let himself be led into the thick of it.

The first conversation was with a cluster of merchants, eager to discuss the new trade routes. The blockades caused by the conflict with the Yrudyen had crippled exports, but now, with safe passage secured, the city could finally reconnect with the rest of Uzlia. There was talk of widening the main road, securing new caravans, stationing additional guards along key junctions, and expanding the railways that climbed the mountains and allowed the transportation of precious materials mined far beyond the city.

Alucard listened carefully, offering measured nods and sharp, precise answers. He let Zalith handle most of the social pleasantries, but when numbers were mentioned— the cost of infrastructure, the balancing of imports against local goods—he stepped in, cutting through the uncertainty with clear, logical direction.

From trade, the topic shifted to employment.

A group of blacksmiths and labourers approached, their voices carrying the weight of concern. With the demons and werewolves settling in, what would that mean for the city's existing workforce? Would Eimwood's human citizens be cast aside?

Zalith fielded their doubts gracefully, laying out plans for cooperative workforces, construction contracts for new housing, and city expansions that would require more workers than ever before. Alucard added to it, outlining tax incentives, ensuring that no existing businesses would be disrupted. He explained that they weren't replacing Eimwood's citizens—they were fortifying them.

The mood shifted. Relief settled in, cautious but real.

And then another drink.

And another.

The hours bled together in a blur of voices, flickering candlelight, and the clink of glasses and silverware.

Talk of farmland came next, led by a wiry older man with dirt-stained hands and a stubborn glint in his eye. With the conflicts settling, there would be land to reclaim, soil to till, homes to build beyond the city's edge. They needed guarantees, promises that the expansion wouldn't be seized by the Lords or encroached upon by forces unknown. Alucard gave them what they needed: clear answers, firm reassurances, the kind of certainty that put worried minds at ease.

More drinks.

More conversation.

The evening deepened, but neither of them felt its weight despite having told each other that they'd only spend a few hours here.

Lamps burned low, their golden glow spilling over cobblestone. Somewhere in the square, a fiddle struck up a livelier tune, laughter rising with it. Someone passed Zalith a whiskey glass filled nearly to the brim, and Alucard found another slipped into his own hand before he could think to refuse.

The vampire glanced at Zalith. His mate was laughing, lips curled in an amused smirk, eyes bright with both liquor and victory—seeing the demon so content after all the dismay and paranoia made him smile wider.

As the last glow of sunset bled into the horizon, the city burned with lamplight and laughter.

Alucard and Zalith moved through the crowd, offering brief nods and parting gestures to those who still had the energy to acknowledge them. The air was thick with the remnants of revelry: spilt ale soaking into cobblestone, the lingering sweetness of roasted nuts and mulled wine, and the low murmur of voices slurred with exhaustion.

As Alucard passed the faces of merchants, labourers, soldiers, and seamstresses—people who had spent years uncertain of their city's fate—he could see that this moment belonged to them. Their Lords had given them something to believe in again.

They walked past drunken clusters of citizens draped over wooden benches, their heads lolling back in spent laughter. A few still swayed to the music, boots scuffing lazily against the stone. A handful of guards nursed half-empty bottles, keeping an eye on the city square with far less rigidity than usual.

Alucard breathed in the night air, cool against the fading warmth of the day, and let himself savour it. It had been a long time since he'd felt this…settled. His gaze flicked to Zalith; the demon walked with an easy, confident stride, hands relaxed at his sides, his usual smirk still playing at his lips. His dark eyes glowed faintly under the gas lamps, alight with something Alucard hadn't seen in too long.

Zalith felt like himself again.

After everything they had lost—after everything they had fought to hold on to— seeing him like this felt like its own kind of victory.

By the time they reached their horses, most of the celebration had blurred into a distant hum behind them. Alucard ran a hand down the side of his stallion's neck, feeling the steady warmth of it beneath his glove, then pulled himself into the saddle.

Zalith followed, swinging onto his own horse, and for a moment, they simply sat there, looking out over the city—the lantern-lit streets, the curling ribbons still hanging from balconies, the last flickers of celebration echoing from the main square.

A good night.

A good start to their new rule.

With a light tap of his reins, the vampire turned his horse towards home. "Vhat's our next step?" he asked curiously. "Ve should vink about a new city council, vight? A government, maybe."

Zalith nodded. "We'll start with a council. I think we should have representatives for each people—humans, demons, werewolves, and the elves, too. And we'll need to pick out a mayor."

"Zhat's a good idea. Ve'll need aldermen—some landowners, invluential vigures, and some merchants. Somevone to vepresent Oklens, and anozzer to vepresent Bauvell."

"A head of trade, a head of security, a head of law," Zalith continued with a small sigh. "We'll figure it all out. I'll ask Idina to send over a list of candidates."

Alucard nodded, setting his eyes on the city gates.

But that was when he caught it.

The scent of blood.

He brought his horse to a halt, and so did Zalith.

They shot each other a glance, a glance that wordlessly told each other they'd picked up the same smell.

And they both knew the same thing.

Something was wrong.

Chapter Fourteen

— ⸱ † ⸱ —

Cloaked and Hooded

| **Alucard** |
| *Uzlia Isles, Yrudberg, Eimwood City* |

Without faltering, Alucard grabbed Zalith's wrist and dematerialized them both into vermillion smoke. He raced into the air and followed the scent of blood to the end of the river, where it flowed out through a grate and under the city walls. When he landed, he stared at the grate—the iron bars had been melted away, and a flurry of muddy footprints spread from the riverbank, along the cobblestone path, and behind the rows of houses and stores.

The blood they'd smelled was splattered up the wall and over the bricks of the house behind them, and lying in the alley was a dead merchant.

"Fuck," Zalith grunted.

Alucard frowned, noticing a black shimmer on the grate bars. He stepped over the short wall—

"Be careful," his fiancé said cautiously.

The vampire slid down to the riverbank. He moved towards the grate, and when he reached it, he dragged his fingers over the melted metal. A black, soot-like powder clung to his skin, and when he inhaled, capturing the scent, his frown thickened. "Is elv ethos," he said, looking up at Zalith. "Dark…" he paused and sniffed again. "And old—very old. Is zhe kind of ethos zhat some beings draw vrom Erich's moon."

Zalith's frown deepened with worry. He swiftly summoned an izuret, taking Alucard's hand with his free one and helping him up from the bank. "Tell your friends to go to as many of my demons as possible. Tell them that we might have an incursion."

The izuret nodded and immediately disappeared.

"I'll get my vampires to 'elp get people to zheir 'omes," Alucard said and quickly sent a message to the vampires he had in Uzlia.

"Come on," Zalith then said, hurriedly following the muddy footprints.

Alucard trailed behind him, focusing his senses, searching for elf auras, but he couldn't detect anything other than Eimwood's citizens, his arriving vampires, and Zalith's patrolling demons.

The footsteps took them through the winding alleyways, around the back of more houses, and near the city gates…but that was where they stopped.

Zalith and Alucard halted. There were still no auras, no sign of who had entered the city. And although there weren't footsteps, there *were* mud trails up the side of the house they stood beside.

"I'll go up," Alucard said. "You should go to zhe streets and be veady in case anyving 'appens."

The demon looked hesitant. "I don't want to leave you."

"I'll be okay. Ve 'ave backup zhis time. And ve can't visk anyvone else dying; ve've only just been accepted 'ere, and ve can't avvord to lose zhis place."

Zalith stared at him for a moment, but he knew just as well as Alucard did that they had to ensure the people felt safe and defended. "Okay," he said reluctantly. He kissed his lips, and then he disappeared down a winding alley, heading for the street.

Alucard looked up, his eyes following the mud trails on the bricks, and then he vanished into vermillion smoke and reappeared on the roof—

The moment he saw the cloaked, hooded figure crouching behind the chimney and watching the street below, he lunged and grabbed it. The woman squirmed in his grip, but he pinned her down on the tiles and held one hand over her mouth, silencing her as he pulled her hood away.

Grey skin, sharp ears, and yellow eyes.

Orrivain.

Alucard snarled at her. "'Ow many of you are 'ere?"

She scowled up at him.

Hoping that he wasn't further than a mile away—and that nobody would take the chance to attempt peering into his mind—Alucard reached for Zalith's mind. Thankfully, he wasn't far away at all. "*Zaliv, zhere's an Orrivain Elv on zhe voof,*" he told him telepathically.

"*Don't kill them,*" his mate replied. "*Subdue only.*"

The vampire glared down at her and hissed, baring his fangs. "If you try to scream or call vor 'elp, I vill tear your 'ead vrom your body. Understood?" he growled.

Her eyes widened a little.

And then Alucard slowly moved his hand from over her mouth.

She didn't scream; she just exhaled raggedly.

"'Ow many of you are 'ere?" he demanded.

"Just…me," she grunted.

That was a lie.

Alucard gripped a fistful of her silvery hair. "I can tell vhen you lie—I advise you not to do zhat again."

She winced and closed her eyes. "I-I don't know. A lot!"

"Take a guess."

With another grunt, she exclaimed, "I-I don't know! M-maybe—"

A horrified scream pierced the air, and the smell of human blood followed.

And then another scream, a yell, a cry, a snarl—the light laughter and chatter burst into fearful shouts and terrified yelps, and the calmness of the evening withered into panic and confusion.

Alucard crashed his fist into the elf's face, knocking her out, and then he leapt off the rooftop and landed in the midst of chaos on the street. People were running in every direction, some grabbing others, fleeing into buildings. The vampire stood there, frantically scanning the crowd with his eyes—and then he saw them. Cloaked and hooded just like the woman he'd left above.

"There's more of them," came Zalith's voice. *"I need you to make your way to me."*

With a snarl, Alucard pushed his way through the crowd and grabbed the first elf he reached. He mercilessly slammed the man's head against the wall, but only enough to render him unconscious. And then he grabbed the elf who tried to come to his aid; he smacked the side of his head, and when the man's body fell and landed beside the other, the vampire replied to Zalith, *"I'll be zhere as vast as I can."*

A screaming woman snatched Alucard's attention. He spun around, his eyes finding her immediately. An elf was dragging her along the street by her hair, and when her husband tried to help, another elf grabbed him and brought a knife to his throat—

Alucard grabbed the nearest object—a metal tankard half-filled with beer—and launched it through the crowd. It collided with the second elf's head, and as the elf collapsed, his blade slashed across the side of the human man's face—but the man didn't react. He scrambled to his feet and ran after his wife.

The vampire followed.

Alucard pushed through the chaos, and when he caught up to the couple, he tore the elf away from the woman's husband, who was trying to fight the elf; the vampire struck the elf hard, knocking him out cold.

The couple cried their thanks as Alucard ushered them into one of the buildings.

"Get zhat seen to," Alucard told the man, and then he turned to face the street.

He knew that he should get to Zalith, but elves were spilling out of the shadows, grabbing people, pulling out knives—Alucard moved to race towards another elf, but there were so many, all seconds from killing the people in their grasp.

Before he took more than a few steps, though, Alucard watched his demons and vampires join the fight. They grabbed the elves, pulling them away from the humans. Some of the citizens got hurt, but none were dead—*yet.*

"Get zhem to savety," he called to the demons. And to the vampires, he said, "Vestrain zhese elves and take zhem to zhe city square."

The demons and vampires nodded obediently and got to work.

Alucard then began making his way to his mate, focusing on his aura. Along the way, he took down every elf he passed, ensuring that not a single person was killed. If anyone else died on the day that he and Zalith officially made their promises as Eimwood's new Lords, it wouldn't look very good for them, would it?

He picked up the pace a little, the smell of blood becoming stronger the closer he got to Zalith, and when he finally emerged on Main Street, he saw his mate through the chaos and bloodshed. Demons, vampires, *and* werewolves were working together to take out the overwhelming number of Orrivain while others were taking the last of the humans to safety. There were a lot more elves than he and Zalith had seen up the mountain, and he wondered whether they had known that he and his mate would check their settlement out. Had they purposely misled them so that they could infiltrate and attack much more easily?

Now wasn't the time for a hypothesis. He pulled an elf away from the werewolf she was about to grab, slammed her against the wall of the closest building, and then moved onto the next and the next and the next, throwing them against walls, through market stalls, and to the ground, kicking the faces of those who didn't fall unconscious from the collisions.

"Alucard," Zalith said in relief once he reached him. "Are you okay?" he asked, dropping the elf he'd just choked into unconsciousness.

The vampire nodded, looking around as their subordinates thinned the enemy's numbers. "Vhere did zhey all come vrom?"

"I don't know, but we weren't the only ones who underestimated our enemy."

"Do you vink zhat Calivarion is 'ere?"

"No. No one has reported seeing him. He's likely watching from a distance."

"Covard," Alucard snarled.

"Yeah," Zalith said. "Come on, let's finish this. The sooner it's over, the sooner we can clean this shit up and interrogate them."

With a nod, Alucard went in the opposite direction to his mate; he moved like a shadow in a storm—quick, ruthless, and relentless. An elf lunged for a demon struggling beneath the weight of a net woven with silver threads. Alucard snatched the elf by the throat mid-strike and slammed him against a cart, the wooden frame splintering on impact; the elf gasped, and a choked, gurgling sound left him before his body went limp.

Alucard ignored the sting when he pulled the silver net away, freeing the demon, and then he moved on.

A flicker of movement—left.

A vampire was cornered against a merchant stall, two elves closing in, their silver blades gleaming in the firelight—the Orrivain had clearly done their research.

Alucard descended upon them in an instant, snatching one by the collar and hurling him through the air; his body collided with a stone pillar, bones cracking beneath the force—he'd need to be healed after this if Zalith wanted them all alive and breathing. The second elf barely had time to react before Alucard grabbed his wrist, twisted the blade free, and drove his boot into his ribs. The impact sent the elf sprawling onto the cobblestones, unconscious.

The vampire stared at Alucard, dazed but alive. "Th-thank you, My Lord."

A snarl cut through the air.

Greymore was fighting off eight elves at once, his claws catching one in the arm, but the others were circling, ready to strike. One had a silvered chain in his grip, prepared to lash it around the werewolf's throat.

Alucard was faster.

He gripped the chain mid-swing, ignoring the agonizing burn of its cold surface, and yanked the elf towards him; he drove his fist into his stomach, and the elf doubled over, gasping for breath before crumpling when Alucard struck him again, a precise blow to the back of the head.

Greymore freed himself from the others, sending some crashing into an overturned cart and the others along the cobblestone road. The last elf made a desperate attempt to run, but Alucard was already on him. He grabbed the elf's head and slammed it against the side of a stone well. The body went slack, and he let it drop.

There were still more.

A demon was pinned beneath a fallen stall, her wings twitching weakly. An elf raised a short spear, poised to drive it into her chest.

Alucard's knife flew before the elf even saw him. The blade struck the elf's wrist, forcing her to drop the spear with a pained cry. Alucard was on her in an instant, grabbing her by the hair and smashing her head against the edge of a broken cart; as the elf sagged, unconscious before her body hit the ground, the vampire swung his cane around, thwacking the head of another elf who'd attempted to creep up from behind, and his body fell, too.

The demon groaned, struggling to push herself up.

Alucard knelt, gripped the edge of the broken wood that had trapped her, and shoved it aside. "Get up," he ordered. "Go."

She didn't hesitate.

And not too long later… it went quiet.

Alucard straightened, scanning the street. The last of the elves lay motionless, some groaning, others unconscious, a few bleeding and being patched up before being restrained, but none were dead. Around him, his and Zalith's forces were regrouping, panting, bloodied but victorious. Some demons were helping the wounded, werewolves were shaking the blood from their fur, their eyes still glowing with adrenaline, and the vampires stood still, eyes cold as they surveyed the aftermath.

With a slow exhale, Alucard rolled his shoulders. Then, through the settling quiet, he caught movement in the distance. Zalith. His mate was striding back towards him, his coat dusty, his knuckles bloodied, but that familiar smirk tugging at his lips.

Alucard met his gaze, and when Zalith reached him, they wrapped their arms around each other.

Zalith beat Alucard to it—"Are you okay?"

The vampire nodded. "Are you?"

"Yeah," he said and leaned out of their hug, glancing around. "Basilan told me that his team have dealt with all the elves on Wispwillow Lane, Duskmire Pass, and Fernvale Avenue. Amira's team are cleaning up in Bauwell."

Alucard nodded again. "Vhat about zhe Yrudyen? Vere zhey attacked?"

Zalith shook his head. "No, thank God. Letha sent an izuret a few minutes ago. I'm going to send reinforcements out there just in case, though. I don't want to risk the Orrivain making any attempts."

The vampire looked around at the devastation. "Vell… vhile no vone else died, all of zhis shit is going to take a vhile to clean up," he muttered.

"I'm sure the people of Eimwood will be much more grateful that we saved their lives instead of their fruit stands," he chuckled, wiping blood from Alucard's cheek.

He scoffed amusedly. "I zon't know, zhey seemed very attached."

With a smile, Zalith put his arm around Alucard's waist and began leading the way down the street. "We need somewhere to put all of these elves until we figure out whether any of them don't agree with their leader. Do you have room at the fort?"

"I do. Ve can transport zhem all zhere soon." He glanced at a demon tending to a werewolf's wounds. "Vhat about Calivarion, zhough? Should ve send people out zhere to see if 'e's near?"

"I've sent a team already."

"Vhat if zhey vind 'im?"

"From what I've heard, I don't think he's going to want to negotiate. But I'll try. I don't want to kill any of them."

Alucard would prefer to negotiate, too. But his interest rested with ensuring that he and Zalith were safe here. He'd kill whoever necessary to protect that safety. "Are any of zhe people dead? Apart vrom zhe vone ve vound."

"No. There are a lot of injuries, but nothing fatal—we've got people who can fix anything. But I'm sure that the guy who did die will upset a lot of people, though it's probably best that we're honest with them."

"Vell, ve *did* save zhe vest of zhe city. Zhat should count vor someving."

"I hope so," Zalith said with a sigh, stopping where his demons were rounding up the restrained elves.

"I told my vampires to take zhe elves to zhe square," Alucard said.

With a nod, Zalith instructed his demons to do the same, and then he took Alucard's hand. "Let's head up there, too." And then he led the way.

Alucard exhaled deeply, calming down from the battle. Things could have gone a lot worse, and he was surprised that only one human ended up dead. He was sure that those facts would convince the people of Eimwood that they were more than capable of living up to their promises, and he hoped that Zalith was right and the Orrivain were just following orders.

But how long would it take to get the answers they were looking for?

Chapter Fifteen

— ≼ ✝ ≽ —

Orders or Ideology?

| **Zalith** |

| *Uzlia Isles, Yrudberg, Eimwood City* |

Elves were spread all over the market square. Zalith eyed each one as he and Alucard walked to the centre, where some of his demons were watching the injured being seen to. Some of the Orrivain were trying to break free from their restraints, while others looked afraid—some were even crying. Clearly, some were eager to fight death, some were ready to accept it, and some were afraid of it.

He halted, pondering for a moment. Should he give the elves a chance to answer his questions themselves, or should he just read their minds? Maybe they'd appreciate the former; he wanted them to know that he wasn't out to kill them, after all.

"Do you vant me to start vith zhis side of zhe square, and you start vith zhat side?" Alucard suggested.

All of the elves were tied up, so they wouldn't be able to hurt anyone. "Yeah," he agreed and kissed his fiancé's lips. He wanted more than that, though—of course he did. The taste of Alucard's kiss sent his instincts into a frenzy, but now wasn't the time. He had to focus. "Let me know if you find anything," he added, stroking his hand down the vampire's arm.

Alucard nodded…but he lingered for a moment. There was desire in his eyes, the same kind that was sizzling inside Zalith. But like him, the vampire knew that they had a job to do. After a smile, Alucard headed to the other side of the square.

Zalith exhaled deeply and approached the first elf. The man was scowling, barely trying to break the ropes tied around his wrists and ankles. When his glower met Zalith, he growled behind the rope around his mouth and huffed through his nose.

The demon crouched in front of him. "I have a few questions for you. I'd appreciate it if you cooperated."

He stared, his eyes brimming with anger.

Zalith pulled the rope away from the man's mouth—

"Demon filth!" he snapped and spat at the ground.

The insult wasn't new; he didn't care. "Were you just following orders, or are you here because you want to kill every human that lives in Uzlia?"

He scoffed, looking Zalith up and down with a disgusted expression. "What the fuck you think, creature?" he barked, his broken Deiganish words edged with a guttural, clipped accent—rough, each syllable carrying the sharp, rolling cadence of someone used to speaking over howling mountain gales.

"I think that despite your loyalty, Calitharion doesn't give a fuck whether you live or die—I think that he sent all of you here to test our strength knowing full well that you likely wouldn't make it out," he said simply.

The man didn't look shaken. "You not know thing about us."

"I know enough," Zalith said, and then he returned the gag to the man's mouth. He moved on to one of the crying elves next. Once he removed the gag, the younger man sniffled and sobbed. "Are you here because you were ordered to be or because—"

"Not answer," he refused, his voice trembling. "No answer!"

Zalith was tempted to search this kid's mind, but not yet. He returned the gag, stood up, and set his sights on one of the wailing elves. Upon reaching her, he crouched, moved the rope from around her mouth, and asked, "Are you here because you were ordered to be or because you believe what Calitharion preaches?"

The woman shook her head, tears streaming down her face. "Let me go!" she pleaded desperately with the same accent as the man. "I not tell anyone!"

He frowned. "Who could you possibly tell?"

She shook her head, looking away from him, and then she started mumbling in a different language—it was likely the native tongue of the Orrivain.

"If you cooperate, I can guarantee your safety," he said firmly.

But she didn't seem at all convinced. After crying in her own language, she met Zalith's gaze for a brief moment. "Leave be," she said tiredly, sniffling. "No answering."

Zalith sighed and stood up. He looked over his shoulder, locating Alucard, but it didn't look like his fiancé was making any progress either. Maybe he should start looking into their minds—it would save a hell of a lot of time. But again…would doing something so invasive affect his chances of convincing these elves of his true intentions?

With a huff, he walked past a few struggling and crying elves, eventually stopping by another man—he barely looked eighteen. The demon crouched, ungagged him, and said, "Answer my questions and I'll guarantee your safety and the safety of everyone who matters to you."

The young elf stared at him, his eyes filled with tears; he stifled a sobbed breath, his exhales ragged.

"Are you here because you're following orders or because you believe what Calitharion is doing is right? Do you believe that everyone other than elves should be exiled from Uzlia?"

For a moment, the boy stared, still struggling to calm his breathing. He then glanced around, his horrified expression thickening with anxiety.

Did he even understand?

"Do you speak Deiganish?" Zalith questioned.

The boy swallowed hard. "Y-yes."

"Then answer me."

He glanced around again—he was nervous, likely about his fellow elves hearing what he had to say.

Zalith grabbed his arm and pulled the elf to his feet. He then tugged him along as he headed for the nearest street exit, and once they were clear of the square, he halted and stared expectantly at the boy.

He trembled, obviously hesitant. But then he shakily said, "Some…we just follow order, yes. Others, they not sure—they…how you say…flip from order to belief? Scared of Calitharion and follower."

"So some of your people are unsure whether they believe the same as Calitharion, and some of you don't believe him at all but are too afraid to resist?" Zalith questioned.

The boy nodded.

"How many feel this way? More than those who follow Calitharion loyally?"

For a few long seconds, the elf pondered, looking away. "Most unsure, but with us who don't want to follow, we more than the true followers."

Zalith focused on the boy's mind, assessing every answer, ensuring that he was being truthful—and he *was*. The demon thought to himself for a moment; if most of the Orrivain were unsure about Calitharion's ideology, then perhaps he could convince them that revolting was possible without it ending in their deaths. "Do you know any of the others who feel the same way or are unsure?"

The boy's nervous expression grew. "Only…ones who come to us. We know each other, but we careful. Ones like us are killed—given to wolves or hung from rope."

Knowing that he was right about the Orrivain made Zalith feel more confident about a treaty—or something of that nature. But the fact that the elves who didn't want to follow Calitharion were being killed made him feel…guilty? No…determined to find a solution *fast*. He despised leaders who forced their people to follow them and their ideology, and the confirmation that Calitharion was a tyrant only intensified his determination to intervene.

But first, he needed to make sure of something else before he shared his offer. "Do any of them have children back at the settlement?"

The boy shook his head. "Calitharion only allow most loyal followers to have family. Rest of us work and hunt and fight."

Zalith wasn't surprised. "If I take you back into that square and tell the rest of your people that I intend to form a treaty—one that will free them from Calitharion—are you going to help convince them to accept my offer?" he asked him. If he could spare locking up the elves who weren't actually their enemy, then he would.

"What you mean to save us?"

"Just as we did with the Yrudyen Elves, we'll offer your people protection and supplies, and you can either keep to your part of Uzlia or live among the people of Eimwood."

The boy frowned and asked, "Live...here?"

Zalith nodded.

"But...what about Calitharion? He will send more to kill us."

He laughed a little. "If he does, he's an idiot. Only one human died tonight, and we captured *all* of his people."

With a conflicted frown, the boy looked towards the square, and then he looked up at Zalith again. "Will you kill him?"

Zalith sighed deeply. "I don't want to kill any of your people, but if he wants war, then we're going to fight back. If he dies in the process, or if killing him ends it and frees your people, then yes."

The boy stared as if he were pondering...and then he nodded slowly. "I can do translation," he offered. "Not all speak your language."

He examined the boy's mind a little deeper; he was afraid and nervous that Calitharion might kill him and his friends, but he wasn't lying, and he was desperate for an escape. Zalith would gladly give that to him and everyone else who wanted it. So he untied the ropes, freeing the elf, and then he gestured towards the square. "Let's go."

For a moment, the boy stared, almost as if he couldn't believe it. He nodded again and turned around, heading for the square.

Zalith walked beside him, and when they emerged into the market, he escorted the boy to the fountain in the centre.

Alucard joined him. "Did you vind anyving?" he asked before his eyes shifted to the boy.

"My suspicions were correct. I'm going to offer safety to those who don't share Calitharion's ideology. This kid is going to translate."

"S-Sylrin," the boy said.

Zalith nodded. "I'm Silas, this is Ezra." He looked at his fiancé. "Did you find anything?"

"Zhe same. Some of zhe elves vant noving to do vith Calivarion but obey out of vear."

With a quiet sigh, Zalith glanced around the square at the Orrivain. He sent a telepathic message to his demons, telling them to be ready to grab anyone who tried to run or attack, and then he cleared his throat. "Listen," he called firmly.

Sylrin began translating.

Zalith continued, "I know that not all of you are here by choice. Some of you follow Calitharion out of obligation, not belief. Some of you are here because you have no other option."

He scanned the crowd, taking in their expressions—some twisted with disgust, others laced with unease. He could feel their hesitation, their silent war between fear and something dangerously close to hope.

The demon went on, "I'm offering you more than survival. I'm offering you freedom. Here in Eimwood, you won't be ruled by fear. You'll have your own choices, your own lives—you can even start your own families—and you won't be left to fend for yourselves; we will give you food, homes, and a future."

He let the words sink in, watching how some of the elves faltered, how the weight of his offer cracked through the walls they had built around themselves. They had a decision to make, and he'd see the truth of it in their minds before they spoke.

"If living among the people of Eimwood isn't something that any of you are comfortable with, and if we cannot secure a treaty with Calitharion or those of you who feel the same way he does, then we will find somewhere in Uzlia that is more suited to your needs, a place that we will protect and supply resources to. But now may be your only chance to come forward because we cannot guarantee what your leader will do next." He paused again, watching as the Orrivain glanced around, as if trying to assure or convince one another. "As for those of you who do not wish to leave Calitharion behind, you will be sent to a safe location until we've resolved this conflict." He saw a fair few angry faces. "And if you come forward in an attempt to deceive us, we *will* know; you're all going to be questioned by somebody who can tell whether you're lying."

Sylrin finished translating.

The Orrivain exchanged stares and glares, some shuffling around, others still trying to break their restraints.

"If you want freedom, now is your chance to come forward," Zalith invited.

Sylrin held his hand out and called, "V-Vaeluna."

Zalith followed the boy's gaze and spotted the woman whose name he said.

The girl looked around Sylrin's age. Golden hair and blue eyes gleamed beneath her hood, and her pale face adorned a nervous expression. But as Sylrin called her name again, she got up. After one of Zalith's demons untied the ropes from around her ankles, she hurried over and collided with Sylrin, who hugged her tightly while she cried.

Vaeluna's acceptance triggered a chain reaction. One by one, and eventually in pairs and more, the Orrivain began rising, walking over to join the others by the fountain once their ankles were untied. A lot of the scowling elves looked astonished at how many of them chose freedom—one man even attempted to stop who might be his wife from leaving, but a demon grabbed him before he could drag her back down to the ground.

By the time elves stopped coming forward, more than three-quarters of them had crowded around the fountain. Zalith finished counting them, and when he realized that he now had eighty-nine new people to provide homes and food for—not to mention all the new werewolves likely arriving tomorrow—he pondered deeply. There were a lot of new houses being built and more on the way; it would take time to house them all comfortably, but at least there were options—makeshift shelters, moored ships, including Alucard's galleon, and there were hotels and many inns being restored and reopened, too. Nobody would be left homeless or hungry.

But before he started finding beds for them, they needed to be questioned. He wasn't taking any chances; he had to be certain that these elves didn't have ulterior motives. "Take everyone to the city hall," he called to his demons. "Ensure that they have blankets and something to sleep on, and give food and water to those who ask for it. I need all of you to watch them, too. I'll be sending Idina over to begin questioning them."

His demons nodded and began escorting the elves away.

"Vhat about zhem?" Alucard asked, nodding to the remaining restrained elves. "Zhe vort?"

"The fort," he confirmed and summoned an izuret. "Tell Idina to head to the city hall and begin questioning the elves; I want to know which of them genuinely want freedom and which of them are trying to deceive us. Tell her that the other demons there will fill her in on what happened and that my best mind-readers are at her disposal."

With a nod, the izuret disappeared.

"Do you vink zhey vere all being truthvul?" his mate asked.

"I really hope so." He huffed, glancing at the elves again. "I hope we don't have another war on the horizon, either."

"Calivarion isn't going to take zhis lightly," the vampire mumbled. "'E devinitely 'as more elves at 'is disposal."

He nodded, and then he looked over his shoulder. "Sylrin," he called.

After a few moments, the boy emerged from the departing crowd with Vaeluna.

Zalith gestured for him to approach, and once the elf was in front of him, he asked, "How many of you are left at the settlement?"

Sylrin drawled, "Um…not many. He keep five with him always for guard, and mothers with children stay. Include children…I think twenty-five…thirty."

"Thank you. I'm sending one of my demons to conduct the interviews—her name is Idina. I need you to translate for her."

"O-okay. Idina," he said with a nod.

"Go," the demon dismissed.

Sylrin hurried off with Vaeluna, rejoining the crowd of Orrivain being led away from the square.

Zalith took hold of Alucard's hand. "Let's take these elves to the fort. When we get back, I need to figure out where to put the others until we have more houses available, and I should probably find some locations where they could set up a new settlement outside of the city. We should also send some izurets to watch the Orrivain still up in that mountain; if they're planning another attack, I want to be ready before they get here."

"I can 'elp," he offered.

He wanted to say yes, but he knew what he was like. The second he had Alucard alone, he'd want to fuck him—and not just once. "It's okay. You should get some rest in case that vampire killer turns up."

"You need to vest, too."

"I will," he assured him, stopping by one of the remaining elves. He waved his hand at Andira, a demon who had stayed behind, and called, "Bring them all over here."

"Yes, sir," she replied.

Zalith set his eyes back on Alucard. "I won't be up all night, I promise. I just need to figure a few things out."

Alucard looked a little hesitant, but he said, "Okay. Zon't overvork yourselv."

The demon smiled at him. "I won't. Besides—" he pulled Alucard closer, "—I don't want to be away from you for too long," he said, smirking at him.

His fiancé smiled at him, but when the Orrivain were delivered by Andira, the vampire glanced at them all and exhaled deeply. "All vight, let's move zhem." He looked at Andira. "Tie zhem all togezzer—link zheir vestraints."

With a nod, she quickly did as he asked.

Once each elf was linked, Alucard grabbed the arm of one of them, offering his free hand to Zalith. When Zalith took his hand, the vampire dematerialized them all into vermillion smoke and raced up into the sky.

Zalith had a lot more work ahead of him, but he was making quick progress. Now he had to figure out his next move. But he had an ever-growing feeling that Calitharion didn't want to be reasoned with. He'd still try, though. Killing him was only a last resort.

Chapter Sixteen

— ⸲ ✝ ⸱ —

The Packs

| **Alucard—*Friday, Tertium 31ˢᵗ, 960(TG)*** |
| ***Rhenovaalis, Atheson, Atheson Coven Sanctum*** |

Despite the long rest he'd gotten last night, Alucard felt exhausted when he landed in Atheson. But the shift from Uzlia's noon sunlight to Atheson's evening sunset was a relief, especially on his eyes. He headed into the Sanctum with Zalith at his side, and Greymore and Danford followed behind him. Before heading to DeiganLupus to meet the wolf packs, he needed to see how the new Fledgelings were doing.

He made his way to the Ebon Chamber, a place where only he could go—he'd not risk the Fledgelings attacking his mate or his friend…or Danford. So when he reached the door, he told the three of them to wait there before pulling it open and stepping inside.

The corridor beyond the threshold was silent, its stone walls swallowing even the faintest echo of Alucard's footsteps. Dim lanterns flickered along the walls, their bluish flames casting long, wavering shadows against the dark stone. The air was cool, heavy with the lingering scent of old wax, humans, and faint traces of blood, well-cleaned but never truly gone.

At the end of the corridor, a lone oak door loomed. Alucard pushed it open and emerged into the Ebon Chamber, a vast, windowless hall. The ceiling arched high overhead, disappearing into gloom untouched by flame. The lanterns here burned lower, steadier, giving the space an almost reverent dimness, as though any brightness would disrupt the solemn purpose of this place.

Along the walls, a series of identical, unmarked black doors lined the perimeter; names meant nothing here. Each one led to a private chamber where the newly turned vampires would rest, recover, and dream of the hunger still coiling in their veins. Once they were ready to be social with their brood kin, they'd be transferred to the Fledgeling Dwelling Space.

The centre of the hall was left open and bare, designed for lessons, training, and discipline. Alucard's gaze swept the room, eyeing the Fledgelings, who stood in stiff, uncertain clusters, their eyes flickering towards him before quickly dropping away. They knew who he was, and they knew to bow their heads.

Lăcrămioara eased through the crowd, bowed her head to him, and approached.

"'Ow are zhey doing?" he asked her.

"Good," she said with a nod. "They've all fed, and I'm starting with teaching them to control their hunger. I think they might be ready to move to the Dwelling Chamber very soon."

"Are zhere any who you vink vill be a problem?"

"I don't think so, but it's hard to tell right now. Once they start adapting and recalling their old selves, some of them might be an issue."

Alucard nodded with a sigh. He knew that some of them might try to refuse their new lives when they remembered who they were before turning, but he knew how to help them, and he'd do so if need be. "All vight. Tell me if zhere are any problems. I'm 'eading to DeiganLupus now, but if anyving 'appens at all, you contact me."

With a firm nod, she said, "Of course, My Lord."

He then turned around and left the hall, swiftly returning to Zalith. After a glance at Greymore and Danford, he led the way through the Sanctum and out into the courtyard. He dematerialized everyone into vermillion smoke and began the journey to DeiganLupus.

"*Is everything okay with your vampires?*" Zalith's voice echoed in his mind.

"*Zhey're vine vor now,*" he replied.

"*Will you be turning more soon?*"

"*I vill, but I zon't know vhen. I'm vaiting vor zhe ozzer covens to gazzer all of zhe 'umans ve need to ensure zhey 'ave at least a 'undred members.*"

"*Let me know if your people need help gathering humans. I can send some demons.*"

"*Vank you,*" he said appreciatively.

They travelled in silence for a while before the sound of crashing waves and seagulls filled the air. DeiganLupus was close.

But then came his mate's voice again, "*How long do you think this meeting will be?*"

"*I zon't know,*" he responded. "*Vhy?*"

"*Because I need to cum in you again.*"

Even in his dematerialized form, Alucard felt a shiver of anticipation spiral through him—and he knew that Zalith was smirking. The flicker of embarrassment that he felt faded fast because Greymore and Danford couldn't see or hear him; all they saw was red mist and glances of the world below.

He felt his nervousness wake, too, but his primal instincts buried it deep, urging him to say, "*Ve shouldn't be too long... but I do 'ave an old bedvoom at zhe estate.*"

"*Then you better show it to me when we're done talking to werewolves.*"

Alucard smiled. "*Okay.*"

And then he reached the docks. The sun was high in the sky, but its light was hidden behind the cityscape and thick smog spewing from distant buildings.

Alucard still landed in the shadows of an alley. He rematerialized everyone—

Danford threw up *again.*

Greymore laughed heartily. "Danny, man... you're really not getting the hang of this flying shit, are you?"

Zalith rolled his eyes.

Alucard huffed irritably. "You need to calm down," he said, watching as the wolf-vampire wiped his mouth with the back of his hand. "If you are panicking or breathing too 'ard vhen ve vly, your body is going to spasm vhen ve revorm."

Danford swallowed hard and nodded, grimacing. "S-sorry."

With a sharp exhale, Alucard took hold of Zalith's hand and led them to the alley entrance. He checked left and right of the dock road; there were a few fishermen preparing to head out to sea, and some ship crewmen smoking, but nobody was on the lookout.

"Zhis vay," he said, turning left.

They headed along the empty dock path, and once they reached the black iron gates, Alucard took them up the long, steep road.

"Just curious," came Greymore's voice. "But why couldn't we land at the estate?"

"All zhe vunes and vards," Alucard answered. "Zhey are designed to keep everyvone and everyving out. Zhe only vay to get in is to know vhere zhe place is." He stopped across the road from a passage that led between a clothing store and a post office, and when he glanced at Zalith, Greymore, and Danford, the three of them looked confused. "I vill show you," he said with a discreet smirk and led them across the road.

He took them into the passage; the space ahead was empty, save for a few old crates and an abandoned, burned carriage—at least that was what it looked like. Alucard stopped at the alley's end and let the three of them look around for a moment... and then he stepped forward, moving past the hidden threshold and into the hidden space inside.

Zalith looked impressed. "Is this the same thing we had around our old house?"

"Similar," Alucard answered. "But zhis type lets you vit a much larger space inside a smaller vone."

The demon smiled at him.

"Oh, damn," came Greymore's voice.

"How does this fit in that tiny alley?" Danford followed.

Alucard took his eyes off them and stared ahead at his estate. It loomed in the distance, a monolith of dark stone and ancient craftsmanship, its silhouette jagged against the shifting air that surrounded it. The towering spires rose like clawed fingers against a sky that wasn't quite a sky at all—just an expanse of rippling distortion, as if the world beyond had been swallowed by a vast, endless mirage.

The estate's façade bore the marks of centuries, but time had not unravelled it. Weathered stone, rich with the scent of damp earth and aged iron, stood unyielding against the quiet pull of decay. The high-arched windows reflected nothing but the shifting barrier around the area, their latticed glass capturing warped glimpses of a world that did not exist beyond the shield.

He led the way towards it. As they drew closer, the details sharpened—intricate carvings etched into the towering double doors, the Nosferatu crest worn smooth by time but still unmistakable, the wrought-iron lanterns casting pools of light that flickered in unnatural ways.

The land around the estate was untouched by the outside world. No roads led here, no signs of life beyond those who belonged; the grass, deep and thick, rustled without a breeze, and the trees stood still, their skeletal branches twisting, frozen as if caught in an eternal dusk.

Above it all, the shield pulsed, a translucent barrier that shimmered like oil on water. It concealed everything within, distorting the air like heat rising from stone, a silent, unbroken veil between his world and the one outside.

Alucard's gaze lingered on it. This was the only place from his past untouched by Damien, the only place that had ever truly been his. Although he hadn't been back in a long time, the way it made him feel hadn't faded, and he held onto the comforting fact of its purity.

The stench of wet dog polluted the air, thickening with every step Alucard took. It clung to the walls, seeped into the very bones of the estate, and by the time he reached the front door, the scent had turned suffocating. He snarled irritably, but he forced himself to swallow the sharp rise of frustration.

Pushing the door open, he stepped inside. The foyer stretched wide before him, steeped in shadows, illuminated only by the dim glow of candle sconces lining the walls. The air was heavy with sound—low murmurs, the occasional burst of laughter, and the shifting of boots against polished stone; voices spilt from every direction, some deep in discussion, others caught in tense, clipped exchanges. He could hear footsteps echoing through the halls, the weight of too many unwelcome bodies settling into his old but still beloved refuge.

His irritation deepened. The scent was everywhere.

He squeezed Zalith's hand and strode forward, his boots clicking softly against the marble floor, veined with deep reds and blacks. He passed the grand staircase, its balustrade carved from dark mahogany, flanked by towering candelabras. A long, rich carpet stretched from the entrance to the far end of the hall, its fabric woven with sigils and patterns long forgotten by the outside world.

But his focus lay ahead. He turned sharply, pushing open the heavy doors of the lounge. The atmosphere inside was different—denser, heavier. The fireplace roared, casting flickering light against the deep-green walls, making the gold inlays shimmer. Velvet drapes pooled against the floor, and the dark wood bookshelves—lined with centuries-old tomes and half-drunk glasses of wine—stood untouched by their current occupants.

And there they were.

A cluster of rugged figures filled the space, some standing, others leaning against furniture, their postures ranging from uneasy to outright wary. They smelled like the wilderness, like damp fur and earth, like something wholly out of place in a house as old and refined as this one.

At the heart of them was Freja. Her blonde hair caught the firelight as she lifted her head, one hand resting over the curve of her stomach. Her expression was unreadable, but her eyes met his, and she nodded in greeting.

Alucard waited until Greymore and Danford stepped into the room, and then he closed the doors behind him.

Danford made his way over to Freja, who called out, summoning the rest of the wolves from around the house. They gradually filed into the lounge, and those who couldn't find space lingered in the hall and the dining room, staring through the wide archway.

With a deep breath, Alucard glanced around at all the scruffy, dirtied faces. Some of them looked and *reeked* like they hadn't bathed in over a week; some had tangles and knots in their hair, others had blood from old meals smeared around their mouths, and others appeared as if they'd willingly rolled around in mud on their way here. He could only hope that if and when they agreed to move to Uzlia, they'd pick up more hygienic habits from Greymore's wolves.

"I'm sure zhat Vreja 'as told you vhy you're all 'ere," the vampire started. "I von't vaste time pitching. Aegisguard 'as become increasingly dangerous since zhe spread of zhe virus and zhe attacks of Liliv's zemons, and ve 'ave secured a place zhat is vree of zhose vings, and entirely 'idden. You all 'ave zhe option to come back vith us under zhe condition zhat you accept Zhomas 'ere as your Prime," he said tonelessly, gesturing to Greymore.

More than one of them loudly questioned, "You mean our Alpha?"

"No," Alucard snapped, silencing the concoction of indiscernible voices. "A Prime verevolf is an Alpha of Alphas. Your packs vill vetain your Alphas, your Betas, etcetera. But your Alphas vill answer to Zhomas, just as all zhe ozzer Alphas under 'im do."

A dark-haired man with a thick, messy beard stepped forward, and at his side was a blonde woman who vaguely resembled Freja—likely her cousin.

The man asked, "What does this mean? It sounds like you're asking us to merge into one massive pack." He scoffed and looked behind him when snarls came from the crowd. "That ain't going to fly."

"Your packs vill not be merging," Alucard muttered. "Your packs vill stay as zhey are, separate, but under Zhomas' vule." He sighed and looked at Greymore. "Can you?"

"Oh, yeah," he said with a nod and moved closer, standing beside him. "I'm not taking over your packs," he assured them firmly. "I've recently become familiar with the way your hierarchy works in this world, and I'm no stranger to how a military works, so think of it this way: I as the Prime am the General. If and when we need to appoint Alpha Kings, they would be the Major Generals. Your Alphas are the Colonels, your Betas are the Captains, and your Gammas are the Sergeants. The rest of you are the squad, all with your respective roles—medics, hunters, patrollers." He paused and glanced at Zalith and Alucard. "And these are our Brigadier Generals."

Alucard listened to their responses. Greymore's explanation seemed to make sense, but there were still people among the crowd who looked unsure and offended.

"What is this place you speak of?" someone called.

Greymore looked to Alucard and Zalith.

"A safe haven," Zalith answered. "You'll be given land to claim as your personal territory, or you can live in the city if you choose. But things will be different. You won't be single packs roaming around doing as you please—to a certain extent, anyway. You will be part of...a kingdom."

Alucard liked that word. Uzlia *was* becoming Zalith's kingdom.

Zalith continued, "You will have responsibilities. When called upon, you will answer. You will follow Greymore without question, and you will follow *us* without question. Protecting this place will be everyone's priority."

Murmurs floated around the room.

"But understand this," the demon called over the chatter. "We are at war with the Numen—we are hunted, and we are hunting them. Our goal is to wipe them from the face of this realm, and their goal is to do the same to us. We'd understand if this is too much, but you've all seen what the false gods have done to Aegisguard in the past two months, and if they aren't stopped, they'll turn this world into a wasteland."

When Zalith paused, Alucard scanned the room with him. Most of the people who appeared convinced before now looked hesitant and anxious.

"It's true that we need an army of our own to destroy them. The greater our numbers, the higher our chances of victory, and the more allies everyone has to watch each other's backs. Keeping you all safe and alive is our highest priority."

"You can trust him," Greymore assured the muttering crowd. "This man was a warlord in the world I came from. He got us out of there despite the odds being impossibly against us—and so did Alucard," he said, gesturing to Zalith and Alucard. "Keeping people alive and safe is one of many things they do best."

Some of the conflicted faces relaxed slightly.

"Like he said, you ain't gotta join us, but as someone who's witnessed what these guys can do, and someone who's been in the middle of a war and God knows how many battles, there's no one else I'd rather fight for or beside," Greymore continued firmly. "Fighting to protect something worth dying for is better than dying out there and being forgotten."

For a few tense moments, the wolves murmured to one another, and eventually, they all diverted their attention to their Alphas.

The Alpha who clung to Freja's cousin was the first to huff and say, "All right. The Veylin Pack accepts your offer." He glanced at the woman. "I am Gheorghe, and this is my mate, Ileana." He gestured to the two barrel-chested men and the broad-shouldered woman behind him. "My Betas, Raduan, Emilian, and Elaina."

And then a hulking woman stepped out of the crowd; her left eye was fogged over, and her ear-length brown hair adorned several long, thin braids that bore small feathers and animal bones. "Othros Pack accepts," she said, her voice orotund; she pulled a short, lithe man against her side, holding him possessively—he looked intimidated but comfortable with her demandingness. "I am Ruxandra, my mate—" she looked down at the man and smiled at him as if he were a long-desired meal, "—Florin." She glanced to her left. "Betas Nicolae, Magda."

Two packs were enough to make Alucard feel relieved. He'd like for *all* of them to accept, but the other two Alphas looked conflicted.

"What do we hunt?" a beefy, bearded but bald man questioned loudly.

"There are deer, rabbits, squirrels, and some boars have been sighted," Zalith replied.

With a deep exhale, the man looked around at those who were obviously his pack, and then he nodded. "The Cinderfell Pack will join. Alpha Vasile—" he gestured to himself, "—no Luna. Sister Betas Irina and Sorina," he said, nodding to the two auburn-haired women at his side; they looked identical save for one of them being wiry and the other close to brawny. "We will require a deep forest territory with good hunting grounds."

"You'll have it," Zalith told him. "You can all tell us what you require once we take you back, and we will do our best to accommodate you."

Alucard then set his eyes on the final Alpha, the willowy man who stood half a foot above the tallest of his pack members. The vampire recognized him—the bright orange hair with white strands here and there, and the gleaming green eyes. That was Crevan Ó Súilleabháin, the son of an ex-Luna werewolf who travelled to Diaráinne and the fox shifter who turned out to be her mate. His mother had worked with Tobias during the same Dor-Sanguian battle that orphaned Elvin.

He looked hesitant—more than anyone else had. And Alucard knew why. His mother was buried on the Grimholt Pack's land, and everyone knew that Crevan was confident that his father would someday come looking for him. Perhaps Alucard could do something to help convince him.

"Crevan," he said.

The orange-white-haired man sharply turned his head, meeting his gaze.

"Your vather is shepherd in Diaráinne, no?"

"He is," he answered.

"If vaiting vor 'im is vhat is keeping you vrom accepting zhis ovver, I vill send somevone to vind 'im vor you. But zhere's no guarantee zhat zhis vill vesult in zhe answers you 'ope vor."

Crevan looked away for a moment, and his pack stared sympathetically at him. But then he stared across the room at Alucard and nodded. "Okay." He glanced at the man beside him. "My Beta, Axandru."

That was all four packs, just as Alucard had hoped. He looked at Zalith and said, "I can 'ave my galleon sent over 'ere to pick zhem all up."

His mate nodded.

"I can stay with them if you want," Greymore offered. "I should probably give them some time to get to know me and vice versa."

"Yeah," Zalith replied. "Wait until the early hours of the morning to move. We don't need anyone seeing a huge crowd of strangers strolling down the street."

Greymore nodded and said, "Got it, boss."

"Zhomas vill stay vith you," Alucard announced. "My ship vill be 'ere to bring you all to your new 'ome—you leave during zhe early hours of tomorrow morning, so make sure you are veady."

Murmured acknowledgements came from the crowd as they began talking again.

Greymore joined them, leaving Alucard and Zalith alone.

"Well, that went better than I expected," Zalith said, sounding relieved.

"Vas looking kind of bad vor a moment at zhe start. Vas a good ving ve brought Zhomas vith us—I zon't 'ave zhe patience to simplify vings sometimes."

The demon chuckled quietly. "Don't I know it—Mr Grumpy."

Zalith hadn't called him that in a *long* time. It made him pout, but he hid an amused smile behind it. "I'm not grumpy," he grumbled.

"No? You sound grumpy to me."

"I'm not. I'm just…tired, I guess."

"From all of the sex?" Zalith asked quietly—he was still smirking, but there was concern in his voice.

Alucard exhaled deeply. "I zon't vink so, no. I just zidn't sleep very vell."

Zalith placed his hand on his arm and guided him closer to the door, away from the crowd. "Why not?" he questioned. "Do you feel restless or frustrated?"

He shrugged. "Kind of."

The demon smiled and pulled him into his embrace. "It's your heat cycle," he murmured. "It becomes more intense over the course of the month; your body is getting more demanding." He nuzzled the side of his face. "I can take care of that for you."

His words sent desire rippling through his body, setting his senses alight.

"Do you still want to show me your old bedroom, or should we head home?" he asked with a sultry hum, discreetly stroking his hand down Alucard's body.

"'Ome," he immediately answered. He didn't want to let four werewolf packs hear him whining and moaning and crying out. That would be a mortifying first impression.

Zalith took his hand and left the lounge with him.

The moment they left the house, Alucard let out a deep sigh before taking in a few breaths of fresh air—no more stench of wet dog and dirt.

But they didn't make it to the edge of the barrier.

With a frustrated groan, Zalith gently grasped Alucard's waist, guided him back, and pinned him against a tree—so fast that Alucard needed a moment to catch up.

"You smell so fucking good," his mate groaned, nuzzling his neck.

Alucard smiled, tilting his head to the side, giving Zalith more room to devour.

And then the demon's hand wandered down his body again. This time, Zalith gripped his crotch and murmured, "I'm not sure I can wait until we get home."

He wanted to agree—his instincts *urged* him to give himself to Zalith, but he didn't want to be seen. "Ve 'ave to," he said and then moaned lightly when his mate softly squeezed his arousal through his trousers.

Zalith grunted reluctantly in response. "Can I fuck you twice?"

Alucard smiled. "Yes."

"What about three times?"

"Maybe."

"Four?" he murmured, squeezing a little tighter.

Alucard couldn't stifle another quiet moan, and the anticipation left no room for shyness. "Yes," he winced.

"Consecutively…or do you need breaks in between?" Zalith asked, smiling against the vampire's neck.

"I zon't know," he answered. "I guess ve'll vind out."

The demon laughed and let go of his crotch. "Then we'd better get home." He took Alucard's hand and began leading the way.

With an excited smile, Alucard followed. Now that he was enthralled with desperation, the fatigue had withered. All he could think about was getting home and letting Zalith give him what his body sorely needed.

Chapter Seventeen

— ⸲ ✝ ⸱ —

Ashes and Slashes

| **Alucard** |
| *Aestrael, Uzlia Isles, Usrul, Castle Reiner* |

The moment they stumbled into the castle, Zalith pinned Alucard against the nearest wall and started kissing him frantically. Alucard smiled between kisses, his hands wandering around the demon's body, and when his mate pulled his cape and coat off for him, the vampire hastily removed Zalith's coat, too.

Once they kicked their shoes off, they kissed a little longer; Zalith took Alucard's hand and swiftly led him through the lounge, the main hall, and to the stairs that led up to their bedroom.

Zalith held him against the wall again, kissing him, his hand stroking down his body until he reached the vampire's crotch. Alucard tensed, humming contently through each kiss as the desperation consumed him. His body cried for more, urging him to beg Zalith to fuck him already. But he wanted to revel in this, to enjoy each kiss, each touch, and each eager breath.

"I'm going to fill you with so much cum," the demon breathed against the vampire's neck, and then he gently bit down on his shoulder.

Alucard moaned quietly, both his mate's words and fangs sending shivers of anticipation through his trembling body. "I'll take as much as you can give me," he replied, his voice thick with desire.

Zalith eased his hand into Alucard's trousers, and as he caressed his arousal, he murmured, "I think that might be too much for you to handle."

"Not vight now," he said, gripping a fistful of the demon's hair. "My body needs as much as can get."

His mate chuckled and started kissing him again. He paused to say, "You're right," and then he eased his tongue into the vampire's mouth.

Alucard's desperation grew, and his body trembled harder—he didn't plan on waiting much longer. He gripped Zalith's arm, and then he began leading the way upstairs, pulling his mate with him as he hurried, letting his instincts take control. Part of him wanted to stop and ask Zalith to fuck him there, but he'd rather be pinned down on their bed.

Halfway up the steps, though, Zalith pulled Alucard to a halt and pushed him against the wall. He smirked before he started kissing the vampire, and they eagerly tore off one another's clothes.

Alucard's heart raced, and his breaths became frenzied. He didn't even try to hide his eagerness. He grasped Zalith's trousers and pulled them down—

The window just above him flung open, and when he looked up in startle, he watched a white owl glide around the tower and towards him.

They both groaned and snarled in response.

"Vhat?" Alucard asked as the bird landed on the bannister.

It looked down at its leg. There was a small piece of rolled parchment attached.

Alucard took it and unrolled it.

"What is it?" Zalith asked.

With a deep sigh, Alucard read it—but the moment he registered the message, all the desire and desperation melted away, and dread replaced it. "Two of my Knights 'ave been killed," he said and pulled his trousers back on.

"Killed by who? The humans?" Zalith questioned worriedly as he started getting dressed, too. "Has the vampire hunter turned up?"

"I zon't know. I 'ave to get to Aveson."

The demon nodded and helped him get his shirt on. "I'll come with you."

Once they were both dressed, Alucard grabbed Zalith's hand and dematerialized into vermillion smoke, taking his mate with him as he raced out of the window and towards Atheson.

Either the Silver Claw had killed his Knights, or the humans had, and he wasn't sure which option aggravated him the most. He'd find out the moment he got to the Coven Sanctum, though, and he was going to kill whoever was responsible.

When he eventually landed and rematerialized in the Atheson Sanctum courtyard, Alucard was struck by fatigue again, and this time, he started feeling disorientated. He stopped for a moment, grasping Zalith's hand, waiting for his body to catch up, and then he headed for the doors.

"Are you okay?" his mate asked quietly.

Alucard nodded, leading the way inside. "I'm just preparing vor zhe shitstorm zhat's vaiting vor me inside."

"We'll figure it out, don't worry," the demon assured him.

"My Lord," came Eyra's voice.

Alucard stopped in the stair hall, where most of the coven were sitting and standing on the spiralling staircase. He watched Eyra emerge from the hall on the right and waited for her to speak.

"It's Lenore and Salvorn," she exclaimed, shaking her head. "Vulpea found them this morning when she arrived and swept the borders."

He dragged his hand over his face with a frustrated snarl. "Vhere are zhe zemons I sent?"

"Searching for a trail, My Lord," Eyra answered.

"And zhe verevolves?"

Eyra hesitated.

Alucard scowled. "Vhere are zhe verevolves I sent over 'ere to *'elp* zhe coven, Eyra?"

She bowed her head shamefully. "We don't trust them, My L—"

He snarled again and sharply turned his head to glare at the rest of the coven. "You all veel zhis vay?"

Not one of them spoke up.

His scowl thickened as he set his eyes back on Eyra.

She bared her fangs towards the coven—

Alucard snatched the woman's throat and made her look at him. "I 'ave 'ad more zhan enough of your disobedience," he growled, baring *his* fangs to her.

"I-I'm sorry, My—"

"You 'ave put zhe security of zhis coven at visk var too many times, and at a time like *zhis*?!" he yelled.

"I'm sorry—I'm sorry, My Lord!" she insisted.

Alucard would usually execute a vampire for putting their coven in as much danger as Eyra had, but he knew that the others didn't need to see that right now. "Lock 'er up in zhe Vithercrypt until I say ozzervise," he said to Evaphene.

With a nod, Evaphene stepped down into the hall, but instead of grabbing Eyra, she stood beside her and Alucard and frowned unsurely. "I…uh—"

"She is no longer Coven Master," Alucard said firmly, and then he glowered at Eyra. "You are Cast Down vrom Aveson Coven Master. You are Veiled until zhe Vampire Council debates your vrongdoings," he stated.

Eyra looked horrified. "M-My Lord, I—"

Alucard continued, "You are entitled to speak to a Praeservare; vone vill arrive bevore your trial."

"B-but—"

"Take 'er," he snapped.

With a nod, Evaphene grabbed Eyra's arm and pulled her away—and Eyra didn't fight back; she knew better than to be any more disobedient than she already had been.

Alucard sighed deeply and turned to face the rest of the coven. "Vhere are zhe verevolves?"

"Coven Mas—I mean… Veiled Eyra had them chased into the city, My Lord. The city guards have captured most of them and locked them up in a non-human compound across the river; I blood-marked the location, and here's all the information I could gather on it," Marius answered, handing him a small notepad. "I think one or two of them are hiding in the surrounding woods, trying to figure out how to help them escape."

"And Lenore and Salvorn's bodies?" he asked, taking the notepad.

"Both were slain with silver, My Lord," Isabeau said. "Salvorn's ashes are in an urn in the Reliquary, and Lenore's body is in the Vitalum."

Alucard huffed, glancing at the information written on the pages. "Stay 'ere and protect zhe Vledgelings. Make sure zhat nobody gets in or out. Understood?"

"Yes, My Lord," the coven replied simultaneously.

He gave Marius his notepad back, and then he turned to Zalith. "Let's go," he said, and the demon followed as he left the Sanctum and crossed the courtyard. "I 'ave to vind Vulpea and see vhat she knows."

Zalith nodded. "Do you know where she is?"

"I can lock on to 'er aura," he said, and then he dematerialized them both into vermillion smoke. He locked on to Vulpea—who was a mile outside the city—and landed not far from her.

The black-haired Paladin vampire was crouched by a river, and she had her hands in the mud.

Alucard frowned as he approached.

She noticed almost immediately, and when she looked over her shoulder and saw him, she shot to her feet and bowed. "My Lord," she said humbly.

"Vhat 'ave you vound?"

"This is where Salvorn was, My Lord—well… his ashes. One of your demons and I gathered as much of him as we could."

"Vhich zemon?"

"Aradia, My Lord. She said that she was one of your Betas."

"And vhat about Lenore?"

"We found her body twenty yards downstream," she answered. "So far, we haven't been able to find a trail, but Lenore's body was covered in slashes. They look as if they were left by a werewolf, but they're… strange, My Lord."

"Strange 'ow?"

"They're not like other werewolf-inflicted wounds."

Alucard huffed and looked around for a moment. He needed to find who was responsible, but he also needed to ensure that his coven was protected and that nobody got in or out of the city. "Zaliv," he said, his eyes landing on his mate. "Could you 'ead to zhe non-'uman compound and get zhe verevolves out? I need zhem back at zhe Coven Sanctum—and if you can also vind zhe vones 'iding in zhe voods, zhat vould be even better."

He nodded. "Which ones?"

"Zhomas lent me zhe Duskvoot Pack—zheir Alpha and Luna are Abel and Temperance." He paused, focusing, attempting to locate and lock on to Marius' blood-mark. "Zhe compound is 'alv a mile vrom 'ere—zhat vay." He pointed across the river at the forest. "Zhere are vences and guards. I can get a team togezzer vor you—"

"I'll be okay, don't worry," the demon assured him.

"Is a 'eavily armed compound, Zaliv," he said worriedly. "Zhey 'ave vifles and poison."

"I know," he said with a small smile. "But you need your vampires and everyone else here. I'll be okay, don't worry—I've dealt with this sort of thing before."

He was reluctant to say yes…but he trusted Zalith; he knew that his mate could handle himself, and the demon was right—he didn't really have the numbers to spare right now. So he nodded and said, "Okay."

"Once I get them to the Sanctum, I'll come back to you," Zalith said firmly.

"Just…please be carevul," Alucard warned him. "Zhe 'umans 'ere are ass'oles."

Zalith laughed a little. "Isn't that always the case?"

"Zhe vones 'ere are more ass'olier zhan usual."

The demon looked amused but nodded. "All right, I'll be back soon—and please be careful." He then adorned his wings and horns and took off, the force of his take-off picking up dust and dirt from the grass.

"Keep looking," Alucard told Vulpea.

"Yes, My Lord," she said and went back to examining the riverbed.

Alucard dematerialized, locking onto Aradia's aura—she was on the other side of the city with Alarian, Calantha, and Velorya. He landed not far from the woman, who was investigating a series of boot prints. "Vhat 'ave you vound?" he called.

The demons immediately turned to face him and bowed humbly.

"We've found several tracks, My Lord," Aradia answered and gestured to the trail. "I was just assigning someone to follow each set of prints."

Alucard looked down at the prints, too. They could very well belong to hunters or random idiots, especially since the bodies were found on the other side of the city—but he wasn't going to take any risks. He'd investigate anything that might be a lead. "Anyving else?" he questioned.

"Corvyn found some non-human blood," Calantha answered. "He's following it."

With a nod, Alucard locked on to Corvyn's aura. "Keep looking," he told them, and then he dematerialized again.

This time, the aura took him to a forest road, and Corvyn had just left it and was prowling into the woods. Alucard landed in the middle of the road, and he followed the man into the trees.

Corvyn didn't notice him until he crouched to investigate some leaf litter. The man shot up to his feet and frowned, looking startled. "My Lord—sorry, I didn't hear you," he said apologetically.

Alucard wasn't aggravated. Very few people could detect his arrival. "Vhat 'ave you vound?"

"There was a struggle not far from here—a lot of tracks in the dirt, like a fight had broken out. I spotted a few drops of blood, and it wasn't human. I haven't been able to determine who or what it belongs to, though."

"Take me to zhe blood."

With a nod, Corvyn walked past Alucard and led the way out of the trees. He took him a few yards down the road, and then he stopped, pointing at his feet.

Alucard set his eyes on the splotches of blood and crouched. He pressed two fingers against it and focused on it. It was eight hours old, ten at most, and it definitely wasn't human, but there was something odd about it. Something was distorting its scent, *and* its aura…like some kind of masking ethos.

Could this blood belong to whoever had killed his Knights? Masking ethos like this was highly sophisticated, and he suspected that the Silver Claw—having slain as many vampires as he had—was likely to use such ethos to keep vampires off his trail.

"Keep vollowing zhe trail. I need to look at Lenore," he said as he stood up, wiping the blood on his trousers.

"Yes, My Lord," Corvyn said, and then he hurried off and returned to his task.

Alucard dissolved into smoke and surged through the air towards the Sanctum. He should go to Alson and check if anyone suspicious had arrived in the city since he'd made sure a record was kept, but right now, that could wait. He needed to see what had killed his Knight.

He landed hard in the Sanctum courtyard, the familiar stone spinning beneath him for half a second before he forced the dizziness aside. He didn't slow. His boots struck the flagstones as he stormed through the main doors of the estate.

Vampires lining the hall paused and bowed; he passed the stair hall and turned right, his cape sweeping behind him as he strode down the corridor, through the lounge, and into the passage leading beneath the Sanctum.

The air cooled the deeper he went, and silence gathered thickly as he descended the narrow steps into the Vitalum. It was quiet as always—low-lit by a constellation of hanging lanterns; alcoves curved into the walls held wide beds and elevated slabs, each space separated by velvet curtains or thin stone partitions. The scent of dried herbs and faint blood lingered in the air, undercut by a sterile sharpness—like old silver and ash. It was a place for recovery… or preparation.

He found Lenore near the far end. Her body lay still atop a low stone platform draped in clean white linen. Her armour had been removed, but the Bloodmenders hadn't scrubbed her dirt-covered, blood-smeared skin as they usually would when preparing a recovered body for Restoration—they knew that Alucard wanted to see the state her killer had left her in.

Deep, ragged gashes carved through Lenore's chest and sides, so clean in some places that the torn flesh looked almost surgical, and others were nothing but ruin. Her long black hair had been brushed and gathered over one shoulder, but there was leaf litter and grass tangled in the strands.

She'd been patrolling the woods, and it didn't look like a quick death; it looked as if she'd fought until she had nothing left. Of course she had.

Alucard's jaw tensed as he stepped closer, the hem of his cape brushing the floor. For a moment, he stared at her, hands at his sides, fingers twitching with the urge to sink his claws into something. But he couldn't act on his anger right now. The entire coven was in danger, and he didn't want anyone else to end up as a pile of ashes or a torn-up corpse.

So he huffed away the rage and edged a little nearer. The slashes mimicked the claws of a werewolf, but they were too clean—*and* too close together. If this *was* the Silver Claw announcing his arrival, these wounds suggested that he was either a runt Omega at the very most… or a *pup*. But a professional vampire hunter who'd taken out Straybloods and Severeds across Scelerisque and Athene couldn't possibly be either of those things.

He eyed one of the deeper wounds and murmured, "Vhat did zhis to you?"

With a deep sigh, his eyes shifted from wound to wound. But once the rage subsided enough to make room in Alucard's mind for more than just anger and hatred, the *obvious* hit him. *How* had she died? What killed her? She wasn't bitten, so it couldn't be werewolf venom. There was no stake, no fire—had fire killed Salvorn, or was it silver? If it had been silver, Vulpea and his demons would have mentioned it. And if there was poison or spell work or anything evident about Lenore's death, the Bloodmenders would have reported it.

Another exhale left him. There were so many questions, but he wouldn't be able to Restore Lenore soon enough to get answers. If the Silver Claw *was* here, then he couldn't waste a single moment. He *would*, however, begin the Restoration process.

"*Vino*," he called.

The door to his left opened, and Bloodmenders Thessaly and Benedric walked out, moving towards him.

"My Lord," they both said gracefully.

"Start preparing 'er vor Vestoration," he ordered.

They nodded.

"Did Salvorn express 'is upon-death vishes?" he then asked.

"One moment, My Lord," Thessaly said and went over to the towering cabinet. She took out a thick book, flipped through it, and then returned it. "Knight Salvorn wishes to remain at Eternal Rest. He changed his mind from Restoration to Eternal Rest a few months ago."

"Do you know vhy?" he asked, concerned.

"He *did* look a little…depressed, My Lord."

Alucard sighed and nodded; it wasn't unheard of for a vampire to decide that Eternal Rest was better than eternal life, but it *was* new for someone as young as Salvorn to feel that way. Still, he'd not question it, nor would he go against Salvorn's wishes. "Make sure 'is urn is engraved."

They both bowed their heads.

Alucard then left the Vitalum and headed back through the Sanctum. Now, he had to find Alson, and he hoped that he'd find a solid lead that he could follow.

Chapter Eighteen

— ⟨ ✝ ⟩ —

Prisoners

| **Zalith** |
| *Atheson, Atheson City Outskirts* |

From the thick bough of an oak tree, Zalith watched the non-human compound in the clearing below. It mirrored the ones he'd encountered during the war in Eltaria—grim, utilitarian, and reeking of manufactured control. The fencing was tall iron, barbed cruelly at the top and electrified by the shimmer of embedded wards. Four stone towers loomed at each corner, manned by human guards in long military coats, rifles slung over their shoulders and revolvers at their hips. The central building squatted low and square, its brickwork stained and windowless, more a containment vault than any structure meant for the living.

He'd seen these places before—*lived through them*—back when his people were hunted, chained, and studied under the guise of wartime necessity, back when entire camps were built to break demons from the inside out. Places like this didn't just kill. They *erased*.

His once steady heart beat a little harder as he surveyed the yard. Shifters in their human forms stood or slumped behind the fence; demons, a witch, and even a siren— she was suffocating, and the guards were enjoying every moment of her suffering. They were all collared with silver so tight that it bit into flesh; the collars shimmered faintly, warded to suppress ethos, will, and instinct.

Most of the trapped beings looked dazed, eyes slow to blink, limbs slack with whatever draught had been forced into them. One woman stared vacantly at her knees. Another man—barefoot and bruised—twitched every few seconds like something inside him was fraying.

Zalith's jaw clenched. His claws flexed at his sides. He'd lost too much to places like this; friends whose names still caught in his throat, colleagues who laughed around firelit tables, men and women who had trusted him to bring them home…only for their bodies to end up inside walls like those.

What lingered now were the ghosts of their screams and the memory of what they looked like when the silver collars came off too late.

He inhaled sharply through his nose, fighting back the despair. *Not this time.*

Zalith scanned the compound, mind sharpening as it moved to strategy—headcount, shifts, the clumsy arc of the patrol routes. These were soldiers, yes, but human ones. Predictable. Imperfect. There were gaps, flaws, and vulnerabilities waiting to be exploited.

Rage flared in his chest like a coal caught in the wind, but he held it steady. If he leapt down now, all he'd gain was another body on the mountain he'd created. But if he planned—if he *waited*—he could gut this place from the inside out and leave not a single prisoner behind.

He *would* get them out.

All of them.

Not having a team with him this time had its pros and cons. He only had himself to consider, but he didn't have backup. There was no room for fucking up—but that wasn't going to happen. He'd seen and sieged enough of these places to know exactly where to strike…allies or not.

Still, he had to be cautious. So he watched, his gaze methodically sweeping across every tower, wall, and patrol. The design was harrowingly familiar, even in a different world. Why wouldn't it be? Humans were nothing if not creatures of repetition. Their arrogance bred patterns…patterns that could be exploited.

He counted seven guards outside the fence. Two walked in laps around the compound's border—one clockwise, the other counterclockwise—guns at the ready, eyes lazily dragging over the same terrain again and again. Another leaned against the southwest tower, a cigarette glowing faintly between his lips; he wasn't watching anything, just listening to the boredom.

The remaining four stood near the inner building, posted at the corners like watchdogs. Zalith's eyes narrowed. Those four were more alert. He clocked their stances, the way they touched their rifles every few seconds out of habit. Ex-soldiers, maybe. But even they weren't immune to complacency; one kept glancing up at the clouds, another chewed his lip, eyes darting too quickly.

A moment later, the patrols passed each other on the north side and gave one another a nod. Routine.

That was it. There. A timing gap.

Roughly every eight minutes, the two walking guards met and turned in opposite directions again, leaving the southeastern edge unwatched for about twelve seconds. It wasn't much, but it was enough. That section of the fence dipped into a depression of old stonework—leftover ruins maybe, or a former livestock trough. No lanterns or footpath. It was forgotten.

Good.

Zalith adjusted slightly on the branch, tilting his head to glance at the sky. The moons would soon be shrouded by clouds; the shadows would stretch deeper along the tree line, cloaking that southeastern blind spot entirely.

That was where he'd start.

He took another long look, just to be sure. He memorized the pace of the guards' strides, the intervals of their glances, even the way their boots struck the ground. One of them had a limp. The smoker finished his cigarette and flicked it into the brush.

Zalith didn't blink.

A low wind stirred the trees around him. He exhaled and let it carry his rage just long enough to think clearly, and then he dropped silently from the branch and melted into the forest shadows, circling south.

The clock had started.

Zalith moved like a shadow between trees, weaving through the underbrush without so much as snapping a twig beneath his boots. The forest floor was damp with yesterday's rain, muffling his steps, and the clouds had just begun covering the moons, lengthening the dark and softening the line where the wild gave way to wire and gunpowder.

He stayed angled along the tree line, circling south, keeping the compound in partial view. The southeastern blind spot was ahead now, just beyond a collapsed stretch of old stone wall half-swallowed by ivy. He descended into a low crouch near the final trees and scanned the ground. The fencing in this corner had sunken unevenly into the soft earth, and the closest floodlamp above flickered feebly, its crystal likely cracked—a blind spot in both light and line of sight.

Perfect.

The demon waited.

Eight minutes.

He could feel the tempo of the guards now. The limping one, rifle heavy at his side, passed almost out of earshot.

Then came the lull. A soft wind stirred the grass.

He moved. Quick, silent strides took him across the last strip of forest and into the tall grass that bordered the compound wall. He crouched, the mist curling faintly at the edges of his coat as he dulled his scent and silenced his breath. Ahead, the old wall rose in uneven slabs—stone just high enough to conceal him. He prowled to it, careful not to disturb the ivy growing wild across it, and peeked up between the gaps.

The guard had already passed.

Zalith slipped over the stone and into the compound's outer border, an unused stretch of dirt and cracked flagstone between the fencing and the main yard. There weren't any sentries, only the quiet buzz of the flickering lantern and the scent of damp moss and gun oil.

He crouched behind a rusted cart and drew in a slow breath. Inside the fence, ten yards ahead, a single guard stood near a small supply shed—alone, bored, distracted by the act of checking his pocket watch and lighting a pipe. Silver bullets glinted in the pouch at his hip, and strange concoctions shimmered. What a fucking hypocrite. These humans hated non-humans, but they'd gladly use the potions and elixirs that mages and seers created.

Zalith tilted his head, watching him.

One step at a time.

He extended his claws and crept forward like fog on cold stone, each step calculated and silent. The guard near the shed was still alone—still blissfully unaware that death was already within striking distance; he'd turned slightly now, exhaling a stream of pipe smoke into the dark air, watching it spiral upward with that distinct human laziness. Relaxed. Arrogant.

The demon scowled, letting the gloom embrace him like an old cloak as he stalked his prey, weaving between the objects scattered along the fence line. When he reached the final crate, the guard shifted his weight, and Zalith halted, waiting. He recalled doing this before—years ago, different uniforms, different faces, the same smell of metal weapons and sweat, the same cold anticipation before the first kill—he hated that he remembered it so well.

But old memories weren't going to impede him.

One more breath.

The guard turned his back.

Zalith struck—he closed the distance in a heartbeat, one clawed hand snapping around the man's mouth, the other driving into his neck. Cartilage gave way. The body jolted once, convulsed, and then went limp. Zalith caught him before he could hit the ground. Slowly and quietly, he dragged the corpse behind the shed and lowered it beside a stack of crates, out of sight, blood pooling in the dirt and steaming faintly in the cold air. The demon crouched over the dead guard, retraced his claws, and began searching the man's coat pockets.

A silver key. A fold-out map of the compound. A small set of warding matches. A flask filled with cheap brandy. He tucked the map into his coat and pocketed the key, and then he paused, remaining crouched beside the still body.

He was proud of it—of the blood, the silence it left behind, and the justice that it brought. He'd never enjoyed killing for the sake of it, but this? *This* was different. These weren't just men. They were the same breed of cowards who collared his kind, who built cages and called them necessary, who stood tall behind weapons and poisons while they starved others in chains.

Killing them wasn't just necessary—it was *deserved.*

The demon left the corpse and melted back into the shadows like the creature they feared he was. His eyes locked on the next guard—the sentry pacing between two lampposts alone. Beyond him, another leaned lazily against a wall, rifle half-slung and eyes unfocused. *Three more before they notice.* That would be enough to fracture the compound's outer ring, enough to unravel them before they even knew that they were being hunted.

Zalith's claws extended once again, gleaming faintly in the lantern light.

The next two guards didn't even see him coming.

He moved like a blade through smoke, silently precise. The first man was pacing between the lampposts, trying to stay awake. A single stroke across his throat ended him, and Zalith caught him before his knees hit the dirt. The second, the one leaning against the wall, was barely upright when the demon struck from behind, claws plunging beneath the ribs, piercing his heart and spine in the blink of an eye.

Three down.

And still no alarm, no cry or gunfire.

He was moving faster now.

With the outer patrol thinned and the murk deeper than ever, Zalith crept towards a squat stone hut nestled against the southern tower, locked but unguarded. A faint symbol had been etched above the lintel—old warding runes, diluted now with age and weather. Human-made. *Pathetic, dirty fucking hypocrites*—every time he saw humans using the things they preached were lesser and unnatural, it made his blood boil. They clutched their purity like a shield, spat on anything not born of their kind, and still laced their defences with stolen power, invoked rites they barely understood, and dared to call *his kind* monsters.

He stifled a snarl and retrieved the silver key from his coat. Twisting the lock open with barely a click, he eased the door open. The supply hut reeked of oil, iron, and cheap ethos. Stored inside were crates of ammunition—some silver-lined, some hollow point— at least these humans hadn't caught word of new demons weak to platinum and rhodium entering Aegisguard. Bundles of rope, lantern fuel, a crate of herbal sedatives used to keep the prisoners compliant… and the smell was familiar—almost harrowing.

Rusted nails, stagnant holy water, charred bone, and chlorine.

In Eltaria, they called it Infirmuseos, but the vials here had Surripio written on them. He knew the sting of it, the suffocating weakness. He'd been shot with many an arrow and cut with blades covered in the drug.

The guards didn't stop at that atrocious narcotic, though. He spotted vials marked with crude symbols, and a half-filled barrel of black sludge that stung his nose even from across the room—hemlock mixed with poppy resin. *That* was how they were keeping every kind of non-human in this place silent.

He pulled a thin rag from a shelf, dipped it in the hemlock mixture, and stuffed it into the barrel's lid. With a flick of one claw, he tore open a ventilation pipe just above the wall and forced the soaked rag inside. It wouldn't kill the guards, but it *would* hinder them; it would make them sluggish and slow to react, dulling their senses just enough to hand him the rest of this place on a platter.

Zalith moved to the back wall and found what he was hoping for—a shelf stacked with signalling devices: bells, flares, and powder whistles. He crushed them all beneath his boot, the chiming snap of crystal and glass echoing dully through the room, and then he left them in the dirt and turned towards the door.

Outside, the wind was shifting. He could smell it—faint silver, blood, and smoke. But no panic.

He stepped out into the dark once more, the scent of rot and hemlock clinging faintly to his coat. Now the compound's systems were compromised; the outer guard ring was broken, their communication was down, and their sedation levels were unpredictable.

It was time to move faster.

However, just before he slipped into the next row of shadows, something caught his attention. A prisoner—a young demon, maybe seventeen, with scorched wounds where her horns should be and a cracked silver collar. She was sitting near the edge of the yard, trembling, *crying*, and her wide, bloodshot eyes were staring at him through the fence.

Zalith couldn't stop moving, nor could he risk sharing comforting words. But their gazes locked long enough for understanding to pass between them.

And then he vanished again into the dark. He slipped through the corridor behind the tower; the map had marked the holding block as a converted carriage barn near the centre of the yard, its windows bricked over, its doors reinforced with steel, and its roof crusted with old warding runes. But the humans had been lazy. The runes were shallow, eroded by rain and carelessness with no proper maintenance or reverence for the old protections.

Typical.

He crouched behind a cart piled with firewood, his eyes narrowing as he counted the guards stationed outside the barn entrance. Two. One pacing, the other leaning against the door, yawning. Both armed but relaxed. Zalith flexed his fingers, stretching out the tension in his knuckles, and then he began prowling.

The first guard was dead before he hit the ground—Zalith's hand twisted at the base of the man's skull, snapping his neck in silence. The second managed a half-choked gasp before Zalith drove him backwards into the barn door and slit his throat with one of his claws, blood slicking the wooden frame. He let the body fall, and then he removed the man's uniform coat. He pressed his palm against the door, eyes flicking over the runes that kept it locked. A spark of power shot through his veins; the dormant sigils flickered once in protest… and then fizzled out with a hiss.

The door creaked open. Inside, it reeked of silver, sweat, and despair. Dozens of prisoners lined the walls, most of them shackled, many collapsed onto the straw-littered floor. They stirred as the door opened, blinking through the haze of whatever drug was in their system.

A woman near the front—older, with scars and sunken eyes—squinted up at him. "… You're… not one of them," she breathed, her voice barely a whisper.

It took Zalith a moment to recognize her. Salome, an Upsilon of the pack he'd come here to liberate. "No," he replied.

And then she seemed to realize who he was, too. "You… you're Zalith."

He nodded as he knelt and wrenched her shackles apart with one violent jerk of his hand. The woman stared at him, stunned as the silver collar clattered to the floor.

Zalith then moved on to the next.

And the next.

And the next.

Some of the prisoners began to rise on shaky legs, others just wept silently. All of them watched him, clearly unsure whether this was real or some final hallucination before death.

Zalith's eyes located Abel, the Duskroot Alpha, sitting in the far corner with Temperance—she wasn't only bleeding and shivering, but she was also pregnant, and like most of the others, the silver collar around her neck was burning the skin beneath it, leaving it sore and blistered.

The demon made his way over and handed the earlier-stolen guard's uniform to the werewolf Alpha. "Get outside. Walk like you belong. Open what you can, but tell everyone to stay put until I tell them to move."

Abel caught the coat, blinking rapidly before turning his drooping head to his Luna. "I-I… I can't leave her."

"She'll be fine. I'll get her out of here," the demon said as he gripped Abel's collar with both hands and pulled it apart, and then he broke the shackles.

The Alpha gawped for a moment… but then he nodded and scrambled to change.

"Stay here," Zalith told Temperance as he pulled her collar off and snapped the chains around her ankles.

She nodded stiffly. "Th-thank you."

Zalith began making his way around the room, removing shackles and collars, and the freed prisoners began shaking each other awake with trembling hands.

Once everyone was free, Zalith turned to the centre of the room and raised his voice—not loud, not urgent, but *final*—"Listen to me. You've been drugged, collared, and weakened, but you're still more powerful than any of them out there. I've silenced the alarms and crippled the patrols. We're all going to get out of here, but you need to stay and work together. Understand?"

A flicker of something passed through the room. Agreement, rage…*hope*. A thread of life returning.

But then a voice bellowed outside—a panicked cry.

They'd found a body.

No alarm was coming, though. He'd made sure of that.

He turned to the scarred demon nearest him. "Get the others to the courtyard, and when the bell doesn't ring, you strike."

The man nodded. "We will."

"You," Zalith snapped, pointing at the most lucid-looking demon. "Your job is to get her to safety," he ordered, turning to point at Temperance. "Do not stop for anything or anyone."

"Yes, sir," the woman said, and then she hurried to the Luna.

Zalith then used the shadows again, slipping out of the barn just as chaos began to take root. Guards were yelling, guns were raised, but the coordination was gone.

And Zalith was already moving towards the next block. There were still more prisoners, and he wasn't leaving until every last collar hit the ground.

Chapter Nineteen

— ⸱ ✝ ⸱ —

A Shard

| **Alucard** |

| *Atheson, Atheson Coven Sanctum* |

Scribe Alson was in The Thornsong Library. He muttered to himself while he hastily read the thick tome laid out on the desk in front of him, and he occasionally glanced at another, thinner book to his right.

"Alson," Alucard said, approaching him.

The Acolyte flinched in startle and swung around in his seat to face him. "Oh, sorry, My Lord. I didn't hear you come in."

"Vhat are you veading?" he questioned, stopping beside him and looking down at the tome—a grimoire covering shifters.

"I was just trying to work out what killed Knight Salvorn and Knight Lenore," he said, looking back down at the aged pages. "And I was looking at the lists—the ones you asked me to compare. Knight Corven-Hale delivered this one early this morning." He slid over a piece of paper so that Alucard could see it, and then the thin book. "And this is the latest from the city."

Alucard started reading over both lists. There were names, ages, and descriptions of what each person looked like, as well as notes as to whether they were human or not.

"If the Silver Claw hunter *has* arrived, and he *was* responsible for our Knights' deaths…and if he *is* a he *and* a werewolf, then we have six people as suspects," Alson continued. "I circled the six."

He looked at each circled name. Tobin, Luke—

"—Lenroy, Oliver, Pascal, and Algernon," Alson listed. "The only one who declared that he was a werewolf was Pascal, but I don't know, there's something fishy about him."

Alucard frowned. "Vhat exactly?"

"Well, he was wearing another werewolf's pelt for starters—M-My Lord, sorry if that sounded rude."

He shook his head and leaned against the desk. "Continue."

"Uh…well, that's where the grimoire comes in. From the descriptions that both the humans you compelled *and* the coven on patrol wrote down, I've been able to determine that Oliver may be a mage—" he pulled the grimoire closer and flipped through it before landing on a page that covered mages, "—he had something with one of these."

He was pointing to a blue crystal, the same crystal that *all* mages adorned somewhere on their person because they stored their staffs or ethos-channelling instruments inside.

"A repono crystal. It was one of his earrings. The humans didn't notice because the other earring is a shaded sapphire, and it looks almost identical to the repono crystal. Most mages don't go through such an effort to hide their crystals, right?" the Acolyte said with a pondering expression.

It wasn't unusual for a mage to want to be discreet, especially when they were on a mission. But did that mean Oliver was in Atheson on mage business? If so, what *was* that business?

Alucard sighed and said, "A mage zidn't do zhis."

"Oh, right—sorry, I'm getting carried away," he said and flipped through the grimoire again. "Okay, so…Algernon had a tattoo—"

"Alson, ve're looking vor a verevolf."

"Y-yes, My Lord, this is related, I promise."

He waited.

Alson continued, "The tattoo was covering up a bite on his arm. Adherent Noctrel managed to get a closer look at him because they were on their way to pick up the humans' list, and they saw it as clear as day."

"'E is bitten verevolf, not born," Alucard mumbled. Could the Silver Claw be a rogue bitten werewolf? That made more sense. If he belonged to a pack or a bloodline, he'd be cautious about starting a war, but he wasn't, was he? He was just killing and killing and killing, taking humans' money—and *that* was another thing that a pack wouldn't do; wolf packs *hated* humans. "Vhere is 'e?"

"Uh…" Alson murmured.

But Alucard still had one of the lists. "Grevemire Vow—"

"Grevemire Row," Alson said at the same time.

The vampire nodded. "Zhe Vellistone 'ouse."

"It's a small hotel, My Lord."

"Vight. Anyvone else?" he asked, looking down at him.

"Well, while I think that Algernon is the biggest suspect, Tobin didn't declare that he's a muto—the lion kind, I think. The grimoire said a telltale sign is how their faces look kinda…lion-like," the Acolyte said.

"Vasn't a muto leo," Alucard said, shaking his head. "Zhe slash marks aren't vide or vhick enough to 'ave been made by zheir claws."

Alson nodded. "Uh… Lenroy didn't declare that he's a sleuth."

A sleuth? The slashes *were* far apart enough… but not as thick as they would be if a sleuth were responsible.

"And Luke said that he was a human, but Adherent Noctrel got a look at his eyes and said that he's an energy vampire," Alson continued, and then he looked up at Alucard. "That's all, My Lord."

He shook his head. "Energy vampire. Who zhe fuck came up vith zhat term?"

"I… well—" the Acolyte flipped through the grimoire, "—well… it would appear that energy vampire is actually a derogatory word, My Lord."

"Mm-hmm," he grumbled. "Zhey are soul leeches."

Alson chuckled a little, staring at the page. "Oh, yeah. Says so right here."

Alucard exhaled deeply. "Keep up zhe good vork," he said, and then he turned towards the door—

"Hey," Zalith said, smirking at him, leaning against the doorframe.

Admittedly surprised, Alucard faltered for a moment… but then he continued and slinked past his mate, leaving the library. "'Ow did vings go?" he asked—the smell of blood clung to the demon, and when he looked at him, he saw streaks of it soaked into Zalith's blazer. It wasn't his, though. It was *all* human. "Did you kill all zhe guards?"

"I did," the demon confirmed, following Alucard through the corridor. "I got the pack out as well as the rest of the non-humans. Temperance needs healing priority. Oh, and one of the Betas is out in the woods looking for the other wolves."

Relieved, Alucard exhaled deeply, untensing his shoulders a little. "Vone of my Bloodmenders knows enough about ozzer species to treat zhe injured," he said as he started leading the way down the spiral staircase.

Zalith, however, didn't let him get far. Before Alucard could descend more than a few steps, a firm hand caught his arm, spun him, and pressed him back against the cool brick wall. Zalith leaned in, his breath warm against Alucard's lips as he kissed him— once… twice… and a third time, slower, deeper, until his tongue slid into the vampire's mouth with a claiming pressure that made Alucard tremble. The moment their tongues met, a fierce pang of desire flared through him, and his body instinctively arched against the demon's, heat flooding his skin, aching for more.

He whimpered softly into the kiss.

Zalith felt it. He *knew* it.

Just as Alucard's hands gripped his coat, ready to pull him closer, Zalith broke the kiss and leaned back slightly—his lips wet, his eyes dark with hunger and amusement.

"Am I going to have to kill that little librarian of yours?" his mate murmured, his voice low and edged with a dangerous playfulness.

Alucard couldn't help the shiver that crawled down his spine. He *loved* it when Zalith got like this—possessive and protective with that spark of jealous hunger in his eyes. It made the heat inside him twist tighter and hotter as he smiled lazily, his gaze flicking down to Zalith's lips. "No, my love," he murmured, his voice like silk. "I belong to you."

Those words roused a pleased smile from the demon, and he leaned into Alucard's ear. "Good boy," he whispered

The praise curled like smoke through Alucard's mind—the sound of it nearly unravelled him. His knees weakened as desperation struck through his body like lightning; he exhaled shakily, his hands clutching at Zalith's sides, and then he groaned quietly when he felt the demon's hips press forward. Zalith slowly ground his crotch against him, letting Alucard feel just how hard he already was beneath the layers of his clothes.

Alucard's head tipped back against the wall, a breathless but hushed whine slipping past his lips before he could stop it, as if Zalith was trying to make whoever heard it jealous. His body throbbed with need, every nerve taut, every inch of skin begging for contact. He *needed* it—he needed Zalith inside him, over him, surrounding him. His heat clawed at the edges of his restraint, and the teasing pressure against him only made it worse.

Zalith leaned in again, letting his breath ghost over Alucard's jaw. "I can feel how much you want it," he murmured darkly, pressing forward again just enough to make Alucard bite back another moan.

He wanted to give in, to take Zalith somewhere and let him do as he pleased. The suggestion almost slipped... but he *couldn't*. He had to tell his body no. He had to tell *Zalith*.... "Ve can't," he said with a groan—it pained him to turn down the chance to get what his body so sorely needed. "Not yet," he then said, and *that* made him feel a little less disappointed. "I need to vind zhis—"

The demon gently gripped Alucard's crotch, smirking, staring into his eyes.

Alucard tensed and stifled a groan as he continued, "—zhis... Silver Claw."

Zalith kissed his lips, his cheek, and then his neck before he pressed his forehead against his and said, "I'm sorry. I can't help it." He sounded almost ashamed.

"No, is okay," Alucard immediately said. He understood why they were both feeling and reacting the way they were, and he knew that if it weren't for him being in heat, Zalith wouldn't be doing anything that might hinder the objective. "I can't eizer." He exhaled deeply, trying to urge the desire to loosen its grip... and his arousal to settle. "Vhen ve're done 'ere," he said firmly, and then he smirked. "You still need to fuck me vour times."

The demon smirked, too. "I think we ought to make it five now."

Amused, Alucard laughed softly. "Six if you 'elp me make sense of someving I'm convlicted about."

Zalith looked intrigued—the gleam of curiosity was narrowly visible behind the hunger in his eyes. "Oh?"

Alucard took his hand. "Is zhis vay," he said, leading the way downstairs.

Once they reached the basement level of the Sanctum, Alucard took Zalith through the Nightvault and into the Vitalum. The Bloodmenders were still cleaning the blood and dirt from Lenore's skin. Alucard sent them away with a wave of his hand, and they retreated towards their quarters.

"Vait," he said, pointing at Thessaly. "Zhere's a verevolf who needs 'ealing." He looked at Zalith. "Vhere did you put zhem?"

"One of you vampires directed me to a guestroom near the stair hall," his mate said.

"Go zhere," he told the Bloodmender. "Treat Temperance virst, and zhen everyvone else."

"Yes, My Lord," she said with a graceful bow. She grabbed one of the field medical kits and headed upstairs.

Benedric bowed, too, and went into his quarters.

"'Ere," Alucard said to Zalith, leading him over to the stone platform where Lenore's body lay. "To start, zhese slashes mimic zhe claws of a verevolf, but zhey're too clean and close togezzer," he said, gesturing to the slashes. "But isn't zhe slashes zhat killed 'er; verevolves zon't 'ave venom in zheir claws—if actually vas a verevolf zhat did zhis. Zhere's no silver, eizer. No poison, no spell vork. Ve zon't know vhat killed 'er."

Zalith moved nearer and examined the slashes. "Are those the only sure ways to kill vampires? Silver, werewolf venom, etcetera?"

He nodded.

"Is it okay if I?" he asked, gesturing to the slashes.

"Mm-hmm."

The demon leaned even closer, practically staring down into one of the wounds; he placed a finger on either side, and then he slowly widened the slash.

Alucard saw it when Zalith did.

That flicker of light.

The vampire took a pair of suture scissors and handed them to him.

Zalith used the scissors to carefully pull a very small shard of something from the gash. He took his other hand away from Lenore's wounds, and he held the scissors in front of himself and Alucard. "I think it's a good idea that your Bloodmenders didn't dig too deep," he said.

It was silver. A tiny but sharp fragment. Triangular, ever so slightly curved.

"Looks like piece of a claw," Alucard mumbled as he took the scissors from Zalith and looked a little closer.

"Be careful," Zalith said.

Alucard gave him an assuring smile and stared at the fragment.

"Silver Claw…silver claws," the demon said with a shrug.

The vampire's eyes shifted to Lenore's wounds again. Was the Silver Claw *not* a werewolf? Now that he thought about it, and now that he had a silver fragment, it added up. Those gashes were far apart enough to have come from a humanoid hand—one with silver claws. *That* was what had killed his Knight, wasn't it? Silver claws. It made perfect sense.

"What are your thoughts?" his mate asked.

"I zon't vink ve're dealing with a verevolf 'ere—maybe zhe Silver Claw isn't a volf at all. Maybe zhe whole volf speculation vas spread to deceive people."

"So, are we dealing with a human? They make up most of the world's vampire hunters," he said with an irritated grunt.

Alucard shook his head. "Lenore is vone of my best Knights—so skilled zhat I've been considering making 'er a Paladin. No 'uman vould be able to do zhis to 'er."

"A demon? Another vampire?"

He glanced at Zalith, ready to shut that suggestion down…but he knew what *Severed* vampires were capable of. Some grew bitter and jealous, and this wouldn't be the first time he'd dealt with a Severed murdering their own kind. However…*silver*. No vampire could touch it without ghastly consequences, let alone wield it, let alone coat their claws in it.

So he shook his head again. "Putting silver on zheir claws vould kill a vampire, or at zhe very least melt zheir 'ands avay." He paused and leaned against the wall. "A zemon? I mean…maybe. Zhe zemons of zhis vorld possess a great disdain vor vampires, but to *zhis* extent? Per'aps vone of Liliv's—but no vaid 'as been veported, and as var as I know, Liliv's cultists zon't go solo."

"Did your little librarian have any demons on that list of his?" Zalith asked, smirking.

"I'd 'ave to go and ask 'im. But if any silver-clawed person vas seen entering zhe city, my people vould 'ave veported."

Zalith shrugged and said, "What if the silver isn't on their claws or nails? It could be a glove or a gauntlet."

Alucard lifted the silver fragment and held it in front of a lantern's glow. The warm light caught on its jagged curve, illuminating the dull sheen of silver fused over the top like a half-melted cap. He turned the scissors slowly, inspecting the pale root still clinging beneath the silvery crust. "Is a nail," he said confidently. "Zhe keratin is still visible under zhe coating—is too vhin to be bone and too organic to be metal. You can even see vhere is cracked vrom the 'eat—gloves zon't burn like zhat."

The demon grinned at him. "You're so fucking hot when you do that."

He frowned. "Do vhat?"

Zalith stroked Alucard's cheek with his fingers. "When you get all scholar-y."

Alucard pouted a little but tried to concentrate. He put the scissors down, making sure the silver fragment stayed clamped in them. "Ve 'ave to go back to Alson."

The demon huffed. "What if he starts flirting with you again?"

"'E vasn't vlirting vith me."

"He certainly was," Zalith teased him.

With a quiet sigh, Alucard took a sterile cloth from a nearby bowl and handed it to his mate. "Vor your 'ands."

Zalith cleaned his hands, and as Alucard directed, he put the cloth into a different bowl. "Thank you," he said.

Alucard grasped his hand and led the way upstairs. "If zhere aren't any ozzer suspicious people on Alson's list, ve're going to talk to Algernon. Verevolf or not, 'e's too shady *not* to question."

The demon nodded in response.

Would he find any demons on Alson's list? He wasn't sure, but the idea of a demon doing this just didn't sit right with him. Was it instinct, or was his lingering suspicion that it was still a werewolf stemmed from the rivalry he'd once had with their species?

Chapter Twenty

— ⸂ ✝ ⸃ —

Wrenhollow Lane

| **Zalith** |
| *Atheson, Atheson Coven Sanctum* |

Zalith watched Alson closely. While he knew that Alucard's vampires simply admired and looked up to him as their creator, he couldn't help but feel protective *and* possessive, even more so since his fiancé was in heat. He wanted to move nearer than the doorframe he was leaning against, but he didn't want to make Alucard uncomfortable.

So he settled for making *Alson* uncomfortable instead. He wanted to make sure that this Scribe—as Alucard had called him—knew that Alucard had a fiancé, that he had a mate, a soon-to-be husband. He wanted to make sure *everyone* knew that Alucard was *his*, and if he had to do more than stand there and glare, then he would.

But his glower was enough right now. He watched Alson squirm every time he glanced his way to see if he was still watching him. The man reminded him of Elvin— small, obviously obsessed with Alucard, eager to please, eager to prove that he was more than met the eye. He wasn't much to look at, though. *Almost* the same brown hair as the dead bard, and a patchy beard that might never become full since he'd been turned as a teenager.

Zalith found that funny. He scoffed amusedly, and when Alson looked at him again, he scowled.

Alson cleared his throat and went back to talking to Alucard. "Um…yeah, none of them were Lilith's as far as anyone could tell, My Lord."

"And zhere vas absolutely *noving* suspicious about any of zhem at all?"

The Scribe shook his head. "Your demons vetted them themselves, My Lord."

With a deep sigh, Alucard nodded. "All vight, vhat about any of zhe ozzer men on zhe list? 'Uman or non-'uman."

Alson nervously shifted his sights to the book—he was clearly trying not to glance at Zalith again. "No, My Lord."

"Maybe I should 'ave ordered vor all of zheir luggage to be searched," Alucard muttered. "Did zhey vecord vhere zhey vere *all* staying?"

He nodded. "Most of them are staying in hotels and inns."

"Vrite me a copy of zhis list—vast," he said.

With a nod, Alson got to work.

Zalith was certain that Alucard was thinking the same thing as him. It would cause an uproar if every single man who'd recently come into the city were searched like a criminal. But how else would they find what they were looking for? Of course, waiting until each suspect left their room was an option, but could they risk waiting around?

"Maybe ve use zhe city law envorcement," Alucard said with a huff, turning his head to look across the room at Zalith. "Spread vumours about somevone smuggling illegal substances."

"It would have to be something that'll scare the city into complying," the demon said. "I'd suggest something relating to the virus, but that's likely going to cause a little *too* much panic."

Alucard nodded in agreement.

"Can I make a suggestion?" Alson asked.

"No," Zalith snapped.

Alucard laughed and looked down at the Scribe. "Vhat?"

Alson shuffled around anxiously, glancing at Zalith again before twiddling his thumbs. "The people here are all pretty afraid of the raiding demons. Maybe we could spread a story about a demon spy being here?"

"That'll make the entire city suspicious of *everyone*," Zalith bit out, tuning the idiot out as he concentrated on his fiancé. "We could have one of the doctors warn the city officials that a new arrival has smallpox, but the test vials weren't labelled correctly or something. Humans are terrified of smallpox outbreaks, and they'll comply with an ordered lockdown while all the new arrivals are searched and tested—the non-humans will comply, too, to keep themselves from being exposed. We can send our people to each suspect's place to search them without revealing who and what we're actually looking for."

Alucard nodded. "Zhat could vork." He asked Alson, "'Ow many new arrivals total?"

"Thirty-two since we started keeping a record, My Lord."

"I 'ave ten zemons 'ere," Alucard told Zalith. "Ve can temporarily put zhe vecovered verevolves on border patrol as vell as a vew more vampires vhile my zemons conduct zhe search," he said, looking at Zalith again. "Zhere's a 'ighly veputable doctor at zhe

Vren'ollow Lane Medical Office. 'Is name is Augustin Vexley. Zhe city vill trust anyving 'e says."

Zalith pondered for a moment. "How soon do you want me to make him share this information?"

"Per'aps vight now. By zhe time zhe news spreads, my zemons vill be veady."

"All right," he replied... but he didn't want to leave Alucard alone. The Silver Claw was in Atheson, and after seeing what he'd done to that other vampire, the last thing he wanted was to risk not being at his fiancé's side if the hunter came after him. "We should stick together, Alucard," he said firmly. "You shouldn't be alone with him out there somewhere."

Alson nodded and opened his mouth to speak, but when Zalith glared at him, he turned away with an anxious frown.

Alucard didn't disagree. "I just need to get Vulpea over 'ere and tell zhe verevolves vhere to go," he said as Alson handed him the copy of the list.

"I'm ready when you are," Zalith said.

As Alucard led the way, the demon followed beside him. When they reached the stair hall, his fiancé took him to a study space, where a few vampires were reading, writing, and crafting. *One* woman sitting in the corner and keeping a watchful eye over them all wasn't a vampire but a demon—Liora, a Beta of Alucard's new pack. Zalith watched Alucard send her to find and replace Vulpea, and then he headed to the guest room.

Most of the werewolves looked a lot better—Alucard's Bloodmender evidently knew exactly what she was doing. Alucard told them of their new task, and by the time he was done assigning a few vampires to assist the wolves on patrol, Vulpea arrived in the courtyard.

"Gazzer everyvone and vait vor me 'ere. I 'ave a new task vor you," he told her.

She bowed and said, "Yes, My Lord." She transformed into a bat and took off.

"Let's go," Alucard said, taking Zalith's hand.

His fiancé dematerialized them into curling vermillion smoke, and when their forms reassembled, they stood in the heart of a gloomy street cloaked in near-midnight hush. The vampire shivered briefly, so Zalith moved his arm around him and pulled him a little closer as he took in their surroundings, the only sound coming from the faint creak of distant shutters in the wind.

The demon's gaze lifted to the worn street sign overhead—Wrenhollow Lane.

At the far end of the narrow street was the medical practice. Three stories tall, its stone façade was darkened with age and soot, ivy clinging to the lower corners like reaching fingers. A brass plaque dulled by time sat beside the door, half-obscured by shadow. Only a few windows glowed faintly, oil lamps burning low behind drawn curtains, casting thin streaks of amber light across the road. Beside it stood the apothecary, its wooden shutters closed tight and a bell hanging crooked above the door.

"Are you sure he'll be here?" Zalith asked as they headed up the street.

"'E alvays vorks late hours," the vampire said with a nod. "My vampires keep close tabs on all zhe important vigures in zhis place."

Smart move. "Better to have him sound the alarm this late, too. Everyone will be too tired to protest."

"Zhere are alvays at least two people in zhe city 'all, too. Vone of zhe chancellors vaits avound vor a certain secretary to vinish papervork each night, so 'e'll be zhere."

Despite the fact that *he* would have made all the same choices, something about seeing Alucard doing just as he would was *very* attractive. He loved how astute his vampire was and seeing him work—whether like this or in battle—was captivating.

He followed Alucard to the door of the medical practice. It was locked, of course— no surprise at this hour—but that hardly mattered. Zalith raised one hand, fingers splayed slightly, and focused. With a subtle tug of his telekinesis, the bolt scraped free from the inside with a soft metallic click. He glanced at Alucard and pushed the door open.

The scent hit him first—aged paper, medicinal herbs, alcohol, and something faintly metallic, like dried blood lingering just beneath the antiseptic tinge. The air was warm but still, as if the building itself was half-asleep, and he felt Alucard relax ever so slightly in his embrace. But the vampire still felt tense, and he looked... anxious?

"Are you okay?" the demon asked quietly.

Alucard nodded. "I'm just tired."

Zalith rubbed his arm. "You should rest after this. It'll give time for word to spread."

"Maybe," he replied.

They stepped into a narrow corridor lined with dark wood panelling, the wallpaper curling faintly at the corners. A single crystal-powered light flickered in a dusty sconce ahead, casting long shadows across the floorboards—yet another thing humans were completely, selfishly hypocritical to use. Beneath a coat rack, a small waiting bench sat with a single overcoat still hanging, as though its owner hadn't yet finished for the night.

Their footsteps were hushed as they passed closed doors on either side—examination rooms, supply closets. He saw Alucard glance into each one... like he was searching for something... but he suspected that it wasn't their target.

Despite his caution, the vampire led confidently, and Zalith kept his senses focused, picking up the faintest thrum of thought from somewhere above. Someone was awake. No... more than one. A lone person in one room, two women in another; it sounded like the loner was writing, the sound of a pen scratching against paper seeping into the quiet, and the women were talking about several patients they'd seen today. Nurses, probably.

The demon and vampire reached the end of the corridor and climbed a narrow staircase, worn slightly in the middle from years of use. On the second floor, the hallway was darker, quieter, but a sliver of light escaped from beneath a door halfway down, and on a nameplate above the frame was the name they were looking for.

Doctor A. Vexley.

Alucard reached for the handle.

And Zalith smirked faintly, looking forward to seeing Alucard work again.

The vampire pushed the door open—

"I keep telling you to knock, Tamsin," the man grunted, not sparing a glance.

Zalith closed the door behind them.

At the same time, Alucard said, "Ve 'ave an appointment."

The man's head snapped up, startled, and the wide-eyed look on his face quickly gave way to a confused frown. "Who are you?" he questioned, putting his pen down. "I don't book appointments at this hour."

"Ve're zhe exception," the vampire said as he moved towards the desk.

Vexley cautiously rose to his feet. "Now, gentlemen…if you need to see a doctor, you need to talk to my—"

Alucard snatched the man's collar and snapped, "Ve need a vavour."

The man held up his hands, panicking…and after he obviously worked out that neither Alucard nor Zalith were human, he looked *horrified.* "L-look…if this is about those non-humans I sent to the compound, I was just doing my job, okay? I *have* to report them or else I'd lose my license."

Zalith's glance shifted to Alucard. Did he know about this? It didn't seem so; the expression on his face was vacant, but he knew how to read his complicated fiancé's eyes. He was *confused*—surprised…maybe even disgusted. Zalith felt the latter. A doctor of all people causing harm when it was their job to—

"'Ow do you live vith yourselv? Is your job to protect and 'eal people—and zon't you dare try zhe whole 'non-'umans aren't people' shit vith me. *You* should know better zhan anyvone zhat zhey *are*," Alucard snarled.

Vexley half-frowned, but he held it back. "Sir, please," he said calmly. "You misunderstand. I have nothing against non-humans, but my nurse…she was the one treating the little boy, and—"

"You sent a *child* to zhe fucking compound?!" Alucard growled, pulling the man closer, baring his fangs.

The doctor's terrified expression thickened, but he kept his voice calm despite it shaking. "I didn't want to—please believe me."

Zalith searched his mind. He wasn't lying, but he wasn't going to stop his fiancé; he was enjoying observing, and he'd rather let his vampire make his own decisions. If he *had* to, though, he'd stop him from killing Vexley. They needed him.

"If you want the one responsible, that's fine by me—you want Nurse Tamsin. She's…" he paused, his eyes momentarily flicking to Alucard's fangs. "She's an awful woman. She prides herself on sending non-humans to that Godforsaken place, and I wouldn't be the first doctor she's gotten fired for not reporting patients. Do you know what they do to people like me? The non-human sympathizers?"

"I can't imagine is anyvhere near as bad as vhat 'appens in zhose compounds."

"They feed us to the lycans," Vexley said, going pale.

Zalith wasn't surprised.

Alucard didn't look shocked, either.

"I'll try to help you, okay? What do you need? Opioids? Sedatives?" the doctor asked desperately. "We've got grim root down in—"

"Ve're not 'ere vor medicine," the vampire interjected, still keeping the man in his intimidating grip.

"S-so…Tamsin? She's down the corridor with—"

"Unvortunately, ve can't trust you vith zhis," Alucard cut him off again, and then he looked at Zalith. "Ve're just going to borrow your mind vor a little vhile."

Vexley panicked as Alucard pulled him towards the demon. "W-what does that mean? What are you doing? Wai—"

Zalith grabbed the side of the man's face and burrowed deep into his mind. "You will go to the city hall and find a chancellor," he instructed as Vexley's eyes went grey. "Tell him that the test results for the latest arrivals have returned, but the nurses mishandled them. The records were mislabelled. You don't know which group it is, but one of them has smallpox. Not the usual strain. This is a *severe variant*—more aggressive, faster-spreading, harder to treat. A full city lockdown must be issued immediately. No one is to leave their homes or rented quarters under any circumstances. Make sure he understands. Do not leave the hall until the lockdown is ordered. And then you will return here and lock yourself in this office under the pretence that you are working desperately to find a treatment. You will do this until I free your mind."

Deadpan, monotone, Vexley replied, "I understand."

The demon took his hand off his face.

Vexley stared aimlessly as he gathered his things, put his glasses on, and left the office.

"How far is the city hall from here?" Zalith asked his fiancé.

"A vivteen-minute valk."

He scoffed amusedly. But he shifted his focus from the desire to make Vexley suffer in small doses for what he'd done to concern for both Alucard and what they'd just learned. "Are you okay, baby?" he asked, rubbing his arm.

Alucard sighed deeply. "Even vhere zhere *are* 'umans who zon't 'ate us, zhere are alvays zhe vones who *do* 'ate us making sure noving changes."

He was right, and it was as upsetting as it was infuriating. "At least the compound is gone," he said, trying to assure him.

The vampire didn't look very comforted by his words, though. "But you vound no children in zhere, did you?"

Zalith didn't want to answer…but he wouldn't lie or keep the truth from him. "I didn't, no."

Alucard huffed—he was clearly trying to keep a despondent frown off his face. "I vant Tamsin."

He wouldn't deny his fiancé *that*, either. "Okay."

The vampire stormed out of the office, and Zalith followed, half-eager to see Alucard kill the bitch who sent children and other non-humans to their deaths and, half-cautious; he was worried that a nurse who clearly despised their kind might be armed, and he was also worried that Alucard might go a little too far. Whatever happened, though, he was there for him.

Alucard was on the hunt—he had that predatory look about him. He'd locked onto his target, and he was speeding up.

Zalith matched his pace, masking his presence just as his fiancé did.

The door up ahead—a bathroom. That was where the voices were coming from.

Alucard didn't hesitate. He burst through the door, the handle slamming into the wall with a sharp crack—bricks split, and a puff of dust scattered across the tiled floor. Before either woman could react, he seized the older one by the arm, catching her just as she finished drying her hands.

Zalith was already moving. In a flash, he closed the distance and grabbed the younger, dark-skinned girl as she turned from the mirror, rouge still clutched in her fingers.

Their hands clamped over mouths in perfect sync.

The girl in Zalith's grip froze, wide-eyed and trembling, tears already slipping down her cheeks. She was terrified—he could feel her pulse hammering against his palm. But the older woman in Alucard's hold didn't cry. She huffed through her nose, eyes narrow and scowling, her face set in a mask of sour defiance.

That was Tamsin.

Zalith kept his hand over the girl's mouth and placed his other on the side of her face—he quickly read her mind, finding anything he could use. "Forget this," he murmured. "We were never here. We didn't grab you. We didn't grab Tamsin. You spoke with her about patients while getting ready. You were doing your makeup, nothing more. Tamsin grew upset when she brought up the non-humans she saw and told Vexley to report. She hates him—you all know that. She stormed out in one of her usual fits, and the door slammed when it hit the wall. You were confused, but you had somewhere to be. A date, remember? You realized you were running late, left your makeup half-done, and walked straight to the bar." He planted the instruction to leave in her head, and then he concluded, "That is what happened."

"That's what happened," she said tonelessly.

"Go," the demon said, letting go of her.

She sluggishly packed her makeup away and left.

Tamsin's scowl had grown colder. She was still struggling in Alucard's grip.

Zalith saw the hunger in his fiancé's eyes—*that* hunger, the hunger for blood, for tearing and slashing, for the satisfaction of a kill. He was fine with it all…except the blood part. He still didn't want his vampire feeding on anyone else, and *that* was something he wasn't hesitant to express.

He pushed the door shut and moved to Alucard. "Wait," he said just as his fiancé was about to sink his fangs into the old woman's throat. "No feeding."

Alucard huffed, glancing down at the woman.

Zalith added, "Draining her is too easy—*too quick.*" His answer was more than just an attempt to remind Alucard of their boundaries. Tamsin deserved to suffer. She wasn't going to escape what she'd done.

His vampire seemed to agree. He pressed two fingers against the centre of the woman's forehead and muttered, "Sleep."

Tamsin's body went limp, and she crumpled to the floor as if she had no bones.

"We'll make sure everyone thinks that she's responsible for fucking up the test results, and that she caught smallpox and died," Zalith said.

Alucard grabbed the old woman's ankle and dragged her towards the door.

Zalith opened it, and once his fiancé left, he followed. Alucard had every right to make Tamsin suffer for what she'd done, and the demon couldn't deny it—he wanted to witness her torment.

Chapter Twenty-One

— ⸱ ✝ ⸱ —

Let Her Eat the Ruin

| Alucard |
| Atheson, Atheson Coven Sanctum |

Deep beneath the Sanctum, the Withercrypt lay still and silent like a buried corpse. Misery clung to every surface, thick as rot, seeping into the cold stone walls and iron bars like a sickness that couldn't be cleansed. The air was damp and bitter, tinged with the tang of old blood and something older—despair, perhaps, or the weight of time measured in screams.

A single hanging crystal provided the place with just enough light to allow any creature without the ability to see in the darkness to make out only distorted shapes. Cells lined the walls in both directions, their gates fashioned of blackened iron—Alucard wouldn't use anything that would harm his people, no matter the crime they'd committed. And if a condemned vampire *did* try to escape, the Wardens would stop them.

To most vampires, the Withercrypt was more than a prison—it was a purgatory of the soul, a place where one's past deeds were left to fester in the dark, where guilt and hunger gnawed louder than any guard's voice. Time did not pass the same down here. It dragged, cold and cruel, and every whisper of movement echoed like judgement.

Alucard wasn't there because of a vampire's crimes, though. He glanced at Warden Maelissa, who bowed humbly, standing guard near Eyra's cell. Dragging Tamsin behind him and with Zalith at his side, he descended to the lower Withercrypt, the place he'd store non-vampires until he was ready to deal with them.

He wasn't going to leave Tamsin waiting, though.

The vampire harshly yanked the woman into the nearest cell, and as she tumbled, she came around with a startled gasp.

Zalith closed the cell door, and Alucard clicked his fingers, waking up the crystal that hung in place of a lantern; very dim light oozed from it, and it hummed quietly.

Tamsin sluggishly but determinedly got up. She swung around to face Alucard and Zalith, and her confused expression thickened with disgust. "How dare you!" She charged forward, but Alucard pushed her away—her back hit the wall, though she managed to stay on her feet, and she spat venomously. "You filthy sinbloods!"

"Sinbloods?" Zalith asked as Tamsin's vulgar insults drowned out.

"Is derogatory—zhere's a vord…uh…" he replied, trying to remember how to say it in Deiganish, keeping his eyes fixed on the shouting woman.

"Slur?" the demon asked.

He nodded. "Slur."

"Well, that's a new one."

"Let me go this instant!" Tamsin then yelled, stomping her foot down.

There it was. Behind the rage and revolt, Alucard saw the fear breaking through the woman's façade. She'd quickly worked out that he and Zalith weren't at all afraid of her, and when she took her eyes off them and glanced around the dark, empty cell, that hint of fear swelled.

"What do you want from me?!" she demanded.

Alucard took a step forward—

Zalith gently grasped his jaw and made him turn his head to look at him. "No feeding," he reminded him, a smirk tugging at his lips, and then he kissed him.

Tamsin exclaimed loudly in disgust. "Ugh! Y-you *disgusting*, impure sodomites!" she screamed, hastily reaching into her pocket.

Alucard had no idea what that word meant, but the snarl that left Zalith assured him that it was yet another slur—he moved faster than the blink of an eye, grabbing Tamsin's wrist before she could take out whatever she'd reached for, and he slammed his other hand against her throat, pinning her against the wall.

"G-get off me, fil—"

"You 'ave a very spitevul mouth on you, zon't you?" he snarled, glaring into her eyes, watching as her anger battled with anxiety. "Per'aps zhat ought to be zhe virst ving I vip off."

A single panicked breath came before she spat, "Heathen! Infidel! *Heretic*! F—"

Alucard slapped the side of her face with a snarl.

The force made Tamsin's head turn. She didn't return her glare to him; she breathed deeply, an astonished expression on her face.

Zalith appeared at Alucard's side. He reached into Tamsin's coat pocket and took out what she'd attempted to. "How original," he muttered, showing Alucard the palm-length silver crucifix.

Tamsin sharply turned her head to glower at Zalith. "The day of Cleansing shall come like a thief in the night, and upon that day the unclean shall burn, their bones shattered beneath the heel of the Chosen," she recited, her voice heavy with contempt.

Alucard snarled and yanked her away from the wall as she began laughing to hide her fearful whimpers.

"The rivers shall run dark with their blood, and no prayer shall stay the hand of justice, for mercy is not given to vermin who walk in flesh!" she shouted and then winced when the vampire forced her down onto the iron chair.

"Vhere is your god now?" he mocked and tightly secured a restraint around one of her wrists.

Tamsin sobbed for a moment and tried to fight back when he grabbed and restrained her other wrist. "Let th-the horn be ssssounded and the flames be raised," she cried, her pathetic attempts to remain calm failing. "L-let the…the ash of the impure f-feed the soil of a-a new dawn!" she continued.

"Is this Letholdus' cult?" Zalith asked with an amused scoff, still holding the silver crucifix.

"How dare you speak his name, unclean f—"

Alucard's fist hit her face this time.

The woman shrieked as her head turned against her will—her body jolted, too, unable to move against the restraints.

"Yes," Alucard replied to his mate, stepping back to stand at his side.

Zalith turned the crucifix over and showed Alucard the verse inscribed on the back. "He shall know them by their taint," he read, "and He will cleanse them in flame without mercy."

"Fucking veligious vanatics," the vampire snarled.

"Tainted!" Tamsin cried out, writhing in the chair. "Tainted! Tainted! The Chosen shall wear no crown, yet their blades shall shine brighter than any sceptre, their cause, righteous in the eyes of the Flame!"

"May I?" Zalith asked politely.

Alucard gestured towards Tamsin and said, "By all means."

"The children of ruin—those born of fang, of claw, of flame and shadow—shall find no shelter, for the fire seeks all!" the woman bellowed as Zalith approached. "Even the stone shall speak—"

Zalith mercilessly stabbed the long end of the crucifix into Tamsin's thigh, and her words exploded into a horrified, agonized scream. "I suppose we could say that her god is kinda with her now," he said amusedly, rejoining Alucard.

He scoffed lightly—a half-chuckle, maybe. But his mind was locking in on the anger, on the desire to make her suffer far more than a crucifix to her leg. However, one thing *did* manage to seep through the rage. Zalith hadn't seen any children in the compound he'd liberated everyone from, and he wondered—no, he *hoped* that wasn't because they'd all been killed.

Usually, he'd ask his mate to look through Tamsin's mind, but she didn't deserve to get off so lightly. So he moved closer, grabbed a fistful of her hair, and made her look up at him. "Vhere do zhey send zhe children?" he growled.

She shook her head, tears streaming down her face. "E-even…even the stone shall speak…their guilt, and the wind—"

"Vhere do zhey send zhe children?!" he yelled, digging his claws into her scalp.

The woman wailed, attempting to pull her arms free. "A-and the wind shall carry their sins into the ears of the faithful!" she insisted.

Alucard snarled—

"Careful, darling," came Zalith's voice—he sounded firm, but there was a hint of amusement. "Don't ask her to think. If she attempts a thought that hasn't come from her silly little book, her skull might crack open from the pressure."

"H-how dare you mock—"

Alucard reached into his coat, pulled out one of his knives, and stabbed it into Tamsin's other leg as he demanded, "Tell me vhere zhose fucking Detainers take zhe children!"

She screamed again. "I-I…I—" The woman wailed and shook her head. "A-and when…when the work—"

The vampire pushed the blade deeper.

Tasmin cried even louder. But she didn't stop. "When the work is…is done, the world…shall breathe clean," she whimpered, her voice barely above a whisper. "Clean…" she exhaled, panting. "And…and the song—"

"Take zhe black jar vrom zhat cupboard," Alucard said, looking over his shoulder at Zalith.

"The song…" Tamsin still went on. "Song…of the *divine*…shall…echo…" she faltered, tilting her head back. "Echo…uncha…unchallenged…once more."

"Here," Zalith said as he handed him the jar. "What is it?"

"Someving zhat vill make 'er vish she'd never been brainvashed into anozzer vlesh puppet with a hymn stuck on vepeat," he snarled, unscrewing the lid.

"Get away from me, filth!" the woman snapped and took a sharp breath. "Nothing will make me speak! I'm doing *His* work, I'm—"

"Open 'er mouth," Alucard said.

Zalith gripped the woman's jaw in one hand and her face with the other. She fought, but the demon effortlessly forced her mouth open.

Alucard pulled the lid off the jar and poured its contents into her mouth—hundreds of tiny black spiders. The woman choked and gagged, and the spiders chirped like crickets as they flooded her body like venom.

"Ew," Zalith murmured.

"Veinburrow spiders," the vampire told him. "Zhey enter zhe bloodstream in smaller doses, but a colony zhis large vill eat 'er vrom zhe inside out in a vew hours."

Zalith grimaced slightly.

And the woman's tear-filled, bloodshot eyes widened as she gagged out a scream.

"'Owever," Alucard then said as he opened the small compartment hidden in the jar's lid. "Zhis…" he continued, taking out the vial of green liquid, "is Hemovex. If you answer my questions vithin zhe next vhirty minutes, zhis vill save your life. If not, ve vill leave you 'ere to veel every single vone of zhe 'undreds of tiny creatures devouring you—oh, and zhey also save zhe 'eart and brain vor last, so you're going to live vhrough pretty much all of zhis." He stepped back and stood beside Zalith, scowling down at her.

Tamsin wailed and cried, gurgled and choked, writhed and thrashed. She started praying again—"I am Yours," she called out, blood trickling from her ears as the spiders did their work. "C-cleanse me…o-or claim me! B-but…but do not *leave* me to *them*!"

"Do you know what I find disappointing about all of this?" Zalith asked casually.

"Vhat?"

"Letholdus is supposed to be the one true god of this world, yet he never shows his face to the people who dedicate their lives to him. He never comes to save people like her," he said, nodding at Tamsin as she screamed.

"He will…His…His fire…will drown…your poison," she choked. "H-He…will let me die *clean*."

"Will he, though?" the demon asked doubtfully. "Your body is full of little impure spiders, you're in the same room as two non-human same sex lovers, and you broke your oath as a healer. Even if Letholdus *did* give a shit about his loyalists, I don't think he'd come for you."

Alucard crossed his arms and impatiently tapped his fingers on his bicep. She wasn't going to be able to fight much longer. The spiders *always* broke their victim.

Tamsin kept wailing, her cries growing hoarse and desperate. "Let…not…their fangs…t-take…what is *Yours*," she grunted, her body convulsing, blood now oozing from her nose and eyes. "G-guard…guard me…in the trial," she pleaded.

Zalith looked at him again with that same curious but casual *but amused* smile. "Do the Numen actually say all of this shit to their followers, or do they just make it all up? And if one of them so happens to be a scribe, they write it down as if it's the word of their god?"

The vampire shrugged, thinking about it. "Vell…I can't speak vor zhe ozzer Numen, but I know zhat Luciver made promises vithout a proxy—"

"Heathens!" the woman screamed, gargling.

They both exhaled deeply, glaring at her.

"This world…this *place*!" she retched and choked. "Impure, filth—oh, great Flame, the things I've seen!" She shrieked. "The Devil…in the eyes of children! S-sapphist parents! D-disgusting…sodomites! H-heretics!" She shook her head, and then she leaned forward, sobbing.

Alucard frowned again and glanced at Zalith. "What is zhat vord she keeps saying?"

"Which one?"

"Sodomite."

"Oh…" his mate replied, sounding hesitant. "She's basically calling us sinners for having sex with each other. It comes from one of those charming little religious tales that people like her cling to—they think it's clever. It's not." He scowled and added, "To be honest, I've read cheap tavern menus more ingenious than that Lethidian bullshit."

Despite having once had a hand in the Lethidian Church to control the Deiganish King, Alucard had never fully read the Lethidian Book of Lore—after all, it was only written in Deiganish, and he hadn't been able to read it at the time. So he didn't know what 'charming tale' Zalith was talking about.

He glanced at the suffering woman, and then he asked Zalith with a frown, "Did you vead zhe Levidian Book of Lore?"

The demon shrugged. "I did a lot of research when I moved to Aegisguard."

Alucard looked at Tamsin again. She was still praying and preaching, so he shifted his sights back to the demon. "Vhat vas zhe tale?"

His mate exhaled through his nose. "The tale is of Sodara and Gomireth—one of the smaller religions in Eltaria had its own version, but it was of Selamir and Gholamir. Supposedly, they were a pair of cities so wicked that the gods wiped them out of existence with fire and brimstone." He shrugged a shoulder. "One version says it was because men slept with men. Another says it was because they were violent, prideful, and inhospitable." His eyes narrowed. "It doesn't matter, though. The pious like her use it as a catch-all excuse to hate anyone who doesn't fuck the way their priests tell them to." He glowered at Tamsin, watching her suffocate on blood and spiders. "It's less a story now and more of a threat—their favourite excuse to burn people alive."

The vampire's scowl returned, deeper this time. Just how many derogatory words were there? Why couldn't people just freely love who they wanted without fear of persecution?

"The story makes me think about Adellum's cult," the demon added, and his tone grew a little sadder. "While most really didn't give a shit about same-sex couples in Eltaria, *that* cult burned people alive for interspecies relationships—they had all sorts of disgusting terms for it, but mixed-blood union was their favourite. If you were a blood-tainter or unionborn, Adellum's cultists would come at you in full force."

"Seems like zhe people of zhis vorld are starting to believe zhe same ving."

"It does," he said with a sigh.

Alucard gently grasped and squeezed Zalith's hand in an attempt to comfort him, whether he needed it or not, and moved closer to Tamsin.

The woman was begging beneath struggled breaths, her body shivering and bloody, her veins bulging as the spiders infested her.

He held the vial of Hemovex a few inches from her face. "Zhe antidote is vight 'ere."

She opened her bloody eyes for a brief moment, and a hesitant but desperate frown flickered across her pale face. She panted heavily, sweating profusely.

"Tell me vhere zhe Detainers took zhe child non-'umans," he said firmly.

Tamsin managed a few more whimpers and groans before she breathlessly said, "Okay."

Alucard waited.

"There's…oh, great Flame…forgive me—"

"Tell me," he growled.

She grimaced and cried, but no sound left her. "Th…there's another compound."

"Where?" Zalith demanded.

The woman twitched and flinched, sobbing. "Down…down by the coast," she wheezed. "They…they've…" she groaned painfully.

Alucard's impatience was getting heavier; reading her mind would be so much simpler, but he *still* wouldn't make this easier for her. She'd earned herself every second of torment. So he grabbed a fistful of her hair and snarled in her face. "Zhey've vhat?"

She winced and wept, her breaths short and struggled. "Th-they came…to the city three months ago," she huffed, blood seeping through her teeth. "They…offered *ten* coronam per child—"

"So zhis isn't all about your god and stupid believs," Alucard scoffed.

Tamsin scowled, but the expression quickly buckled under agony. "They wanted the children."

"Why?" Zalith questioned.

"I-I…don't know," she replied, wearily trying to pull her hands from the restraints.

Alucard hissed. "Vhat are zhey doing to zhem?"

"I don't know," she repeated, gritting her teeth before wailing. "They had a quota!"

"Vhat kind of quota?" the vampire demanded.

"Who…whoever they work for," she spat. "F-fifty non-human kids."

Alucard glanced at his mate. Who would want fifty non-human children if not to kill them? Why the coast and not near civilization where they could easily meet whatever quota they had? He glowered at the woman…but now was probably the time to ask Zalith to step in. "Vill you vind out zhe vest?" he asked, backing away from Tamsin.

Zalith nodded but didn't move closer or touch the woman's face; her mind was as weak as it could be with the veinburrow spiders devouring her.

The vampire waited, crossing his arms again, keeping his hostile glare on Tamsin.

"She doesn't know who the Detainers work for, nor does she know why they want fifty children, but they *did* arrive with a quota three weeks ago," the demon confirmed. "They spread their message to doctors, nurses, and school and nursery staff."

As disgust filled Zalith's voice, the same anger crept into Alucard's glare.

"The compound is at a place called the Bleeding Shore…Mirewharf," Zalith continued. "They have a ship there. They plan to use it to transport the children once their quota is met."

"Vhere's zhe ship taking zhem?"

The demon paused…and then he answered, "Veilmar Coast."

"Zhat's Avalmoor," Alucard snarled.

"Land of the Flame," Tamsin whispered firmly.

"Is Levoldus involved?" the vampire asked Zalith.

His mate shook his head. "She doesn't know." He paused and cast a curious but concerned glance at him. "What's a Detainer?"

"Zhey are…specialist 'unters. Zhey zon't kill zheir target; zhey capture and detain zhem, usually to send off to compounds or deliver alive to whoever 'ired zhem…who zhen do vings I'd vather not vink about. Zhose kinds of people get off on torturing non-'umans, and Detainers love zhe money."

Zalith snarled in disgust, and as he set his eyes back on the woman, he asked Alucard, "If a Numen really wanted children, though, why would they send Detainers? They're just humans, right?"

He nodded and said, "Zhe Numen cower be'ind cults and gullible idiots. If isn't Levoldus, could be an Aegis…or could just be somevone using non-'uman children in useless medicinal practices—vouldn't be zhe virst time I've 'eard of such a ving."

Zalith nodded slowly, his piercing glare still locked on the woman. "The last time she collected her payment, it looked like the Detainers' quota was almost met."

Alucard huffed irritably. He didn't want to let the Detainers leave Atheson with those children, but with the Silver Claw hiding in the city, he couldn't risk leaving or sending a team down to the coast. Though…there *was* Zalith. His mate had saved everyone from that other compound earlier without so much as a scratch on him—but then again, *this* compound was guarded by Detainers, not lazy soldiers.

He sighed and dragged a hand over his face. "Ve can't let zhem leave vith zhose children," he said, looking at the demon. "But ve can't leave zhe city until ve've dealt vith zhis vampire 'unter."

Zalith hummed in agreement, looking as if he were thinking. "Well, nobody will be leaving or coming into the city after Vexley's story gets out, so that should halt any Detainer activity, right?"

"I 'ope so."

"As soon as we can spare the manpower, we'll save those children and kill the Detainers."

"I vant to send somevone out zhere to vatch zhe place," the vampire said, watching as the veinburrow spiders became visible through Tamsin's shin, making easy work of her muscle and bone. "I'm not going to let zhat ship leave zhe shore."

The demon nodded and said, "I can send one of my demons—Virelle; she's a chironex, so she can use the water as cover."

"Vank you."

"P-please," Tamsin then sobbed. "I-I told…told you all I know."

Alucard glanced at the antidote in his hand, and then he scoffed. He returned it to the compartment in the jar lid, and he placed the jar on the floor at her feet. The spiders would return to it once they'd finished their meal.

He took hold of Zalith's hand and headed for the door.

"W-wait!" the woman cried. "Y-you said—"

"I lied," the vampire snarled, leaving the cell with his mate, and then he closed the door behind them.

Just as her god had forsaken her, so too would this place offer no mercy.

Chapter Twenty-Two

— ⸱ ✝ ⸱ —

Midnight Quarantine

| **Alucard—***Saturday, Aprilis 1ˢᵗ, 960(TG)* |
| *Atheson, Atheson Coven Sanctum* |

It was just past Midnight when the governor announced the quarantine. The sheriff sent officers around the city, waking people, sending others home, ensuring that they all understood the reason, and they were terrified.

Alucard and Zalith observed from the top of the city Cathedral. Behind them, Alucard's demons were awaiting his signal; they knew where they were supposed to go and what they had to do…he just hoped that the Silver Claw didn't see through the smallpox façade.

Once the law enforcement began moving from door to door, all wearing beaked and gloved plague garb, Alucard glanced over his shoulder at his pack. They began putting on the same garb, and then they melted into the shadows, heading for the houses and inns they'd been instructed to search.

Alucard turned to ask Zalith if he was ready to go, but when he saw his mate already gazing at him, he hesitated. He knew that look in his eyes, and he wanted to give Zalith exactly what he was obviously thinking about…however, he had to wait—they both did. "Are you veady?" he asked him, trying to ignore the desire.

Zalith's gaze didn't falter, and he smirked for a moment before nodding. "Let's go."

They were after Algernon, the man Alucard had marked as the most suspicious. Cloaked in the cover of night, they slipped through the city's hushed streets, avoiding the flicker of gas lamps and the heavy boots of searching officers. Doctors in plague garb moved like phantoms, but Alucard and Zalith wove between them unnoticed, ghosting past shuttered windows and bolted doors.

Eventually, they reached Grevemire Row.

The street sloped slightly downhill, damp and glistening under the moonlight. Cobblestones shimmered faintly with frost, and the air smelled of soot, old rain, and scorched herbs—likely from what the doctors were burning to ward off contagion. Iron fences lined the crumbling terraces, and lanterns hummed softly above doorways. All was still, yet tension clung to the fog like a held breath.

The Vellistone House lay just ahead, hunched between two taller town homes like an afterthought squeezed into place. Its weather-blackened front bore the faded remnants of once-elegant paintwork, and the brass nameplate by the crooked door was dulled by years of fog and filth.

A narrow wood stair led to the entrance, its railing bent, the top step groaning beneath Alucard's heel. Thin lace curtains hung limp behind the first-floor windows, and the shutters on the upper floors were slightly ajar, swaying just enough to suggest someone—or something—had recently passed by.

The inn looked half-forgotten, the kind of place people checked into and rarely spoke of again. It was the perfect place to hide, to go unseen. Perfect for a hiding hunter.

Alucard stepped through the front door, Zalith close behind. The inn's interior was dim and musty, lit only by the weak glow of a single crystal lamp near the wall. Faint creaks echoed above, but the reception desk sat abandoned.

There was no sign of a keeper nor any sound of movement.

Without pause, the vampire slipped behind the counter and flipped open the guest record book. His eyes scanned the names and found Algernon's signature next to room number seven.

He returned the book and said to his mate, "Should be avound zhe back."

Zalith nodded and followed behind him as they moved down the cramped corridor, passing closed doors and faded portraits, the wood under their boots groaning faintly. The deeper they went, the colder the air became, and the flickering light behind them didn't reach far.

Room Seven waited at the far end of the hall, slouched beside a mummified potted plant. The air reeked of mould, and splintered wood thorned in every direction, like the building itself had been left to decay in silence; the floor felt soft and soggy under the threadbare rug, as if rot had already hollowed out the boards, waiting for the right moment to swallow them whole.

Alucard slowed, keeping his footsteps silent, and then he knocked on the door—even *that* felt soft.

Moments later, the rugged, broad-shouldered man answered, almost yanking it open. Algernon looked like someone who'd spent more nights on the road than in a bed; his torn, sleeveless shirt clung to a frame lined with quiet strength, exposing the faded tattoo on his left upper arm, and it was just as Alson had said. The black artwork was *good*, but this close up, it didn't hide the old bite mark beneath it.

"Aye?" Algernon asked with a Northern-Deiganish accent.

"We're here to ensure that you haven't brought smallpox into the city," Zalith said, standing beside Alucard. "If you'd kindly allow my colleague to make sure you don't have any symptoms, I'll head in and search your room and belongings."

At first, the man looked hostile, but he didn't fight or argue. "Aye, whatever."

Zalith eased between them and went into the room.

Alucard looked Algernon up and down. "Vhere vere you travelling vrom?"

There was that expression—the one people made when they didn't understand what he'd just said to them.

The vampire deadpanned and irritably rephrased, slowing his words, "Vhere vere you bevore you got to Aveson?"

"Ah've been travellin' from DieganLupus, tryin' tae get tae Noridge."

"Vhat's in Noridge?"

"Family."

Alucard glanced at the bite on his arm. "Are you vleeing a pack?"

That was when Algernon tensed up as if he were getting ready to run.

"Answer zhe question—and zon't try to vun. I'll catch you bevore your next breath."

Algernon glanced into the room at Zalith, who was searching his luggage, and then he frowned at Alucard. "Aye," he answered.

"Vhat 'appened?"

He exhaled deeply. "Pack politics, man. Ye've nae idea how hard it is tryin' tae fit in when ye weren't born wi' their blood."

"As a matter of vact, I do."

Algernon frowned.

Alucard then glanced at Zalith.

The demon shook his head and walked towards him.

"'Ave you seen anyvone or anyving suspicious since your arrival?" the vampire asked. "More specivically, ozzer lone volves."

Algernon stepped aside, letting Zalith out of the room. He then crossed his arms, looking conflicted. "Why?"

"Answer the question," Zalith said.

He huffed. "There's a lot o' dodgy folk roamin' this part o' the city. It's where all the non-humans gather. Easier tae blend in somewhere folk dinnae wanna go—'cause it reeks and looks like pure shite."

Alucard asked, "Any verevolves? People vith silver on zheir nails?"

"No' that Ah've seen."

"So you 'aven't seen zhe guy valking avound with anozzer dead verevolf on 'is back?" he asked skeptically.

Algernon tensed up, uncrossing his arms. "Whit did ye jus' say?"

"Pascal," the vampire said.

The man looked horrified. "He's here?" he asked, sounding anxious. "Shite, Ah need tae go, mate. Ah'm cleared, right? Ah've no' got smallpox."

"Who is 'e?" Alucard asked.

"Ah've really got tae—"

"Tell us who he is," Zalith demanded calmly.

Algernon exhaled deeply, nervously scratching the hidden bite on his arm. "The guy that did this tae me—he's been obsessed since the day Ah met him eight years back. Ah didnae think he'd care if Ah left that pack; he was always threatenin' tae boot me out, but he's been followin' me for months."

Alucard's frown thickened with suspicion... but it didn't line up with what he already knew about the Silver Claw. The vampire hunter hadn't come from DeiganLupus— unless he had and was making his way through Rhenovaalis in search of Algernon and was taking out vampires along the way. "You know 'im vell, zhen?"

"Aye," he mumbled.

"Does 'e kill vampires?"

"Ah cannae say Ah know. He didnae leave the pack much—but then again, Ah barely ever left the cavern he made me stay in."

Alucard glanced at Zalith. "Ve should go and see Pascal."

The demon nodded in agreement.

"Please dinnae tell him Ah'm here. Ah need tae go before he tracks me doon."

"Do you actually have family in Noridge, or is that your cover story for the doctors and law enforcement currently searching the city?" Zalith asked tonelessly.

Algernon dragged his hand over the back of his head; it looked like he was considering whether or not he should lie. But he shook his head and said, "Ah've got nae family out there—nae family anywhere. Ah'm just tryin' tae start somewhere new. Ah'm sure the two o' ye know what it's like bein' around humans."

Alucard and Zalith glanced at one another—he was sure his mate was thinking the same thing, and the demon's nod told him that Algernon was telling the truth. But they couldn't waste another moment.

"Please, mate," Algernon pleaded. "Ah've got money—Ah'll pay ye, just gie me an hour's head start."

"Are you avoiding pack life, or are you just avoiding Pascal's pack?" Zalith asked.

Algernon pretty much squirmed around as if he were desperate for a piss. "Are ye the werewolf polis or somethin'? Come on, Ah need tae go."

"Just answer the question—we're on a clock just as much as you are," the demon snapped irritably.

"Just Pascal's pack, awright? Can Ah go noo?"

Alucard said, "Zhere's an estate just outside zhe city—you can see vrom zhe top vloor of zhis place. If you vant zhat new start vith zhe savety of a new pack, go to zhe estate and tell zhem zhat Aleksei sent you."

The man frowned. "Whit?"

Zalith said, "Estate on the hill, huge werewolf pack always welcoming new members—"

"Bitten or born," Alucard added.

"—You'll be safe from Pascal. You just need to be ready and willing to fight for the pack and its allies' cause," the demon continued.

Algernon looked as if he was struggling to process what he'd heard.

"Now, if you don't mind, we have somewhere else to be," Zalith finalized.

"Ve're going to see Pascal now," Alucard told the werewolf. "I'd suggest you make your move—vhether to zhe estate or an unguarded exit—vhile Pascal is distracted."

The man managed a stiff nod.

Zalith then brushed Alucard's hand with his fingertips as they turned around. The demon led the way through the inn. "He sounded a lot like our coachman," he said with a small laugh.

"Maybe Clint and Algernon are vrom zhe same part of DeiganLupus," he suggested.

"Maybe," he said with a nod, and once they stepped outside, he asked, "Where is Pascal staying?"

Alucard took the folded list out of his inside pocket. "Miller's End, a bed and breakfast called Zhe Sleepy Badger." He looked left and then right; he hadn't mapped *every* street in this city, but he knew where Miller's Close was, so Miller's End couldn't be far from it. "Zhis vay," he said, taking hold of Zalith's hand.

The vampire and demon walked in silence to the end of Grevemire Row, passing a few garb-wearing officials searching homes and inspecting people. Alucard wasn't ashamed to admit that seeing the humans of this city so terrified brought him a moment of fleeting pleasure, especially after learning about the Detainers taking non-human children.

When they turned left, they emerged into the small fish market. The place lay dormant, its canvas stalls sagging like wilted flowers, the scent of brine and blood still clinging to the cobbles. Empty crates were stacked against crumbling walls, and a few gulls loitered in the rafters, silent for once beneath the shroud of night.

Both Alucard and Zalith grimaced as they crossed a narrow stone bridge, its slick surface wet with grime and mud. Below, the stream that wound through this part of the city had long since turned to sludge—black, oily water dragging itself under the platform as if it resented being looked at.

On the other side, Miller's Close waited, a hollow courtyard of crooked houses, some patched together with scrap wood and cloth. Clotheslines drooped between cracked chimneys, and lamplight flickered behind thin curtains, but most windows remained dark, shuttered against the world.

Alucard's jaw tensed. This was the only place in the city where non-humans could live without being hunted, and still, it reeked of neglect and the city's hatred. The safety it offered was a cage, not a sanctuary, and it made his blood boil. He wanted to help them, but this wasn't Uzlia; he and Zalith couldn't just funnel money into the city hall and tell the governor to fix places like this. He hoped, however, that once his coven had control of this city—or at least the fear of its human population—the non-humans would have more protection and fairer treatment. *That* would be his goal for this place once everything else was dealt with.

"What's on your mind?" Zalith suddenly asked.

He glanced at his mate as they walked through the courtyard. "Zhis place," he said with a sigh. "Sometimes…I vink about vhat vings might be like if Year Zero never 'appened. Living as someving only spoken about in volklore sounds much safer zhan vhat vings are like now."

"I don't know if it would be safer," the demon said with a small chuckle. "People are superstitious even when we *are* around."

"I suppose so," he said, leaving the courtyard and emerging onto another filthy street. "But at least people vere avraid zhat zheir neighbour might be a verevolf bevore. Now, veels like people 'ope zhat zheir suspicions are vight so zhat zhey can skin zheir neighbour alive in vront of zhe whole city, take all of zheir land and property, and label zhemselves a 'ero vor killing zhe single mother zemon who did noving but vant to vind a safe place vor 'er children." He huffed and looked at Zalith. "Sorry, I zon't mean to sour zhe mood. Places like zhese…zhey make me angry."

Zalith squeezed his hand. "I understand. I've seen my fair share of violence."

Alucard exhaled deeply and set his eyes on the street sign. *This* was Miller's End. He stopped walking and looked up and down the road. There weren't any beak-masked men around, and he hoped that was because they hadn't yet reached this part of the city; if they had, there was a chance that Pascal had already left.

"Is that the place?" Zalith asked, nodding to the right.

The vampire set his eyes on a small café-like building; the paint on its crooked sign had long since peeled, but the name The Sleepy Badger could still be made out beneath layers of muck. A few cloudy lanterns flickered weakly outside the front door, and the windows were fogged with condensation, hinting at a meagre warmth within. Cracks ran through the stonework, the door hung slightly askew on rusted hinges, and the scent of stale tea and smoke oozed through the frame.

"Zhat's zhe place," he confirmed and started leading the way over there.

Zalith pushed the door open, the hinges creaking sharply in the stillness, and Alucard followed him in. The air was thick with cheap tobacco, sour tea leaves, and the lingering tang of dried fish; the café space to the right sat abandoned with half-drunk mugs and cold plates of stew littering the few tables, chairs pushed back in haste. It was evident that the patrons had cleared out fast after the quarantine announcement.

The reception desk stood empty beneath a wall-mounted clock that had stopped ticking. Alucard stepped behind the counter, flipping open the leather-bound guest record resting there.

"Voom Vhree," he said, putting the book down.

He took Zalith's hand and led the way up the stairs. The boards creaked as they reached the second floor, and the hallway was shrouded in complete darkness; the wallpaper peeled in long curls that fluttered with every draft, and the air was thick—a pungent mix of sweat, damp wood, and wet fur. There were obviously other werewolves here; their scent clung to the hall like glue.

They passed a few shut doors, each one marked with a number scrawled onto tarnished metal plates, and once they reached Room Three, Alucard knocked.

Faint movement stirred on the other side... the floorboards creaked, something heavy was shifted, and then the door opened.

"What?" the man grumbled through his thick beard, but then he scowled. "You ain't doctors—you ain't even human. What the fuck do you want?"

Alucard exhaled deeply. "I'll check zhe voom, you check 'is mind," he said to Zalith and shoved past Pascal.

"You can't just—"

Zalith grabbed Pascal's collar and pinned him against the wall before he could finish.

While the demon read the man's thoughts, Alucard began searching the room. There wasn't much luggage at all—just a single suitcase, and inside were clothes, money, and an old fiction novel. Pascal had clearly moved something before he opened the door, though, and Alucard's eyes landed on the wardrobe. Scrapes marred the wooden flooring around it, suggesting that it had been moved, so he went over to it and pulled it away from the wall.

He didn't find what he'd been hoping to, though. There were no silver claws or gauntlets, just a stash of jewels and money. The vampire rolled his eyes and returned to the door—he didn't care where Pascal's treasures had come from; he just wanted to find the vampire hunter.

"Nothing," Zalith said when the vampire joined him in the hallway. "Though he did rob a carriage a few days ago."

"I know. I vound 'is stash."

"It was a human's carriage."

"Good," Alucard muttered. "Did 'e 'ide or burn zhe ving?"

"Burned," the demon said.

"At least no vone vill immediately point zheir vingers at non-'umans," he muttered.

Zalith shoved Pascal back into the room and pulled the door shut before the man could say anything. "Where to now?"

He took out the list as they walked downstairs. "Vell, zhese vere zhe only two I vanted to question myselv. My zemons are dealing vith zhe vest. If zhey zon't vind zhe Silver Claw or at least bring in suspects, I'm going to 'ave to viden zhe search."

"Widen it how?"

"Maybe zhis guy set up outside Aveson somevhere—var avay enough zhat even my patrols von't detect 'im. But my people 'ave alveady set up a very vide patrol area, so I'm almost certain zhat zhis 'unter is in zhe city somevhere." He put the paper away. "If 'e some'ow managed to slip in unseen, my people vill 'ave to start searching tunnels and sewers and shit," he grumbled. "Or maybe 'e's somevhere protected. Zhe 'umans 'ired 'im, avter all. Per'aps I should get somevone to search zhe government buildings."

"Who's your most human-looking demon?" Zalith asked, laughing softly.

"Hmm... probably Vhett."

"Vhett?"

Alucard frowned. "Vh... Vhett," he said again, but he was sure that Zalith was teasing him.

"Oh, Rhett?"

He pouted. "Yes."

Zalith moved his arm around his waist and pulled him closer. "So, should we go back to the Sanctum and wait for your demons to report?"

Alucard nodded. "Lenore should be veady vor me to Vestore by now, so I can do zhat vhile ve vait."

"Restore?"

"Like I did vith Velix, but she isn't ashes, so is a little more complicated."

The demon looked surprised. "I thought Restoring someone from ashes would be the more complicated option."

"Zhe Bloodmenders 'ave to vepair 'er vounds bevore she can be Vestored, or she'd just die again," he said with a shrug.

"I suppose that makes sense," his mate said.

Alucard stopped walking and took hold of Zalith's hand. "Are you veady?"

He nodded.

The vampire dematerialized them into vermillion smoke and raced towards the Sanctum. He could only hope that his demons would uncover something useful—anything that might give this chaos a shape. But more than that, he hoped Lenore had answers waiting for him.

Chapter Twenty-Three

— ⸨ † ⸩ —

Savouring Time

| **Zalith** |

| *Atheson, Atheson Coven Sanctum* |

Captivating, irresistible, *devouring*.

That was Alucard's scent.

In the room Alucard had called his Rest Space, Zalith lay with him on the couch, arms wrapped tightly around the vampire's body, his face buried against the curve of his neck. Every breath inhaled that maddening fragrance—dark, sweet, aching with heat. His desire boiled hot, nearly suffocating, and he wasn't sure what he craved more: another lungful of that intoxicating scent…or to be buried deep inside him.

His body, caught between reverence and hunger, didn't know which would ruin him faster. Should he give in…or should he hold on? Should he let his hands wander the vampire's body, should he make sure Alucard knew what he wanted? Or should he just lie there, ready to give himself to his fiancé should he ask?

The demon inhaled again, and a quiet, longing hum escaped him. He was getting hard just thinking about sliding his dick inside Alucard, about hearing him moan, feeling him fidget and tighten. It was all he wanted right now, and it was becoming more and more of a struggle with each passing moment.

How long would it be until they had to head down to the Vitalum so that Alucard could Restore Lenore? He didn't want to waste whatever time they had until then. He should make the most of this, shouldn't he?

"Do you vant someving to eat?" Alucard suddenly asked.

Zalith frowned and asked, "Why?"

"Zon't you need to eat? 'As been a vhile since you 'ad anyving."

"Oh…" he said with a frown, turning his head a little to glance at the vampire's face. Now that he thought about it, he couldn't actually remember when he'd last eaten. Was it at the Eimwood City Celebration? Or later than that? He couldn't attempt to recall when, either; all he could think about was how much he wanted to fuck Alucard.

"Should ve send an izuret to get someving vrom somevhere?"

He pressed his face back against Alucard's neck and closed his eyes. "I'll take whatever you're offering," he replied and then inhaled his scent quietly, letting himself become lost in it again.

"Maybe ve can get someving vrom Lupa," Alucard suggested.

It took him a moment to comprehend what his fiancé just said…and then he replied, "Sure."

"Vhat do you vant?"

His smile grew as he exhaled and hummed. "Anything," he replied—but then he quickly said, "You."

Alucard rested his head on his. "Not yet," he said amusedly. "Vhat about pasta?"

He hummed in agreement…but his hand was slowly trailing down the vampire's body—he couldn't help it, he couldn't even begin to fight it. His body needed it, and he was desperate to oblige.

"Ve could get tortellini or someving," the vampire said.

Zalith *tried* to agree, but it wasn't a 'yes' or a 'sure' that left him…it was, "I just *really* need to fuck you."

Alucard didn't immediately reply; he fiddled with the demon's hair—maybe he was thinking. A few moments later, though, just as Zalith's hand traced over the vampire's abs, he grasped the demon's wrist. But he didn't push him away or tell him to stop. He guided Zalith's hand down to his crotch.

A sharp thrill surged through Zalith as he gripped the bulge between Alucard's legs, fingers closing eagerly around it. The vampire tensed beneath his touch, and Zalith moved without hesitation, sliding into his lap with a hungry grin. He kissed him hard, letting their mouths tangle as his hands slipped down to unfasten Alucard's trousers.

When he eased his hand inside and wrapped his fingers around his fiancé's thickening length, a pleased hum escaped the vampire. Feeling Alucard harden in his grasp only worsened the aching pressure in Zalith's gut. He didn't want to restrain it. He couldn't.

With a growl of anticipation, he pulled Alucard up from the couch and guided him across the room. Their bodies stayed close, breath hot and shallow, until they reached the desk. Alucard turned without needing to be told, bracing his hands on the wood and arching slightly—obedient, wanting, *perfect.*

Zalith shoved the vampire's trousers down and then hastily unbuckled his own belt, his heart pounding against his ribs like it wanted out. Every breath carried that maddening scent—that ethereal, heat-laced pull that made his head swim. He reached into his vault, retrieved the lube, and squeezed some onto his fingers, not bothering to be neat about it. The bottle clattered aside as he stepped closer, one hand spreading Alucard while the fingers of his other pressed inside.

The vampire moaned, soft and trembling, and Zalith hummed low in his throat like a predator who'd just tasted something sweet. He leaned down, lips brushing the back of Alucard's neck.

He couldn't wait a moment longer.

The demon lined himself up and eased forward, holding his breath as the heat of Alucard's body welcomed him in, and then he groaned contently. Tight muscles resisted at first, clenching instinctively around him, and Zalith could feel every stretch, every slow surrender around the thick length of him. It was *addictive*.

Every inch deeper made his restraint fray. His claws dug gently into Alucard's hips as the vampire's body adjusted, stretching beautifully to take him. The resistance, the give, the way Alucard fit around him like he was meant to—it wrung a groan from deep in Zalith's chest, and every taut line of tension along his spine melted into pure, pulsing need, making him grip harder, reverent and possessive all at once.

The vampire shuddered, his fingers tightening on the desk as a moan escaped him, eager and utterly obedient. It lit something feral inside Zalith. He began to thrust—slow at first, drawing himself out only to push back in with a pleasing force. Alucard's body accepted him, and the sound of his soft, broken whines only pushed Zalith further into instinct. He thrusted harder, *faster*. The desk creaked beneath them, but he didn't care. The room felt like it was shrinking around them, heat clinging to the air, tension winding tighter with every breath.

Zalith pressed his chest to Alucard's back, his mouth grazing the nape of his neck as he used one hand to spread the vampire's legs a little wider.

Alucard whimpered in response, his body yielding to every push, every demanding thrust. Zalith's grip tightened again, his mind nearly gone to primal instinct—but somewhere in the haze, he still felt it: the connection, the bond, the unrelenting desire not just to take, but to give his mate everything.

That was when he felt it—that sudden and familiar bone-deep compulsion to give Alucard's body something it couldn't take. It struck him hard and fast, like a surge of hunger knotted low within him. A need not just to rut, not just to satisfy—but to fill. To breed. To give his mate something permanent, something that would stay long after this moment burned out.

It wasn't possible. He knew that.

Alucard couldn't bear the weight of what Zalith's body was begging to give him, but the knowledge didn't matter right now. The heat, the scent, the way Alucard gripped him, stretching around him with every thrust—it fed that drive until it drowned out everything else.

His thoughts frayed, unravelled into demand, desire, and desperation.

All he could feel was the wet slide of pheromone-damp skin, the shudder of Alucard's body under his hands, and the perfect, maddening pull of his fiancé's warmth around him. Zalith's rhythm faltered for half a second before it returned with aggression, the sound of flesh and breath filling the space between groans and sharp, hungry moans—

Someone knocked on the door.

A desperate but aggravated cry escaped Alucard as Zalith stopped, his own frustrated snarl breaking his pleasured hums.

"My Lord, I—" the man who entered the room stopped, frozen, eyes wide. "Uh…I'm sorry, I—"

Despite tensing, Alucard didn't push Zalith away. "Vhat?!" he snapped.

Zalith's protective, possessive instincts intensified. He leaned forward, resting an arm beside Alucard, covering most of his face—*hiding* him from prying eyes.

"I-I just came to tell you that Algernon is with the rest of the wolves, and—"

The demon snarled again and resumed thrusting.

Alucard dug his claws into the desk and whined pleasurably, and then he snarled as he lowered his head. "Get out!" he exclaimed.

The man left swiftly, closing the door behind him.

Zalith growled low in his throat, the sound dark and guttural, vibrating against Alucard's back. He dragged a hand down the vampire's side, fingers trailing over damp skin until he reached his thigh. With a firm grip, he lifted and pressed his mate's foot against his own, forcing Alucard to spread wider, just enough to open him up even more.

The shift was perfect. *Devastating.*

He drove forward, plunging the full length of his dick inside in one powerful thrust.

Alucard cried out a ragged, desperate sound that tore from his throat like a plea. His arm flung back instinctively as he collapsed onto the desk, fingers clutching Zalith's wrist in a tight, trembling grip as his body tensed beneath him, his forehead hitting his other arm. Every muscle quivered with pressure and aspiration, his name a broken gasp from his lips, "Zaliv—!"

The demon groaned at the way Alucard's walls clamped down, fluttering in that telltale way just before climax. He could feel his mate unravelling around him, burning and pulsing, each tight squeeze dragging him closer to the edge.

Zalith didn't hold back.

He slammed into him harder, more desperate now, hips snapping with as much precision as he could manage, his breath coming in ragged gasps against Alucard's nape. The sound of their bodies filled the space around them, a rhythm of longing and surrender, wet and breathless.

And then Alucard's whole body stiffened, a strangled cry escaping him as he clenched hard around Zalith's dick, the rush of his climax painting the desk beneath them.

Zalith moaned loudly, the sudden tightness threatening to undo him right there. His rhythm faltered for a beat, every instinct screaming at him to give in. The pleasure surged through him like fire, and he hissed between his teeth as he fought to hold himself back— just a little longer, just a little *deeper*.

He growled once more and seized the vampire's hips with both hands, holding him still as he drove himself as deep as Alucard's body would allow, the stretch and heat drawing a sharp gasp from both of them. He came *hard*; rapture surged through him, and he held Alucard tightly, overwhelmed by the sensation of warmth spreading deep into his mate. Alucard's body constricted around him in soft, rhythmic pulses, drawing every drop of cum from him. Zalith could feel the way Alucard responded, the way his body welcomed him, held him, almost as if it didn't want to let him go.

Even as the last tremors of his orgasm faded, Zalith stayed buried deep, his grip tightening even more at Alucard's hips. His body knew what it wanted—what it *needed*—despite the futility of it. No pregnancy would come from this, no life would take root in the warmth he'd just filled, but that didn't stop the primal part of him from aching for it, from wanting to keep every drop inside until it *took*.

But then Alucard let go of his wrist—

Zalith snarled instinctively, pressing one hand down on Alucard's back, making sure that he stayed where he was. "Don't move," he murmured. "Let me stay inside you. Let it spread deeper… even if your body doesn't know what to do with it, *mine* does."

Alucard let out a soft, obedient whine—eager, breathless, and utterly content. His body melted under Zalith's hold, yielding without resistance, as if offering himself all over again. He didn't speak, he didn't need to; the way he relaxed into him said everything.

"There you go," the demon purred possessively, stroking his fingertips down Alucard's back. "My good little vampire—you always know who you belong to."

The vampire responded with another hushed moan, gripping the edge of the desk, his eyes shut but a delighted gleam to his face.

Zalith stayed buried for a moment longer, savouring the warmth wrapped tight around him. Then, slowly, he began to ease out, dragging each inch from Alucard's body with a low, satisfied breath. But when he caught sight of the soft trickle of white slipping free, something primal surged again. He thrust forward once more, slower this time, deep enough to push the cum back inside.

Alucard whined once more, weaker this time, *exhausted*—but still obedient.

"Not yet," the demon said, his voice low, almost a growl as he leaned in close. "Keep it in, vampire. Let it settle." And then his hand slid down to Alucard's thigh, guiding it inward. "Close your legs for me." Only once the vampire obeyed did he slowly ease out, watching with dark satisfaction as his cum stayed where it belonged.

He then curled his fingers around Alucard's shoulder and gave a gentle tug, coaxing him upright.

His fiancé complied without resistance, rising to stand and leaning back against Zalith's chest, his body pliant, still trembling in the aftermath.

The demon wrapped an arm around him and nuzzled into the curve of his neck, breathing in the heady, addictive scent that only Alucard carried. "You feel so different," he whispered, letting the fulfilment devour him.

Alucard hummed before a deep exhale, his weight softening against the demon's hold, his tension unravelling as he melted into him, claimed, calmed, and safe. "Divverent…'ow?" he murmured, breathless.

Zalith dragged his tongue along Alucard's neck, groaning softly as the intoxicating taste of his pheromones hit his tongue like honeyed fire. "Better," he answered. He pressed a slow kiss beneath Alucard's jaw, and then he whispered with a husky, reverent edge, "Better than any man I've ever touched." Because it was true. Whatever Alucard was—whatever strange, beautiful thing lived in his blood and heat—it stirred something new in Zalith. Something feral. He'd never felt instincts so strong, so maddeningly specific. And he never wanted them to stop.

Alucard tilted his head to the side, giving Zalith more space to kiss and taste. "Zhat velt so fucking good," he breathed, reaching his hand back and stroking Zalith's thigh. "*Still*…veels so good."

The demon smiled, his lips tracing Alucard's neck. "Can you feel my cum inside you?" he asked with a prideful smirk—and he didn't have to look at the vampire's face to know that it had gone red. "What does it feel like?" he whispered as he brushed his fingers down his fiancé's thigh, still holding him close, still keeping him exactly where he wanted him.

"Veels…I zon't know," he said shyly.

Zalith nuzzled the side of his face again. "You can tell me," he urged softly.

Alucard fidgeted, and Zalith could feel how sensitive he still was.

His mate frowned slightly, as if he were trying to figure out how to put the sensation into words. "Is…varm, and…'eavy." He paused. "Is like…I can still…*veel* moving inside me…like is trying to go deeper." He exhaled slowly, fidgeting again. "My body zoesn't vant to let go."

Zalith's gaze darkened, watching his mate's flushed face with hunger. "And?" he asked, his smirk growing.

A pleased hum carried upon Alucard's sigh. "I veel vull," he murmured. "Is like…I'm meant to 'old all in until—" He cut himself off, but the heat in his eyes said the rest.

The demon grinned and pressed a kiss behind his ear. "Good," he growled. "I'll keep filling you, vampire." He *loved* that Alucard's heat cycle took away some of his shyness, that it let him say things he'd usually be too nervous to say aloud.

Alucard smiled with a huff—he was clearly still exhausted.

Zalith slowly turned his fiancé to face him. For a moment, he gazed at him, taking in his beautiful face, his captivating eyes, and his tempting lips, and then he kissed him softly before pressing their foreheads together. "If we weren't waiting on your vampires, I'd fuck you again right now—my dick wants it," he said, pressing his crotch against Alucard's, letting him feel his arousal.

The vampire smiled, too—and that adorable shyness gleamed across his face for a moment; it looked like he wanted to give in, but he said, "Ve'll 'ave plenty of time vonce all of zhis is over."

Zalith knew that Alucard needed to rest, so he did his best to calm down. He kissed him again before helping him pull up his trousers, and then he put his own back on. He guided his fiancé to the couch, letting him relax while he cleaned the table, and when he lay down on the couch with him, he moved as close as he could get and nuzzled the vampire's neck.

For a while, they lazed in silence. The occasional sound came from outside or above the room; Alucard's people were all hard at work, and although he *did* want an end to come to this Silver Claw business, the part of him that wanted to keep claiming Alucard's undivided attention was stronger.

He needed to resist, though—just for a little while. He could appreciate the satisfaction he'd got just now. *And* he could focus on more than just the consuming need for sex. Alucard had offered to have an izuret bring him food, and it reminded him that his vampire needed to eat, too—to *feed*.

Zalith fiddled with Alucard's shirt buttons and asked, "Do you want blood?"

Alucard stroked his fingers down the demon's arm. "Zhat sounds veally good."

The demon was about to sit up…but he didn't want to tear himself away from the intoxicating scent. He instead offered his wrist to Alucard and asked, "Is this okay?" If it wasn't, he'd give him his neck, of course.

"Yes," the vampire said, gently grasping his wrist, and then he bit down.

Zalith groaned pleasurably as Alucard's venom hit his bloodstream and surged through his body. He eagerly pressed his face against his neck, another pleased sigh escaping him. "I want all of you," he murmured, letting the scent and sensation devour him entirely.

Alucard hummed in delight, and once he pulled his fangs from Zalith's wrist, he slowly dragged his tongue over the wounds.

The demon caressed his fiancé's cheek with his thumb. But just as he opened his mouth to ask him if he wanted more, someone knocked on the door again. He snarled irritably in response; when Alucard told whoever it was to come in, the demon protectively tightened his embrace around his mate.

"My Lord—" It was a woman this time. "—The Bloodmenders are ready for you."

"All vight. Tell zhem I'll be down in a vew minutes," Alucard replied.

With a nod, she left the room.

Zalith didn't loosen his grip. "I need a minute," he said.

"Zhat's okay."

He inhaled Alucard's scent, kissed his neck, and savoured what might be the last moment he got to enjoy him like this for a while—unguarded, breathless, and utterly his. Every inch of the vampire's body pressed to his, steeped in the mingled scents of sex and something only Zalith could smell: bond and belonging.

The demon dragged his lips across Alucard's skin, tasting the sweetness of pheromones. He didn't want to let go, he didn't want to move. Not when he had this, his mate trembling in his arms, filled with his cum, trusting him without a word… because out there, beyond this moment, the world was still cruel and cold. But here… *here*, Zalith had everything he wanted.

And he'd keep hold of it a little longer.

Chapter Twenty-Four

—⟨ † ⟩—

Restore

| **Alucard** |
| *Atheson, Atheson Coven Sanctum* |

Lenore was just over a century old. It wouldn't take much to Restore her, Alucard just hoped that there wasn't any more silver in her body—if there was, though, the Bloodmenders would have found it.

"Everything is ready, My Lord," Benedric said with a bow.

Alucard nodded and watched him head over to the supply closet to help Thessaly tidy up the equipment.

"Do you have to give her blood?" Zalith asked—he sounded curious… but there was a possessive tint to his voice.

"Sort of," he replied as he moved closer to the platform that the Knight lay upon. He placed his hand on her chest and focused, reaching into her with his ethos. As his ethos ensnared her dead heart, he clenched his other fist, using his claws to cut his skin. Then, he held his fist above her mouth, letting his blood drip into it, and muttered, *"Expergiscere."*

Lenore's body responded with the faintest aura, a reply to his power, an acceptance of his command. All that was left to do was wait.

Alucard took his hand off the Knight and let the wounds on his other palm heal.

"What's that language you keep speaking?" Zalith asked curiously. "I still hear you speaking it in your sleep sometimes," he added with a small chuckle.

He turned to face his mate, but he didn't have an answer—well… not right away. As he frowned, he said, "I vink…Zamien called True Speech." His frown thickened. "'E spoke zhe same language when 'e vound me avter I killed Ada." The memory was a blur, the same kind of distorted mess that festered in place of his stolen, buried memories. "I guess 'e zidn't vant me knowing zhat," he said with a shrug, refusing the biting grasp of dismay that came when he thought about Damien.

Zalith pulled him closer and hugged him. "You don't have to think about him."

Alucard rested his head on his mate's shoulder. "Vhat do I say in my sleep?"

He laughed and said, "I honestly couldn't repeat any of it."

The vampire laughed softly, too.

"Why is it called True Speech?" the demon then asked.

He had to search the storm of obscured memories again. It was more of a struggle this time, though—he was scouring for more than a word or two, after all.

"It's okay if you can't remember," Zalith assured him.

"I *vant* to," he replied determinedly. "Is zhe only vay I'm going to get zhese memories back, vight?"

The demon's embrace tightened. "Don't push yourself, though."

He exhaled deeply and nuzzled his mate's neck, still sifting through the haze. Words, incantations, spells, wards…and there—*that* was what it was. "Is an ancient language," he started, focusing on a memory over four centuries old, a memory from when he was a child. "Liliv called zhe Language of zhe Gods—is zhe only language somebody can use to speak to zhem or summon zhem, vhich is probably vhy nobody knows 'ow to speak or vecognize." He paused again. "A lot of zhe vitches in zhe Diabolus spoke True Speech," he recalled. "I just…knew, zhough—vas like an instinct."

Zalith fiddled with his hair. "Well, you have Numen blood, so it would make sense that you were born knowing it, right?" he suggested.

That *did* make sense. "Probably," he agreed.

The demon trailed his fingers down Alucard's back. "Actually, there *is* something you say quite a lot."

Alucard frowned again. "Vhat?"

Zalith hummed as if he were thinking. "It's like…non…nonesol—no, nonesolus."

He didn't know what that meant. If it were True Speech, he'd understand, wouldn't he? Unless Zalith was pronouncing it wrong.

"Do you want me to show you?" his mate suggested.

His curiosity made him nod, and he leaned out of Zalith's embrace.

The demon pressed his forehead against Alucard's, and then he placed his hand on the side of his face.

Alucard closed his eyes, allowing Zalith into his mind completely.

He saw himself lying in bed, and Zalith had his arms around him. But he was mumbling—nonsense at first, like he was trying to figure something out.

And then he said it.

"Non es solus."

"*Non es solus*," he repeated as Zalith retreated from his mind.

"What does it mean?" the demon asked.

What *did* it mean? His frown returned…but he knew how to get an answer. True Speech was complicated, like a living thing—sentient in a strange, impossible way. He had to *ask* for its permission to understand, he had to welcome it. But he couldn't do that himself. True Speech needed a vessel, a page, something to speak for it.

"Can you say?" he asked Zalith.

His mate's curious expression grew. "I'll try," he chuckled. "How does it sound again?"

"*Non es solus*," he said slowly.

With a nod, he repeated, "*Non es solus*."

Alucard heard the same words, but he *felt* their true meaning. "You're…not alone," he translated.

"That's what it means?"

He nodded.

Zalith looked a little bewildered. "Why do you say that in your sleep?"

"I zon't know," he said and glanced at Lenore—she was still Restoring.

Zalith kept a perplexed expression but pulled Alucard back into his embrace.

"I vink—" he said, seeking an answer in the mirage, "—my mother said to me."

Zalith kissed his head. "Well, she was right. You're not alone anymore."

He smiled as he nuzzled his neck. "And neizer are you."

The demon kissed him again.

Alucard lifted his head so that he could kiss his mate's lips, but a quiet gasp came from Lenore, so he turned to face her.

Zalith didn't let go of him; he dragged his hands down the vampire's body when he turned, and he softly held his waist.

"Lenore?" Alucard asked.

The Knight blinked slowly, and as she raised a hand to her head, she groaned deeply.

"You 'ave been Vestored," he told her.

She groaned again before her dull grey eyes met his. "M-M…My Lord?"

"*Da*," he replied.

Lenore exhaled, and her eyes shifted to Zalith. "Where am I?"

"Zhe Sanctum Vitalum."

She looked around, stiffly turning her head.

Alucard clicked his fingers and held out his hand.

Bloodmender Benedric hurried over and handed Alucard a tincture bottle of blood.

"Drvink zhis," he said to Lenore, handing it to her.

She slowly took the bottle…and then she pressed the rim against her bottom lip. Gradually, she poured the blood into her mouth; she hummed in relief, her eyes rolling back as her stiff body started waking from its slumber.

Alucard took the empty bottle from her and handed it back to Benedric. He caught Zalith's intrigued gaze. "Vhen I Vestore a vampire, zhey're in zhis sort of starved state, but zhey're not like me; zhey zon't get zhat…reserved burst of energy so zhat zhey can veed to vepair zhemselves," he explained. "Usually, zhey'd need at least two 'umans to complete zhe Vestoration, but I give zhem zhat," he said, gesturing to the bottle that Benedric was holding. "Is Aegis blood."

The demon smirked amusedly. "Did you bleed out an entire Aegis?"

"I did."

Zalith seemed surprised, like he'd expected Alucard to say no to his tease.

"Zhat's a story vor anozzer time," he said, smiling at him—it also reminded him that he and Zalith still needed to hunt an Aegis so that he could create some protective clothing, but that was something to think about once this Silver Claw business was over. He shifted his gaze and attention back to Lenore. "I need to ask you some questions. Are you veeling up to zhat?"

Lenore exhaled again and nodded. "Can I sit up?"

"'Elp 'er," he said to Benedric.

"Yes, My Lord," he said before tucking the bottle into his pocket. He helped the Knight sit up, and then he backed off with a bow—still, he lingered, as he should.

"Did you see who attacked you?" Alucard asked.

She frowned, thinking. "I…well…I…."

"Take your time," he assured her. "Start vrom zhe beginning, vetrace your steps."

Lenore closed her eyes. "I was…patrolling the East River." She furrowed her brow, tapping her fingers on the platform. "It…wasn't a beast, My Lord."

"Vhat did zhis, zhen?"

"I…remember seeing silver—I felt it."

"Claws?" he asked.

She nodded stiffly. "Definitely a person's hand, My Lord—but they were *strong*. They…pinned me on my stomach before I had a chance to fight."

"You zidn't see zhem when zhey cut you?"

Lenore shook her head. "It was all so fast." She opened her eyes, donning an ashamed stare. "I'm sorry, My Lord. I let you down."

Alucard sighed but shook his head. "You zidn't let me down, Lenore."

Her face lit up slightly.

"Is zhere anyving else you can vemember? Any veature, any detail."

She closed her eyes again, that struggled expression returning.

Alucard waited…and waited. He glanced at Zalith, who was gazing at him with hunger in his eyes, and it sent a shiver of desperation through him. His body immediately reacted to his mate's stare, urging him to give himself to him again. But he had to resist. He had to get whatever he could out of Lenore.

"There was—"

He sharply turned his head, ripping his attention from Zalith, telling his body no.

"—Something," she said, opening her eyes to look at him. "There was no scent, but there *was* an aura…type of feeling."

"Vhat did zhe aura veel like?"

"Well…almost like a werewolf, but not a werewolf at the same time. It was a trace of werewolf."

A hybrid? "Vhat else vas vith zhat aura?"

"It was…like Greymore," she said, her frown lifting.

"What do you mean like Greymore?" Zalith questioned.

Her stare shifted to him, and then back to Alucard.

The vampire nodded, letting her know that she could answer him.

"Greymore has this sort of overpowering…ethos feeling—something new. It's like I can *feel* the existence of his strength. That was what this aura felt like."

Alucard pondered. Lenore was right about Greymore's aura; he'd felt it, too, but *he* knew that it was the aura of a Prime—at least part of it. There was a lot of mystery to Greymore, but that was curiosity for a different time. If what Lenore felt was powerful strength entangled with a faint werewolf aura, then it was likely that her attacker was a stronger type of werewolf—perhaps even a different species of lycan.

"They had…there was this sort of yellow to their eyes," Lenore added.

Powerful, strong, a trace of werewolf…and yellow in its eyes. "Loup-garou," he said, turning his head to look at Zalith.

The demon's expression deepened with concern. "I remember you telling me about loup-garou."

Alucard sighed and said, "Vell, at least ve can narrow our search options."

"Searching for the aura?"

"Loup-garou are very good at 'iding zheir aura and covering zheir tracks. But 'e von't be above ground. Zhere's a vull moon coming, and zhey veel zhe invluence more zhan any ozzer lycan; 'e could unintentionally shivt at any point, and zhat vould expose 'im to us." He paused as dread crept in. "Zhey become much stronger two days bevore and avter zhe vull moon, and even more so zhe day bevore. Zhe day *of* zhe moon is vhen zhey're almost tvice as dangerous, so is likely zhat 'e is vaiting vor zhe vull moon to attack my coven."

"So we need to find him before that happens," Zalith said firmly. "When is the full moon?"

"Two days."

He huffed and nodded. "I'll get some more of my demons over here to help."

Alucard felt conflicted. "But vhat about zhe elves? Vhat if Calivarion decides to attack?"

Zalith crossed his arms, clearly thinking. "How long is your ship going to take to get those new packs to Uzlia?"

"If zhey leave vhen I told zhem to, zhey should be zhere in zhe next tventy-vour hours."

"Once they get there, Greymore can put them to work. They can replace some of my demons until we deal with this. Until then, we can keep searching," he suggested.

Alucard nodded, and then he looked at Lenore. "You need to vest vor a vew hours."

"I can help, My Lord," she insisted.

But he shook his head. "Vest, Lenore," he said firmly. "At least vour hours. You 'aven't vinished Vestoring."

She didn't protest. "Yes, My Lord," she said with a bow of her head.

"'Elp 'er to 'er coffin," he told Benedric.

The Bloodmender took Lenore's arm as she got up and let her lean her weight on him. He helped her to the end of the Vitalum and up the stairs.

Alucard sighed and turned to face Zalith. "Vell, zhis just got a whole lot more complicated," he muttered.

Zalith pulled him into his embrace again and nuzzled his head. "We'll get it done, don't worry," he said…and then he inhaled quietly and hummed contently before he added, "We'll find him before he kills anyone else."

"I 'ope so," he grumbled, sinking into the demon's embrace.

"We will," he assured him.

The vampire exhaled and closed his eyes, trying to relax and calm his mind. "I can get zhe city plans vrom zhe city 'all. Zhey'll show me all zhe tunnels and underground passages."

Zalith kissed his head. "Are we going now?"

"I'll get somevone to vetch zhem—Evaphene is vone of my vaster Ad'erents, so I'll probably send 'er. Zhe city is still under quarantine, so she can slip in zhere easily."

He felt Zalith smirk against his head.

"I know where I'd like to slip in easily," his mate murmured.

Alucard smiled, but he couldn't cave this time. He needed to focus. He needed to be ready no matter how aggressively his body urged him to give in to instinct. "Later," he said. He couldn't deny it entirely, but postponing it was enough for now. With a final glance at Zalith, he turned, leading them both back through the corridor and towards his Rest Space, where the tension between them would be waiting…unresolved, but far from forgotten.

Chapter Twenty-Five

— ⪤ ✝ ⪥ —

He Who Must Stay, He Who Must Defend

| **Alucard** |

| ***Atheson, Atheson Coven Sanctum*** |

Evaphene didn't take long to fetch the plans from the city hall. Once Alucard had them, he started examining every passage and tunnel that ran under Atheson; he took note of each grate, drain, and manhole—any place that the loup-garou could use to retreat and hide. But it looked like a maze down there, one that even a vampire could become lost in if they didn't retain every direction they went in.

He flipped the pages, eyes skimming the mapped routes, weighing decisions—who to send where, how to split their forces—but focus eluded him. Every calculation warred with the gnawing demands of his own body, with the slow-burning ache that pulsed just beneath his skin.

And Zalith wasn't helping. His mate lay stretched beside him on the couch, lips brushing his neck in slow nuzzles, hips shifting just enough to grind against him. Alucard didn't stop him. He couldn't. That subtle friction, Zalith's gradually hardening arousal pressing against his thigh—it was maddeningly soothing. A gentle torment. And despite his best efforts, he found himself sinking into the warmth of it, surrendering inch by inch.

With his free hand, he grabbed his pen from the cushion beside him and started noting down small groups of vampires and which paths they'd search; most of the tunnels on the map were marked with letters and numbers, likely to keep workmen from getting lost, and he hoped that the same symbols would be painted onto the walls. He didn't want to send a lone vampire to confirm that suspicion, though.

He turned his head to look down at Zalith. "Can I send an izuret to check zhe tunnels vor symbols?"

Zalith didn't answer.

"Zaliv?"

"Huh?"

Alucard smiled a little. "Can I send an izuret to check zhe tunnels vor symbols?"

"Oh. Yeah, that's okay," he replied, and then he lazily flicked his hand.

In a puff of yellow smoke, one of the wide-eyed, leathery-winged creatures appeared and gave them both an enthusiastic wave.

"Come 'ere," Alucard invited, gesturing for the izuret to float closer.

It did as he asked.

"See zhis?" he asked, pointing to the symbols on the map. "I need you to go to zhis grate." He pointed to one of the grates. "You vill vind along zhe east vall; vill be 'ard to miss because zhe ground is covered in sludge."

The creature nodded.

"Go inside to zhis crossvoad. I need you to tell me if zhese symbols are on each of zhe vour passage openings. Understand?"

For a moment, the izuret examined the map, and then it looked at Alucard and nodded with a squeak.

"*Multumesc*," the vampire said.

It saluted, and then it disappeared.

Alucard put the maps aside and noted down a few more of his vampires' names.

"We're not traipsing through muddy tunnels, are we?" Zalith questioned.

"Ve von't be searching, but ve *vill* be going vonce zhe loup-garou is located. I'd vather deal with 'im down zhere avay vrom zhe Sanctum and city."

Zalith huffed quietly and then kissed Alucard's neck. "We should probably find ourselves some of those…tall boots that cowboys wear."

Alucard laughed softly. "You mean buckaroo boots?"

"That's what they're called?"

"Vone of many terms. Viding boots, Vellington boots—even vopers, but zhose are shorter, so zhey'd do us no good."

The demon smirked against his neck. "How do you know that?"

He shrugged as he put his notebook aside. "Vell, I told you zhat I spent a lot of time in Nevastus at vone point. Zhat vasn't alvays exclusively zhe Citadel."

Zalith's smirk grew. "Were you an outlaw, vampire?"

"I guess zhat's vhat zhey'd call us…but no—vell…maybe. I zidn't attack carriages and murder travellers if zhat's vhat you mean. I vas chasing a Diabolus lead, and a lot of vings 'appened along zhe vay."

"What things?" he asked curiously before licking the vampire's neck. "You taste so good."

Alucard smiled again. "Bounties, criminal gangs, cow vhieves—zhat sort of ving."

Zalith chuckled. "Oh, so you were the good guy?"

"Sometimes."

The demon stroked his fingers to Alucard's cheek and then to the back of his neck. "Do you still have your boots?"

"Somevhere." He paused, thinking back a decade or so. "Ve 'ad zhis sort of save'ouse on zhe border of Yruulens. Is still zhere as var as I know."

Zalith hummed quietly, fiddling with Alucard's hair. "Maybe we should go someday—just to make sure."

"Maybe," he said amusedly. "As vor now, zhough, ve can send somevone to pick up some suitable vootvear vor zhe tunnels."

He nodded in agreement. "We can send another izuret," he said as he summoned another.

The creature appeared and grinned at them.

Alucard waited, expecting Zalith to give it orders, but his mate was distracted, still nuzzling his neck. So, he told it, "Go to Clarimond in Ansby—zhat's in Dor-Sanguis. She's vone of my zemons. You'll vind 'er in zhe town zhere. Ask 'er to go to a shoemaker and pick up two pairs of viding boots." He looked down at Zalith. "Vhat size are you?"

Zalith smirked against his neck again and murmured, "A little over nine inches."

He frowned. That didn't sound right. "Are you sure?"

"You tell me. You're the one moaning and whining when it's inside you."

Alucard pouted as fluster and embarrassment shot through him.

The izuret held its small hands to its mouth, hiding a giggle.

"Your shoe size," the vampire grumbled.

"Oh…I always have to have them custom-made. Cobblers don't usually stock my size—I'm too tall," he said amusedly.

A smile broke through Alucard's fluster. "I deal vith zhat a lot, too. Is because 'umans are small, stupid, vragile vings. Zheir cobblers zon't usually bovver vith anyving past size nine—zhey'd probably break zheir ankles if zhey tried vearing anyving over zhat."

Zalith laughed quietly as he stroked his fingers down Alucard's body. "Shoes aren't the only thing that run small on humans," he said, his voice low and suggestive. He then leaned into the vampire's ear. "But you already know that I've never had that problem…not with size, and certainly not with girth."

Alucard tensed up, a shiver of anticipation electrifying through him—and it intensified when the demon's fingertips brushed his crotch.

"You feel it every time, don't you, vampire?" his fingers gently gripped the bulge in Alucard's trousers. "The stretch…the way your body fights to take it all—and how much you love it," he murmured, easing his fingers around the vampire's already-stiffened shaft.

He stifled a moan because he remembered that there was an izuret in the room…just waiting for him to finish giving his order.

"I can feel your pre-cum, Alucard," Zalith taunted, dragging his thumb over the swollen head of his dick through the fabric, now warm and damp where it clung to him.

Alucard breathed out a stifled moan, trying to resist. He reluctantly shifted his sights to the creature and said, "Just…vind a cobbler who sells shoes vor non-'umans." He paused when Zalith's grip tightened, making him stifle another groan, and then he grabbed his notebook and flipped to a new page. He wrote it down as he told the izuret, "Tell 'im ve need as close as zhe cobbler 'as in stock to a slightly vider vidth with eleven-point two inches length."

The izuret nodded.

Alucard looked at Zalith. "*Shoe* size."

He smirked at him, withdrawing his hand; his thumb glistened faintly as he brought it to his mouth and sucked it slowly, his tongue pressing against the pad, never once breaking eye contact with Alucard. After a satisfied hum, he answered, "Wide width, eleven-point eight length."

Flustered and enticed, Alucard grasped desperately at his focus; he wrote the numbers down, and then he handed the paper to the izuret. "Noving smaller zhan zhose measurements—and ve vant viding boots or Vellington boots. If zhe cobbler zoesn't 'ave eizer, tell 'im ve need anyving at least shin 'igh. Understood?"

The izuret chirped as it nodded, and then it disappeared.

Zalith kissed the vampire's neck as he fiddled with his trouser buttons. "Can I put my dick inside you?"

He wanted to say yes—he very nearly did. But he still had work to do. "Not yet," he struggled to say. "I still 'ave to vigure zhese tunnels out."

The demon grinned against his neck.

"Zon't," Alucard warned him.

He chuckled and kissed him.

The vampire flipped back to the page he'd been noting down vampire teams on. Currently, the coven had thirty members able to fight, excluding Lenore, who needed to recover, Lăcrămioara, who needed to protect the Fledgelings, and Lysandra, who was waiting to be relocated to another city with Rosaline. But then there was Eyra; she was now Veiled, so that meant there were only twenty-eight capable fighters.

"Are you okay?" Zalith suddenly asked.

Alucard sighed deeply. "So much 'as 'appened in zhe past vew days. I need to Dignivy a new Coven Master because Eyra is Veiled, and I need to get zhe Vampire Council to send an Inquisitor to judge 'er."

Zalith trailed his fingers up Alucard's body and to the side of his neck. "I have a question," he said, sounding curious.

"Mm-hmm," the vampire replied, staring at the page.

"What's the difference between both vampire councils? Or are they the same?"

"Vone of zhe councils is my personal vone—is made up of most of zhe Coven Masters; zhey 'elp me make decisions vor each coven. Zhe ozzer is zhe vone zhat deals vith vampire crimes. Is convusing, I know. I've vhought about a new title vor vone of zhem, but zhere are many more important vings to deal vith vight now."

The demon nodded and kissed his neck again. "Who are you going to make Master of this coven?"

He thought about it, tapping his pen against his notebook. "I zon't know," he said with a huff. "Maybe Vasmus... but 'e's a Vhisper, very good to 'ave in zhe vield."

"Whisper?"

"Zhey are uh... espionage—spies of sorts. Zhey're like Orin."

"Oh," he replied... and then licked his neck with a pleased purr.

A shiver ran through Alucard, but he did his best to remain focused. "Ve're sending Crowell to 'elp Tyrus and Orin 'unt Lucious vonce Eimvood is safe, aren't ve? So can't be 'im, eizer."

Zalith replied with a hum and a quiet inhale.

"Noctrel is vone of my best Ad'erents; zhey 'ave a very sharp eye, and zhey're Skyborne—zhat's a vampire who aged enough to evolve zhe ability to vly."

The demon chuckled. "All of these titles—vampires are really sophisticated over here, aren't they?"

"I 'ave a very specivic system," he said proudly. "'Elps everyvone keep track of each ozzer."

Zalith pressed his forehead against the side of Alucard's face and murmured, "With the way it's growing, this demon army of mine might need your expertise with titles and ranks."

"Zhat's a good idea," he said—he was admittedly surprised that his mate was able to manifest such a thought while clearly completely infatuated.

The demon licked his neck again, and then he leaned into his ear. "You should probably change your trousers," he teased him eagerly. "And when you do, we might as well take advantage of your ass being out; it needs to be filled with my cum again."

Anticipation raced through Alucard, making him smile. He enjoyed Zalith's persistence—and so did his body. It urged him once again to say yes, and this time... maybe he sh—

An izuret burst from a huge, ungraceful cloud of blue smoke and started chirping and squeaking and flailing its hands around.

The vampire stared at it, trying to make sense of what it was saying.

And Zalith sighed deeply against Alucard's neck.

"Slow down," Alucard interjected.

After a deep, squeaking huff, the izuret slowed just enough for its words to make sense—and it told them exactly what Alucard had been worried about.

Orrivain Elves had been spotted taking position outside of Eimwood.

Zalith sat up. "How many?"

The izuret told him that twenty-two elves had been seen outside the walls from all angles, but there was no sign of Calitharion. The elves were armed and armoured, and each of them had vargrs—some even had two or three.

"Fuck," Zalith grunted as he shifted away from Alucard. "The Yrudyen?" he asked the izuret, pulling his blazer on.

It told him that no Orrivain had been seen near the Yrudyen settlement.

Zalith then looked at Alucard.

However, Alucard felt conflicted. He wanted to go with him and protect their city, but what if he left and the Silver Claw attacked the coven? He was sending vampires beneath the city to find him, and he didn't want to leave and not be there if they found him—or worse, *he* found *them*.

"I need to stay 'ere," he said guiltily. "I can't leave zhe coven vhile 'e's out zhere."

Zalith frowned hesitantly, and worry settled in his eyes. "Aren't we waiting to do anything until my demons can get here and help?"

"Ve *are*, but zhere's no telling vhether zhe loup-garou vill decide to attack bevore zhen. I 'ave to be 'ere if zhat 'appens."

The demon's worry visibly grew, and he dragged his hand down the side of his face.

"I'll be okay, Zaliv," he tried to assure him. "I 'ave a whole coven to back me up."

"I know, I just—" he raked a hand through his hair, gripping it for a second as if it might anchor him, "—I can't...*not* be here, Alucard, especially when there's some hunter going around killing vampires with silver nails or claws," he forced out, jaw clenched.

Alucard took his hand—

"I can send for Greymore; one of my demons can get him here."

The vampire shook his head and said, "Zhomas is vith zhe new packs. I zon't vink vill be a good impression if 'e suddenly 'as to abandon zhem."

Zalith exhaled deeply, gripping Alucard's hand tightly. "I'll get Tyrus over here, then. I need to know that you're safe or I'm not going to be able to focus."

"But 'e's vorking on vinding Lucious."

"That can wait for a few days. They're still gathering information; they haven't left Aegisguard yet."

He wouldn't say no; he didn't want him to be worrying constantly, so much that it affected his ability to fight and protect. And Zalith was right. Tyrus and Orin hadn't yet left for the pocket world that Lucious was hiding in; they were waiting for Crowell. So he nodded, and then he added, "You could send Zanvord, too. Vorking vith zhe coven vill be a good lesson vor 'im."

The demon's worry didn't entirely fade—in fact, it barely faded at all. But he sighed deeply, looked down at Alucard's hand, and said, "All right." He then lifted his head and stared at the vampire. "*Please* tell me if anything happens while I'm dealing with the elves, even if it's just some tiny change or a suspicion or something—just…keep me updated, okay?"

Alucard nodded, placing his left hand over Zalith's, which was still clasped around his right. "I'll tell you everyving if anyving changes," he promised, and then he kissed his lips. "Go," he insisted. "I'll vait 'ere until Tyrus arrives."

Zalith still didn't move, though. His frown thickened, and he squeezed Alucard's hand *even* tighter. He looked like he was going to say something, but whatever it was, he held it back and turned his head away for a moment. Another exhale…one more sigh…and he murmured, "Okay."

The vampire gently gripped the demon's shoulder and pulled him into his embrace. "I love you," he said quietly. "Be carevul…and make sure zhis is zhe end of Calivarion's vule. No tyrant deserves to lead anyvone."

"I couldn't agree more," Zalith said, holding him firmly. "As soon as it's done, I'll be back."

"I know. Just zon't vush."

Zalith pressed his forehead against Alucard's. Hesitation remained on his face, and his eyes were filled with worry…and longing. The demon kissed his lips, caressed the back of his head, and then sighed one last time. "I love you," he said, his voice hushed. "I'll see you in a little while, okay?"

Alucard smiled at him. "I'll see you soon."

The demon got up, but just as he was about to walk, he stopped, turned, and leaned down to kiss Alucard again. Then, he pulled himself away and headed for the door while he told the lingering izuret to send Tyrus and Danford to the Sanctum.

As he watched his mate leave, Alucard began to feel a cold emptiness in his chest. He didn't want him to go, but he knew just as well as Zalith did that they couldn't do both things at once. Eimwood and its people were just as important as the covens, and they deserved equal attention.

When the door shut, finalizing Zalith's departure, Alucard leaned back on the couch with a deep exhale. He sank into the emptiness for a moment, and the urge to run after his mate was *strong*, but he did his best to focus on what needed doing—other than what his *body* insisted needed doing.

For now, he had a vampire hunter to kill, and Zalith had a tyrant to deal with. Once that was all over, he'd surrender to his instincts…and to Zalith.

Chapter Twenty-Six

— ⸱ ✝ ⸱ —

Veiled Atrocities

| **Alucard** |
| *Atheson, Atheson Coven Sanctum* |

awn was approaching. Danford was sitting awkwardly at the table by the door, and Tyrus sat across the room in one of the armchairs—and he hadn't taken his eyes off Alucard since he got there.

Alucard didn't let it distract him, though. After the izuret returned and told him that the tunnels were all marked with the same symbols as they were on the map, he started planning more efficient routes.

When he looked at the very last page, it revealed ancient catacombs, and old notes on the side mentioned that only a quarter or so of them had been mapped because they became too dangerous, were flooded, or collapsed. Could the loup-garou be hiding down there? Those tunnels were the deepest of the underground system; moonlight would never reach them, so it was the *perfect* hiding place.

He tapped his pen against his thigh, pondering. There was a bygone grate not far from the Sanctum, so if the search began during daylight, he'd be able to get those of his vampires who couldn't walk in the sun into the tunnels using the cover of the walls and trees, and those who *could* walk during the day could gain access through the several other entrances he'd marked.

The vampire noted down the last of his vampires. He then shifted his attention to the demons Zalith planned to send over to help. His mate hadn't told him who he'd be sending yet or how many, so he couldn't exactly make a fully-fledged plan involving them. But if enough were joining the hunt, he thought it might be best to put one with each of the vampire groups.

He wrote it... but he slowed when he heard Tyrus inhale deeply but quietly.

Alucard glanced at him. He was *still* staring, like he was searching for an answer, like he was very submerged in thought. Or maybe he was captivated.

The latter made Alucard feel uncomfortable, and so did the staring. He wasn't sure how much longer he could put up with it. Although he knew that Tyrus respected him as Zalith's mate—or was at least *supposed* to—there was still a part of him that felt as if the allocer demon wasn't his to treat like a subordinate. Tyrus *did* work for Zalith, after all, not *him*. Alucard had his own pack, and Tyrus wasn't a part of it.

He shifted his focus back to his work, reading over his plans. Judging from all the passages and pathways, it would take all day to search for the Silver Claw—perhaps even longer. But with him and maybe even Zalith there, too, they'd cut that time down by a few hours. However, he wasn't sure whenZalith would be back, and—

"Are you trans?" Tyrus suddenly asked. "Sorry."

Alucard looked over at him and frowned. "Vhat?"

The allocer demon shook his head and finally broke his stare. "Never mind."

He kept his frown but went back to reading his notes. While he read his vampires' names, though, he lost his focus. What the hell kind of question was that? As far as he was aware, he'd never said or done anything that might make someone assume or wonder…so why had Tyrus just asked? Was it the way he looked? The way he spoke?

Slowly, he turned his head—Tyrus was staring again.

But Alucard didn't hesitate. "Vhy are you asking zhat?"

Tyrus shrugged. "I don't know. You're in heat, and it's confusing me," he answered with a small laugh.

He tapped his pen on his thigh again. Why would that make him think he was transgender? Surely, he wasn't the first demon in heat whom Tyrus had been around…unless he was. Still, he asked, "Vhy?"

"Because you're a man…and yet for some reason, your scent isn't fully male. There's a faint trace of what heat smells like on a woman. I didn't mean any offence— sorry if it sounded that way. I just didn't know what else it could mean."

Alucard's frown thickened. He wasn't sure how to take that or what to do with it. Not fully male? As far as he was aware, he'd been a man all his life. Maybe Tyrus was mistaken; maybe he just didn't know what the scent of a Numen-blooded demon was like. That was the only explanation that made sense to him.

"Is because I 'ave Numen blood," he told him.

Tyrus nodded once as he said, "Oh, okay."

The vampire exhaled quietly and reorganized the maps before placing them on the couch beside him. He leaned back a little, relaxing as he put his notebook aside, too. All that was left to do now was wait. But he still hated the silence, especially when he had one person staring at him and another fidgeting nervously in the same room.

He sighed and stood up, heading for the door.

"Do you want me to go with you?" Tyrus called.

"No," Alucard grumbled. He left his Rest space, closing the doors behind him. But when he stepped into the hall, he halted. He didn't know where he was going, he just needed to get up and walk around.

He descended the steps into the stair hall. Every vampire had retreated to their coffins—save for Lysandra, who he could hear in the lounge. He made his way down the corridor, and when he stepped into the room, Lysandra turned to face him, as did the man she was talking to.

"My Lord," she greeted. Her wounds had healed, and she looked much better.

"Uh…sir—sorry, I don't know what to call you," the man said nervously—a werewolf, one from the Duskroot Pack.

"Vhat are you doing 'ere?" Alucard questioned him.

Lysandra bowed her head and said, "Sorry, that'd be my doing. I saw him wandering the halls looking for a bathroom. I showed him to the one through the study space, and then we just got to talking."

"We're very grateful for your and Zalith's help, sir," the man said, and then he stood up, holding his hand out. "I'm Mortimer, one of the pack's Iotas."

Alucard didn't want to shake his hand. He ignored it, walking over to one of the tables. As he leaned against it, he asked Lysandra, "Do you or Vosaline 'ave any preverence as to vhere I velocate you?"

"Oh…um…well," she started, glancing at Mortimer as he sat back down. "Rosaline talks a lot about Boszorkány. She says that it's very beautiful there, and a lot of the Miréfalle districts are non-human friendly."

He nodded in response. "If you vant to be moved to Mirévalle, you vill need to join zhe coven, Lysandra. Zhey do not take kindly to Straybloods in zheir territory." He folded his arms. "If you and Vosaline vish to vemain outside of coven life, zhere are a vew places I know of vhere Straybloods live but ignore vone anozzer."

She looked like she was thinking. "Are any of them in Boszorkány?"

Alucard felt hesitant to answer, but if Lysandra desired to remain a Strayblood, he wouldn't force her to seek out a coven. He *would*, however, warn her of the dangers. "Zhere's no coven in Vhéloix, but zhere's a town on zhe border—Volérine—vhere a verevolf pack makes up zhe majority of zhe population; Cupitors are ovten sent into zhe city to pick up supplies zhat zhe town zoesn't 'ave."

"Oh…" she said disappointedly.

He sighed and fidgeted—he was starting to notice more and more that he was growing increasingly frustrated, and he was certain of what the reason for it was. But he did his best to ignore it. "Zhere's Vontisère in Chantrevaux," he told her. "Sits at zhe junction of zhe Rhévin and Sahléa vivers, so is a big vishing location. Is a lot of narrow streets, so you vill both be vine to 'unt. But vhile same-sex couples are not illegal, zhere are public indecency laws zhat could cause you problems outside of closed doors."

Lysandra laughed a little. "Well, Fontisère sounds better than most other places I've heard stories about. At least Rosaline and I won't be hanged for loving each other. I'm sure we can refrain ourselves from upsetting the public with it."

"Humans are so awful," Mortimer chimed in with a sigh. "They mock us, fear us, and call us unnatural when they're still choking on their own backward prejudices. We're centuries ahead of them socially—it's laughable."

"Honestly, we are," Lysandra agreed. "They fear what they don't understand, shame what they secretly crave, and call it righteousness. It's *exhausting*."

"I'm sure you've faced your fair share of discrimination," Mortimer said.

Alucard snapped his gaze to him, realizing he'd zoned out a little. "Vhat?"

"Well… you're a homosexual, too… aren't you?" the Iota asked unsurely.

The vampire cringed. "Zon't use zhat vord."

"Oh, sorry," he said, looking nervous. "I-I'm still kinda new to this whole queer thing," he added with a quiet chuckle.

"Or zhat vone," Alucard grumbled.

"Gay," Lysandra corrected Mortimer. "And Rosaline and I are sapphists—or the more recent term that's flying around: lesbians."

"R-right," he said with a nod. "Sorry, sir."

Alucard rolled his eyes. "So, Vontisère?" he asked Lysandra.

"I think so," she said. "I should make sure that Rosaline is okay with it first, though."

"You can't go to zhe city vight now, nor can she leave because of zhe quarantine. I zon't vant to scare 'er vith a zemon messenger, eizer. Vonce zhe quarantine is over, I'll send somevone to vetch 'er."

"Thank you, My Lord," she said with a smile.

He half nodded, his thoughts drifting again. If he could speak into Zalith's mind right now, he might just ask him if one of them could go to the other so that he could relieve the frustration, but it was probably a good thing that he couldn't because leaving his vampires would be a terrible mistake, as would his mate leaving Eimwood.

But he wanted to see him. What if he found a mirror and spoke to him through it?

No. He had to focus.

With a quiet sigh, he tried to urge his attention elsewhere, and his eyes landed on Mortimer. "Vhy aren't you on border patrol?" he questioned. The city may be under quarantine, and there may be a very strong suspicion that the Silver Claw was hiding beneath the streets, but that didn't mean anyone could let their guard down, especially with Lilith's demons still sweeping the realm—they could turn up here again at any time.

"Oh, Alpha Abel has me assigned to Luna Temperance," he answered. "She's due any time now, and he wants to make sure that someone is with her in case it happens while he's away."

Fair enough—he gave a nod in response. It made him think about Freja, though. She was only a few months along, but still…pregnancy changed things, especially for werewolves. Maybe taking Danford away from her so often was a little selfish of him. Well…no. Danford had a job, and Freja understood that. Alucard also knew Freja, and if she really had a problem with it, she wouldn't hesitate to say so. More likely, she was glad Danford was learning to manage his new abilities and spending more time among vampires—after all, he was one of them now…almost.

He shifted his sights to Lysandra. "Vhere are you vesting? Not zhe Nightvault, I assume."

"I…hadn't actually thought about it, My Lord. I've been spending most of my time here."

"Zhe ozzer vampires zon't 'ave a problem vith you," he assured her. "Eyra vill be causing no more trouble, eizer."

"I know, I just…well…gosh, this is embarrassing," she said, shaking her head. "I'm just incredibly afraid of being alone…and of empty spaces…and large buildings."

Mortimer nodded and said, "She didn't want to be alone, sir. It's why I'm here—well, why I stayed after she directed me to the bathroom."

"I'm sorry, My Lord," she said ashamedly, hiding her face. "It's not that I hate the place you've given us vampires, it's just…not for me."

Alucard shook his head. He understood in a way; after four centuries, the idea of willingly walking into any space that remotely resembled the catacombs where he grew up made him feel sick—and it was only *now* that he wasn't so distracted that he realized…*that* was exactly what he was going to do. The tunnels under the city would be lightless, narrow, and a twisting, turning labyrinth.

He tensed up ever so slightly, his heart quickening for a moment. How could he have been such an idiot? He'd very nearly let himself walk into a place where he'd be absolutely no use to anyone—in fact, he'd be a burden. Even with Zalith at his side, he'd not be able to conquer *that* fear.

But he wasn't trapped in a narrow passage right now, and he wouldn't lose his composure around his subordinates, so he exhaled deeply and shook his head again, dismissing the looming trepidation. "Zhere's noving to be sorry vor, nor should you be embarrassed," he replied. "If vill make you veel more comvortable, zhere are a vew empty private vaults on zhe virst vloor. Some of zhem aren't much larger zhan zhe coffin inside—*or*…zhere's zhe Vledgeling Dvelling Space. Zhere's alvays movement and noise down zhere."

Lysandra sighed in relief. "Thank you, My Lord—that would be perfect."

"I vouldn't advise *you* to 'ead down zhere," he said to Mortimer. "Zhe Vledgelings vill tear you apart even if you're poison to zhem."

The Iota went a little pale and laughed nervously. "Yeah, I don't plan on it."

"I can take you down zhere vhen you're veady," Alucard said to Lysandra.

She smiled appreciatively at him, and then she looked at Mortimer. "Thanks for sitting with me, I really appreciate it."

He nodded. "Yeah, no problem. I'll be with the other wolves if you need me again."

Lysandra got up, and so did Mortimer.

"Vollow us," Alucard said to the Iota.

They left the lounge and headed to the stair hall. After dropping Mortimer off at the guest room, Alucard led Lysandra around the curved corridor and down the stairs. He took her through the Ebon Chamber and to the Fledgeling Dwelling Space, where Lăcrămioara was comforting the sleeping Fledgelings—*all* of them. He was glad to see that they'd progressed quickly.

"My Lord," the brood nurse said respectfully when he stepped into the room.

The moment they laid their glowing eyes on him, the Fledgelings began crawling and fumbling towards Alucard. He didn't shoo them away, though; he let them gather at his feet, some murmuring indistinct words, others droning or clicking—they hadn't found their voices yet, or their individuality. But in time, they'd regain their independence. Right now, they were like infants.

He let them linger a few moments longer, and then he pointed at Lăcrămioara and said, "Go."

The Fledgelings, one by one, scurried away.

Alucard set his eyes on the brood nurse. "Lysandra vill be vesting 'ere zhis morning."

Lăcrămioara nodded. "Of course. There are some coffins over there," she said to Lysandra, gesturing to the coffins against the left wall. "The Fledgelings haven't begun learning to sleep in them yet."

"Uh... actually, the Nesting Circle is okay—if that's all right," she said, gesturing to the sunken circular sleeping area where all of the Fledgelings were huddled together.

Alucard was beginning to wonder whether Lysandra had ever been properly weaned out of whichever Dwelling Space she'd been taught in. "Lysandra, vhen vere you turned?" he asked.

"Oh... well..." she drawled, sounding hesitant.

"Tell me," he said, firmer this time.

She lowered her head again. "You... weren't supposed to find out, My Lord."

He frowned at her. "Vhat?"

"I wasn't meant to—"

"Tell me vhat I vant to know," he demanded.

Some of the Fledgelings stirred, but Lăcrămioara lulled them back to sleep.

Lysandra took a deep breath. "It was Eyra, My Lord."

"Vhy am I not fucking surprised?" he muttered. He grabbed her arm and pulled her out of the room, closing the door behind them. "Tell me exactly vhat 'appened."

She nodded, still hiding her face.

"Look at me."

Lysandra did as he told her and lifted her head, her nervous gaze meeting his irritated glare. "It was four months ago, My Lord."

He dragged his hand over his face with a frustrated sigh.

"We met in the city—Lainwright's Cocktail Bar; it's in the Dunstrowe District. She was just…really nice back then. I didn't even realize that she was a vampire until she fed on me."

Why was Eyra in a cocktail bar in the city? Why was she attacking and feeding on humans at her pleasure? And *why* had she turned one? How many people had she done this to before and after Lysandra? He snarled and tried focusing on one problem at a time. "Did she teach you avter she turned you?"

"Well…she taught me how to feed safely, but that's about it."

"So you veren't veaned out of zhe Dvelling Space?"

"Um—"

"Vere zhere ozzer Vledgelings in zhere vith you at zhe time?"

"Well—"

"'Ow many ozzer people 'as Eyra turned?"

Lysandra started tearing up.

Alucard sighed and placed his hand on her shoulder. "Is not your vault, and I'm not angry vith you. I'm angry vith Eyra."

She exhaled deeply and nodded as he took his hand away. "There were four others, My Lord—um…Camilla…Dorothee, Lilly, and Hanna."

"Vhere are zhey?"

Lysandra pouted sadly. "Dorothee starved," she mumbled, her voice breaking. "Lilly was just gone one morning. Hanna walked out into the sun the second she got the chance." Tears now trickled down her face. "Camilla left when I was Severed—I don't know where she went." She wiped her face and took a deep breath. "Eyra Severed me because I started seeing Rosaline." A pause. "We didn't even get to bury them or put them into urns because Eyra scattered Dorothee and Hanna's ashes."

He scowled skeptically. "Vhat exactly did Eyra attempt turning you all vor?"

"I don't know, honestly. We thought it might be a…well, a sex fetish thing at first, but she isn't into women at all—not like that." She wiped more tears away. "I mean we saw her with a few of the Adherent men, so we kinda just assumed that she wanted us for something else."

"Vhich men?"

"Um…one of them was definitely Knight Corven-Hale because Lilly had a crush on him and wouldn't stop talking about him. And then I think one of the others was Knight Salvorn."

Salvorn was dead, so Corven-Hale was Alucard's next stop. *Somebody* must have noticed Eyra's activities, and he hoped that the Knight would tell him what Lysandra couldn't.

"Go and vest," he told her, gesturing to the Fledgeling Dwelling Space. It was now clear why she wanted to join the newly turned. Not only had she evidently not received the proper training, care, or attention, but she'd lost her brood sisters. One thing Fledgelings heavily relied on during their first months was their brood kin, and without *hers*, Lysandra's fears of being alone made perfect sense.

With a bow, Lysandra headed into the room and closed the door behind her.

Alucard made his way up to the third floor—the Nocturne Wing. He found and knocked on Corven-Hale's door; the creak of a coffin lid came moments later, followed by heavy footsteps…and then the door opened.

The Knight looked surprised to see him. "My Lord," he said with a bow, wide-eyed.

"'As been brought to my attention zhat you spent a lot of time vith Eyra," he started, keeping his eyes fixed on the barrel-chested man and his voice vacant.

"Yes, My Lord," he answered firmly.

"I've also been invormed zhat Eyra 'as turned several vomen vithout my knowledge. Vould you 'appen to know anyving about zhat?"

That was when Corven-Hale faltered; he opened his mouth to speak but hesitated as if he was expecting a blow to the face—Alucard knew that look too well, that reaction…because he'd reacted in the same way for centuries.

"Tell me vhat you know," he ordered—his orders negated any other vampire's.

Corven-Hale fiddled with his moustache for a moment. "She ordered Salvorn and me not to speak of it."

"Speak."

He bowed his head. "Salvorn and I witnessed the way she treated those women, My Lord. She practically love-bombed them, giving them purpose and praise. But she'd withdraw the very moment they showed independence; she punished and shamed them until they crawled back—it was very upsetting to watch, My Lord. Her cycle kept them confused and dependent, and they were constantly seeking her approval." He paused and sighed deeply. "After Dorothee began refusing blood, Veiled Eyra's treatment got much worse; she became more abusive than manipulative."

Alucard was all too familiar with what he was hearing, but he kept hold of his composure. He needed all of the details to ensure that Eyra paid for everything she'd done.

"Veiled Eyra began force-feeding Dorothee. I only know that Dorothee began throwing the blood up afterwards because Lilly told me, My Lord." He lifted his head to look at Alucard, his eyes filled with guilt and regret. "Salvorn and I wanted to tell you what was going on here, but as I said, Veiled Eyra compelled us not to speak of it. Salvorn did try to break the compulsion, but—"

He nodded. He knew what happened when a vampire tried to defy a Coven Master's strict orders. "Vhat 'appened to zhe ozzer vomen?"

"Veiled Eyra became livid when she found Dorothee. We don't know where she took her body, but she rushed to the city to find a replacement, and that was when Hanna walked out into the sunlight." He huffed and insisted, "I tried to stop her, My Lord. But she was already ash by the time I reached her."

"Is not your vault," he said. "Vhat about Lilly?"

Corven-Hale hesitated again—but only for a few moments. "I…I had to get her out of here, My Lord. I know that I shouldn't have taken—"

"As var as I'm concerned, in zhis situation, getting 'er avay vas zhe vight ving."

He exhaled in relief.

"Vhere is she now?" Alucard asked. "Eyra isn't going to get to 'er ever again."

The Knight nodded. "I couldn't risk keeping her in the city because Veiled Eyra spent too much time there. I took her to Antamont. There's a young Strayblood living in an abandoned crypt just outside of a small village; he's taking care of her."

At least Lilly was safe—or as safe as she could be. A covenless Fledgeling, especially one that hadn't received the proper training, was either a disaster waiting to happen or another slaying added to some random hunter's list. But he was certain that she wouldn't want to return to this coven. Perhaps he could find her another one.

"As for Camilla, I have no idea where she went, My Lord," Corven-Hale continued. "We assumed that she went with Lysandra, but after her return the other day, I think that maybe she managed to get out of Atheson."

Alucard sighed and said, "You vill likely 'ave to vepeat all of zhis to zhe Vampire Council vhen is time vor Eyra to be tried."

"Of course, My Lord. They all deserve justice." He then frowned worriedly. "Is Lysandra going to be okay?"

"She's going to 'ave to go vhrough zhe Vledgeling process again, but yes."

"If I can help in any way, let me know."

With a nod, Alucard turned around and headed for the stairs. Eyra's list of treachery was getting worse and worse, and he wondered whether this was the end of it. He had a strong suspicion that it was not. What else had she been doing here? A part of him even suspected that Lilith's demons hadn't stormed this place at all. What if Eyra was responsible for everything she'd reported as demon activity?

He huffed angrily, making his way back towards his Rest Space. It was time to get an Inquisitor to the Sanctum. Eyra would answer for everything she'd done, and he'd make sure that *nothing* like this ever happened again.

Chapter Twenty-Seven

— ⸲ ✝ ⸱ —

Conflict's End

| Zalith |
| *Aestrael, Uzlia Isles, Yrudberg, Eimwood City* |

Just as the izuret had said, twenty-two armed, armoured elves were positioned strategically outside of Eimwood's walls. While Zalith had been prepared for *them*, there were a lot more vargr than he and Alucard had counted at the Orrivain settlement. Calitharion wasn't with his soldiers, and Zalith worried that might mean he was heading for the Yrudyen settlement, and he could very well have vargr with him.

Zalith had more than enough people who could take care of the forces surrounding the city, but what he *didn't* have right now were enough werewolves guarding the Yrudyen—not enough to deal with a potential pack of vargr.

He turned to Silvannus, one of Tyrus' Betas. "Go and tell fifteen of the werewolves to meet me by the city gates. Then go and regroup with the rest of the demons and grab those elves. Kill the vargr if you have to; if you can get their collars off without any risk at all to *anyone*, then do so, and if they flee, let them." Those hounds may be with the Orrivain, but the beasts were cursed and chained, and he knew that Alucard would give the same order. He didn't want to kill innocent animals that had no choice but to follow their masters.

"Yes, sir," the orange-eyed man said, and then he leapt down from the wall.

Zalith remained for a moment, eyeing the positioned elves that he could see from his vantage point. His eyes then shifted to the forest; he could see the *very* distant glow of the Yrudyen settlement. There wasn't smoke or the glows of ethos attacks, and he hadn't received word from the werewolves guarding the place, so he hoped that either Calitharion was cowering back in Orrivain territory, or he hadn't yet reached or initiated his attack. Whichever it was, Zalith needed to get out there—he had to make sure.

He turned, and then he quickly disappeared and reappeared in the street below. Using the space between the Astral Plane and this world, he navigated his way to the city gates in moments. And then he waited.

The demon summoned an izuret, and when it appeared in a puff of blue smoke, he told it, "Go to Alucard and tell him that my demons are going to apprehend the elves surrounding the city while I head to the Yrudyen settlement with some werewolves to make sure that Calitharion isn't using this as a distraction to attack them."

With a nod, the creature disappeared.

Zalith caught movement up ahead; he watched as the fifteen werewolves he'd asked for raced towards him. He immediately recognized Mirelda, the Theta of Greymore's original Eltarian pack, and Cassimir, the Iota. Seliora, the Gamma originally from Freja's pack, was among the group, too…as was Peris, an Omega who joined Greymore's pack after they defeated the Hemlock Hollow Pack. He hoped she wouldn't be a hindrance.

The rest of them came from other Nefastian packs loyal to Greymore. Zalith already knew that the Enforcers of the Ember Mountain Pack—Edras, Lazran, Callixene, and Annelith—were *very* capable, as were Veyric and Iscar, Epsilons of the Lament Grove Pack. He'd never seen Rowain and Ophelyne fight before, but they were Betas of the Cypress Creek Pack, which Greymore had praised for its capabilities. And the last was Davoren, whom the demon rolled his eyes at. That man was a well-known troublemaker, and he came from a repulsive pack—the Pure Moon Pack, as they had boastfully called themselves. They were disgraceful, but Davoren was a Zeta, a rare type of werewolf, and unfortunately, Greymore's top fighter.

They came to a halt in front of Zalith, and Davoren took the lead.

"Reporting for duty," the purple-eyed man said with a lazy salute.

Zalith rolled his eyes again. "The Orrivain leader is possibly at the Yrudyen settlement. We need to get there immediately. Let's move," he said, and as the wolves shifted and began racing to the forest, he returned to the space between the Astral Plane and this world—but he couldn't travel as fast as he usually would; he had to keep the wolves close.

As he hurried to the settlement, Zalith's focus moved back to Alucard. He knew that his fiancé would tell him if anything happened while he was dealing with this elf shit, but he couldn't help but worry about him—he *always* worried about him. The Silver Claw was dangerous, more than they'd assumed. What if he surfaced and ambushed Alucard? What if he wasn't working alone and had allies?

He huffed and tried to concentrate on what he was doing. Alucard was capable, and Tyrus was also there to assist if needed. And the sooner the Orrivain were dealt with, the sooner Zalith could return to his vampire.

When Zalith reached the outskirts of the Yrudyen settlement, he stopped behind the cover of a massive oak tree and waited for the wolves. He took out his pocket watch—it took fifteen minutes to get here, much longer than he'd have liked, but there was no sign of Calitharion or any vargrs.

Yet.

He waited, focusing his senses. Every aura coming from the Yrudyen settlement was calm; not one felt distressed or corrupted. He located the auras of the five werewolves guarding the place, and they felt just as calm. There was no scent of blood or ethos in the air, and when he reached beyond the settlement and as close to the mountains as he could, scouring for scent, sound, and aura, Zalith found nothing.

But that wasn't evidence enough that the Orrivain weren't here. They could shroud themselves, after all.

To be sure, he'd send an izuret to check out the mountain. So he summoned one, and the creature appeared in a puff of orange smoke and waved its hand at him.

"Go to—"

A blur of white slammed into him, knocking him clean off his feet. The silence was shattered—vicious snarling erupted, cut through by a shrill, panicked screech. Zalith struck a tree with a grunt but forced himself upright in time to witness the izuret writhing in the blood-slick jaws of a mutilated vargr, its small frame flailing as the beast shook it like a ragdoll.

Blood painted the ground in violent bursts, and rage detonated in Zalith's chest.

The demon launched forward with a snarl, claws unsheathed, instincts igniting like fire. He seized the vargr by its throat and slammed it back; his other hand caught its lower jaw, and with a sickening rip, he tore it from the beast's head. The vargr yelped and dropped the izuret, staggering, but Zalith didn't give it the chance to recover. He drove his claws straight into its chest, his hand punching through twisted muscle and bone, and gripped its heart. He tore it from its body with a furious growl, and then he dropped the lifeless beast.

He hurried to the izuret. It lay in the grass, bloodied, its tiny body torn and mangled. It squeaked and panted painfully, staring up at him as he crouched beside it. His heart ached, and he tried to place his hand over the bleeding gashes, but he knew that there was nothing he could do for it—nothing to *save* it.

"I'm so sorry," he said sadly, using his ethos to take its pain away.

The creature's frantic heartbeat began to slow, its trembling limbs falling still. It stared up at him, wide-eyed with that same unwavering trust that all izurets had...even as life drained from its body. And when its eyes dulled to grey and its chest gave one final, shuddering rise, its aura flickered...and vanished.

Zalith scowled, the sorrow and guilt twisting inside him. He took his hand off the izuret, staring down at it for a moment, and then he slowly raised his glare towards the darkness of the forest. The Orrivain were here. As much as he wanted to summon another izuret to take its comrade home, he wouldn't risk another's life. Instead, he gently moved the lifeless creature into the cover of a bush. He'd come back for it once it was safe.

He stood up, wiping his bloody hands on his trousers, breathing deeply, the anger lingering.

The wolves were nearing. He sensed their auras, he heard their movements, and when he turned to face the sound, he set his eyes on them.

"W-what happened?" Peris asked as the wolves came to a halt.

Zalith pointed at the dead vargr. "This is what you're all looking for. Scour every inch of the surrounding forest, and when you find the wolves already stationed here, tell them to do the same. If you find these things or any Orrivain Elves, subdue them or kill them if you must. I don't want a single one of them getting into this settlement."

The wolves nodded, and then they dispersed, fanning into the woods.

Zalith lingered only a moment longer, his gaze returning to the bush where the izuret's body lay hidden beneath ferns and shadow. Then, jaw tight, he turned back towards the tree line.

He moved quietly, a blur of shadow and silent breath. The forest whispered around him; branches creaked in the wind, frost cracked faintly beneath his boots, and somewhere, a bird called once before falling still. It didn't look like the settlement had been breached, but he needed to be sure. He took a careful step forward, preparing to break from the woods—

But something shifted to his right.

Zalith froze.

Barely a breath passed before he slowly turned his head, narrowing his eyes. A faint glint—glass catching moonlight—flickered through the lattice of branches. He stepped sideways, weaving around a gnarled trunk to get a better angle.

There. Nestled high in the boughs of a thick pine, crouched against the trunk with a spyglass raised to his eye, was an Orrivain Elf. His pale features were half-shadowed beneath his hood, and he was utterly still, watching the Yrudyen settlement like a hawk.

Zalith's eyes darkened. He didn't hesitate.

The demon soundlessly scaled a nearby tree, keeping to the opposite side of the elf's perch. His claws aided his ascent without so much as a scrape of bark, and from his new vantage, he leapt.

The elf didn't have time to gasp.

Zalith collided with him, one arm wrapping around his chest, the other clamping over his mouth to stifle the cry. They dropped from the branch, landing hard in the undergrowth; the impact knocked the wind from the elf's lungs, and before he could recover, Zalith twisted, locking a firm hold around his neck. He tightened his grip, choking the man into a deep sleep—his body went slack a moment later.

The demon exhaled slowly, brushing pine needles from his shoulder. He could've killed the elf. It would've been cleaner, but not smarter. Not if he wanted peace and to prove his offer was more than just words.

He shoved the unconscious body aside and pushed to his feet, sweeping more leaves and dirt from his blazer as his gaze shifted through the trees.

Now he saw what the elf had been watching.

A cloaked Orrivain was dragging a Yrudyen guard behind a hut.

Zalith scowled and slipped into the shadows of the trees. No sound accompanied his steps as he crept forward. His wings and horns appeared when he passed the village threshold, and he folded his wings against his back. When he was close enough, he surged out of the shadows and snatched the cloaked figure by the throat. The Orrivain barely had time to grunt before Zalith slammed him against the hut wall and squeezed. The elf's legs kicked feebly and then stilled as his eyes rolled back. Zalith lowered the limp form gently to the ground, unconscious but alive.

He dropped to one knee beside the fallen Yrudyen. A young woman. Her aura was steady…but she was *dead*. No heartbeat, no pulse—her neck was snapped. So why did she read as living?

He frowned confusedly. Some kind of Orrivain ethos?

The demon looked up, and the settlement unfolded in grim silence. Drag marks scored the dirt, shallow and erratic. A fallen spear lay across a patch of flattened grass, and not far from it, a boot half-buried in the soil. The telltale signs of struggle and capture.

Zalith slipped back into the darkness, moving quickly but silently from cover to cover. He spotted another collapsed body beside a stack of chopped wood behind one of the larger huts; the emanating aura insisted that they were alive, so he made his way over.

He knelt by the fallen man. Another Yrudyen guard with bruises around his neck. He'd clearly put up a fight, but he was dead, too.

Before Zalith could attempt to make sense of it, more movement snatched his attention. A muffled noise came from inside the hut beside him, the sound of something being overturned, the sound of someone struggling. He crept to the side, peering in through the cracked window. Another Orrivain stood over a restrained Yrudyen woman, his dagger raised, her wrists bound and mouth gagged as she kicked and squirmed in vain.

He had mere seconds—

Zalith vaulted soundlessly through the open window. The Orrivain spun, eyes wide—but it was too late. The demon was already behind him. One hand clamped over the elf's mouth, the other twisted his head in a brutal jerk. His neck snapped clean, and the elf crumpled like a rag. With a huff, Zalith let the body fall, panting softly through his nose as he turned his eyes to the bound Yrudyen woman, who was terrified but alive. He quickly freed her, telling her, "You're okay now."

She murmured her thanks, trembling, crying.

"How long ago did he get here?" he questioned, pointing at the dead Orrivain.

The woman didn't answer, though. She shook her head, frantically wiping her tears away as she rocked back and forth.

"I need to know how long they've been here," he insisted.

"I-I d-don't know," she wept. "He just…he just came in here—"

"When?"

She whimpered, holding her hands over her face. "I don't know."

Zalith huffed through his nose and focused. Despite the woman's trembling form and the tears streaking down her face, her aura pulsed with perfect equilibrium, no pain or panic.

Why?

Something was off.

Something was *interfering*.

His gaze swept the room and landed on the dead Orrivain. He crouched beside the corpse and searched the pockets; his fingers brushed against something icy, *bitingly* cold, cold enough to make even him shiver. He wrapped his fingers around it and pulled it free.

A crystal? Kite-shaped. Translucent white, rimmed with a thin band of silver etched in runes he didn't recognize. It hummed softly in his palm, vibrating with an odd, low frequency, and as it did, he felt it again…that *same* artificial, veiled aura radiating from the woman beside him.

His eyes narrowed. "What is this?" he asked as he turned the object towards her.

She glanced at it, winced, and quickly turned her head away.

He didn't push. He didn't need a name for it. The thing was clearly designed to mask or falsify aura readings, disrupting his ability to sense who was in danger and who wasn't. That meant he couldn't trust what he felt from *anyone* in the village. He'd have to assume the worst. He'd have to assume they all needed help.

The demon extended a hand, summoning an izuret. "Go to the city. Find Silvannus," he instructed firmly. "Tell him I need ten demons here—now. The village is under attack. They need to quietly sweep the place and take out the Orrivain without risking the Yrudyen."

With a salute, the izuret vanished without a sound.

Zalith stood up, still holding the crystal. Whatever the Orrivain were planning, they were doing it carefully and quietly. But not for much longer. "Is Queen Syllia here?" he asked the woman.

She sniffled, still crying but not as terrified as before. "S-she…she's in the Sacred Tree," she answered.

Zalith nodded. "Stay here and hide. This will all be over soon."

With a nod, she scrambled across the floor and scurried under her bed.

The demon left through the window and took cover in the shadows again. He was certain that Syllia was Calitharion's main target; perhaps the Orrivain were taking the rest of the village out to make it easier for their leader to reach the queen, or maybe Calitharion was already with her.

He prowled to the Sacred Tree; the heart of the settlement loomed ahead, its massive roots crawling over the earth like ancient limbs, and its towering trunk glowing faintly with the soft, otherworldly light only the oldest of trees possessed. Zalith kept low, his senses razor-sharp despite knowing that he'd get nothing but calm in every corner of this place. But just as he was about to reach one of the massive roots, he caught the glint of metal past a slanted hut.

Two figures. One standing, blade raised, and the other kneeling.

Zalith recognized the silver-blue hair of the kneeling man.

That was Vaelien.

The demon moved fast, a blur through the dark. He grabbed the Orrivain from behind and slammed him into the wall of the hut with enough force to daze, then struck hard at the base of his skull. The elf crumpled, unconscious before he hit the ground.

Vaelien gasped, clutching his chest. "Y-you!" he exclaimed, sounding more angrily astonished than grateful.

Zalith raised a hand to silence him. "You're lucky I was here," he snarled quietly. "Go and find cover. Wait for my demons to get here."

But Vaelien shook his head, his hair falling across his bruised brow. "My Queen is in danger. I refuse to hide—"

The demon growled irritably. "And if you're killed before you reach her, how does that help her? You're injured. Let my people handle this."

"It's my duty."

"It's your pride," he snapped, voice low but edged with warning—he hadn't liked this guy the first time they crossed paths, and that feeling hadn't changed *at all*. "If you want to protect her, stay alive until reinforcements arrive."

Vaelien hesitated, teeth clenched…but after a glance at his bruised wrists and his snapped bow, he finally nodded. "Fine. But if your people don't come fast, I'm going in whether you like it or not."

"They'll be here," he said, already stepping back into the shadows.

He moved again, reaching the huge root and following it towards the tree's trunk. Even without the Orrivain's strange crystals, Zalith wouldn't be able to hear what was going on inside—the hum of ethos oozing from the tree was far too disorientating. Though he didn't need to hear to know that Syllia was in danger.

The demon narrowed his eyes, recalling the interior layout from the last time he was inside. Just above the eastern curve of the trunk, nestled in a thick cradle of bark, was a natural window-like gap, a small opening that let in pale light during the day. Zalith circled around the back of the Sacred Tree, stepping softly over roots and fallen leaves until he spotted it.

There. The gap was small but large enough to see through.

Zalith made his way up, his claws and carpal talons digging into the gnarled grooves for support—if he used his wings to fly, he'd be heard. The climb was swift and silent, and when he reached the gap, he peered through. Inside, the atmosphere was heavy with ethos and tension. Calitharion stood near the centre of the chamber; like Syllia, he was taller than his subordinates; his jet-black hair fell to his ankles, and he wore a crown of bones and teeth on his head. Beside him, two other Orrivain Elves flanked the room, both armed and watching with grins on their faces.

And in the middle, bound to a chair with glimmering silver rope, sat Queen Syllia.

Her pale face was set in a defiant scowl, her platinum eyes burning with contempt. She wasn't crying, nor was she begging. Zalith could see it clearly—she wasn't afraid.

Calitharion, however, was seething. "You've disgraced the bloodline of Khila and spat on the blessings of Aresphis, you disgusting, whore bitch!" he roared, his voice echoing through the chamber. "Allying with demons and human filth! What madness has poisoned your mind?!"

Syllia lifted her chin. "Khila wished for unity, Tharion. You twist her words into excuses for your cruelty. The longer you force your people to follow the old ways, the quicker your race will die out."

That earned her a vicious backhand. The sound of the slap cracked through the air, and Syllia's head snapped to the side. But she didn't cry out. She turned her glare back on Calitharion, blood trickling from her lip.

Calitharion's voice deepened, trembling with religious fervour, "You will be sacrificed for your betrayal. The gods demand atonement, and I will send them every single one of your weak, pathetic followers." He unsheathed a long, ceremonial dagger from his belt—silver-edged with grooves carved into the blade for channelling blood. He stepped nearer to Syllia, eyes wild with glee. "And I can't tell you how long I've waited for this moment. Your traitorous bloodline ends *here*." He lifted the blade—

Zalith prepared to attack—

A crack of fire erupted outside the tree, followed by shouts and the whoosh of something large toppling into flame. The sacred hum of the tree was broken by the chaos rising beyond its bark.

Zalith recognized that sound—it was demon fire. His reinforcements had arrived.

Calitharion's eyes narrowed as he turned his head towards the door. "What fucking now?" he hissed. He turned to the Orrivain flanking the doorway. "Go. See what's happening, and do not return until it's dealt with."

The two soldiers nodded and swiftly exited.

As soon as the door shut behind them, Zalith disappeared and reappeared behind Calitharion—

But the man swung around and slashed Zalith's arm with his blade before the demon could grab him.

Zalith backed off, the cut burning—but why? He wasn't susceptible to silver. As he snarled at Calitharion, he glanced at the wound. It was sizzling, not healing, bleeding profusely.

Calitharion let out a cold, humourless laugh as he stepped forward, his blade glinting in the firelight. "So, you're the filthy demon leader she's been grovelling to."

He snarled again. "And you'd know about filth, wouldn't you?" he muttered, watching the man as he started circling him, holding onto his knife and waving it about as if it was going to save him. "Hoarding your people up in those mountains, denying them every basic need and simple right of existence, deciding who does and who doesn't get to have children." He scoffed and gestured to Calitharion's crown, saying, "Wearing fucking bones." And then he turned around, facing the man. "Do you want to know how easy it was to get them to turn their backs on you? I asked them *one* question. That was all it took, and they left you behind without a second thought."

The Moonwarden stopped prowling, gritting his teeth, tightening his grip on his blade's hilt—and then he lunged, blade aiming for Zalith.

But the demon dodged to the side and swiftly grabbed Calitharion's arm. When he tried to pull it behind the man's back, though, the elf broke free and swung around, his blade missing Zalith's face by mere inches.

"It's a saevulca!" Syllia shouted, worry in her voice. "He'll kill you, Silas!"

Zalith snarled, watching as Calitharion steadied himself. His wrist was still bleeding and burning; he didn't know what a saevulca was, but Syllia's warning made him think that his wound wasn't going to heal.

"I'm going to kill you in front of this whore," Calitharion growled, pointing his blade towards Syllia. "I'm going to kill *her*... and then I'm going to tear that disgusting city apart!"

Zalith didn't answer. The only reply Calitharion deserved was the one his broken body would deliver to the forest floor.

The Moonwarden lunged again with a furious shout, blade slicing through the air, silver glinting like lightning in a storm. But Zalith was faster. He shifted just enough to let the blade whistle past him, the heat of its cursed edge brushing his cheek, and then he ducked low, surged forward, and slammed his palm into Calitharion's chest. The elf staggered, coughing, yet not down. He spun, slashing wildly—but Zalith caught his wrist.

As soon as they connected, Zalith's claws tightened like a vice. Calitharion bared his teeth, struggling, but the demon shifted behind him, twisting the elf's arm. Slowly, he turned the blade inward.

Calitharion's eyes widened. "Don't—"

Zalith's voice was a whisper against his ear, "How about we deliver *you* to your gods?" And with a final growl, he forced Calitharion's hand, driving the blade into the elf's gut.

The saevulca sank in to the hilt.

Calitharion gasped a wet, choking sound and staggered; his knees buckled, and blood blackened with the blade's curse poured down his robes as the weapon clattered to the ground.

Zalith let Calitharion's body drop and turned to Syllia, her wide, silver eyes shimmering with unspoken gratitude. He crossed the room, untied the ropes, and steadied her as she stood. But before he could say a word, she surged forward, her arms sweeping around his shoulders—then her lips were on his.

He immediately but gently pushed her away and said with a chuckle, "I'm engaged." He wasn't completely shocked; this kind of thing had happened a lot in the past. But he *did* feel bad for leading her on. He knew that she wanted him.

Syllia didn't look disappointed, though. She giggled and said, "She doesn't have to know." She gripped his blazer and tried to pull him closer.

But he carefully gripped her wrist and pulled her hand away. "But *I* will," he said with another small laugh. "I'm sorry." He then said, "Stay here. I'm going to make sure that the rest of the Orrivain have been dealt with."

Instead of backing away, though, she smirked and reached for his crotch—

He swatted her hand away. "What did I just say?" he said, chuckling again but becoming irritated.

She pouted and crossed her arms.

Zalith headed for the door, wiping his mouth as he left the tree. He knew that Alucard would smell her on him, and he knew how his fiancé would react—everything would be heightened because he was in heat. But Zalith would explain what happened; he'd make sure his vampire understood.

When he stepped outside, he was met with the relieving sight of the captured Orrivain all lying in the centre of the village, surrounded by demons and werewolves, and the rest of his reinforcements were tending to the wounded Yrudyen.

Davoren hurried over to him. "The vargrs are dealt with, sir. Most of them fled; we only had to kill six."

"Good. Help with the rest of the injured and guard this place until I say otherwise."

"Got it, boss." He hurried back to join his packmates.

"You," Zalith said, waving over one of the demons—Julius, Nymeris' Beta.

"Sir," the dark-haired man said, swiftly appearing in front of him.

"Take all of these Orrivain to Alucard's fort. He knows the way," he instructed, pointing to Branden, Nymeris' other Beta. "Find the mothers with children back in the Orrivain territory; send someone to collect them. Once you have them all, take them to Idina but stay with them; if they don't want to accept my offer, send them to the fort, too. I'll figure out what to do with them later."

"Yes, sir," Julius said with a nod before going to Branden.

Zalith exhaled deeply and looked down at his wrist. It wasn't bleeding anymore, but the wound was still there. He snarled irritably, pulling his sleeve down to cover it, and then he headed for the woods.

He located the dead izuret, and as he crouched beside its tiny body, guilt washed over him again. Although these little creatures often annoyed him, they meant so much to him. They were the only connection he really had left to his mother—the izurets were *hers*, and she'd loved them with all her heart. He loved them, too, and the fact that one had just died because of him…it made his heart ache.

With a sullen sigh, he summoned another.

The izuret saluted, but the moment it saw its fallen comrade, it squeaked unsurely and floated closer. It nudged the dead creature's arm…and when it didn't respond, the izuret wailed painfully.

"I'm sorry," Zalith told it quietly.

With a despondent chirp, the izuret acknowledged his apology.

"Can you take him to his family, please?"

It nodded, hanging its head.

"They can take all the time they need to grieve."

With another nod, the izuret picked up its lifeless comrade, and then it disappeared.

Zalith sighed deeply, standing up. The guilt still weighed heavily on his shoulders, but there wasn't much else he could do; he'd managed to save its body to send back to its family, and he'd ensured that it didn't die in agony. He just wished that he could have saved it.

He adorned his wings again, and then he took off. Once he'd checked on the city, he was heading straight back to Atheson. The Orrivain problem was pretty much over. He'd figure out what to do with the remaining elves later.

Chapter Twenty-Eight

— ⸱ ✝ ⸱ —

Reclaim

| **Alucard** |

| ***Rhenovaalis, Atheson, Atheson Coven Sanctum*** |

Alucard stirred at the sound of Zalith's muffled voice. His eyes opened to darkness—not the kind that unsettled or disoriented him, but one he knew intimately. He hadn't indulged in the comfort of this darkness for years; it was familiar and embracing, a quiet that dulled the world's edges and let only what he wanted seep through… and this time, it let in Zalith.

"*Where's Alucard?*" came the demon's voice.

The vampire reached up and gripped the handle above him. He pushed the casket lid open, and as the peace and silence faded away, the world quickly raced back into existence—but he didn't care about that. As he sat up, he set his eyes on Zalith, who was making his way over to him.

"Hi," his mate said, smiling. "What are you doing in there?" he then asked with a light chuckle, stopping by the casket.

"I needed some vest—avay vrom all zhe noise… and vrom zhe vrustration," he said, taking Zalith's hand when he offered it to him. "Vhen I'm inside, zhe whole vorld is kind of blocked out."

Zalith nodded in response, and then he gestured down at the floor. "What's that for?"

He glanced down at the thin layer of earth that surrounded the casket and stretched beneath the platform it lay on. "Zhat's soil… vrom Dor-Sanguis," he said quietly. "Ve zon't *need* to 'ave, but… 'elps, keeps us grounded—connected." His fingers brushed Zalith's knuckles. "Is symbolic, mostly… but zhere is ethos in, too; a kind of tezher zhat keeps me and vampires strong, stops us vrom slipping too var avay vhen ve vest too long." He smiled faintly, though it didn't quite reach his eyes. "Besides, vhen you live vorever, sometimes you vant to veel like part of you is still buried somevhere vamiliar— some part of me still vants to vest, you know?"

With another nod, the demon said, "Yeah, I understand that very well."

Alucard then leaned in, intending to kiss him—but he paused. Something was off. No…something was *wrong*. There, faint but undeniable, clinging to Zalith's lips—the scent of someone else. Not just their presence, but the trace of a kiss. It hit him like a silver bullet. A possessive flicker of heat surged through his chest, twisting into a scowl before he could stop it. The feral urge to find and destroy whoever had touched his mate simmered beneath his skin.

But it wasn't just Zalith's lips. The scent of someone else was *all over* his mate.

His scowl thickened as he asked, "Did…somebody touch you?"

"Yes," he replied.

Alucard's instincts intensified.

"But it was out of nowhere. Syllia grabbed me, and I pushed her away and told her that I'm engaged, but she didn't seem to care. She tried to grab my dick, and I left after that."

He huffed irritably. "She's lucky I vasn't zhere."

"She sure is," he agreed

The vampire exhaled slowly, the weight of his jealousy and frustration lifting the moment Zalith's scent enveloped him again. He was here now. That was all that mattered. He leaned in and pressed a kiss to his mate's lips.

Zalith responded with a low hum, his hands finding Alucard's waist as the vampire stepped forward, guiding him away from Tyrus and Danford's view; the couch in the shadowed corner of the room offered enough privacy from them; he didn't care that they were nearby—he just didn't want them watching.

Their mouths met again, each kiss growing more frantic. Alucard clutched Zalith's collar as his body flooded with warmth, the familiar burn of his heat reigniting like a match struck in dry air. Every brush of their lips, every breath they shared only heightened it.

He pushed Zalith back onto the couch, following him down, straddling his lap without hesitation. The vampire's hands roamed up Zalith's chest, his mouth trailing fevered kisses from jaw to throat as the demon hummed in delight, tightening his grip on Alucard's waist, and a low growl escaped the vampire as the need to remind the world— no, to remind *Zalith* of who he belonged to pulsed through every instinct he had.

As he pulled Zalith's blazer off, he leaned into the demon's ear and murmured, "No vone else gets to touch you." He lightly bit his mate's neck, making the demon groan pleasurably. "You belong to *me*."

Zalith hummed contently as he nuzzled Alucard's neck. "I do," he purred.

Alucard smiled in satisfaction, but he wanted more than words. He let his mate kiss his neck while he unbuttoned his shirt—when he pulled it from Zalith's body, though, the scent of blood managed to break through the desire and determination, and his eyes wandered down to the demon's wrist.

"Vhat 'appened?" he asked, gently grasping Zalith's hand and lifting his arm to get a closer look at the unhealed gash.

"What?" the demon mumbled, still nuzzling his neck.

He couldn't help but smile when Zalith kissed along his jawline, but then he turned his head and lifted the demon's arm even closer, ensuring that Zalith could see it. "Your vrist."

"Oh…I don't care," he said with a small laugh and started kissing him again.

Alucard's concern withered with every pass of Zalith's tongue against his own, burned away by the heat building between them like a storm about to break. The scent, the taste—everything was too much and not enough, and the urgency clawing at him refused to be ignored.

Their kisses turned feverish, mouths colliding with growing desperation. Fingers tugged, slipped under fabric, and tore at buttons without care for seams or stitches. Clothes fell to the floor in a trail of surrender until there was nothing left between them but skin and the promise of more.

The vampire broke the kiss with a ragged breath. "Turn avound," he ordered.

Zalith smirked and obeyed, climbing onto the couch and bracing his arms on the backrest, his posture tilting slightly forward beneath the vampire's gaze. Alucard's hands slid over his mate's back, lingering at the curve of his spine, admiring the view he now had all to himself—his demon, laid bare and ready.

He didn't waste time.

As soon as Zalith handed him the lube, something in him snapped, the thinnest thread of restraint giving way to a deeper hunger. His heat pulsed through him like fire in his veins, flooding every nerve, every thought, every breath with desire. He hastily poured lube onto his fingers, not bothering with slow tenderness. He needed to be inside.

He pushed one finger into the demon's ass, then another, scissoring them open roughly as his eyes dragged down Zalith's spine; Zalith's moan sent a shiver through him, like his mate was urging him for more. Alucard's dick throbbed, already slick from his own arousal, and his breath came hard and fast against the demon's skin. He added a third finger, working quickly now, desperation consuming him—and Zalith's pleased hums made it worse.

Zalith shuddered with a content groan beneath him, but Alucard barely registered it. He pulled his fingers free and lined himself up without hesitation, a growl curling in his throat as his hips surged forward. The first push made him moan in relief; it was tight and hot yet still not enough. He grabbed Zalith's hips, fingers digging into his mate's skin as he drove the rest of the way in.

The stretch burned through him like lightning, his body strung taut with the need to move, to fuck, *to claim*. He gave a shallow thrust, then another, the rhythm already building as his instincts roared beneath his skin. His lips brushed Zalith's shoulder, but it wasn't out of affection, it was *possession*. His claws raked along Zalith's sides, anchoring him as his hips snapped forward again, harder this time, chasing the release that his heat demanded.

Zalith moaned roughly, unmistakably pleased.

The sound went straight to Alucard's spine, igniting something wild within him. He thrusted again, rewarded by another breathless moan, then a sharper one when he adjusted his angle and hit that spot that made Zalith jolt against the couch.

Alucard gritted his teeth, a groan upon his exhale as he gripped tighter. He didn't slow down. The feel of Zalith around him was maddening, and the scent of him was everywhere. His heat had made him hypersensitive, everything more intense: the wet drag of friction, the way Zalith's hips rocked back to meet his every thrust.

His hands slid up Zalith's torso, one flattening between his shoulder blades to keep him down, the other bracing his own balance as he began to fuck him aggressively. Each thrust was forceful, driven by pure instinct and the need to satisfy the aching demand clawing through his veins.

Zalith became louder, panting between each moan, the sounds breaking apart when Alucard slammed into him just right. It spurred the vampire on; he adjusted his grip, pinned Zalith's wrists to the cushion, and bore down, his pace punishing, his movements eager and relentless.

Alucard's fangs scraped against his own lip as he snarled softly through the rhythm, the taste of blood mixing with the scent of sex. His hips snapped again, harder, deeper, chasing climax but not yet ready for it, not until he'd wrung every sound and drop of pleasure from his mate's body.

Zalith's voice cracked around a moan—and then Alucard heard it, gasped like a prayer through gritted teeth. "Alucard—" the demon whined.

The sound of his name from Zalith's lips lit a fire behind his ribs, something primal that stole his breath. He growled almost savagely, thrusting with renewed force. His movements turned erratic and wild, the pace no longer measured but desperate.

He could feel Zalith tightening around him, every moan tumbling shamelessly free. Alucard's name came again, slurred between panting gasps, and he drank it in like a man starved, drunk on the sound, the scent, and the way Zalith writhed beneath him.

The pressure in his spine twisted tightly, dragging a snarl from his throat. He buried his dick to the hilt and ground his hips forward, chasing friction, dragging pleasure through his nerves. One hand gripped Zalith's hair, pulling his head back just enough to bare the column of his throat—Alucard didn't bite, he didn't even kiss, he just hovered there, breathing him in, trembling with restraint even as his body betrayed him.

The heat was cresting now, almost blinding.

He fucked eagerly, every movement brutal, and when Zalith moaned his name *again*, shattered and reverent, Alucard broke.

Pleasure slammed through him, his whole body locking as he climaxed, his cum spilling into his mate with a delighted cry. His claws scored across Zalith's hips, his fangs bared in the air, and his vision blurred with the force of it. He stayed buried deep, rocking through the aftershocks, pulse racing, muscles trembling with the overwhelming rush.

But Zalith didn't give him long.

The moment Alucard began to soften, Zalith moved swiftly. He pulled free, his hands guiding Alucard up and then forward, flipping their positions with no warning and no room for protest. Alucard barely had time to brace his arms against the backrest, his breath still ragged when he felt Zalith behind him—larger, hotter, breath gusting across his back like a furnace.

The wet sound of lube followed. Zalith's claws dragged lightly down Alucard's spine as he worked his own dick in hand, coating it, his movements rough with urgency. Then a hand gripped Alucard's hip while the other spread him open.

And then Zalith pressed in.

Alucard whined, his eyes fluttering shut as the demon's thick tip breached him. His body was still aching, still sensitive, and every inch that Zalith pushed inside made him tremble. The stretch burned, not unkindly, but enough to pull a low, shuddering groan from him.

Zalith didn't hesitate. He eased deeper, the slide smooth but insistent, his breath stuttering as he sank into the vampire's heat. Alucard clung to the couch cushion, his claws sinking into the fabric while Zalith seated himself fully inside him, panting like he'd been holding it back for too long.

The switch in power was sudden and overwhelming, his mate fucking him now, claiming him in return, their bodies damp with lube and the desire that pulsed between them like a second heartbeat.

Alucard was given no time to adjust before Zalith pulled back and thrust in again, setting a rhythm of his own—one that promised no gentleness.

Zalith fucked into him with a wild and unrelenting force, each thrust sending a fresh wave of sensation through Alucard's already trembling body. He was still overstimulated in the best way; his own cum was smeared between them, thick and warm, pushed out from Zalith's body with every hard, punishing stroke. And it was *harder* than before, rougher than anything Alucard had given him. It wasn't just craving, it was Zalith proving something, claiming control, driving into him with a dominance that left no room for doubt: *this* was Zalith's pace now. His rhythm. His show of power. And Alucard *loved* it. He loved being taken like this, being shown where the power shifted when Zalith wanted it to. It thrilled something dark and deep inside him; it made him ache in ways that had nothing to do with heat and everything to do with surrender.

And that surrender made what came next hit even harder.

It wasn't just the physical mess, though that was part of it; the wet heat sliding down Zalith's thighs, soaking Alucard's hole with each thrust that pressed it back into him. No, it was the *awareness* of it, knowing that *he'd* done that, that he'd emptied himself into his mate, marked him in a way no scent or scar could rival. And now Zalith was fucking him back with his own cum clinging to his dick, dripping from the demon, spreading more of it with every slam of his hips. It was possessive in a way that made Alucard's pulse thunder. *He* had filled him—and Zalith was giving it back, every thrust a reminder that Alucard had already claimed him, and Zalith was claiming *him* in return.

Zalith's growled words came next, breathless—"Fuck…I can feel your cum dripping out of me."

It undid him.

Alucard groaned loud, his hips jerking involuntarily, his body tightening around the thickness inside him as that image took hold in his mind—Zalith stretched open, full of his cum, still wet from it, and now rutting into him with the evidence of it slicking every inch of skin they touched. It made Alucard's head spin. A claiming, and a return, a loop of need and fulfilment, sealed with heat and cum.

He could feel it still leaking, wet between his thighs, dripping lazily from where their bodies met. The sensation was enthralling and gorgeous, making his already-sensitive body twitch with every shift. Zalith's dick moved through the mess with relentless force, spreading it deeper, dragging every thrust through the heat that Alucard had left inside him. It made the stretch more intense, the friction wetter, as if he were being fucked open all over again—bred again without pause, without mercy.

And he *loved* it.

It fed something buried deep in his bones, something starved. His body ached to be filled like this, used like this, and Zalith—still hard, still fucking into him with a rhythm that hadn't faltered—seemed just as hungry, as if Alucard's cum inside him only made him *need* more.

And Alucard wanted to take it. *All* of it.

Zalith's pace changed, subtle at first, but Alucard felt it. The way his thrusts grew rougher and less measured, the way his breathing and moans stuttered against the back of his neck, teeth gritted, growls slipping free from his throat without restraint. The tension building behind every movement was unmistakable. He was close.

Alucard's body responded before his mind could catch up. He shifted beneath him, spreading his legs wider, lowering his chest against the back of the couch, offering himself, taking more, *inviting* it. His spine curved in a perfect line of submission, every part of him ready to be filled.

Zalith snarled, the sound frayed, and then he drove into him one final time—deep and hard and desperate.

And then he came, whining loudly.

Alucard felt it immediately—the first hot pulse spilling deep, followed by another, and another, and another, thick and *endless*. He cried out in sheer delight, his heart racing. Zalith's hips twitched against him, grinding forward through the waves of it, his entire body pressed flush to Alucard's back as he emptied himself with a strained, half-broken moan. His claws gripped Alucard's waist, holding him still as if afraid he'd slip away before it was done.

The vampire whined, tightening around the sensation, around the way Zalith filled him so completely that it almost hurt. He shuddered through it, eyes closing as the pressure built and overflowed, their combined release starting to leak out even before Zalith had finished.

It was too much.

And still, Alucard held himself open, taking every last drop that his mate gave, panting, humming—and when Zalith nuzzled the back of his neck, they both moaned quietly.

"Sorry," came Tyrus' voice. "Sir—"

Zalith protectively leaned his arm forward to cover Alucard's face from view and snarled quietly—it sent an electrifying jolt of pleasure through Alucard's trembling body, and as he rested his forehead down on the cushion, he couldn't help but groan upon his deep exhale.

"There's someone with a message for Alucard," Tyrus said.

The demon just waved him off dismissively, and the man left.

Zalith leaned in, his breath hot against the back of Alucard's neck as he nuzzled slowly, lazily, like a predator savouring what was his. His lips ghosted over his skin— once, twice—then parted just beside Alucard's ear. "You're mine," he growled, his voice still trembling with afterglow.

A slow, satisfied smile curved across Alucard's lips. He pushed back into him, grinding down onto the still-hard dick buried deep inside him, groaning at the way it throbbed at the motion. "I am," he breathed, submissive and *willing*.

The demon then slowly pulled his dick from Alucard's ass.

Alucard inhaled a sharp breath at the sensation, too much and not enough, the stretch easing only to be replaced by a wet, pleasing slide. As Zalith slipped free, the mess they'd made followed. Hot and thick, a slow pour of cum spilled out of him, both his own and Zalith's, mingled together and leaking freely down the insides of his thighs.

He moaned shakily, his body shivering at the feeling of it. It made him hum, a hum that turned into a whine as the wet heat trailed from him. The ache of being stretched so wide lingered; knowing that he'd been fucked open and filled until he couldn't hold it anymore kept him panting, it kept him struggling to stifle moans, and so did knowing that Zalith had emptied himself deep, that his body was now releasing it in lazy, messy drips, marking the space between them with the aftermath of something carnal.

He fucking *loved* how ruined he felt; he loved that his mate could still see the proof of what they'd done dripping from him, seeping from a body that had welcomed it. Every shift of his hips made more of it spill out, and still he didn't move away, letting it happen, revelling in it, in the warmth and the weight and the utter surrender of it all.

He was claimed. Used. *Marked.*

And he'd never felt more sated.

He stayed where he was, panting, shaking, trying to calm himself, his chest still pressed to the back of the couch, legs spread, body open and leaking. His overstimulated muscles twitched, every slow drip that slid down his thighs making him shiver with delight.

Zalith's clawed thumb then dragged slowly around the vampire's used hole, smearing the slick mess with a pleasing sort of reverence. Alucard moaned meekly, his hips jerking slightly at the contact, the stimulation exquisite and sinful.

"Look at you," Zalith purred. "So full. So fucking *good* for me."

The praise made Alucard moan a compliant noise, his head dropping further against the cushions. He *loved* when Zalith talked like that, when his voice curled around those words like a promise, like a reward. And then Zalith gradually pushed the tip of one finger back inside him, slipping easily past the loosened ring of muscle. The pressure made more of their cum spill out around it, warm and wet, forcing Alucard to moan again—half from pleasure, half from the sheer *humiliation* of how much he enjoyed it.

Zalith curled his finger slightly, watching the way Alucard clenched around it, as if his body didn't want to let him go. "Do you want me to fuck you again?" he whispered.

Alucard bit down on a groan, his body trembling under the weight of those words, that finger, the slow drag of pleasure starting to spark again through his nerves. He didn't need to speak. His body said *yes* with every flutter, every arch, every shiver beneath Zalith's hand.

He pushed back, a slow roll of his hips, guiding Zalith's finger deeper, inviting it, *needing* it. The reaction earned him a low growl from his mate, sending a fresh jolt of heat up his spine. He didn't have to look to know that Zalith was watching him, drinking in the sight of him still open and dripping, craving more.

Another finger slid in beside the first.

And then a third.

Alucard whined, his hands tightening against the couch cushions as the strain returned, not as sharp as before, but just as pleasing. His hole fluttered around the intrusion, greedy and wet, the mess of their cum making the slide effortless. He could feel it leak out around Zalith's fingers with every motion, and it only made him push back harder, wanting all of it again.

He couldn't get enough of this. The way Zalith filled him, even now. The way his fingers curled just so, working him open with slow thrusts that made his thighs tremble, not gentle but indulgent and possessive, erotic in a way that made Alucard feel dizzy and grounded all at once. He again clenched around those fingers, his whole body responding, hips rolling to meet each thrust. The sound of it filled the room, louder now, wetter with every curl and drag of Zalith's fingers inside him. His hole ached from the overstimulation, and still it *welcomed* it—he welcomed *him*.

"*Mine*," Zalith said.

Alucard couldn't stifle the whine of agreement that immediately followed, and he felt it in every stroke, every messy slide of their cum spilling down his thighs, every shiver that ran through his core as Zalith drove his fingers deeper.

He was already used. Already claimed.

And he was going to cum again.

Zalith didn't stop.

His fingers kept working in and out, thrusting deep, curling to graze the spot that made Alucard wince every time. The vampire's heart raced frantically, his thighs trembled, muscles taut, every nerve lit up with an edge of overstimulation that blurred the line between too much and *not enough*.

He gritted his teeth, forehead pressed to the couch as his hips rocked helplessly into each push, chasing the friction and the pressure and the way Zalith's fingers filled him so perfectly. He was burning again—lower this time, tighter, the sensation winding through his body. Every thrust dragged it closer until his body was shaking almost violently.

And then Zalith pressed his palm down against Alucard's lower back, holding him there, open and pinned while his fingers drove deeper, faster, relentless now.

Alucard cried out.

His back arched, his whole body locking as the orgasm hit, abrupt and intense, wrung out of him with no mercy. He came *hard*, untouched, spilling across the couch in thick, pulsing ropes as his body clamped around Zalith's fingers. The pleasure tore through him, overbearing, too much. He moaned through it, trembling, gasping for breath as everything inside him gave way.

Zalith didn't pull back right away. He kept his fingers deep, letting Alucard ride it out, feeling the way he twitched around him.

And Alucard let him…because there was nothing he wanted more than to be taken apart like this.

But when the pleasure began fading, he slumped forward, chest heaving, every limb loose and shivering. His skin was flushed, sticky, glowing with the heat of exertion, release, and pheromones. His hole still fluttered weakly around Zalith's fingers, oversensitive, aching, but finally, *finally* beginning to settle.

He only realized that the demon had withdrawn when he felt his warm hands on him, guiding him to move. Zalith turned him gently, coaxing him back onto the couch where the evidence of their pleasure had already soaked the cushions. Alucard let himself be lowered, his spine hitting the ruined fabric, his legs spread lazily, and his mind fogged with the weight of exhaustion and the lingering burn of his heat. Before he could settle fully, though, Zalith climbed into his lap and straddled him.

Their bodies slid together.

Zalith didn't speak. He leaned in and kissed him, their tongues sliding, teeth grazing. It felt claiming—*reclaiming*. Their mouths moved together in something hot and heavy, slow but spiralling quickly into more as Zalith rolled his hips over Alucard's spent dick, grinding against him, stirring sparks from the embers that hadn't quite cooled.

Alucard moaned softly into the kiss. His body answered the way it always did now—instinct tightening its grip on him, urging him to go again, to *take* again. Even with the trembling in his limbs and the dull ache in his thighs, he could feel himself hardening, rising to the friction and the taste of Zalith's mouth, the scent of sex still thick between them.

He wanted to keep going. Fuck, he *needed* to.

But somewhere beneath the heat, buried deep under the fog of hormones and overstimulation, a single thought managed to slip through the cracks.

There was a message. Someone had come by earlier and said they needed to speak with him. Now, in the quiet between peaks of pleasure, that memory resurfaced just enough to pull at him. He should really get up. He should find out what it was….

Zalith shifted in his lap again, grinding down harder, mouth trailing to his neck.

Alucard's head tipped back with a groan.

…But not yet.

Just a little longer.

Their mouths stayed locked, breaths mingling between each kiss. Zalith moved slowly over him, lazily, like he had no intention of going anywhere. One hand slid between them, fingers wrapping around Alucard's dick—half-hard, twitching with renewed interest, coaxed by touch and heat and everything they'd already shared.

Alucard moaned into the kiss, his hips giving a weak thrust upward. The pleasure sparked; he could *feel* it building again, a slow thrum just beneath the skin.

But so was the fatigue.

His body was heavy, his muscles liquid, his thighs still trembling from the last orgasm. His dick responded, but the rest of him lagged behind, every movement slowed by the weight of exhaustion. Zalith's touch was good—*too* good—but the pleasure no longer outpaced the ache in his bones.

Still, he kissed him. He kissed him because he *wanted* to, because every brush of Zalith's lips continued stirring something deeper. But after a minute, Alucard let the kiss break, panting softly, forehead resting against Zalith's.

"Vait," he murmured, his voice hoarse and thick with wear. "I need a minute."

Zalith stopped but smirked. He didn't pull away. His hand left Alucard's shaft with a final, gentle squeeze, but he stayed right where he was, thighs bracketing Alucard's hips. Instead of teasing further, he dipped his head and began to affectionately nuzzle along Alucard's neck; the soft drag of his lips over exhaustion-damp skin, the occasional flick of his tongue or brush of his fangs—it soothed rather than stirred.

Alucard exhaled and closed his eyes, his hands settling on Zalith's hips.

Just a moment to breathe. To *rest*. He let the weight of Zalith on him be enough.

"I think you need a new couch," Zalith then said amusedly.

Alucard smiled through an exhausted huff. "I vink so, too."

Zalith dragged his tongue up the vampire's neck and groaned in delight before nuzzling the side of his face. He licked his jawline, his throat, his shoulder—he devoured Alucard like a starved beast, humming and moaning with each taste.

The vampire exhaled again, tilting his head back, giving his mate more skin to indulge. As much as he wanted to stay there, though, there was still work to be done. "Ve should…probably shower," he mumbled.

His mate responded with a pleased hum, licking his neck again. "I'm not done yet."

Alucard smiled, and a content sigh left him as the demon licked his throat again. He'd let Zalith do as he pleased just a little while longer. Just a few more licks, just a few more kisses…and then it would be time to leave their solitude and return to the world outside.

Chapter Twenty-Nine

Ache

Water cascaded over Alucard, washing away everything but the fatigue. Zalith still clung to him, nuzzling his neck while he carefully massaged shampoo into the vampire's hair. Alucard didn't mind it at all—he could become lost in his mate's affection, and he was letting it devour him.

But the smell of blood pulled him from the serenity. He opened his eyes and looked down at Zalith's wrist. That wound was still there; he was still bleeding—the water had opened the cut.

"You're still bleeding, Zaliv," he said worriedly.

He moved his head just enough to look down, too. "Oh…yeah."

"Can I see?" Alucard asked.

Zalith nodded and lifted his arm.

Alucard held the demon's wrist and examined the wound. It looked fresh, as if it had just been cut, and there was no sign that it was healing. "Vhat did zhis?"

His mate exhaled deeply as he went back to nuzzling his neck. "Something…I don't know." He groaned quietly. "Uh…say…no, saevulca."

"Saevulca?" he repeated, his worry growing.

"Mm-hmm."

The vampire leaned his head back against the wall, trying to look at Zalith's face. "Zhis could 'ave killed you, you know," he said with a frown. "A saevulca prevents any vound vrom 'ealing—ever."

Zalith pressed his face closer to Alucard's neck as he murmured, "Oh…." He then kissed there, then his cheek, and eventually reached his lips.

Alucard couldn't help but smile, though he kept hold of Zalith's wrist. He kissed him for a few moments before using his free hand to gently push the demon back. "Let me 'eal you," he said firmly. "Or you'll get a scar. I'm sure you zon't vant zhat."

The demon smiled at him, eyes half-lidded and hazy with affection. He looked *entranced*. "Thank you," he murmured, his voice tinged with reverence, before lowering his head again to resume nuzzling at Alucard's neck slowly, savouring every inch of exposed skin.

Alucard loosened his grip on Zalith's wrist, but only to trade one hold for another. His hand slid up, curling around the demon's jaw, fingers firm as he tilted Zalith's face upward. Their eyes met for a moment…then Alucard gently pried his mate's mouth open with the pad of his thumb. His other hand twisted into Zalith's hair and tugged, just enough to bring him close again, lips brushing against his neck where his pulse beat slow and steady beneath the skin. "Bite," he told him.

Zalith did as he was told. He bit down softly at first, but when Alucard moaned pleasurably, and the demon groaned in response to his pouring blood, he sank his fangs in deeper, drinking desperately, humming in satisfaction. He grasped Alucard's shampoo-covered hair, pulling as he pressed his body against his, still downing his blood with greedy, moan-filled gulps.

Alucard winced delightedly, Zalith's venom spreading through his veins, ensnaring him. But at the rate his mate was drinking him, he'd be out cold in a matter of minutes. So he gently grasped the demon's jaw and pulled him away, a pleased moan escaping him when the demon's fangs slipped from his neck.

"Every part of you tastes so good," Zalith said, his lips bloody, crimson trickling down his chin—his dazed expression was thicker, the blood high taking over. He pressed his face against Alucard's cheek, groaning again, now grinding his crotch against Alucard's thigh.

The vampire smiled, but his eyes were on Zalith's wrist. He watched the wound heal, and once it was gone, he dragged his fingers down the demon's back. "Tell me vhat 'appened vith zhe elves."

Zalith grunted, his face returning to Alucard's neck. He licked the wounds his fangs had left, and then he stroked his face around to the other side. "I killed Calitharion," he murmured. "The rest of the elves…I sent them to your fort, but I sent the mothers and children to Idina. We'll deal with them later."

"Good," he said—his answer gave him some relief. At least the elf business was over with. All that was left now was what he'd come to Atheson to do. "I vink I'm going to make Noctrel zhe Coven Master 'ere."

The demon didn't reply—not immediately. After a few kisses to Alucard's neck, he murmured, "Who?"

Amused, Alucard rested his head against Zalith's. "Zon't vorry."

Zalith hummed and mumbled, "Just…let me take you."

He wanted to give in. As Zalith's hands roamed his body, he tensed up, tilting his head, giving the demon more room to indulge. His mate started sucking his neck, and Alucard melted beneath the touch, his head tipping to the side, water streaming over his skin. The hot spray from the shower soaked them both, washing the mess away, but it did nothing to cool the heat between them. Zalith's mouth was relentless—lips and tongue dragging along Alucard's neck, sucking at the sensitive place just beneath his jaw, fangs grazing without biting.

Then Zalith's hand moved. It slid down between their soaked bodies, possessively wrapping around Alucard's dick.

Alucard tensed and grunted as pleasure crashed through him like a thunderclap—no build-up, no warning. His dick twitched once in Zalith's fist, and he came *immediately*, intensely, his whole body locking as he spilled between them. Hot ropes of cum splattered against his belly and thigh before the water could carry it away; his knees nearly gave way, his hand flying to grip Zalith's shoulder for support as a hoarse moan ripped from his throat.

It should've ended there.

But it didn't.

Zalith didn't stop. His hand kept moving with slow, steady strokes that coaxed sparks from nerves that should've been spent. His mouth stayed at Alucard's neck, tongue flicking over the wet skin, sucking marks into his pale throat, lips dragging over every sensitive spot he could find.

The afterglow wasn't fading, though. It *twisted*, getting tighter, stoked by whatever power Zalith was channelling into his touch. Heat pulsed low in Alucard's body again. His shaft, still trembling from the last orgasm, hardened again almost instantly.

What was he *doing* to him?

Alucard's moan was soft and shaky, his body already shivering under the hot spray. Pleasure started rising again, faster than before, overwhelming. He couldn't catch his breath, he couldn't think. All he could feel was Zalith's hand stroking him, mouth dragging fire down his throat, and the unbearable pressure mounting.

Then he came *again*.

It was weaker this time—less fluid, less force—but no less intense. His back hit the slick tiles with a dull sound as he cried out, water rushing down his chest, cum spilling in pale threads over Zalith's fingers before the stream rinsed it away.

But Zalith kept going.

He stroked him through it, into it, *past* it, drawing out sensation until it blurred into something too sharp to name. Alucard gasped, thighs trembling, dick twitching with oversensitive pulses as the strokes continued. His balls ached, his whole body gone tight and hot and overstimulated, and still, *still* Zalith was coaxing pleasure from him like his body didn't know how to say no.

Alucard felt it again—the pressure building, his dick hardening even as it hurt, desire still spiralling inside him with nowhere to go. He didn't even know if he *could* cum, but he felt the surge start, his muscles contracting, pleasure rolling in thick, unbearable waves.

It was too much.

He sobbed out a breath, his moans collapsing into broken noise, his hands slipping uselessly against Zalith's chest as he came a third time, thin, watery spurts that barely left his body before the water washed them away. His shaft throbbed but barely twitched now, his strength draining fast.

"Z-Zaliv—" he choked, voice wrecked, "I can't...."

But he didn't push him away. He didn't mean it. Even as the exhaustion dragged at him, he leaned into the demon's touch, trembling and ravaged under the hot spray, aching for more even as his body screamed for rest.

He looked down for a moment, and he saw the almost-gold vein-like glows on Zalith's hands, spidering up his wrists—they were spreading from his crotch, too, pulsing as he ground his dick against Alucard's leg. He'd only seen them once, and Zalith had been in his demon form. Was he losing his control? Was he letting his incubus nature break through the walls he kept it behind?

Alucard tilted his head back with a choked moan, the painful pleasure writhing through him, stealing the breath from his lungs. He *loved* it—the pressure, the heat that wasn't just physical but *dangerous*. Zalith was letting go—just a little, but exactly enough to let Alucard taste the power that he usually kept buried.

The thought that his mate—so strong, so carefully restrained—was beginning to unravel because of him made Alucard tremble. He wanted that...to feel the weight of everything Zalith held back, to be trusted with it, *marked* by it. He craved the moment instinct would take over, and that deep, starved thing inside Zalith would stop being polite about wanting him.

He wanted to be the reason the demon lost control.

Zalith hadn't stopped. He said nothing, he just kissed lower, his mouth dragging along Alucard's throat to his collarbone, tongue swirling against water-slick skin while his hand kept working Alucard's dick. There was no space to recover, no reprieve, only the steady pressure, the constant touch, Zalith's palm wet with rinsewater and leftover desire, dragging Alucard's body into a cycle that it no longer had the strength to resist.

Another orgasm rose—hazy and desperate, even less cum now, just pulsing contractions that wracked his body and made his knees bend. The vampire groaned, the sound cracked and half-choked, the side of his face pressing against the cool tile as the release hit.

The demon dragged on.

Alucard whimpered, pleased but exhausted.

It was *too much*. His shaft twitched in Zalith's grip, hypersensitive and aching, his thighs shaking beneath him. His muscles burned from holding himself up, and the sharp flicks of pleasure were becoming unbearable—sparks across tender nerves that no longer knew the difference between bliss and pain.

Still, Zalith *wouldn't stop*.

His pace remained slow, torturous, each pass of his hand drawing a fresh, helpless twitch from Alucard's abused dick. The vampire gasped, shoulders trembling violently, fingers scrabbling at the wall to keep upright. The tile beneath his claws cracked.

He came again—barely more than a tremble and a sob, no cum left, just spasms that tore through him like a punishment. His hips jerked once, involuntarily, his whole body trying to escape even as another orgasm rolled in before the last had finished fading.

"Please," he whispered despite the part of him that wanted more, the word lost in the spray. His claws *dug* into the tile, panting, twitching, his body wet and flushed and coming apart in Zalith's hand.

Zalith only responded with pleased hums, clearly drinking it all in, *feasting*.

Alucard moaned weakly at the idea—Zalith was feeding off him, and he wanted to keep giving...but could he? The ache in his dick was a constant throb now, tender and hot, pulsing between half-hardened and flaccid with no time to recover. And still the pressure built. His whole body tried to flinch away from the touch, but he couldn't—not completely. Every time Zalith dragged his palm up his shaft, Alucard moaned *again*, a sharp, stuttering sound that collapsed into a near-whimper.

His claws left long gouges in the wall.

Another orgasm crashed through him, full-body and violent, even though there was nothing left to give. His voice broke on the moan that followed, sounding almost like a plea. Overwhelmed. Stripped down to pure sensation.

He was fidgeting now, twitching forward, then away, caught in the space between craving and overload, nerves short-circuiting with every touch.

He couldn't take it.

He couldn't take *another*.

The vampire managed to raise a hand—he grasped Zalith's wrist as he panted, "Stop." He winced as the demon let go of his shaft. "I can't...again."

"Sorry," Zalith said with a quiet laugh, pressing his face against Alucard's cheek. "You just taste so fucking good." He licked his neck before asking, "Are you okay?"

Alucard didn't answer right away. He was shaking—subtly, uncontrollably. His thighs felt like they'd been hollowed out, nothing but water and fire left in their place. Every breath stuttered through him as if his lungs had forgotten how to pull in air without trembling. His dick twitched weakly, aching and red, too sensitive to even brush against Zalith's skin without flinching.

He didn't feel like he'd *just* climaxed, he felt like he'd been milked dry.

His balls throbbed faintly from the inside, empty and sore, and there was a persistent dull cramp in his lower abdomen, like his body had tried to produce more than it physically could. Even the tightness in his core felt like it had been stretched beyond reason, clenching involuntarily with each aftershock.

Cum no longer dripped from him. There was nothing left but the memory of release, the throbbing ache of his hole, and the constant echo of orgasm still rippling through his body like a fading earthquake. His muscles twitched with fatigue, small, involuntary spasms in his thighs, his stomach, even his fingers. He sagged against the wall, soaked in exhaustion and water, drained of everything but the soft, slow thump of his heart and the warmth of Zalith still pressed close.

"I...I'm vine," he murmured, his voice barely more than a whisper. "Just...tired."

Zalith laughed quietly again, but Alucard heard it—the victory in that laugh.

The vampire groaned. His limbs wouldn't stop trembling. His claws stayed in the wall because pulling them free took more strength than he currently had. He let his head roll to the side to meet Zalith's shoulder, eyes half-lidded and glazed. Heat still pulsed faintly through his blood, but it was distant now, muted under the weight of being *so completely spent*.

His mate nuzzled him gently, no teasing now, just slow affection.

Alucard leaned into it, unable to do much else. He didn't think he could walk...but he didn't even care.

"Sorry," Zalith whispered again and kissed his neck. "I got carried away."

He couldn't muster a smile this time, or an answer. All Alucard could do was breathe...and tremble.

"I'll take care of you, baby," the demon promised and started washing the shampoo from Alucard's hair.

The warmth of the water poured over him in heavy waves, and Zalith's fingers threaded through his scalp, gradual and steady. It should've been grounding, but Alucard's awareness drifted, distant as if he were floating inside his own skin. He blinked once, slowly, and the world tilted. And then it steadied. He wasn't sure how much time passed between that blink and the next.

Zalith kept moving, his gentle hands guiding him under the water, tilting his head, rinsing the last of the shampoo, blood, and cum away. Alucard slouched forward with the motion, forehead brushing Zalith's chest as his balance swayed. His knees felt loose. His spine was only upright because the demon's arms were there.

Another blink.

Zalith was speaking—something quiet, soft, meant only for him—but the words came through muffled. He tried to nod and wasn't sure if he succeeded.

By the time the water shut off, Alucard's body was humming with a low ache from scalp to heel. His legs barely held him up.

"I've got you," Zalith said, his voice closer now.

One arm looped around Alucard's waist, the other steadying his chest. He let himself be turned, guided, and *lifted*. He wasn't even sure his feet touched the floor as the demon led him out of the shower. His skin was flushed, water-slick, and shivering despite the heat. His dick throbbed faintly with dull ache, his thighs ached from strain, and his core still spasmed now and then with the memory of orgasm. There was nothing left to give.

He sagged into Zalith's arms as the towel wrapped around him, heavy and soft and still somehow *too much*. Everything felt too much, but his mate didn't let go. He helped him dry off, and then he eased the robe around him before leading him out of the bathroom.

"Get out," Zalith called.

Alucard lifted his head to see Tyrus and Danford leaving the lounge-like part of the room. Zalith then guided him to the couch—the *clean* couch—and sat down with him.

The moment Alucard's weight sank into the cushions, a soft, involuntary noise escaped him. His body felt like it was burning. His thighs protested the bend, his overstretched core throbbed with a dull, echoing soreness, and the raw sensitivity between his legs flared all over again from the shift in position. Even the softness of the cushions felt like too much.

He winced slightly as his hips settled, every muscle trembling in quiet rebellion. The hollowness pulsed deep in his body where Zalith had been, and he was too tender to want anything more—but he felt *everything*. The wet stretch, the soreness, the ghost of fingers and thick inches and thrusts and the endless spill of cum that had wrung him out until nothing was left.

It was overwhelming in every way. He loved it. He craved it.

But he also craved…*this*.

Now, after it all, he felt safe. Zalith stayed against him, anchoring him even as his body trembled and throbbed in the aftermath of being thoroughly used and gently cared for.

"I love you," Zalith said as he rested his head on the vampire's shoulder.

Alucard smiled. "I love you," he murmured tiredly.

The demon started nuzzling his neck again, but at the same time, he caressed the vampire's hair. "You should get some sleep. It's past bedtime back home."

He was right. When was the last time he *had* gotten some actual sleep? He closed his eyes, trying to sink into the relief of Zalith's embrace. The ache of his body slowly faded away, and the fatigue grew heavier and heavier and—

Someone knocked on the door.

Alucard snarled irritably as he opened his eyes and glared at it. "Vhat?!" he called.

The door opened, and a small vampire stepped in. Her black hair had dyed streaks of red, and her lips were painted a deep purple. "My Lord," she said humbly but sounded a little rushed. "The werewolf Luna has gone into labour. Bloodmender Thessaly asked me to inform you."

That was who she was—it took Alucard a moment to see through the haze of fatigue. Votary Elspethia, Thessaly's student. *She* was learning to become a Bloodmender.

"Are zhe Vledgelings and younger Acolytes vesting?" he asked her.

"Yes, My Lord."

"Make sure zhere are guards on zhe doors; I zon't vant somevone vandering in zhere and getting torn apart by territorial verevolves."

She nodded and once again said, "Yes, My Lord." She didn't leave.

"Vhat?" Alucard grumbled.

"Liora asked me to tell you that the demons found nothing in the city, My Lord."

He sighed deeply. That *had* to mean that the Silver Claw was underground, then. "Vight. *Multumesc.*"

With a bow, Elspethia left the room.

Alucard huffed and rested his head on Zalith's.

"Yes, My Lord," Zalith mocked amusedly and kissed his neck. "Anything for you, My Lord."

He rolled his eyes, smiling a little. "Stop."

"So sorry, My Lord," he teased.

Alucard huffed and closed his eyes. "I should Dignivy Noctrel," he muttered.

"Right now?"

"Zhe sooner zhe better." He exhaled deeply, sinking back into the comfort of his mate. "I need to tell Lysandra zhat she can't leave zhis coven yet, too."

"Why can't she leave?"

"I vound out zhat Eyra vas turning people be'ind my back. Lilly, vone of zhe surviving Vledgelings, is safe in Antamont, but zhe abandoned crypt she's staying in vith anozzer Strayblood von't be a sanctuary vorever."

"Why was she turning people behind your back?"

He shifted around uncomfortably. "Corven-'ale explained; she vas pretty much doing vhat Zamien did to me—I zon't…vant to get into zhat, zhough."

Zalith caressed his hair affectionately. "You don't have to, it's okay."

With a quiet sigh, he turned his head and nuzzled the demon's hair, taking in his grounding scent. "Camilla is missing, Dorovhee starved 'erselv, and 'anna is dead, too—she valked into zhe sun." He huffed again. "Zhey veren't given zhe proper lessons, and Lysandra lost 'er brood sisters. Vledgelings 'eavily vely on zheir brood kin in zhe virst vew months, so she never learned 'ow to vunction vithout virst learning to become independent. I'm going to 'ave to 'ave 'er go vhrough zhe Vledgeling process all over again. But I suppose zhat could be a good ving," he said, thinking aloud. "She vants to turn 'er vife, so she could be turned at zhe same time; zhey could learn togezzer."

The demon smiled against his neck. "Look at you…the thoughtful Lord Vampire."

Alucard scoffed a laugh. "I care about all of my vampires."

"I know you do, and I love that about you, baby." He kissed his neck again. "You're going to be such a dad, you know."

His smile grew. He feared he'd be a terrible parent, and although he was still anxious, hearing Zalith say that *did* encourage him a little. "So vill you," he replied.

"Hmm…maybe," he murmured, pressing his face against his neck as much as he possibly could. "You're going to make a really amazing husband, too," he told him with that flirty, seductive tone. "You give me everything I need, and everything I *want*."

Flustered, Alucard hid his face. "I veally can't vait to be your 'usband, and vor you to be mine."

Zalith playfully nipped his neck, making him flinch. "I just hope you're ready for what I'm going to do to you the second we get away from that altar."

He felt his face turn redder, and excitement flickered through him, too. "I'll be veady," he murmured.

"You might regret saying that," he said amusedly.

"I von't."

The demon laughed a little. "We'll see."

He pouted in response, but he let the silence fall around them. It was calming.

Zalith then asked, "What about the missing vampire? Are you going to send people to look for her?"

He thought about it. "I'd like to, but I zon't 'ave zhe people to spare vight now. Maybe vonce ve've dealt vith zhe Silver Claw."

"Understandable," he said before softly dragging his tongue over Alucard's skin. "Do you want more blood?"

Blood would probably alleviate some of the fatigue, but what Zalith had taken from him needed to remain in the his system to ensure that the saevulca wound healed entirely and remained that way. "Later," he said with a nod.

"Are you sure?"

"Mm-hmm." He kissed what he could reach of Zalith's head. "Vank you."

Zalith responded with a hum.

Alucard glanced around the room. He wanted to rest…and he wanted to Dignify Noctrel, but he didn't want to get up yet. So he reached over Zalith and grabbed the maps and his notebook. He'd finished planning routes and teams; all that was left to do now was send them down there. However, it was dawn, which meant he couldn't send a little under half of his vampires out now—they weren't all Day Walkers, after all.

Maybe some rest wouldn't be such a bad thing. However, he didn't have a bed here. This Coven Sanctum was *old*; the last time he'd spent more than half a day here was over a century ago, when he slept in his caskets much more often than a bed. Of course, there was always the couch…but it wasn't exactly *big*.

He glanced around the room for a moment. Going home wasn't an option, nor was staying in an inn in the city. There was only one option, really.

"Zaliv?" he asked quietly.

His mate didn't reply.

Alucard laughed a little and nudged his mate. "Zaliv."

"Huh?" the demon replied. "Oh…what?"

"Do you vant to sleep vith me?"

Zalith grinned against his neck. "Ready to go again?"

He laughed once more. "No, not like zhat. *Sleep*. Vest."

The demon hummed as if he were thinking. "Sure," he answered.

"I zon't 'ave a bed 'ere, zhough. Vill 'ave to be in my casket."

Zalith hummed again, sounding suggestive. "Us, together, in a cramped, dark space? I don't know, darling…things might escalate beyond sleep."

His smile grew. "Sleep virst," he said firmly.

After a hushed chuckle, Zalith said, "Okay."

Alucard took his hand, but the moment he shifted to rise, a deep, lingering ache flared through his body. His legs trembled beneath him, muscles protesting with sharp, spent twitches; his thighs burned faintly, and his lower abdomen clenched with that same low, hollow soreness that came from too many orgasms too close together. Even the simple motion of standing made his overstimulated dick throb with overbearing sensitivity, a dull pulse that reminded him of every time Zalith had pushed him over the edge.

He winced and let Zalith's hand steady him, because *walking* suddenly felt like a challenge. Or maybe a mistake.

Zalith laughed in satisfaction as he helped him stand. "It looks like you really *could* use some sleep." He scooped him up in his arms and carried him into the other section of the room.

Alucard huffed, embarrassed and flustered. "Vhatever," he muttered.

The demon smirked as he took him to his casket, and then he gently placed him inside before climbing in and lying beside him. "Should I close the lid?"

"Only if you're okay vith zhat. You von't be able to sense zhe vorld outside at all— vell…I zon't know about zhat, actually. I zon't know if ozzer zemons vork zhe vay I do."

"Well, I suppose we'll find out," Zalith said as he reached up for the handle, and then he pulled the lid shut.

Alucard exhaled deeply as he slowly turned onto his side and rested his head on Zalith's chest. He felt the demon wrap his arms around him and nuzzle his hair, and then he closed his eyes, letting himself relax.

"When will we know it's time to wake up?" his mate asked curiously.

"I 'ave zhis sort of…body clock," he said as Zalith's captivating, *calming* scent wrapped around him, pulling him deeper into repose. "Vill know vhen to vake me up."

Zalith kissed his head. "Okay. Get some rest, baby."

After a deep exhale, Alucard surrendered entirely, hoping that once he woke, his body would have healed.

Chapter Thirty

— ⟨ ✝ ⟩ —

Demons and Vampires

| **Alucard** |

| *Atheson, Atheson Coven Sanctum* |

Alucard woke with a sharp breath.

"What is it?" Zalith immediately asked.

Nothing. It was nothing. Just…*calming* nothing. Embracing darkness.

"Noving," he replied contently, closing his eyes again.

Zalith caressed his hair with one hand and stroked his back with the other. "Is it time to get up?" he asked curiously.

It *was*. That was why he woke so suddenly. "Yes," he said with a deep sigh.

"What if we open the lid and the house is on fire?"

Alucard pouted—he knew that he was joking, but…. He reached up and pushed the lid open a mere inch, letting the outside world ooze in for a moment. Everything was fine, though. No panic, no noise at all other than the light chatter of waking vampires. And it was raining. Storming.

He closed the lid and nuzzled into Zalith's chest. The cushion-lined interior of his casket cradled him with that familiar comfort, its satin embrace tailored perfectly to his frame. The warmth between him and his mate was amplified by the enclosed space, a gentle caress of velvet heat and quiet closeness.

The next thing he became aware of was his body. It was trembling anymore. The ache was gone. When he moved a little, there was no sting, no soreness clinging to muscle or bone. He bent his knee and dragged his left leg up along Zalith's body, a silent reassurance that he was whole again.

Relief was subtle, but it settled deep; an unconscious tension melted from his shoulders as he adjusted his position, his body sliding against warm skin and the soft give of silk. He could feel the steady press of Zalith beside him, wrapped with him in the private, dark haven he had always relied on for rest—and now, for more than that.

"How often did you sleep in caskets before you met me?" Zalith asked curiously.

"Not all zhe time, but a lot," he said, feeling himself dozing off again. He opened his eyes, lifting his head to rest on Zalith's shoulder. "Vas mostly to 'eal—I vecover vaster because my body goes into zhis state of vest," he explained slowly. "Not comatose like vhen I lose too much blood; I can still vake up vhen I vant to. But is almost…like I'm disconnected vrom zhe vorld—in 'ere…is kind of like my own space…or plane of existence. Does zhat make sense?"

He nodded. "Yeah, it does." He kissed his forehead. "It's peaceful."

Alucard smiled, letting himself enjoy their solitude for a while longer.

"Did you finish looking at those maps while I was gone?"

"I did," he answered—but then he frowned. "Tyrus asked me someving veird, zhough."

"What?" Zalith asked, sounding irritated—*possessive.*

Alucard's frown thickened. "'E asked me if I vas transgender."

"…Why?" he questioned.

"I zon't know. 'E said someving about 'ow I'm in 'eat and my scent isn't vully male, and zhat zhere's a trace or someving of vhat 'eat smells like on a voman."

Zalith shrugged lightly. "Well, he's not wrong—but I still don't think he should have asked."

His expression grew more confused with each passing moment. It wasn't just the fact that *two* demons said that his heat scent was abnormal, but also the way he was feeling. Did *all* male demons feel this way when they were in heat? Did they all feel the deep, instinctual desire to be bred? That didn't make sense now that he thought about it. Shouldn't *he* be the one constantly fucking Zalith? Shouldn't *he* be desperate to attempt breeding his mate rather than the other way around?

"Shouldn't…vell…*I'm* zhe vone in 'eat, so shouldn't I be zhe vone who vants to fuck *you* all zhe time?" he asked.

"Maybe it's my fault."

"Vhy? Because you are incubus?"

"Yeah. Not because of what it does to you but because you're in heat, and all I want is to fuck you. So that's what we've been doing…mostly."

He nodded slowly. While *that* made sense, the desire to be bred didn't…unless that was just part of what Zalith explained. It was, after all, an incubus' natural duty to create offspring—well, Alucard assumed so because that was what succubi did.

"Zhat makes sense," he replied, closing his eyes again. "I'm enjoying zhis, zhough. I vas just curious."

The demon stroked his fingers down Alucard's body and circled them around his crotch. "Is this you telling me that you're receptive again?" he laughed.

Alucard pouted. "You're not vunny."

"Yes I am," he teased.

"Vhatever," he grumbled.

Zalith lightly gripped and squeezed his shaft. "Do I need to fuck the grumpy out of you, vampire?" he asked, his tone turning flirtatious.

He exhaled deeply, his mate's touch effortlessly arousing him. As much as he wanted to agree…he knew that he shouldn't—they needed to get up. There was a lot to do now that dusk was upon them. "Not vight now," he said with a sigh, as much as it frustrated him. "Ve need to get up."

The demon didn't let go, though.

He knew what Zalith was going to say. "Vonce zhe Silver Claw is dead, you can fuck me as much as you vant," he told him, slowly prying the demon's hand from his crotch. "Vight now, zhough, ve 'ave a vampire 'unter to deal vith."

Zalith smirked as Alucard pushed himself up. "I really love it when you're bossy," he murmured.

Alucard pouted again and pushed the casket lid open. "Zhen get up and get dressed."

"Yes, My Lord," he teased.

With a huff to hide his amused smile, Alucard got out of the casket, and when Zalith gently slapped his ass as he followed, the vampire let a laugh escape him.

They took their bathrobes off and quickly got dressed. Zalith shot a suggestive glance at the ruined couch, making Alucard's face red with fluster; the demon took his hand and led the way through the room, and the vampire grabbed the maps and his notebook as they passed the surviving couch. The izuret had delivered their new shoes while they were sleeping, so Alucard grabbed those, too.

The Sanctum was buzzing with activity, the noise mounting as Alucard stepped into the communal hall. A loud crack of thunder cut through the calm, but the rumbling soon faded. Every socializing vampire greeted him with humble bows and nods, others raising their blood-filled chalices. Alucard responded with his own nods, and every smile he got in return added to his contentment.

"They all really love you, don't they?" Zalith said with an amused but adoring smile.

Alucard nodded, taking him down the wide, spiralled staircase. "Apart vrom zhe odd Eyra or two," he muttered. "I zon't know vhether zhey do zhese silly vings in an attempt to earn more vavour vrom me or because some part of zheir 'umanness still exists."

"Humanness?" his mate questioned.

"I've crveated a lot of vampires in vour centuries," he began, leading him towards the lounge, where most of the noise came from. "Ninety-nine percent of zhem 'ave turned as zhey should and grown as zhey should, but zhere 'ave been zhe occasional vew who some'ow deviate, like someving vent vrong. Zhey eizer vetain or slowly vedevelop zhe vorst parts of 'umanity: gveed, selvishness, pride, zhat sort of ving. Zhey lose zhe vespect vor who and vhat zhey are, and zhe people avound zhem."

"Very human," Zalith agreed with a grunt.

When Alucard got to the lounge, the lively chatter quickly turned into several groups of 'My Lord' and 'Good evening, My Lord', followed by bows and tilting of heads.

"Vhere is Noctrel?" Alucard asked.

The crowd swiftly turned to look in the same direction.

"Here, My Lord," Noctrel said, rising from the armchair they'd been sitting in and placing their chalice of blood on the coffee table. "Do you need me to return to my shift early? I'd be happy to."

He shook his head, keeping hold of Zalith's hand as he headed over to them. "Eyra is Veiled," he called, ensuring the entire room heard him, and then he stopped in front of the Adherent vampire. "Every coven needs a leader zhey can trust, and a leader powervul enough to ensure zheir savety in my absence. So, I'm Dignivying Noctrel to Coven Master." He glanced around the room.

Everyone bowed their heads in understanding and agreement.

Alucard then set his eyes back on Noctrel. "I know you vill do a much better job zhan Eyra. 'Owever, you must leave Eyra to zhe Council. An Inquisitor vill arrive to judge 'er during zhe veek."

Noctrel bowed their head. "Thank you. I won't let you down, My Lord."

"I know," he said with a nod, and then he turned to the room again. "Make sure zhe entire coven knows."

On his word, three vampires hurried out of the room to spread the news.

"Tell everyvone to gazzer in zhe Noctuary in ten minutes," Alucard ordered.

Three more vampires left the room.

He looked at Noctrel one last time. "You can 'ead up to zhe Eldergloam vhen you're veady. 'Ave Odette clean out Eyra's stuff. She is problem student, and she needs a chance to prove 'erselv. Make 'er your Votary vor now. Let 'er see 'ow zhe coven vunctions."

They nodded and said, "Of course, My Lord."

"Send Drusilda and 'alvarn, too," he added. "I need everyvone vor zhis mission."

With a final bow of their head, Noctrel left the room.

"Are they your commanders?" Zalith asked as Alucard began leading the way again.

"Drusilda is zhe Vice Matron, zhe second-in-command—she vas also an Executor of zhe Sanguinari Vite—and 'alvarn is zhe Night Steward, who is vhird-in-command."

"Sanguinari Rite?"

"Is anozzer division of zhe Nosveratu—a sort of mercenary-type situation. I vill tell you more at anozzer time if you vant."

Zalith nodded and smiled at him and squeezed his hand. "It really is quite impressive how you remember all of this."

"Vell, you vemember zhe names of all your zemons, so is not *zhat* impressive."

"*You* remember all of their ranks and such. I know it's going to take me a while to get used to whatever we come up with once we hand out new titles."

Alucard glanced at him. "So, zhat's someving you devinitely vant to do?"

He nodded. "It'll help classify them all a lot more—what they're capable of, what their specialties are, ectcetera."

"Vell, I can 'elp you, vor sure."

"Thank you, baby," he said and kissed his cheek.

Alucard turned right into the curved corridor beside the stair hall. He stopped by the door to the guest room, where Sentinels Anselric and Edricus were on guard. "Is everyving vine in zhere?" he asked, and then he quietly told Zalith, "Zhis is Anselric and Edricus, Sentinels; zhey guard most of zhe Sanctum."

The twin vampires nodded to his question in unison, their greying hair catching the lantern light and gleaming like silver thread. They were near-identical in every way— eerily so—the only distinction between them the short, neatly trimmed goatee that marked Anselric apart from his brother.

"Elspethia updated us three minutes ago, My Lord," Anselric said.

"The Luna has had triplets," Edricus continued. "Though Thessaly thinks another may be on the way."

Alucard exhaled deeply. "Ve need to get zhese volves back to Uzlia," he said to Zalith. "Zhe last ving I need is pups vunning avound zhis place."

"Well, the elves are dealt with," Zalith said, walking at his side as they began walking to the Noctuary. "I can get a lot more demons over here to help; they can replace the wolves—I'll do it now."

"Zhat's probably best," he agreed, pushing open the Noctuary doors. "I'll 'ave to get a ship 'ere to pick up zhe volves." And that reminded him…. "'As your zemon veported anyving about zhe compound?"

"Not yet," his mate replied.

He hoped that the Silver Claw would be dealt with in time, *before* those Detainers reached their quota. If he had the forces to spare, he'd send people to liberate that compound right now, but he didn't. This bounty hunter needed to die.

A few vampires were already waiting in the Noctuary. The windowless room was lit dimly by the runes carved into the vaulted ceiling and the flickering candelabras, and the rumble of thunder echoed beyond the walls.

Alucard took Zalith to the stage at the back of the room and sat on the couch with him, sighing deeply. Despite his deep rest, he was already beginning to feel tired again. Maybe it was because of the sudden shift in time; perhaps his body was still trying to catch up with it.

Zalith leaned his head on his shoulder. "Do you think we'll find the guy?"

"I 'ope so."

The demon nuzzled his neck, but only for a moment...and not long later, he did it again. He was clearly trying his best not to linger.

Alucard didn't mind, though. He moved his hand to the back of Zalith's head and pulled him closer, letting him know that it was fine.

The coven began filing into the hall, and Zalith's demons didn't long follow. Within a matter of minutes, *everyone* was present, standing before the stage and awaiting orders.

First, Alucard's eyes swept the crowd, counting how many demons Zalith had summoned—there were twenty-one of them, almost as many as the Duskroot wolves.

"Tell me about your zemons," he murmured to his mate, taking out his notebook.

Zalith turned his head to look out at the crowd. "They're Elyndar's." He paused for a moment. "The one that belonged to Alegan—well...Erasmus, but then Alegan took over before I went to fight him."

He nodded. "I vemember zhem."

"The redhead with the one red eye is Olivienne—she's one of the Betas. The other Beta is the bald guy, green eyes—Osbern." He pointed to another man with spiked black hair, burns on the right side of his face, and a greyed-out eye. "Oh, and that's Brannoc. He was next in line to be Alpha after Alegan. He's a little sour about it, but he works closely with Elyndar."

"Vhat kind of zemon is 'e?" he asked curiously, noting everything down.

"Asynari."

Alucard nodded slowly. Asynari demons fed on sacrifice and martyrdom; every feed powered them for *decades*. There was no question as to why he was next in line for Alpha. "Olivienne and Osbern?"

"Olivienne is nureliad, and Osbern is carovar."

A feeder of hope and joy, and a feeder of physical and emotional pain. Carovar demons were much stronger than nureliads, able to cause pain from a single touch, but he'd find a use for Olivienne.

Zalith continued, "We have three ymbruen demons—Thalric, Royandra, and Sorrelle, though Sorrelle is part skarrix. Five malisite demons—Aldric, Elewaln, Roderic, Odessae, and Halvene. Two valefar—Mirilden and Cadwell. Four craventh demons—Nerilitha, Wilmot, Jossian, and Anwenna. And then three skarrix—Merrion, Eldan, and Briallen...it looks like Celandria tagged along, too; she's dating Merrion or something; Idina noted it down for me."

Alucard started assigning Zalith's demons to certain teams. The groups with released Fledgelings needed the additional help more than the others, so he added more demons to those. Once he was done, he tore the page out and waved Vulpea forward.

She stepped up onto the stage.

He handed her the page. "Start sorting everyvone into zhese groups."

"Yes, My Lord," she said and got to work.

"Ve're starting our search vor zhe Silver Claw," he then called.

Every vampire and demon set their eyes on him, waiting.

"You're all being sorted into groups, and each group vill be searching a specivic part of zhe underground tunnels. You are looking vor a loup-garou. Vor zhose of you who do not know, a loup-garou is a vogue Alpha verevolf. Zhey are very vast and very strong, vhich is vhy you vill all 'ave at least two zemons vith you—zhey are 'ere to 'elp ensure nobody is killed by zhis ving. Loup-garou are bipedal, and zhey can vemain in zheir volf vorm vor much longer zhan an average verevolf. You must *all* be very cautious."

The sorted groups began mumbled to one another…but the vampires and demons gave each other either unsure or hostile stares.

"I veally 'ope I zon't 'ave to tell you to vork togezzer—"

"Do as he says," Zalith called.

The demons lost their conflicted expressions, instead looking obedient.

Alucard hoped that was all it would take. "Vulpea 'as told you who is leading your team. Use zhis time to discuss voles and positions." He waved Vulpea over again and handed her the maps. "Put zhese on zhat table."

"Yes, My Lord," she said, taking them from him.

"Look over zhese maps, vemember zhe passages you 'ave been assigned to," he called, watching as everyone followed the Paladin to the table.

"We're heading down there too, right?" Zalith asked.

Although the idea of being in those narrow, lightless tunnels made Alucard feel sick, he nodded stiffly. He had to focus on his vampires, on protecting them from something that would wipe them *all* out. His dedication to protect them had to outweigh his traumatizing fear of dark catacombs and endless labyrinths.

"Are you okay?" his mate asked quietly.

He nodded again. "Just…zhe tunnels," he said—he wasn't going to lie.

Zalith squeezed his hand. "You don't have to go down there; you can stay here if you want; I can go with them."

Alucard wanted to accept his offer, but how would that make him look? Staying back while he sent his coven down into the dark, hunting for a monster that was hunting them, a monster that could end their lives in a heartbeat. No. He was going, too. His fear wasn't going to stop him.

"I'll be okay," he assured him…but he frowned nervously—he turned away from his coven to hide his face in case any of them were looking. "Just…stay vith me," he requested, his voice barely above a whisper. "I can't be alone down zhere."

The demon pulled him into his embrace and held him tightly. "Don't worry. I'll be right there with you."

He rested his head on his mate's shoulder. "Ve 'ave to vind zhis guy—*tonight*."

"We will," Zalith said firmly. "He won't live to see the morning."

Chapter Thirty-One

━ ⟨ ✝ ⟩ ━

Tunnels, Catacombs, Memories

| **Alucard** |

| *Atheson, Atheson Coven Sanctum* |

Everyone was getting ready to head underground.

Alucard pulled his new boots on, dragging his movements out as if it would give him the time he needed to fully prepare—or prepare as much as he could. The sooner he got down there and found the loup-garou, though, the sooner it would all be over, and the sooner he could return to the surface.

He sighed deeply, watching the demons and vampires file out of the Sanctum and into the courtyard. Once Zalith had his boots on, he took his mate's hand and followed the groups outside. There were ten of them, eleven if he included himself, Zalith, Tyrus, Danford, and Roderic, one of the malisite demons. He *did* feel nervous leaving the Sanctum with only the Duskroot wolves to protect it and the new Fledgelings inside, but he knew that the pack was capable, and so was Lăcrămioara.

Alucard stopped by the fountain, and everyone turned to face him. "You vill 'ead to your designated entrances to zhe underground system. Stick to zhe paths, be *very* carevul, and do exactly as your group leaders say. If you vind *anyving* at all zhat even vemotely vesembles tracks, you tell me; your zemon allies 'ave access to izurets. Zhe moment you vind zhe Silver Claw, you back off and vait vor me. Understood?"

The crowd called their agreements.

"Let's move," he said, turning and heading for the gates.

As the groups dispersed, Alucard stopped outside the gates and held out his free hand. When Tyrus moved to take it, the vampire grabbed his wrist instead; Danford grasped Tyrus' arm, and Roderic grabbed his. Alucard then dematerialized them all into vermillion smoke and travelled to the grate he'd assigned himself to.

When he landed and rematerialized, though… he hesitated so fiercely that the fatigue had no chance at grasping him. His gaze locked onto the grimy, rusted grate bars, the darkness beyond pressing outward like the maw of a beast. It loomed before him, promising no physical harm, only the venom of old memories that he had long tried to bury, memories that would claw at him the moment he stepped inside.

He didn't want to go in.

But he had to.

Drawing a shallow breath, he moved forward, following behind Tyrus, Roderic, and Danford, stepping into a blackness so heavy that it swallowed the world behind him. No lanterns, no faint traces of moonlight, only the damp, suffocating gloom pressing close against his skin—and despite the fact that he could see clearly, the despair and dismay still lingered in the air, threatening to lash out at any moment.

He exhaled deeply, his eyes shifting from Tyrus, Roderic, and Danford to the sludge-covered walls. His every step was slow and careful, his boots splashing quietly through stagnant puddles left by the runoff from the city above. He spotted the symbols carved into the surface, old markers of the city's maintenance tunnels; the numbers and shapes matched what he had studied in the maps and blueprints. Good. They were exactly where they needed to be.

Zalith then lightly squeezed his hand, a silent reminder that he wasn't alone. The vampire squeezed back once, forcing himself to keep moving deeper into the throat of the underground. He'd keep hold of the fact that these *weren't* the catacombs he'd grown up in, that these weren't the corridors of Damien's castle. This was just a system beneath Atheson.

Tyrus suddenly stopped, holding up his hand before they reached the fork in the tunnel.

Danford halted immediately, and Roderic moments later.

Zalith joined Tyrus but kept Alucard behind him, holding his hand firmly.

Alucard focused his senses, searching for whatever alerted the allocer demon…but there was nothing other than the auras of rodents, the sound of dripping water, and the horrifying, *intensifying* stench of filthy water and sewage. Thankfully, though, he'd mapped himself a tunnel that wouldn't take him through years' worth of human waste.

"Something to the left," Tyrus whispered. "Not sure what."

"Yeah, I felt it, too," Roderic agreed.

The allocer demon extended his left arm and drew two fingers slowly down the inside of it. A muted pulse of silver light spilled from his palm, mist curling outward and thickening as it touched the stale air. Within seconds, the mist twisted and took form—a spectre-like tiger, black as night with glistening platinum stripes, its body slightly translucent, as if caught between this world and another.

Alucard watched, briefly distracted by the sight. That had to be Tyrus' familiar. All allocer demons possessed the potential to summon one, but mastering the craft was rare. He had heard it required exceptional control, something few allocers ever achieved.

But what was to the left?

Tyrus sent his familiar in that direction, and then he looked to Zalith and Alucard.

And Zalith looked to Alucard.

But the vampire was trying to detect what Tyrus and Roderic had. Was his simmering anxiety affecting his concentration? Or were Tyrus and Roderic wrong? "Vhat did you sense?" he asked them.

"It was really faint," Roderic answered.

Alucard waited, glaring at him.

The malisite demon glanced at Zalith—he had that look about his face...that hesitant, almost *offended* expression.

Zalith *scowled* at him, growling under his breath.

Roderic straightened, quietly clearing his throat. "Like a whisper," he said.

Tyrus rolled his eyes. "Somebody just used ethos," he explained, keeping his voice hushed. "For half a second, if that. It wasn't demon or vampire."

Alucard pondered, shifting his sights to the left tunnel again. If *he* hadn't felt it.... "Did you veel zhe same ving?" he asked his mate.

Zalith shook his head.

"Is a diversion," Alucard deduced.

"How'd you come to that conclusion?" Roderic questioned—and again, there was that condescending tone.

Alucard's glare turned into a scowl.

Tyrus looked to Zalith.

And Zalith rolled his eyes and nodded.

The allocer demon slammed his fist into Roderic's face.

Roderic stumbled back and tripped, landing in the filth-laden water, missing Danford by inches—the wolf-vampire stepped aside just in time.

"Watch yourself," Tyrus snarled at Roderic.

Alucard huffed and said, "Zhe vact zhat Zaliv and I zidn't veel zhe ethos means zhat whoever used isn't strong enough to convuse our senses. Somevone zoesn't vant us going onvard or to zhe vight."

"Tyrus, take him and go forward," Zalith instructed.

With a nod, Tyrus crossed the fork, and Roderic scurried after him.

"Let's go," Zalith then said to Danford, also squeezing Alucard's hand.

The three of them headed right.

"Was it the loo...loop-gar-ow?" the wolf-vampire asked.

"Loup-garou," Alucard corrected. "Maybe," he answered straight after. "'E could 'ave shivted, or 'e could 'ave used an enchantment or someving along zhose lines."

"It'd make sense if he has enchanted weapons," Zalith agreed with a nod. "A lot of the hunters we dealt with in Eltaria were particularly fond of lingering pain inducers."

Alucard snarled under his breath as they navigated a curving, dipping tunnel. "'Umans," he muttered.

"James was hit by one of those," Danford mumbled sadly. "I wouldn't wish it on anyone—except the human who did it to him."

Though he didn't care... Alucard wasn't only attempting to tolerate Danford, but he was also doing his best to keep himself from letting the anxiety creep in. "Who vas James?"

Danford looked a little flustered, and Zalith seemed surprised. Evidently, they were both adjusting to the fact that Alucard was *trying*.

"He was one of my close friends," Danford answered; his voice echoed slightly, swallowed by the damp chill of the tunnel. "We were together for a while, but when I started working solo more often, he couldn't handle only seeing me once in a while." As he spoke, he moved carefully down the crumbling, sunken steps, each one slimy with moss and worn thin by time; the walls around them wept moisture, streaking the stone with dark trails, and the air grew colder the deeper they descended. "We crossed paths more often during the retreat," he added, his voice softening. "But... he's gone now."

Alucard nodded once, holding Zalith's hand tighter when they reached the bottom of the steps, emerging into a long, narrow tunnel that appeared to go on forever. "Ve've all lost a lot of people," he mumbled, still trying to fight the trauma-triggered instincts urging him to flee. "Vhat matters is zhat ve survived, and zhe people ve lost vill stay vith us vorever."

Zalith moved his arm around him and hugged him as he kissed his head.

The vampire let himself sink into the assuring embrace—his mate was there with him; he'd be okay; those catacombs were in the past.

They continued onwards, following the route Alucard had mapped out earlier.

A damp, bone-deep freeze clung to Alucard's clothes and seeped into his skin, making him huff and shiver; Zalith's embrace only helped so much. Every footstep was muffled by the oppressive weight of the earth above them, and the narrowness of the tunnel seemed to tighten with each passing moment, the ceiling bowing lower, the walls pressing just a little closer. Even the sound of everyone's breathing felt muted now, swallowed by the heavy gloom, as if the darkness was drawing the life from the air.

Alucard fought the instinct to turn back, every nerve in his body panicking. The stench of ancient rot was thick in his nose, a grim reminder of those long-ago catacombs he'd once called a prison. His hand stayed tight in Zalith's, the demon's presence tethering him... but it was getting harder.

Still, they pressed on, each step slightly heavier, the silence growing denser until even their heartbeats felt too loud—Alucard could hear Danford's racing pulse, and he could feel Zalith's steady one.

A sudden puff of green smoke startled Alucard—he flinched violently, stumbling into Zalith, who caught him.

It was just an izuret.

The vampire sighed and stared at it as Zalith helped him straighten.

With quiet chirps, the creature told him that Drusilda's team had found scat by their second turning and more fifty feet down.

Zalith looked just as disgusted as Alucard felt.

The vampire grimaced and mumbled, "Vell, 'e's marking 'is territory."

"That's a good sign," Danford said.

"Drusilda's team is 'alv a mile avay," Alucard said as he thought. "Eizer zhe scat is anozzer intended misdirection, or zhe ethos Tyrus sensed earlier vas meant to make us vink ve should go zhis vay."

"Do you think he's that smart?" Zalith asked.

"If 'e's been 'unting vampires, zhen 'e must know 'ow to mislead and attract zhem. But 'e vasn't prepared vor *us*…so I vink is zhe vormer. 'E knows 'e's dealing vith a coven, so 'e'd be prepared vor zhem to come looking vor 'im. Zhe smartest ving to do vould be to split zhe coven up as var vrom each ozzer as possible; zhe scat and aura are pervect vays to do zhat," he explained, still pondering—the thinking was definitely helping him focus more on the mission. "Zhe territorial marks are meant to lead vampires avay vrom each ozzer, and zhe aura vas very likely meant to draw us in."

"Do we go back?" Zalith asked.

He considered it…but under the urge to flee, his instincts were telling him to continue following *this* tunnel. "No," he replied, and then he turned to the izuret. "Tell zhem to turn avound and vollow Voute B instead."

With a salute, the izuret disappeared.

"I veel like zhere's someving 'ere," he said to Zalith and nodded at Danford, telling him to proceed.

The wolf-vampire did as he was told.

Zalith didn't question him.

Alucard focused again, every sense on high alert. Loup-garou were *very* good at hiding their aura, yes…but if this one was alluding even *him*, then it was definitely more of a threat than normal. Experienced, perhaps older. Those things made it deadlier. But he'd faced things far worse than a loup-garou—even if it *was* wearing silver on its claws—and with Zalith at his side, he knew that once they found this vampire killer, they'd make short work of it.

"I see the end," Danford said quietly. "It looks like—"

Another izuret abruptly appeared.

This time, it didn't shock Alucard as much, but it did throw him off a little.

"Vhat?" he mumbled, still walking.

It squeaked and clicked, telling him that Theremond's group found several tracks in the mud—pawprints twice the size of a hand.

Genuine tracks…or another 'clue' intending to mislead vampires?

Alucard slowed to a halt once they reached the end of the tunnel. "Vere zhere any grates or 'oles letting moonlight shine in avound zhe area?"

The izuret tapped its chin before nodding frantically.

"Loup-garou get careless vhen vunning vrom zhe moon. Tell zhem to keep vollowing zhe tracks—but *carevully*."

After another nod, the izuret vanished.

"Um…do we go back?" Danford asked.

Alucard looked around. It *seemed* like a dead end…until he looked up. Half-hidden under century-old grime and cobwebs was a hatch.

A hatch.

He couldn't stop the flash of memory that struck him—something he'd forgotten, something that had been stolen from him. When he was a child, he found himself at the end of a tunnel…staring up at a hatch. It was the only way out that he'd thought he'd found in that place since birth.

And there was something else.

Someone else.

"Aleksei…" came a silky, purring voice.

Familiar but strange, greeting like an old friend…but *cold* and misleading.

"Aleksei…."

"Aleksei—"

Alucard flinched and gasped in shock, sharply turning his head and setting his wide eyes on…

A cat? Wings, horns, red eyes.

"What are you doing down here?" the cat asked with a frown, swaying its tail.

Alucard climbed down off a crate. "Vhat are you doing 'ere?"

It purred deeply. "I was trying to catch that man for you."

Man…. That was right. He'd been tailing a man he'd seen sneaking around the catacombs.

Alucard hadn't seen Gossamer anywhere while in pursuit. "I vas chasing 'im."

"Were you? Oh…."

"Vhere did you come vrom? Is a dead end," he asked skeptically.

"I am like you, Aleksei. I was in the shadows."

Was that true?

"Did you get to see his face?" the cat asked. "I couldn't get close enough."

Alucard stiffly shook his head.

The cat mewed a huff. "Perhaps we will succeed next time."

"Alucard?" Zalith's voice cut through the haze.

He snapped out of it, taking his eyes off the hatch to meet his mate's confused stare.

"Are you okay?"

The vampire frowned. "I…" he drawled and looked up at the hatch again. "I vas vemembering someving."

Zalith moved closer. "One of your memories?" he asked, keeping his voice hushed.

He nodded. "I vas…in a tunnel like zhis—zhe Diabolus catacombs." He glanced around before returning his sights to the hatch. "Zhere vas a cat."

"A cat?"

The vampire nodded. "Vas…'ad a name," he muttered frustratedly, trying to recall it. "Vas…odd name."

Zalith rubbed his arm. "Don't push yourself, baby. It'll come to you."

He sighed and shifted his sights to Danford. "Get up zhere and open zhat."

Danford looked up…grimaced…and nodded. "Okay," he said as he hesitantly gripped the slimy ladder, and he started climbing.

Alucard exhaled again and urged Zalith nearer to himself. "At least zhe memory isn't traumatizing, I suppose."

He kissed his head and teased him, "Is that where your cat obsession started?"

He thought about the cat—that strange creature. "Vas a katsie," he said, certain. "What's a katsie?"

"Is zhis sort of…guiding spirit—an astral. Supposedly, zhey vind people who need zhem zhe most and guide zhem out of life-vhreatening situations."

"So, he helped you get away from the Diabolus?"

That didn't sound right. Thinking about the cat filled him with a peculiar sense of distrust. He'd been skeptical of that cat. Was it because katsie only assisted those who they could benefit from? Had that cat needed something from him?

But what?

He sighed and shook his head. "I zon't know."

Zalith pulled him into his embrace. "It's all right."

A loud clank snatched Alucard's attention. He looked up and watched as Danford grunted and huffed, pushing the hatch upwards.

"Gross," the wolf-vampire muttered.

That was when it struck him.

"Gossamer," Alucard said. It felt like another piece had fit into the never-ending puzzle of lost memories.

"What's Gossamer?" Zalith asked.

"Zhe cat," he said. "Vas called Gossamer."

The demon scoffed amusedly. "Was he transparent?"

"No," he said with a light shrug. "'Ad...black vur, and zhese...big ved eyes zhat kind of looked like Liliv's."

"Sounds spooky," Zalith murmured...dragging his face down the side of Alucard's until he reached his neck.

Maybe *that* was why he hadn't trusted the katsie.

Was it?

Yes...that *was* it. At some point, he'd suspected that Gossamer had been sent by Lilith—perhaps it even *was* Lilith.

And then he asked himself: who had he been following before the cat interrupted?

Once again, he turned his attention to the hatch and watched as Danford climbed back down the ladder, grunting as the slime oozed through his fingers.

Gossamer.

Gossamer.

He concentrated on the name, on the cat...and the *tunnel.*

And the distorted memory echoed inside his head.

"Did you get to see his face?" the katsie asked. "I couldn't get close enough."

Alucard stiffly shook his head.

The katsie mewed a huff. "Perhaps we will succeed next time."

He eyed the cat for a moment, trying to decide whether he wanted to continue his suspicious interrogation or ask Gossamer for other answers. It didn't take long for him to decide, though. "'E vas talking about me."

"You?"

"Yes."

"Are you certain?"

"Yes."

"Absolutely?"

"Yes!" he snarled. "'E vas talking about 'ow I zidn't kill Simion, and 'ow I saw zhe vitual vith Dargana."

"What ritual?"

Alucard felt reluctant to answer, and he wasn't sure why. Suspicion? Hesitation?

The cat frowned. "Aleksei?"

"I zidn't 'ear 'im go vhrough zhat." He pointed at the hatch. "Vhere did 'e go?"

Gossamer opened its mouth to speak, but the clicking of approaching heels made the cat's eyes widen fully. "Be strong, Aleksei," it said, and then it disappeared into smoke.

Alucard froze, and his breath caught in his throat. The tap of heels echoed down the corridor.... He knew that unmistakable sound.

Lilith was coming.

Alucard looked away, dismissing the memory, focusing instead on Zalith's affection. He didn't want to remember the rest.

"It doesn't look like there's anything up there. It's sort of a low loft," Danford said. "I saw some old crates, but other than that, it's just spiders and dead rats."

The vampire frowned. He wasn't sure whether he felt embarrassed or confused—maybe it was both. Was *this* why his instincts had led him down this tunnel? Were they leading him to uncover another piece of his past?

No. There had to be *something* else.

"Zaliv," he murmured as he gently pushed Zalith away.

"Hmm?" he replied, dazed.

"I need to see vhat's up zhere."

Zalith glanced at the hatch. "I can come with—"

"Is okay; I zon't vant you to get slime all over your 'ands."

"But what about *your* hands?"

"I von't be climbing," he said with a small laugh.

The vampire vanished into vermillion smoke, reappearing a moment later in his horned owl form—it was too narrow to navigate this space as smoke alone. He beat his wings once, ascending through the open hatch, and once inside, he shifted again, this time into his fox form; he wasn't about to crawl around on his hands and knees. Low and soundless, he scampered across the floorboards towards the rows of crates, his eyes scanning for anything disturbed.

Most of the crates were thick with dust, cobwebs clinging to the corners, the wood stained with years of filth. But one stood out, the dust smudged by recent handprints. He leapt lightly onto the box, his claws clicking softly against the old wood, and he quickly found the latch. A deft nudge of his paw unclipped it.

He hopped over to the next crate and pried the lid open, his ears twitching at the faint creak. Inside was a grim arsenal: a worn leather medical bag, a belt heavy with silver bullets and blades, a scattering of silver stakes, coils of hemlock-soaked rope, several glass bottles filled with blessed water, and sanctified religious items.

The Silver Claw's hidden cache.

"Alucard?" Zalith called quietly.

He spoke into his mate's mind, "*Zhere's veapons up 'ere,*" he answered, still looking around. The hatch had been covered in settled, almost solidified muck. Sure, he wasn't an expert in how filth aged, but he was almost certain that even a loup-garou couldn't make slime, gunge, and cobwebs look *that* natural. There had to be some other way the Silver Claw had accessed this place.

"Are you coming back down?" the demon asked—he was worried.

"*I'm just looking avound. I'm okay, zhough.*"

He weaved through the crates, nose twitching as he sniffed for anything out of place. The faint scent of disturbed dust and fresh stone caught his attention, and he slowed, his glowing eyes narrowing on a stack near the far wall. Unlike the rest, those boxes weren't blanketed in the heavy layers of frothing sludge and silky strands. They looked newer—no, not newer…*moved.*

Padding closer, Alucard wedged his small fox body between two crates and pushed. His claws scrabbled slightly against the wood, and with a soft grunt—well, a soft *squeak*—he managed to heave one aside just enough to slip through. Dust puffed into the air, and tucked against the wall where the crate had been was another hatch. This one was clean, almost startlingly so; the metal frame looked almost polished compared to everything else.

He crouched, sniffing it. There, a faint smell of old sweat and leather, a scent trail so weak that it had to be days old. But it was proof. Someone had been using this.

"Alucard?" Zalith's voice reached him again, this time edged with concern, as if he'd already called for him more than once.

Alucard flicked his tail, swivelling his head to look back. Zalith stood halfway up the ladder, his broad shoulders framed by the open hatch, his gaze locked onto him. "*I vound anozzer 'atch,*" he spoke into the demon's mind. "*Might lead us closer to vherever zhe 'unter is 'oled up.*" He crept closer, nose nearly touching the hatch's seam, ears twitching for the slightest sound beyond it.

This was where they needed to go. Whatever waited below would take them to the Silver Claw. He was certain of it.

He looked back at Zalith again and telepathically said, "*Zhis is zhe vay ve need to go—down zhis 'atch.*"

Zalith stared in its direction, and the concerned expression on his face contorted into a hesitant frown. "I don't know, Alucard. What if he's waiting down there for us?"

If he *was*, Alucard couldn't tell. Even as he focused his senses again, all he felt beneath his paws and beyond was empty stillness. The last thing he wanted was to walk into a trap, so he headed back to his mate. "*Maybe ve can vind a vay avound.*"

The demon scooped Alucard up in one arm and carried him down the ladder as he said, "There was a turning back the way we came; maybe it'll lead us around to wherever that other hatch would've taken us."

Once Zalith stood on the ground, Alucard morphed into vermillion smoke and re-emerged as his normal self. "I just 'ope 'e zoesn't 'ave a whole arsenal vaiting vor us. Zhe shit I saw up in zhat crawlspace vas very provessional equipment."

Zalith held his hand and led the way.

Danford hurried behind them. "What do we do if he does?"

"'E's equipped to kill vampires, not zemons," Alucard said as they headed up the eroded steps. "Ve can get all zhe zemons to us." He looked at Zalith. "Zhey are all Lilidian, vight?"

"Yeah."

"Zhe silver von't avvect zhem." He huffed and shook his head. "Ve need to vind 'im tonight; I 'ope zhat vhen ve *do* vind 'im, 'e unintentionally shivts; 'e'll lose 'is vocus, and zhat vill give us a vindow to kill 'im vast."

"Or we could just light him on fire," Zalith laughed.

"Zhat's zhe *last* ving ve should do. You could bring zhe entire tunnel system down."

"You're right," he said amusedly. "I just want it over with so I can take you home and fuck you in our own bed," he murmured, leaning closer to Alucard's neck.

He smiled as the demon pressed his body against his, making him sidestep a little when they reached the top of the slope. But he couldn't lose his focus, nor could he allow Zalith to lose his. "I do, too. But *vight now*, you need to vocus."

Zalith purred, "Yes, My Lord," and straightened himself.

The vampire shifted his stare to Danford, who quickly looked away with a flustered expression.

Alucard rolled his eyes and said, "Let's go."

With a nod, Danford took the lead again, heading around the curve, following the tunnel that Zalith had suggested.

Would they find the Silver Claw waiting at the end of this passage, or would they be forced to lose themselves in a labyrinth of endless corridors and wynds? Alucard hoped for the former. Yet, just as instinct had led him to the hidden hatch, it now whispered of a long and winding hunt ahead.

But was that hunt leading him to his enemy…or would it take him deeper into the shadows of his forgotten past?

Chapter Thirty-Two

— ⊰ † ⊱ —

In the Walls

| Zalith |
| Atheson, Atheson City Vaults |

How long had they been walking?

Zalith took a glimpse at his pocket watch, half to check the time, half to try and distract himself for a moment from Alucard's enthralling scent. The curved tunnel was now taking them down, coiled like a massive serpent, slowly swallowing them deeper and deeper. Surely by now they'd reached the same level that the hatch had been on.

He glanced at Alucard. The moment he set his eyes on his fiancé, his instincts grew wilder than they already were. All he could think about were all the ways he wanted to fuck him, all the ways he wanted to get lost in him. It would be so easy to grab him, undress him, and *take* him. But that small piece of lingering common sense guided him away from those thoughts—for now, at least. There was a loup-garou to find.

Another izuret appeared with an update regarding another trail. There'd been so many of them in the past thirty minutes that everything behind them had long been proved a distraction. He trusted Alucard's senses, and he was confident that his vampire was leading them in the right direction, so he was ready at a moment's notice to summon his demons.

Danford lifted his hand and gave a sharp, familiar signal—they were nearing the end of the twisting passage.

Zalith exhaled silently in relief; he was beginning to think that they might never escape the turn.

Once the slope came to a gradual end, the even stone ground stretched onwards for what he might usually consider an annoying length of empty path, but after that painfully slow descent, he welcomed it. The water that had been flowing down either side of the slope spilled into a small grate, and down here, there was no grime or filth, only cobwebs, dust, and the weakening scent of stagnant water.

His eyes lowered to the ground. There weren't any tracks—no paw or footprints—but the dust *had* been swept all over the place. If this passage were as undisturbed as it first appeared, the dust would be like a blanket of frost beneath their boots, wouldn't it?

He spoke into Alucard's mind, *"He's been covering his tracks down here."*

"Evidently, not too vell," the vampire replied.

Danford glanced back at them.

Zalith gave him a silent command, telling him to look down with a slant of his hand. He did as he was told, and after seeing the shifted dust, he nodded in understanding.

The three of them slowed ever so slightly.

Zalith tightened his grip on Alucard's hand, concern rising in his chest, eclipsing the lingering heat of his desires. His instincts shifted with it—no longer driven by desire but by the need to protect. As the end of the narrow passage came into view, he scanned the shadows for any further signs—stray fur, a fleck of silver-painted nail—but found nothing.

They turned left and found a staircase climbing upward. Stone at first, cold and damp underfoot, but soon the steps gave way to worn wood. With every stride they took, the air grew thicker, the scent of old rot settling deeper into Zalith's lungs. When they reached the landing, the air felt almost normal again, a subtle shift that made the back of Zalith's neck prickle.

The stairs took them into what must have once been a wine cellar—large, empty, and abandoned long ago; the space yawned around them, wide and hollow, its rows of crumbling wooden racks sagging under their own weight. On the ceiling in the far-left corner, Zalith spotted what looked like the hatch that Alucard had found up in that crawlspace earlier. Once again, his fiancé was right; his instincts were just as extraordinary as the rest of him.

Now wasn't the time to get lost in the sheer idea of the man he loved, though. He paused, scanning the room, keeping Alucard close.

Danford stopped, too. He knew better than to investigate until he was told.

Much like in the tunnel, the dust here was swirled unevenly across the floor, disturbed in unnatural patterns. It wasn't the thick, settled blanket of a forgotten place; it had been swept and marred by someone trying to hide their movements…and it was fresh enough that Zalith could still smell the faint trace of displaced earth and humanoid sweat beneath the musty rot.

Zalith flexed his grip on Alucard's hand without thinking, drawing him even closer. Every instinct he had screamed for *extreme* caution now. He stretched his senses outward, inhaling deeply through his nose. Under the heavy scent of a bygone era, he caught something softer, faint but distinct.

Voices.

A whispering murmur, light and reverent, carried on the stale air from above.

"O Lord of Fire and Judgement, cleanse us of this plague! Spare the faithful, scourge the wicked! Deliver us from the rot of the unclean, O Merciful Flame; burn their sin from our midst!"

The desperate voices grew louder, and to Zalith, it sounded all too familiar.

"Shield us beneath Thy gaze, O Lord; let not the vermin's disease touch the Chosen! Purge the blight from our streets, O Righteous One! Smite the carriers of sin! We are Yours, O Pure One! Deliver us from the touch of the defiled!"

Praying.

Humans were such moronic little things. Their 'God' didn't give a fuck about them, and their pleas for him to lift the smallpox outbreak—fake or not—were landing on deaf ears, ears that would *never* listen. But they'd never listen to reason, either. Pathetic.

The demon frowned, and when he saw Alucard staring up—listening, perhaps—he tilted his head slightly and did the same.

"Raise Your sword against the corrupters, O Lord! Preserve the faithful! Turn Thy wrath upon the vermin, O Just One, and make whole the flock that serves You!"

And then the voices repeated over and over and over, *"Spare us, O Flame, and scourge the unclean!"*

Zalith rolled his eyes when Alucard did, but they'd both clearly come to the same conclusion.

"Church," they said into one another's minds at the same time.

Danford turned his head to look at them and mouthed the same word.

The demon nodded.

What better place for a hunter to hide than underneath the one place a vampire could never go?

As he signed to Danford, alerting him that the Silver Claw was very likely nearby, he spoke into Alucard's mind, *"He's got to be close."*

Alucard replied, *"You go levt, I go vight?"*

He shook his head, fear and desperation ensnaring him in a thorn-sharp grip. *"We should stay together,"* he said. *"Even Danford."* He signed *that* to the wolf-vampire, too. If they split up, the loup-garou would have the advantage.

Together, the three of them prowled the edges of the room, Zalith keeping a protective hold on Alucard's hand as they moved. They searched behind every shelf, barrel, and crate, leaving nothing unchecked; they peered under the crooked stairs that led up to an old door trimmed with tarnished silver; Zalith's eyes narrowed at the sight, a flicker of unease darting through him. If there was silver on the door, there could be more hidden in the walls or supports… and Alucard was vulnerable to it. He squeezed his fiancé's hand a little tighter, keeping him close.

They continued on, checking a small two-step-down room cluttered with dusty wine bottles and crumbling Books of Lore; they searched the supply closet, the collapsed remains of a vestibule with no way through, and even beneath the tangle of old support beams and planks straining to keep the groaning ceiling above them intact.

The humans' cult-like praying droned on, grating against Zalith's ears. The mindless repetition irked him, and so did the utter volume of it. Their voices swelled and echoed through the stone, loud enough to drown out anything else. No scrape or telltale whisper of the loup-garou's presence would reach them through that wall of noise if it came.

If they weren't trying to keep themselves hidden right now, Zalith would do something to shut them up—well…he *could* still do that…but that might alert the Silver Claw. It wasn't worth the risk.

Almost.

Danford waved his hand, catching Alucard's and Zalith's attention. He pointed to a hole tucked into the shadows beside the vestibule doorway, visible only from the angle the wolf-vampire had taken beside the stairs. Bricks had been clawed out and torn free; crumbled stone and trails of dust were hastily brushed aside to make it seem part of the collapsed entrance. Whatever made that gap had worked slowly at first…and then grew reckless—reckless enough to leave a glaring trail straight to its hiding place.

It had to be the Silver Claw. It made sense. Loup-garou turned at unpredictable times this close to the full moon; for now, the hunter held the advantage, hidden in this revolting place, free to strike without warning, but if he shifted and rampaged, the situation would change. His sanctuary would become his tomb, and the ones he stalked would turn their hunt on him.

Zalith felt Alucard move. He swiftly grasped the vampire's shoulder with his free hand, keeping him where he was. He already knew what his fiancé was going to say, so he shook his head and spoke into his mind, *"You're not going in there alone, Alucard."*

For a fleeting moment, it looked like Alucard might disagree…but he frowned instead and set his eyes back on the hole.

"I'll get Tyrus to come back. He can send his familiar in," he told him.

The vampire nodded in response.

Zalith telepathically summoned the allocer demon. *"He'll be here soon,"* he said to his vampire. He signed to Danford: I've called for Tyrus.

Danford moved closer to them both and waited.

The demon kept his eyes locked on the hole in the wall. He could see into the darkness beyond—but something was wrong. It wasn't normal. Usually, his vision in the dark was sharp, distorted only by subtle shifts in hue. But this? A strange glow pulsed at the centre with deeper shadows clinging around the edges like oil.

He didn't need to guess the cause. Alucard found weapons hidden in the crawlspace, and Zalith caught a glimpse of the contents—bottles of blessed water, sanctified objects, the kind that twisted a Lilidian demon's senses, making darkness deceptive and light treacherous. He wasn't surprised, though. Any hunter knew that blessed items were their dearest ally in a fight against vampires.

The Silver Claw was *definitely* in there—there wasn't a single doubt about it.

The humans' praying suddenly went silent, and scurrying footsteps echoed from above, followed by the slam of a door. Thankfully, they were finished for the night.

Tyrus arrived promptly, and Roderic lagged shortly behind him.

Zalith hadn't asked for Roderic, but it made sense for Tyrus to bring him. He was just going to have to refrain from breaking his face if he so much as *looked* at Alucard the wrong way. However, he tried to set his hostility and protective instincts aside for a moment; he gestured his hand towards the hole in the wall, silently instructing Tyrus to search it.

The allocer demon summoned his tiger familiar and sent it through the hole.

They waited, all watching the gap.

But when Zalith glanced at his fiancé, he saw that expression on his pale face again— he was thinking…*recalling*. "*What is it?*" he asked telepathically.

Alucard didn't answer right away. He frowned…looked down…and then set his eyes back on the hole with a muted exhale. "*Just vemembering more of zhe same memory vrom earlier.*"

"*With Gossamer?*"

He nodded.

"*What did you remember?*" He knew that he should be focusing on the mission, but he couldn't help it. His worry for Alucard had him on edge, and talking to him— just *hearing* his voice, spoken or projected—was a comfort, an assurance, and the desire played a part, too. He longed for any part of his vampire, even his words.

"*I zon't know if 'appened at zhe same time or zhe same day or vhatever, but I vemember zhat katsie…coming vhrough a 'ole in zhe vall—smaller zhan zhat vone—*" he nodded at the torn-out wall, "*—but still. And I vas in zhe voom zhat zhe priestesses alvays kept me locked up in.*"

He was curious, but he was also upset for him. With his free hand, he rubbed the vampire's arm, and he asked him, "*Was he trying to help you find a way out or something?*" But he remembered asking something similar earlier, and Alucard told him that he didn't know if the cat was trying to help. His conflicting feelings were making it hard for him to think, to *focus* on anything at all. Yet he attempted to concentrate on both his mate *and* the mission at the same time.

Perhaps with his body warring with his mind and heart, he ought to prioritize a single thing at a time.

"*I vink…Gossamer taught me 'ow to turn to smoke,*" the vampire revealed.

That was indeed intriguing, and it was then that Zalith's mind—already fraying under the pull of duty, desire, and the aching urge to drown in Alucard—abandoned reason and fixated on him completely.

"*Really?*" he replied, his eyes abandoning the gap and locking on Alucard.

"'*E 'elped—*" he paused for a moment, his frown thickening, "*—no … just Gossamer. Not 'e.*" He exhaled again, his eyes still fixed on the gap in the wall. "*Anyvay … 'elped me escape vrom zhat cell vhrough zhe same gap.*"

His curiosity increased. Just as Alucard had obviously been made to believe, *he* thought that it was Damien who took his fiancé away from the Diabolus. Had it been Gossamer, this strange katsie that Alucard's tortured mind had been triggered to recall? He asked, "*So, Gossamer was the one who got you out of there?*"

However, Alucard shook his head. "*Zhere vas no vay out—not zhat I knew of, and Gossamer never mentioned zhat. But I vound zhis sort of … library.*"

Zalith frowned—

Tyrus' familiar slipped soundlessly from the wall and returned to the allocer demon's side. A moment later, he relayed the message to those who understood, signing: A humanoid-shaped distortion, two hundred feet away.

When they were using stealth in Eltaria, the motion for 'distortion' always meant that there was an anomaly, highly likely caused by ethos or ethos-repelling materials.

Or in this case, a lycan who could hide itself from detection.

He asked Alucard, "*Would the loup-garou show up as a blurred mass to a creature that sees everything either as alive or inanimate?*"

The vampire appeared unsure. "*Is possible, yes,*" he replied. "*Looks like zhe voundations of zhe church are in zhat vall; is pervect cover.*"

Zalith was tired of all the tunnels and cramped spaces and hatches and holes in the walls. What was next?

No room for frustration. No room for anger.

Concentrate.

He gave Tyrus a gesture of his hand, signing, telling him that he was discussing a plan with Alucard. Then, he spoke into his fiancé's mind again, "*How do we draw him out of there if we can't use fire and don't want to risk him shifting?*"

Alucard was thinking.

Danford signed with his hands: Blood?

"*Vhat are you saying to each ozzer?*" the vampire abruptly asked.

"*It's a sort of … snappy sign language we used back in Eltaria. We found ourselves in a lot of situations like this, only we were the ones being hunted.*"

Alucard nodded again.

"*Would blood lure it out?*" the demon asked.

"Maybe...but vould 'ave to be mine. I'd 'ave to play zhe vole of zhe unsuspecting victim."

No. He wasn't going to let Alucard be used as bait. *"Absolutely not,"* he said firmly.

"Ve need a vampire. But I can't ask vone of my coven, Zaliv."

He understood...however, he was firm on his answer. Alucard would not be wolf bait. *"Can't you use the one you like the least?"* he suggested—sure, it sounded awful, and he *did* feel bad about saying it, but he'd rather it be a coven member than the man he loved.

Alucard looked guiltily conflicted...and his gaze slowly shifted to Danford.

Zalith stifled an amused smile.

Danford looked confused.

The demon signed to him, telling him that they needed him to be bait.

His wary expression thickened with fear...and he signed: Really?

Zalith signed back: We need you to cut yourself and play dumb until the wolf comes out. We'll grab him before he gets too close.

Danford still looked horrified.

Tyrus then signed: You'll be fine. We've got this handled.

The wolf-vampire's trepidation-thick frown didn't lift entirely, but he *did* exhale deeply and nod.

Zalith gestured to himself and Alucard as he signed: We'll be behind you on your right.

Tyrus nodded at Roderic, signing: We'll be on your left.

Danford nodded nervously.

Zalith led Alucard to the far-right corner and took cover in the narrow gap between the staircase and the wall; they'd be out of the loup-garou's line of sight when it emerged from the gap *and* the vestibule doorframe. He looked across the room, watching as Tyrus and Roderic crouched behind a stack of crates, and then he set his sights on Danford, holding Alucard's hand tightly.

The wolf-vampire stayed standing where he was for a moment, breathing unsteadily, dragging a hand over his face as he glanced around the room. Finally, he sat on one of the crates with his back to the vestibule. He cut his palm with his claws and loudly exclaimed, "Ah, shit."

A muffled sound came from the wall.

Zalith scowled, focusing, pushing every other need and thought aside. His first priority was protecting his fiancé, and his second was ensuring that the loup-garou didn't kill Danford, leaving his wife a widow and his unborn child or children without a father. Killing the vampire hunter was tied with saving Danford, actually. He'd do his best to reach the conclusion he wanted.

More muffled sounds.

Rustling.

A deep, echoing exhale.

Movement.

Zalith kept calm, ensuring not to give the loup-garou any sign that Danford wasn't alone. He waited…and waited…the air growing thick with tension.

And then soft footfall.

From the vestibule…came a woman—she wasn't wearing *a thing*. She was easily close to six feet tall with long, loose curls of pale blonde hair catching what little light touched the cellar. Her nails glinted as she walked, each one coated in a thin layer of silver.

Strangely, *harrowingly*…she looked like Ada. She had those piss-coloured eyes that Alucard had once described, and around them, a vibrant yellow outlined iris.

It was *her*. That woman was the one who attacked Alucard's Knights, and *she* was the Silver Claw.

His eyes should have shot to Danford, but they shifted to Alucard; he worried that his vampire might be horrified by the woman's ghostly similarity to someone he'd spent so much of his life fighting and avoiding.

But Alucard didn't appear uncomfortable. He met Zalith's gaze for a fleeting moment before staring at the woman again.

Zalith did the same. He watched her prowl nearer to Danford, tilting her head as if trying to understand something, sniffing, smirking. She flexed her nails, their silver coating glinting as her irises glowed brighter and brighter, and she licked her lips like a starved animal.

Not yet.

She edged closer, reaching towards the wolf-vampire, who continued his oblivious charade, tending to his bleeding palm.

Zalith exchanged a sign with Tyrus: On three.

Three…

       Two…

              One…

                    All four of them burst from their hiding places at once, lunging for the woman. They moved fast—

But she was just as quick. She veered straight for Danford, claws flashing, and he flung himself against the wall to avoid being gutted.

Tyrus and Roderic caught one of her arms, Zalith and Alucard the other, wrenching her back with their combined strength. But she twisted violently, ripping herself half-free; Roderic lost his grip with a grunt, and she drove her foot up into his groin. He cried out, the force of the blow hurling him across the room.

Danford lunged in without hesitation, seizing her wrist before she could rip at Tyrus' throat.

Zalith saw the opening and struck, releasing her arm with one hand to go for her neck.

The second he let go, she tore herself free.

There was no time to recover, nothing he could do to stop her as she viciously threw *everyone* across the room.

Zalith's body slammed into the stone wall with bone-rattling force, knocking the breath from his lungs.

The sharp tang of blood filled the air, and a deafening roar ripped through the cellar, making the ground shudder.

In mere seconds, the woman was gone, and a towering beast stood in her place.

Shit.

Chapter Thirty-Three

— ‹ † › —

Only Blood

| **Alucard** |

| *Atheson, Atheson City Vaults* |

Sharp, stinging pain tore through Alucard's body, radiating out from one side in burning twinges. He grunted, trying to catch his breath, only to realize that he was sprawled on the floor, pinned awkwardly on his right side. The world spun wildly around him, and through the relentless ringing in his ears, he caught the muffled sounds of snarls and shouting somewhere behind him.

He tried to lift his head to glance over his shoulder—the movement sent another searing jolt through his side, and a stifled cry escaped him, his vision blurring. The smell of blood was thick now, iron and salt heavy in the back of his throat.

Gritting his teeth, he tried to push himself up, but his right arm was trapped beneath him, useless, and when he pressed his left hand against the ground, it slid through something slick and warm. He collapsed back down with a wet, sickening thump.

His heart raced frantically, each beat hammering against his ribs. His breath was shallow, panicked bursts, fire seeming to rage through his veins.

And then he saw it.

Blood.

Everywhere.

A dark puddle oozed from beneath him, spreading and soaking into his clothes, painting his free hand in deep, glistening red. The wound itself remained hidden, shielded by the way he lay crumpled on his injured side—but there was no mistaking the source. It was *his*.

"Alucard!" Zalith's voice reached him, anxious and distorted with horror.

The murk at the edges of Alucard's vision began to close in, the pain fading as cold ensnared his body, though the wound remained burning hot. He knew this feeling, this debilitating weakness.

It was silver.

Zalith reached him—he was barely visible through the blur. "Alucard?!" he insisted again, placing his hands on him, panting, looking him up and down frantically. "What do I do?" he exclaimed, panicking.

He could feel the silver lingering in his wounds; he wasn't going to be able to do anything unless it was removed.

But the demon worked that out before he spoke. His mate carefully turned him onto his back; he said something, sounding dismayed and terrified at the same time; his voice was no more than a strange, contorting whisper.

Alucard closed his eyes and grimaced as the burning got worse; he felt the twinging sting of Zalith's claws, he felt him removing each piece of silver, and although it took some of the burning away, it was still unbearable.

"Just…more," the demon's voice cut through the haze, words missing.

The vampire let his head turn to the side, the dizziness cursing him with nausea. When he opened his eyes, though, the world was slowly coming back to him. He saw a mass of clashing figures—the largest had to be the loup-garou, and the rest must be Zalith's demons. He just hoped that none of them were his coven.

"Alucard?" Zalith asked, his voice clearer.

He turned his head, meeting his mate's anxious stare, and he already knew what he was going to say. Zalith wanted to get him out of here; he was going to tell his demons to stay behind and fight the loup-garou. But Alucard knew as well as Zalith did that the Silver Claw would slaughter every one of them, and then she'd chase after him and Zalith—she might even leave the demons the moment Zalith attempted to escape with him.

And his coven was still in these tunnels. He couldn't leave them.

Zalith tried picking him up—

"No," he grunted before wincing, the sharp pain electrifying through him.

"I need to get you out of here," he persisted, trying again.

But Alucard pushed his arm away—as much as his drained strength would allow, anyway. He set his eyes back on the battle, watching as Tyrus and *seven* others tried fighting the loup-garou, but she was lightning-fast, avoiding their claws and knives, and she even managed to duck under a blast of sizzling ethos.

Roderic was dead in the corner, torn apart.

Thalric was bleeding out, too many wounds for his body to heal at once.

And Briallen had just been launched and collided with the wall—her bones broke loudly, and she cried out in agony.

Alucard resisted Zalith's eager arms again, his eyes locked on Cadwell, who was racing to Briallen's aid. His sight shot to the loup-garou—she shoved the other demons away with a ferocious roar, and then she went for Cadwell. The vampire put all his strength into quickly raising his hand; he didn't have anything at his disposal right now other than his lost blood. Fog wouldn't help, but he had to try *something*. He concentrated on his blood, still part of him despite having left his body, and he focused on what he wanted from it—what he *needed* from it.

And then it happened.

Something he knew he could do, buried under the haze of his recovering memories.

Globes of blood lifted from the stone floor, shimmering like molten rubies. In the span of a heartbeat, they twisted and hardened, becoming razor-thin and blade-sharp, gleaming with that eerie luciferium shine. They shot forward, dozens of crimson knives racing in the direction his glare was locked onto—*the loup-garou*—following a command he merely thought in his mind.

The blades struck, burying deep into the monstrous wolf's right side—two in her arm, three in her leg, and another piercing the thick muscle of her neck. She howled a sound that shook the walls and wrenched the blood-forged knives free with savage, jerking movements as she turned, rage flashing in her golden eyes.

But Alucard wasn't going to let her kill anyone else.

As Zalith finally hoisted him up, Alucard seized what little strength he had left and gave a final silent command. His blood—still gleaming in thin, floating veins—shifted and dissolved into thick, swirling fog.

The room plunged into distortion. Black mist flooded the cellar, threaded with silver and red embers that caught and flickered like dying stars. Within the storm, sound dulled to a faint, underwater roar—muted growls, muffled yells. Silence wrapped around them like a second skin.

Through the fog, Alucard's vision stayed clear, and by force of will, he granted Zalith's demons the same clarity.

The loup-garou stumbled blindly, snapping at phantoms, her senses smothered by power she clearly hadn't encountered before. She whirled, confused, fury bleeding into desperation as the contorted world swallowed her.

With Alucard cradled against him, Zalith barked an order, his fading voice cutting through the fog like a blade. His demons responded instantly, gathering their fallen and sprinting for the same cellar stairs that Zalith was hastily climbing, carrying the vampire up to the silver door.

The heavy beat of thundering boots was all Alucard could hear now. All his vision faded, no longer able to see the raging monster, blinded by the sheer weight of his depleted ethos. But he was in Zalith's arms, and he knew that his mate would get everyone to safety.

But....

Alucard couldn't let the weakness take him yet. He didn't possess what he needed to tell the entire coven…but their group leaders would be enough. Using the last of his reserves, he reached out to his vampires, and he told them to retreat.

And that was it.

He had nothing left.

The silver, the wounds, his desire to save as many people as he could…it had taken everything from him, and there wasn't a thing he could do to stop the darkness from devouring him.

| **Zalith—*Sunday, Aprilis 2nd, 960(TG)* |**
| ***Atheson, Atheson Coven Sanctum* |**

Zalith stared down at Alucard, barely blinking.

The demon sat rigidly on the couch, his fiancé's head resting in his lap, the vampire's body unsettlingly still beside him, hidden under a blanket. Every shallow rise and fall of Alucard's chest was a fragile tether Zalith clung to, but his heart twisted painfully with each slow inhale and exhale that passed without change.

He dragged in a shaky breath, trying and failing to calm himself. He'd painstakingly removed the remaining splinters of silver from Alucard's wounds; the torn flesh had knit itself back together, but he showed no sign of waking. His life force, while no longer bleeding out, still flickered faint and frail, like a candle fighting a cold wind.

Zalith's hand moved in slow, endless motions through Alucard's crimson hair, refusing to look away for even a heartbeat, as if watching would will him back to consciousness. He pressed his wrist to Alucard's mouth once…twice…and again across hours that stretched unbearably long, each one feeling like it should have cracked the sky with its weight.

Guilt gnawed at him, sharper than any deadly metal or monstrous claws could. He should have been smarter, he should have held back, he should have waited for a better moment instead of lunging for the kill like a reckless, blood-drunk fool. But his mind hadn't been clear—not since Alucard's heat had first begun to burn through the air between them. The pheromones clung to his senses, tangling with every instinct he had. His incubus nature—his *demon* nature—had made it almost impossible to think of anything but protecting, claiming, and keeping Alucard close. Even now, that same primal pull muddled the edges of his thoughts, urging him to *touch*, to *hold*, to *take*…when what Alucard needed was calm, clear-headed control.

And he had failed him.

Zalith bowed his head slightly, his forehead brushing the soft, tangled strands of Alucard's hair, breathing him in like a plea he didn't dare speak aloud. He'd like to tell himself that he'd not fail like this again; however, he knew it was a lie, a useless statement. He'd not be able to concentrate. He really shouldn't have let himself follow Alucard into this Silver Claw business. But it wasn't just his desires urging him to cling to his fiancé like this. He was still paranoid. There was no point in denying it. He was still afraid that if he wasn't with his vampire every moment of every day, someone would take him from him…someone would *kill* him.

The demon huffed at the harrowing thought, closing his eyes, breathing in Alucard's scent again—but then he lifted his head, shaking it, trying to fight the warring thoughts, the conflicting emotions and clashing reactions. Fear, *need*, anxiety, *desire*, horror, *desperation*.

He couldn't think straight. Concentration was too far for him to reach.

It wasn't a foreign feeling…hating what he was. And *right now*, he hated it more than he might ever have.

Alucard needed him. *He* needed to figure out how to help him wake up. He'd done it before—he'd had the *time* before. Now, though, time wasn't on either of their side. That loup-garou could turn up at any moment; it could tear through even the extra security he'd surrounded the Sanctum with. And if it got in *here*, Zalith was afraid that he might not be able to kill it fast enough, if at all.

He huffed again, closing his eyes tightly, grasping aimlessly in his head. There had to be *something*.

"Come on," he grunted to himself, gritting his teeth.

It was hard…but he pried his gaze away from his vampire. His eyes took in the room for the first time since he'd gotten back to the Sanctum. It was dark and silent. No sound came from any direction; maybe that was because his senses were focused entirely on Alucard. He needed to pull *those* away, too. He could still smell him…feel him. His instincts wanted more than that.

His eyes darted about the place, from books to lamps to artwork…to the torn, bloody clothes he'd taken off his fiancé and the soaked rags he'd used to clean his skin…and then to the archway that led into the other part of the room.

It took a moment for his thoughts to let him, but he recalled what Alucard said earlier: when he rested in his casket, his body went into a state of rest; it helped him heal, to recover faster. And Zalith asked himself, would helping him into that state help him recover…even if he was comatose from blood loss?

The demon held tightly onto the idea as he carefully got off the couch; he moved quickly, heading into the other room and to Alucard's casket. He lifted the lid, hurried back to his fiancé, and gently scooped him up, keeping the blanket around him. When he returned to the casket, he slowly lowered the vampire inside.

And then he stared down at him again.

At first, it was his desire that urged him to climb in and lie beside him, but the anxiety and dismay of seeing the man he loved like this buried those instincts deeper and deeper, and the desperation for solutions surfaced.

A healer? A doctor?

No. Even if he knew where to find either of those people *fast*, he wasn't sure it would work, not after what he'd learned when Alucard had succumbed to the Eltaria-Aegisguard portal while taking vampires through it. And if he kept giving him his blood, it would deteriorate Alucard's human likeness, making things worse for him when he eventually woke. He didn't want to do that to him.

But…thinking about *that* helped him recover something else he'd learned a long, *long* time ago: mate-bonded demons healed faster when they were together. He'd witnessed it during the war.

He and Alucard had only imprinted on one another, though. They hadn't sealed that bond yet.

Would it still work?

He had to try.

The demon pulled his shirt off—it worked through skin-to-skin contact. He climbed into the casket, and after he lay beside Alucard, he pulled the lid shut, sealing them away from the outside world. Darkness embraced them, and for a moment, Zalith just stared at his vampire. He kept every desire other than that to heal and protect Alucard at bay, refusing to let them creep in, and pulled the blanket over himself, moving closer to his fiancé. Slowly and carefully, he eased his arm around him, pressing as much of his body against his as he could…and then he waited.

Was there any way for him to tell whether it was working? Was he supposed to feel something? Some sort of connection? His ethos waking and working? Because there was just…nothing. Only fear and desperation.

So maybe he was wrong. Maybe they *did* have to be bonded.

The thought made him angry—no, it made him *furious* at the situation…and at himself. Why hadn't he and Alucard bonded yet? Why hadn't he said something, especially after proposing to him? He knew that Alucard likely didn't know of it; his fiancé hadn't even known what imprinting was until it happened. If he *had* brought it up, if he'd taken a moment or two to *think*, then maybe his vampire would have recovered already. Maybe their bond would have healed him wholly and swiftly.

But…there they were…unbonded, one of them bordering death while the other lay there in anxious, despairing frustration.

Zalith huffed before nuzzling Alucard's neck—he didn't deserve the indulgence, but he couldn't keep fighting it. His worry was starting to eat away at every part of him. It tore at the aggravation, savagely mauled the anger and despair, and buried the panic and anxiety as if storing it for later, waiting for the right moment to dig it up and let it loose again.

He sighed deeply but softly, closing his eyes, ever so slightly tightening his embrace around his mate. "I'm sorry," he murmured, the sadness only lingering remnants now. Though the longing overtaking everything else wasn't sexual desire, it was the desire to just *hear* Alucard again, to see life on his face, to see no struggle or fatigue, and to feel more than still coldness from his soft skin. "I need you to wake up," he pleaded, his voice a whisper laced with a conflicting combination of emotions and reason.

But he wasn't going to overanalyze himself. He knew what he wanted and needed right now, and it was only for the man he loved to open his eyes and say his name.

Chapter Thirty-Four

— ⸱ ✝ ⸱ —

Not One, Not the Other

| Alucard |
| *The Darkness* |

Gossamer was with Alucard in the library—the place the katsie had helped him find. At first, he'd thought that the cat had helped him for *his* sake, but in this memory, there was a lingering suspicion, just like before. The katsie had its own agenda.

But still, Alucard was demanding answers from the priestess suspended mid-air by strange red ethos. He was asking about his mother. Whatever point this was in his life exactly, he knew that his mother had been killed, but he didn't have her murderer's name.

Why would he suspect Lilith at the time? He looked up to her, desired her approval, longed to work at her side…just as they'd made him believe his mother had—he was convinced that this was the life she wanted for him.

Was it?

Just like Gossamer's ulterior motives, though, this memory of his wasn't just helping him recall the questions he'd had as a child: what bloodline did his mother come from, who was she, what did Erichdian mean, what was a Meridian witch?

His mother was a Cruossorem demon, but not purely—she was three-quarters witch—and Gossamer said that he was something new, something else entirely.

Still, *that* wasn't what he was remembering—not solely.

It wasn't about Gossamer.

Was it?

No.

No?

It was a memory of a time he'd been desperate for the truth, desperate for answers to the endless list of questions that had grown over the five years he'd spent locked up in those catacombs, hearing whispers among the priestesses and the other kids. Most of them thought him a freak, a disgusting abomination, a strange monstrosity. Gossamer had told him that he was *different*, though, a word that triggered his undying desire for an answer as to why, a word he'd never heard used to describe him until the katsie found him.

But the cult and its supply of children didn't say those cruel things because he was the only offspring born with Lucifer's blood.

They murmured about the way he looked. Not just the fading scales, not just the claws, not just the fangs—not even his eyes or ears.

It was his *face*.

His *body*.

His voice.

It was who he was beneath the demon, beneath the creature created for rituals and destruction.

And in that library, when he'd been questioning that priestess, when his frustration had finally cracked through the haze of confusion and doubt, he understood why he'd been asking all along.

He remembered it—inspection—the daily ritual where the priestesses paraded the children out like livestock, ensuring they met Brânduśa's harsh, unyielding standards. He remembered standing there, watching them sort the others. Boys to one side. Girls to the other.

And him?

He hadn't belonged to either.

He hadn't been placed among the girls or the boys. He'd been left hovering at the edges, unspoken for, unseen, the sole occupant of a category no one acknowledged.

Not male. Not female.

Just…him.

It had been in that moment that he'd asked himself: was that what Gossamer meant when it said he was different?

And as his confusion grew, he'd asked himself one other question, a question that filled him with *dread*.

Would he have to choose? Would he have to decide whether he'd stand with the girls or with the boys? And worse…would somebody *make* him choose?

That was when the recollection slipped from his grasp, though. The library faded, the hall of children dissipated like smoke in a bitter breeze, and he was left in darkness— a familiar place. Endless black, an inch-deep layer of water at his feet. It was the same place his dreams often took him to…and his rage. It was the place where he'd seen those three mirrors, the place where Lucifer had attempted to reach him.

What was he going to see this time?

A creeping memory.

Begging to be recalled.

So he let it wrap around him, he let it seep into him…and he was there again—in that cell with that katsie. Only this time, it wasn't accompanying him to dig up answers. This time, Gossamer was teaching him again. Not to turn to vermillion smoke but to find *this place*.

Gossamer had given him a gift—a crystal. It told him that it would help him determine what time of day it was because the catacombs allowed no light in, no hint at the outside world.

But if the priestesses found it, they'd punish him, and he'd likely never be able to see Gossamer again or return to the library.

So the katsie taught him how to hide it.

He closed his eyes, letting the memory take hold, letting it unfold around him as if he were living in that moment again.

He—

No…they.

Not male. Not female.

They.

They clasped their hand shut around the crystal…but when they looked down at themself, there wasn't anywhere to store it. Their clothes were torn and bloody, barely hanging onto their body. No shoes, no pockets. "I 'ave novhere to—"

"You already have a place," Gossamer interjected.

"Vhat…place?"

The cat seemed to hesitate. "Well…you may."

They waited.

"A place within yourself. A part of you. Just as you did to access your ethos, you must do to find this place. Ask your ethos to provide you with somewhere to hide things, to store things…and if you possess a place, it will open, and you can put the stone within."

Aleksei frowned, thinking about it…and then they tried. They reached inward, grasping onto their ethos—something that was gradually becoming easier to do. Once they found their power, they focused, requesting that it give them somewhere to hide this stone, somewhere where the priestesses wouldn't find it, somewhere safe and only known to Aleksei.

A strange crackling sound sliced the silence, and flickering light became visible through Aleksei's eyelids. They opened their eyes, setting their sights on the peculiar glow in front of them. It was like an open wound in the air, only there was no blood, and inside, there was just darkness—endless darkness.

"That's it, Aleksei," the cat gasped, sounding impressed. "Such a fast learner...such great potential." It sounded happy, relieved. "Oh, yes...." But then it purred loudly before saying, "Place the stone inside."

Aleksei felt hesitant at first. The tear looked a lot like a ritual, the kind of thing that they saw the priestesses conjure up. But...Gossamer wouldn't make them do something that would hurt them, would it?

"It is perfectly safe, Aleksei—for you," the cat said, still purring. "The space inside the darkness is yours. It is you."

They glanced at the cat, and then they slowly moved their hand towards the tear. Their fingers passed through. An unusual sensation wrapped around their hand...and then their wrist. It was like...nothingness. There was no cold, no warmth, no feeling at all. There was no smell, either. Nothing to see, nothing to hear. Just nothing.

Yet it felt right. It felt familiar. Like a part of them.

As the familiar comfort welcomed them like the shadows, Aleksei placed the glowing blue stone inside.

"It will be just as easy to take it out again," the cat said. "But not in that room. The silver door will continue to prevent you from using your ethos. That hole in the wall, however, is all you need. You can reach through and create another rift, just as you are able to dematerialize."

Aleksei nodded in understanding.

"You can close it the same way—ask your ethos to seal the rift shut."

That took a little more effort. At first, Aleksei thought that all they had to do was reverse the ethos, but that did nothing other than make them feel strange. So they did exactly as Gossamer said, asking their ethos to close the opening and seal the rift shut, protecting what sat inside.

And their ethos complied. The rift closed with a tiny flash of light and a small crackle.

"Good," the cat purred. "Now go, Aleksei. "And do not get caught."

Aleksei almost did as it said. But they hadn't forgotten. "Vhat about zhat man?"

"What man?"

"Zhe vone I vas vollowing."

"Oh..." the cat said with a nod, glancing in the direction the man had gone. "I will try to find him and see what he is up to. Do not worry about him, Aleksei. You must get back before anyone notices."

They nodded stiffly. "Vill you tell me if you vind 'im? 'E zidn't seem like zhe ozzers."

Gossamer nodded. "Of course." And then it purred. "Stick to the shadows, Aleksei, just as I have taught you."

"Okay," Aleksei said, and then they turned around.

As they disappeared into the dark, though, they looked over their shoulder. The cat didn't move from where it was; it didn't jump down and go after the man, nor did it look in Aleksei's direction; it just… sat and stared aimlessly.

Why? Why wasn't it going after him?

Just as Aleksei was about to stop and question it, though, the cat glided down to the rubble-covered ground and hurried in the direction the man had gone.

And Aleksei continued on their way back to their room. They'd learned yet another ability, and they were excited to see what Gossamer would teach them next.

That was where the memory faded.

But Alucard had already learned enough—*too much.*

He wasn't concerned about what had dragged him into the darkness this time. He wasn't asking if the people he cared for were still alive. He wasn't even panicking that the loup-garou might have seen through his ethos and torn everyone apart.

His fear sat elsewhere.

It gnawed at him in the shape of a single, dismaying question: what would Zalith think of him now?

What would anyone think of him?

He hadn't always been a man—could he even call himself that at all?

Once, he had been something else. Something that didn't make sense. Something that didn't fit into any neat classification that the world demanded.

He was something *other.*

And maybe he always had been—maybe he always was.

That was why Tyrus had asked that question, why Zalith told him that he was different—better than any man he'd ever touched. Because he *was* different; he was strange and nameless, standing always at the edge, belonging to no one side, and no one word.

He didn't remember when he'd changed… if at all.

No… he *had.* He'd chosen at some point despite the dread he felt as a child. But why? When? *How?*

That didn't matter right now. What mattered was the question: how was he going to tell Zalith? …Would he tell him at all?

The vampire scowled, glancing around the endless dark. What if this newfound truth revolted Zalith? What if learning that he was… *different* made him uncomfortable? What if Zalith decided that he didn't want him anymore? Because he was gay—he wanted a *man.* But Alucard wasn't one, was he?

He was just… *nothing.*

He was just….

Cold.

It was only now that he'd realized there'd been no sensation in his body; he felt it only when the bitterness of an unseen breeze scraped against his skin.

The vampire wrapped his arms around himself, standing there, ensnared in the worry and confusion that had struck him. As if bleeding out in an old church cellar wasn't terrible enough. *Now* he had *this* to add to the weight on his shoulders, to add to the twinging ache in his heart.

He and Zalith were supposed to be getting married. Would that still happen if he told his fiancé what he'd just learned? Would the revelation cut between them like a fine talon through flesh, leaving it to slowly bleed until there was nothing left? Only despair and memories.

The cold came again. It brushed down his right side, sending shivers up his spine.

But there was warmth, too. Comforting and *devouring*, spreading from the other side of his body. Gradually, it banished the chill; it sent everything overwhelming Alucard far, *far* away.

And then the darkness shifted. He was no longer standing; there was no longer water at his feet. He couldn't move, but it wasn't the kind of stillness that made his aching heart beat harder. That warmth remained, keeping him grounded, helping ease the pain of unseen wounds.

"Alucard?"

Zalith.

He wanted to respond, to tell his mate that he was awake. But the dread crept back in, wrapping thorns around every inch of him. Anxiety flared in his chest, forcing him to take a low, shuddering breath, and he could feel the scars on his back throbbing. He'd been laying on his back for too long again; his scars were irritated.

"Baby?" came Zalith's voice again.

Alucard felt the demon's warm hand trail across his chest, settling on the side of his neck. The urge to open his eyes and meet Zalith's gaze grew with every passing moment, but so did the worry and despair attached to his recovered memory.

"Hey?" Zalith asked anxiously.

He didn't want to scare him—not after what just happened beneath that church. His mate's feelings were more important than his own. So he opened his eyes. At first, he was ensnared in darkness again, but when he looked slightly to his left, his gaze landed on the man he loved. The man who might not love him after he learned what he was.

"Hey, baby," the demon said with a relieved, affectionate smile, gently stroking the vampire's cheek. He was propped up on his arm, staring down at him, his dark eyes a comforting sight. "How are you feeling?"

Terrified. Despaired. Deceived. Even a little nauseous.

"Tired," he answered. He could feel the lingering ache, the 'I need to sleep for a century' kind of fatigue. But he didn't even have a day, let alone a hundred years. And that made him ask, "'Ow long vas I out?"

"A little over thirteen hours."

The dread intensified, the fear for his relationship and that for his coven combining.

"Everyone's okay, though. Don't worry," the demon said quietly. "I lost two demons…but all of your vampires are okay."

Alucard didn't have the strength to do math, to work out exactly what time it was. He knew that the day of the full moon was approaching—mere hours away, maybe less, maybe more. But it was still coming. If they didn't stop the Silver Claw before then, she'd be nearly impossible to kill, and she could slaughter his entire coven before sunrise.

He tried to sit up, but Zalith made him stay where he was.

"You need to rest," he said worriedly.

The vampire shook his head. "Zhe vull moon vill be 'ere soon. Ve need to come up vith a plan; ve need to vind out vhat we missed, and zhen—"

"I've already got Tyrus working with Alson and a few other vampires who offered to help," Zalith said with an assuring tone. "They're finding whatever they can."

He frowned at him. "Ve vound all ve could about zhe Silver Claw."

Zalith nodded. "But not about who she is behind that name."

Alucard's frown thickened a little. "Vhat did you vind?"

"I don't know yet; I haven't left your side." He fiddled with Alucard's hair, gazing down at him. "But she looked like Ada—*almost* a mirror reflection, if I'm being honest. Anyway, I told them to find out what they could about Ada's direct bloodline and whatever other bloodlines they broke off into. I've spared most of my best intelligence demons, including Orin. We should have *some* answers soon."

Should? That didn't settle Alucard. His coven was in even more danger than they had been thirteen hours ago. "Ve can't vait avound, Zaliv. Vhat if zhey zon't vind anyving?"

"They *will*," he said with a nod, caressing the side of his face. "I can get one of them in here right now if you want…but I think we should stay in here a little longer so you can heal some more."

He stared up at him for a moment, his mind racing, his heart even more so—he wasn't only torn between rest and strategize, though. It was still there…that dread, that confusion and dismay about who and what he was.

With a huff, he looked away, trying to calm his mind.

"It'll be okay," Zalith said. "Just focus on recovering…please?"

He closed his eyes, still fighting the overbearing cascade of thoughts and emotions, demanding the space he needed to reach out. "*Alson,*" he spoke into the Scribe's mind.

"*'Ave you vound anyving out about zhe loup-garou?*" And at the same time, he said to Zalith, "Okay."

The demon rested his head on his shoulder and hugged him tightly.

Alson's reply came not long later, "*W-we're working on it, My Lord. I'm compiling everything, and—*"

"*So, you 'ave vound someving?*"

"*We have, My Lord. Should I bring to you what we have so far? We're still waiting on a few of the demons to come back, though—it's um...O...Orin? He's leading them.*"

They *had* found some information. Alucard wanted to know what it was, but it was probably best to do as Zalith said and rest. That'd give the demons time to return, possibly with more to reveal. "*Vait vor zhe zemons to get back.*"

"*Yes, My Lord.*"

Alucard then severed the telepathic link and turned his head to the side, resting it against Zalith's. He let himself sink into his mate's calming embrace—he even smiled faintly when he felt the demon nuzzling his neck. But as the silence enveloped them, the shroud of despair brought by his recently recovered memory fell over him.

Zalith hummed and murmured, "Do you want blood?" He paused and kissed his neck. "I gave you some earlier a few times, but I didn't want to affect your human form like last time."

He appreciated that. If he'd begun returning to his true form, he'd be down in the city gorging right now. "Vank you," he said, pondering.

"Here, baby," the demon murmured, his hand gliding slowly up Alucard's side, lingering with a reverence that made him tremble, even now. Then Zalith offered his wrist with a small tilt of his hand.

Alucard reached for it, his fingers curling gently around his arm, and drew it towards his mouth. But just before their skin met, Zalith pulled away with a soft, teasing tug.

"Wait," he whispered.

He shifted onto his back and gently guided Alucard to follow, easing him down until he lay draped over the demon's chest. Zalith's body was warm beneath him, a solid comfort. He smiled up at Alucard, and Alucard found himself smiling back despite the dismay.

Zalith caressed the back of the vampire's head, fingers threading through his hair, and he guided Alucard to his throat.

The vampire didn't hesitate—he couldn't help it. He let his lips brush against Zalith's skin first, savouring the pulse beneath, the rich heat of life thrumming just for him. His fangs urged him to bite, a shiver racing through his body as instinct took hold.

He bit down, making Zalith flinch and groan delightedly.

The blood flowed instantly, flooding Alucard's mouth with a taste so potent, so *perfect* that he nearly moaned. Every ache in his muscles and every thread of exhaustion tangled inside him dissolved under that first rush. He drank deeply, each pull sending waves of relief through his exhausted body. His mind, so clouded with doubts and the jagged chaos of the past few days, quieted—not silenced entirely, but smoothed over, lulled by the steady, anchoring presence of the demon beneath him. For a moment, there was no fear, no past clawing at the edges of his thoughts. There was only this, the bond between them, the blood, the warmth of skin against skin, and the knowledge that, for now, he was exactly where he needed to be.

Chapter Thirty-Five

— ⸲ ✝ ⸴ —

Loup-Garou, Thaernari, and...?

| Alucard |

| *Atheson, Atheson Coven Sanctum* |

Peaceful rest couldn't last forever, especially not now. As much as Alucard wanted to lie there beside the man he loved, as much as he wanted to stay lost in his mate's warmth and the embracing darkness of his casket, he couldn't afford to let the hours slip away. The full moon was at the threshold, and the clock was ticking.

The vampire shifted lightly under the weight of Zalith's body, and he smiled when the demon kissed his neck. Zalith's affection chased away the despair—for now, at least. Alucard couldn't let anything slow him down; he couldn't become distracted. The only thing he couldn't bury, though, was the lingering desire. But maybe that was a good thing. Letting the demands of his heat burn within him helped him escape the overbearing emotions that his recovered memory burdened him with.

"No," Zalith drawled, complaining as Alucard shifted again. "Don't go."

Alucard ran his fingers through the demon's hair and down his back. The softness of Zalith's skin flared his instincts, but he wouldn't give in. "Ve need to get veady to kill zhe loup-garou," he said as he reached for the casket handle.

Zalith groaned and tightened his arms around him.

The vampire gripped the handle and said, "Zhe sooner zhat bitch is dead, zhe sooner ve can go 'ome."

His mate purred against his neck, "I *love* it when you get all serious and angry."

Alucard smiled but used his other hand to gently ease Zalith off him. "Come on," he said as he lifted the lid.

Although he groaned in response, Zalith followed him out of the casket.

The vampire kept hold of the blanket, wrapping it around himself as he headed for the wardrobe—Zalith had taken his bloody clothes off, and it was *freezing* in this room.

He took out some new clothes, and as he hastily dressed, he glanced at the demon, who was buttoning his own shirt.

"Is Tyrus in zhe library vith Alson?"

Zalith nodded, moving towards him. "I'm going to warn you, though—if that little half-bearded vampire starts flirting with you again, I might have to take his eyes out."

Undeniably amused, Alucard smiled a little.

The demon placed one hand on the side of his neck and said, "Hold on." He licked his own thumb and then gently rubbed Alucard's lip with it. "You had some blood on your lip," he told him, smirking as he took his thumb away.

"Vank you," he said and pulled his blazer on.

Zalith took hold of his hand and began leading the way across the room.

Alucard led him across the communal hall, through the hallway, and to the Thornsong Library, where not only Alson and Tyrus were working but a crowd of people, too—some of Zalith's demons, and most of his vampires.

"What have you got?" Zalith asked, stopping by Tyrus.

Tyrus' eyes were on Alucard for a moment.

Alucard scowled a little. Not only did Tyrus have a job to do and a question to answer, but the vampire was admittedly aggravated—and upset—about the question the allocer had asked him earlier, especially after the memory he'd just relived.

"So, Ada Ardelean's bloodline began about four hundred years ago," Alson started.

Tyrus snapped out of it, glancing down at the Scribe. "That means around sixteen generations have been created since then. Orin sent some updates, and at the moment, we've recorded six different werewolf lines."

"Most of them are of Dor-Sanguian descent," Alson said and waved someone over.

Fledgeling Esphyllia scurried through the crowd with a large leather-bound book and several smaller books clutched against her chest. She dropped them onto Alson's table and hastily opened the larger one first. "Here, sir," she said to the Scribe.

Alucard stared down at the pages. The book was written in Dor-Sanguian. "You learned zhis language?" he questioned.

The Scribe nodded. "Some of it. I wanted to read the books in here that are written in it—I-I hope that's okay."

Alucard didn't have a problem with it—in fact, a part of him was glad that someone else was able to understand his native language, a tongue that had become almost extinct. But when he glanced at Zalith, he saw that irritated, *hostile* glare on his face, and the demon tightened his grip on his hand.

Alson continued, "So, Kardos—the Aegis who created Ada—had a brother, Thalis."

"Who created the first werewolves in Eltaria," Tyrus said.

"They created werewolves *together*—"

"At first," the allocer added.

"But it says here—" Alson pointed to a large section of text, "—that Thalis *also* created a few werewolves *here*. This is an old story about how Kardos and Thalis had a disagreement not even a year after creating the first wolves." He tapped the page, glancing up at Alucard.

"What does this have to do with the loup-garou?" Zalith muttered.

"Well, the brothers were in disagreement about what werewolves should and shouldn't be capable of. Thalis' first…design, I guess we could call it, was *extremely* powerful—"

Tyrus interjected again, "Likely where Greymore's unique appearance and power comes from."

"—while Kardos' first design paled in comparison—that would be Ada. *So*, Kardos tried to create something that would shadow his brother's first wolf. *That's* when the loup-garou come in. Kardos wanted to create a wolf that would outgrow the pack hierarchy that had developed among the first wolves. It took him a few tries—and that's where several other old bloodlines began and evolved into all these other kinds of wolves—that doesn't matter right now, I know—but he got there in the end, and the first loup-garou was created." He flipped the page.

"Apparently, the first loup-garou and one of Thalis' Aegisguardian wolves were fated," Tyrus said before the Scribe could.

"That was something neither Aegis thought about," Alson chuckled. "You can't breed fate out of anything."

Tyrus continued with a small eye roll, "They started the Veyne Bloodline, a combination of their surnames, Velcanar and Seradyne. As said, since then, over two dozen generations have been born; if this loup-garou really is related to Ada, then somewhere among those generations, a Veyne loup-garou must have had children with one of Ada's direct descendants, but we don't know which—"

"But *two* generations ago—"

"Two generations ago—" Tyrus said louder, cutting Alson off, "—Orin managed to find out that Mihăilă Veyne-Blood, the son of Nocturne King Nechifor Veyne-Blood, the ruler of Dor-San—"

"Dor-Sanguis' Deep Luna Vorests, I know," Alucard impatiently interrupted—he hadn't known Nechifor's bloodline name, though.

Tyrus nodded. "He married Sânziana, the Thaernari Elf Princess."

"They brought elf blood into the Veyne loup-garou line," Alson said, worriedly.

Alucard nodded. "Zhat's vhy zhe Silver Claw isn't susceptible to silver," he said to Zalith. "And 'er strength makes sense—she's velated to a Nocturne King and zhe princess of an elv bloodline."

Zalith crossed his arms but stepped closer to Alucard, ensuring that their shoulders were touching now that their hands weren't. "So, Veyne or Veyne-Blood is the hunter's surname?" He didn't look at Alson—he was asking Tyrus.

"It seems that way, sir, yes," the allocer answered. "Orin's on it."

"Thaernari Elves—what do we know?" he then questioned.

"Zhey're an ancient Dor-Sanguian species," Alucard said.

Alson nodded and took one of the smaller books that Esphyllia had brought over. "They're uh... forest-dwelling, but they're kinda more fungal and bone-like than planty. Usually, they have like... antlers and stuff, but their blood is apparently very easily tainted through interspecies breeding, and since this elf and loup-garou had a kid, and *that* kid had the loup-garou we're dealing with, it's likely that the immunity to silver is the only thing she inherited. Although there is a sort of regeneration ability that she *might* have inherited—it's like a fifty-fifty situation—but she could possibly be able to heal herself even faster by absorbing the vitality from like... decaying things."

Alucard dragged his hand over his face. "Do ve 'ave devinite answer as to vhether or not ve *are* dealing vith zhis elv-loup-garou 'ybrid?" But the signs were there: immunity to silver, enough strength to fight off even him and Zalith. How had nobody else worked any of this out? Why didn't the stories of the Silver Claw mention anything about what they were now learning?

Zalith was evidently thinking the exact same thing. He asked before Alson could answer Alucard's question, "Why was none of this information recorded by the people who heard stories and shit about this hunter?"

"Is possible zhat she killed anyvone who saw vhat she vas veally capable of," Alucard said with a sigh. "A 'unter like 'er vouldn't vant 'er targets to know vhat to prepare vor." He sighed and looked at Tyrus. "So, is zhere devinite answer?"

Tyrus half-nodded. "Orin's hunting for it," he said, looking at Alucard. "He's tracked down Sânziana; that's how we know all of this bloodline information. She said that Mihăilă left Dor-Sanguis a few months after she gave birth to their daughter, Amechiția. Mihăilă wanted a son, and Sânziana had complications after having their daughter or something—those details don't matter. It's likely that Amechiția is our loup-garou's mother."

Alson said, "Orin is trying to track *her* down, but he—"

"He hasn't gotten that far yet," Tyrus interrupted him again.

Alucard glanced at the clock standing between two bookshelves, only just able to see it through the crowd of muttering, reading vampires and demons. "Ve 'ave less zhan seven hours now." He looked at Zalith. "Do you vink Orin vill vind out in time?"

Zalith glanced at Tyrus. "Does he have any leads?"

The allocer shook his head. "Only Sânziana. Her daughter cut contact after meeting a man, but she doesn't know whether this guy was werewolf or human or something else."

"Vhich means zhis loup-garou could 'ave even more vesistances and abilities zhat ve're not avare of," Alucard snarled frustratedly.

"Well, loup-garou are very egotistical, it seems," Zalith said. "Would one of them marry beneath them? Or have a child with someone they thought was inferior?"

Alucard exhaled deeply. "Only if vate vas involved."

"Are non-humans and humans often fated to one another?"

"More ovten zhan vone might vink."

Zalith nodded slowly. "So, what are the odds?"

Alucard thought about it. "I'd say…vivteen to eighty-vive—but…" he paused, pondering again, "someving as powervul as a loup-garou against vate lowers zhat."

"Then I think we should assume that this loup-garou has another non-human heritage."

With a frown on his face, Alucard slowly sank onto the couch—his legs were starting to feel tired. "Did anyvone notice anyving about 'er ozzer zhan zhe vact zhat she almost killed everyvone?" he mumbled.

Zalith sat beside him. "Nobody reported anything."

"I saw how Roderic died, sir," Tyrus said. "When he lost his grip, I heard him try to summon his influence, but the woman's eyes kind of…pulsed for less than half a second—I thought it was the light coming from that door. Now that I think about it, though, it was almost as if she saw what Roderic was going to do before he did it. She knew exactly how to stop him."

"Vhat kind of pulse?" Alucard questioned.

Tyrus crossed his arms. "It was like…when a drop of water hits a puddle's surface— a ripple, almost."

Zalith looked at the vampire. "Does that sound like anything you know of?"

He frowned again, thinking…. "I zon't know," he answered, shaking his head. "Zhere are a lot of non-'umans whose eyes veact in some vay vhen zhey use ethos. Is too much to narrow down."

"I suppose we'll have to go on what we've got," the demon said, both worry and confliction in his voice.

Alucard looked at Alson. "Tell everyvone to start vesearching all non-'umans whose eyes veact vhen zhey use ethos."

The Scribe nodded and got up, disappearing into the crowd while he called out Alucard's order.

"Ve can try to narrow down in zhe time ve 'ave," he said to Zalith. "And 'ope zhat Orin can get us a devinite answer about zhis loup-garou's bloodline."

Zalith nodded and rested his head on his shoulder. "Can we hypothesize what her weaknesses are based on what we already know?"

"Vell, I vead somevhere zhat a lot of elves are susceptible to necromancy ethos, but ve zon't 'ave any necromancers among us, do ve?"

The demon shook his head.

"Zhere's um… Veybane Oil," he said…though he was hesitant.

"Feybane Oil?" Zalith questioned, sounding intrigued.

He nodded.

"Why do you sound unsure about it?" he asked, clearly concerned.

"Is just…pretty barbaric," the vampire said with a sigh. Yes, this bitch had killed his vampires and was out to destroy the entire coven, and he wanted her dead so that she couldn't harm another, but he involuntarily felt *unnerved* about using the oil. He didn't have to search deep to figure out why, though. He'd seen what that oil could do, and the result looked far too similar to the things Damien and Lilith had done to *him*.

Zalith's voice snatched his attention, "Barbaric how?"

He glanced at him before leaning back, trying to relax, but the fatigue was getting worse. "Is made vrom evernight lilies, golden cordyceps, and ground iron. Zhe lilies put zhe elv into zhis sort of sleep, and zhe cordyceps takes avay all of zheir perception, but zhey still veel everyving vhile zhe iron burns zhem alive," he explained, grimacing lightly.

Tyrus huffed and said, "I've heard about golden cordyceps. It's used a lot to erase memories, but it has some nasty side effects."

"Can we get our hands on some?" Zalith asked.

Alucard did his best to bury the idea of comparison in the same grave as the despair of his memories. "Zhere might be some in zhe veapons vault, or all of zhe components vill be in zhe alchemy supply closet." He shifted, resting one leg over the other. "Ve 'ave a Vitreophage 'ere who can make zhe oil quickly."

"Vitreophage?" his mate repeated.

"Zhe vampire vesponsible vor cveating anyving alchemy-velated vor zhe coven."

"Oh."

"Give me a second," Alucard said, and then he focused, reaching out to the Vitreophage. "*Virelka,*" he said into her mind.

"*Y-yes, My Lord?*" she replied.

"*Do ve 'ave Veybane Oil?*"

"*Let me check.*"

"Zhere's iron, of course," Alucard then said. "Ve 'ave iron veapons in zhe vault."

"*We have one five-hundred-millimetre bottle, My Lord,*" came Virelka's voice.

"Ve do 'ave zhe oil," he told Zalith as he said to Virelka, "*Multumesc,*" and severed the telepathic link.

"What do we do?" Tyrus asked. "Cover the weapons in oil?"

"Zhat's probably zhe best idea vor most of zhe zemons. But now zhat ve know more, ve shouldn't vace 'er in a small space, especially not a tunnel or cellar."

Zalith frowned. "Get her out into an open area?"

He nodded. "Exposing 'er to zhe moonlight, making 'er shivt—zhat zoesn't matter; she's alveady powervul. Ve just need to do zhis bevore zhe day of zhe vull moon. Getting 'er outside gives us more voom to attack and vetreat."

"Do you think she's going to let us lead her out from wherever she's hiding, though?" Tyrus asked. "She already kicked our asses. Why would we go looking for her again if not with a better plan?"

"Ego," Zalith said firmly. "You said it yourself; she kicked our asses, and she's probably under the impression that she'll kick them again. She kills vampires for a living, so she likely thinks that she knows everything about them." He turned his gaze to Alucard. "She looked pretty confused when you hurt and blinded her."

Alucard shook his head. "Zhat could be zhe very ving zhat outweighs 'er ego. Vas like she's *never* been 'urt *at all*. She's going to be cautious now."

"But she got a fatal hit off on you—well, fatal if you were just a vampire," Tyrus said to Alucard. "She probably thinks you're dead."

He thought about it for a moment. He admittedly felt embarrassed about the fact that he'd been incapacitated so quickly and easily; being in heat was wildly distracting, but he didn't feel as though it was *so* focus-stealing that it could have gotten him killed. However, *that* shouldn't be what he was concentrating on. "Vell, vhether she vinks I'm dead or not, ve 'ave no idea vhere she moved to. She vouldn't be in zhat cellar anymore—she might not even be in zhe tunnels at all."

"Nymeris is searching the tunnels with her familiar," Zalith said as he moved his arm around Alucard. "When was her last report?" he asked Tyrus.

"Two hours ago, sir—she's searched a little over seventy percent of what's on the maps, and now she's reached the lower catacombs. I could go and help her if you don't need me here anymore."

Zalith nodded.

Tyrus swiftly left the room.

"As for the city, it's still under quarantine," Zalith then said. "If she were there, our people would have spotted her."

With a deep exhale, Alucard tried his best to relax. But how could he? He had but hours left to find and kill this loup-garou before it went on a rampage and destroyed his entire Atheson coven.

Zalith nuzzled his neck.

A desire-ridden chill ran down Alucard's back. *Not now.* He looked around the library, searching for something to distract himself with. But that was when he noticed them—the demons…glancing at him, some dragging gazes away that might have been locked onto him since he stepped into the room. It made him uncomfortable, forcing him to look away.

Maybe they should head down to the weapons vault and start gathering up what iron was available. Or maybe…maybe he should use this time to recover more. He was *still* tired; his legs felt heavy, like he'd been on his feet non-stop for a decade.

Why? He didn't feel this exhausted the last time his body went comatose, or the time before that…or *any* previous time at all.

He sighed again. He didn't know what to put it down to, and he was too tired to try.

"Do you want to eat me a little more?" Zalith murmured seductively.

Alucard glanced down at what he could see of his face. "Vhat?"

"My blood," he said with a small laugh, still nuzzling his neck. "Do you want more?"

Perhaps *that* would help. But if he took more, Zalith would get weaker. "I can't," he replied, resting his head against the demon's.

"You *can*," his mate said, his voice barely a whisper. "You put your teeth in me, and then you suck out my blood."

He laughed softly. "If I do zhat vight now, you vill get veaker, Zaliv."

"I'd rather be weaker if it means that you're stronger…and feeling better."

"I'll be okay, zon't vorry," he tried to assure him.

Zalith hummed in response, nuzzling a little closer. "Can we go back to your room?"

He glanced around again. More demons tore their stares away—stares just like Tyrus'. They were all wondering the same thing, weren't they? They wanted to know what he was. But he didn't know the answer to that anymore, and he wasn't sure whether he wanted it or not, no matter how desperate he might have been as a child.

"Let's go," he said, taking Zalith's hand.

They got up and left the library.

Zalith clung to him, close enough that their bodies met but they weren't stumbling over one another. Instead of his silent indulging, though, the demon asked, "Are you okay, baby?"

He nodded. "I just need a little more vest. I'm vorried about all of zhis, too. I guess I'm overvhelmed."

"Is there anything I can do to help?" he asked, and although he was clearly flirting, there was concern in his voice.

His body said yes, his heart said maybe…but his mind said *don't do it*. He knew that having sex would at least relieve the frustration and demands of his body, but it would take away from what little energy he had right now—and he was sure that they wouldn't stop at only once; they'd go again…and maybe even again after that.

"Lie down vith me," he answered, pushing the door to his resting space open.

"I can do that—"

"No sex," he said firmly, taking Zalith to the couch.

Zalith groaned…but he didn't plead. "You're right," he said, sitting beside him. "I'm sorry, it's just—"

"I know," he said softly, slowly settling his body against Zalith's, resting his head on his chest. "Is 'ard vor me, too." Though he was certain that it was much harder for his mate, the incubus, the demon who needed sex to survive.

The demon kissed his head and started rubbing his arm. "We'll kill her, don't worry." He *nuzzled* his head. "I'm not going to let her hurt you again, nor will I let her kill any of your vampires."

A small smile broke his tired face as he closed his eyes and let the comfort of Zalith's embrace devour him. "Vank you vor 'elping me vith all of zhis."

Zalith hummed quietly. "I'm always here for you baby, no matter what it is."

His smile grew, and to the calming beat of his mate's heart and the pleasing, relieving scent of him, Alucard *finally* felt his tense, tired body surrendering, *alleviating*. This time, maybe the rest and quiet would give him the strength he needed. He just hoped that those overbearing thoughts didn't take this silence as an invitation to intrude.

To his relief, though, it was something else that came to mind.

He needed to hunt an Aegis.

"Zaliv?"

"Hmm?"

"Ve still need to vind and kill an Aegis so I can make zhat protective clothing."

The demon sighed heavily. "I know. I'm just afraid that something's going to happen to you. An Aegis is a whole lot more dangerous than a loup-garou."

"I know, but you saw me take down Boreas in Avalmoor. Killing zhe Aegis is vhat I vas born to do. Ve'll be okay. Zhe 'ard part is *vinding* vone, not killing vone," he tried to assure him.

Zalith huffed. "I trust you, baby…I just…" he paused and sighed again.

"I can get my people to tell me vhich Aegis are vhere, and ve can go vrom zhere, no? I 'ave Mărioara and Gheorghiță; zhey lead zhe team searching vor and vatching Aegis; I can get zhem to send me vegular updates. Ve'll pick zhe least dangerous of zhem all—some of zhem are actually so veak zhat you'd vink is a joke."

He scoffed a laugh. "Well, let's hope we can find one of *them*, then."

Alucard nodded in agreement and relaxed. He was tired, and he didn't want to talk about hunting and killing and working anymore. Right now, he just wanted to rest.

Chapter Thirty-Six

Tyrus and Nymeris

| Tyrus |
| *Atheson, Atheson City Vaults* |

Descending into the tunnels, Tyrus honed his focus, narrowing the world to the subtle thread of Nymeris' familiar aura. It shimmered faintly at the edge of his awareness, elusive but there. He latched onto it, pushing everything else aside.

The air thickened as he moved deeper; the walls narrowed, the stone around him damp and choked with the scent of mildew. His boots echoed as he walked, quiet enough not to draw attention but loud enough to remind anything lurking that he didn't fear the dark.

When he reached the catacombs, he passed rusted sconces, broken bricks, and passages that branched off like skeletal ribs, once burial paths and now just forgotten arteries beneath the city's skin. He navigated them swiftly, every step taking him closer to the aura's pull, and every breath tightened the tension in his chest. Something had disturbed the flow of the space; faint tremors in the air, unsettled dust in the corners. Someone had been here recently, and it wasn't Nymeris.

He readied himself for potential confrontation, hoping that it wasn't the loup-garou. He knew that Nymeris could handle herself, but he'd seen what that monster could do, and the idea of his ex-Beta being torn apart unnerved him—no, it made him anxious. She was more than an old subordinate; she was a friend, and he didn't want to see her slaughtered.

So he picked up the pace. Nymeris' aura was getting stronger now, but whatever had drawn her this far… it hadn't left—it was with her, clashing with her aura.

It had a scent. Faint. Wet dust and old fabric.

That wasn't the loup-garou.

So what the hell was it?

He moved faster, his footfalls sharper, echoing off the stone in clipped bursts. The tunnel thinned before flaring open again, and he turned left into a lower passage where the place grew colder and vaulted.

More scent. Blood. Burnt silk. Something was definitely dead.

At the end of the corridor, an arched doorway led into a crypt. Tyrus slipped through it silently, ready to attack—

But he didn't have to.

In the gloom of the forgotten chamber, surrounded by shattered stone coffins and torn sigils, was Nymeris. She stood over the twitching remains of a massive, spider-like beast, her blades slick with crimson and her expression cool. The creature was grotesque, its body bloated and black with limbs that bent in every angle, each one lined with fine hairs like cracked velvet. Its face wasn't like that of a spider at all, but vaguely humanoid, a warped mimicry of a woman's mouth split open too wide, fangs embedded in rotted flesh. Tattered white robes still clung to parts of its body, as if it had once masqueraded as a priestess...or devoured one. Now, it lay slumped across broken altar stones, steaming from deep slashes across its abdomen.

Nymeris straightened, exhaling once through her nose as she wiped blood from her jaw with the back of her hand. Her eyes—shard-like and iridescent orange—glinted in the dim light that came from the dying flicker of charged ethos by one of the coffins, burning what looked like *huge* spider eggs. Her pale skin bore glowing scars, winding across her arms like ritual markings, and her long white braids were tied back in a high knot, still swinging with the force of her last strike.

Tyrus stood still for a moment, relieved. He wasn't surprised, not really. He used to fight at her side; she was his best Beta before she was reassigned and given leadership of her own pack. But it was still impressive to see her take down another beast.

Nymeris turned to face him, smiling a little as a streak of black blood curved down her cheekbone; she looked half glad to see him and half shocked.

Tyrus took one look at the mangled creature behind her and gave a low whistle. "Still showing off, I see." He stepped closer, boots crunching lightly over broken stone and half-dried ichor. "Nicely done, though." His eyes flicked over her—no obvious wounds, no shaking in her hands—but he still tilted his head a little, one brow raised. "You okay?"

With a nod, she wiped the blood from her face; she gave a small shrug, eyes flicking briefly to the floor before meeting his again. "I figured I'd save you the trouble." There was a glint of dry humour behind her words—subtle, but unmistakably her. "I know how much you hate huge insects."

"Who told you that?" he asked with a laugh.

She cleaned her swords with her coat before sheathing them, one on either side of her belt. "Nobody, but I saw enough when we were dealing with Cecil's giant cockroach council, and I recall you standing at a 'tactical distance' when we were clearing out that arachnoid nest back in Nefastus so the compound could be built."

Tyrus ran a hand over the back of his neck. "All right, fine. *Tactical distance* may have been more like the next building over." His lips twitched—he *was* a little embarrassed, but he wasn't going to turn red-faced about it. If there was anyone he didn't mind knowing his fears, it was the person he'd been able to rely on for *years* to watch his back. "I was prioritizing survival—and dignity."

Nymeris gave him a look, all quiet amusement and purposeful innocence. "Mm. Is that what we're calling shrieking and climbing onto the supply cart now?"

Tyrus barked a laugh, unable to stop it. "I didn't *shriek*, I was just surprised to see them all pouring out of those holes—and that cart was extremely defensible, thank you. Perfect vantage point."

She shook her head, but her smile lingered. After a brief pause, she nodded back towards the shadowed tunnel behind her. "I was heading that way, but these things were nesting in the side passage. I didn't want to risk getting flanked later." She adjusted the straps of her blades on her belt, the confidence still there but tempered by a flicker of hesitation. "Sorry I slowed down."

He waved it off instantly, more serious now. "It's fine. I figured you'd run into something this far underground; it's why I suggested you for this job in the first place. I knew you'd handle it."

Nymeris smiled appreciatively. "Well, I'm grateful. Ever since the promotion, I've been trying to find an opportunity to prove to the boss that I'm up to it, you know?"

"He wouldn't have signed off on the suggestion if he didn't think you were ready," he assured her, walking towards her. "You get all of them?" he then asked as he stopped in front of her and glanced around the crypt.

She followed his glance and gave a thoughtful hum. "I *think* I got all of them," she said, drawing the word out just enough to sound suspicious. "Unless there's still one hiding somewhere. You know, waiting. Something with too many legs and a personal vendetta." She nudged his arm lightly with her elbow. "Maybe it's watching you right now, knitting a Tyrus-sized web to store you inside for dinner later."

Tyrus gave her a sidelong look. "That sounds exactly like something a giant spider with a human face would be doing." He took a half-step back and glanced up at the ceiling. "If a single leg of that thing twitches—" he nodded at the dead creature, "—I'm setting this whole crypt on fire. I'll write it off as tactical cremation."

Nymeris grinned. "Very professional."

"I try." He rolled his shoulders and gestured tunnel she'd indicated. "Come on, spider-whisperer. Let's finish mapping this place before your hairy little friends catch up."

She nodded and took the lead, summoning her spectre-like snake familiar; just like Tyrus' tiger, it shimmered with hints of silver, and it hissed as it formed and oozed to the rubble-covered floor. "Scout ahead again," she told it, and then it slithered off. "How are things back at the Sanctum?" she asked, looking over her shoulder at him.

"Tense," he answered. "Everyone's getting restless trying to find out who and what this loup-garou is. A lot of the new demons are finding it hard to accept Alucard, though. I had to punch Roderic earlier before he died. I'm surprised Zalith hasn't mauled any of them yet."

"Elyndar's pack?"

He nodded.

Nymeris looked ahead again, stepping over a few chunks of fallen stone. "I've learned a lot about the demons of this realm," she started. "They definitely clung onto the rules and expectations of demon society despite having to assimilate with humans to survive. I've also heard chatter among my own pack, and apparently, when Alegan led Elyndar's pack, he was *extremely* old-world, and he even adopted some of the humans' religious beliefs, one being that only man and woman should lie together. So, of course, his pack had all of that drilled into them. But under Elyndar, I'm sure all of the brainwashing will fade. They'll come to respect the boss as much as we do, too. I think they just need time." She glanced back at him for half a moment as she added, "Some of them are probably still bitter about the packmates they lost in the initial takeover, too."

With another nod, he said, "I understand that, at least. We all know what it's like to lose people."

"What still kinda baffles me is the fact that some of them have all these problems with one thing or another but choose to stay—the boss gave them a choice, and they still have one." She shook her head. "I don't know. Maybe I haven't learned everything about Aegisguardian demons."

He followed her down a narrow set of stone steps. "One thing that doesn't seem to be different from race to race is misery loves company," he said with a sigh.

"And here I thought non-humans as a whole were socially centuries ahead of humans," she muttered, slowing as they approached a fork in their path.

Tyrus gave a quiet snort. "Some are. Some just like to pretend they are." He glanced ahead, scanning the dim paths and stopping beside Nymeris when she halted. "There's always going to be someone who prefers the past—grudges, bad routines, all of it. It's familiar. It doesn't matter if they're demon, human, werewolf, or something in between with a superiority complex…people cling to what they know, even if it's rotting." He checked left and then right. "Progress makes noise, and some people hate noise." He glanced at her. "At least *we're* evolved, though."

"All we can do is hope they'll catch up soon," she mumbled. "So, how do you want to tackle this?"

He stared down each path—the left sloped downward, slick with moisture; the right narrowed sharply, already half-choked by roots; the centre was wide and dark with air that smelled faintly disturbed. He didn't like the idea of splitting up, not with the loup-garou still unaccounted for. Nymeris could hold her own—he'd never doubted that—but still, the thought sat wrong in his gut. Dragging their feet wouldn't help, either. They needed to map this place *fast*.

His jaw shifted slightly as he made the call, "We'll send our familiars—yours left and mine right." He pointed forward. "We take the centre."

Nymeris nodded without hesitation, already reaching out and summoning her familiar back.

Tyrus manifested his tiger with a quiet breath, and it stood beside him.

Silence.

They waited.

He took his eyes off the tunnel and looked at Nymeris for a moment. He hadn't seen very much of her lately, not since everyone got to Uzlia, and he was glad to have the chance to work with her again. He missed the banter, and he missed working with someone so capable—not that the rest of his pack weren't good at their jobs, Nymeris just had a particular way of approaching situations, something he'd never underestimate or fail to appreciate. Above *that*, though, he'd missed *her*.

"So," he said, breaking the silence, "since you know I don't like bugs, I think it's only fair that you tell me something *you* don't like."

"Me?" she asked with a quiet laugh—she sounded a little nervous. "It's stupid."

He laughed, too. "Come on," he encouraged her.

Nymeris sighed and shrugged. "Mannequins."

Tyrus frowned, stifling another laugh. "Mannequins?"

"See? It *is* stupid."

He chuckled and said, "I didn't say it was stupid, I just haven't heard it before."

She sighed and shook her head. "They just…it's like they resemble people in only the *worst* ways—they're too smooth and stiff and always watching with eyes that they don't have," she explained with a grimace. "They *look* like people from a distance, but then not enough up close. And the silence." She shivered. "I just…can't."

Tyrus thought about it for a moment. It made sense…in a way. "Have you ever had a run-in with a mannequin?"

"Did you *see* where I was assigned when we got to Eimwood, Tyrus?"

"You were patrolling in the woods with Ruthven, right?"

"Near one of the city walls," she said with a nod, cringing. "There was a pit out there, maybe fifty feet from the tree line. Ruthven found it. It was *filled* with discarded mannequins—literally hundreds of the things," she exclaimed. "I'd always never been huge about them…or dolls, but after seeing *that*? I'd rather have been up in that cellar with the loup-garou than see another goddamn mannequin, and I'm *not* joking."

"Why were they in a pit?"

"Beats me," she muttered. "Maybe one of Cecil's cockroach buddies had a fetish." She turned her head and frowned at him. "Did you know that one of his little councilmen—Bertram, I think—had a doorknob fetish?"

"What?"

"They found maybe a thousand doorknobs stashed in his estate basement, and even a few door handles, too. I would not be surprised if that pit belonged to one of them."

"What was he even doing with them?" he questioned but then frowned. "Not butt things…."

She laughed and shook her head. "I honestly don't know. But considering they found a whole room of laceless shoes in the house of one of the other councilmen, I think it's safe to assume that they either all had weird fetishes or just hoarded stuff for whatever reason. I'm not a giant bug-person specialist, though."

His frown thickened. "Laceless shoes…."

"Maybe he ate the laces, and maybe Bertram ate the doors that the knobs were attached to, and maybe whoever put those mannequins out there ate the clothes off of them," she suggested.

"I wonder if there's clothing-moth people—they're probably hideous."

Nymeris shivered. "I don't even want to think about it," she said as her familiar returned, slithering along the ground of the tunnel ahead of them. She placed her hand on the spectral snake when it lifted its head. "He explored maybe a hundred feet, but it looks like it goes on for much longer."

Tyrus nodded. "All right, I'll send Kubra left, and you send Veshka right."

She chuckled softly as she instructed her familiar to search the right tunnel. "So, you remember his name."

"Of course. I remember a lot of things," he said as he sent his tiger left.

The two of them stepped into the central tunnel, walking side by side, the echoes of their steps swallowed by the dark.

"Like what?" she asked curiously.

"Well…." Tyrus glanced at her as they stepped over more rubble, and he pulled a protruding clump of vines out of her way. "You always hated the cold, even though Amira swore you were just being dramatic."

Nymeris let out a quiet laugh under her breath.

"And you used to hum when you were nervous. Mostly under your breath, but Cillian always noticed. He thought it meant you were about to snap someone's neck."

"I was *usually* just thinking," she muttered, cheeks faintly flushed.

He grinned. "That's what I told him."

They walked a few more steps before he added, "Also, when I'd let one of you guys lead the mission, you used to braid your hair differently depending on how much you trusted who I chose. You always had it knotted tight when Ruthven was in charge."

Nymeris was clearly trying not to smile too much. "That's ridiculous."

"Is it?" Tyrus said, brows raised. "Because I've seen at least three different braid patterns since we got to Uzlia."

She laughed softly, the sound echoing lightly through the stone tunnel. "All right, fine," she said, nudging his arm with her elbow. "Since we're apparently trading memories now… I remember something about *you*."

He gave her a cautious glance. "This feels like a trap."

She grinned, eyes flicking ahead. "You remember that job in Aeldrin's Hollow? The one where Cillian got stuck in the well?"

"Vividly."

"Well, while we were trying to pull him out, *you* fell in. Backwards."

Tyrus groaned. "Here we go." He exhaled sharply through his nose. "I *descended with intent*."

"I distinctly remember you shouting, 'I slipped on purpose to assess the depth,' while flailing."

"It *was* a depth assessment," he said, lifting his chin just a bit. "And a structural test. If I recall, that well didn't collapse under me, which means it passed."

"Uh-huh. And then you refused help getting out because you said it was a 'training opportunity.'"

He shrugged. "I stand by that. Builds initiative."

She looked at him, amused. "You were lucky you're the Alpha."

"You *know* I'd do it again," he said, feigning solemnity. "For the mission."

Nymeris held up her hands, still smiling. "Truce."

"Temporary truce," he muttered, though the warmth never left his voice.

They walked in silence for a while longer. But when they passed beneath a low, crumbling archway, its edges scorched and half-choked with old mortar, it became clear that the passage had once been sealed.

Beyond it lay a wide, forgotten chamber.

As they stepped into the space, the air got colder. Ancient stone coffins lined the walls in broken rows, their lids cracked or missing entirely. Scattered bones littered the floor like a battlefield long lost to time, and in the centre of the room lay the massive, long-dead corpse of a creature twisted by age and decay. Its skin had mummified against its ribs, the shape of it unrecognizable but unmistakably wrong.

Nymeris slowed to a halt. Tyrus did too, scanning the shadows while she reached into her coat and pulled out a handful of folded papers. She flipped through them quickly, her brow furrowing.

"What is it?" he asked, eyes still tracking the edges of the room.

She frowned. "The map from those city plans… it stops at the end of the tunnel we just came from."

Tyrus glanced at the papers—she'd drawn up a very rough copy of the mapped tunnels. "You're sure?" he asked despite knowing that it was very unlikely she was wrong, but maybe the *maps* were incomplete.

Nymeris shook her head. "I looked over those maps a dozen times. They definitely ended at that tunnel."

He set his eyes on the archway at the end of the chamber. "Well, it looks like it goes on much further than this room." He looked at her again. "We should continue. The loup-garou could be that way."

She nodded and said, "Agreed."

They crossed the chamber in silence, their boots crunching over debris and brittle bones. Tyrus kept his senses sharp, scanning every corner, every shadow, but his thoughts tugged back towards Nymeris. He missed talking to her—*really* talking. The easy rhythm, the shared shorthand. But now wasn't the best time to start another conversation. One wrong sound could carry too far down these old halls. The loup-garou could still be down here.

So instead, he stayed quiet and near.

The tunnel was narrower than the last, thick with the kind of cold that didn't feel natural. It clung to the back of his throat and settled along his bones. The stone underfoot changed, too; it was no longer the rough city-hewn texture of the older catacombs, but smoother.

Tyrus slowed slightly, his hands drifting into their combat-ready grasp. Something wasn't right. There was no rot or smell of decay. The walls were too clean, the silence too complete.

He glanced at Nymeris. She didn't say a word, but the slight tension in her shoulders and the way her hand hovered near the hilt at her belt told him everything.

She felt it too.

He stopped for a beat and scanned the corridor. There was nothing…yet his instincts twisted tight. This wasn't just some forgotten passage. The air had changed—*he could feel it*. He drew in a breath and immediately regretted it. It tasted foul, a rot that wasn't quite flesh, not quite mildew—it was sour and acidic, like meat left to stew in vinegar.

Ahead, the tunnel began to curve, the stone underfoot softening subtly as if the moisture clinging to the floor had a *film* to it, slippery and *slimy*. There was a sound now, too…but distant, barely audible behind their breathing. A wet, sucking drag, like something immense pulling itself slowly across the ground.

Nymeris slowed beside him.

Neither of them spoke.

The faint flicker of bioluminescent fungus appeared along the walls, green and sickly, pulsing like a heartbeat; the light reflected off veins in the stone—no... *trails*. Trails left by a massive and soft-bodied thing, wet with mucous that glistened as it dried.

That smell grew stronger.

And now... voices. Not loud or clear, just a slow, whispering blend of syllables and breath, like someone speaking from beneath water, backwards, or through cracked, too-wide jaws, the kind of sound that made Tyrus' skin tighten and his mind instinctively shy away, as if understanding it might invite something closer.

His instincts flared, urging him to be cautious—more than usual. They were getting close to whatever he was sensing. He glanced at Nymeris, who had her hands near the hilts of her blades. They moved cautiously as the whispering deepened, clinging to the walls and curling between breaths like a sound trying to wear a voice.

At the end of the tunnel, the path opened into a wider hall-like space—no door, just the crumbled remains of what might have once been a seal. Tyrus raised a hand, slowing them. A mound of collapsed rock lay just to the right, dark with moisture and sagging in places with moss or worse. He motioned to it, and the two of them dropped low behind it.

Tyrus risked a glance... and he froze.

The hall beyond was vast, part natural cavern, part rotted ruin, the walls dripping with slime veined with glowing fungus that pulsed dully in time with the low, wet sounds echoing off the stone. Old pipes and ventilation shafts jutted like bones from the ceiling, warped by age, many of them cracked wide open.

From those pipes... came man-sized slugs, each one glistening, pale and bloated; they oozed through the vents, dragging themselves down the curved walls and along the floor in lazy undulations. Their skin shimmered with translucent slime, showing hints of bones or half-digested remains inside. And all of them were carrying something. Some lugged squealing pigs, bleating goats, a half-conscious deer. Others pulled humans, still alive, barely conscious, bound in cords of half-dried mucus. One of the creatures gurgled as it passed, its mouth parting in a slit that revealed barbed ridges instead of teeth.

But it was what waited at the centre of the room that made Tyrus' stomach clench.

The queen.

If the others were revolting, *she* was monstrous. She was easily the size of a carriage, her mass coiled in the middle of the hall like a mound of glistening fat. Her mouth was a vertical slit as tall as a man, twitching as she shifted; her skin bulged and rippled with feeding tubes and twitching veins, and her belly was ringed with smaller mouths that sucked air like dying lungs.

As Tyrus watched, two of the smaller slugs brought a barely-moving pair of humans to her, one young and one old, both panicking, both trying to yell through the slime gagging their mouths. The queen uncoiled, lifted herself slightly, and swallowed the first whole, the body vanishing in moments. The second screamed louder—but was then gone, devoured faster than a breath.

The remaining captives—livestock and people alike—were wrapped in mucus, cocooned like insect prey; the slugs weaved and spun layers of thick, sticky slime over their victims, storing them against the walls.

Tyrus pulled back behind the rubble, jaw clenched. The stench was unbearable, hot and acidic like bile poured over spoiled meat. The sound of slime stretching and bones cracking echoed through the air—it was like some sort of sick orchestra…a performance that struck all the senses of its viewers.

Nymeris leaned against the stone, one hand over her mouth. Her face was pale. "She's eating them *alive*," she whispered hoarsely.

Tyrus didn't answer. He couldn't. He was still trying not to gag. But once the disgust passed just enough, he muttered, "Reminds me of Varana."

She held back a laugh and shook her head. "You dated her, though."

"Barely."

"But you still got up close and personal—you were practically in that huge, slobbering mouth," she teased and nodded to the giant queen slug.

Tyrus grimaced, glancing at the slug as it drooled a fresh pool of sludge. "Yeah. Starting to think I made it out of that one easier than I deserved."

Nymeris exhaled sharply, part laugh, part shudder. "How the hell are we supposed to get through that?"

He looked at her. "We kill them."

She raised an eyebrow, still a little pale. "All of them?"

"That or we end up wrapped in snot and served for dinner," he said, motioning towards the cocoons strung along the chamber walls.

Nymeris peered around the rubble again, watching the smaller slugs weave more mucus over a goat that had started screaming. "What happens if we get slimed? That stuff looks like it *hardens*."

Tyrus narrowed his eyes. "Then we don't get slimed."

She gave him a flat look. "Tactical brilliance."

He smirked. "Thank you."

Nymeris ducked back into cover, breathing through her mouth now. "We still can't risk using fire; I don't wanna blow the place up and ourselves with it. I could use my devouring ethos, but it's only good for one or two targets at a time. If I try to trap more, it could ignite…and we both know what happens if it does."

Tyrus nodded slowly, thinking. His gaze flicked back to the pipes overhead, corroded and veined with sludge and rust. Some still dripped steadily, feeding the damp that clung to every surface. "We don't go through them," he said finally. "We flush them."

Nymeris blinked. "What, like…drown them?"

"Not drown, *disrupt*." He pointed upward. "Those sewer channels, some of them are still active, or at least connected to the main flow works. If we can breach one of the primary lines or divert the pressure, we might be able to flood part of the nest. That'll scatter them and break their formation."

She followed his gaze. "You think they'll retreat?"

"I think they'll panic. Or protect the queen. Either way, it gives us an opening. There has to be another way out on the other side, too; there's always at least two exits for safety reasons."

"It might work. There was that small valve chamber back the way we came; it was half-collapsed, but some of the pressure mechanisms were intact. If we can reroute the flow through the side vents, it'll hit this hall low and fast."

Tyrus looked at her with something close to a grin. "See? That's why I missed working with you."

She rolled her eyes, but the corner of her mouth curved. "Come on, then. Let's go crack some plumbing."

They moved quickly, doubling back the way they came. The further they got from the nest, the easier it was to breathe; the whispering faded into a low murmur behind them, though the stench still clung to their clothes like a curse.

The valve chamber sat just beyond the last half-collapsed fork—a cramped, half-buried room lined with rusting pipes, moss-slicked walls, and shattered stone tiles. One of the older main lines jutted from the wall at a crooked angle, still fitted with a corroded wheel mostly hidden under debris.

Nymeris stepped in first, her eyes already scanning the mechanisms. "This is it. Pressure lines are collapsed, but the flow gate is intact."

Tyrus tested the ground with his boot, checking for sink. "We don't need perfect, just ugly."

She pulled a small pry tool from her belt and crouched beside the main wheel.

"As resourceful as ever, huh?" he teased.

Nymeris rolled her eyes. "I like to be prepared."

Tyrus smiled just a little. "It's a good thing that you are."

She smirked smugly as she said, "I'm certain you miss always having some silly little piece of metal that can do things no ethos can."

"I'd be lying if I said I didn't."

Nymeris kept her smirk but focused on the task at hand. "If I breach this one and twist the auxiliary valve there—" she pointed to a half-sunk one beneath a stone slab, "—we should reroute the old runoff straight into the nesting chamber."

"Do it."

She nodded once and got to work. The chamber filled with the sound of creaking metal, scraping brick, and the occasional grunt as Nymeris threw her weight into the stuck valve. Tyrus kept watch at the door, hands ready to fight, ears tuned for the sound of slithering bodies.

A hard clang echoed behind him. Then came the rush. From somewhere deep within the walls, pipes groaned… and then they roared as stagnant water under ancient pressure was suddenly freed. The floor vibrated, and dust spewed from the cracks in the ceiling.

Nymeris stood, slightly breathless, her hands wet and filthy. "That's our cue."

They ran back through the fork, boots slapping wet stone, the distant rumble now a thunderous, surging growl. As they neared the chamber, a flood burst from the left wall vent, a gushing wave of black, foaming water tearing across the floor like a beast unchained.

Tyrus grabbed Nymeris by the arm and pulled her behind a low ridge of stone as the first torrent slammed into the nest. Shrieks erupted, wet and high-pitched, the giant slugs convulsing as their nest was drowned in its own filth. The smaller slugs recoiled, slipping across the drenched ground, their bodies no longer graceful but panicked and blind.

The queen reared, belching thick, snotting liquid as her mass shifted violently in the rising water.

"Now!" Tyrus blurted.

He vaulted with Nymeris over the rubble, sprinting into the chaos. Water churned around their calves, warm and foul, but they pushed forward, cutting a path through the writhing creatures.

Nymeris unsheathed one of her blades and sliced through the nearest slug, bile spraying as it collapsed. "Go high!" she barked, pointing to a raised ridge that looped behind the queen.

They dashed for it—Nymeris was as agile as always, even with the slick terrain; she drew the attention of two more of the man-sized slugs trying to regroup while Tyrus leapt over slimy rubble up onto the ridge, and once Nymeris executed the slugs, he held out his hand and grabbed hold of hers, helping her up.

Behind them, the queen shrieked again, her feeding mouths snapping blindly as her defenders tried to shield her. She let out a wet, guttural roar, and her massive bulk shifted, rippling with strength no creature that bloated should possess. Thick, veined tentacles unfurled from beneath her slime-slick mass, lashing upward to the ridge.

Tyrus spotted the movement an instant too late.

One of the limbs snapped towards Nymeris, fast and whip-like.

Without hesitation, Tyrus moved—he shoved her aside, and the tentacle constricted tightly around his torso instead, crushing the air from his lungs as it dragged him in the direction of the writhing pit. He dug his claws into the stone, boots scraping, trying to anchor himself, but it was no use. That disgusting thing was *strong*, and he was sliding fast.

"Tyrus!" Nymeris panicked. She hit the edge of the ridge in a blink, her blades gleaming wet in the flickering glow of the bioluminescent slime. With one hand, she dropped her sword and grabbed the front of his coat to stop his slide, and with the other, she brought her weapon down on the tentacle, slicing deep.

The queen screamed, and the room rumbled. Her tentacle convulsed and snapped free, leaving a spray of acidic mucus across the stone.

Tyrus coughed, staggered up with Nymeris still gripping his arm, and as she grabbed her sword, they ran for it, sprinting along the ridge as the nest behind them roared and screamed and writhed. Smaller slugs surged after them, hissing and skidding through the flooding tunnel, their bodies thudding against the walls as they gained speed.

"Don't stop!" Tyrus insisted, his throat burning as they splashed through the rising water and shifting rubble.

They hurried down from the ridge and into the tunnel's narrowing passage, the grotesque chorus of the hive booming behind them; their boots pounded through ankle-deep water, lungs burning, muscles screaming.

Tyrus saw the chamber just ahead—a wide, rounded junction space with arched tunnel mouths leading off in multiple directions, some blocked by rusted iron gates, others collapsed entirely. The centre was slightly raised, an old drainage lip circling the floor. They burst into it together, splashing up onto the drier stone. He spun just in time to see that the tunnel they'd burst from had a pair of iron-bar doors half-embedded into the walls, pushed open ages ago and left to rust.

And beyond it were the slugs—*dozens* of them.

He bolted forward and slammed the gate shut, the metal shrieking in protest. The second door followed, teeth grinding into place. He rammed the latch bar down with both hands just as the first slug slammed against the other side with a wet, thunderous crack.

The gate shuddered.

Nymeris stepped beside him, swords raised, panting hard, but the creatures couldn't break through. They slammed, writhed, clawed, and spewed, but the bars, twisted as they were, held firm.

Both demons stood there in silence for a moment, soaked to the bone and breathless.

Tyrus exhaled hard and leaned his back against the wall, eyes still locked on the gate. "You good?"

Nymeris nodded. "You?"

He gave a tight, crooked grin. "Been worse."

Behind the gate, the slugs screeched and howled, bile hitting the floor, snotty ooze running like thick blood through the bars.

"Let's just hope one of these tunnels leads to a way out," he said, nodding at the two open passages. "Kubra found nothing but dead ends."

She focused for a moment—she was connecting with her familiar. "Veshka found a manhole, but that's it. No sign of the loup-garou, either."

Tyrus exhaled deeply and moved away from the bars. "Thanks for saving my ass," he laughed. "What would you do without me?"

She laughed, too, as they turned their backs to the slugs. "I'm sure Silvannus and Basilan would start brawling with each other over your spot while Cillian tries ass-kissing the boss for it. I'd rather be back with those slugs than watch either of those things happen."

"Maybe I should start writing down names for a successor, and who I want to work where in case of my untimely death," he said with an amused scoff.

"That's probably a good idea since you won't have me around all the time to save you anymore, huh?" she said with a smirk, sheathing her swords.

He waved his hand, summoning his familiar back. "Oh, I don't know about that; maybe I'll swap some names around," he joked.

She summoned hers back, too. "Swap as many names as you like, Tyrus," she said challengingly. "No one's gonna live up to me—I mean, have you seen *any* of them with a sword? They're like babies holding butter knives."

Tyrus chortled. "Are you saying I'm bad at training?"

"No, I'm saying that *they're* bad at learning."

"Oh, so you're saying I'm bad at picking capable Betas?" he questioned with a chuckle, watching the slugs give up and begin slithering back down the tunnel.

She shrugged, holding out her hand as her snake returned, and she instructed it to search the second pathway. "No, I just don't think they value the use of any weapon that isn't enchanted or magical in some way—ethosical, I mean."

Tyrus sighed as he sent his tiger with it; he began leading the way. "Fine, I'll retrain them," he quipped. He knew that it was an issue if his Betas, the people he was supposed to rely on completely, weren't prepared for a situation where ethos would be useless.

"Sorry if I sound patronizing," she said quietly. "I don't mean it in that way."

"Oh, I know, don't worry. Sorry if *I* sound like a weak leader; I don't mean it in that way, either."

"Even if you did, I don't think you're a weak leader. You've gotten everyone out of countless dangerous situations, Tyrus. A lot of them would be dead without you."

"You're right. I *am* incredible."

"Well...I wouldn't go *that* far," she teased him.

"I don't know..." he drawled. "I was picking up on some admiration."

"I suppose you can call it that," she mumbled.

Tyrus glanced at her, catching the way she looked away, her cheeks just tinged with pink. Something about it tugged at his chest—not hard, just enough to knock the wind loose. His voice softened a touch as he said, "Well…I appreciate it. And you, Nymeris."

She shifted her sights back to him, and she seemed surprised.

"I always know I can count on you," he added simply. "Not just for the sword stuff. All of it."

Nymeris shrugged lightly. "You don't have to thank me." But then she scoffed and said, "I think we do, however, both have to pray to whatever gods are listening that there's a way out at the end of one of these tunnels because I am *not* walking through that slug nest again."

"I hear you. I think I've reached my giant bug tolerance limit for the day."

She laughed in response, and they continued in silence.

Tyrus kept his senses focused, but a smile lingered on his face. He was glad he'd gotten the chance to work with her again—despite the circumstances—and there was a part of him that almost felt as if he didn't want this to be over as swiftly as he knew it would be. But they had a job to do, and he *hoped* that once it was complete, he'd get to spend a little time with Nymeris that didn't involve giant slugs and loup-garou.

For now, though, it was time to focus on finishing the job.

Chapter Thirty-Seven

─ ⟨ † ⟩ ─

Four Generations Ago

| **Alucard** |
| *Atheson, Atheson Coven Sanctum* |

Writing down the things he remembered was supposed to help Alucard process it, but he couldn't write it—not because Zalith was nuzzling his neck and might see, though; it was because a part of him didn't even want to process it. He didn't want to accept that it was real, that what he'd remembered was even a memory at all.

But it was.

And now he was slowly losing his grip on who and what he was.

Tyrus' question made sense, and so did what Zalith said about the scent he was giving off while in heat. It wasn't because he had Numen blood, it wasn't because he was something that neither of them had been around before—well... it *was*, but not in the way he originally thought.

It answered another question, too. He didn't understand why he'd been feeling the way he had when he and Zalith had sex recently, why he felt the yearning desire to be bred, to be able to give his mate children, but now he was almost certain that he knew the reason.

He wasn't a man, was he? And he wasn't a woman, either. So what was he? Was he both? Neither? Something else entirely?

With a frustrated, despair-ridden sigh, he closed his memory journal and placed it aside, dragging his fingers along the smooth black leather for a moment. He wasn't going to try convincing himself that he'd misunderstood what he'd seen because he'd *felt* it, too. He knew that it was the truth, and he knew that he should be asking himself how and when he'd decided that he was a man—maybe he hadn't made the choice himself, just as he'd feared when he was a child. But he couldn't sit there and wonder under the weight of everything he was feeling... and with the man he loved so close to him.

He closed his eyes, leaning his head back. He felt his mate press his face against his neck with a quiet hum, and he responded with a soft exhale, slowly resting his head on Zalith's. Should he tell him? Maybe he could help him make sense of it—or maybe it would drive him away. But he didn't like keeping things from him. What if Zalith found out after they got married and felt as if he'd purposely lied to trap him?

What would Zalith even think?

There wasn't really a way to tell, was there?

Was there?

Alucard frowned, glancing down at what he could see of his mate's face. Could he somehow get Zalith's potential reaction out of him without giving away the reason why he was asking for it?

He thought about *how* he'd find out. The first question would probably be the easiest; when he started trying to narrow it down, though, things would get harder. But he needed to know. If he wasn't prepared at all, he knew that he'd never be able to tell Zalith himself. He knew what he was like. He'd leave it until the demon somehow discovered the truth alone, and things would explode.

But then he scowled at himself. Asking would mean that he was accepting what he learned. *Did* he accept it? No. No? He didn't want to. Yet he knew that there wasn't much more reason to doubt what his memory revealed. Zalith had removed all of the distortion and shroud that Lilith and Damien had riddled his mind with. Everything that had come to him since then and everything that would *still* come was only the truth.

He wasn't a man.

Never had been, never would be.

That fact alone terrified him. It strangled him, *suffocated* him, and it dragged him so far down into a pit of despair and dismay that he knew there was no way back. It almost made him wish that Zalith had never freed his memories, but he wouldn't take that back. The truth had changed his life and set him free in more ways than one. This time, though, he'd recalled a memory that felt more like a curse—it wasn't the *worst*, but…it was still mortifying.

He sighed, looking down at Zalith again. If he left it now, he'd leave it forever. So he shoved his way through the doubt and pulled whatever words together that he could find. "Zaliv, I—"

An izuret appeared in a puff of blue smoke and chirped triumphantly.

Alucard took his eyes off his mate and stared at the creature, a confliction of relief and aggravation ensnaring his racing heart.

The creature was holding a white bowl with a metal lid over the top, and it was wearing leather gloves…to avoid getting its skin burned? Weren't izurets fireproof?

He held his hand out to it. "*Multumesc.*"

As it floated over and handed Alucard the bowl, it repeated the word to him, though it sounded more like a question.

"Means vank you in Dor-Sanguian," he replied.

The creature grinned curiously and asked him how to say goodbye.

"*La revedere.*"

After repeating the word, the izuret looked like it was going to disappear, but instead, its eyes widened, and it enthusiastically pointed to its right ear—it was wearing a small golden hoop earring. Then, it started pointing at Alucard, telling him that they matched.

Alucard smiled and said, "I suppose ve do."

The creature floated closer and held its gloved hand out. It told him that its name was Pompom.

"*Salut*, Pompom," he said, shaking her hand. "Alucard."

Pompom held her hands to her face, looking a little flustered. But when Zalith adjusted ever so slightly, the izuret told Alucard that she should be getting back.

Alucard nodded and said, "*La revedere.*"

After repeating, Pompom disappeared.

The vampire looked down at Zalith. "Zaliv," he said.

He didn't respond.

"Zaliv," he said again, moving his shoulder a little.

"Huh?" the demon murmured.

"Your vood is 'ere," he said, offering the bowl to him.

"I'm not hungry," he purred before licking Alucard's neck.

Alucard tried pulling him away with his free hand. "You need to eat someving, my love. 'As been nearly two days."

He groaned loudly.

"*Now.*"

With a huff... and after another lick of Alucard's skin, the demon gradually turned and sat up. "What is it?"

"Lobster visotto," he said, lifting the lid and offering him a fork.

Zalith huffed again, but he started eating.

Alucard watched him, though his mind once again attempted to find the words to ask Zalith something that might tell him how he'd react to his latest memory. Maybe he should just start somewhere simple. "Zaliv?"

"Hmm?" he replied, still eating.

"'Ow do you... veel about transgender people?" he mumbled.

Zalith laughed a little and asked, "Is this about what Tyrus said?" He smiled at him and continued, "Don't listen to him. He's fine."

Alucard shrugged. "I just vant to know vhat you vink."

"I don't really think. I don't know. They're people," he said with another quiet laugh. "I don't have any opinions."

That only really answered a fraction of what he wanted to know. "Vhat about… vell, vould you be attracted to somevone who vas transgender? Sexually."

"Probably," he said with a shrug. "I've kinda seen it all."

The vampire nodded slowly. Had Zalith seen something like *him*, though?

What even was he?

Was he transgender?

No… because he wasn't even male or female as a child. So what did that make him?

He sighed quietly, resting his head on Zalith's shoulder.

"Why are you so worried?" his mate then asked, sounding both concerned and curious.

"I'm not vorried," he assured him, moving his head so that he could nuzzle his neck. "I'm just curious, I guess. I've been vinking about Tyrus' stupid question and vondering if every ozzer zemon in zhat voom vas vondering zhe same."

Zalith chuckled amusedly and said, "Who cares?"

"A lot of zhese new zemons of yours vink being vith me is var beneath you because I'm Disavowed," he grumbled sadly. "And I know zhat non-'umans aren't as judgemental as 'umans, but I'm sure zhere vould be some who'd vink I'm even less vorthy to be your mate *and* viancé if I vas transgender—and vanks to Tyrus, ve now know zhat some if not all of zhem vink I am." Although he was trying to avoid telling Zalith why he was really asking, his answer was genuine. He *did* worry about his fiancé's reputation because when—and if—he told him about this, it was likely going to cause *many* of the new demons to question their Apex's leadership.

The demon finished eating and put the bowl aside. "I don't care about what they think," he said, moving his arm around Alucard and pulling him closer. "I only care about *my* opinion, which is that you're an incredible person—and incredibly hot," he continued, smirking down at him. "If they can't handle something stupid and trivial like this, then they really need to re-evaluate their lives."

He was right. There was no logical reason at all to be a bigot. But there would always be people who found some shitty little way to justify their hatred. He didn't want to think about it anymore, though. If he asked Zalith how he'd feel if his mate turned out to be… whatever he was… then he'd probably tell him the real reason behind his questions without meaning to.

With a small nod, he closed his eyes and relaxed. "I guess is better zhat zhey're just staring and vinking instead of lunging and trying to cling to me like ticks."

"Who clung to you?" he questioned possessively, tightening his embrace.

Alucard smiled. "You."

"Oh," he said with a smirk and kissed his head. "Good."

The vampire's smile grew as he focused on the moment—Zalith's affection…his captivating scent. He let it envelope him, indulging just the way his mate did, pressing his face against his neck. Despite knowing that he needed to rest, he couldn't help but give in just a little, just for a moment. It pushed away any other emotion, focusing solely on the cravings that his heat gave him, and as the desire for sex quickly intensified, he pressed more of his body against Zalith's—and he could feel him giving in, too.

Neither of them fought very hard to resist.

Alucard climbed into Zalith's lap with barely a breath between them, straddling him. His arms wound around the demon's shoulders as their mouths frantically collided; fingers slipped beneath cloth, clawed at seams, and tugged and tore as they struggled to get closer, faster, baring skin wherever they could reach.

He felt Zalith's dick hardening beneath him, thick against his own arousal, and the feel of it sent a pulse through his spine. His body begged to be taken—to be bent and filled—but his instincts wanted something else. Right now, *he* needed to be the one claiming.

With a sharp huff, Alucard yanked Zalith's trousers down, taking a fast-fleeting second to enjoy the sight before rising to his feet. He grabbed his mate's waist, demanding rather than guiding, and hauled him upright. Their breaths tangled, hot and fast, as he steered Zalith towards the wall. The moment the demon turned, Alucard pressed up behind him, one hand flat against Zalith's back, the other snatching the lube from the nearby table. He smothered his fingers quickly and brought them down between Zalith's cheeks, working the cool gel into him as his heart raced. He could feel Zalith twitch against the touch, and he felt himself shaking with restraint as his desire pressed hard and aching against his thigh.

Zalith groaned excitedly, bracing himself against the wall as Alucard worked him open, messy and determined. The vampire's fingers pushed in deeper, twisting just enough to make the demon moan quietly, though not long enough to savour it. He couldn't wait. His heat clawed at him from the inside; he needed relief, he needed to sink into his mate and *own* him.

He pulled his hand away, already reaching for himself, slicking his dick with the remnants of lube and whatever patience he still had. He stepped in close, his chest flush to Zalith's back, and thrusted into him in one smooth, forceful push.

Zalith's moan cracked through the air like lightning.

Alucard's hands slid to Zalith's hips, fingers digging in as he pulled back and drove forward again, harder, making the demon moan louder. He pressed his mouth to Zalith's neck, biting, kissing, and tasting his skin; he growled against the demon's shoulder, thrusting into him, deeper and rougher as each second raced by.

His mate moaned delightedly, his claws cutting into the wall. "Harder," he pleaded, and when the vampire obeyed, he whined Alucard's name.

A shiver ran down the vampire's back, making him groan as he thrusted desperately. He didn't want to stop, he didn't want to let go; he wanted to fuck Zalith until his legs gave out, until he was marked and trembling with the weight of it.

Each plunge sent a shudder through Alucard's limbs, like something buried deep in his body was finally being fed—finally being *heard*. His heat had been a gnawing ache for hours, tightening in his spine and throat, but now it began to melt, soothed by every wet, pulsing slide into Zalith's body.

Alucard bit down again, not hard enough to break skin this time. He just wanted to hush his moans as they grew louder, as the pleasure mounted inside him—he needed to hold on, he needed to draw this out as long as he could manage.

Zalith trembled beneath him, his voice rasping low and rough through the warmth of his breath. "That's it, baby," he growled. "Take everything you need from me."

The vampire couldn't help but bite harder, whether that was what his mate meant or not. He whined in delight, and his body snapped forward with a sharper thrust, grinding in and holding there, hips flush to the demon's ass, chest heaving as Zalith's hot, sweet blood poured into his mouth. The demon's words lingered—they were permission and praise, they made him lose control just a little, and once he gulped down only a few mouthfuls, he fucked the demon even harder, driven by the growing throb of pleasure and the heavy drag of dominance setting into his bones.

Every muscle moved with that single-minded purpose; his pace grew frantic and *ruthless* until his whole body trembled from the force of it. He was getting close. His fingers clawed at Zalith's hips as he pulled him back with every thrust, breath ragged, heart pounding. The need to let go tore through him like fire, demanding that he do as it ordered, demanding he do what his body was made for.

And Zalith, ever patient and perfectly wicked, tipped his head back just enough to murmur, "Fill me up, Alucard." He moaned longingly. "Give me your cum."

Alucard whined contently in response—he was *too* close, and he could feel it coiling deep within, rising faster with every movement. But he didn't want to finish yet; not before Zalith, not before he'd given him everything he deserved.

His claws dug into the demon's waist, holding him still, trying to slow his rhythm even as his hips bucked on instinct. He had to *wait*... he had to hold on just a little longer. But then Zalith's moans and groans grew thicker, and he aggressively pushed back against him, pulling Alucard in deeper, clenching around him in a way that shattered what little resolve the vampire had left.

The next thrust was a mistake—it was driven by instinct.

Alucard's breath caught violently, his body locking as he slammed in one final time and came with a broken gasp, spilling deep inside his mate. Pleasure roared through him, overwhelming, almost punishing. His forehead dropped to Zalith's shoulder, fangs bared in a silent cry as he shook, thrusting weakly through the aftershocks even as guilt flickered under the edge of bliss.

He hadn't waited, he hadn't lasted, and he hadn't given Zalith what he meant to—not fully. But it was so *relieving*, so completely devouring that it left him trembling against him, his chest rising and falling like he'd run miles. His heart still pounded, but it was quieter now. His body was satisfied. *Fed*.

Zalith turned his head and murmured, "Good boy." He clenched again and pushed back ever so slightly, easing Alucard back in entirely. "Your cum feels almost as good as it tastes."

Alucard shuddered, groaning softly against his back, too spent to answer, yet already aching to start again. But as the heat ebbed, a flicker of frustration curled at the edge of his mind. He hadn't meant to finish so soon…and he realized…he never really did. Once again, though…he couldn't make Zalith cum. No matter how hard he tried, no matter how deep he fucked him or how much his body burned to please, it was never enough. Not in that way. The climax should have satisfied him—well, it did—but there was a bitter little ache, a deep, irritating disappointment that he hadn't been able to pull his mate over the edge, that no matter how aggressive he let himself get, no matter how much Zalith *said* he loved it, Alucard had never made him cum just from this, just from being inside him.

It shouldn't matter. Zalith never complained. If anything, he always sounded proud, like he *enjoyed* how undone Alucard became.

But it still lingered enough to dull the afterglow.

Before the weight of that thought could settle deeper, Zalith turned and caught his waist.

"My turn," the demon murmured, his lips brushing Alucard's temple. "Let me finish inside you."

Alucard had no time to catch his breath before Zalith eased him away from the wall and guided him down onto the couch. He let it happen, docile and pliant in the demon's hands.

Zalith slid Alucard's thighs apart, kneeling between them as he reached for the lube. The demon's fingers worked fast, rubbing the viscous liquid into his hole in slow circles that made the vampire's overstimulated body twitch. His legs quivered, still loose from his orgasm, and Zalith smiled at the way his body responded, ready to serve.

And then he pushed in.

Alucard whined as Zalith's thick dick pressed deep…and Zalith didn't hold back. He buried himself with a pleasured growl, both hands gripping Alucard's hips, and once he was as far as the vampire's trembling body would allow, he started thrusting, long, asserting plunges that made the couch creak beneath them.

He leaned into Alucard's ear, gripping a fistful of his hair. "Do you feel that?" he murmured, pushing his dick deeper with every thrust as Alucard's body submitted, as it loosened and welcomed the demon in completely. "That's where I belong," he purred, and then he gently bit the vampire's neck.

Alucard moaned, his back arching. He *could* feel it—he could feel *all* of him, he could feel himself stretching to take it, to hold it. His instincts almost immediately switched from needing to cum inside Zalith to needing Zalith to cum inside him. He didn't have the space to question it, though. All he could think about was the intensifying need to be bred.

Zalith grew aggressive, his pace becoming erratic, like his body had felt that shift in Alucard, too. His grip tightened, possessive, and his breathing turned ragged as his hips thrusted forward in a desperate rhythm. Alucard could barely breathe through it. Every push struck something sensitive, and yet he didn't want it to end. His fingers grasped the couch's edge, his limbs trembling, and his chest heaving.

And then he felt that sudden, primal change in Zalith's rhythm, the way his claws dug in, the growl that spilled hot against Alucard's skin. The demon came with a loud, pleased moan, burying himself deep as his dick throbbed inside him. Alucard whined when he felt the heat of it pouring into him, flooding him in wave after wave. The pressure and the warmth combined with the sensation of being so thoroughly filled—it all collided in his chest and left him shaking.

His body welcomed it greedily, just as it did every time before, and now, finally, it had what it needed—Zalith's cum deep inside him, claiming him, soothing that ache that nothing else ever could. And it made Alucard feel complete.

The vampire let out a satisfied but tired moan as he let himself melt into it all—Zalith's weight above him, the soft sound of breathless groans between them, and the dull throb of overworked muscles and pleased nerves.

Zalith's voice murmured a moment later, warm against his throat, "It feels so fucking good to cum inside you." He kissed and then licked his neck.

All Alucard could do was moan meekly in response. The fatigue was returning *fast*.

The demon pulled out *slowly*, stroking his fingers down Alucard's body, and then he lay on the couch with him, resting his head on the vampire's chest.

With a deep exhale, Alucard closed his eyes and relaxed, letting the warmth of his mate ensnare him. The satisfaction and the bloodlust left him free of thought and emotion, allowing him to rest and recover. He needed as much of that as he could get.

But he evidently wasn't going to get it yet.

Another izuret appeared, chirping to announce its presence.

Alucard didn't look at it. He was too tired.

"What?" Zalith asked.

The creature told them that Orin had sent it.

Alucard *had* to open his eyes to look.

It explained that Orin had dug up not only the Silver Claw's real name but also what species she was a combination of.

"What's a kheviran?" Zalith questioned.

The izuret opened its mouth to answer—

"Zhey're *said* to be zhe strongest kind of seer," Alucard grumbled irritably.

"Said to be?"

"People vink zhat zhey 'ave powers of premonition, but zhey're actually just veally skilled at spotting zhe slightest muscle tvitch or indication zhat somevone is about to say or do someving. Zhey are mentalists mostly, but sometimes, you vind vones like zhis loup-garou who 'ave mastered zhe art of seeing physical signs."

Zalith sighed quietly and asked the izuret, "What's her name?"

It answered: Accalia Veyne. Four generations ago, her pure-blooded loup-garou great-great-grandmother had a child with Thûravok Kaelvurn, a kheviran and personal advisor to King Willarion IV of DeiganLupus, but when Queen Vorticia inherited the crown, Thûravok disappeared. There was a rumour among the Veyne family that Accalia's great-grandfather killed him because kheviran can steal each other's power by eating their hearts, and the rumour suggested that since then, every new generation had done the same to their parents.

"Did 'e vind zhe Ada connection?" Alucard asked.

The creature nodded and told them that Accalia's great-grandmother was the Ardelean-blooded ancestor and Nocturne Queen, and her great-grandfather was the loup-garou-kheviran.

"Zhat explains a lot, I suppose," he mumbled.

It held up a finger, and with a matter-of-fact tone, it added that Accalia's father was a full-blooded loup-garou.

Alucard exhaled deeply.

"So, we're dealing with an Ada-blooded loup-garou-thaernari-kheviran," Zalith said. "That's a mouthful." He looked at Alucard. "Does that give her any other resistances or weaknesses we don't already know about?"

He shook his head. "Zhere's noving special about a kheviran—not in zhat sense. Zhe Ada connection explains 'er strength, as does zhe Nocturne loup-garou line. But ve've seen vhat she's capable of, and like Tyrus said, she vinks I'm dead, so ve'll 'ave zhat advantage."

"And the Feybane Oil," the demon added.

Alucard nodded.

Zalith then said to the izuret, "Tell Orin to head back to Uzlia."

With a salute, the creature disappeared.

The demon sighed deeply, tightening his embrace around Alucard. "I suppose her great-grandmother being the Ada link is better than it being her mother. The further back, the weaker, right?"

"Depends on 'ow diluted 'er great grandmothers line vas. But considering 'ow Accalia looks a lot like Ada, zhe line 'as to still be pretty strong."

Zalith sighed once more and said, "I'm sorry you have to deal with her again—she might not be Ada, but this is all still connected to her."

Alucard shrugged. "I killed Ada, so 'er descendant von't be much 'arder to deal vith; she's just stronger because she's a loup-garou, and zhe vull moon is in a vew hours."

"Yeah, but… didn't you lose control when you killed Ada? We can't risk letting that happen again," he said worriedly.

He wasn't wrong. When he killed Ada, he'd let the darkest parts of himself take control. Damien had to pull him out of it, and now that Damien's runes were gone, Alucard knew that he was at even greater risk of succumbing to it again.

The vampire shook his head and closed his eyes. "I know. I von't let zhat 'appen."

Zalith kissed his neck. "We have enough people to deal with her. It's not just you alone this time."

That *did* assure him, and so did the fact that he had so much to lose. Back then, he thought he'd lost everything—well, he *had*. But now, he had more than he could have ever dreamt of… if he didn't lose it because of his recovered memories, that was.

He dismissed the thought with a huff. "Ve should start planning. Everyvone needs to be veady vor vhen Nymeris and Tyrus veport back."

"We should," Zalith said, but he sounded hesitant.

Alucard knew why. He also had his own reasons for feeling reluctant to get up, but they *had* to. They needed to get this over with. "Come on," he said, pulling Zalith with him as he sat up.

The demon's face went straight to his neck, though. "Can't I just… cum in you one more time?"

Although he smiled—albeit fainter than usual—the struggle that Alucard felt to resist wasn't as powerful as before… and he knew the reason for that, too. There it was again… that lingering disappointment, that *embarrassment*… the feeling of failure. And with it came the dismay of not knowing what he was. Right now, the idea of sex made him feel… inferior? That was probably the best way to describe it. Zalith made him orgasm without any effort at all—he didn't ever need to try harder than usual. But *Alucard*? He just couldn't do the same for him… and he wondered if that was because he wasn't really a man.

He tried dismissing it all. "Later," he said, handing Zalith his trousers.

Zalith groaned but started getting dressed.

As he pulled his clothes on, too, Alucard attempted to focus on the mission. There wasn't room for anything else. Accalia needed to be stopped, and he wouldn't retreat to rest again until it was done.

Chapter Thirty-Eight

Archers

It felt almost impossible to concentrate. Zalith couldn't keep still. He shifted restlessly against the library doorframe; he leaned, crossed his arms, and even pushed off again, only to find himself drawn back into place, hovering just behind Alucard. His vampire stood before the assembled crowd, his voice steady and commanding—*and hot as fuck*—as he spoke about strategy, as if the heat curling beneath his skin wasn't enough to drive anyone mad. Zalith admired that strength. But it made everything harder.

His gaze swept the room again, catching the flickers of attention in every face. The demons were listening, yes, but some stared too long and intently. Every time Zalith saw it, that possessive fire in his chest flared so much hotter than usual, his jaw tightened, and his claws flexed against his arms. He wanted to lunge, to bare his fangs and make it clear that anyone caught scenting Alucard's heat too deeply would not live to even *think* about acting on it. He wanted blood. He wanted the air to reek of fear, not lust.

And if even one of them took a single step too close…he wouldn't hesitate.

But he had to control himself for the sake of the mission.

So he stood there, taut and silent, fighting to hold back the monster inside him…because Alucard needed him to, and that was the only thing stronger than instinct.

He set his sights back on Alucard, attempting to listen, too.

"Zhe only vay to counter 'er ability to predict our movements vould be to move in groups *and* to be as vast as possible," the vampire explained. "If 'er vhaernari blood is strong enough, zhere's zhe possibility zhat she in'erited zhe ability to 'eal vaster using decaying vings, vhich vould mean ve're likely to vind 'er someplace vith easy and a lot of access to dead or dying vings."

"Like…bodies?" Danford asked, glancing around the room. "Could she be in a graveyard?"

"Maybe," Alucard said, crossing his arms. "Vhat's zhe graveyard or cemetery situation 'ere?"

One of the vampires—no…the Coven Master, Noctrel—stepped forward. "It's to the west of the city, My Lord," they answered. "No church. There are quite a few crypts, and one of the larger ones is partly caved in."

Alucard glanced at Zalith as he said, "She could be zhere."

Zalith took his glare off the crowd and nodded. "It's possible."

"Did anyone see the thing leave the tunnels and head in that direction?"

Zalith's glower immediately shot to the man who asked.

Cadwell, a valefar demon. There was anger in his green eyes, and it looked like he was trying to hold back. When his sight flicked to Zalith, though, he frowned, startled, and lowered his head. "Sorry. I don't mean to be disrespectful."

Another man scoffed.

When Zalith's eyes shot to *him*—Aldric, someone who was frequently seen hanging around with Roderic—the guy didn't back down, nor did he look afraid.

"Roderic got torn apart, and Thalric bled out all over the place!" Aldric exclaimed, shaking his head. "Briallen almost died, too. And why? Because *that thing*—" he pointed at Alucard, "—led us all down there and—"

Zalith moved without hesitation. In less than a breath, he was across the room, his hand closing around Aldric's throat. He wrenched the valefar out of the crowd and slammed a fist into his face—bone cracked, and Aldric's body flew backward, crashing into the bookshelf behind him with a hollow thud. Shelves splintered, books spilled, and the man crumpled to the floor in a heap.

Shocked murmurs rippled through the room, but they died quickly.

Zalith turned, his eyes like fire sweeping across the gathering. Any demon who met his gaze immediately looked away, heads bowing in silence.

"If anyone refers to my fiancé as anything other than that or my mate, " he paused and nodded towards Aldric's motionless body, "they'll join him."

Silence held for a heartbeat…then came a chorus of quiet, immediate affirmations. The message had been received.

Zalith hissed angrily, and then he returned to Alucard's side. "Sorry about the mess."

"Is okay," Alucard said as the demon took hold of his hand.

"You two," Zalith snapped at Elewaln and Wilmot, the two demons closest to Aldric. And then he asked Alucard, "Can they throw him in the Withercrypt?"

His fiancé nodded. "Show zhem vhere to take 'im," he instructed one of the Wardens who'd been down by Eyra's cell.

Zalith nodded at his two demons, telling them to follow her. "Clean that up," he then told Merrion, one of the skarrix demons.

"Yes, sir," he said and started cleaning up the fallen shelves and books.

"Anyway," Zalith mumbled and looked to Alucard.

"To answer Cadvell's question: no, Accalia vas not seen entering zhe cemetery. But vor all ve know, zhose tunnels and catacombs could lead to any of zhe many crypts. Zhe maps ve got vrom zhe city 'all only showed vhat vas built and vhat vas mapped vhile zhey vere being built."

"Nymeris and Tyrus should be back any time now," Zalith said, trying just that little bit harder to focus on the mission.

This time, Cadwell raised his hand.

"What?" Zalith muttered.

"Sorry, it's just…if they'd found the loup-garou or unmapped tunnels, they would have told us, right?"

"Ve asked only vor zhem to search vor zhe loup-garou. If zhey did vind unmapped tunnels, ve'll ask about zhem vhen zhey veturn, and if zhere *are* some zhat lead to zhe cemetery, zhere is a very 'igh chance zhat she is zhere."

Cadwell nodded in response.

"Zhe veapons?" Alucard asked the vampire beside him.

"Vitreophage Virelka is almost done, My Lord," she replied.

"Everyvone vill 'ave some sort of veapon covered vith Veybane Oil. Since zhis voman isn't vully elv, zhe oil vill likely not be as evvective, so vill take a 'igher dose to knock 'er out. *Zhat* should be our goal instead of vighting 'er 'ead-on." He looked around the room. "Is anyvone at least *good* with a bow?"

No one raised their voice.

Zalith was conflicted about answering. His mother made him take archery lessons as a kid hoping that it would help him make some friends—it hadn't—but a few classes didn't exactly make him 'at least good', but even if it did, he'd still be hesitant about offering himself up. He knew that Alucard was trying to find people to remain distant from the fight, likely to fire Feybane Oil-covered arrows at the loup-garou; he didn't want to be away from his fiancé, though…even if he could be more helpful in another position.

There was someone else, though—someone who should have put their hand up immediately. His eyes shifted to *Danford*, and when he scowled, the wolf-vampire tensed, and his eye widened.

"Uh…I…I'm pretty okay, I guess," Danford said.

And then a vampire said, "I, uh…I used to hunt."

"Same," Olivienne said.

"And me," Brannoc followed. "Mostly long range."

Nerilitha raised her hand and said, "I used to watch my dad at his archery lessons. I don't have physical training myself, but I have what I've seen."

Alucard nodded and said to the vampire who answered, "Cenric, take zhose vour down to zhe veapons vault." He looked around the room, frowning.

"Uh... Vaultwright Berengar isn't here, My Lord," Cenric said as Danford and the three demons followed him towards Alucard.

"Zhen vhere is 'e?"

"He left the library a little while before you came back."

"I think he went to help Vitreophage Virelka, My Lord," Isabeau said.

Alucard nodded and waved the archers off.

Zalith felt a little bad about not speaking up, but he knew that he'd be much more use in the middle of the battle, and four was a good number of archers—they didn't need a fifth, especially since he wasn't a professional.

"Vifles?" Alucard asked.

A few people raised their hands.

Alucard pointed to one of the vampires and said, "Go to zhe veapons vault, too."

With a nod, the woman led Osbern, Royandra, Wilmot, and Eldan out of the room, along with one of the Sentinels Zalith remembered from earlier—Edricus.

"Does anyvone 'ave any ozzer veapon skills?" Alucard asked, looking around at who remained. "You vhree—" he pointed to three vampires standing beside the table that Alson was sitting at, "—go and get your knives oiled."

The three of them looked almost identical, all with the same shade of brown hair—he recognized one of them, Esphyllia, from earlier; she'd handed books to Alson.

"Zhey're Caylinne, Esphyllia, and Oswyn," Alucard told him, obviously having seen him watching them as they walked past him and left the library. "Zhey're triplets vrom Scelerisque. Zhey came to Aveson a vew years ago with a travelling circus; zhey vere very good knive vhrowers and blade dancers. Esphyllia vas attacked zhe night bevore zhey vere meant to travel 'ome; Drusilda vound 'er, ovvered to turn 'er to save 'er life, and she accepted. Vhen 'er siblings learned about vhat 'appened, zhey asked to be turned, too. I zidn't see vhy not."

Zalith smiled and murmured into his ear, "I love that you have such a soft side, you know." He resisted the urge to nuzzle his neck, though. Not while he was addressing his whole coven and half a pack of demons.

Alucard gave him a small smile in response before focusing on the crowd again. "Zhe Duskvoot verevolf pack vill stay 'ere to guard zhe Sanctum, and zhe vest of zhe zemons vill be part of zhe close combat attack team."

The demons all agreed without hesitation. Evidently, they'd all learned to respect Alucard.

Good.

Before the room was dismissed, though, Tyrus and Nymeris stepped in.

And a *revolting* stench filled the air.

Zalith turned his head, both his nose and eyes finding the allocer demons.

Everyone else set their sights on them, too.

"Vhat zhe fuck is zhat smell?" Alucard snarled.

Tyrus and Nymeris looked at their own and each other's slime-smothered clothes.

"Uh…we kind of stumbled into a giant slug nest," Nymeris said.

Tyrus chuckled, wiping his hands on his blazer. "It was unavoidable—"

"—And we didn't want to waste time washing off before reporting back," Nymeris said, glancing at Tyrus. "We didn't leave a mess on our way through the house, though."

"It's not wet…or anything," Tyrus added.

Zalith rolled his eyes.

And so did Alucard. "You vinished searching zhe tunnels?" he questioned irritably.

They nodded.

"We didn't find her. Sorry," Nymeris said.

Tyrus continued, "We found some unmapped tunnels, but she wasn't there, either."

"Vhere did zhe unmapped tunnels lead?" Alucard asked.

"They were a lot like the mapped catacombs," Tyrus answered. "Most of them were collapsed, so we couldn't follow them to their ends."

"Did any lead west?" Zalith asked.

Nymeris nodded. "Two, but one was collapsed barely a hundred feet from the fork we came to, and the other was flooded…maybe a ten-or-so-minute walk from the fork."

"Could she have swum through the flooded tunnel?" Zalith asked his fiancé.

"Is possible, especially if she vanted to make extra sure zhat she vasn't vollowed."

"Should we send someone to scout out the cemetery?"

"Zhose two," he agreed, gesturing to Tyrus and Nymeris. "Zheir vamiliars are undetectable."

With a nod, Zalith said to the allocers, "There's a cemetery to the west of the city. Search the crypts and anywhere else where she could hide from the moonlight. If and as soon as you find her, report back."

They bowed their heads and left the room.

"You can go," Alucard said to the crowd. "Make sure you are all prepared vor zhe vight a'ead of us."

Everyone called their agreements and filed out of the library.

Zalith turned to face his fiancé, who glanced at the clock. "We've still got five hours," he assured him, placing his hand on the vampire's shoulder. "We'll find her."

Alucard exhaled deeply and nodded.

But he didn't look convinced.

No…it wasn't that. It almost looked like his mind was drifting elsewhere, and Zalith was only just noticing because he wasn't entirely lost in his mate's devouring scent. "What's wrong?" he asked worriedly.

He shook his head. "Noving. I'm just avraid ve're going to vun out of time."

Zalith pulled his fiancé into his embrace. "We won't," he tried to convince him. "And even if by some slim chance we do, I'll call *all* of my demons over here if I have to. I won't let her kill anyone else."

Alucard relaxed in his arms. "I just…vish I'd been 'ere to stop 'er vrom killing Salvorn. Is my job to protect *all* vampires."

"It's not your fault, Alucard," he said quietly, caressing his hair. "You couldn't have known that she'd attack when she did—you didn't even know that she was in Atheson."

"But I knew zhat she vas coming 'ere."

"Still, you did everything you could—and I'm sure that no one blames you, either. You have so many covens, and you have your own life, too. You can't be everywhere all at once. That's why you have Coven Masters, right?"

Alucard sighed deeply. "I guess so. I've lost so many of zhem vecently."

"I know," he murmured, holding him tighter. "But that also wasn't your fault. We're going to war with the Numen, and all of our people knew what they were signing up for when they chose to join our fight." He said that…yet he was still broken about being chased from his home. He tried to hold on, though. They were rebuilding, and he was living up to his promises as best as he could. "And we have other enemies," he continued, feeling Alucard nuzzle his neck. "That's just…part of being who we are, I suppose. Our people know *that*, too. They also know that we'll do our very best to protect them; if they didn't believe that, they wouldn't still be here."

His fiancé exhaled quietly against his neck. "I guess I just…veel bad—I veel bad about everyving and everyvone." There was sadness in his voice. "I 'ave zhese…moments when I vink about zhem all. Not just zhe people who died vecently but all zhe people who died bevore. I vink about Tobias, I vink about Elvin, I vink about all zhe people ve lost vhen ve 'ad to vlee vrom Nevastus…and now I'm vinking about zhe people ve've lost to zhis fucking 'unter."

Zalith's heart started aching. He knew how his vampire felt because he went through the same thing—he experienced those same doubtful moments. It was a heavy, suffocating kind of sorrow, a clawing sense of guilt. So many people had trusted him to protect them, and they'd joined the mountain of bodies that lay at his feet, a mountain he'd built with his own hands, the result of all his failures. He knew that Alucard had a mountain of dead, too…but thinking about it…*hearing* about it dismayed him. He hated knowing that the man he loved was in *any* kind of pain. But was there anything he could do to help soothe it this time?

"I'm sorry, baby," he said, rubbing his back. "I know I keep saying it, but none of that was your fault."

Alucard huffed sadly—he was clearly frustrated. "*Vas* my vault, zhough," he murmured, his voice breaking a little. "I killed Tobias—I drvank 'im dry vith no 'esitation vhatsoever—"

"You were dying, Alucard—"

"I killed Elvin and 'is girlvriend and an unborn child zhat 'e zidn't even know 'e 'ad—"

"Damien made you do that," he insisted, trying his best to comfort him, both with his words and his hands, still holding him.

The vampire shook his head. "Elvin trusted me, and I killed 'im like 'e vas noving—I *acted* like 'e vas noving—"

"Alucard," he said, gently pulling back so that he could see him, and when he saw the tears trickling down his face, his heart hurt a whole lot more. "You had no choice in either of those situations. You didn't *want* to kill them, and I'm sure that they both knew that—and if you somehow had a chance to speak to them, I'm certain they'd tell you that they don't blame you for what you did."

"I'd blame me," he murmured despondently.

Zalith frowned sadly. "Stop being so hard on yourself, baby," he said quietly, using his thumbs to wipe the tears from his face, and then he gently pulled him closer and kissed his forehead. "None of that and none of this is your fault."

His fiancé still didn't look convinced—not entirely—but his tears stopped falling, and some of the dismay on his face was buried beneath a tired stare. He leaned nearer, resting his body against Zalith's. "I'm sorry," he mumbled.

"For what?"

"Vor zhis."

He frowned again. "For crying?"

The vampire nodded stiffly.

Zalith kissed his head and hugged him tightly. "You don't need to be sorry for that. You could cry for hours and I'd still be here with you." He kissed his head again. "There's nothing to be sorry for or embarrassed about. I love you, and I'm here, okay? For anything. You can cry to me, you can let all your frustration out and tell me why you had such a shitty day or such a good day—you can tell me why someone pisses you off or why you want to rip someone's head off," he said with a small laugh. "There's nothing you can't tell me."

Alucard's embrace got a little firmer. It seemed as though he was going to speak, but he hesitated.

He wouldn't urge him to tell him whatever it was, though. He'd let him be sad, and he'd hold him through it.

And he'd try his utmost best to resist the overwhelming urge to let himself sink into his fiancé's heat.

But he was succumbing to it already. Every second he spent standing there holding his mate…the stronger the desire grew.

He couldn't let it win, though—not right now. Alucard needed *him*, not sex. So he slowly guided him away from where they stood, steering him gently towards the couch in the corner of the library. He helped him sit, and then he settled beside him, moving his arm around him as Alucard rested his head on his chest.

"You know," he then said quietly, glancing down at him, "when I was fifteen, my mother forced me into archery lessons." He exhaled a short breath through his nose. "She thought if I got out more and made friends, maybe I'd stop being so…*annoyingly tender-spirited.* Her words, not mine." The ghost of a smile tugged at his mouth. "She sent me to this little archery academy that sat between our town and the next. The students were a group of boys pretending to be warriors, and the instructors were these two old seers who fought in quite a few battles in their time."

He paused, recalling the memory while he fiddled with Alucard's hair.

"On the first day, they asked us to show our form. So I do what I've seen in books, line up my stance, pull back the string like I mean it…and it snaps straight into my mouth." He looked down at Alucard again, and as he met the vampire's gaze, he tapped the edge of his lower lip. "I split it clean open and bled all over my shirt. One boy fainted, and another asked if he could *keep* the arrow because it had 'real demon blood' on it— he was some kid from a local wolf pack; he had this weird obsession with demons. I think his name was Greg or something…Gregorian…I don't know."

A flicker of amusement broke through Alucard's despondent stare.

Zalith continued, "The instructor just grunted and said, 'Well, lad, at least you're committed,'" he mimicked in that dry, croaky tone that most old men had back then. "I spent the rest of the day sitting on a stump holding a rag to my face while they shot hay bales. It healed almost immediately, but I was too embarrassed to go back over there." He affectionately stroked the vampire's cheek. "I didn't make a single friend that day. But I did ruin any hope my mother had of me joining something respectable. I tried faking a hand tremble for the next lesson. She didn't fall for it, of course, and she made me go for six more months."

"You tried to vake an injury?" his fiancé questioned.

"Yeah, it was pretty stupid—I felt like such an idiot when my mother told me that demons don't get that kind of thing unless they had a limb cut off and it's still growing back. It was Xurian who convinced me it would work, and I was desperate," he said with a chuckle. "Six months of lessons didn't make me anywhere near much of an archer, though. At that point, I'd gotten good enough with mind manipulation that I just sat around and made the instructors think that I'd participated—my mother made sure to have them tell her whether I was actually learning or not."

"I zon't blame you," he mumbled, now resting his head on Zalith's shoulder. "I never took lessons because I vouldn't ever need zhe skill. I 'unted 'umans, not vabbits and deer. Vasn't a very appealing 'obby, eizer."

"Well, at least some people took their lessons seriously or we wouldn't have archers tonight," he said with a quiet laugh.

"Vankvully," Alucard agreed.

Zalith kissed his head again and asked, "Do you want to go back to your room?"

"Mm-hmm," his fiancé replied.

The demon took hold of his hand and stood up, pulling him with him. He began leading the way back to Alucard's private space in the Sanctum, still trying to resist the pull of his mate's heat. Tyrus and Nymeris could return at any moment, and if they'd found out that Accalia *was* in the cemetery, it would be time to move out. He needed to ensure that he was ready, and Alucard, too. There was no room for distraction anymore…no matter how tempting it was.

Chapter Thirty-Nine

— ⸲ ✝ ⸱ —

The Cemetery

| **Tyrus** |
| *Atheson, Atheson Cemetery* |

The hardening slime covering Tyrus' clothes reeked. It was like rotten meat topped with decaying fruit stuffed into a month-old corpse and sprinkled with the saliva of someone who'd just licked a sewer pipe. His eyes watered, his mouth tasted it—it was in his *pores*.

He didn't gag, but he made a sound that translated to *what the actual fuck?* as he scraped at the gunk clinging to his forearm, stumbling past a fallen headstone and through the cemetery gates. It peeled off in cotton-like strings, crusty yet somehow wet, like someone had weaponized jellyfish. His familiar gave him a look from a safe distance, her tail low and eyes wide, as if to say '*You brought this on yourself*', and Nymeris' snake followed even further away, weaving through overgrown grass and forgotten graves.

As he glanced at Nymeris, he exhaled sharply through his nose. "I'm burning these clothes. And maybe my skin."

She looked just as revolted, wiping the strange substance from her coat, but she laughed softly. "We should probably consider ourselves lucky that we didn't get any of it on the walls or carpets of the Sanctum; I'm sure the boss would have burned our skin for us." She then pointed at one of the sunken crypts, and her familiar slithered towards it.

Tyrus huffed and tried to focus on his surroundings. The cemetery sprawled out around them, quiet and dense with fog, the kind that softened everything into vague outlines. Cracked headstones leaned at odd angles, and statues loomed from the mist like they were half-forgotten caretakers. The scent of damp stone and dead plants hung low in the air, barely breaking through the stench of hardened slime. It wasn't abandoned exactly; someone had kept it passably clean, but it had the look of a place no one had truly cared about in a while.

The moons overhead cast kaleidoscopic sheens across the crypts, like light escaping through the mesmerizing stained-glass windows of an ancient church.

"Do you remember that old cathedral we were hiding in? The one in Roselake," Nymeris asked quietly, easing her hands into her pockets as she walked a little closer to him. "With that weird, creaky staircase—"

"Oh, yeah," he said with a small chuckle, commanding his familiar to search the next crypt, half collapsed and devoured by overgrown weeds. "Ancretta got her foot stuck between two of the steps, and three of us almost fell down trying to get her out."

"And then Ebaniel found that stash of really old wine."

"Greymore and his guys caught some hares…or squirrels, I don't know."

"I think both," she said with a smirk, but there was sadness beneath it.

Despite his own smile, a familiar ache settled in his chest. They'd lost too many during their escape from Adellum and the humans. Roselake had been one of the last places where grief hadn't suffocated everything. For a few nights, they'd shared more than fear and silence—wine dulled the edge of survival just enough for laughter to return, for old stories to resurface, and for the dead to be remembered without breaking apart. After they left that cathedral, though, things unravelled fast. No more warmth, no more room to breathe. Just blood, frost, and the slow, brutal narrowing of hope.

Nymeris' gaze stayed on the mist drifting between the crypts. "I still have the cork from one of those bottles," she told him. "It smelled like dust and ash, but it was the first time in weeks I didn't feel like I was going to break down and cry." She paused and looked up at him with a faint, fragile smile. "You made that dumb toast. Do you remember? Something about dying warm and tipsy instead of cold and hungry."

He scoffed amusedly. "I sort of remember. But that was the point, right?"

She smiled and said, "Yeah, it was."

"I *vividly* remember Lunabeth throwing up all over Greymore's shoes, though."

"He was so drunk that he just stared at it for a moment," she cringed.

"And then he forgot about it and went back to drinking." He gestured to an old, vine-ensnared stone bench and said, "I think we should sit here and let our familiars do the job this time; these crypts seem a lot narrower than the tunnels, and I'd rather get covered in more slime than come face-to-face with that loup-garou in one of them."

She nodded in agreement, sitting when he did. "Veshka is almost done with the first one—he hasn't found anything."

"Kubra's found nothing but spiders," he mumbled. Even seeing a bug through his familiar's hazy sight made him shiver.

Nymeris turned to face him, and she looked curious. "Where *did* your bug phobia come from? I mean…what made you realize that you hated them? I'd say *scared* of them, but I don't want to embarrass you." She grinned at him.

He leaned back, crossing his arms—he *was* embarrassed, but he wouldn't show it. "I was on a mission in the Wraithshade Jungle," he said, tone flat but eyes distant, the memory unsettling him. "It was dense, trees so tall they blocked the sun, really thick air with fog and heat. We were tracking some rogue bloodcasters, and we figured that they were using the ruins there to siphon magic off the old ley lines. We set up camp near a river because we thought it was a good spot. But it was a little *too* quiet. The next morning, two of the guys couldn't stand; they said their backs were killing them." He shifted his stance, arms still crossed like a shield. "It turned out that we'd pitched right in the middle of a hatching ground—some kind of winged insect…big things, translucent wings, all teeth and legs. They laid eggs under the skin, and the larvae…." He exhaled through his nose. "They started eating their way out of the guys' backs. Screaming, blood, bile, the works. One of them got dragged into the river trying to rip them out, and the other—well, we ended him quick." He looked at Nymeris and shrugged, "So yeah. Not a fan of bugs."

She was cringing again. "Okay, the origin story of *your* fear is a lot scarier than mine," she said with a nervous chuckle.

"Well, you never know what those mannequins might be up to, so I think your fear is still valid," he said amusedly.

Nymeris smiled but then looked over her shoulder.

Tyrus glanced in the same direction and watched as Veshka slithered from the first crypt and headed to the next. But then he caught sight of one of the crumbling statues, and as he set his eyes back on Nymeris, he smirked. "Are you afraid of statues, too?" he teased her, but he *was* curious.

Her cheeks turned red, and she tried to scoff to hide the reaction, but the sound came out as more of a choke. She shook her head, rolled her eyes, and said, "Maybe, okay? Just the people-looking ones, though—the *old* ones with most of their facial features faded away. They're just really creepy." She finally met his gaze and asked, "I mean, how would *you* feel if you saw some faceless, man-sized bug just standing there without any way to tell whether it's looking at you or not?"

He smiled at her fluster and laughed softly. "Well, bug faces are hideous, so I'd probably feel better than usual about it."

"You're right. I don't think I've seen a single bug face that didn't make me think 'ew'," she mumbled.

Tyrus glanced to his right, commanding his familiar into the next crypt.

"You got a dog, didn't you?" Nymeris asked.

"I did," he said with a nod, turning to face her again. "Vesta. She's a Drydenan Shepherd. I have a dog sitter to look after her when I'm away, which has been a lot lately, so I feel pretty bad."

"I'm sure she understands."

"I just don't want her to think I'm abandoning her, you know?"

"Is she a puppy still?"

"Yeah, just a few months."

"Well, if she grows up with a steady routine, even one that includes you being away, she'll adapt to it. Dogs are ridiculously smart; they learn patterns fast. If she's got someone looking after her, and she knows you always come back, she won't feel abandoned. It just becomes normal for her."

He smiled at her again. "How do you know so much about dogs?"

She shrugged. "I love dogs. I've just never really had the time to get one, I suppose. Well…that and the fact that I know I'd struggle a little. I sketch a lot in my downtime, and it's very easy for me to lose track of time."

"That's fair," he said.

"I'd love to meet Vesta, though."

"You're welcome to visit her whenever—or both of us," he chuckled.

A flustered expression returned to her face as she looked down at her lap and said, "I'll probably take you up on that—maybe once we're done here, before you leave with Orin."

"I should have a day or two to rest, maybe longer. I'll be waiting around for Orin and Crowell. Orin won't take long, but I don't really know Crowell."

"Yeah, neither do I. I've only seen him maybe two or three times, and…well, he looks kind of creepy—is that rude of me to say?"

He laughed and asked, "But Orin doesn't?"

She went to reply but chose not to—not right away. With a sigh, she glanced away, and then she frowned at him. "Okay, yes…Orin is a *little* creepy-looking, sure…but I've been working with him for over two decades, so I've gotten used to him. Besides, his eyes don't glow like these kinda…weird, haunted lanterns—it's like when a little bit of light hits certain animals' eyes, and they just stare into your soul or something." She was getting flustered again, her words coming faster. "And at least I know that when Orin looks at me, he isn't planning on floating in my window at night and feasting on me."

"Or so you think."

Nymeris laughed a little. "Orin can't float…can he?"

"I don't know, but I wouldn't be surprised. He's weird. I mean, credit where it's due, but he's weird."

She frowned curiously. "What do *you* find weird about him?"

He hesitated. "I shouldn't say, actually."

Nymeris pouted. "Oh, come on. We're all friends," she said amusedly.

Tyrus was still reluctant to say anything; he knew that he shouldn't be talking shit to her about someone who outranked her—it didn't set the right tone—and he also took his job very seriously. What he *could* say, though, was, "Well, he's a seir demon for starters."

"Yeah…that's a good point. I guess he really could be anywhere at any time, and no one would know. He could even be here right now…" she drawled as if to unsettle him.

"Wouldn't be the first time," he said with a roll of his eyes.

She frowned again. "Does he *actually* watch people or are you kidding with me?"

He shrugged—he didn't want to answer, he didn't even want to think about it. Half the things he knew about Orin…he wished he *didn't* know.

Nymeris laughed. "Okay, *now* he might be just as creepy as Crowell to me."

"He's not a problem, though," he assured her. "So don't worry about him too much."

"I'll try."

He didn't want to talk about Orin anymore. "How's your sister doing?" he asked, changing the subject.

"Oh, Azariah's doing good," she said with a smile and a nod. "She's been dating Ambrose, and things seem to be looking up for her…." She paused and tilted her head a little. "You know how bad her last relationship went."

Unfortunately, he *did* know—he knew *very well* since he was one of the three people who had to clean up the mess. "Really?" he responded. "I thought she said she didn't want to date a werewolf."

She shrugged. "If this guy is good enough to change her mind, then maybe this one will work out."

"Well, I hope so. That would be good for her."

Nymeris nodded.

"Did you two end up finding that recipe you were looking for?"

With another laugh, she said, "We did, actually. It was in one of those stupid little journals that she insisted on getting from the house before we had to run; she *still* writes everything down these days."

"Well, it's good that you found it. You'll have to do some cooking for me one of these days."

She smiled shyly, looking down at her lap for a moment. "I'd like that. What do you like?"

"Pretty much anything—you can surprise me." His smile grew a little. "Maybe I can cook for you one day, too."

Despite the deepening flush on her face, she nodded and quietly said, "Yeah, that'd be nice." She then went to say something else, but she frowned and looked over her shoulder at one of the crypts. "Wait…."

"What is it?" he asked, looking in the same direction.

"What did the loup-garou look like when you found it in that wall?"

"Just a mass of energy—a humanoid-shaped distortion." He frowned in concern. "Did Veshka find something?"

She nodded stiffly. "In that crypt back there. I think it's her."

Tyrus summoned Kubra and sent her into the same crypt. He focused on his familiar, seeing through its eyes, and when he saw the mass of energy, he nodded, too. "That's her," he confirmed. "We should get back and tell Zalith." He called his tiger and stood up. "Come on."

Nymeris followed at his side, and once their familiars returned, they stepped into the space between the real world and the Astral Plane.

As they raced back to the Sanctum, Tyrus stole a glance at Nymeris. The more time he spent with her, the more he realized how much he really did miss her. *Would* he have the chance to spend a few days with her before he left for the pocket world, or was this it? He wasn't certain. But he *was* tempted to ask Zalith for a day or two of downtime before moving on to the next mission because he *did* want to do the things he and Nymeris had just talked about.

But was that silly? He loved his job, and he was dedicated to it. Would it make him look bad and unreliable if he asked for time off to spend with a woman he liked? Would he even have to specify why he wanted to take a day or two? He wouldn't lie if he were asked, though.

He wouldn't overthink it right now. There were still things to be done.

Chapter Forty

— ⸱ ✝ ⸱ —

Book Clubs and Bards

| **Alucard** |

| *Atheson, Atheson Coven Sanctum* |

Dismay still lingered, the same despair that had ensnared Alucard not long ago. He *was* starting to feel better, lying on the couch in Zalith's arms and away from possible prying eyes. The last thing he'd wanted was to start crying like an idiot, but when he let the melancholy in, it was never gentle with him.

But as the pain surrounding the loss of people who trusted him retreated, it was only fitting that something would rise to replace it. Old memories, things he'd recently recovered.

No. He wouldn't let it dig its claws in this time.

"Vas zhere a 'obby you enjoyed when you vere younger?" he asked curiously, trying to focus on his love for hearing about Zalith's past rather than letting the torment of his own devour him.

The demon hummed quietly for a moment. "I loved doing calligraphy, and I went to quite a few book clubs, too."

"Vere mystery novels also your vavourite back zhen?"

"They were," he said with a nod. "Back when I thought I could socialize like a normal person, there was this one book club I went to every fourth evening. It was some candlelit salon; three humans, two demons, and one werewolf, Phoebe or something, who kept pretending to have read everything there was to read at the time." He paused, and then he added dryly, "She once said 'Crime and Punishment' was an uplifting tale of personal growth. It went downhill from there."

"Vhat vas 'Crime and Punishment' about?"

"Just some silly little novel about a court jester stealing from the king or something. It was stupid, but everyone else loved it." His lip twitched, and then he continued, "Anyway, one night we were discussing 'The Hollow Hour', which was, in my opinion, another terrible story—it was this small-village mystery where the killer hides in the priest's confession booth. One of the humans in the club, Edric, kept insisting that it was the innkeeper; he wouldn't shut up about it. He wouldn't even let anyone finish a sentence without saying, '*No no, trust me, it's the innkeeper. It's always the innkeeper.*'" The demon lifted a hand. "So, naturally, I snapped and spoiled the ending—I lost my temper a lot when I was younger. I told them exactly how the killer was the priest's twin brother, who'd faked his own death in chapter three. Edric looked like I'd kicked his soul out of his body." He laughed a little. "I apologized, and then I added that if he interrupted me again, I'd eat him." He shrugged with mock innocence. "The book club never ran late after that. But they *did* start bringing stronger wine, and Phoebe stopped insisting that she'd read everything in the world."

Alucard laughed, nuzzling Zalith's neck.

"Things stayed tolerable after that," his mate said, fiddling with Alucard's hair. "Quieter. I started bringing pastries, and I even caught Edric whispering to someone that I had a surprisingly nuanced take on murder, which I did, and still do."

The vampire smiled and murmured, "You do."

Zalith traced a line down the side of Alucard's face. "I tolerated the next two books— some nonsense about poisoned corsets and twins who swapped places during eclipses. Entertaining, but barely coherent. Then we read 'The Winter Veil Murders'." A flicker of something almost fond touched his voice. "That one was actually good. It was set in a storm-shrouded mountain village, and the killer was picking off guests in an abandoned lodge. It was all about atmosphere and pacing—subtle clues, sharp dialogue. I finished it in a single night and considered rereading it."

"Sounds intervesting," Alucard said quietly. "Did zhe club like as much as you?"

He nodded. "They did." He paused, exhaling deeply. "And then Leanan joined."

Alucard was certain that he was about to hear some six-century-old drama, and that kind of excited him, mostly because he wanted to hear how Zalith dealt with it.

"She was this snooty noblewoman from the city. She introduced herself with, '*I only read books where the killer is the main character, or where everyone dies at the end.*' Which is fine, you know—taste. I respect that. But then she picked up 'The Winter Veil Murders' and said, '*This would've been better if the killer was a cursed librarian who seduced people into overdue returns.*'" He blinked slowly. "She rewrote the ending. Verbally. For forty-five minutes. With charts."

"Charts?" Alucard scoffed amusedly.

"She also insisted that we stop calling it a book club and start calling it a narrative soul circle."

He scoffed again, laughing more. "Narrative soul circle?"

Zalith's expression flattened. "I walked out mid-scone when the others started agreeing with her insane ideas."

"I vould 'ave valked out, too."

The demon sighed, fiddling with his hair again. "I tried joining another club a few towns over, but it turned out to be a romance reading group where they passed around scented scarves and voted on which suitor had the best wrists." He paused again, shaking his head. "I went home and reread 'The Winter Veil Murders' in the dark—alone, as the author intended. I mean, when the author's note tells you *not* to read it alone, you know that it's going to be just that little bit more thrilling."

Alucard smiled again. He loved hearing the contentment in Zalith's voice, and he wanted to hear more.

Zalith exhaled through his nose and continued, "After that, I got stubborn. I told myself I wouldn't let Leanan and the narrative soul circle ruin books for me. So I tried again. The next club met in a bakery basement and only read books with animal protagonists; I sat through three chapters of a mystery narrated by a clairvoyant goose before I realized I'd made a mistake."

The vampire laughed with him.

"After that was the tavern group. It was promising at first—an older crowd, quiet, smelled like ink and pipe smoke—but it turned out to be a front for some kind of cult. They didn't discuss the books so much as channel the author, whom they believed had written instructions for dark rituals between the lines of the story. I left when someone tried to summon a supposed spirit from within the pages through interpretive dance." He rolled his eyes and muttered, "I can't even count how many people back then were convinced of similar nonsense."

"I zon't know, Zaliv…maybe you should 'ave set someving on vire and made zhem vink zhey vere now cursed vor getting zhe vitual vrong."

"I very nearly did." He sighed, still fiddling with his hair. "The next one met in the attic of a clockmaker's shop. I thought they were serious—they dressed in black, carried notebooks—it looked promising…until I realized none of them had actually read the books, they just memorized the summaries and argued about subtext they'd invented. One woman told me the plot twist in 'Murder on the Solstice Bridge' was a metaphor for reincarnation through pastry." He went quiet for a moment, frowning, and then added, "The worst part is, she made a very convincing argument."

"Did she suggest zhey vere veincarnated as pies or someving?"

"Something like that," he chuckled.

Alucard smiled, staring across the room. "Did you ever vind a good club?"

"I did," he said with a nod. "It was a small group—six of us. No one lied about reading or brought charts or interrupted. We picked one book a month, shared notes, kept it civil, funny when it counted. Even Edric came once. He stayed quiet the whole time; I think he might've been scared of me, but I didn't mind." He paused again, like he was thinking. "That one felt right, kinda like the book club version of a pack. I stayed with them for years. The only reason I left was…" He trailed off for a breath. "Well, the usual. Demon things. War. Deadlines. Something caught fire. You know how it goes." His expression tilted into something faintly self-deprecating. "I still think about it. I hope they kept reading."

"Maybe you should vind some book clubs to join in Eimvood—vell…I'm sure all of zhe members vould be ass-kissing you, so maybe not. Vone of zhe surrounding countries, zhough. I vouldn't mind vlying you zhere."

The demon shrugged. "I'm fine for now, but maybe one day."

He was expecting that answer—he knew that Zalith was still hesitant about leaving Uzlia and was only in Atheson because the situation was dire.

"Were you ever in any kind of club or group or anything?" the demon asked.

"Not zhat I can vemember—I could 'ave been," he said with a shrug.

Zalith slowly caressed his cheek. "What would you have liked to be in?"

He thought about it for a moment. "Maybe…not a band or an orchestra, but vith a group of people who liked making music as much as I did."

"I can see that for you—it would be very nice," he said with a light nod.

Alucard shrugged. "I 'aven't played since ve levt Nevastus. I miss zhe violin you got vor me back vhen ve virst started dating," he mumbled sadly.

"We can get you a new one if you want," Zalith suggested.

"Maybe," he said with a sigh. "Zhat vone vas just veally special to me."

"I know, baby," he murmured, fiddling with his fringe affectionately. "I hope we can get it back one day."

"Me too," he mumbled, but he was sure that it either wouldn't be possible or that if it *was*, by the time they got there, the dust and elements would have made it unplayable.

With a quiet sigh, he moved around, making himself a little more comfortable. He draped one arm across his chest, the other tangled lazily in Zalith's fingers. The room was peacefully quiet, lit only by the low flicker of candlelight, and for what felt like once in a long while, the world beyond the walls went still.

Zalith chuckled softly to himself.

Alucard tilted his head, narrowing his eyes. "Vhat?"

"I was just thinking about the time Xurian got kicked out of a tavern for trying to perform at open stage night."

The vampire smiled amusedly. "Vhat 'appened?"

"Twenty-five…maybe thirty years ago, he walks into this tavern with a second-hand guitar and this ridiculous feathered jacket—like he was born to be famous. He told me he was going to 'move the crowd.'"

Alucard raised an eyebrow. "And did 'e?"

Zalith gave a wolfish smile. "Well, yes. But not in the way he wanted. It turned out that it *wasn't* open stage night; he'd just walked on during someone else's scheduled set."

He laughed.

"He strutted right up in the middle of a poetry reading. He interrupted this poor half-elf's deeply personal, tragic love piece; he sat down and started tuning his guitar like it was all part of the act. I mean…the elf *had* hidden behind the curtain for a moment to wipe his tears, so I could see why my brother thought it was someone else's turn, but still."

Alucard's laughter didn't stop—he could imagine the embarrassment and uproar.

"The staff were *not* amused, and the crowd booed him before he even played the first note. Someone threw a pastry—I think it was still warm. They tossed him out into the street before the chorus."

"Did 'e ever go back?"

"Not to *that* tavern. But he still insists it was a misunderstanding and claims the booing was part of the energy of the place."

Alucard shook his head. "Did your brover ever 'ave a good experience vith 'is music?" he asked curiously, though he felt bad for Xurian. And in a way…it also reminded him of Elvin. That bard had experienced one too many booing crowds and pastry-throwing patrons, just as Zalith's brother appeared to have.

Zalith sighed and replied, "He did about four times out of ten—usually not with people who were artistically inclined enough to know that he kinda sucked most of the time."

"Vell, at least zhere vas some good to outveigh zhe bad." He started fiddling with his engagement ring. "You know, Elvin actually managed to captivate an audience vonce."

The demon scoffed lightly. "That's surprising."

Alucard's smile slowly faded, but he wouldn't let the guilt and sorrow creep in. "Ve vere in Dombrava—a Dor-Sanguian city in Vinsemoore—and 'e'd charmed 'is vay into a tiny vheatre. 'E stood in zhe corner of zhe tavern stage and sang zhis awvul ballad about vorbidden love and blood debts. Vas *terrible*, but zhe crowd loved zhe whole ving. Some even cried."

Zalith chuckled as he nuzzled Alucard's neck. "Crying in agony, I'd assume."

He smiled amusedly and continued, "Avtervard, zhis man approached 'im and said 'e vorked vor a play'ouse in Lunegarde, vone of Dor-Sanguis' largest cities. 'E asked if Elvin vould consider vriting scripts and said 'e 'ad veal promise. Elvin vas overjoyed; 'e spent vhree days bragging about, planned out costumes and cast lists…" he paused and sighed. "Turned out zhat zhe whole ving vas a scam. Zhe guy vas looking vor vriters desperate enough to pay vor zheir own staging; 'e told Elvin vas standard practice—'e just needed a 'production deposit'." His jaw clenched subtly. "Elvin 'anded over everyving 'e'd saved. 'E laughed zhe whole ving off and said vas a lesson in narrative betrayal or someving, but I vink zhat broke someving in 'im." He looked down at his hands, still fiddling with his rings. "'E carried zhat stupid script avound all zhe time… vaiting vor anozzer opportunity." He scowled sadly, unable to fight off the guilt—it was far too heavy.

Zalith gently shifted closer, his hand stroking Alucard's.

The vampire exhaled slowly, sinking a little further into Zalith's embrace. "I vink zhat 'e and your brover might 'ave liked each ozzer. Zhey'd probably piss vone anozzer off 'ere and zhere, but still."

"Oh, I don't know," he chuckled. "My brother is kind of mean sometimes."

"'Ow vas 'e mean?"

"I don't know, just in a rich person way, I guess? Pretentious and entitled, maybe—at times. He liked to pretend that he was different than our family and tried to be relatable to the people who weren't so well-off. But he wasn't very good at hiding it sometimes."

"'Ow many people did 'e piss off vith 'is pretending?"

"A lot at first because he'd do his best to hide it, but our family was fairly well-known, obviously, so it would never last long. He stopped hiding it eventually, but he still tried to fit in. We had fun, though. I sometimes preferred the places we'd go to over a lot of the more expensive ones uptown."

Alucard frowned curiously. "What vas vone of your vunnest nights at vone of zhose places?"

"Hmm…" Zalith hummed, nuzzling further into his neck. "One time, we were standing on the bar counter, and I slipped, but I grabbed Xurian and took him down with me," he laughed.

The vampire laughed, too. "Vhat did you slip on?"

"I don't know… beer or something. We were drunk and acting really stupid."

Alucard huffed, casting a slow glance around the room. "Maybe ve should get drvunk and act veally stupid."

Zalith didn't answer right away. He leaned nearer, his hand moving in a slow path down Alucard's body, not hurried or teasing but possessive. "I don't know…" he murmured. "I might get a little handsy."

That touch alone sent a ripple of pleasure curling up Alucard's spine. His body responded before he had time to think—heat twisting low, that familiar ache beginning to stir now that grief had loosened its grip. His skin felt too warm, sensitive even beneath his shirt. He let his head tip back against the couch, a smile tugging at his lips. "Maybe I vant you to get 'andsy," he replied quietly, giving in.

The moment stretched between them, desire bleeding in to replace the sorrow, rising slowly, insistently, until it pressed against the edges of Alucard's restraint. His instincts unfurled, the flickering need of his heat licking at his skin with every slow brush of Zalith's fingers.

Zalith's hand kept moving, tracing idle paths down his chest and side with the kind of touch that knew exactly what it was doing. "I wouldn't mind," he purred.

Alucard shrugged, the yearning intensifying with every passing moment. "Maybe zhere's some century-old alcohol avound 'ere somevhere."

"Maybe…" Zalith's tone was amused, low against his ear. "But I don't know if I feel like getting sick right now."

The vampire tensed as Zalith's fingers curved lightly along his waist; the warmth between his thighs was growing, his thoughts muddling around it. "Maybe…" he said, eyes slipping half shut, "vill distract us vrom vanting to 'ave sex all zhe time."

Zalith chuckled, his voice dark and indulgent, "For two minutes, maybe."

That teasing touch was beginning to drive him mad. Alucard shivered and let his eyes fall fully closed, the flicker of old grief pushed to the farthest corner of his mind. It wouldn't devour him tonight. His body was aching, begging as if it had been starved for decades.

He breathed out slowly, and then he caught Zalith's wrist in his hand—firm, but not rough—and guided it lower, pressing it down over the growing bulge between his legs. "Maybe…" the vampire murmured, "…ve should skip zhe alcohol."

Zalith exhaled softly, pleased, and curled his fingers around Alucard's shaft, slowly increasing the pressure, his voice a near-growl as he said, "I like the sound of that."

The demon's hand lingered, palming Alucard's arousal; his thumb traced a teasing path along the shape of him, pressing just enough to make the vampire's hips twitch.

Zalith leaned in, his lips grazing Alucard's ear as he murmured, "You feel like you're burning."

Alucard didn't answer. His pulse quickened, his breath unsteady as heat shot through him like a fire stoked too close to the edge. Zalith's hand shifted lower, fingers brushing beneath the waistband, and Alucard let out a soft groan—half warning, half encouragement.

The demon withdrew just enough to catch Alucard's gaze, and then he smirked. "Come here," he whispered.

Alucard obeyed without hesitation, sliding into Zalith's lap—one knee braced to either side, his body settling against the demon's. Zalith's hands found his waist immediately, pulling him in; their mouths crashed together, their tongues tangling frantically.

Zalith's fingers made quick work of the vampire's shirt, eagerly unfastening each button, and Alucard barely noticed until the fabric slipped down his shoulders, baring his skin to the air and to Zalith's touch.

He groaned into the kiss, the desire flaring brighter every time his mate touched him. Despite how many times Zalith had already claimed him today, he felt as if he'd been starved of pleasure and satisfaction for *years*. But his hunger was finally being sated, and he couldn't help but moan desperately when the demon's hands reached his bare waist.

And yet, when Zalith's hand slipped into his trousers and wrapped around his arousal, a flicker of hesitation struck him. It wasn't shame, not quite fear, but a creeping, quiet unease. The desire didn't vanish, but it blurred at the edges, dimmed by the memory that still hadn't settled, the one that told him—without question—that he'd never really been the boy he was told he was… that he wasn't the man he thought he'd grown to be.

Would Zalith still touch him like this if he truly understood what that meant? Would he still want him, would he still worship him with this same reverent hunger? Zalith had said that he'd seen everything… but he'd never even met a blood-child of the Numen before him, so how could he possibly understand?

Alucard's fingers curled tightly against Zalith's shoulder. He didn't want to hide it. Not from him. But the words—what even *were* the words?

His breath trembled as he broke the kiss, and when Zalith pulled back, confused but gentle, Alucard stared at him, unsure where to begin, but knowing he had to try.

"What's wrong?" the demon asked.

Alucard frowned. "Noving… I just—"

A knock came at the door.

"What?!" Zalith snarled angrily.

Alucard quickly pulled his shirt back over his shoulders and turned his head to glare at the door. He watched as it opened, and Tyrus and Nymeris stepped in.

"We searched the cemetery, sir," Tyrus said quickly. "The loup-garou is holed up in one of the deeper crypts. It's near the far end of the cemetery that borders the forest—it has the name Saint Monroe carved into the archway entrance."

Zalith huffed frustratedly.

Alucard felt the same way, but his desperation to kill the Silver Claw and protect his coven grew and quickly outweighed the desire for sex—and the need to tell Zalith what he'd remembered. "Get everyvone veady," he said as he climbed off Zalith and stood up. "Vind Noctrel and tell zhem to get zhe coven veady. Ve leave in tventy minutes. And get yourselves cleaned up—you veek."

With a nod each, the two allocer demons left the room.

Zalith's hand found Alucard's again, his fingers grasping around his with a firm, possessive warmth as he drew him back in. "Twenty minutes is more than enough time for me to fuck you," he murmured, smirking as he pulled Alucard down into his lap once more.

Alucard didn't resist. He melted into it, sliding his arms around Zalith's shoulders. The hardness beneath him stirred something deep, a pulse of desire that spread through his hips like fire. His instincts stirred at once, coaxing him to give in, to let Zalith take him, to surrender to what his body craved.

And when their lips met, he nearly did.

The kiss sent a shiver through him, and his body pressed down without thinking, seeking friction, seeking heat. His dick was already half-hard again, throbbing faintly against the front of Zalith's trousers.

But he knew he couldn't.

"Not yet," he breathed, the words barely a whisper, pulled from him with effort. They felt strange on his tongue; his body wanted to beg for the opposite.

Zalith groaned in frustration, dragging his hands up Alucard's bare chest with a slow, lingering touch. There was a wildness behind his eyes now—dangerous, intense—but he didn't press. "Okay," he said lowly, "but we're making up for all of this lost time as soon as we're done killing that loup-garou." One hand slid higher and pinched Alucard's nipple.

The vampire flinched, his mouth parting in protest, but it turned into a pout instead.

His mate laughed under his breath, clearly pleased, and let his fingers trail down to the vampire's waist—a tease, a promise. "I suppose we should get ready for war," he said, voice still thick with hunger. But his hands remained where they were, as if ready to change the plan the moment Alucard did.

As much as Alucard wanted to change his mind, though, he pulled away from Zalith and started buttoning his shirt up. "Is less zhan vour hours until zhe day of zhe vull moon. Ve need to vork vast."

Zalith got up with a deep groan and straightened his clothes. But when he gently grabbed Alucard's waist and pulled him closer, it wasn't desire and hunger that lingered in the demon's eyes anymore. He looked *worried*. "I know I can't ask you to stay behind, I just…it sounds selfish, I know, but with you being in heat, it's hard for me to focus— if anything happened to you because of me *again*, I—"

"I'll be okay, Zaliv," he tried to assure him. "Ve veren't prepared zhe virst time, but ve 'ave everyvone vith us now; ve 'ave a plan, and ve know vhat ve're up against."

He exhaled deeply, resting his forehead against Alucard's. "I know. But I can't stop worrying about you. What if she springs something else on us that we had no idea about? I don't…I don't want to see you hurt again."

"Our people vound out everyving about 'er, so zhere's noving ve aren't prepared vor. All ve 'ave to do is 'it 'er a vew times vith Veybane Oil and is over vor 'er."

Zalith huffed and mumbled, "We'll just have to hope our archers are good enough."

"I trust zhem—I trust everyvone ve've assigned veapons to, so zon't vorry. Zhis bitch von't see zhe light of anozzer moon."

The worry didn't lift from Zalith's face—not all of it—but he did settle a little. "Just stay close to me, please."

Alucard nodded. "I vill."

Chapter Forty-One

— ⸰ ✝ ⸰ —

Once Hunter, Now Hunted

| **Alucard** |
| *Atheson, Atheson City Cemetery* |

Everyone was ready and waiting in the courtyard. The archers had coated their arrows in Feybane Oil, and the blades of every other weapon gleamed with the same deadly sheen. Vampires waited behind Noctrel, and demons stood ready around Tyrus and Nymeris.

Alucard stood by the fountain with his mate at his side. "Zaliv and I vill lead Tyrus and 'is team inside zhe crypt," Alucard called. "Nymeris and 'er team vill take positions a 'undred veet vrom zhe south exit. Noctrel, you and your team vill take positions at zhe east. Drusilda, your team vill take positions at zhe vest, and 'alvarn's team vill cover zhe north. You all know vhat you 'ave to do, no?"

The crowd called their confirmations.

"Archers, you know your positions, *da*?"

Danford, Olivienne, Brannoc, Nerilitha, and Cenric nodded, clasping their bows.

With a huff, Alucard looked over his shoulder at Lăcrămioara, who stood in the estate doorway with Lysandra at her side. He knew that having the brood nurse join the hunt would benefit them greatly, but he wasn't going to leave the Fledgelings unguarded. Besides, he had a powerful group of vampires already—they'd get this done.

"Let's move," he called.

On his word, everyone departed, racing off towards the cemetery to take position.

Alucard went to follow, but Zalith gently grasped his hand.

"Are you sure you're ready?" he asked worriedly. "You didn't get much rest."

"I'm veally okay, Zaliv. Zon't vorry about me," he insisted calmly.

Zalith exhaled…but nodded. "Okay. Just promise me you'll take cover once you've flooded the cemetery with fog."

"I vill, I promise." He then dematerialized them both into vermillion smoke and raced to the cemetery.

When he landed behind the cover of a towering headstone, Tyrus' team quickly joined him and Zalith.

The cemetery stretched out in shadowed rows, a sea of weathered stones and cold marble statues half-swallowed by a thin veil of fog; the air smelled faintly of damp stone and wilted flowers, and despite its age, the cemetery had been kept just neat enough to avoid the look of abandonment, though the vines curling around the rusted fence suggested it had been a while since anyone cared deeply.

Above them, the silver moon was inches close to being full, its silvery light now managing to break through the shadow of its crimson cousin. Most nights, the red moon cloaked it almost entirely, but tonight, its white sheen bled visibly into the kaleidoscopic glow that bathed everything it touched.

The light clung to the fog like breath on glass, softening the world into ghostly silhouettes. Beyond the cemetery gates, the city stood quiet and still, its usual glow diffused behind clouded windows and silent lamps. The lockdown had muted it all; not a single carriage wheel or drunken voice in the distance, just the eerie hush that followed a fake plague warning... and a deeper tension that hummed beneath it.

Alucard could feel them—the others. Vampires and demons moving through the cemetery, keeping low, positioning themselves among statues and family plots. Their presence brushed against his senses like pressure in the air, silent coordination, waiting.

"Remember the plan," Zalith said lowly. "We go in, we find her, and we force her out into the open. Do not let her grab you or pull you into a fight. We flee only."

Everyone nodded.

"Let's go," the vampire muttered, and he began leading the way to the Saint Monroe crypt.

The arched entrance was half-collapsed, and vines spewed from the cracks, thick, tangled things that looked more like veins than plant life. The crypt itself slouched beneath a shallow rise of earth, its weatherworn structure marked by crumbling stonework and an iron gate clinging to its hinges; the engraved name was nearly erased by time, the letters soft and shallow under centuries of rot and neglect.

It hadn't been visited in decades—that much was obvious. No flowers, no offerings, not even the faintest sign of mourning, just the warped remnants of old lantern hooks and crumbling angelic statues, their faces worn into ghoulish blanks. Dead leaves and bones cluttered the threshold, and near the base of the steps, Alucard caught sight of several small corpses—rats, dried and shrivelled, their limbs twisted as if they'd died in pain. One of them was little more than skin pulled tight around a broken jaw.

The smell hit him before he reached the arch.

Rotting moss, and the scent of long-sealed air that hadn't been clean in years. But beneath that was something else, barely there, only noticed because Alucard was aware of what to search for: the stale, metallic tang of necromancy. It threaded through the stench like blood laced with spoiled incense, and ensnared within that was the unmistakable reek of wet, filthy fur.

He slowed his pace, and when he halted, everyone stopped behind him. *"She's devinitely 'ere,"* he said into his mate's mind.

Zalith passed the message on, signing to their team.

"Ve 'ave to move single vile."

The demon passed that on, too.

And then Alucard pressed on.

He stepped inside, the stone beneath his boots colder than it had any right to be. The air thickened instantly, heavy with mildew, old dust, and the unmistakable stench of disturbed death. The crypt interior had once been orderly, family coffins arranged in alcoves and along raised platforms, but time and something far less natural had ravaged the space. Most of the caskets were open, their lids either rotted away or forced aside; some were splintered entirely, shattered from within or pried apart carelessly. Bones lay scattered—ribcages half-intact, femurs stripped of their ends, finger bones crushed beneath drag marks smeared across the floor.

Alucard crouched near one of the smears. The tracks weren't new... but they weren't ancient either. Flesh had clung to these bones when they were pulled free, and judging by the angle, the force, and the mess, it hadn't been clean. It had been *eager.*

And the further they moved in, the worse it got.

The scent of necromancy intensified, and the walls themselves felt heavier, as though the crypt no longer belonged to the dead but to a parasitic entity.

Alucard stopped again. Ahead, near the rear of the crypt, was a jagged hole in the wall. The stone had been crumbled from the other side, clawed and gouged out in chunks, and its edges were darkened by soot or old ichor, hard to tell in the dimness. But it looked just like the hole they'd found in the church cellar.

A tunnel stretched beyond, veering down and into the blackness beneath the cemetery.

Another catacomb.

The sight of it made Alucard tense up, every instinct in his body recoiling before his mind could reason it away. The tunnel looked too familiar—the same old bricks, the shadows within stretching long and deep, just like the ones that had nearly swallowed him when he was a child.

He didn't want to look at it, let alone step into it. But what would that say about him if he hesitated now? If he, the mate of the one leading these demons—*a Numen's heir*— let fear claim him in front of the others? And over something as simple as a tunnel?

He forced his jaw to unclench, steadying the urge to exhale and react. One wrong sound might carry. One breath too loud, and the loup-garou would know they were coming.

So he shoved the fear aside and slipped through the opening.

The walls were narrow, close enough that his shoulder occasionally brushed them; the air grew denser, stirring old scents left to rot beneath the city. As the tunnel sloped downward, the footing grew uneven, clumps of half-crushed bone underfoot, rock worn by claw or heel, he wasn't sure which.

And then came the sounds. Distant at first, barely audible beneath the weight of silence.

A sharp *crack*, followed by a slower, wetter one.

The low shuffle of something moving.

And a noise no creature should make: a *chew*. A *rip*. The wet slide of something being devoured.

Alucard stopped briefly and glanced behind him, confirming that Zalith understood the same thing he did.

The loup-garou was close.

It sounded like she was feeding... and the sharp, sour trace of necromantic residue told him something else: she was healing. It had to be the Thaernari trait, the ability to feed on the long-dead and use it to mend. If that was the case, if she'd already absorbed enough from the crypt's ancient corpses, then the damage they'd done to her before might mean nothing now, and with the full moon so near, she'd be faster, stronger, and harder to stop.

Still, this time, they were prepared. They had a plan. They had numbers. They knew what she was susceptible to, and they weren't walking in blind. If Tyrus was right, if she truly believed that Alucard was dead, then they had one more advantage: the element of shock.

He clung to that thought as he pressed deeper into the catacomb, keeping his breathing even and his footsteps light. The walls seemed to close in the farther they went, and the foul air clung to him like wet silk. His senses were pulled taut, every faint noise and flicker of scent carving new tension into his bones, but he fought off the anxiety. This wasn't a passage in the place he'd spent his childhood; this passage was taking him to the biggest threat his Atheson coven had faced in decades, and he was going to put an end to it.

At last, the tunnel opened.

They emerged into a wide, round chamber. The ceiling domed overhead, ribbed with age-darkened supports, and in the centre yawned a gaping hole in the floor, black as pitch. A spiralled staircase had once descended into the depths, but it was mostly gone now, shattered into jagged fragments that clung to the walls like broken teeth.

Alucard lifted a hand to slow the others, and then he crept closer to the edge. He leaned forward just enough to peer down into the darkness....

And there she was.

Accalia Veyne. The Silver Claw. The loup-garou.

In her *massive* wolf form, she knelt on powerful haunches below, a hulking, bipedal mass of fur and muscle. Her claws were slick with ancient blood, buried deep in a pile of half-rotted, half-mummified corpses. She tore into them greedily, jaws cracking bones, snarling low between gulps. Strips of dried skin hung from her claws, and when she turned her head just slightly, her glowing yellow eyes swept over the chamber like a predator still hungry despite the pile at her feet.

Alucard watched her devour another limb like a dog tearing apart cooked poultry. Her strength was returning—he could feel it in the air, humming like static.

Time was running out.

He spoke into Zalith's mind, "*Tell six of zhem to take positions avound zhis gap, 'ugging zhe valls so zhat she von't see zhem if she looks up.*"

Zalith signed the command.

Six demons silently took position, using the shadows to remain invisible to the monster below.

"*I vill crveate smoke. Vhile she is convused, you, me, Tyrus, and vhree ozzers vill move down zhere. I vill zhen clear zhe smoke. If she zoesn't vlee vhen she sees us, ve attack until she does, and zhen ve all chase 'er out of zhe crypt. But considering 'ow I vounded 'er, I suspect zhat she'll choose to vun on 'er own.*"

His mate passed everything on.

Alucard then turned his head, his eyes locking with Zalith's. He didn't need to speak to ask him if he was ready—they'd fought side by side long enough to say and answer with mere looks.

Zalith nodded once.

The vampire set his eyes on the feasting loup-garou again...and then he drew his claws across his wrist. Blood welled instantly, and with a sharp, focused breath, he commanded it outward, twisting it into thick fog that burst down into the chamber.

It flooded the space in a heartbeat, curling around the bodies and ensnaring the loup-garou. She roared and thrashed, staggering back from the corpses as her senses were choked by the dense, ember-laced distortion, and Alucard leapt, leading Zalith and his demons down through the shattered gap.

The moment their boots struck stone and they took position, Alucard recalled the fog. The blood surged back into his body, clearing the chamber just as the loup-garou spun to face them—snarling, wide-eyed, fangs bared.

She didn't hesitate.

With a guttural roar, she lunged. Her claws shot out, seizing one of Zalith's demons by the collar and yanking him clean off the floor. Another rushed to intervene, only to be struck aside with brutal force, his body cracking into the stone wall with a sharp, wet thud.

But then Zalith stepped forward, his hand ablaze with radiant white fire. With a sudden thrust, he slammed the burning flames into her arm. The loup-garou shrieked and dropped the demon immediately, her fur blackened, flesh curling beneath the searing flame as she stumbled backward, growling and clutching at the burn—but the fire didn't devour her; she managed to extinguish it, another benefit of her lineage.

Alucard moved like instinct. He lifted his arm, blood already pouring to his palm, shaping itself into glimmering, jagged blades. But just as he prepared to strike, the loup-garou looked at him.

Their eyes locked.

And for a split second, something shifted in hers. Recognition. *Fear.*

She snarled again, but this time, it wasn't a challenge.

It was retreat.

With a violent leap, she launched herself upward, claws tearing into the fractured remnants of the stairwell. Stone splintered beneath her as she vaulted through the gap they'd descended from, disappearing into the dark beyond.

"Stay and help them," Zalith ordered the third demon, pointing to the two the loup-garou had managed to injure.

And then he, Alucard, and Tyrus hurried up towards the tunnel, following behind the other demons as they chased the monster through the passage, feet pounding against the stone floor, the sounds of pursuit echoing like war drums through the cramped, ancient catacomb.

Alucard kept close to Zalith's side; he could feel the fatigue tightening its grip, a familiar side-effect of blood magic. But he didn't let it stop him. He continued his pursuit, his fangs bared in concentration. The loup-garou's scent lingered ahead—musky, feral, and now tainted with the acrid bite of burned flesh. He could hear her movements, too: the scrape of claws, the crash of shattered debris, the desperate rhythm of her retreat.

But she didn't veer right when she should have—she didn't leave the crypt the same way they'd come in. She darted past and deeper into the cramped burial place; the tunnel twisted and narrowed, and then it opened again just before they saw the faint shimmer of moonlight bleeding in ahead. The beast burst through the western exit like a cannon blast, stone and dirt flinging up in her wake as she tore across the overgrown grounds.

Alucard and the demons emerged seconds later—the vampire spotted her silhouette under the kaleidoscopic light of the moons, bounding low and fast through the tall, brittle grass. Her form was nothing but blur and muscle, but her path was clear.

She was heading straight for the forest.

He snarled, picking up the pace even as Drusilda and her team joined the chase; he wasn't going to let her vanish into the trees, not after the bodies she'd left behind, not after how many of his vampires she'd torn apart, and not after learning who she truly was.

But she didn't reach the wall.

And Alucard didn't need to dematerialize to catch up to her.

The distant explosions of firing rifles cut through the silence. Bullets hit the ground at the loup-garou's feet as she skidded to a halt—she managed to avoid them all, but she wasn't fast enough to dodge the rain of arrows.

She roared furiously as only one of five arrows embedded in her burned forearm.

But one was enough.

"Now!" Alucard and Zalith commanded simultaneously.

Every demon and vampire sprinted from their posts to join the onslaught, merging before the loup-garou could pull the arrow free. Alucard once again drew his blood and ensnared the cemetery-turned-battlefield in thick, gleaming fog, blinding the loup-garou and giving his allies the huge upper hand he hoped would end this quickly.

Zalith then urged him towards one of the towering headstones. Alucard ducked behind the wide curve of it, and the demon crouched beside him. Cracks spiderwebbed through the stone from age and weather, but it held firm as he took cover in its shadow.

"Stay here," Zalith said firmly.

Alucard nodded.

The demon lingered a second longer, his gaze flicking to the slight tremor in Alucard's bloodied fingers.

"I'm vine," the vampire assured him. It wasn't a lie—not really.

Zalith hesitated…but only for a breath. He nodded and peeled away, charging into the fog-drenched chaos with white fire licking at his fingertips.

The battlefield erupted.

Gunfire cracked across the cemetery, bullets sparking off stone and splintered wood, some slicing past the loup-garou's limbs, others embedding uselessly in the earth. Arrows hissed through the fog, some thudding into her, others missing entirely. She roared, spinning wildly as the blindness overtook her, lashing out at anything that moved.

One vampire was caught in her sweeping arm and flung across the field like a rag doll. A demon screamed as her silver claws slashed across his shoulder, cutting deep, sizzling the wound with a cursed, searing burn. Two more rushed her from behind, trying to pin her down, but she kicked one aside and grabbed the other by the throat, slamming him into a headstone that cracked in two.

Then Zalith appeared through the fog. A streak of white flame roared across the field—beautiful, blinding—and struck the loup-garou's leg dead on.

She screamed as the fire crawled up her thigh, a hungry light against the blood and fur, and for a moment, Alucard thought it might take hold, that it might finally burn her down to ash.

But she snarled through gritted teeth, slammed her claws into the earth, and rolled hard, dragging herself through the churned mud and grass until the flame was smothered. Her fur smoked, scorched—but she was far from finished. She stilled, crouched low, her claws dug deep into the dirt. Her limbs trembled, muscles tight with fury and pain, but her eyes gleamed brightly, and yellow light cracked through the ground beneath her.

Alucard's heart stuttered.

Veins of glowing gold split the soil like lightning frozen mid-burst, snaking between headstones, crawling under graves long forgotten. The cemetery trembled faintly and then violently, and from the disturbed earth, hands began to emerge.

Skeletal. Rotten.

The dead were rising.

"Fuck," Alucard snarled.

She wasn't just fast and impossible to burn. She'd inherited necromancy, too.

All around them, graves split open with sickening cracks. Corpses dragged themselves from the soil, some half-mummified, others little more than skeletons held together by scraps of tendon and cloth. A nearby vampire screamed as one latched onto her leg; another demon was yanked backwards, toppling into the dirt as bony fingers wrapped around his throat.

And the chaos intensified.

Most of their force broke formation, scattering to defend themselves against the sudden undead surge. Steel rang out against bone. Spells ignited the fog in flashes of blue and silver and crimson, and cries of warning and pain echoed through the mist. Skyborne vampires had no choice but to grab their struggling Fellkin and lift them away from the corpses, pulling them out of reach.

Zalith held the line with Tyrus, Nymeris, and two others, throwing themselves back at the loup-garou, trying to restrain her again as she let out another furious howl.

And Alucard—

His focus shattered.

A cold grip clamped around his ankle, and when he looked down, his eyes met the hollow sockets of a skull—a corpse clawed its way out of the dirt at his feet, its jaw twisted, one arm already loose at the elbow but still grasping him with relentless strength. Its mouth opened in a silent groan, and it kept pulling.

Alucard snarled and slammed his heel down, crushing the skull beneath his boot with a wet crack. Bone splintered, and the half-risen corpse went still, twitching once before falling limp. He yanked his other leg free, teeth gritted as dead fingers scraped along his calf. He then straightened sharply, eyes snapping back to the battlefield.

The undead were still crawling out of their graves, one after another—bone, rot, and rags reeking of ethos and damp soil. The cemetery had become a necromancer's stage, and Accalia was pulling every string.

Zalith moved like lightning, caught between the loup-garou's lunges and the corpses swarming from all sides. White fire flashed from his hands, searing through reanimated bodies—but the moment one fell, another seemed to rise.

The archers and riflemen had turned their aim from the massive wolf to the undead, picking off the shambling threats before they could tear into packmates and allies. Silver bullets, oil-dipped arrowheads, screams and snarls filling the fog like music from a dirge.

Still crouched behind the headstone, Alucard forced himself to focus. He reached inward, calling for his blood again, pulling it to his palm, feeling it stubbornly slide from his veins. He had to do more than just sit there. He had to *strike*.

The fog would hold a little longer. He just needed one clean shot, one perfect throw.

But his hand trembled weakly. His chest tightened with the strain, his heartbeat jagged, his breath ragged. Every muscle in his body felt heavier, as if the ground beneath him was making another attempt to drag him down. The fog was costing him; it coiled sluggishly now, its silver-red glow dimming.

He was losing too much blood. He was losing it too fast.

And yet, he didn't let go. He *couldn't*. Not while Zalith was still fighting, not while the loup-garou was still standing.

He grasped the edge of the headstone, claws digging into it as he hissed between gritted teeth, trying to steady his trembling limbs. His vision blurred around the edges, dimmed by strain and blood loss, but he kept his eyes on Zalith.

His mate surged forward, conjuring more fire—but before he could unleash it, the loup-garou grabbed a wounded vampire and hurled him like a ragdoll. The body collided with Zalith mid-cast, and the two rolled across the blood-slicked grass.

Tyrus was already there, dragging both to their feet, but Accalia wasn't waiting. She tore through the fray like a possessed beast, snarling, roaring, shrieking when a silver bullet ripped into her arm. But it barely slowed her. Even burned and slashed with wounds crisscrossing her monstrous body, she moved like nothing could kill her.

And she charged *straight* for Zalith.

Alucard lurched upright—he couldn't use his blood, but that didn't mean he couldn't do more than just stand there and keep the place ensnared in fog. He reached into his coat and pulled out one of his revolvers, aimed at the charging beast, lining up the shot as best he could…and fired—

The shot cracked like thunder, the bullet spiralling through the mist; it struck the loup-garou's arm and burrowed deep. She staggered mid-sprint, a shriek tearing from her throat—then the bullet detonated. Blood and shredded muscle burst across the grass and headstones. Her arm was gone, reduced to ruin.

Before she could recover, Tyrus and the vampire triplets slammed into her flank. Steel flashed. Claws raked. Blades pierced her gut and dragged down through her ribs. Blood sprayed in thick arcs, but she only screamed louder, her flailing limbs crushing one of the triplets beneath her.

More vampires surged from the fog, demons in tow, piling onto her like a pack of wolves. They drove her back in a tangle of snarling bodies and silver-tipped blades.

But it wasn't enough.

With a feral roar, she ripped free. Bodies flew, crashing into gravestones, skidding across the mud. Her blood drenched the earth, but she didn't falter. Her one remaining arm flexed, cords of muscle twitching with renewed power. Her eyes burned like coals, alive with wrath, and the rage on her face was almost feral in its joy.

Then her gaze snapped to Tyrus, who'd barely pushed to his feet, still grappling with two reanimated corpses clawing at his back.

Zalith raised his hand, white fire blazing in a radiant arc. The corpses ignited instantly, disintegrating in a flash of blinding heat, and then he hurled a second blast towards Accalia—

The fire collided with her shoulder, burning through fur and flesh. She howled, stumbling.

But even *that* wasn't enough.

She lunged again and slammed into Tyrus with full force, launching him across the cemetery. He hit the ground *hard*, rolling through bone-littered mud until he disappeared behind a crooked statue.

And then she turned again, her blood-slick mouth twisting into a snarl, and she charged at Zalith.

Alucard's heart slammed against his ribs. He reached for more fog, trying to thicken it, trying to blind her again. But his ethos faltered, and the cemetery started spinning. His blood no longer responded like it should; the fog was thinning, becoming useless. He couldn't hold it much longer.

But just as the weakness began to win, his legs going numb, one hand gripping the headstone to keep himself upright, a single arrow sliced through the fog. It shimmered silver as it flew, trailing Feybane residue in its wake, and before the loup-garou could reach Zalith, it struck true—it buried clean through her eye.

She shrieked furiously, the sound ripping through the cemetery, a howl of agony so loud that it cracked the stillness like lightning. Her momentum faltered, her clawed feet skidding in the torn grass as she stumbled back, pawing at her face with bloodied fingers. Her jaws snapped wildly, her weight teetering.

Alucard didn't waste the opening.

He tightened his grip on the headstone, keeping himself on his feet, and forced his free hand forward. The bloody ground under Accalia rumbled, and before the loup-garou could react, a single thin luciferium crystal erupted beneath her, a jagged spike of glimmering red-black bursting from the soil and impaling her through the left side of her torso. It punched through her ribs and out her back, locking her in place mid-scream.

Her limbs thrashed, but she couldn't escape.

Alucard tried to summon the charge, he tried to detonate the crystal while she was pinned, but he had nothing left. The blood in his veins felt distant, and his breath stammered; he staggered once, and then he crumpled behind the headstone, darkness biting at the edge of his vision. He couldn't stand any longer, but he could see—he watched Zalith move in.

Vampires and demons surged after him, pouring through the thinning fog like a tidal wave. Zalith reached Accalia first, grabbing her by the throat with burning hands. Others swarmed her limbs, slashing and tearing, dodging her frenzied strikes as she tried to free herself. She fought like a cornered beast—thrashing, howling, raking silver claws through flesh and bone.

They didn't stop. It took effort, it took blood, but they tore her apart, claw by claw, limb by limb. They ripped her from the luciferium spike, forced her to the ground, and silenced her screams.

And finally, once he tore her head off, Zalith sent the loup-garou's body up in white flames.

The undead corpses crumbled as the source of their reanimation withered, and as the remnants of Alucard's fog dissipated, silence ensnared the battlefield.

And Alucard—still slumped behind the stone—finally let himself succumb to the fatigue. He slid down, resting his shoulder against the headstone, leaning his weight onto it. The hunter was dead, and his vampires were safe.

How many had he lost, though?

He edged forward, peering around the headstone. Zalith was rushing over, and behind him, demons and vampires were helping each other up and tending to wounds. He couldn't see any lifeless allies, but he couldn't really see much of anything. The world was still spinning, and his vision was blurring. He'd overdone it again, too much for how little rest he'd gotten. But it was necessary. It was the only way to ensure that Accalia didn't leave this place and kill any more of his vampires.

"Alucard," Zalith urged worriedly, kneeling in front of him and gently grasping his shoulders. "Are you okay?" He caressed the side of Alucard's face.

He nodded and exhaled deeply.

Zalith pulled him into his embrace. "She's dead," he told him quietly. "It's over."

A relieved sigh left him. "I guess 'er Vhaernari blood vas stronger zhan ve suspected," he mumbled. "And I 'ad no idea zhat zhose elves 'ad necromancy abilities; elves are usually susceptible to zhat shit."

"It doesn't matter now," his mate said softly, caressing the back of his head. "I've ordered my demons to get everyone back to the Sanctum. We didn't lose anyone, but some of them were badly injured."

Alucard nodded, closing his eyes for a moment.

Zalith then chuckled a little. "One eye, and Danford still managed to take hers."

The vampire laughed quietly, sliding—albeit struggling a little—his revolver back into its holster. "A lucky shot?"

"Maybe," he murmured, now stroking Alucard's back. "Can you stand?"

With another nod, the vampire tried to get up, but he stumbled, and Zalith had to help him. "I should vest," he mumbled.

"You should," the demon said firmly. "Let me take you back to the Sanctum."

Alucard didn't argue. If he tried to dematerialize in his current state, it would drain what little strength he had left; the last thing he needed was to lose consciousness mid-flight and crash headfirst into a rooftop.

Zalith shifted into his demon form, wings unfurling with a low, leathery rustle. He swept Alucard into his arms, holding him close against his chest. Then, with one powerful beat of his wings, he soared upward, cutting through the misty night.

Alucard rested his head against his mate's shoulder, the heat of Zalith's body seeping into his own, easing the ache in his limbs. The cemetery shrank beneath them, bathed in moonlight and lingering fog, but the dread that had settled there no longer followed him.

The danger was over, and he could finally rest. No more chasing a ghost in the dark, no more fearing who her claws might kill next. The Silver Claw—*Accalia*—was dead, and with her, another piece of Ada's cursed legacy had been buried for good.

His eyelids drifted shut as the wind rushed past them. Zalith would get him to safety.

And for the first time since the Silver Claw first showed up, Alucard allowed himself to truly relax.

Chapter Forty-Two

— ‹ † › —

Connection

| Tyrus—Monday, Aprilis 3ʳᵈ, 960(TG) |
| Atheson, Atheson Coven Sanctum |

Tyrus stared up at the ceiling, moonlight spilling through the cracks in the drawn curtains. The Nocturne Wing was quieter than the rest of the Sanctum—peaceful, even. That stillness dulled the edge of his pain, though only slightly. It had been a long time since he'd been wounded by silver, long enough that he'd half-forgotten the way it burned, not just through flesh but deep into bone. The ache was different, *harsher*.

He let out a slow breath and dragged a hand over his face before resting it on the empty pillow beside him. There wasn't a bed in the room Alucard had assigned him, but the couch he was stretched across was better than expected, soft and plush, as if it were embracing him. It even had a faint but sweet scent, roses and amber, perhaps. Though if he had the choice, he'd be recovering at home.

But he wasn't about to leave. Zalith still needed him. The loup-garou was dead, but the compound was still on the coast, full of non-human children who needed to be rescued. And he hadn't forgotten about Lucious either. He was still going to find him, and he suspected that after they tied things up in Atheson, he'd be travelling to that pocket world with Orin and Crowell—*finally*.

The Bloodmenders had done what they could for him, but silver slowed the healing. He'd be benched for a few days whether he liked it or not. Still, he could be useful. There were always ways to help, and there were always a few humans who needed killing.

He took a long drag of his cigarette, holding the smoke in his lungs before exhaling slowly. The haze drifted towards the ceiling, soft and aimless. He tapped the ash into the tray and closed his eyes for a breath of quiet.

Then came a knock at the door.

He didn't startle; he just opened his eyes and said, "Come in," as he stubbed the cigarette out.

The door opened, and Nymeris stepped in. "Hi," she said with a smile—there was sympathy in her tone, and it was accompanied by worry.

"Oh, hey," he said, sitting up as much as the healing gashes along his chest would let him. He was admittedly embarrassed to be seen like this, especially in front of her.

"I heard that the Bloodmenders finished patching you up," she said, lingering by the door. "How are you feeling?"

He looked down at his bandaged chest and shrugged with a scoff. "Oh, you know... dealing with it. Just another day on the job, I suppose."

She smiled amusedly. "That was a pretty nasty hit you took, though. I mean, giant slugs and hostile demons are one thing, but a *huge* werewolf monster with silver for claws?"

"First time for everything," he said with a quiet chuckle, settling deeper into the couch and resting one arm along the cushions. He tilted his head towards her. "You can have a seat if you want."

Nymeris hesitated just a fraction, enough to catch his attention. But then she nodded and stepped inside, gently closing the door behind her. She moved around the low coffee table and lowered herself beside him, her movements careful, like she wasn't sure how close was too close.

For a moment, neither of them spoke.

She looked at him.

He looked right back.

Something passed between them—unspoken, a little uncertain. But not unwelcome.

Then her gaze shifted downward to his bruised, bandaged chest. "Did they tell you how long it'll take to heal?"

"Could be a day... could be two. Maybe longer. They're gonna take another look later when they're done seeing to everyone else. It was mayhem in the Vitalum."

She nodded, fingers fidgeting lightly in her lap. Her eyes flicked to his face, then away again, glancing around the quiet, shadowed room. "I saw Cadwell. He's not doing great. Sorrelle and Royandra had to drag Briallen out—she wouldn't stop hovering or let the healers work."

Tyrus breathed out a slow sigh, watching her profile, the way she avoided his gaze like she wasn't quite sure she wanted to be caught in it. "Yeah," he said, his voice softer now. "If it were *my* partner on the edge like that... I'd probably be just as stubborn."

She didn't answer right away, but he saw the corners of her mouth twitch. It was like some sort of shared understanding, and the distance between them didn't feel so distant anymore.

"Can I get you anything?" she asked, her eyes finally meeting his again. "The izurets are being sent on food runs."

"I'm not really hungry right now, but thank you."

She nodded and looked away.

"But I could go for a drink if you wanna have one with me," he said with another light chuckle.

Nymeris smiled and said, "Well, lucky for us, there's a small bar just across the hall. What do you want? I'll go grab it."

"I don't know—surprise me," he said with a smile.

She nodded and got up. "I'll be right back."

"Okay," he said, watching her leave.

He leaned back into the cushions, exhaling slowly and ignoring the dull throb beneath his bandages. Seeing Nymeris had helped…more than he wanted to admit. He wasn't used to anyone being able to distract him like that, not enough to ease the sting of silver-inflicted wounds. The pain was still there, but with her around, it faded into the background. It was manageable, quieter.

She hadn't fussed, she hadn't hovered, nor had she treated him like something fragile, and he appreciated that. He appreciated *her*. She didn't have to check on him— not when there were a dozen others in worse shape. But she had. She'd come anyway, just to see how he was doing, and that…it meant more than he was used to. He found himself smiling faintly, eyes still on the door she'd just walked through.

But then his gaze dropped to the ashtray, and his smile faded. He'd missed working with Nymeris. He realized that now…he *really* realized it after crawling through catacombs and fighting side by side again. She hadn't just been his best fighter and his most reliable Beta; she'd been his *friend*. She still was.

And now…something was shifting.

He wanted more.

That made him feel stupid, though. Risky, even. From a professional standpoint, the idea was a bad one—they were both Alphas now, from different packs, and relationships in their line of work didn't just *complicate* things, they endangered them. If it didn't work out, the fallout wouldn't be private. It would ripple through everything—missions, assignments, the people they led.

And Zalith? Zalith would be *furious*. Not because of the feelings but because it meant that Tyrus would become a liability he'd have to factor for; he'd have to go out of his way to ensure that Nymeris and he weren't assigned to work together, and that was the last thing he wanted to be.

But…none of that discouraged him—not really…not entirely. He felt something between them. It was more than just the wish for her company, more than the desire for conversation and familiarity. After being away from her for so long and finally seeing her again—finally *being* with her again—something inside him seemed to wake up. It was like finding something he'd spent months hunting for, like he'd been searching for an answer and eventually found it in the most unexpected place.

He didn't want to ignore it. Whatever this feeling was, whatever this *connection* was, it deserved more of his attention—*Nymeris* deserved more of his attention.

The door then opened again, and Nymeris returned with a bottle of reddish-brown liquid and two glasses. "I found this cognac," she said, sitting beside him. "The guy sitting in there said it was good."

Tyrus nodded. "I suppose we'll be the judge of that."

She smiled and poured them both a glass. "Well, here's to slain loup-garou and flooded giant slug nests," she said amusedly.

He laughed and clinked his glass with hers. "And to a cemetery full of resurrected corpses."

She giggled and sipped from her drink.

As he tried the cognac, Tyrus raised his eyebrows in surprise. "Huh…it's actually pretty good."

Nymeris picked up the bottle and read the label on the back. "Oh, it has the little Nosferatu sigil—Vraja Vitæ Distilling Co., since seven-fifty-seven."

Tyrus glanced at it. "I heard that Alucard owns wine companies or something."

"It says that it was aged in oak for *seven decades*, and then it was sealed in glass in eight-eighty-three."

He huffed a laugh and took another sip. "So, we're drinking…hundred and forty-year-old cognac," he said, swirling the liquid around in his glass.

"One hundred and forty-seven, to be exact," she said matter-of-factly, putting the bottle down. "It's probably so expensive."

"Well, they get all that money from somewhere," he chuckled. "Have you had it before?"

She turned the bottle so that she could see the label again. "Not this cognac, but I think I *did* try one of this company's wines back in Nefastus. *That* was pretty good, too."

He finished his drink and placed his glass on the table. "Do you miss Nefastus?"

Nymeris leaned back into the cushions, staring at her drink. "I mean…yeah, kinda. It wasn't like Andora—it wasn't very much like Chronia, to be honest. But it did have this sort of…not familiarity, because we didn't have all those balloon airship things flying about," she paused and laughed. "You get what I'm trying to say, right? Just something about the people and the way they talk…maybe even how some of the houses looked…and the docks." She shrugged her shoulders. "I don't know." She exhaled through her nose and turned her head to look at him. "Do *you* miss it?"

"Sometimes. It was where we all settled—or at least tried to—after we got everyone out of Eltaria, so it kinda…stuck. I mean, I didn't really spend long there since I was away working most of the time, but I *did* like where I was living."

"Do you like Uzlia?"

"Yeah," he said with a nod. "It's…different—in a good way. It's kinda this sort of…if Nefastus and an Elven country clashed together and merged."

She smiled and said, "It feels…I don't want to sound silly and say magical, but it just has that aura. *And* the humans get on with us non-humans a lot better than anywhere else I've seen in this world."

"Which is definitely a surprise," he concurred.

Nymeris finished her drink, and then she giggled. "You know what I find funny?"

"What?"

"*Ethos.*"

He chuckled. "What about it?"

"Just…the word. It's really interesting to me how some things here are the same as Eltaria, or *very* similar, but also not really at the same time. Like magic. They *do* use that word here, but not in the way we do—well…*did.*"

"Yeah. When I first heard someone say 'my ethos', I admit, I was confused as hell. Ethos is the credibility of writing or something—or shared values, right?"

"Not anymore," she chuckled.

"Clearly," he said amusedly.

Tyrus watched her set her glass down, her fingers brushing the rim for a second longer than necessary.

"Ethosical," she said sarcastically.

He scoffed a laugh. "Yeah, that one gets me."

"Surely, there are other terms."

"If there are, I haven't heard them."

"Maybe we ought to ask around," she suggested, but she didn't sound serious.

"Maybe," he said.

A small silence then settled between them.

Tyrus leaned back a little, the quiet stretching just enough to feel intentional. "…You know what I miss most?" he said after a pause. "Having people around all the time. I used to complain about it—about not getting enough space. But now that everyone's scattered, and half the people I knew are either dead or transferred somewhere else, I kind of get it. The silence isn't always peace."

She rested her hands in her lap and turned her head slowly; her brows drew together just a bit, like she wasn't sure what to say yet, but she was listening.

He let out a soft breath and tilted his head. "Back in Eltaria, I used to sneak off between missions. Not to escape command, but to meet up with this family we'd helped relocate. A couple of kids, an older couple running the house. They insisted on feeding me every time. It was loud, always someone talking, laughing, spilling something. I'd stay longer than I meant to every time." His mouth twitched faintly. "I haven't really thought about that in years." He then looked back at her.

Her expression had softened; something in her eyes was warm and familiar, like the kind of look someone gave when they were reading between the lines.

Tyrus hesitated and leaned forward just slightly, one arm still resting along the back of the couch. "It's just nice," he said quietly, "having someone here who makes the place feel a little less empty."

Her lips parted like she might say something, but nothing came out—just a breath and a blink.

Their eyes locked again, a stare that neither of them broke.

Until Nymeris glanced down at her hands and said, "I feel the same." She smiled but didn't shift her gaze. "It's been hard…all of this moving around, hunting people down, fighting monsters and creatures and whatever else. All of these new demons…none of them really take a moment to breathe and acknowledge the people around them as more than just packmates or colleagues." Then she took a brief look at him; sadness lingered in her iridescent orange eyes, glooming their shine. "It's not like how it was in Eltaria. We all know each other; we know each other's lives and hobbies and all of that. And I get it, we're still fighting for peace, but I miss that connection."

Tyrus watched her as she spoke, his focus narrowing in on the subtle strain in her voice, the ache underneath her words. Her honesty sat heavily between them, not uncomfortable but real in a way that very few people dared to be anymore, not in their line of work, and not with everything they'd seen.

"I know what you mean," he said sympathetically. "Back in Eltaria, even when things were bad, we still found time to be people, not just soldiers or enforcers or whatever titles we've got now. You knew who had a temper, who baked, and who played music in their downtime. It mattered." He paused, lowering his gaze to her hands, still resting in her lap, fingers gently laced together like she was holding herself in place. "I don't think that kind of connection is gone," he added quietly as he set his eyes on her face again. "I think some of us are just…waiting for the right people to bring it back, or the right time."

When she looked up at him again, the despondent gleam in her eyes hadn't vanished, but it *was* softer. "I think some of us are too scared to get attached again. We lost Eltaria, we lost Nefastus, and I won't lie…I sometimes worry that we might lose Uzlia, too."

His gaze flickered to her hands again. The urge to reach out rose like a whisper inside him; it wasn't impulsive…it just felt right. He hesitated for a second, unsure if it would be too much, but the need to comfort her—or at least try to—was stronger. So, slowly, he extended his hand, letting his fingers graze hers before he gently took her hand in his. Her skin was cool from the glass she'd held, but soft, her sorrow causing them to tremble.

She didn't pull away.

His thumb brushed lightly over hers. "We might," he replied honestly. "We've lost before. We've bled for things that didn't hold. But not everything ends in loss, Nymeris, and not everything worth keeping survives just by luck. We fight for it, just like we did back then."

She didn't reply right away. It looked like she was thinking, but then her cheeks reddened slightly when she glanced towards him. And then she shifted closer.

Tyrus kept hold of her hand as she moved, their knees now touching. Her honesty had hit him hard…because he felt it too. That fear of investing, of letting himself believe something might last this time.

He turned slightly and lifted his arm, gradually moving his hand from hers to rest gently against her arm. He guided her closer, letting his touch speak for him as much as his words did. When her head settled against his shoulder, he exhaled, some tension slipping from his chest.

Nymeris sighed quietly, tucked close, her breath softening against the side of his neck. "But what if this is just another in between?" she murmured. "What if we're only safe here until the next enemy shows up, or the next city falls?"

He looked down at her, the top of her hair brushing his jaw. His voice dropped to something lower, more certain as he said, "Then we hold the line again. You, me, everyone we've still got. And we keep doing that until something finally holds for good." He paused. "I'm not walking away this time. I'm tired of starting over. Aren't you?"

She didn't answer, but the slight shift in her body, the way she relaxed a little more against him, said enough.

Tyrus let his head settle gently atop hers. For a moment, he just breathed her in— her presence, her calm, her warmth. A soft, smoky sweetness lingered in the air around her: plum blossom and smoked vanilla, like a quiet fire blooming in early spring. It wrapped around him, subtle but impossible to ignore, and it made him feel like he'd stumbled into something sacred.

When she started lightly rubbing her thumb over his hand, though, he paused. The tenderness of it caught him off guard. He wanted to keep holding her; he wanted to stay in this moment a little longer, and more than that, he wanted what came next…whatever it was. But after years of dismissing closeness in favour of practicality, he wasn't sure if this pull in his chest was a sudden need or something deeper finally surfacing.

Maybe it didn't matter just yet.

He tucked the feeling away for now and glanced down at her with a crooked grin. "Do you remember when Ruthven convinced everyone that sewer eels were good luck and made us carry them in our boots before every mission for a month?"

Nymeris started laughing. "Oh my God—of course I do. She told us they heightened reflexes."

"And somehow, Cillian actually believed her," he added. "He swore his reaction time was better—until one wriggled up his leg mid-fight and he screamed so loud it gave away our position."

She laughed harder, and he smiled at the sound, letting the tension from before melt into a light and familiar comfort.

"See?" he said, giving her a nudge with his shoulder. "That's the real reason we need more downtime. No one's started any eel rituals here yet. Standards are slipping."

Nymeris kept laughing, shaking her head as she sat up straight. "I'm sure that Ruthven would find *far* too many good luck charms and reflex enhancers if she got more than a week in Uzlia."

He chuckled and poured them both another glass of cognac. "I'm surprised we didn't come across any eels down in those catacombs."

"I'd rather have dealt with eels than giant slugs."

"Yeah…we came out of there smelling pretty bad."

Nymeris sipped from her drink. "At least we weren't wrapped up and eaten."

Tyrus shivered. "I don't even want to think about it."

She giggled, sipped from her drink again, and then cleared her throat. "I'm supposed to be down in the lounge soon; we're working out what to do about that compound on the coast."

"Yeah," he said with a nod. "What time?"

Nymeris frowned in concern. "Well…I don't think the boss expects you to join the mission—in fact, I think he mentioned your name when he was talking about who needed to stay here and recover."

He shook his head. "I'm not just gonna lie around here and be useless."

Her frown thickened, but she looked a little amused. "Nobody thinks you're useless, Tyrus. The fact that he's concerned enough to tell you to rest just shows how much the boss values you."

He finished his drink and put his glass down. "I'll be fine," he insisted, getting up.

But Nymeris gently grabbed his shoulder and made him stay seated. "You need to stay here," she said softly, this time with more worry in her voice. "The guards at that place have things that could really, *really* hurt you right now. You know that."

"I'll be healed up faster than you know it," he said with a small laugh. "It'll be okay."

She didn't take her hand off his shoulder. "No, it won't," she said firmly. "One wrong move and those wounds could open, and then you'll be out of commission for even longer." She tapped his shoulder as she added, "Besides, it's an order, and I honestly don't think that now is a good time to irritate the boss…if you know what I mean."

He sighed, rubbing a hand down his face. "Yeah…you're right."

Nymeris reached for the cognac bottle again—

Tyrus stood and started towards the door.

"Tyrus," she said, her tone edged with disapproval as she followed after him.

"I'm fine," he muttered, grabbing the handle.

But the moment her hand touched the side of his face, he stopped cold. The gentle weight of her palm, followed by the word 'sleep', told him that he wasn't going anywhere. The fatigue he'd been holding at bay surged through him all at once, like a dam finally cracking, intensifying under Nymeris' ethos.

His legs gave up. She caught him.

"I'm sorry," she whispered, lowering him to the couch. "It's for your own good, Tyrus."

As the world darkened, a mess of emotions tumbled through him. Surprise. Frustration. The urge to fight it off. But just before the pull of sleep dragged him under, one last thought flickered through the haze—

That was hot as hell.

Chapter Forty-Three

— ⸲ † ⸲ —

The Requisite of Rest

| Zalith |
| Atheson, Atheson Coven Sanctum |

While Alucard rested and recovered in the calming silence of his casket, Zalith lay beside him. He didn't refrain from getting lost in his fiancé's intoxicating scent—he didn't need to be careful about becoming distracted anymore. The Silver Claw was dead, the vampires were safe, and so was *his* vampire.

He inhaled quietly, the pheromones urging him to do more than nuzzle and hold; the craving grew heavier with each breath, but as much as he'd like to give in and claim his mate again, he knew that Alucard needed to rest. These past few days had taken a huge toll on him, and the last thing Zalith wanted to do was make it even worse.

So he settled for being as close as he could right now.

With a quiet, content hum, he pressed his face against Alucard's neck, and he couldn't help but slowly drag his tongue along his skin. He felt the vampire move a little, and when Alucard stroked his hand down the demon's arm, Zalith tensed up for a moment. He hoped that single touch would quickly lead to what he longed for, but his fiancé went still again seconds later.

He was disappointed, yes, but he also understood. Alucard needed to rest, not only because of the problem they'd solved hours earlier but because of the problem that remained. That compound was still standing; Detainers were still capturing and holding non-human children, and they needed to be rescued.

As much as Zalith tried focusing on that, though…he couldn't. He just wanted to touch and taste and feel and devour. His mind and body wouldn't allow anything else.

The demon inhaled deeply but quietly, and a hushed, desire-ridden groan escaped him as he breathed out. He trailed his fingertips across Alucard's bare chest, down to his abs, and then along his waist. He'd not venture any lower, though. Not until his vampire had gotten his rest.

Another jolt of anticipation shot through Zalith when Alucard moved again. His fiancé turned his head a little, pressing his cheek against his, and he exhaled softly, stroking the demon's arm.

"Tell me a story," the vampire murmured sleepily. "Maybe…about vone of zhe most dangerous voes you vaced in Eltaria—not…war-velated, zhough. I zon't vant you to be sad."

"Hmm…" he pondered, and then he laughed a little. "I don't know. My mother."

Alucard laughed, too. "No, I mean…like a loup-garou or a troll or someving."

Zalith exhaled slowly, focusing on the way Alucard's hand traced lazy, half-conscious lines over his arm. He shut his eyes for a moment, trying to ease the spiralling heat twisting low inside him. "There…was a job years ago—maybe a century or so, actually," he started, recalling the memory. "I had to deliver an alliance proposal to a desert clan of shapeshifters out near the Ediris Wastes. It was neutral ground, supposedly. Me and a couple of demons phased to the nearest town since my father and I had visited before, and then we had to fly the rest of the journey—or close enough for the clan to not see us and get spooked."

The vampire nodded stiffly, listening.

"Halfway there, a sandstorm forced us down because one of the guys—I think his name was Ichabod or something—he didn't heal as quickly as the rest of us; his species of demon didn't recover well from tiny wounds made by grains of sand. But when we landed, we also couldn't see more than ten feet ahead. There was sand in my ears, eyes, mouth, and I felt like I was trying to breathe inside a furnace. One of the others was convinced that he was going to start vomiting up pure sand at one point."

Alucard hummed softly in amusement, his cheek still pressed against Zalith's.

"We tried to wait it out," Zalith went on. "But the wind lasted for hours. We wandered around a little, trying to retrace our steps." He paused and scoffed a laugh. "And *that* was when we found remains."

"Vemains?"

He nodded. "They were just bones, half-buried and all stripped clean. But there was also a drag trail, like something massive had slithered across the dunes. We didn't hear it or smell it until it struck—a sand-skin wyrm. It was a giant thing; it moved like smoke, hid like a shadow. I didn't even see the coils until I was halfway in its trap. It had paralyzing venom in its bite; if you got so much as nicked, you'd drop in seconds. Lucky for me, it missed. It got a piece of my boot, though; it burned straight through the leather."

His fiancé laughed quietly again.

"I tried flying, but it was a stupid idea. The sand had gotten thicker in the air, and a lot of it was sharp as fuck and cut into my wings, and I hit the ground hard. The wyrm had bitten Abijah, and the others were trying to help him, so the thing came for me again, and it almost had me. The only reason I lived was because I drove one of my glaives into its inner jaw when it lunged. I lodged it in there, and the stupid thing tried to swallow me anyway." He smiled faintly, shifting his hand to rest over Alucard's waist. "After Abijah could walk again, it took another two hours for us to crawl out of the storm with bleeding wings, not to mention the glaive wound in my ribs. But I got one of the wyrm's scales— I still have it. It's sort of black and gold. It's in my vault; I can show you sometime."

"Zhat sounds good," Alucard said. "Do you still 'ave zhose glaives?"

He chuckled. "I think so."

"I vant to see zhose, too."

"Why?" he asked amusedly.

"Because you 'ardly ever use veapons. I'm curious."

The demon smiled. "I'll see if I can find them sometime."

"Okay," Alucard murmured as his fingers stilled against the demon's skin, and his breathing slowed into a rhythm that suggested deeper rest.

But Zalith knew better. The heat was still there, thick in the vampire's blood, just under the surface. He could feel it... and he wasn't sure how much more of this closeness he could take without giving in.

"Are Ichabod and Abijah still avound?" his fiancé asked quietly, his voice a sleepy murmur against his skin.

Zalith took in a slow breath, letting the vampire's scent flood his senses. "No..." he exhaled. "They were my father's subordinates, loyal to the end. They stayed behind when he did." His voice dropped with the weight of it, soft and almost bitter. "He gave us the time we needed to get away."

"I'm sorry, my love," Alucard whispered, stroking his hand down Zalith's arm in a gesture meant to soothe.

The demon gave a small shrug, not quite ready to rise from that ache just yet. Instead, he leaned in, dragging his tongue along the pale curve of Alucard's throat. "You taste really good," he purred, his voice thick with instinct.

Alucard tilted his head back a little, exposing more of his neck with a sly smile. "Do I?"

He groaned eagerly and licked again. "You do."

The vampire ran his fingers down the demon's back. "You can keep tasting me," he teased with a velvety murmur. "Maybe... *every* inch of me."

Zalith's restraint wavered immediately... but he knew better than to let desire override care. Alucard was still healing, and as much as the sight and sound and smell of him stirred every possessive, desperate urge in his chest, he refused to risk slowing his recovery.

That didn't mean either of them had to starve, though.

He dipped lower, letting his breath fan against Alucard's throat before dragging his tongue in a slow line up the column of his neck; the vampire's skin tasted like pure bliss, making him hum contently. When he reached Alucard's ear, he nipped at the lobe, gentle but just sharp enough to make his fiancé twitch, and then he murmured, "Can I suck your dick?"

"Yes." The answer came so fast that it was more a gasp than a word.

Zalith's lips curved in a faint, wicked smile. He slid his hand down, tracing the defined plane of Alucard's stomach before gripping his bulge through his trousers, already hard beneath his palm. He began to stroke him through the fabric, slow, teasing pressure; his other hand braced beside Alucard's head, muscles taut as he leaned in and captured the vampire's mouth, his tongue claiming his in a hungry kiss thick with anticipation.

Their mouths clung to each other for only a few breaths more before Alucard reached up and shoved the casket lid open. Zalith moved with him, grasping his fiancé's arms as he rose and pulling him upright; he backed them towards the nearest wall, lips never straying far from Alucard's, trading kiss after desperate kiss as quiet groans escaped him.

The second Alucard's back touched the wall, Zalith's hands dropped, fumbling with his belt in a flurry of motion. The buckle clinked open, the demon yanked Alucard's trousers low with no ceremony, and then he sank to his knees with reverence and hunger, fingers curling around Alucard's dick like he'd been starving for it—because he *had*. The vampire was already achingly hard, flushed, perfect. Zalith stroked him slowly at first, dragging his thumb over the tip to spread the bead of pre-cum before leaning in and parting his lips around it.

A low, delighted sound left him the moment Alucard's taste hit his tongue, divine and addictive and *his*. He hummed in contentment, the vibration coaxing a pleased breath from above. Alucard's hand threaded into his hair, and when Zalith eased more of his dick into his mouth—inch by inch, greedy but careful—they both groaned in tandem, the shared pleasure sparking something hot and possessive in the demon's chest.

Zalith worked his mouth deeper, his jaw relaxing as he took Alucard further in, tongue dragging along the underside with just enough pressure to make the vampire moan a little louder. The sound only spurred Zalith on, each hum and breathy sigh like praise poured straight into his veins.

He began to move faster, letting his lips stretch wetly around Alucard's shaft as one hand braced against the vampire's thigh and the other stroked what his mouth couldn't reach. The scent of him—sharp and dark and so *deeply Alucard*—made Zalith's head spin. He *needed* to make him cum, to taste it, to take every drop down like it was owed to him.

Zalith moaned around him; he could feel the tension beginning to build in Alucard's body, he could sense the way his breath caught, hips twitching ever so slightly. *Good.* He wanted to feel his mate unravel. He wanted to make him forget everything but this— his mouth, his hands, his *willingness* to give, to serve, to *please*.

Alucard's fingers tightened in his hair, and Zalith felt the subtle shift in his breathing, the way it quickened, the way it grew shallower—the telltale signs of his climax nearing were deliciously familiar. Zalith moaned again, greedily, and hollowed his cheeks as he sucked harder, faster, his hand stroking in rhythm with his mouth. Alucard's hips jerked, barely restrained, and then he let out a stuttering groan as he came—hot and sudden, spilling over Zalith's tongue in thick pulses.

Zalith swallowed instinctively, his throat working around each surge of release, and still Alucard kept cumming, his voice trembling with strained pleasure. The taste flooded the demon's senses, rich and heavy, laced with that delightful potency of heat. He drank it all down like a gift, humming in blissed-out satisfaction, his eyes fluttering shut. Alucard tasted *divine*—he always had… but right now, it was much more intense.

By the time it tapered off, Alucard was trembling faintly against the wall, his chest rising and falling with shallow breaths. Zalith finally drew back, slowly licking him clean, and then he pressed a soft kiss just above the sensitive tip before looking up.

His lips were slick, his voice low and reverent as he murmured, "You're so fucking perfect." He licked his lips. "I could drink from you forever."

Alucard smiled and stroked the side of his face. "Lucky vor you, you *can*."

He smiled, too, and then he kissed his way up his body. As he nuzzled the side of the vampire's face, he possessively whispered, "You're right. You're mine—" he kissed his cheek, "—for all eternity."

The vampire hummed contently. "I am."

"Good," he said firmly, and then he pulled Alucard's trousers up.

Zalith remained close, but his hunger had shifted. It was no longer frantic, just smouldering beneath the surface. He dipped his head, unable to resist the temptation, and ran his tongue slowly along Alucard's neck—once, then again on the other side. The vampire's scent was intoxicating, thick with pheromones and warmth, coaxing another low sound from deep in Zalith's throat. He didn't fight it. He *never* did with Alucard.

But as he pressed his forehead to Alucard's and met his gaze, the haze of lust parted just enough to let concern seep in. Alucard's eyes were heavy-lidded, his pale skin even paler than usual. He looked worn down, fragile in a way only Zalith ever got to see.

"Do you want blood?" he asked softly, his thumb brushing along Alucard's jaw.

The vampire blinked slowly, considering, then gave a small nod. "Vank you," he murmured, voice faintly slurred.

Zalith smiled gently and slid his hand behind Alucard's head, guiding him close. The bite came swiftly—no hesitation, only the press of fangs and the immediate rush of delight as venom spread beneath his skin. The demon groaned, his head tilting back with a quiet sigh of pleasure.

Alucard drank slowly… but after only a few gulps, he began to pull away.

Zalith kept him there with a soft but firm touch. "It's okay, baby. You can take more."

His vampire gave a small hum of appreciation; he started drinking again, still slow, still with a pleased murmur with every gradual swallow.

The demon caressed and fiddled with his crimson hair, waiting patiently, sinking further into the venom-induced high as he fed the man he loved.

No more than a minute later, Alucard stopped. He pulled his fangs from Zalith's neck, licked the wound, and pressed his forehead against the demon's cheek. "Vank you," he said once more.

Zalith kissed his head. "You're welcome." He then guided him over to the couch and relaxed with him. "How are you feeling?"

Alucard exhaled deeply, resting his head on Zalith's shoulder. "A little better," he answered. "I'll be vine in anozzer hour or two, and zhen ve can go to zhe compound."

Hesitation ensnared Zalith, and his protective instincts outweighed the lingering desire to become lost in his mate's scent again. "I think you should stay here and let me handle it, Alucard." The moment those words left his mouth, desperation struck, and so did the possessiveness; he didn't want to be apart from Alucard…but he knew it was for the best. So he ignored everything but the concern and continued, "You've had barely any rest since the loup-garou stuff started; I don't want you to get any worse."

"I'll be okay," he tried to assure him. "Zhe blood vill 'elp."

Zalith gently caressed his head. "I know, but you need more than a few hours to relax. We dealt with Accalia, so you don't have to worry anymore," he said softly. "I can deal with that compound; I managed just fine with the first one."

The vampire sighed quietly. "I know, I just…I veel like some of zhis is my vault. I vas so vocused on zhis coven zhat I zidn't pay attention to any of zhe ozzer non-'umans in zhe city."

He shook his head. "I know it might sound cruel, but they're not your responsibility. Your vampires come first—and you had no idea what was going on, anyway."

"I should 'ave, zhough. I'm alvays very vhorough vhen gazzering invormation on zhe places I plan to settle covens; I zon't know 'ow I missed zhis."

"Baby, don't be so hard on yourself," he murmured, trying to comfort him, absentmindedly fiddling with his hair. "What matters is that you found out *now* while we can still help. We've already liberated one compound; this one won't be any different."

"Zhis vone is guarded by Detainers, Zaliv," he said, a hint of anxiety in his tired voice. "Zhey're more dangerous zhan 'ired soldiers."

Zalith felt him tense up against him.

"If zhey captured you, zhey…I zon't…vant to vink about zhe vings zhey'd do," he murmured sadly. "And I know zhat you can 'andle yourselv—I zon't doubt you or your abilities at all—I'm just…avraid. I've seen vhat zhey do to people like us."

He gently rubbed the vampire's cheek with his thumb. "I'll have backup with me this time, so I won't be alone." He didn't know very much about Detainers at all, but he noted Alucard's warning; he should probably try to find out what he could before it was time to leave. "Can you tell me about them? What to expect."

Alucard exhaled deeply. "Zhey're alvays prepared vor any situation," he said, his voice still heavy with worry. "Zhey've devinitely learned or at least 'eard by now zhat silver isn't evvective against all zemons. Zhey'll 'ave done zheir vesearch. Zhese guys value zhe money over everyving else, so zhey make sure to deliver zheir targets just as zhey vere asked; zhey stun and paralyze you, making impossible vor you to vight back—zhey even use zhese metal nets and cages and traps and shit. And considering zhat zhey 'ave been paying zhe locals to deliver children makes obvious zhat zhey're earning a *vortune* vor zhis job, so zhat compound is going to be *very* 'eavily guarded." He scoffed and added, "Ten coronam per child? Most 'unters zon't even get ten coronam vor a bounty. But vor *vivty* children? Most people zon't see zhat kind of money in zheir whole life, and I veally zon't vink somevone vould pay zhat much just so zhey can torture non-'umans to death. Zhey vant zhem vor someving else, and *zhat* just makes zhis whole ving even more dangerous."

Zalith felt more and more disgusted with each revelation and every unanswered question. Who exactly wanted these children if not a Numen? What were their plans? Was Atheson the only place this faceless employer had sent Detainers to? He scowled at the idea and said, "Then we find whoever's paying these guys and kill them."

"I zon't vink zhat's going to be easy. Vith 'ow much money zhis employer seems to 'ave, I'm sure zhat zhey've taken a lot of precautions. Ve'd need to send people to track zhem down."

"Then that's what we'll do. We save the kids, we destroy the compound, and we get whatever we can out of the Detainers. We'll go from there," he said firmly.

Alucard tightened his embrace around him. "Ve'll 'ave to vigure out who ve can spare vight now."

He kissed the vampire's head. "I'll look into it once we're done here in Atheson."

"Okay."

A small silence fell between them.

"I still want you to stay here while I deal with the compound, though," Zalith said.

"I vant to 'elp you, Zaliv," he insisted quietly.

He guided his hand down to Alucard's back and started gently rubbing it. "I know you do, but staying here to rest where it's safe *will* be helping me—knowing that you're okay and recovering will help me focus better; if you're there with me, I'm going to be too worried about you getting hurt." He traced his fingers along the vampire's shoulders. "And don't get me started on how much of a distraction you being in heat is," he added with an amused chuckle.

Alucard exhaled deeply and slowly. "I know," he mumbled. "I guess I just…zon't vant to look veak in vront of your zemons and my coven. I know zhat some of zhe newer zemons still vink I zon't deserve to be vith you."

"I can just tell them that you're off dealing with something else. It's not really their business what you are and aren't doing."

He shrugged and said, "I vorry most about 'ow zhat makes *you* look, zhough."

Zalith laughed quietly. "Well, if *I* don't care, *you* shouldn't, either."

Alucard nodded slightly. "I know—I try not to, is just 'ard sometimes vhen I see zhem looking at me veird."

"You should do that thing that people do when they have stage fright and imagine them all in their underwear," he suggested, smirking.

The vampire scoffed amusedly. "I'm sure you zon't vant me vinking about anyvone ozzer zhan you in zheir undervear."

"What kind?" he asked, his smirk growing.

"Zhe kind you usually vear."

"Which ones?"

"None," the vampire murmured, amused.

Zalith huffed a laugh. "You're right; those are my favourite."

Alucard tilted his head and asked, "Vhy do you 'ardly vear zhem?"

He gave a lazy shrug. "They're uncomfortable. No one makes them for someone of my size—at least not a pair that are wearable for more than an hour or so before it starts feeling like my dick is in a vice."

The vampire laughed a little.

"*But*," he continued, stroking his fingertips down the vampire's body, "sometimes, wearing undergarments is sexier than just being naked."

"Vell, maybe you should show me an example or two someday," Alucard flirted. "Vor no longer zhan an hour, of course."

"Maybe if you behave yourself," he teased him.

Alucard smiled as he slowly lifted his head from Zalith's chest and nuzzled his neck. "Vhen do I not?"

"You're right. You are pretty well-behaved."

"I am," he murmured.

Zalith smirked again. "So you're going to be good and stay here and sleep while I go and deal with those Detainers?"

Alucard huffed, but he still sounded amused. "Vine," he mumbled.

"Good boy," he said and kissed his head.

They lay there for a little while longer. Zalith pulled Alucard closer so that he could nuzzle his head, breathing in his scent, but he tried to keep himself from sinking too far.

Though it was quickly devouring him, and he knew that if he didn't pull away soon, he'd lose his focus, unable to think about anything but his desires.

So he inhaled one last time, kissed the vampire's head, and then carefully sat up straight. "Come on," he said, rubbing Alucard's arm. "Let's get you to bed."

Alucard groaned but sat up, too.

"Couch or casket?" he asked amusedly.

"Casket," he mumbled. "I'll vecover vaster."

Zalith kissed his lips and took hold of his hand. "Do you want a blanket?" he asked as he stood up and led his fiancé towards his casket.

He shook his head. "I'll be okay."

The demon stopped by the casket and turned to face Alucard, smiling at him. "In you get," he said but placed his hands on the vampire's waist and pulled him closer.

Alucard glanced at the casket; he looked hesitant for a moment, but he nodded and went to get in.

Zalith, however, urged his fiancé's body against his, smirked at him, and kissed his lips. "Make sure you stay in bed until I'm back," he murmured and softly stroked his thumb across the vampire's bottom lip.

He smiled and turned his head ever so slightly, clearly trying to hide his fluster. "I vill," he said quietly.

Despite promising himself that it would be just one last kiss, Zalith lingered, his mouth brushing tenderly against Alucard's before the moment stretched and deepened. He eased his tongue past the vampire's lips, slow and reverent, and Alucard met each gentle stroke with his own, matching the affection.

The moment he felt the arousal intensifying, though, Zalith gently pulled away. "I'll be back as soon as I can, okay?"

Alucard's worried frown returned, but he nodded and mumbled, "Okay." And then he grasped Zalith's hand. "Please be carevul."

He allowed himself to kiss his fiancé just once more. "I will. I love you."

The vampire smiled softly and said, "I love you, too."

Alucard climbed into the casket, and when he sat down, Zalith leaned closer and kissed his head. Once the vampire lay back, the demon smiled down at him, and despite the growing urge to climb in with him, he helped Alucard close the lid.

And then he exhaled deeply, grabbing his shirt from the dresser and pulling it on. The urges and instincts intensified by the second, but he grasped onto what he knew he had to do. Those children needed saving, and whoever was paying the Detainers to capture them was going to die.

Chapter Forty-Four

— ⸱ † ⸱ —

Mirewharf

| Zalith |

| *Atheson, Sablemoore, The Bleeding Shore* |

The scent of brine and rot clung thick in the air as Zalith crouched near the cliff's edge, the wind dragging salt through his hair and stinging his eyes. Below, the Bleeding Shore stretched out like a festering wound, crude structures half-swallowed by black, bubbling mud, the skeletal remains of the Mirewharf dock jutting from the bank like broken ribs.

At the centre stood the compound: makeshift, ugly, but fortified like a warfront. Barbed fences encircled it in layered rings, and glints of metal traps glistened faintly in the murk below; wires, mines, alchemical snares, and things that crackled softly with latent energy. Beyond it, a transport vessel loomed at the dock, iron-scaled and still, its hull stained red along the waterline. Even from this distance, Zalith could feel the power coiled inside it—cages, sigils, weapons, and containment wards.

He could sense the children inside the tents that spread across the mud—tents that were thrown over silver cages; the fabric was likely enchanted, perhaps emitting whatever the kids were drugged with. The metals and wards made it hard for him to determine just how many children there were, though. What he *could* tell was that none of the kids were fully conscious, just small, flickering pulses of life, their ethos suppressed, their minds barely tethered.

His claws bit into the soil.

The demons he'd brought with him examined Virelle's map in silence, taking note of every trap, ward, and mine that she'd located. Around them, the air was tainted with flickers of anxiety; they'd all seen similar places in Eltaria; some had even experienced what it was like to be trapped inside, and Zalith didn't fault them for their worry. He knew that they'd compose themselves when it was time to attack.

Zalith's eyes burned as he scanned the perimeter. Just as his fiancé had warned him, this wasn't like the last facility; there were no slouching soldiers or careless gaps. Detainers, trained to subdue and kill anything non-human, no hesitation, no fear. He observed the weapons slung across their backs: charged spears, null-rifles, vials strapped to belts with seals that would eat through ethos like acid. Blades made of silver, rhodium, platinum, gold, and even iron. They were prepared for *everything*.

His stomach twisted as the memories of places like these flooded into his mind. The same coldness, the same smell of punishment and machinery pretending to be order. And the fact that this compound was filled with children made it worse. The atrocity of human cruelty knew no bounds.

He exhaled slowly through his nose, fighting the instinct to leap down and tear the entire place apart and let his rage take hold of him.

And yet…even as he catalogued each threat and marked every route in and out, his thoughts flicked to Alucard. He hated being away from him. His fiancé had looked too pale and drained before he left; there was a hollowness in his eyes that hadn't been there before. He'd said he'd be fine, but…Zalith wasn't sure whether he fully believed him. He knew Alucard too well; he always tried to hide his pain and fatigue.

Zalith only hoped that by the time this was over, Alucard would have recovered a little, that the colour had returned to his face, and the exhaustion in his eyes had lifted. He'd given his vampire blood, and he'd managed to convince him to rest while he took care of this compound. Would that be enough, though? If it wasn't, then he'd do whatever else was necessary to ensure that Alucard recuperated *entirely*.

But another anxious thought crept in. What if, when he got back, he found Alucard in a worse state? Or what if something happened while he wasn't there to help him?

He swallowed hard and tried to refocus, forcing the fear back down where it belonged. Alucard would be okay. Nothing would happen. The Sanctum was protected. But those children? Their lives needed saving *here*.

After one last look at the area surrounding the compound, he turned to the demons behind him. "We do this quietly. Move in pairs. Allie, you and Eren are responsible for capturing one of the Detainers; grab one and retreat to this location."

They both nodded and said, "Yes, sir."

"Everyone else, kill the Detainers and only extract the children once you've cleared a path. No risks, no exceptions." However, he turned his head and said, "Nymeris, I want you to focus on getting the children out, though. If you see an opening that isn't going to risk you or any children, take it."

Each demon nodded.

And Nymeris said, "Understood, boss."

"Let's move," Zalith commanded.

The demons slipped over the cliff's edge in silence.

Zalith led the descent, boots barely brushing the rock face as he followed a jagged, sloping ledge obscured by overgrown ferns and sea-wet moss. The cliff wall was slick with salt spray, but none of them faltered. Behind him, the others moved in pairs as ordered, their expressions determined and fearless.

The mist drifted around them, thick enough to shroud their silhouettes. Far below, the dull thrum of ethos wards pulsed along the compound's perimeter, barely visible but detectable in the way the air trembled faintly against his skin.

Zalith paused halfway down, crouched in the rock's natural dip, and gestured with two fingers towards a lower outcrop. Two demons broke off and glided into position, following the outer perimeter where coils of barbed ward-wire ringed the makeshift compound. A second team split towards the northern flank, where a rusted storage shack was hunched in the mud.

No sound but breath and the distant caw of a carrion bird.

Zalith turned his eyes to the docked transport vessel. The glow of containment runes flickered along its hull, active and likely rigged with proximity wards. Judging by the sheer intensity of those wards, he'd bet that the Detainers would be taking the children through unsafe waters, channels that no one dared to sail. How else would they avoid pirates and law enforcement?

He continued downward, boots touching soft, sucking mud as he reached the shoreline. The scent here was worse—sea rot layered with old blood and scorched alchemicals. He scanned the compound's outermost guards: two Detainers patrolling the east gate, their armour painted matte black but made of patchwork metal, likely each type poisonous to non-humans; the weapons strapped to their backs hummed faintly with charge, clearly equipped to deal with anything.

Zalith's jaw tensed. Their formation was tight, but he'd dealt with places like this before, and so had his demons. Those at his side right now were Tyrus', his best fighters; they knew better than most what the compounds were like.

He crouched low, his hand sweeping the soil. All pairs were nearly in place.

For a moment, his eyes shifted from the pair he'd been watching. He could see inside one of the tents; there were at least five kids stuffed into the tiny space, all immobile, lying on the muddy ground, their breathing struggled and their small bodies twitching and convulsing. Some were bloody, others were pale, and most were so malnourished that they'd be mistaken for corpses.

He scowled, clenching his fists—but he needed to focus. The Detainers *were* going to die, he just needed to be tactical about it. His anger could wait.

With a quiet huff, his eyes darted from each demon pair. They were all ready.

Zalith moved first.

While the others held their positions, he slinked to the west side of the compound, where a collapsed section of fencing lay half-submerged in mud. It looked like someone had patched it recently, but not well; the wards were faint, and the binding sigils were uneven. Either the job had been rushed, or they assumed that no one would be insane enough to come in from the swamp side—or at all.

Their mistake.

He slid through the breach without a sound. His boots sank an inch into the wet earth, but he didn't slow. The shadows clung to him as he crept along the side of a storage unit, ducking beneath a row of hanging chains that jingled faintly in the wind. A single Detainer stood nearby, facing away, rifle slung casually over one shoulder as he scanned the perimeter.

Zalith was behind him in two heartbeats.

One hand snapped over the man's mouth, and he drove the other through the gap in his armour right beneath the ribs. Ignoring the sting of blended metal, the demon twisted *hard* until the body went limp. No sound escaped. Zalith dragged the corpse behind the storage unit and slipped deeper inside.

The compound's interior layout was little more than tarpaulin tunnels stretched between prefab sheds and temporary barracks. Crystal-lit floodlamps lined the narrow passages, bathing everything in a harsh, sterile blue. The scent of blood was stronger, not fresh but recent enough.

Zalith passed the first tent-covered cage. The bars were patchwork metal, just like the Detainers' armour, and the space inside was narrow, barely big enough for the children to move. And that unnerving reek of chlorine, stagnant holy water, rusted nails, and charred bone clashed with the smell of hemlock and poppy resin.

He was right. The tents were soaked in Infirmuseos—*Surripio*—and a disorienting concoction that made it impossible for the children to do more than lie there, slipping in and out of consciousness. They likely had no idea where they were or how long they'd been here.

The demon crouched to look through the bars. One child—an elven girl by the look of her ears and faintly glowing half-lidded eyes—was breathing, but slow. The rugged boy beside her looked worse, covered in claw marks of his own doing, a result of an anxious, stressed werewolf pup—he'd seen it enough to recognize it. A demon child was shivering, clearly starved and succumbing to it, and the fourth, a girl covered in snake scales, was trying to speak, her jaw moving but no discernible words leaving it.

A snarl almost left Zalith, but he held it back and stood up. He couldn't start freeing them yet, not until the path was clear.

Something crackled faintly—a voice from a communication rune embedded in the wall nearby. Detainer chatter, crisp and controlled, coordinating rotations, using sickening terms and jokes to refer to each child.

Zalith flattened against the wall, eyes sharp, already recalculating routes. Another set of guards passed just ahead, walking in formation with silver-inlaid staves.

He let them go.

His eyes shifted from the locations of his demons.

Finnik signed: Eastern ward disabled. Ready on your signal.

Zalith exhaled once through his nose and set his sights on his first target—

A sudden flash flickered at the compound's northern perimeter—a crystalline ping rang out, a deep, unnatural crack followed, and the ground split with a pulse of blinding light.

Zalith froze mid-step as the explosion tore through the northern access path, flinging debris and a plume of acidic smoke into the air. A shockwave rippled through the mud and fencing, making him stumble, and for a second, the whole compound went still.

But then came the sound he'd dreaded.

Alarms.

Sirens howled from mounted pylons. A web of red ward light lit up overhead, flashing through the fog like bleeding veins. Floodlamps surged to life, cutting across the camp in stark beams. The entire place stirred like a wasp's nest, Detainers pouring from barracks, shouting orders in clipped voices.

Zalith's heart surged, but his body remained still, his eyes flaring with fury...and guilt. He didn't know who had set off that explosion, and through the chaos of running Detainers and swirling, light-ridden mist, he couldn't see his demons. Wherever they were, though, he couldn't leave them confused. So he focused, sending them all a telepathic order to continue; he couldn't use exact words, but they'd know what to do.

And moments later, through the haze and disorder, he saw the shadows of a duo, and then another. He watched as his demons broke formation, emerging from every corner of the perimeter; spells flared, metal and claws clashed. One Detainer barely managed to turn before Sara blurred through the smoke; she vanished mid-lunge and reappeared behind him in the same breath, and her claws slid through the back of his ribcage like silk. She tore out his heart without a word, and the man collapsed, eyes already glazed, confusion etched across his face like he'd forgotten where he was.

Behind her, Finnik stepped through a veil of unravelling shadow, his velmorae demon aura shifting in pale ribbons around his limbs. He raised one hand, and the Detainer charging at him staggered, suddenly gasping, disoriented and overwhelmed. Finnik's glamour bent the light, making him seem ten feet tall and wreathed in silver flame; the man fired his rifle wildly, his shots glancing off illusions before Finnik cut his throat with an elegant flick of a curved blade.

A sharp crack rang out from the east barracks—Chrisan had arrived. The thornvek demon smashed through a barricade of crates, bark-armoured and bristling with thorns that pulsed with venom. He let out a guttural growl and slammed both fists into the ground, and in an instant, a web of thorned roots erupted beneath a squad of Detainers, skewering one through the leg, another through the spine. They screamed and thrashed, but the brambles only twisted deeper, blooming wickedly as they drank in spilled blood.

"Path clear!" Chrisan shouted over the din, his barkskin already knitting over a gunshot wound in his side.

To the west, Reenah crouched low near the containment sheds, her fingers painting glyphs in the dirt faster than most could blink. Glowing runes snaked outward from her hands—anti-ethos brands laced with lunar threads. A Detainer raised a null-blade and rushed her, but she looked up just once, eyes glimmering. "Collapse," she whispered.

The ground under the Detainer's feet glowed and then detonated in a burst of compressed force. He hit the wall behind him and didn't get back up. Reenah didn't wait. Her next rune had already begun to spread, crawling beneath the nearest cage to destabilize the locks.

Zalith moved like a blade loosed from a sheath. He darted through the now-blazing passages, cutting down two more Detainers in a blur of bloody claws and barely restrained rage. The cages ahead of him shook from the growing chaos, the children inside stirring, dazed and terrified.

He ducked behind a storage unit as a cluster of Detainers passed, moving to reinforce the docks. His eyes flicked towards the transport ship; guards were dragging limp bodies up the gangplank. They were already trying to flee with the children.

That wasn't going to happen.

Zalith pushed off the wall and sprang forward. "Cut them off!" he yelled, pointing at the dock.

At once, four demons broke from cover, two leaping down from the rooftops, two emerging from the mist.

A Detainer managed to fire off a single shot—the silver bullet scraped Danrel's arm—before Sara materialized in front of him and opened his throat without slowing, and his body tumbled over the edge of the dock with a splash.

West broke through the chaos immediately, seeing to Danrel.

Zalith darted towards a crooked holding shed, ramming the heel of his boot into the door. It splintered, and he burst inside. More cages, more children; some blinked up at him, hardly aware, their silver chains pulling taut as they flinched. He scowled and slashed through the locks, and then he tossed white flames at the sigil in the corner of the room, burning away its numbing effect.

The oppressive ethos fog dropped instantly. A few of the children whimpered and pressed themselves into corners, but one—a pale-horned boy with blood crusted under one eye—stared at Zalith like he'd just seen the sun for the first time.

"Stay here," Zalith said firmly. "Don't move until a woman comes for you—her name is Nymeris; she has white hair and orange eyes. Understood?"

Some of the trembling children nodded and grasped each other's hands.

The sound of gunfire cracked just beyond the wall.

Zalith looked over his shoulder. He needed to get back out there. "Stay here," he said once again, and then he hurried back outside.

"Boss!" came Nicki's voice.

He stopped just outside the door, and Nicki skidded to a halt beside him.

"They're bottlenecking near the docks," she huffed, panting. "Finnik and Reenah are pinching from the left."

With a nod, Zalith rushed for the docks.

Chrisan emerged from the smoke, covered in blood. He ran beside Zalith as he told him, "I've got roots laced under the gangplank. Give me the word, I'll rip it in half."

"Not yet," Zalith replied. "Let them try. We make it hurt."

He grunted in response, and then he disappeared with Nicki, rejoining the fight.

Zalith emerged from the thickening smoke.

The docks had become a killing field.

Finnik's illusions shimmered across the surface of the pier, flickering forms that drew fire in all directions. Detainers shouted over each other, trying to regroup, but it was useless; half of them were firing at ghosts, while Reenah slipped in through their blind spots, carving suppression runes into the boards beneath their feet—one Detainer stepped onto a marked spot and vanished in a shriek of imploding light, and the man beside him quickly followed, devoured by the ash that his comrade turned into.

Chrisan then surged from beneath the dock, rising with a roar as bramble-thorns shot upward like spears, skewering the last two soldiers near the gangplank. He turned, body steaming from a rune blast, and shouted, "Now?!"

Zalith halted just behind the last row of holding crates, grabbing the crossbow-wielding woman who was just about to fire at Reenah. He tore her throat out, and then he sharply turned his head, setting his sights on the ship.

Three Detainers remained, dragging a pair of unconscious children to the vessel. One turned and raised a flame rifle—

Zalith vanished from the spot and reappeared mid-air, dropped from a rooftop, and landed on the Detainer's back, the man's bones crunching under the impact. The demon tore the rifle free, drove it into the man's chest, and pulled the trigger.

"Chrisan," he then called, eyes locked on the ship. "Now!"

With a guttural bellow, the thornvek demon slammed his fists to the dock. The roots writhed and snapped, and then they surged—the gangplank cracked in half, swallowed whole by thick, barbed vines that wrapped around the support beams and dragged them screaming into the mire. The last two Detainers barely had time to shout before the dock beneath them gave way completely.

The children tumbled from their arms into the waiting hands of Nicki and Finnik.

But just as the two demons grabbed the children, the deck beneath them began to hum, snatching Zalith's attention. A low, unnatural sound pulsed from deep within the hull of the transport vessel—too steady to be mechanical, too rhythmic to be ignored. And for one breath, everything around it stilled: the children's whimpers, the roar of the fire, even the wind off the Bleeding Shore.

That was when Zalith felt it.

Ethos. Foul, dense, and laced with corruption.

"Off the dock—now!" West bellowed.

"The ship's rigged!" Sara's voice followed.

And then came West's again, "Back away!"

Zalith grabbed the child nearest to him as he adorned his demon form; Reenah wrapped her arms around another stumbling near the gangplank, and Chrisan yanked Nicki back by the collar just as the air warped, distorting with a deep, deafening boom.

The explosion hit a heartbeat later.

The ship detonated, folding inward in a violent implosion of pressure and heat before flinging itself apart in a halo of white fire. The blast swallowed the dock in seconds, shattering wood and steel into molten debris that rained down in glowing arcs. Flame washed over the compound's edge, kicking up mud, salt, blood, and smoke in one choking wave.

Zalith was thrown back by the shockwave—he only just had time to wrap his wings around himself and the child in his grip before he hit the ground, skidding through muck and shattered glass before slamming into the side of a holding shed. His ears rang, and his vision narrowed, but he forced himself up. He had to.

"Are you okay?" he asked the boy whose arms were wrapped around his leg, trembling and crying.

The kid stiffly looked up at him and nodded.

"Go," he said as he weakly ushered the child in the direction of the other kids, who were being rushed to a hole in the fence by Sara and Nymeris.

Zalith staggered through the haze, wiping blood from his forehead, hissing irritably as the cuts all over his body stung. He reached out, searching for his demons' auras, and he found them all grouped behind some shattered crates.

He lurched forward a little, gripping one of the crates to keep himself standing. The ache and weakness were familiar; he knew he'd been hit by rhodium. But he didn't care. "Status," he said with a huff, his eyes shifting from demon to demon.

Finnik was sprawled on the ground. "A little scorched but still pretty," he said with a pain-ridden grin while West saw to the silver burns spread across his chest. The three kids he'd saved from the chaos stayed close, clinging to him like kittens to a mother cat.

Reenah raised her hand, sat leaning against a crooked post. "G-good, boss," she said, holding up a bloody thumb, and she nodded at the ash-covered elf girl beside her. "I got her out."

"Dock's gone, boss," Chrisan said, perched on a half-sunken barrel. "Those fuckers offed themselves."

"Sara's getting the kids out with Nymeris," Nicki said, wrapping a piece of torn fabric around a burn on her arm.

"Danrel?" Zalith questioned—the guy wasn't there.

West glanced up at Zalith, shook his head, and returned to his healing duties.

"He couldn't get away in time," Chrisan told him. "The silver."

Zalith snarled angrily.

"I can see to those burns in a sec," West said.

"I'm fine," Zalith muttered, glancing around. The fires were still burning, and ash fell like snow. His eyes found the crater where the dock had been—only scorched mud and charred splinters remained. There was no trace of the Detainers or who sent them; the explosion had done exactly what it was meant to: erase everything. Whoever was behind this had no intention of letting the truth survive.

But the children *had*.

"Did we lose any of the kids?" he asked.

"No," Nicki said, shaking her head. "Some of them are a little banged up, but it's nothing we can't fix."

Zalith looked around again, searching for Allie and Eren. The thick smoke was clearing, shoved away by the biting wind; his vision remained hazed—he knew it wouldn't clear until his body started recovering from the rhodium damage—but after a few minutes, he spotted Allie, and she was dragging an unconscious Detainer through the mud.

With a furious snarl, Zalith stormed across the battlefield as fast as his injuries would allow. When he reached Allie, he snatched the collar of the man in her grip.

"H-he's out, boss," she said, letting go of the Detainer.

Zalith huffed and dropped the man into the mud. He glanced over at the children…and then he noticed—"Where's Eren?"

Allie exhaled sharply, looking away as tears washed away thin trails of dirt and ash from her face. "He—" she stammered and shook her head. "A mine—he didn't see it."

He sighed deeply, the guilt returning. *Eren* had set off that explosion. But Zalith wouldn't stand there and try to figure out why now. The compound was destroyed, the kids were safe, and the Detainers were dead. However, for all he knew, more could be on the way, and he didn't want to be here if and when they arrived—not with the vulnerable kids, and not with his injured demons.

"All right, get the kids to the Sanctum." He paused, exhaling. "Is there anything left of Eren to take to his friends and family?"

She wiped a tear away. "No, sir—I'm sorry."

After another, disappointed sigh, he nodded and said, "Take this piece of shit back, too," as he kicked the unconscious Detainer. "Take him down into the Withercrypt and tear the armour off, take his skin with it if need be." He'd interrogate him once he was back at the Sanctum and sure that Alucard was okay.

"Yes, sir," Allie said and started dragging the man in Sara's direction, where Nymeris and the terrified children were.

Zalith headed back to the others, who were still being healed by West. Once they were stable enough to travel, he'd get them back to the safety of the estate, too. *A lot* of people had been hurt these past few days, and too many had died. It made him dread what was to come—loup-garou and specialist hunters weren't anywhere near as dangerous as a Numen, and he worried how many people he was going to lose when it was time to face Lilith.

He didn't want to let the worry consume him, though. After all, his people had never faced a loup-garou before, or Detainers—or a loup-garou with the ancient lineage of the Silver Claw. What they *were* familiar with were demons, and it would be demons that they'd be fighting. They'd also be going through extensive training beforehand.

As much as he might try to focus on the plan, though, he couldn't ignore the sharp sting of each recent loss, and *all* of those who came before. The best thing he could do now was take everything he'd learned and ensure that it was used to better prepare his army for what was coming.

And Eren, Danrel, Thalric, and Roderic would be remembered.

Chapter Forty-Five

— ⸺ ✝ ⸻ —

After the Battle

| Alucard |
| *Atheson, Atheson Coven Sanctum* |

Quiet tapping woke Alucard. He frowned as he opened his eyes, taking in the familiar, calming darkness around him. The first thing he noticed was the fatigue—it was *gone*. He finally felt as if he'd gotten some proper rest; his limbs didn't feel like lead, his head wasn't aching, and he could relax.

But frustration quickly engulfed him—restlessness, desperation. Still, he'd rather feel *this* way than be weighed down by exhaustion.

"*Alucard?*" came Zalith's voice.

That must be where the tapping came from. It was Zalith, and the moment he acknowledged that fact, the frustration and desire transformed into *hunger*, the longing to sate what he needed.

He reached up and slowly lifted the casket lid, and he was greeted by his mate's relieved smile.

"Hey," the demon said as he took Alucard's hand and helped him out of the casket. "How are you feeling?"

"Better," he answered, pulling Zalith closer. He pressed his body against his and nuzzled his neck, but among the enthralling scent of bergamot, sandalwood, and white sage was the faint smell of blood—*Zalith's* blood.

As concern clashed with desire, Alucard leaned back so that he could get a better look at his mate. His clothes were torn, dirtied with dried mud and blood, and through the rips and tears, he could see healing wounds.

"Vhat 'appened?" he asked worriedly.

"I'm okay, don't worry," the demon assured him, pulling him into his embrace. "We got all of the children out, and we managed to grab one of the Detainers." He paused, nuzzling Alucard's neck. "He's in the Withercrypt. The cell key is on the table."

"You killed all zhe ozzers?"

"Kind of."

"Kind of?"

"Well, the ones we didn't kill took care of the rest themselves—either that, or their employer did. Their own ship exploded, likely to erase any trace of the operation. But we'll get what we can out of the one we managed to grab."

Alucard nodded, his eyes fluttering shut as he let himself melt into Zalith's arms. The moment he did, that slow, familiar ache crept back in—yearning, desire, the pull of his mate's body against his. He gave in easily.

He tilted his head back, exposing his throat in a silent offering as the demon's lips brushed against his skin. Zalith kissed a path along the curve of his neck, soft and lingering, and when his tongue finally dragged over the line of Alucard's pulse, a quiet hum escaped him. Anticipation coiled through his chest like a slow-blooming fire.

"I missed you," Zalith murmured, his voice dark and warm, just before licking him again, slower this time.

The vampire smiled and tilted his head further to the side, giving Zalith more to touch, more to take. "I missed you, too." His fingers trailed up the demon's spine, but ash and dried mud scratched at his skin—reminders of the battlefield, the filth of blood and smoke not yet washed away. He grimaced lightly and curled his hand into the front of Zalith's shirt instead, fisting the fabric. "You should shower, my love," he murmured, brushing their noses together. "I'll get you some clean clothes."

Zalith let out a soft exhale, more of a growl than a breath. "No," he mumbled, mouth already finding its way back to Alucard's throat like he couldn't bear even the thought of letting go.

Alucard huffed a quiet laugh but let himself be guided without resistance. Zalith backed him slowly towards the wall, his hands never leaving Alucard's waist, and when the vampire's back met the cool stone, Zalith caught his mouth in a deep kiss laced with heat and something far more desperate than simple longing.

The kiss deepened, gradually at first but intensifying with hunger. Zalith's mouth moved with the kind of restrained fervour that made Alucard shudder, like he'd been holding back all night and had finally decided to indulge. Their lips parted only to reconnect harder, wetter, tongues sliding together in a way that left no space for breath or thought.

Alucard gripped his mate's shirt tighter, grounding himself in the heat of him. He should have resisted; he should have told Zalith to rest, to clean the blood and grime from his body; instead, he moaned softly into the kiss, his thighs instinctively tensing as the ache inside him flared hot again. He was in heat, and every inch of Zalith pressed against him made it worse in the best possible way.

The demon's hand slid up his side, his fingers splayed possessively wide, before drifting lower.

And lower.

And lower…until his palm pressed against the front of Alucard's trousers. The vampire groaned into his mouth, hips twitching faintly as Zalith's fingers began to move, slow strokes over his already-growing bulge. Even through the fabric, the pressure made his knees weaken.

"You're already hard," Zalith murmured between kisses, his lips stroking Alucard's cheek. "How long were you waiting?"

Alucard's head tipped back against the wall as he closed his eyes. "I—" He tried to answer, but the words dissolved into a shaky moan as Zalith's touch grew more insistent, his fingers rubbing and gently squeezing his shaft, making his back arch.

It had only been a few hours, and already he was craving this, craving *him*. But it wasn't just the heat coursing through him, though that made his skin feel fevered and thin; it was the pull in his chest, the ache in his ribs that only eased when Zalith was close. He needed to feel him. He needed to be wanted and touched…devoured and *claimed*.

"I missed you," Alucard whispered again, almost breathless now. "Even…if is stupid…I did."

Zalith answered not with words but with another kiss, rougher than before, his hand never stopping its slow rhythm between the vampire's legs.

And Alucard let himself be enthralled by it. His body yielded completely, his mind quieting beneath the tide of touch and scent and the low, possessive growl of the one he belonged to.

The demon's hand slowed, and then it stilled entirely, his palm resting heavy against Alucard's arousal. He leaned in, breath hot against the vampire's ear, and nuzzled once before speaking, his voice low, almost cruel in its calm—"You want more, don't you?" He paused, smirking against Alucard's ear. "I can feel how badly your body wants it."

Alucard swallowed, his hands fisting tighter in Zalith's shirt. He nodded faintly, already trembling beneath the surface.

Zalith grinned before he kissed just beneath the vampire's ear, and then he let his voice dip deeper and darker as he murmured, "Do you want me inside you?"

A desperate wince left Alucard's lips. He could hardly think. The feeling of Zalith pressed against him, the scent of blood and ash and heat, the desperation in his body—it was overwhelming. "Yes," he whispered, almost shamefully fast. "I vant…you."

The demon's grip on his waist tightened. "How badly?"

Alucard tipped his head forward against Zalith's shoulder. "So bad…zhat everyving 'urts."

Zalith let out a quiet, pleased growl and kissed him again, this time biting softly at his lower lip. "That's what I wanted to hear," he purred and pressed his face against the vampire's neck once more. "You're always…so fucking good when you beg for it," he groaned, grinding his crotch against Alucard's thigh.

The vampire whimpered, and Zalith pulled him away from the wall just long enough to turn him, pressing his chest flat against the stone. His mate leaned in behind him, now grinding against his ass, letting Alucard feel the hard press of his dick through his ash-covered trousers.

"Keep your hands on the wall," the demon ordered, his tone dangerous and possessive, the kind of demanding that made Alucard tremble.

Alucard obeyed without hesitation, palms flat, his body already arching back to meet him, desperate and willing to take him, ready to serve, ready to submit. He didn't care that he was now covered in ash, too, or that the room still smelled faintly of fire and iron. All that mattered was Zalith—his touch, his weight behind him, pressing closer.

Zalith's hands didn't waste time. One slid down Alucard's hip while the other reached for his belt, unbuckling it. The sound of the leather slipping loose and the soft clink of the buckle echoed in the still room like a promise, intensifying the anticipation. Alucard didn't move; he breathed harder, his body trembling, his heart racing.

The demon tugged his trousers down just enough to bare his hips, ass, and thighs, all flushed with heat and already slick with a faint sheen of pheromones. Alucard winced softly at the exposure, the cool air of the room dragging a shiver from him, but it was nothing compared to the burn of desperation threading through him.

He felt Zalith's hand on him again, now skin to skin, stroking once, slow and heavy, as if to remind him who he belonged to. The demon then stepped back, and a moment later, Alucard heard the soft click of a vial uncapping, and then the warm, wet sound of oil being poured over fingers. He hummed at the familiar, faintly herbal scent, and again when Zalith's free hand gripped his hip. The first slick touch pressed between his cheeks, and he moaned as a finger pushed inside, sending a wave of relief crashing through the thirst that had been building for hours.

Alucard then whimpered pleasurably, his back arching just a little more as a second finger joined the first, curling expertly. He tried to bite back another sound, but it escaped anyway—a soft, broken moan against the wall.

"I can feel how badly your body wants this," Zalith growled, leaning in to mouth at his shoulder. "You're soaking my fingers, baby."

The vampire whimpered again, his voice ragged as he pleaded, "Fuck me…please."

Zalith hummed a satisfied sound as he withdrew his fingers slowly, leaving Alucard empty long enough to make him whine desperately. The demon then reached down; Alucard felt him stroke himself once before pressing the thick head of his dick against his hole. Alucard's entire body tensed, and then it melted with a shudder as Zalith began to push in—slow at first, stretching him open inch by inch.

Alucard moaned, high and breathless as the pressure built and Zalith kept going. The stretch was deep, overwhelming, but it was everything he'd been craving, everything he'd been burning for.

The demon's hips pressed forward again, slow and steady, the head of his dick sliding deeper—until Alucard felt something different…a new pressure, firmer and tighter. It wasn't pain exactly, but it made him wince, his body clenching instinctively around the intrusion.

He tensed up, confused by the sudden resistance, by the almost locked sensation that halted the demon's advance. "Z-Zaliv—?" he moaned.

Zalith groaned low in his throat, his fingers flexing against Alucard's hips as he held him still. "Shh…you're okay," he murmured, his voice rough but reassuring. He leaned in slightly, his breath brushing over Alucard's skin. "It's your second hole. It always grips me like that the first time…just let it open for me."

Alucard closed his eyes, heat rushing through his body at the words. He hadn't even known that part of him existed, but somehow, the explanation made sense. His instincts responded before his thoughts did, and with a trembling exhale, he relaxed.

With a groan of approval, Zalith pushed deeper, the stretch stealing the vampire's breath. Inch by inch, he filled him until their bodies pressed flush, the demon fully sheathed inside. The sensation was overwhelming—tight and deep, so complete that it bordered on maddening.

"Vhy…'aven't I velt zhat bevore?" he breathed.

Zalith hummed pleasurably and whispered into his ear, "Because I relax your body for you. But I wanted you to feel it this time." He pressed a slow kiss just beneath Alucard's ear. "That second hole—it's the deepest part of you, the place that only *I* get to touch. It's where you hold me the tightest." His hand smoothed up Alucard's back as he rocked into him gently, teasingly, and then, without warning, he pulled back and thrusted in hard.

Alucard moaned, loud and helpless as pleasure shot through him like lightning. The pressure and the rhythm blurred together into something heady and consuming, the world narrowing to the stretch of his mate inside him and the low, primal sounds Zalith made as he claimed him.

Zalith's next thrust was harder, *sharper*, and it knocked a breathless sound from Alucard's throat. He didn't have time to brace before the next came, then another, each one deep and punishing, grinding into the perfect spot that made Alucard cry out. He whined, head falling forward, forehead pressed to the wall as the demon fucked into him with growing force. Zalith's hands were bruising on his hips, dragging him back with every thrust, forcing him to take it, to feel every inch. The slap of their bodies echoed quietly in the enclosed room, accompanied only by Alucard's ragged breaths and the hushed rhythm of Zalith's growls behind him.

His body took it greedily. The heat roared through him, turning every nerve hypersensitive. Pheromones slicked the insides of his thighs, thick and heady, only making it worse. The harder Zalith went, the more he wanted it, the more he *needed* it. His body arched into every movement, hips rocking back to meet each thrust as if it were instinct.

"*Zaliv*—" he moaned, the name torn from his lips like a plea. His voice was hoarse, trembling, but he didn't care. His mate's dick filled him over and over, stretching him wide and setting his nerves alight.

Zalith snarled something under his breath—wordless, wild—and fucked him harder, faster. The collision of skin against skin turned wetter, loud and relentless. Alucard's legs threatened to give out more than once, but Zalith held him steady, one hand moving up to grip his shoulder, pulling him back into every brutal thrust like he was trying to claim the heat right out of him.

Another desperate cry slipped from Alucard's mouth, and this time, he couldn't stop shaking. Pressure was building fast inside him, everything tightening, his dick untouched but painfully hard, smearing the stone wall with every sharp rut forward. He couldn't think, he couldn't breathe. All he could do was feel Zalith's aggressive thrusts and take each one eagerly, *willingly*.

The vampire shifted his foot wider, spreading his legs further to give Zalith deeper access, and the demon rewarded him with a loud, desperate whine, hips snapping forward like he'd just been invited to lose control.

His mate's rhythm turned feral after that. Every plunge slammed brutally, dragging broken sounds from Alucard's throat as his body submitted entirely, helpless to do anything but take it. Soaked noises filled the room, his own arousal dripping down his thighs as the wet sound of Zalith driving into him over and over pushed him nearer to the edge.

Alucard's mind blurred, his body trembled, knees close to buckling, eyes fluttering shut as the burn inside twisted into something sharper—hot, unbearable, close. His dick throbbed untouched beneath him, aching with pressure, leaking steadily as each grind of Zalith's hips urged him closer to his peak.

Zalith was moaning with almost every breath now—so was Alucard. The demon fucked harder and faster, aggression and desperation devouring them both.

Alucard came first. His orgasm tore through him like a snap of flame, wracking his body with wave after wave of heat and pleasure. He cried out, forehead pressed to the wall, body convulsing as he spilled across the stone in thick, shuddering pulses.

Zalith didn't stop. He kept fucking him through it, dragging out every twitch, every tremble. Alucard was still moaning when he felt Zalith stiffen behind him, one final, devastating thrust burying him to the hilt. The demon whined as he came, buried deep inside, his dick pulsing as he flooded into his mate in thick, searing waves. His hips jerked once, twice, and then stilled, his breath ragged against the back of Alucard's neck.

For a long moment, they just breathed, their skin flushed with heat, the only sound their shared panting and the slow drip of cum sliding down Alucard's thighs.

Zalith didn't pull out. He wrapped his arms around Alucard's chest instead, pressing their bodies together as if he needed the contact to calm the animal still snarling beneath his skin. "Alucard," he breathed.

The demon's fingers gradually stroked down Alucard's body; when they graced the vampire's sensitive shaft, Alucard flinched softly and winced as pleasure shot through him. Zalith hummed in satisfaction, still holding him there, his chest pressed to his back and his breath unsteady against Alucard's neck. His dick throbbed faintly inside him with the last slow pulse of release, but he didn't move; he held him, his arms wrapped tight around his body as if he wasn't ready to let go yet.

Alucard didn't mind. He let himself breathe, deep and slow, melting into the warmth of it. His legs were trembling, his thighs soaked, and his mind still hazy from the force of it all. But he needed it…and he'd got it.

Zalith's nose brushed against the side of his neck and trailed down to his shoulder, where he pressed a kiss to the fang marks scarred onto Alucard's skin.

"You've…made a mess of me," Alucard muttered, still catching his breath but a faint smile on his lips. "I can't veel my legs."

His mate huffed a quiet laugh. "That's not my fault. You're the one who spread them wider," he murmured, his voice thick with satisfaction.

Alucard groaned, pressing his forehead to the wall. "Zon't make me vegret zhat alveady."

The demon pressed another soft kiss to his shoulder. "You couldn't if you tried."

He was right. When Zalith took him like that, when the demon became aggressive and possessive, Alucard couldn't help but submit to him—he *loved* submitting.

With a hesitant groan, Zalith finally but reluctantly pulled out, and Alucard couldn't stifle the disappointed whine at the loss, his body twitching slightly with oversensitivity. The demon reached for Alucard's trousers and gently pulled them back up, careful, almost tender, and then he helped the vampire turn around, catching him before his legs gave out completely.

Alucard leaned into him, arms loosely wrapping around Zalith's neck as the demon supported him easily.

He could still feel it. Zalith's cum. Thick and warm, still deep inside him. The awareness pulsed low in his abdomen, a strange, soft pressure that shouldn't have been as comforting as it was. Without thinking, his hand drifted down, fingers stroking faintly over his stomach as if trying to soothe it. He didn't fully understand the impulse, but it felt…right, like his body was holding something important.

Zalith clearly noticed the motion but didn't call him out. He just kissed the side of his head and held him tighter.

"You're still vilthy," Alucard muttered, teasing him and trying to distract himself. "Zhere's…ash in your 'air…and mud on your vace."

Zalith grinned. "You didn't seem to mind when I had you pinned to the wall."

Alucard narrowed his eyes, but it was faint and slow, his expression too relaxed to be truly annoyed. "You're insuvverable."

"Mm-hmm…and you're still hard, darling, even after all of that." The demon slid a hand between them, his palm resting lazily over the bulge forming again beneath the fabric of Alucard's trousers. "Heat isn't going to give you a break. Maybe we should deal with it." He gently squeezed the vampire's arousal.

Alucard groaned again, ridden with desire. "Zon't start someving unless you plan to carry me to zhe shower again when ve're done."

Zalith's eyes glinted. "Tempting," he murmured, but he didn't start kissing and undressing him. He gently lifted him, his arms sliding beneath the vampire's thighs.

Alucard made a soft noise of protest as he was picked up, but he didn't fight it; he let his head fall against Zalith's shoulder, his body loose, his chest warm with the feeling of safety. Even now with the evidence of their mating still resting inside him, Alucard felt…calm…claimed, and wanted. Fangs and fire aside, *that* was the part he craved most.

But…*of course*…with the soft silence that fell between them, that embarrassment returned, that dismaying feeling of not knowing. He couldn't make Zalith cum the way he'd just made *him* cum; Alucard couldn't do *any* of that. And the feeling of inferiority intensified.

He wouldn't let it devour him, though. He wouldn't let it ruin the moment.

"You should probably hire a cleaner," Zalith said with a quiet laugh as he carried Alucard into the bathroom.

The vampire huffed softly as the demon let him down, his legs still weak, and he caught the edge of the shower wall for balance. "I should," he muttered, brushing damp hair from his face. "Vould 'elp to 'ave somevone clean avound zhis place."

His mate chuckled and stepped closer, taking off his ruined clothes. "We should keep one on standby. They can get the room ready for when I fuck you again."

Alucard gave him a look, but it was softened by amusement. "Later," he murmured, reaching to caress his cheek as the demon began undressing him next. His thumb ghosted over a smudge of dirt beneath Zalith's eye. "Let's vash you virst."

The demon leaned in and kissed him, slow and unhurried, and then he took his hand and gently guided him into the shower.

They stepped beneath the warm spray, water trailing over their flushed skin. Alucard turned the dial until the temperature settled just right, the heat soaking into his aching muscles. Zalith stood still in front of him, hair matted and clumped with ash and dried mud, streaks of blood still smeared down his arms.

Without a word, Alucard reached for the shampoo and worked it into his hands; he stepped behind the demon, fingertips threading gently through his hair. He massaged the lather in slow circles, claws lightly grazing Zalith's scalp. Gray suds streaked down his mate's back, the water swirling with grime at their feet as the filth of battle and sweatless pheromones was washed away.

Zalith let his eyes close, head tilting forward slightly under the vampire's touch.

Alucard didn't rush. He stood there with his fingers in his mate's hair, washing the world off him. "Is everyvone else okay?" he asked quietly.

The demon exhaled deeply. "We lost Eren and Danrel," he mumbled guiltily. "I thought about doing something to help everyone remember those we've lost, but I don't have any ideas right now."

He wanted to ask what happened, and he thought about coming up with some suggestions, but he didn't want to drag Zalith deeper into the despair that he was obviously fighting. "I'm sorry," he said, massaging his mate's head, and when he unintentionally soothed the place where Zalith's horns would be, the demon moaned softly.

"You're going to make me hard again," Zalith purred.

Alucard smiled, and the part of him that wanted that to happen urged him to keep going, but he knew better. He stroked his hands down Zalith's back instead and rubbed the last of the shampoo into his skin, washing some of the dirt away. "Ve can go 'ome soon," he told him. "Ve still 'ave to interrogate zhat Detainer, but I zon't 'ave to vait 'ere vor Eyra to be judged, and Lăcrămioara is taking care of zhe Vledgelings. I need to tell Lysandra zhat she needs to go vhrough Vledgeling training again, but zhat von't take long; I zon't need to turn 'er vife because Lysandra isn't a Day Valker—vell...unless zhey both vant Vosaline to be vone—" He stopped and shook his head. "Sorry. I'm vinking aloud."

"No, it's okay. I like listening to you."

His smile grew a little as he washed the shampoo from Zalith's hair. "I may 'ave to go to Antamont and vind Lilly; I vant to try and 'elp 'er and maybe zhe Strayblood she's vith." He grabbed some soap and began washing the demon's skin. "Vhat do ve do if zhe Detainer zoesn't know anyving zhat can 'elp us vind zhe person who vanted zhose children?"

The demon hummed for a second. "I don't know. Somebody has to know something. But if whoever wanted these kids is desperate enough, they'll likely target someplace else. I can spare some demons to scour the world and look for similar activity."

Alucard nodded. "Okay."

"We should start looking for the parents and families."

He frowned slightly, feeling a little despondent—he'd been through something just like this. "Vhat if zheir vamilies are dead?"

"Then we take them to Eimwood and ensure they find new homes," he said firmly.

Alucard finished washing the demon, so he turned him to face him. "I vink ve should ovver zhe vamilies savety, too—invite zhem to Uzlia."

Zalith smiled at him, caressing the side of his face. "We should."

He moved closer and rested his head on Zalith's shoulder. "Ve can try to tie everyving up 'ere bevore ve go. Shouldn't take too long. I can send zemons into zhe city to look vor zhe vamilies."

"All right," the demon murmured, caressing his head.

With a deep exhale, Alucard let any remaining tension leave his body. There was still work ahead—there always was—but for now, the worst had passed.

Chapter Forty-Six

— ⸓ ✝ ⸓ —

Now, But Not Always

| **Alucard** |
| *Atheson, Atheson Coven Sanctum* |

The city quarantine wasn't over yet, but the Oakley Quarter had been marked clear, so Alucard sent Nymeris and Danford to fetch Rosaline. While he waited, he headed down to the Dwelling Space, where Lăcrămioara was teaching a few of the Fledgelings to rest in coffins.

Lysandra was in the Nesting Circle with some of the others. This time, a little over half of the Fledgelings raced to him and began murmuring and droning. Lăcrămioara had made a lot of progress already.

"Lysandra," he called.

She sat up, and she almost seemed to hesitate for a moment before standing and making her way over. "Y-yes, My Lord?"

Alucard looked down at the Fledgelings and pointed to the Nesting Circle as he said, "Go."

The Fledgelings did as they were told.

He then led Lysandra out of the room and pulled the door shut behind him. "I've sent two of my people to get Vosaline," he said, stopping a few feet from the door. "You vere intervested in being moved to Vontisère in Chantrevaux, no?"

She nodded. "That's right."

"I can 'ave a place prepared vor you zhere, but virst, you vill need to go vhrough Vledgeling training again alongside your vife."

Lysandra looked confused for a moment, but she didn't ask why. "I understand," she said. "Eyra didn't exactly teach me everything I needed, I know."

He half-nodded. "You're not a Day Valker, so you and Vosaline vill need to decide vhether or not *she* vill be vone."

"Will she be here soon?" she asked eagerly.

"Any minute," he answered. "She'll be taken to zhe lounge. You can go and vait up zhere and talk to 'er about Vontisère, Vledgeling training, and vhether or not she'll be a Day Valker. Vonce you 'ave come to your decisions, I'll be in my voom. If you need more time, zhough, and I'm not 'ere anymore, you can send an owl."

"Yes, My Lord," she said with a smile and a bow of her head. "Thank you." She stopped mid-step, though. "Oh… did you find Lilly or Camilla?"

"I know vhere Lilly is, but not Camilla. I vill likely send somevone to vind 'er now zhat zhe Silver Claw is dead."

"Is Lilly okay?" she asked worriedly.

"She's in Antamont with anozzer vampire. I'm going to vind 'er and try to 'elp 'er."

She looked relieved. "Well… I'm sure that Rosaline wouldn't mind if she came with us—i-if that's even a good idea. I mean it's better if we stick together, right? Even Camilla… if you found her."

"I vill talk to Lilly about zhat, and Camilla if I vind 'er—and *you* should talk to your vife about zhat, too."

"I will," she said contently. Then, after another bow, she turned around and hurried out of the Ebon Chamber and upstairs.

Alucard headed that way, too, but he didn't rush. Now that the vampire hunter was dead, and since he'd turned many people from the city into Fledgelings, he felt almost ready to head back to Uzlia, especially since Lăcrămioara was making fast work of training the new vampires—and with their ties to the city, the humans might take to the coven's presence rather than threaten and hunt them. But he wouldn't let his guard down. He'd leave the Duskroot Pack here to help protect the Sanctum.

He climbed the steps, making his way up to the second floor. His instincts flared almost immediately when he locked on to Zalith's scent; he walked a little faster, unable to fight the urge to get as close as he could—but he had to remember that there was still work to be done. He couldn't become distracted.

When he stepped into the room, he set his eyes on his mate, who was sitting on the couch with a leather-bound book in his lap and a pen in his hand. He smiled at the vampire, watching him walk over, but he frowned mere seconds later.

"Why do you smell like that?"

Alucard frowned as well, sitting beside him. "Like vhat?"

"Like vampires… and humans—mixed together."

He laughed a little, shuffling closer and resting his head on the demon's shoulder. "*Zhat* is vhat Vledgelings smell like—I smell like zhem because I 'ad to go down to zhe Dvelling Space to speak to Lysandra. Zhey're all veborn vith zhe instinct to vemain close to zheir crveator."

"Did they touch you?" he asked possessively.

"No, zhey just crawled avound at my veet."

"But they touched your feet?"

"My *shoes*," Alucard clarified with a faint smirk.

Zalith's gaze dropped to the vampire's boots, and he *glared* at them as if they'd personally offended him. Then, without a word, he snapped his book shut, set it aside, and reached for Alucard. His hands were firm but gentle as he grasped his arms, guiding him down onto the couch and pinning him there. Alucard let him, amused, smiling faintly as his mate hovered over him, looking him up and down as if searching for incriminating evidence.

When Zalith leaned in and nuzzled at his neck, Alucard exhaled softly and reached up to drag his fingers through his mate's hair. Zalith began to press his body subtly against him, rubbing along his sides, chest, and throat.

At first, Alucard thought he was teasing him, maybe about to start grinding on him, working him up...but it didn't feel like that. The demon's touch wasn't focused on his crotch or any one spot. It was something else.

"Vhat are you doing?" he asked curiously.

Zalith growled low against his throat, then licked a slow line along the side of his neck before nuzzling into the other. "Getting rid of that awful smell," he muttered darkly. "You're *mine*, not theirs."

Alucard chuckled softly, letting his eyes drift shut as the demon continued his slow, possessive work. He didn't fight it. He didn't want to. He liked when Zalith got jealous, and he liked when he displayed his devotion like this.

Now he understood. The scent of Zalith deepened around him, rich and intoxicating. It sank into his clothes and clung to his skin, threading through every breath he took. His mate wasn't just touching him; he was *marking* him, erasing anything that didn't belong, drowning out every trace of scent but their own...and it was enough to arouse Alucard.

He tried to fight it. This wasn't about sex—he knew that. This was Zalith claiming him, covering him, making him his again. But even knowing that, it took effort not to give in to the growing ache. As strong as it was, though, he wouldn't let himself move unless Zalith wanted to take it further.

Not long later, though, Zalith stopped with a grunt and a huff. He lifted his body a little, just enough for him to look down, clearly examining Alucard again, and then he met the vampire's gaze.

"Better?" Alucard asked amusedly.

"Yes," the demon said, his irritated glower slowly lifting. He kissed the vampire's lips, smiled, and then returned to nuzzling his neck.

Alucard sank into the comfort of Zalith's embrace, caressing his mate's hair while he breathed in his scent. "Vhat vere you vorking on?" he asked quietly.

Zalith didn't answer right away. He hummed softly, pressing his face against the vampire's neck. "I was trying to figure out the whole…new ranks and roles thing for the demon army."

"Did you make much progress?"

"Sort of," he mumbled.

Alucard waited for him to continue…. But after a short silence, he asked, "Sort of?"

"Mm-hmm." He paused. "I couldn't figure out rank or title names, but I worked out *how* I want to differentiate them."

"Do you vant me to take a look and 'elp you vith zhe vank titles?"

Zalith smiled against his neck. "Later," he murmured. "Thank you."

The vampire started fiddling with his hair. "I 'ad a vhought, actually. Verevolves 'ave packs, and vampires 'ave covens, but vith zemons, zhey *also* 'ave packs. Maybe zhey should 'ave some ozzer term," he suggested. "I could vink of someving."

His mate replied with a hum.

"I vink zhat you should also vink about appointing new Alphas. Zhe numbers are growing vast, and—"

"Alucard," Zalith interjected.

"Vhat?"

"Shut up," he said playfully, laughing a little.

The vampire pouted but smiled half a second later—it *was* funny. So he did as Zalith asked and rested the side of his head against his. He wanted to see what the demon had come up with, but the longer he lay there, the faster his curiosity turned into conflicting desire. His body was demanding that he give it what it needed, but his mind was starting to convince him otherwise.

Now that he wasn't exhausted, he could *actually* think, but that was more a regret than a relief. Planning and hypothesizing weren't the only things that came back to him; the questions returned, the dismay and confusion poured in, and so did the despair of not knowing what he was.

He still needed to tell Zalith. Maybe he could help him understand it. Or perhaps he could help him recover more of his memories faster. He wanted to know when and why he'd chosen to be a man—if he could even call himself that.

With a sharp huff, he looked up at the ceiling. He wasn't going to let all of that consume him again. "Zaliv?" he asked quietly.

Zalith responded with a murmured hum.

If he let himself try to figure out how to say it, he'd hesitate, so he just focused on the memory and started, "You vemember vhen I vas telling you about Gossamer, vight?"

The demon made another sound.

"Vell…I vemembered someving else vrom avound zhe time zhe cat vas teaching me, and I zon't veally…I zon't 'ave all zhe answers, I'm still trying to vemember, but I vink zhat—"

A knock at the door interrupted him.

He turned his head—

"You think what?" Zalith asked, sounding more focused now.

The hesitation quickly rose—he couldn't stop it. Despite Zalith's answers to his questions earlier, he still worried that his mate might not be comfortable with what he needed to tell him. But he tried anyway. "I vink zhat…I zon't vink I vas alvays a man," he murmured despondently, his heart beating faster as anxiety swallowed him. He'd said it, and he dreaded what Zalith might say in response.

"What do you mean?" There was confusion in his voice.

He fidgeted a little, trying to grasp on to whatever courage he could find. "I—"

Whoever was at the door knocked again.

"One minute," Zalith called irritably, and then he propped himself up on his arm and looked down at Alucard. He looked curious, but still a little confused.

Alucard's anxiety intensified; he looked away for a moment, attempting to find his voice and ignore the fear and worry…and then he turned his head to meet the demon's gaze again. "I vasn't…a boy vhen I vas a child," he said sadly. "I vemembered zhat I vas searching vor answers as a child, and I vhought zhat I vas trying to vind out vhat kind of zemon I vas and vhat my mother vas, but I vasn't." He pouted and looked away again. "I vas trying to vind out vhy every ozzer child vas convused and disgusted by me, and vhy zhe priestesses vhought zhe same—I vanted to know vhy zhey never grouped me vith zhe ozzer boys or zhe girls; I vas just…levt standing zhere on zhe sidelines. And I vemember being *avraid* of 'aving to choose to be vone or zhe ozzer." He scowled almost shamefully—he didn't want to look at Zalith; he didn't want to see the expression on his face. "I zon't even vemember choosing," he murmured despondently.

"How is that possible?" Zalith asked—he sounded more confused now.

"I zon't know," he answered quietly. "I vas vinking zhat…maybe zhat's vhy you and Tyrus said I 'ave zhis sort of voman smell vight now—I vhought *zhat* might be because I 'ave Numen blood." He paused, tempted to glance at Zalith, but he couldn't. After an exhale, he continued, "Maybe I vas like zhat as a child because of zhe Numen part of me…or maybe because I'm not vully Numen." He then scowled in despair, the trauma of his past beginning to ensnare him. "Or maybe zhey all did someving to me— maybe Liliv did someving. Vouldn't be zhe virst time."

"Did something to make you a boy?"

"No. To make me neizer."

"But how are you a man now, then?"

"I zon't know. I can't vemember anyving else, and I zon't know vhen I vill."

Zalith started fiddling with his hair. "Well, I don't really know what to say other than something that's probably a little insensitive right now because I know you're upset, but either way, I'm not bothered by this."

He slowly turned his head to meet Zalith's gaze again. The demon didn't look repulsed, nor did he seem confused anymore. He looked…fine, relaxed…like he'd accepted it. *Had he?* The vampire still felt anxious, he still felt dismayed and ashamed…and he wanted to know what else Zalith might have said. So he asked, "Vhat…insensitive ving vere you going to say?"

The demon laughed and gently stroked his thumb along Alucard's bottom lip. "That I'd still fuck you regardless."

Alucard smiled faintly—he *was* amused, and he appreciated the fact that Zalith was trying to lighten the mood…but the anxiety didn't fade completely despite his mate's responses. "You're not…just saying zhat because I'm in 'eat, are you? Vhat if vonce I'm not anymore, you vind me disgusting?" he mumbled sadly.

"No, not at all," he said, caressing the side of his face. "In fact, I think you're hotter for being honest and letting me know," he flirted.

The vampire's smile grew a little more, and his anxiety finally started withering. He still didn't understand why he was different as a child, or when and why he'd become a man, but Zalith's reaction had been the part that mattered most, and now that he knew his mate didn't find him revolting and wasn't any less attracted to him, he felt like he could relax. Maybe he'd remember the rest eventually, but right now, he just wanted to let the demon's reassurance comfort him.

Zalith kissed his lips, smiled at him, and said, "We should see who's at the door."

He nodded, and when Zalith sat up, so did he.

The demon leaned into his ear and whispered, "I'm going to fuck you again once they're gone, by the way."

Alucard smiled, both excited and flustered, and then he called, "Come in."

"I will, don't worry," his mate murmured.

He pouted for half a moment before turning deadpan, facing the opening door.

Sentinel Edricus stepped in…with his hands behind his back, and he seemed hesitant. "Sorry to disturb you, My Lord, but—" he pulled his hands around to reveal an unconscious, snoring izuret covered in crimson, "—this creature flew in through one of the lounge windows and collided with a wine decanter. Anselric has sent someone to clean up the mess, and I sent an order to the distillery to replace what this thing consumed." He looked down at the izuret, which hiccupped in its sleep.

Zalith rolled his eyes and huffed irritably. "Leave him in the hall and get one of my demons to call his family to come and take him home. I'll talk to him about it later."

Edricus nodded as he reached into his pocket and pulled out a piece of wine-covered paper. "I found this tucked inside one of its wings."

Alucard held his hand out.

The Sentinel made his way over and handed it to him.

"*Multumesc*," he thanked.

With a bow, Edricus left the room, taking the izuret with him.

Alucard unfolded the damp paper. Some of the ink was smudged, but it was readable. "Is vrom Zhomas. Zhe new volf packs arrived in Eimvood not long ago."

Zalith grunted in response.

"Ve can send zhem to Anburidge vor now; zhere's plenty of voom, no?

"Yeah," he said with a nod, leaning closer.

"Oh, I need to send somevone to vind Creven's vather."

"Who?"

"Vone of zhe new Alphas."

"Oh…right," he murmured, nuzzling Alucard's neck.

"I vant to vind 'im vast, so I vill probably send a zemon and a verevolf," he pondered.

"Mm-hmm," Zalith hummed and dragged his tongue slowly across Alucard's neck.

A shiver chased down the vampire's spine, sinking deep, and anticipation electrified through him. His body reacted instantly, warming, heart beating faster, nerves sparking under every place Zalith touched, and his mind didn't take long to follow. The flicker of worry he'd held not long ago burned to ash under the heat of his mate's mouth, taking with it the whispers of anxiety and hesitation.

When Zalith licked him again, slower this time, one hand stroking over his chest, Alucard's restraint melted completely. He let his instincts take over. There was no other thought or feeling other than the aching relief of being wanted exactly as he was.

He smiled softly and lay back, sinking into the cushions, letting his body settle beneath his mate. Zalith followed, draping over him, still nuzzling at his throat, tongue tracing the hollow beneath his jaw; the demon's hips shifted, pressing down, making the vampire groan quietly in content as he began to grind against him. Each slow, heavy drag of his clothed dick against Alucard's made the vampire fidget, the friction intoxicating. Zalith kept licking and kissing along his neck as his hips moved, creating just enough stimulation to make it impossible to think about anything else.

Alucard arched into him, fingers curling in Zalith's hair as heat bloomed low within him again. The demon's hand moved lower, trailing over his ribs and stomach, then back up, teasing without rushing. Alucard moaned softly, his legs parting slightly without conscious thought, his body already begging to be touched more directly. But Zalith took his time, grinding in a steady, maddening rhythm, keeping him suspended in that sweet, slow descent into desire.

The demon then growled quietly and gently bit Alucard's neck. "You have no idea what you do to me," he murmured before biting again, harder this time.

He couldn't stifle a moan in response.

Zalith aggressively rubbed his crotch against Alucard's, his hard dick pressing firmly against his thigh. "Every inch of you makes me so fucking hard," he groaned.

The vampire smiled, warmth pooling in his chest as he locked one leg around Zalith's waist, pulling him closer.

Zalith growled softly and dipped his head, his mouth latching onto Alucard's neck with a slow, sucking pressure. His hand slid lower, dragging across the vampire's stomach before gently grasping his arousal through his trousers. The eager huff he let out against Alucard's skin made him shiver, and a moan slipped from his lips as he buried his fingers in his mate's hair, gripping tight.

And then came another knock.

Alucard's eyes snapped open, his head jerking towards the door with an irritated snarl.

Zalith didn't even look. "Ignore it," he muttered, mouth still against Alucard's throat as he sucked harder, nipping just beneath his jaw.

The vampire laughed under his breath, exasperated but already melting again. He tilted his head back to give Zalith more room, letting the demon drag his lips lower, across his collarbone and then over the curve of his shoulder, licking and biting as if he were making a map of everywhere he planned to devour.

Alucard let himself sink into it—into the rhythm, the scent, the feel of Zalith's body against his. The demon peeled his shirt off first, and then he pulled Alucard's open, pressing kisses to every newly bared inch of skin. Alucard's trousers were unbuttoned next, tugged down slowly, Zalith's knuckles grazing along his thighs. The demon shed the rest of his own clothes in between kisses, lips never straying far from Alucard's chest, neck, and mouth.

Soon they were both naked, skin against skin, heat growing with each press and drag of their bodies.

Another knock.

Zalith froze.

Alucard blinked at the ceiling in disbelief.

With a sound that was more growl than sigh, Zalith reached blindly for the nearest pillow and hurled it, and it hit the door with a dull thump.

Alucard scoffed a laugh. "Zaliv—"

"I don't care." The demon leaned back down, biting lightly at his chest. "If it's not a fire..." he paused to bite, "...or your Fledgelings dying, they can wait." He bit again.

Alucard smiled as he looked down at him. "And if is a vire?"

Zalith didn't stop kissing him. "We're fireproof. I'll keep fucking you."

He settled back over the vampire, his body radiating warmth; the weight of him, the closeness—it was grounding but maddeningly arousing, especially when Zalith began to move again. His hips rolled in a slow, grinding rhythm, his shaft dragging along Alucard's. There was no more teasing in Zalith's movements now, just determination.

Alucard moaned eagerly, arching into him as their dicks slid together, slick between their stomachs. His fingers roamed Zalith's back, claws grazing muscle, feeling every shift and flex beneath his hands. Every thrust sent a pulse of heat through him, the ache inside growing again with impossible speed.

The demon kissed him deeply, one hand curled under Alucard's thigh, lifting it to his waist again, and he rutted against him harder, grinding into the space between his legs like he needed to mark every inch of him. The friction and the tension built at once, intoxicating and overwhelming.

Alucard was lost in it—in the scent of him, in the way his mate held him like he couldn't stand the idea of letting go. His own dick throbbed desperately, leaking steadily, every drag against Zalith's sending sparks up his spine. He wanted to be taken— he *needed* it. And Zalith was right there, breath ragged against his cheek, dick hard and heavy as it slid between his thighs.

The demon paused for only a few seconds, eagerly grabbing the lube, pouring some onto his fingers, and then massaging it into Alucard's ass, and then he shifted his weight, dragging his shaft back and pressing its tip between Alucard's thighs, lining up perfectly. He stopped for a heartbeat, long enough to stroke a hand down Alucard's side, to feel the tremble already starting beneath his skin, and then he pushed in.

Alucard whined loudly, his back arching as he was filled again, slow and deep, the thick inches of his mate's dick easing him open in one smooth, devastating thrust.

There was no hesitation. Zalith thrusted hard in that precise way, the way that made Alucard's voice crack on the first moan. The demon angled his hips just enough to catch that spot inside him again and again, and Alucard knew immediately what he was doing.

He wanted him loud.

Zalith moved aggressively, grinding in at the end of each thrust just to make Alucard cry out. And he did. He couldn't help it. Every time Zalith drove in, the pressure sent his voice tumbling out in broken, shameless sounds that echoed off the walls. He clung to him, legs locked around his waist, claws digging into his shoulders. Pheromones slicked their skin, the air between them thick with it. The demon growled low in his throat, fucking him harder in response, his dick hitting so deep that it made Alucard's whole body jolt.

The vampire cried out, his hips twitching with every brutal grind. He could feel the way Zalith's muscles flexed with every push, he heard the pleased moans that told him his mate was enjoying every sound he pulled from him. The demon's mouth found his throat again, biting this time, nipping without breaking skin, and it only made Alucard moan louder.

And then Zalith shifted again, only slightly, but it was enough. The next thrust was angled *perfectly*, catching that spot inside Alucard with aggressive accuracy, and then again, and again, and again, faster, harder. Alucard's breath caught and then stuttered into a moan that turned sharp at the edges.

He felt it gathering too fast.

Zalith knew exactly what he was doing.

The rhythm changed—not rougher, but more focused, more intentional, every thrust designed to tear the climax out of him before he could prepare for it. Alucard's body shook, his hands scrabbling at Zalith's back, trying to brace himself, but the heat was too much, the friction too good, and his mate was hitting so *deep*, so pleasingly forceful, right where he needed—

And then it broke.

Alucard came with a sudden, startled whine, loud and helpless as his body tensed and shuddered beneath Zalith. His climax hit fast and violent, painting between them in thick, hot pulses, his dick untouched, his mind blanked completely.

He didn't have time to recover before Zalith slammed in one final time, burying himself with a possessive growl and then a pleased moan. Alucard felt the warmth flood his body as Zalith came inside him, filling him deeply, holding him close.

They stayed like that for a moment—bodies tangled, skin slick, breath mingling between them—before Zalith lifted his head and kissed his lips. It was slow, lasting only seconds, giving Alucard no time to respond; Zalith's lips broke away and began to trail lower, down the curve of the vampire's jaw, across the line of his throat, and along the centre of his chest. The demon's hands moved, too, stroking Alucard's sides with the same gentle care he'd used when pinning him down, only now there was no urgency…just heat, reverence, and the afterglow of satisfaction.

Zalith gradually pulled out as he descended, and Alucard winced at the emptiness, his body twitching from the overstimulated sensation, and from the feeling of his mate's cum slowly dripping from him in the wake of it. His fingers drifted through the demon's hair, and he tightened his grip when he felt Zalith drag his tongue over his stomach, humming in satisfaction as he licked the climax from his still-sensitive skin, a slow trail over the inside of Alucard's thigh before pressing a kiss to his hipbone.

The cool air against damp skin made Alucard shiver faintly as he watched Zalith move beside him. His mate stretched out on the couch with a low exhale and wrapped his arm around Alucard's waist, pulling him close without a word. Alucard turned into him easily, curling against his chest, letting the warmth of Zalith's body bleed into his own.

Each sound of the room faded; the distant world outside was muffled and irrelevant. All that remained was the slow, steady rhythm of their breathing, the soft brush of Zalith's fingers across his back, and the faint scent of spent heat and skin.

Alucard let his eyes drift shut. He was still aching in a delightfully satisfying way, still a little flushed, but there was no tension in him anymore. For once, his thoughts didn't spiral. He didn't question what Zalith might think of who he'd been, or what he didn't understand right now. Though the answers hadn't all come yet, one truth settled steadily in his chest: Zalith accepted him.

Chapter Forty-Seven

⚊ ⋞ ✝ ⋟ ⚊

Legion, Covenant, Kingdom

| Alucard |
| Atheson, Atheson Coven Sanctum |

Despite how much he wanted to just lie in silence, Alucard had work to do. There were still things that needed tying up before he and Zalith headed back to Uzlia.

"Zaliv," he murmured.

The demon stirred softly, still nuzzling his neck.

"I need to see who's at zhe door."

Zalith groaned.

Alucard smiled and carefully eased his mate off him. When he sat up, though, Zalith tried to pull him back down again.

"No," the demon grumbled.

"Vill only be a vew minutes," he told him amusedly, peeling Zalith's hand from his shoulder.

The demon groaned again but didn't make another attempt to stop him; he stayed where he was, lying on his side with his head resting on one of the cushions—still naked.

As he got up, Alucard pulled his trousers back on. Once he buttoned his shirt, he headed over to the door, and he opened it to find Danford sitting in his private library.

The wolf-vampire looked a little flustered.

"Vhat?" Alucard muttered.

"Uh…Rosaline's in the lounge with Lysandra," he told him.

He nodded, but just as he was about to turn and head back into the room, he stopped. "Go and vind vone of zhe zemons and get zhem to take you to Diaráinne." He recalled where Crevan's father was last seen. "In Draíocht, zhere's a small varming village, Sléibhe. Zhere are only non-'umans living zhere, but you vill still need to be carevul, vhich is vhy I vant a zemon vith you."

Danford nodded as he slowly stood up.

"Zhe man you are looking vor is called Séamus Ó Súilleabháin. 'E is shepherd, and 'e is sionnach—a Diaráinnish vox shivter. Ask vor 'im only by name, zhough; sionnaigh are very vare, and people may vink you 'ave ill intentions if you start asking avound vor vone."

"What do I do when I find him?"

"Tell 'im zhat 'is son, Crevan, is 'oping zhat 'e'd leave Diaráinne and join 'im. Zon't mention Uzlia, eizer; tell 'im zhat Crevan is still in Dor-Sanguis. I zon't vant you to vorce 'im to go vith you, zhough. Zhe choice is entirely 'is. And if 'e does agree to go, convince 'im to let you take 'im now or as soon as possible. Ve'll likely be leaving zhis place bevore midnight, so if you can't get 'im 'ere bevore zhen, just 'ead to Uzlia and land in Anburidge vhere all zhe new volf packs vill be staying. 'E can veunite vith 'is son zhere."

Danford nodded again and turned—

"'Ow is Vreja?" Alucard asked.

He stopped, facing him again. "Oh, she's good," he said with a small smile. "Pepper is really protective, though—oh, that's the bulldog's name. He bit Greymore when he went to go and check on Freja."

Alucard couldn't stifle an amused smirk.

"She's going for a check-up on Wednesday at that Albany clinic; we should be able to tell how many babies we're gonna have then."

He nodded slightly. "Do you 'ave a guess?"

Danford chuckled a little, sounding nervous. "I don't know. Uh…maybe three—no more than five…I hope."

"Vell, is a vivty-vivty chance betveen 'aving vone and two or more."

The wolf-vampire dragged his hand over the back of his neck. "I'm hoping for one, to be honest," he said, but then he lowered his hand. "Maybe we'll know on Wednesday."

Alucard glanced over his shoulder into the room; Zalith was still lying on the couch, but he had his eyes fixed on him, and he looked *hungry*. The demon's expression sent a shiver up his spine, but he did his best to resist the urge to go to him and let his instincts take control again.

"If you can't vind Séamus bevore Tuesday evening, you can come back so you zon't miss zhe appointment," he said, setting his eyes back on Danford.

He smiled appreciatively. "Thank you."

Alucard then said, "Go now," and headed back into the room. He closed the door behind him, smiled at his mate, and joined him on the couch.

Zalith immediately pressed his body against his, getting close and nuzzling his neck. "You seem to know a lot about Crevan's father," he murmured, sounding curious.

"I 'ave alvays made a 'abit of vinding out vhat I can about people who may become my allies, but mostly just verevolves in general—especially zhe Dor-Sanguian vones."

The demon kissed his neck and said, "That makes sense."

Alucard leaned back, letting himself relax. But he could already feel the pull, that intensifying need. He needed to rest, and he was hungry, but the latter would definitely lead to sex, so he thought it best to wait.

Instead, he reached past Zalith and took the leather-bound book he'd been writing in. "So, did you vinish deciding 'ow you vant to divverentiate zhe zemons?" he asked as he opened it.

Zalith responded with a quiet hum, one that didn't sound like a yes or a no.

The vampire started reading through the pages. His mate was not only meticulous in his notes, but the structure he'd laid out was very tactical in its logic; it was a perfect hierarchy, and a brilliant strategy. All that was left to do was title each rank and skill level.

"Zhis is all veally good, you know," he said, glancing at what he could see of the demon's face. "Is zhis everyvone, or do you plan on adding a vew more?"

His mate kissed his neck again, lingering for a moment. "I think that's it."

He nodded, reading through Zalith's notes again. "Vell, ve should start with calling zhe packs someving ozzer zhan packs, no?"

"Mm."

Alucard pondered. "Vell…hmm…legion? No…zhat vould be good instead of army," he suggested.

Zalith licked his throat before murmuring, "That sounds good."

The vampire reached for the pen and noted it down. "As vor pack…maybe someving like covenant could vork. I know sounds a little like coven, but I veel is better zhan pack."

"I like it," his mate purred.

Alucard smiled when Zalith started sucking his neck again. "I can vead vhrough all of zhis a vew times and come up vith some ideas to show you."

"Mm-hmm."

He rested his head on Zalith's, and then he got to work, letting the silence settle around them.

However, that silence was interrupted.

Alucard didn't know how long had passed, but the sudden end felt too soon.

Zalith snarled angrily in response and irritably repositioned himself, lying on his back and resting his head in Alucard's lap.

The vampire smiled down at him, putting the book aside. "Vhat?" he called.

Nymeris stepped into the room this time. "Oh, sorry," she said, her face turning red.

"Vhat do you vant?" Alucard questioned as he let his instincts take hold for a moment; he possessively placed his hand on Zalith's head, fiddling with his hair.

"Um…I just wanted to ask for permission to…well, to pursue a relationship with Tyrus." She held her arms behind her back, straightening up, staring confidently now. "I know that we're both Alphas, but we've known each other a *long* time, so if things didn't work out, we'd be completely fine just being friends again. It wouldn't affect how we work together…or anything like that," she explained, pleading her case firmly.

Zalith snarled again. "I don't care," he grumbled and rolled over, nuzzling Alucard's waist.

Alucard laughed a little, still fiddling with his hair. It probably wasn't his place to respond and question—he didn't exactly feel like it was—but his mate, Nymeris' superior, was far too distracted. And if Nymeris gave him the same look as those other demons, he'd not intrude on Zalith's authority. "I vink is okay," he told her.

Her face lit up a little.

"As long as your packs von't vight."

She shook her head. "I have been teaching them to be respectful. I know that some of them are still hung up on how things used to work for them when they were with their previous Alpha, but I'll keep them in line." She stammered after a pause, "S-sir," she added, nodding her head respectfully.

The vampire looked down at Zalith.

His mate didn't say anything, he just started slowly untucking his shirt from his belt.

"Just zon't let zhis become an issue."

Nymeris nodded again. "I won't—thank you." She turned to leave, but then she spun on her heel to face him again. "Sorry, this isn't related, but I was curious…as to whether there were other terms to use instead of ethosical—in certain situations, like…ethosical object or…'This crime scene looks ethosical.' That sort of thing."

Alucard thought about it. There'd been many a situation where using the word 'ethosical' had felt odd, especially since ethos wasn't always involved in every non-human situation. "Vell, bevore Year Zero, zhe vord 'Arcana' vas used a lot. I zon't know exactly vhen zhe term died out, zhough."

"Oh…well…I kind of like that more. Is…it okay to start using it again?"

He shrugged. "Sure. But expect to 'ave to explain vhat you mean to a lot of people."

"Thank you, sir," she said, and then she left, pulling the door shut behind her.

Alucard then looked down at his mate again.

Zalith lifted Alucard's shirt, licked his waist, and then started sucking his skin.

The vampire exhaled a content sigh, tilting his head back. He let himself relax again, but when he glanced at the clock, he saw that it would soon be sunrise. There were still things to do, things he didn't want to leave too long.

He looked down at Zalith and caressed the side of his face. "I should go to Antamont soon to look vor Lilly. Do you vant to come vith me?"

Zalith gradually loosened his possessive, lingering kiss and asked, "When?" before resuming his quest to give Alucard yet another love bite.

"Maybe vonce ve know vhich of zhe non-'uman children and vamilies are moving to Uzlia...and avter I've turned Lysandra's vife." He ran his fingers through the demon's hair. "But...maybe you should 'ead back to Uzlia vith zhem, actually. You should check on zhe Orrivain situation."

The demon grunted stubbornly, and his fangs pinched Alucard's skin.

He flinched lightly.

"Sorry," Zalith murmured and continued.

"Is okay," he said quietly. "You can come vith me."

His mate hummed in response, sounding satisfied.

"I 'ave to speak to Corven-'ale again and see if 'e missed any details zhat might 'elp me vind Camilla, too."

"Corven who?" the demon grumbled possessively.

"Vone of my Knights, zhe vone who vitnessed vhat Eyra vas doing be'ind my back."

Zalith grunted in response.

"Zon't vorry, 'e's not like Alson," he said amusedly.

"Good," he muttered.

He smiled, glancing at the clock again. "Do you vant me to vun zhese ideas by you bevore ve go?" he asked, grabbing the book.

"Sure."

Alucard flipped through the pages until he found Zalith's notes. "Vell, ve agreed on Legion instead of army, and covenant instead of pack. Zhough I vhought about 'ow not all zemons are cut out to be vighters—ve'd also need zemons vor voles outside of vighting, no? So...maybe, as a collective, ve should rever to every zemon under your command as zhe Kingdom or Zemon Kingdom."

Zalith hummed quietly. "Kingdom is good."

He circled the word, marking it as the name they'd use. Then, he said, "So, your vank is pretty much vhat Zhomas' is if ve vere talking in verevolf terms, but ve're obviously not going to be calling you a Prime." He paused to smile contently in response to Zalith kissing another spot and starting to work on a new love bite. "Zhere are a vew vords zhat mean zhe same ving, but my vavourite is Zeniv."

His mate hummed a laugh. "Because it sounds like my name?"

Alucard pouted embarrassedly. "Maybe," he mumbled.

The demon kissed just below one of his abs. "I like it," he told him.

With a quiet exhale, Alucard smiled again, letting the embarrassment fade. "I vink zhat Sovereign vould be a good veplacement vor Apex, but if you vant to keep Apex, zhat's okay."

Zalith didn't answer. He was too busy sucking the place he'd kissed.

Alucard looked down at him. "Vhat do you vant to do?"

"Hmm?" he responded, halted for a moment. "Oh...Sovereign sounds good."

"I also vhought about a vank above zhat vor vhen zhe Kingdom grows even bigger, and at zhe vate is growing vight now, I veel von't be long until ve can start using zhat."

His mate hummed again.

"Do you like zhe sound of Invernarch? Vor a leader of several Sovereigns, just like a Sovereign vill vule over several Alphas."

He nodded ever so slightly.

Alucard made note of Zalith's confirmations. "Alpha can stay zhe same, and Beta—unless you vant new titles vor zhose."

Zalith shook his head.

"Okay." He flipped the page. "Vor zhis overseer zhat carries out zhe Alpha's orders—zhe war leader—I vink 'arbinger could vork."

"Mm-hmm."

"Cravengar vor zhe zemon varrior commander?"

He nodded.

"I vhought maybe 'exer vould be good vor zhe ethos master and keeper of covenant traditions."

"I like that," the demon murmured.

Alucard smiled again. "Sentry vor zhe overseer of internal avvairs?"

"That's the one that handles loyalty and justice, isn't it?"

"Yes."

"Okay, yeah—I like that."

The vampire nodded and said, "Maybe Veylarch vor zhe interrogators, Ignivar vor zhe vitual and general advisor, and Voxiren vor zhe messengers?"

Zalith hummed in approval.

"As vor zhe 'ealers, zhere are ozzer ideas, but I vhought zhat Sangralux sounded zhe best—sounds like blood."

The demon smiled against his skin. "That's my favourite so far."

Alucard fiddled with his hair. "Mine, too." He then flipped the page. "Nightvender vor zhe trackers and scouts?"

He hummed again.

"And vhat about Lorepyre vor zhe 'istory and knowledge keeper?"

"That's good," he agreed.

After noting it down, he said, "I vink ve can keep Vhrall as a collective term vor zhese more common vanks—zhe vighters, vorkers, and new initiates—but I came up vith singular names to better devine zhem vhen need be."

Zalith dragged his tongue along Alucard's stomach. "You're so cute."

He laughed a little and continued, "So, zhe varriors I vink could be called Lupivex, and I added in someving of my own, but if you zon't like, I can vemove." He waited a moment, but Zalith didn't say anything. "I vhought zhat since some zemons are more aggressive zhan ozzers, maybe ve separate zhose into a new vank—'owler, per'aps?"

The demon nodded. "Sounds good." He started licking him again.

"Vexari vor Vhralls who 'ave completed zhe physical tvaining and are now learning strategy, and Milivex vor zhe Vhralls yet to vinish zhe physical tvaining. Oh, and Vexling vor new initiates, who 'ave to learn zhe vay of covenant life bevore zhey start tvaining."

Zalith kissed Alucard's waist. "Perfect." He turned onto his back and smirked up at him, and then he started fiddling with his crucifix. "I love the way your mind works, baby," he said softly.

Alucard smiled, admittedly a little flustered.

The demon caressed his cheek. "I could listen to you for hours."

"Even if all I talk about is animals?"

"Yes."

"Or dragons?"

"Mm-hmm."

"Vell, maybe I vill tell you everyving I know about zhose vings someday."

"I'd like that."

"I vhought about vhat you said about a vay to 'elp everyvone vemember zhose zhey've lost, too." He paused, stroking Zalith's cheek. "Vhat about a memorial? A statue or a monument carved with zhe names of zhose who 'ave passed? Maybe in zhe city or someving—per'aps even a private space on vone of zhe ozzer islands."

Zalith smiled appreciatively. "That's a really good idea, baby. We can look into it."

He smiled, too, and fiddled with the demon's fringe. "Vhen should ve start veorganizing zhe packs?"

He stroked his hand down the vampire's body and exhaled deeply. "I'll get Tyrus and Orin to make a start later. Let's just…lie here a little longer before we get back to work."

Alucard nodded, caressing his hair. "Okay."

Zalith smiled, and once the vampire lay down beside him, the demon cuddled up to him and sighed contently.

There was still work to be done, but Alucard felt no guilt in enjoying the peace for just a little while longer.

Chapter Forty-Eight

— ⸻ ✝ ⸻ —

The Smallest Hint

| **Zalith** |

| *Atheson, Atheson Coven Sanctum* |

It was hard to focus, but Zalith did his best as he followed Alucard down into the Withercrypt. His clothes felt like a prison meant to keep his urges locked inside, and his mind was fogged, not with thought but desire. Every breath pulled in more of Alucard's scent, heavy with heat and thick with pheromones that clung to his skin like silk and sin. It gnawed at his control, sharpening his instincts to a single point: claim, protect, fuck. His thoughts tripped over themselves trying to stay ahead of it.

As they passed through the archway towards the lower level, a voice called out—Eyra, pleading. The demon didn't register what she said, and Alucard didn't stop; his fiancé ignored her completely, his expression cold and distant. Zalith might not know the full story, but he knew enough. Eyra had crossed a line. She'd acted recklessly, endangered Alucard and the coven by making choices that weren't hers to make. Whatever punishment she was facing, she'd earned it.

If Zalith's instincts weren't clawing at him to grab his mate and haul him back to safety, to smear that scent all over him until no one else could dare breathe it in, he might've cared more about the details. But right now, his self-control was stretched thin. And Alucard, walking just ahead, smelled like a promise he wasn't allowed to touch.

He couldn't keep his hands to himself, and he gave in just a little, reaching out, his fingers curling gently around Alucard's. The vampire's skin was warm and soft, enough to satisfy him for now, and when their eyes met, even for just a second, Zalith's heart fluttered—no, it lurched, as if it forgot how to beat for a breath. He loved him so much, and he wanted him, almost painfully so. But the urge to simply hold him warred against the more primal pull to take him again, and the lines between affection and desire blurred; he couldn't tell which one he was chasing.

Another voice cut through the fog of pheromones and instinct, sharp enough to drag Zalith's attention sideways. They were in the Lower Withercrypt; he hadn't even realized until he heard Aldric's pleas rise from one of the cells, strained and desperate.

"Boss, please," the man called out, his fingers gripping the bars. "I'm sorry. I was out of line."

Zalith didn't bother looking at him. Just like Eyra, Aldric was exactly where he belonged—behind reinforced bars and blessed wards. The apology rang hollow. No plea could erase the venom he'd spat at Alucard, and Zalith still remembered every word. He'd struck the man once, but even that had felt far too lenient.

He kept walking, gaze fixed ahead, his hand tightening around Alucard's.

But Aldric wasn't done. "Boss," he tried again, louder now, reaching out of his cell as Zalith and Alucard passed it. "I wasn't thinking straight, all right? I didn't mean it like that. I was angry, I—"

Zalith's steps didn't slow.

Behind him, Aldric's desperation cracked. "I served you," he snarled, the plea in his voice souring to bitterness. "*Fought* for you—for the *cause*. You know I'm loyal. I just...I thought I was protecting you." He paused and snarled again. "From *him*."

That stopped Zalith cold. His head turned slightly, just enough to glance over his shoulder, but past Aldric, never at him.

Aldric stiffened, but his pride snapped louder than his caution. "He's Disavowed!" he hissed bitterly. "You know what that means. I was just following demon law— *our* law. His kind aren't even supposed to *look* at us; how can you let him into your bed? I was trying to save you from the shame of it."

Zalith didn't speak. He just smiled, his eyes still not meeting Aldric's—he'd not give him the satisfaction of attention. And then he turned to the only person in the room who mattered. "Can the Wardens gag him?" he calmly asked his fiancé.

Alucard's reply was immediate, laced with cold delight, "Gladly."

Moments later, footsteps echoed down the crypt stairs. Two vampires emerged from the shadows, cloaked in black, expressions unreadable beneath the faint glint of warded goggles.

"Wardens Maelissa and Lucaniel," Alucard introduced to him.

Lucaniel, the bald man with several gem-studded nose piercings, was carrying a leather muzzle rigged with iron buckles and thin metal bars—antique, but effective, designed for silence.

He recognized Maelissa; she'd been guarding Eyra's cell when he and Alucard brought Tamsin in for interrogation. The woman's dark skin seemed to shimmer crimson in the faint crystal light, and her silvery-blonde hair reflected it like moonlight on water. She took an iron key from her pocket, and when she eased it into the cell's lock, it hummed quietly and pulsed orange.

Aldric backed away from the bars, but there was nowhere to go.

The Wardens entered the cell without a word.

Lucaniel grabbed him by the collar, and Maelissa pinned his arms back. Aldric shouted once, but it was muffled instantly as the gag was forced into place, strapped tight around his head. The moment the final buckle snapped, the crypt went still again.

Zalith didn't look back. He resumed walking, matching Alucard's pace as they moved towards the end of the Withercrypt, leaving the sound of muffled, useless fury behind them like dust. But he could feel the *very* faint tenseness in his fiancé's grip. "Are you okay?" he asked quietly.

Alucard nodded, slowing as they approached the Detainer's cell.

The demon brought them to another halt, though. He placed his hands on Alucard's shoulders and gazed at him. There was a hint of dismay in his eyes, and Zalith hated that he understood why. He pulled his vampire into his embrace and rubbed his back with one hand. "Don't listen to that piece of shit," he said softly. "I never cared about any of that, and neither did any of my demons. You know that, right?" He'd never stop trying to assure him, no matter how many times he had to say it.

With a weak huff, Alucard nodded again. "I know. Is just…I can't pretend zoesn't bovver me vhen I 'ear zhem say zhat—just…veminds me of vings Zamien said."

He stroked his hand up the vampire's back and caressed his head, holding him tighter. "I'm sorry, baby," he murmured and kissed his forehead. "But none of that matters. Honestly, anyone still clinging to that cultish, archaic bullshit needs to grow up and catch up with reality. The gods don't give a fuck and haven't for centuries; there's no 'divine law' holding it together anymore. At this point, the only reason to keep following it is pure, stubborn bigotry."

Alucard leaned into him, nuzzling the side of his face. "Vhat are you going to do about 'im?"

Zalith thought about it, watching as the Warden vampires locked Aldric's cell and left the Withercrypt in silence. He didn't want Aldric rejoining the pack and spreading hatred, but killing him wasn't a good idea right now; it wouldn't send the type of message he wanted to send. There *were* options, though. "Did you happen to come up with a word for the demon version of Veiled?"

"Exactly like Veiled?"

"Well…with the punishment either being exile or demotion, execution in extreme cases," he explained.

Alucard didn't answer right away—maybe he was thinking. He inhaled quietly, and it sent a shiver down Zalith's spine, urging the desire within him to break the little control he had over it.

"Scourged?" the vampire then suggested.

Zalith smiled and said, "Scourged it is. That's what we do with Aldric."

"So...you vill need a council?"

He laughed a little. "Yeah. It'll probably be a good idea to take a page out of your book and form a personal council *and* one like your Vampire Council."

"Vell, zhat actually veminds me zhat I need to come up vith a new name vor my personal council so is easier to tell zhem apart vrom zhe actual Vampire Council."

Zalith smiled, stroking his fingers through the vampire's hair. He knew that they were supposed to be interrogating the Detainer, but he couldn't help but indulge his love for both Alucard's creative mind and his captivating voice. "Any ideas?"

"Hmm...vell, my personal council alvays kept anyving ve spoke about betveen me and zhemselves unless told ozzervise, so...I guess...Silent Vite could vork."

The demon hummed and said, "I like how dark that sounds. *Very* mysterious."

His fiancé laughed a little. "I'll call zhem Vitekeepers singularly."

"Even *more* mysterious," he teased him.

"I just 'ave to choose new members. I'll do zhat later, zhough. *Your* council...vhat about zhe Zenith's Delegation? You could call each member a Delegate or Zenith's Delegate," he suggested with a pondering tone.

"I like that."

"And someving like zhe Vampire Council...maybe just someving simple, too...like zhe Zemon Crucible."

He tightened his embrace around him. "That's perfect. Thank you."

"You're velcome," he murmured, smiling against his cheek.

Zalith then leaned back and kissed his lips. He felt the desire creeping in again, and it was *so strong*, urging him to pin Alucard against the wall—maybe he could fuck him here...or even in one of the cells. But he had to resist...as hard as it was, and as hard as he could feel himself quickly becoming.

He took his fiancé's hand and turned around, walking towards the Detainer's cell. "Let's find out what this man knows."

"Should I get zhe veinburrow spiders?" Alucard asked.

"Keep them on standby," he said, taking the key from his pocket.

When Zalith opened the cell door, the Detainer lifted his head with a low, weary grunt. He was strapped tightly to the steel chair, his body slumped but still conscious. Blood had dried in thick, dark crusts around the raw wounds that Allie had left behind; just as instructed, she'd torn the armour from him piece by piece, stripping away skin and muscle in the process. The black-painted metal lay discarded in the corner, twisted and glinting, half-submerged in a dark puddle that hadn't yet dried.

"I'd offer you a choice between the easy way and the hard way, but we both know how this ends," Zalith said, releasing Alucard's hand and stepping forward. "And I'm not about to waste the opportunity to make you suffer for what you did to those children," he snarled, and then he crashed his fist into the side of the man's face. Bone crunched beneath the blow, and a spray of blood, teeth, and spit hit the stone floor.

The man grunted and muttered, *"De sou... léo típota, ánte gamísou!"*

With an aggravated snarl, Zalith hit him again and then backed off a little, turning his head to look at Alucard. "What's he saying?"

The vampire shook his head. "I zon't know. I vink 'e's speaking Avheek. I zon't know enough to translate."

Zalith huffed irritably and grabbed the man's face—

"Zhey all take anti-ethos elixirs," Alucard told him.

That just aggravated him more. He let go of the man's face and instead gripped his jaw. The Detainer tried to fight and yell, but Zalith opened his mouth and searched for signs that he'd recently drank an elixir, but there was no blue staining on his tongue or teeth. He let go and tore the sleeve of the man's shirt away, revealing his arm, and then he did the same with the other. When he saw the needle track marks on the Detainer's skin, he let go and backed off again.

"Ve can bleed zhat out of 'im," Alucard said.

"Ti les?" the man blurted. *"Ti ennoeís?!"*

Zalith snarled angrily and smashed his fist against the man's jaw, breaking it with a loud *crack*.

The man yelped and started groaning painfully.

"Do you have the equipment to do that here?" the demon asked his fiancé.

"Virelka 'as everyving," he said with a nod. "Vill take at least vhree hours, zhough."

"We have other things that need doing, right? We can kill some time that way."

"Ve can talk to Corven-'ale about Camilla. Maybe I can start looking vor Lilly, too."

With a nod, Zalith took his hand and began leading the way. As much as he wanted the answers so that he could stop the Detainers and whoever they were working for from harming any more children, he knew that there was nothing he could do other than wait. The answers would come soon, and in the meantime, he hoped that he could help Alucard bring an end to the last of his work in Rhenovaalis.

| **Alucard** |
| *Atheson, Atheson Coven Sanctum* |

That odd feeling of fatigue was coming back. Alucard could feel it slowly tightening around him like a serpent strangling the life from its prey.

He did his best to ignore it. If he paid it no mind, maybe it would ease up, maybe his body would burn it away just as it had been since he'd entered heat. But he couldn't let either feeling consume him right now. He needed to find Camilla, and he had to get to Lilly before she was discovered.

Corven-Hale opened his door when Alucard knocked. "Oh, good morning, My Lord," he said with a bow, and then he stood upright, fiddling with his moustache. "Is everything okay?" His eyes flicked to Zalith for a moment.

"You vitnessed a lot of Eyra's interactions with Camilla and zhe ozzers," he started, watching as Corven-Hale's eyes darkened with dismay. "Is zhere anyving you 'eard zhat might give even zhe smallest 'int as to vhere Camilla might 'ave gone?"

The Knight shook his head. "There was nothing like that, My Lord. She was just gone when Lysandra was."

"*Anyving*," Alucard insisted. "Maybe she spoke to zhe ozzers about vhere she came vrom or places she vanted to go—maybe she spoke about vamily or vriends."

He frowned, the expression thickening with each passing second. "It's…hard to recall anything but the abuse, My Lord. I—"

"I can help," Zalith interjected, shifting his gaze to Alucard. "If you're okay with that."

"My viancé can look into your mind and try to 'elp you vemember, but only vith your permission," Alucard said.

Corven-Hale didn't hesitate. "Of course," he said, stepping aside and inviting them into his gloomy room.

They walked to the couch, where Alucard made Zalith sit, and Corven-Hale sat beside him. Alucard sat on the arm beside the demon and observed.

"You don't have to do anything," Zalith told the Knight.

Corven-Hale nodded.

"Just velax," Alucard told him.

He nodded again.

Zalith placed his fingers on the side of Corven-Hale's face.

The Knight grunted in response, and he closed his eyes, the other side of his face twitching slightly.

"Should I start from the beginning?" Zalith asked.

"Yes," Alucard said with a nod.

"Do you want to see, too?"

He immediately shook his head and said, "No." He exhaled deeply. "Vill make me vink of Zamien."

"Okay," his mate said softly, brushing his free hand over his. "He first saw the five women when Eyra took him and Salvorn to her room, just over three months ago. He was surprised to see them, and he planned to immediately inform you, but Eyra ordered him and Salvorn never to speak of it." He paused and looked back at Alucard. "Eyra didn't exactly look shocked or anxious. Maybe she wanted someone to share her little secret with."

"Is possible," he mumbled. "Did 'e make attempts to tell me? Coven Masters can compel ozzers vith orders, but zhere are vays to get past zhat—zhough zhey're not videly known vor obvious veasons."

Zalith faced Corven-Hale again. "Hmm…he attempted a letter, but when he tried to write anything that would implicate Eyra, his hand started burning."

Alucard huffed. "Okay. You can keep going."

The demon nodded. "Eyra was sleeping with both of them, but after they witnessed how she was treating the women, they tried to pull away from her. Eyra didn't take that very well, of course, and threatened to hurt the women more if either Salvorn or Corven-Hale, as she put it, abandoned her."

With a deep sigh, Alucard leaned back, resting against the wall.

"Salvorn was distant, but Corven-Hale started spending time around the women; he seemed worried for them."

"Zhat vas vhen 'e got closer to zhem."

"Yeah—mostly Camilla and Lilly. He didn't interact with them much at first, but he did hear some of the things they'd mumble while they were still learning to speak." He paused for a moment. "He learned a lot about Lilly, but not so much about Camilla. Should I just focus on Camilla?"

Alucard thought about it for a moment. He *did* want to know more about Lilly in case he ended up needing the information for when he went looking for her, too. "Vhat did 'e learn about Lilly?"

"Small things at first," Zalith murmured, narrowing his eyes. "Bits of memory that surfaced while she was still trying to understand herself. Her accent, for one—he noticed it wasn't local—he thought it was older, maybe northern coast." He paused again. "She had a sister; she'd mention her sometimes, not by name but through broken phrases, saying that she'd be worried or that she used to sing when Lilly cried. There was grief behind it, and guilt. Corven-Hale assumed the sister was still human."

Alucard's brow furrowed slightly. Could the sister be connected?

"She loved peaches; she mentioned them more than once, saying that she used to buy them from an old man with a crooked cart and stained gloves, same vendor every week, apparently. When Corven-Hale started speaking to her, she'd mention it all the time. He brought her peaches from that guy a few times to try and help her." The demon paused again and looked at Alucard. "I think Corven-Hale is half the reason Lilly found herself again. She seems to be the first who recovered."

The vampire nodded slowly. "Lysandra did say zhat Lilly 'ad a crush on 'im."

"It looks like he reciprocated that attraction," he said as he looked at the Knight again. "Lilly used to love romance novels; he overheard a title in her mumbles once, so he found a copy and started reading to her. She loved the sound of rain, so he took her out onto one of the balconies at one point and let her experience rainfall again. But Corven-Hale suspected Eyra saw that because the next day, she started treating Lilly worse than the others."

Alucard didn't want to hear specifics about the abuse. He'd lived centuries through it. "Is zhere any veason 'e specivically chose Antamont?"

Zalith didn't immediately answer—he was clearly searching. "He knew there was a vampire who could help keep her safe; he's been living undiscovered there for a little under three decades."

"Zhe Strayblood, vight?"

"Yeah. His name is Emilien Vautrin. He was a tailor here in the city twenty-six years ago."

Alucard sighed. "Anozzer turned vithout my knowing?"

"Unfortunately," Zalith confirmed. "Maybe Eyra's defiance rubbed off on other coven members. But it appears that it was an accident. Emilien was Corven-Hale's personal tailor. Corven-Hale went to pick up an order one evening but didn't know that his Votary was following him."

"Vheremond. 'E vas an eager student."

Zalith nodded. "He thought that Corven-Hale and Emilien's little friendly hug and handshake were an attempt on Corven-Hale's life. He attacked Emilien, Corven-Hale had to stop him, and the only way to save Emilien was to turn him. Emilien didn't want to join the coven, so Corven-Hale helped him get to Antamont. They reconnected maybe ten or so years ago, and Corven-Hale trusted him to take care of Lilly."

Alucard dragged a hand over his face. "I vonder 'ow many more people 'ave been turned vithout my knowledge."

"Corven-Hale doesn't know of any."

"Zhere are many ozzers who could." He huffed and said, "Zhat's not zhe point of zhis, anyvay. Vhat about Camilla?"

Zalith nodded and focused. "She was harder to read. Corven-Hale didn't get close to her like he did Lilly, but he still overheard things. Camilla spoke less in the beginning, more muttering than talking. The first word she repeated often was 'why.' Not in a confused way or out of fear, it was more like bitterness, like everything about her new existence offended her." He tilted his head slightly, eyes distant as he continued to sift. "She would say strange things sometimes, like 'I was meant to be married by now,' or 'She said I'd be in silk, not this.' Things that didn't make sense to Corven-Hale but sounded like echoes of some old, stolen life. She wasn't trying to remember; it was more like the pieces were forcing their way back."

Alucard remained quiet, brows slightly drawn.

The demon's gaze narrowed. "She mentioned someone…called Thaleus, but only once—maybe it was *something* rather than someone. Corven-Hale couldn't tell. But she said that she hoped Thaleus would still be as beautiful as she remembered when Hell let her leave. Then she went silent for a week after that." He looked at Alucard again. "Does Thaleus mean anything to you?"

He thought about it. "I zon't vink so, but I can ask Alson to look zhe vord up."

Zalith rolled his eyes. "I'm sure he'll be thrilled to help you out."

Alucard scoffed amusedly. "Zon't vorry about 'im."

"I'm not worried, he's just annoying and ugly."

Shaking his head, Alucard flicked Zalith's shoulder. "Keep looking."

"Yes, sir," he said with an amused smile.

Alucard then quickly sent Alson a telepathic order, telling him to look up Thaleus and find out whether it's a place or not.

"Camilla talked to the others sometimes," Zalith continued. "Nothing sweet, more like quiet alliances. She asked Dorothee if she remembered what her house smelled like, asked Hanna if she still believed in anything, and told Lysandra that her eyes were too kind, and it would get her killed. She said to Lilly: 'You'll break before you bend, and that's going to be a problem.' She was angry, but she wasn't loud or reckless about it. She kept it controlled. Everything about her felt like it was trying not to boil over." He glanced towards Alucard again. "And she hated Eyra. That much Corven-Hale could feel."

"Did 'e catch anyving about 'er desire to leave?"

Zalith concentrated again, shifting his gaze to Corven-Hale. "They all started whispering about wanting to leave, and they'd come up with little plans here and there. It was mostly Lilly, and Corven-Hale suspected that it played a part in Eyra's increased cruelty towards her, too. Camilla suggested looking for *you*."

He sighed deeply as guilt flooded in. They were only Fledgelings, so they had no idea how to contact him. "Maybe zhat's vhere she is—out zhere…looking vor me still."

The demon squeezed his hand and said, "This isn't your fault, baby. You trusted Eyra, and she shit all over that. You had no reason to suspect that any Coven Master would go rogue."

Alucard nodded stiffly, but despite Zalith's words being fact, he still felt like he could have done something. What if Camilla had been searching for him and had died while doing so? "Is zhere anyving else?" he mumbled, trying to focus on the task.

Zalith hummed quietly, pondering. "It looks like the other Knight couldn't handle it all as well as Corven-Hale did. He decided just a month after getting involved that he'd rather stay dead if he were to die."

"Vhessaly did tell me zhat Salvorn changed 'is death vishes," he said with a deep exhale. "All makes sense now."

"That's everything," Zalith said and let go of Corven-Hale.

The moment his mind was freed, Corven-Hale gasped for air and flinched back, his eyes wide, his fangs bared.

"You're vine," Alucard told him with an assuring tone.

Corven-Hale still looked wildly confused, but after a few panting breaths, he nodded and calmed down. "W-was there anything helpful, My Lord?"

Alucard stood up with Zalith and said, "*Da*, zhere vas. *Multumesc*."

The Knight's expression quickly became a relieved one. "Do you know where to look for Camilla?"

"Maybe," he said, but then he frowned. "Vhy zidn't you tell me about Emilien?"

Corven-Hale bowed his head shamefully. "I apologize, My Lord," he said, sounding both nervous and ashamed. "Theremond was a good Votary; he made an honest mistake, and I take full responsibility. He was only trying to protect me. I didn't want that to affect his learning and coven rank."

"You should 'ave told me zhis tventy-six years ago, Corven-'ale."

"I know, My Lord. I'm very sorry, and I won't make excuses for myself. I did not know better back then; I now realize that I wasn't ready for the position that I was given, and—"

"You're going to vind out if anyvone else 'as turned somevone vithout my knowledge, dating back to vhen zhis coven vas virst vormed. Ask *everyvone*. Vrite down your vindings, even if you discover zhat no vone else 'as turned somevone. Understand?"

"Y-yes, My Lord. I'll start right away."

"Tell me zhe exact location of zhe crypt vhere Lilly and Emilien are."

"It's a village in Græsholde called Vardeskov. The cemetery is next to the forest; some of it spreads past the tree line. Emilien's crypt is partly buried in earth and grass; it was abandoned a long time ago. It's warded to keep people away, but it's not very strong—the seer he hired wasn't very skilled, but he was all Emilien could afford. It won't work on you, My Lord, but you'll be able to see it, right?"

"I vill. Anyving else?"

He shook his head. "That's all."

Alucard nodded and headed for the door. "Ve'll vind out vrom Eyra if she turned anyvone else bevore zhose vour vomen."

"Now?"

He contemplated for a moment. Lilly was in Antamont, and he needed to get to her before she was discovered—he didn't want to risk that happening even if Corven-Hale thought it was unlikely. They may or may not have a lead on Camilla; there was nothing else to do but wait and see if Alson turned anything up. And the demons he'd sent to retrieve the families of the stolen children weren't yet back.

So… Antamont or Eyra?

"Eyra isn't going anyvhere. Ve need to vind Lilly."

Zalith nodded as they left Corven-Hale's room. "Lead the way."

Chapter Forty-Nine

— ⟨ † ⟩ —

Emilien and Lilly

| Alucard |

| *Rhenovaalis, Antamont, Græsholde, Vardeskov Cemetery* |

Vardeskov was shrouded in gloom despite the rising sun. The shadows of the trees seemed to stretch intentionally to keep the still village hidden. Alucard heard no sound behind him as he and Zalith moved further away, their eyes focused on the abandoned cemetery. If he couldn't feel the human auras, it would be easy to mistake that place as long forgotten, too.

The grass beneath their boots had withered in the dark, crunching and breaking like it was covered in frost. It smelled like sweet flowers and damp earth, a cold breeze spreading the scent of the sycamore maple trees through the miserable atmosphere, almost as if it were attempting to give the place something to hope for.

Alucard didn't like it at all. This place…it made him feel uneasy, reminding him of the aftermath of war—silent, locked in despair. But there was no war here, so why did Vardeskov suggest that its life had been drained away?

"Are you okay?" Zalith asked quietly as they approached the cemetery gates.

He nodded. "Is just kind of creepy 'ere."

"I was thinking the same thing," the demon said with a chuckle. "And that it vaguely reminds me of the one in Atheson."

"Vell, at least zhere aren't any loup-garou and undead valking avound."

"Yet."

Alucard smiled amusedly as he pulled open the crooked iron gate, its rusted hinges groaning low beneath his touch. The shadows beyond were thick, knotted branches overhead blotting out any attempt at light breaking through. He tightened his grip on Zalith's hand and stepped forward, eyes narrowing as he followed the sunken stone path.

He focused, searching for the aura of a ward, and it didn't take long to find. "Zhis vay," he murmured, guiding Zalith to the right and across a patch of brittle, dead grass.

They slipped between two crumbling crypts, the path narrowing. Fallen statues watched their passage with hollow, moss-laced eyes, and the trees beyond loomed like guards, limbs outstretched, casting murkiness that refused to move with the cold, biting wind.

"Zhis Strayblood ve're looking vor 'as zhe same name as vone of zhe Veylin Pack's Betas," Alucard said quietly.

Zalith nodded and said, "Well, at least they won't be around each other to get confused."

"Ve're going to be dealing vith zhat sort of ving *a lot* soon—your Legion is growing vast."

"Well, we have all those new ranks to help with the confusion, I suppose."

That was a good point. "Zhat's true."

They went quiet again, the rustling of leaves very faint upon a whistling breeze.

Beyond the tree line, the vampire and demon crossed a fenced plot where long-dead flowers lay shrivelled beneath a thin layer of ash-dusted soil. And then Alucard saw it: the half-sunken crypt nestled against a slope, its presence all but consumed by the surrounding dark. The ward around it pulsed faintly, weak and unstable, carelessly applied. Symbols had been scrawled onto the trunks of three leaning trees, their glow dulled but still visible, threadbare traces of ethos that barely held. The seer that Emilien had hired hadn't even tried to mask the hum of it, nor the low flicker of light beneath the runes.

Twenty-six years, and somehow, the Strayblood inside had remained hidden. It was pure, impossible luck.

"Are you sure he's even alive in there? Anyone could have seen this ward," Zalith said as they neared the entrance.

"If Corven-'ale said 'e is, zhen 'e must be."

He crouched, still holding the demon's hand tightly as he eased in through the sunken doorway, and Zalith followed. The hardened soil inside dipped down, leading deeper into the crypt, eventually breaking away to reveal limestone steps.

They could stand now, the ceiling getting higher with each step they took. But that was when the smell of human blood hit. Evidently, all that ward was doing was hiding scent, but its range didn't reach far at all.

The deeper Alucard descended, though, the narrower the passage became, and the dirt and moss covering the bricks began fading. Blood, darkness, and the type of cold that oozed into his skin and made it feel like ice was flooding his veins. Old bricks, crumbling and cracked—they were even the same shade of brown.

Alucard stopped, his body tensing, his heart racing. This time, it wasn't a memory that came flooding back. It was only the fear, and his instincts urged him to turn back. But he couldn't, nor did he want to. He needed to find Lilly and right Eyra's wrong. And letting the fear of tunnels and catacombs rule him forever wasn't something he was willing to do. He didn't need to worry about the Diabolus or where he'd been raised anymore. All of that was over and gone. There weren't any cultists waiting at the bottom of these stairs.

"Hey?" came Zalith's voice.

The vampire snapped out of it, looking over his shoulder at his mate, who was squeezing his hand a little firmer.

"Do you need to turn back?"

He exhaled deeply. "No, I'm okay."

"Are you sure?"

Alucard nodded, and then he continued, his steps lighter but unhesitating.

The staircase stretched on for nearly a minute, descending into a wide, dust-choked chamber. Two coffins rested within, one on either side, shrouded in layers of moss and fine cobwebs. But these weren't vampire resting places. He could smell the decay of ancient human corpses within, a century old at least.

At the far end of the room, a rusted doorway stood open, its iron bars hanging by a single hinge that groaned faintly in the still air. Alucard moved towards it, extending his senses, searching for the presence of the two vampires reportedly sheltering here.

But the next chamber held no signs of reborn life, only death.

Several human corpses were scattered across the room, some barely more than husks, others bloated and half-drained, each older than the last, as if used and discarded over time. A pattern emerged, though—intentional, methodical; it looked like a Fledgeling had been feeding under instruction, practising.

That had to be Lilly.

Alucard let his gaze drift slowly across the room as Zalith let go of his hand and crossed to the far side

The demon stopped beside the freshest corpse. "Maybe twelve hours old," he murmured, studying the body with a faint frown. "But something about it doesn't smell right."

He noticed it at the same moment. Each corpse bore the same sickly green veining beneath the skin, as if something unnatural had bloomed just under the surface. The air carried a faint, earthy scent, like moss and spoiled roots, threaded through the copper tang of old blood and the sweeter rot of decaying flesh.

Dread struck Alucard when realization did. He knew what to look for now, but the idea made him feel sick. It made him feel *awful*.

"What is it?" Zalith asked, rejoining him.

Instead of searching for vampire auras, Alucard scoured the space around them for *decaying* half-life, and his senses urged him into the next chamber. "Zhis vay," he said, taking Zalith's hand and heading for the closed door.

"What's that green shit on the bodies, Alucard?" the demon asked worriedly, pulling him away from the door.

"Is Virosis-Animara," he answered and pushed the door open. "'Umans get vhen zhey eat animals invected vith mycoriaspore."

"What's mycoriaspore?"

Alucard didn't answer, though—he stopped as soon as he stepped into the room. Huddled in the far-left corner were two vampires, both shivering and groaning, clinging to one another.

Lilly and Emilien.

"Wait," Zalith insisted—he kept hold of Alucard's hand and stood anchored by the doorway, stopping the vampire from getting any closer to them. "What's wrong with them?"

"I need to 'elp zhem, Zaliv," he urged, trying to pull free.

"What's wrong with them?" he repeated. "I don't want you getting sick."

"Zhey might 'ave 'emal Dissonance; is vhat 'appens vhen vampires drvink invected blood—is not contagious."

Zalith looked hesitant. He didn't let go of Alucard's hand, but he *did* move with him when he hurried to Lilly and Emilien.

"Emilien?" Alucard asked as he crouched beside the shivering man and gently shook his arm.

The man groaned a little louder.

So did Lilly when Alucard nudged her, too.

With a huff, Alucard stood up. "Is a lot easier vhen zhere's just vone of zhem," he mumbled, stepping back.

"What do you mean? What's easier?" the demon questioned, sounding more worried by the second.

"Ve 'ave to separate zhem so I can cure zhem, but zhey're going to vight to stay togezzer. Zhe invection gives zhe 'ost zhis sort of...'ivemind Syndrome—zhey 'ave an instinct to move as vone."

Zalith nodded slowly, setting his eyes back on Lilly and Emilien. "And how do you cure them?"

"My blood."

The demon sighed deeply. "Do they have to bite you?"

"No, zhey just 'ave to drvink."

His hesitance clearly grew, but he gave a stiff nod.

Alucard rolled up his sleeve—

"Just...wait," Zalith insisted as he gently snatched Alucard's wrist.

He watched as his mate reached into his vault with his free hand and pulled out a wine glass with a dragon-carved stem.

"Use this," the demon said, handing it to him.

Alucard took it and admired it for a moment. "Vhat's zhis?"

"It's just part of one of my mother's sets," he said, and he sounded sad.

The vampire smiled and said, "Is veally beautivul."

A small smile banished a fraction of Zalith's despondent stare. "Yeah, it is."

"I vill take care of zhis," he assured him.

And then he looked down at Lilly and Emilien. They were still trembling and groaning painfully, holding onto one another harder than before—their nails were digging into one another's skin. He knew that it was going to be hard to separate them and *keep* them separated, and it would be much more difficult to feed his blood to one of them while the other was still infected. But he had Zalith to help him. *That* would hopefully make it easier.

"You need to 'old zhis," he said, giving the glass back to Zalith.

Zalith held it, waiting, shifting his concerned gaze from Alucard to the vampires and back to Alucard again. "What if they attack you, Alucard?" he asked. "What if they *hurt* you?"

"I 'ave you to 'elp me," he tried to assure him as he held his wrist over the glass and then used his claws to cut it. He took a glimpse at Lilly and Emilien, but neither reacted— he knew what that meant, too. "Looks like zhey're only in zhe virst stage, so zhey von't need much."

"How do you know?"

"Zhey're 'iding avay. Zhe invection makes sure zhat zhey stay somevhere dark and safe vhile spreads."

The demon grimaced a little.

Once the glass was filled an inch, Alucard wrapped his hand around his wrist and waited for the cut to heal. Then, he took the glass and placed it on a ledge near the infected vampires. "Ve 'ave to grab zhem at zhe same time and pull zhem avay vrom each ozzer. Vonce I give Emilien zhe blood, 'e'll pass out a vew seconds later. Zhen I can give to Lilly."

"All right," Zalith said with a nod.

Alucard crouched by Emilien, and Zalith by Lilly. The vampire steadied his breath and gave Zalith a sharp nod, and then they moved at once.

The moment they seized them, both Emilien and Lilly let out piercing, inhuman screeches that echoed through the stone chamber like iron dragged against glass. They thrashed violently, their limbs jerking in uncoordinated spasms as they fought to stay together—hands reaching, clawing at empty air, blood-flecked teeth bared.

Alucard gritted his jaw, wrapping his arms around Emilien's chest and hauling him back. The force of it wasn't difficult; he could've thrown Emilien across the room if he'd wanted to, but he didn't. He didn't want to hurt him. He shifted his grip, twisted Emilien's arms behind his back, and pressed him hard against the wall.

"Calm down," he hissed under his breath, more to himself than the infected vampire.

Emilien snarled and snapped at the air, his crimson eyes wild, glowing faintly with a sick, fungal green.

Alucard reached for the wine glass with one hand, grabbed it from the ledge, and quickly tipped it towards Emilien's lips. It took a few moments—he had to wait until the man widened his jaw to screech, and then he poured the blood in. The moment it touched his tongue, Emilien choked and gagged; his body jerked one last time…and then he sagged in Alucard's arms, the tension draining all at once. The man's breathing slowed, his eyes gradually shut, and he was finally unconscious.

On the other side of the chamber, Lilly shrieked louder, her voice high and shattering, like a beast whose tether had been violently severed. She fought Zalith like her limbs weren't even her own, but the demon held firm, arms locked around her, his strength unshakable.

Alucard carefully laid Emilien down, and then he grabbed the glass again, what little was left sloshing in the bottom as he crossed the chamber and joined Zalith. With the demon holding her still, Alucard pressed the rim of the glass to Lilly's lips.

Her head jerked, but she drank—reflexively at first, but then greedily, like something inside her recognized what it was.

Moments later, her body stilled, and she, too, slumped into unconsciousness.

Zalith lowered her to the floor. "Is that it?" he asked, wiping his hands on his trousers.

Alucard nodded, glancing back at Emilien as he gave Zalith the wine glass back. "Zhey'll be asleep vor a vew hours. I 'ave a coven 'ere in Antamont; I can get some of zhem over 'ere to 'elp. Zhey can take zhem to zhe Sanctum, and vhile ve vait vor zhem to vake up, ve can probably go and talk to Eyra back in Aveson."

"Are they going to be okay at this other Sanctum?" he asked, sending the glass back to his vault.

"Zhey vill. Vould likely be a problem if eizer of zhem vere Severed, but zhey're not. And zhey'll be contained, too," he explained as he sent a telepathic message to Eske, the Antamont Coven Master.

Zalith took hold of his hand and pulled him closer, taking a wary glance at the unconscious vampires. "What about the infection? It could spread from wherever they picked it up."

"Zhat's—"

An izuret suddenly appeared in a cloud of yellow smoke, and it immediately told Alucard that Inquisitor Sanchia had arrived at the Atheson Coven Sanctum with Praeservare Adelaide.

Alucard nodded and waved his hand dismissively. "*Multumesc.*"

With a nod, the creature disappeared.

"Anyvay…zhe invection. Zhat's probably vhy zhat village back zhere vas so quiet. Zhey're probably eizer all dead or dying. Ve can make sure vonce 'elp gets 'ere, and if zhey *are* invected, I'll burn zhe whole place down. I'll also get somevone to investigate 'ow zhe mycoriaspore grew in zhe virst place."

The demon nodded. "You still didn't tell me what mycoriaspore is."

"Is a sort of vungus zhat grows on vegetation exposed to dark ethos, usually zhe kind levt be'ind by unstable necromancy or unsuccessvul blood vituals."

"Maybe the same seer who made that pathetic ward caused it."

"Is possible. I can ask Emilien vor 'is details vhen 'e vakes up."

"Okay," he said, and then he pulled Alucard into his embrace.

Alucard eased into the demon's arms, letting the tension drain from his limbs. For now, he allowed himself the quiet comfort of Zalith's warmth—the steady rise and fall of his chest, and his enthralling scent. Eske would arrive soon enough, but until then, he'd cling to these brief moments of stillness…and try to ignore the way his instincts clawed just beneath his skin, urging him to want more.

Chapter Fifty

— ⸲ † ⸱ —

New Instructions

| **Tyrus** |
| *Rhenovaalis, Atheson, Atheson Coven Sanctum* |

So many things hit Tyrus at once. The second he woke, the dull throb in his head made him groan, and the confusion made him feel dizzy for a moment. He hadn't forgotten what happened, though—he knew why he'd passed out, and as he opened his eyes, the thought of it made him scowl. He was aggravated because he couldn't escape the fact that he thought Nymeris was hot for doing it, but he was also annoyed because she shouldn't really be knocking out her superior.

He sighed, slowly sitting up, and he pulled the blanket that had been placed over him away so that he could examine his wounds. As he lifted the bandages, he saw fading scars, and the lingering ache was gone. His first relieved thought was that he could join the mission to take down the Detainer compound, but only seconds later did he realize that it was over. He could feel the auras of not only his fellow demons in the Sanctum but those of many non-human children, too.

He'd slept through the entire thing, hadn't he? Sunlight was creeping in through the curtains, so he'd evidently been asleep for the rest of the early morning.

The door opened a few minutes later, and Nymeris walked in holding two cups of coffee. As soon as she saw him, their gazes locked, and she stopped in her tracks, her eyes widening. He was surprised to see her—he was surprised by her a lot lately.

"Oh…um…I brought you some coffee," she said, a hint of nervousness in her voice.

"To wire me up before you knock me out again?" he asked with an irritated but amused scoff.

"You gave me no choice, Tyrus," she said with a shrug as she walked over to him and placed the cups on the table. "I had to make sure that you got enough rest. Your body needed to heal. Going into battle was the last thing you should've been doing."

"I know, but you didn't have to do that."

"You weren't going to listen to me. I know what you're like."

He sighed and said, "Well, warn me first at least." He watched her sit beside him. "Don't think you can get your way all the time by doing this, either," he added firmly.

Nymeris frowned—she looked both guilty and anxious—and turned away, staring down at the coffee. "I'm sorry. I made a bad call."

Tyrus picked up one of the cups and took a sip. "Blackbird and Flint?" he asked in an attempt to change the subject. He didn't want her beating herself up about it; she *had* done it for his own good, after all.

She nodded and said, "I remember you ordering it a few times when we had time for breaks here and there out in the field."

"Thank you," he said and took another sip. "How did the mission go?"

Nymeris sat up straight and picked up the other cup. "Well, we got all of the kids out of there, but we lost Eren and Danrel—I'm sorry," she said sadly.

That made him feel even worse about not being there. If he had been, then he could have helped. But he wasn't, and two demons he'd known for decades were dead. "Have their families been notified yet?"

She nodded. "We've handled all of that, don't worry. Belle's gone back to Eimwood to be with her mother."

Tyrus looked down at his cup, his grip tightening just slightly. He didn't want to let the melancholy devour him *or* Nymeris. "Do you…remember Danrel used to bring those terrible biscuits to briefings? He'd say they were a 'family recipe.' I don't think any of us ever finished one." Reminiscing had always helped them cope with loss in Eltaria; maybe it would help now, too.

Nymeris gave a small, sad smile. "He knew. He just liked having something to share."

He huffed quietly, but there was no humour in it. "And Eren never shut up about wanting to retire somewhere warm. He said he was going to open a damn fruit stall."

"He talked about it right up until the week before we left Eltaria." Nymeris glanced at the wall, her expression distant. "He even had a name picked out. Something cheesy. Sun-something."

"Sunbloom."

"Yeah, Sunbloom."

"Maybe Belle will still do it. I know they talked about partnering up a few times."

"Maybe," she murmured.

A silence settled between them, heavy but not uncomfortable.

After a few moments, Tyrus asked, "Did they go quickly?"

Nymeris didn't answer right away. "Eren…well, he set off a ward-mine, so it was instant for him." She hesitated. "Danrel was shot first, and the silver made him too slow to get out of the radius of a huge explosion."

He sighed deeply, shaking his head as the guilt grew heavier. "We need to figure out a way for our people to be resistant to silver."

"I don't think that's possible," she said despondently.

Tyrus laughed just a little. "Not with that attitude."

She shrugged and said, "I suppose there's a million books in that library. Maybe we should start looking."

"You get a head start and let me know what you find," he replied. He really wasn't one for reading, and if there *was* a way to resist silver in those books, Alucard would have found it, wouldn't he? He was vulnerable to silver, too—and it was *his* library.

Nymeris laughed softly, and then she sipped from her coffee. She put the cup down and traced the rim for a moment, a short silence stretching between them…before she turned her head to look at him again. "I was reading something earlier, actually…."

He leaned back, letting himself relax. "What were you reading?"

She exhaled sharply. "Don't make fun of me," she warned him.

Tyrus held his hands up, amused.

"After we talked about Crowell and Orin, I felt kinda…I don't know, unsettled. So I read one of those demonology books—more specifically about seir demons." She paused and shuffled around. "Does…he really eat people?"

He laughed again, longer this time. All the things he'd had to cover up for Orin at Zalith's behest came flooding back to him, and he fought off a grimace and the urge to cringe. And like he always did—like he always *had* to, he chuckled and lied, "Of course not."

She frowned, either confused or unconvinced—it was hard to tell. "Then how does he survive?"

Tyrus had to think fast. He shrugged and sipped from his coffee. "He's kind of a vegetarian, I suppose. He only eats animals."

"Raw?"

"Only when he's in a hurry."

Nymeris looked like she was pondering. "So he just…grabs a deer…and starts chewing on it?"

"Pretty much. Maybe he'll add some hot sauce if he's feeling adventurous."

She giggled in response.

Tyrus smiled as he took another sip of his coffee; he loved the way she giggled.

"I had a brief conversation with Alucard, too," she added.

"Oh?"

"He said that…before Year Zero, people used the word Arcana a lot instead of ethosical. I thought that maybe we can start using it again in situations where saying ethosical sounds weird and annoying," she said with an amused smile.

He nodded. "Yeah, I definitely like that more than ethosical."

"Then it's settled," she said firmly.

"I'll pass it on," he said with a chuckle.

Nymeris smiled in response, and once she finished her drink, she put the cup down and repositioned herself, crossing one leg and leaning her shoulder against the cushions. "I'm uh…going back to Eimwood once things have been wrapped up here—I mean, we *all* are. But I'm staying." She sounded disappointed. "I haven't been given a new assignment yet."

"Well, I'll still have a day or two in the city, so you can still come and meet Vesta. We might even have time to cook for each other."

Nymeris smiled shyly and nodded. "Yeah. We should probably make the most of it, huh? You'll be away a while again, won't you?"

He sighed deeply, gently swirling around what little remained of his coffee. "At least a few months, could be longer. I don't know how well Crowell works or if he'll even get on with me and Orin, but I suppose we'll find out."

She nodded, looking down at her lap for a moment. "Maybe we should…well…no, never mind."

"What?" he asked curiously.

"Nothing, I just…" she drawled and hesitated.

"You can tell me," he assured her.

She huffed and glanced at him, her shy expression having grown shyer. "Well, if you were comfortable with the idea—and it's totally okay if you're not, I won't be offended or anything—but I was thinking that…maybe we could check out one of those new restaurants. A few have been reopening since the bosses started helping fix the city up, and I've been meaning to try at least one, so we could go together or something," she murmured, twiddling her fingers.

Tyrus blinked. It wasn't a huge ask, not really, and yet it caught him completely off guard. Nymeris wasn't exactly timid, but she didn't usually offer things like this, not unless she meant them. And the way she said it—quiet, hesitant, like the idea had been sitting on her tongue for a while—hit him harder than he expected.

His first feeling was surprise, and then something warmer pushed in right behind it, a thought he'd let linger earlier, a thought that clashed with another. He wanted what this might be leading to—what a part of him *hoped* it was leading too—but the part of him that had grown used to prioritizing duty over social life still made him question whether what he felt was a simple desire for momentary comfort or the wish for something that lasted much longer.

Maybe she *did* feel the same way, or at least similarly.

He looked at her fingers, which were still fidgeting in her lap…and a flicker of an unfamiliar sensation stirred in his chest. Nervousness, maybe even anticipation. She wanted to spend time with him, not out of duty or convenience but because *she wanted to*, and with so little time left before they both scattered off to different corners of the world again, the idea of sharing something—*just one normal thing*—suddenly meant more than it probably should.

Tyrus smiled softly, setting his cup down on the low table in front of them. "Yeah," he said, his voice quiet but steady. "I'd really like that."

Her gaze lifted, and their eyes met for a moment that felt just a second too long.

"I mean, if we're both going to be stuck apart for a while," he added, trying to keep it light but honest, "it seems fair to stockpile a few good memories first."

Nymeris' smile grew. "There's a little family restaurant in Bauwell called The Verdant Table—it's on Oakenfire Street, that place with mostly Elven places. It serves these sort of Elven dishes but with a Nefastian twist. Laria says that the Wildroot Burgers are amazing, or the Elderflower Fried Chicken."

"Do they taste floral?"

"Actually, no," she said, shaking her head. "I think that's the Nefastian part. The food looks really pretty and smells very Elvish, but it actually tastes very much like what we used to eat in Nefastus."

"Good because I hate the way lavender tastes; I can only imagine what wildroot must taste like," he laughed. "But I'm more than willing to try."

"You know what *I* hate the taste of? Roses." She shook her head. "People say they taste like strawberries and green apples, but all I taste is soap."

He laughed and asked, "Who says that?"

"My sister, my mother, *her* mother—the family tree goes on."

Tyrus couldn't help but laugh again. "Well, maybe you should all get some type of scientific study done because roses do not taste like strawberries and green apples."

"They insist and insist—I gave up trying to convince them. I just avoid anything flowery, to be honest. I guess I'm just one of those people who think that flowers should be left for the animals and insects."

He went to reply, but before he could, someone knocked on the door. At first, he felt irritated because they were having a private moment, but they weren't, really, were they? So he calmly called, "Come in."

One of the vampires stepped into the room—Anselric or Edricus. Tyrus couldn't remember which of the twins had the beard.

"Lord Alucard and Zalith asked me to deliver this to you," the grey-haired man said as he walked over and held out a leather-bound book. "Zalith asked me to relay these instructions," he continued, giving Tyrus the book. "He said that you've been assigned a new rank; it used to be called Apex, but as of today, it has been renamed Sovereign. You'll be ruling over these Alphas and their covenants—covenant is the new name for pack. The Alphas are as follows: Nymeris, Asahel, Tavion, Selah, and Silvannus, whom Zalith has instructed to be promoted to Alpha of your current covenant. He has also requested that you assist your new Alphas in reorganizing their covenants following this new ranking system," he explained.

Tyrus wasn't surprised at all—he expected it. With the rate that Zalith's numbers were growing, it was inevitable that a new structure would form. He took the book and said, "Thank you."

The man nodded. "There's also breakfast in the Noctuary; you're free to help yourselves if and when you want."

"Thanks," Tyrus said again.

Then, the man left the room.

Nymeris laughed a little. "Well…I suppose I should start calling you Sovereign Tyrus now, huh?"

He smirked. "I like the sound of that. But no, you can call me Tyrus."

She smiled and leaned closer, looking at the information as he did. "That's a lot of new ranks," she said and flipped the page. "It's going to take a while to reorganize everyone." Then she frowned at him. "Do you think he expects you to have it done before you have to leave?"

As he skim-read the details, he said, "I think if he did, he would have most likely specified."

"Okay, good. I'm sure we're not the only ones who need a few days without any work."

"I think even Zalith and Alucard are going to be taking some downtime," he said, closing the book. "Anyway, do you want to go and get breakfast? I'm starving."

"Yeah, that sounds good."

Tyrus finished the last of his coffee, and then he stood up. "Maybe we can take a closer look at this while we eat," he said as he tapped the book with his knuckles.

Nymeris handed him a clean shirt and blazer. "They said you can use anything in here," she said, glancing around the room.

"Thanks," he said and pulled the shirt on. He took the blazer and held it over his arm, and then he followed her to the door.

Things in Atheson were coming to an end. He still felt the weight of guilt and sorrow for those who'd died here, but they hadn't died for nothing, and he'd try to hold onto that fact…and the comfort that being with Nymeris gave him.

Tyrus and Nymeris' story continues in the Numenverse Tether Story, THE KEEPER'S REALM.

Chapter Fifty-One

A Tale of Bieláňski and Woe

| **Alucard** |
| *Atheson, Atheson Coven Sanctum* |

Eyra stared up at Alucard from the cell floor, her crimson eyes rimmed red and glossy with tears. She'd been crying for a while now—he could tell by the streaks of ruined makeup trailing down her cheeks like ink bleeding through parchment. One eye still held the shape of a winged line, and the other was smudged so badly that it looked bruised.

Her hands trembled as she reached for the bars, fingertips streaked with black from where she'd rubbed at her face too many times. One of her earrings was missing, and a faint red mark curved beneath her lobe, like she'd tugged it free herself in a fit of panic or restless guilt. Her dress was torn along the hem and snagged at the shoulder; a piece of silver thread hung there, catching the flickering crystal light in dull flashes.

She hadn't noticed Inquisitor Sanchia lingering in the shadows, her red eyes glowing in the dark like fireflies, nor had she spotted Praeservare Adelaide, who waited not far from the stairs. The Veiled vampire just pleaded with Alucard again, words tumbling out between ragged breaths, the same desperate refrain she'd clung to for the last several minutes: that she hadn't done anything wrong, that she didn't understand why she was there.

Over and over and over.

But Alucard didn't move. He simply watched her, silent and cold, because it was painfully clear: she had no idea that he knew, no idea that he'd uncovered the truth about the women she'd turned.

"P-please, My Lord," she cried, shaking her head. "I'll never disobey you again. I made a mistake with the wolves, but now I know—I *understand*."

"*Do* you?" he snarled.

Eyra frowned. "I-I do, My Lord. The wolves are our allies, and—"

"I know about Lysandra, Camilla, Lilly, Dorovhee, and 'anna."

The dismayed expression on Eyra's face contorted into horror.

"I vill give you only vone chance to be 'onest vith me, Eyra," Alucard warned her firmly. "'Ave you or ozzer Vellkin turned anyvone else be'ind my back?"

She hesitated, looking down at her lap.

Her reaction made the answer pretty clear.

"Yes, My Lord," she mumbled nervously.

"Vhen, 'ow many, and vhy?"

Eyra took a deep breath. "I just wanted to help the coven, My Lord. The more of us there are, the safer we'll be. I—"

He shook his head and cut her off, "If zhat vere zhe case, you vouldn't be love-bombing zhem and 'iding zhem vrom me."

She turned her head again.

"Start by telling me 'ow many people 'ave been turned vithout my knowledge and vhere zhey are now," Alucard demanded.

After a deep exhale, Eyra looked up at him again. "What's going to happen to me, My Lord?"

"Tell me vhat I vant to know," he growled impatiently.

Her horrified expression grew. "I started turning humans myself seven years ago, My lord. I believe…thirty-five, including Lysandra, Lilly, Camilla, Hanna, and Dorothee. Nobody else has turned anyone."

Alucard sighed deeply and glanced at Inquisitor Sanchia, who stood silent and still like a form carved out of the Withercrypt's stone walls. The vampire's eyes then shifted to Zalith, who was leaning against the wall beside him. His mate was probably thinking the same thing: Eyra was a liability and had been for almost a decade; she couldn't remain in this coven or *any* coven, and leaving her to wander could be just as dangerous. He was almost certain of what the Vampire Council's decision would be once the Inquisitor returned to them with what she heard, and Alucard guiltlessly awaited it. There probably wouldn't even be a trial; her sentence may very well come immediately.

He set his eyes back on Eyra. "Vhere are zhey now?" he questioned.

"I…didn't keep track of them once they left the Sanctum, My Lord."

Another deep, irritated sigh escaped him. "Vere any of zhem killed in zhe city?"

She lowered her head in shame. "Yes, My—"

"'Ow many?"

Eyra huffed sharply, as if she were trying to hold back tears. "Twelve, My Lord."

He tensed a little, his anger rising. "Vecently?"

She shook her head. "Just…over the course of the last seven years."

Alucard dragged his hand over his face. He relaxed the slightest bit when Zalith's fingers entwined with his, and he let the demon's warmth soothe him. "You know as vell as *every ozzer vampire* zhat turning people vithout my knowledge is against zhe law—zhe law zhat I very clearly stated *several* times, zhe law zhat vas crveated to protect our kind and ensure our survival, especially in a time like zhis."

"I-I know, My Lord," she said shakily, crying again. "I'm sorry! Please just give me another chance—I'll prove that I can be trusted!"

He shook his head. "You've 'ad var too many chances, Eyra. I can't trust you, and I can't allow somevone I zon't trust to be avound my people."

The tears fell heavier, and she shuddered with a wince. "B-but…My Lord," she sniffled. "Just…I can explain!"

"You can explain to zhe Council. Zhey vill properly judge your crimes and carry out zheir chosen punishment."

"They'll kill me!" she cried, reaching out through the bars.

Alucard stepped back to avoid her grasping hands.

And Wardens Maelissa and Lucaniel stepped forward.

But Alucard held his hand towards them, ordering them to stay put at the other end of the Withercrypt, and then he set his eyes on Eyra again.

"Please," she sobbed, curling into a ball on the stone ground. "I didn't mean for any of this to happen. I was just…trying to find him again."

That was when Alucard's irritated, tired expression broke for a fleeting moment. "Vind who?"

Eyra closed her eyes, her tears washing away her makeup. "Mærek," she murmured, her voice barely a whisper but thick with pain.

Alucard waited for her to elaborate.

After a few moments of sniffling and trembling, Eyra opened her eyes again and stared aimlessly across the dark room. "My dear Mærek," she drawled, almost a hum. "We found each other…sixty-seven years ago—it was like…fate." She paused, her eyes closing again. "Destiny…like it is for werewolves, the other part of my soul just like it is for you—for demons. We just knew." A pause and a deep, shaky breath. "He travelled from the Mountains of Duskvale." She dragged a whimsical sigh. "Such a beautiful valley, Bieláňski. His family lived there for centuries. It was a sacred place, forbidden to outsiders, but he invited me in."

Although he was growing impatient, Alucard didn't stop her.

She scowled painfully, both fury and despair raging in her dimming eyes. "He was taken from me."

He frowned, listening.

"The Athene War of Independence," she said bitterly.

Zalith frowned and quietly asked Alucard, "Athene War?"

"Avhene vas under Sahranic vule since zhe mid vive 'undreds; Avheek people vere slaughtered, tortured, and enslaved in vetaliation vor vebellion on zhe Island of Kyoneía. Zhis drew 'uge outvage across Rhenovaalis."

"The Sahranic Dominion were *cowards*!" Eyra interrupted, crying still. "They had to call in Sulianh Voshed from Eshkunda because they couldn't hold their own against the rebellion!" she exclaimed as if citing from a history book. "Of course, Sulianh sent his pathetic excuse for a son and their armies, and Athene was devastated—Bieláňski Valley went with it." She sniffled, wiping her face with her dress.

Zalith sighed. "What does this have to do with you betraying Alucard?"

Eyra looked offended, but she didn't snap back. She lowered her head, taking a deep, trembling breath. "My darling Mærek joined the fight when the Deiganish, Boszorkian, and Ascelans came to help with their big army ships. They destroyed the Sahranic-Eshkundan fleet, and everything was working out *so well*. The Ripperton Protocol recognized Athene as an independent state, and then it was declared a Kingdom in nine seventeen." She scoffed, baring her fangs. "Good old Crown Heir Leontes of Brückenthal was made the first king, and everyone was so happy about it. But kings are greedy fuckers." She snarled. "Mærek and his family were restoring their valley—I'd go there every other week to help out and be with him. But I wasn't there when Leontes and his men stormed the place." Her scowl deepened, a conflicting storm of anger, despair, and sorrow smothering her wet, makeup-smeared face. "They wanted the rare metals that formed beneath the crystal rivers. They already knew that Mærek's family wouldn't sell, so they just…slaughtered them." She hissed through her teeth. "And they just…covered it up. Nobody knew what happened—nobody knew that Mærek and his family were up there, no one gave a shit! One of the war heroes they so passionately claimed to love and appreciate was killed over some fucking metal!" she screamed, and then she wailed, sobbing into her hands.

Alucard stifled a sigh and glanced at Zalith.

His mate gave him the same look.

Was this actually going anywhere? Was she trying to make them feel sorry for her in an attempt to have her imminent sentence postponed or cancelled altogether?

He exhaled deeply. "Eyra. Zhe point."

She frantically wiped her face, sniffling sharply. "I-I went to Bieláňski Valley. I tried to save him, but…it was too late." She hid her face in her hands for a few moments.

Alucard frowned irritably. "Did you turn 'im into a ghoul?"

Eyra shook her head. "It was too late even for that—n-not that I would. I know that's breaking the law, My Lord."

"Ghoul?" Zalith whispered.

"Vampire blood and venom can sometimes 'alv-turn a vecently-deceased 'uman, but turns zhem into zhis vabid, mindless monster."

The demon nodded once.

"But I just…I *knew*," she insisted, her voice becoming slightly higher. "I stayed by his body until midnight, and I buried him in our favourite spot. Even though he wasn't alive anymore, I could still feel his soul…like he'd waited for me to come. And once I buried him, I swear…I felt him leave. He passed on."

Alucard huffed quietly. He was quite sure that he knew where this was headed.

"He'd come back to me," Eyra insisted. "We're destined to be together in *every* life." She stood up, a determined expression sending her scowls and frowns running. "I waited two decades—a little longer than two, but I waited. And then I started looking. I *had* to."

"And zhat's vhy you started turning people."

Eyra nodded stiffly. "I searched Duskvale first. All of the villages and settlements." She exhaled deeply. "I felt a connection—I…I *thought* I felt that connection—"

"And you turned everyvone you velt a connection vith."

"Yes, My Lord. I didn't want to risk it happening again; I didn't want a repeat of Bielański. I thought that…if I immediately turned Mærek's reincarnation, he'd not only remember me faster, but we'd escape the risk of history repeating—b-but I asked to turn them; I didn't force the gift on anyone."

Alucard crossed his arms. "So vhat changed? Vhy Lysandra and Camilla and zhe ozzers?"

Eyra lowered her head again and slowly sank to the floor. "I became more and more impatient over the years, and that eventually turned into…well…I—"

"You became jealous, no?" he muttered. "Lysandra and Vosaline."

She sighed…and nodded. "I was witnessing love *everywhere*, but I was still hunting for my own. I know that it was wrong of me—selfish—and…I take responsibility."

"Vor vhat? Tell me vhat you did, Eyra. I need to 'ear you admit."

"Y-yes, My Lord," she mumbled, sounding hesitant. "I became…I *am* bitter and cruel. The first time I did it, I was in a cocktail bar in the city. I saw a couple, and they were *so* in love. They were engaged." She exhaled, shuffling around. "I *hated* it—I hated *them*. So I followed them when they left. I was stalking them at first, planning on killing them both, but my selfishness suggested something more satisfying, something that might help me escape the heartbreak for a while." Another huff, another shake of her head. "I turned the girl. I did it quickly, the wrong way. She became frenzied, and she killed him. When she came to moments later and saw what she'd done, she cut her own throat with his knife."

Alucard clenched his jaw and turned his head, both scowling and grimacing. It wasn't unlike a vampire to hunt humans regardless of whether they were married, engaged, parents, etcetera, but what Eyra did wasn't about the hunt or the need to feed. It had been about her desire to make others suffer. He didn't give a fuck about humans, but he *did* give a fuck about the kind of activity that could quickly spread and cause problems for a coven.

If Eyra was a Strayblood hunting in a city that wasn't host to a vampire coven, then what she'd done to that couple wouldn't matter. Straybloods could do as they pleased. But when she'd joined this coven, she'd taken a pledge *not* to do this sort of thing; she'd sworn to refrain from any hunting and searching for suffering and pain; she'd sworn to avoid doing *anything* that would implicate the coven. But she'd been risking every single vampire under her care for *years*. That couldn't be ignored.

"'Ow many people 'ave you done zhis to, Eyra?" he questioned angrily, setting his scowl back on her—and *that* was when he saw the guilt fading; it was only for a moment, but he noticed what very well looked like a mask Eyra was wearing. "'Ow many of zhe vhirty-vive people you turned vere couples?"

Complete guilt painted her face now. "Twenty-six."

His scowl grew thicker. "Eizer you are *very* bad at simple math, or you are lying to me, Eyra. Your numbers zon't add up."

She huffed, irritation cutting through her ashamed visage. "I don't know, My Lord. I'm sorry. A lot of it is a blur. I was so broken and focused on finding Mærek that I spent half my days trying to remember what happened yesterday and the day before."

He gripped a fistful of his hair, aggravation and frustration quickly devouring him, and this time, Zalith's attempt to comfort him by grasping his hand didn't help. "Zhe crimes just keep piling up, Eyra. Did you 'onestly not stop to vink just vor a moment about vhat might 'appen to zhe coven? To *you*? Vhat if you did vind Mærek, and zhen you vere caught? Vampires zon't veincarnate. You'd never see 'im again."

Eyra stared at him wide-eyed for a moment, like she was trying to understand what she'd just heard. And then she started crying *again*. "I'm never going to see him again anyway!" she wailed, digging her nails into her forehead. "I know what happens next, I know there's nothing I can do to save myself—maybe I don't even deserve to be saved. I just…wish that I could have at least *seen* him one last time. He's out there…and whether he knows it or not, he's *waiting* for me." She paused, sobbing, tears dripping through her fingers. "But he'll never find me."

Alucard sighed heavily. He didn't know what exactly he was feeling right now, but it definitely wasn't sympathy or sorrow. A tragic romance story wasn't going to influence his *or* the Inquisitor's decisions. In their centuries of work, he and the Vampire Council had heard many a woe-is-me tale, and this wasn't the first time he'd heard a vampire tell the story of reincarnation and meeting their human or mortal lover again.

Had he witnessed the phenomenon? Yes.

But was Eyra's way of going about it justified? No. Not at all. Not in this circumstance. If she wanted to search for her past lover, she could have very easily become a Strayblood. Of course, it would have been a first for a Coven Master to leave, but he'd understand.

She hadn't taken that path, though, and it was too late to go back.

Alucard looked at Zalith, and then his gaze moved to the lingering Inquisitor.

Sanchia gave a nod, letting him know that she'd received enough information to pass on to the Council.

He looked at Maelissa.

The Warden made her way over, pulling a vial from her pocket. She removed the cork and crouched by Eyra's cell door. "Wrist," she said.

Eyra scowled at her.

"Now," Alucard snarled.

The Veiled vampire huffed but held her arm through the bars.

Maelissa used a small blade to cut Eyra's wrist. She filled the vial with blood, pressed the cork into the top, and then pushed Eyra's arm back through the bars. After she gave the vial to Sanchia, she returned to her post beside Lucaniel.

Alucard's sights returned to the Inquisitor.

She held up six fingers, slipped the vial into her pocket, and then she left, heading upstairs in silence.

"Your trial vill be in six hours," Alucard told Eyra.

Eyra started breathing raggedly. "W-what? B-but, My Lord, I told you everything!"

"You did," he said tonelessly. "And you also told Inquisitor Sanchia. Your openness 'as granted you a trial instead of an immediate decision—if you *vere* given an immediate sentence, I vould 'ave executed you myselv."

Her eyes went wide, and despite her snow-white skin, she became paler.

"Your be'aviour endangered zhis coven. You could 'ave gotten *everyvone* killed. Zhere is no coming back vrom zhat. You 'ave six hours to vigure out just 'ow many people you turned and killed since Mærek's death—and zon't answer vith 'I zon't know'. Zhe Council are novhere near as patient as I am."

Eyra winced.

Alucard held his arm towards Praeservare Adelaide, who stepped closer. "Discuss your case vith Adelaide," he said to the Veiled vampire. "Zhe more cooperative you are, zhe better your chances of still existing avter zhis vill be."

Adelaide tucked her ash-blonde ringlets behind her ears as she stopped in front of Eyra's cell. "I have no doubt there is much for us to discuss. It is not my place to exonerate you, but rather to advocate on your behalf. Rest assured, I shall do everything in my power to see the Council hears and understands every detail and every reason," she said almost tonelessly, looking down at Eyra.

Alucard then turned around and took Zalith's hand. Ignoring Eyra's pleas, he headed for the stairs. He didn't want to see her or hear her voice anymore. She'd been nothing but an annoyance and danger, and he just wanted it all over with.

He sighed, climbing the steps as the demon followed behind him.

Zalith's hand slid down and gripped his ass, his touch lingering on the right side as he gave a teasing squeeze. "You're so hot when you get all bossy and serious," he murmured, his voice low and reverent against Alucard's skin as his hand dipped forward, fingertips brushing along the sensitive inside of his thigh.

The words, the touch...Alucard couldn't help the shiver that spiralled through him, sharp and warm like a spark igniting in his spine. He didn't try to resist it. Instead, he stopped halfway up the stairs, a quiet, content hum escaping him as Zalith pressed him gently but firmly against the wall. The chill of the bricks seeped through his clothes, searing against his chest and almost cruel against his cheek, but it only made the heat building beneath his skin burn hotter.

"And yet..." Zalith whispered, leaning into Alucard's ear as his fingertips lightly stroked his balls through the fabric of his trousers, "you're so submissive...so eager to be taken."

Alucard groaned softly as the demon's fingers traced upward and gripped his bulge, stroking with that perfect, teasing pressure. The vampire's knees tensed, but he didn't pull away. His clawtips cut into the stone as pleasure enthralled him—he could feel Zalith purposely intensifying his light touches, and only moments later, it made him slightly spread his legs as if to invite the demon in deeper.

But Zalith wasn't inside him.

Yet.

Zalith started tightening his grip, squeezing Alucard's bulge harder, enough to make him moan, and then he licked the side of the vampire's face. "Is there time for me to fill your ass?" he asked before gently biting his neck.

He didn't care whether there was or not. "Yes," he breathed, tensing as Zalith's fingers caressed his hardening shaft.

"Good," the demon said.

The moment Zalith took his hand and demandingly led the way upstairs, Alucard meekly but eagerly followed, his body *screaming* for what his mate promised. And when Zalith smirked over his shoulder at him, Alucard felt his dick throb. There were only seconds to wait until he got what he desperately needed.

But those seconds felt like a century.

Chapter Fifty-Two

— ⸲ ✝ ⸱ —

Somewhere in Vharakaal

| Alucard |
| *Atheson, Atheson Coven Sanctum* |

Just as he and Zalith stepped out of the shower, a knock echoed from the door of Alucard's Resting Space. He sighed quietly, the sound barely more than a breath. Whoever it was…they could wait.

He reached for the towel and began drying his hair. The warmth from the steam still clung to his skin, and for now, the desire that had gnawed at him had quieted. It wasn't gone entirely, but it stilled—it was sated…at least for now.

The vampire smiled as he felt Zalith behind him, the gentle pull of his arms wrapping around his waist making him murmur quietly and contently. His mate's body was warm and damp against his back, the sensation almost enough to convince the longing to return. Zalith leaned in and nuzzled the curve of his neck, exhaling a pleased hum that sent a soft wave of delight through the vampire's chest.

Alucard let himself lean into it, reaching back to thread his fingers through Zalith's wet hair, slow and fond; all that mattered right now was the hush of their breath, the lingering heat of the shower, and the quiet peace of simply being held.

But then came another knock.

He rolled his eyes. Although he ignored it, he focused for a moment, ensuring that it wasn't anything or anyone important…but it was Corven-Hale and Lysandra. They could wait. Whatever news they had couldn't be dire.

Zalith kissed the back of his neck, his hands gradually sliding down from Alucard's waist to his thighs. And then he leaned into his ear—

Another knock.

Alucard huffed irritably.

The demon laughed quietly. "So many people want you, darling," he murmured, his lips brushing Alucard's cheek. "But you belong to *me*." He kissed him, his hands slipping under Alucard's towel and up his thighs. "I'll remind them of that if I have to."

He wanted him to, and so did his body. The anticipation electrified through him when the demon's fingers trailed around his thighs and to his crotch. He tensed up, closing his eyes as he leaned his head back, resting it on Zalith's shoulder.

But yet another knock came, and it made Alucard snarl frustratedly.

His mate laughed again before playfully biting his ear. "Should we see what they want, or should I fuck you again?"

Alucard managed a half smile through his irritated glare. "Is everyvone I've been vaiting to 'ear vrom," he said with a sigh. "I should see vhat zhey vound."

Zalith kissed him again. "All right. But you should probably get dressed first." He squeezed his ass. "I don't want them seeing what's mine."

The vampire's smile lingered this time. He *loved* when Zalith got possessive. "Okay," he said obediently.

After handing Alucard his shirt, Zalith leaned back against the wall, arms folded, his eyes heavy with quiet desire as he watched the vampire dry off and begin to dress. His gaze was weighty but soft, unashamed in its appreciation. It made Alucard's skin tingle, not with embarrassment but with a rising heat that hadn't yet fully faded.

Alucard tried not to fluster, though he was certain there was a trace of red on his cheeks. He turned his back slightly as he towelled off his chest and shoulders, his breath shallow from more than just exertion. The feel of Zalith's eyes on him stirred something that hadn't quite cooled—an ache in his lower stomach, a warmth lingering between his thighs, a dull hunger that still clung to his spine. Even pulling the fabric over his skin felt oddly arousing; the friction of cloth on freshly marked skin only deepened the flush of awareness across his body.

Zalith didn't speak. He watched, and that silence only made it worse. Or better. Alucard couldn't tell.

He pulled the shirt on, fingers quickly moving to the buttons

But his hands slowed. He wasn't sure why… but something tugged at the edge of his awareness—a flicker… a shadow.

Then he looked up and caught sight of himself in the mirror.

His fingers froze against the fourth button.

At first, he only saw the mess of damp red hair and flushed skin, his neck marked with Zalith's proud claim, dark love bites that would linger for *days*.

His gaze drifted upward.

His jaw.

His cheeks.

The slope of his nose.

The shape of his mouth.

Something looked…off.

Or not off, exactly…just…softer than he expected.

He frowned and leaned in a little, subtly shifting his posture. There it was again. A slight roundness to his cheeks that he didn't remember noticing before. His chin, while still narrow and refined, lacked the sharpness he instinctively expected. And his mouth—it was too full. Too soft at the edges, delicate in a way that didn't match the picture he had of himself in his mind.

He glanced at Zalith.

The demon's face was striking, strong, unmistakably masculine. High, sculpted cheekbones. A jaw cut like stone. Even in stillness, there was weight to him—structure, presence, edge.

Alucard's reflection, by comparison, seemed…blurred, almost like he'd stepped into someone else's frame. Was he just imagining it? Was he only seeing it now because of what he'd learned about his childhood? He looked down at his hands again—slender, long-fingered. Not unfamiliar. But even they seemed smaller now, somehow. Less certain. Less fixed.

His thoughts spiralled, uninvited. Tyrus had asked if he was trans; he hadn't meant anything by it, nor had he said it cruelly…but still, he'd said it. And Zalith, too…Zalith said that his heat scent reminded him faintly of what a woman's smelled like. Subtle, but present, like an undertone in a familiar song.

Was he overthinking it?

He might have dismissed it…if he hadn't learned what he had—that he'd once been physically ambiguous, that he hadn't always been male, not in the way others were. He'd made a choice at some point in his life. But now that certainty felt less like a pillar and more like a ledge.

Maybe he was just looking too hard, reading too deeply, seeing things that weren't there. Or maybe…now that he knew, he was finally starting to see what had always been there.

He blinked and turned his head away from the mirror, his throat tightening. His fingers resumed their slow movement over the buttons, but the feeling had shifted. He no longer felt like he was dressing his body; it felt like he was just…inhabiting it, a feeling that had haunted him for four centuries, a feeling that had imprisoned him until Zalith showed him that the scars on his back didn't change the way he felt about him.

Would it be the same this time, though? His mate may have said that he'd seen everything, that he wasn't bothered by what he'd remembered. But what if Zalith started noticing the same thing? The way he didn't possess that sharp, perfect structure.

But no man looked the same—they didn't all have flawless jawlines and cheekbones, they didn't all look strikingly, perfectly masculine.

Did they?

"What's wrong?" Zalith asked.

Snapping out of his thoughts, Alucard's gaze met the demon's. "Vhat?"

His mate chuckled amusedly, unfolding his arms. "I said, what's wrong?" he asked as he stepped closer and placed his hands on Alucard's waist.

Alucard smiled at him—without hesitation, he let the demands of his body flood in and take over, immediately banishing everything else; he still tried to keep the commanding instincts from urging him to give in, though. "Noving," he assured him and tied his last button. "I vas just vinking about vhat everyvone is about to tell me. I veally 'ope ve zon't 'ave to sidetrack again. I just vant to tie up everyving zhat needs tying up and go 'ome." He looked down at the demon's thin gold chain as he fiddled with it. "I miss our bed."

Zalith ran his fingers through his hair, and then he took one of the towels and started drying it a little more. "I miss it, too," he said softly. "I miss how it smells of both of us, I miss that fur throw, and I miss waking up to you next to me—I miss being able to just admire you."

The fluster returned, clashing with the simmering heat inside him. "'Opevully, ve can be in our own bed again tonight."

"I hope so," Zalith said as he stopped drying the vampire's hair. "Because I also miss fucking you in it."

Alucard had to look away again, hiding his flustered pout. "I miss zhat, too," he murmured.

Zalith kissed his forehead, and then he handed him a comb. "I'll get dressed and join you out there in a few minutes."

With a nod, Alucard faced the mirror—but the moment his eyes caught his reflection, the doubt slithered back in. That same subtle wrongness crept beneath his skin, soft as breath and just as inescapable. He looked away before it could take root again and dragged the comb slowly through the damp strands of his hair.

His gaze wandered. It always did when Zalith was nearby.

Across the room, his mate lifted his shirt from the chair and slid it over his shoulders. The fabric pulled tight across his back as he stretched his arms through the sleeves, muscles shifting beneath smooth skin; his shoulders flexed, and Alucard's hand stilled mid-comb.

He watched.

The way Zalith rolled his shoulders and adjusted the shirt made something low in his stomach stir. There was strength in every motion—not just brute power but the practiced kind, the kind that came from confidence and control. His mate's hips rolled slightly as he fastened his belt, slow and unhurried, like he knew exactly what he was doing to him.

And he probably did.

Alucard exhaled softly through his nose, the comb forgotten in his fingers. The flutter of uncertainty that had clung to him a moment ago began to blur under the returning pull of desire. The sharp lines of Zalith's waist, the way his abdomen tensed when he reached down to pull his trouser leg straight—it was all too easy to fixate on.

The vampire bit the inside of his cheek and glanced away, only to glance back again a second later. Heat shot up his spine, demanding, persistent. The sight of Zalith like this always lit something in him, something that had nothing to do with dominance or submission, nothing to do with control. It was simpler than that. It was the ache of being bound to someone who could undo him with a glance.

And right now, Zalith wasn't even looking at him. He didn't need to.

Alucard swallowed and combed another stroke through his hair, slower this time, the heat climbing its way back into his blood. And then one more gradual stroke, trying not to stare…but Zalith bent to retrieve his discarded boots, and the stretch of his back and the quiet strength in his arms made Alucard's grip on the comb falter.

"You're supposed to be seeing who's at the door," the demon said without turning, voice edged with amusement but thick with seduction. "Not eyeing me like you're ready to take my dick again."

Alucard stiffened slightly, embarrassed that he'd been caught. He cleared his throat softly and resumed combing, though the warmth on his face betrayed him. "I'll see you in zhere," he said, putting the comb down.

Zalith responded with a quiet, "Mm-hmm."

The vampire headed into the other part of the room; when he reached the door, he took a deep breath…and opened it.

Corven-Hale was the first to notice—he was standing mere feet from the door. He bowed humbly.

Lysandra and Alson noticed seconds later, taking their eyes off the books lined along one of the shelves and turning to face the open door.

Alucard stepped aside and gestured into the room with his arm, inviting them all in.

All three vampires filed inside.

After closing the door, Alucard leaned against the table. "So?" he asked.

Corven-Hale sat in the armchair, and Lysandra and Alson sat on the couch.

The Knight started, "I spoke to every Fellkin, My Lord. No one else has turned or made attempts to turn humans without your knowledge."

Alucard was relieved to hear that. No vampire would lie to the Knights of the coven, and Corven-Hale had always been very efficient at his job.

"Is there anything else you'd like me to do, My Lord?"

"Eyra's trial is in vive hours. Make sure you 'ave all zhe vacts veady to share."

He nodded and bowed his head. "Of course, My Lord."

Alucard then shifted his gaze to Lysandra.

She looked excited. "Rosaline and I talked, and we decided that she *should* be a Day Walker. We think things will be much easier for us if one of us can go out during the day—you know, just in case there's an emergency or anything like that."

Zalith then walked into the room, and Alucard's eyes shot to him. He watched as his mate approached and joined him; the demon took hold of and squeezed his hand, and then he smiled at him before he started eyeing the vampires.

"We also agreed on being relocated to Fontisère," Lysandra added.

"Good," Alucard replied. "As vor Lilly, ve vound 'er with a Strayblood—Emilien." He looked at Corven-Hale.

The Knight lowered his head. "Emilien was a tailor in Atheson City twenty-six years ago," he told the room. "Theremond almost killed him in what was an honest mistake. I saved his life by turning him, but he did not want to join coven life. I helped him get to Antamont."

"At least you gave him a choice," Lysandra mumbled.

Alucard got back to the point, "You suggested zhat Lilly go vith you and Vosaline. If Emilien vants to stay vith Lilly, and Lilly vants to join you and your vife, you both need to decide vhether or not Emilien vill be velcome."

"I don't think that'll be an issue," Lysandra said. "What about Camilla?"

Alson's hand shot up.

Zalith snarled almost silently, but it was just enough for Alucard to hear.

Stifling a smirk, Alucard asked the Scribe, "Vhat?"

"That word you asked me to search for, My Lord—Thaleus."

He waited.

"It's a place in Eshkunda."

Alucard frowned. The name wasn't familiar.

"In Vharakaal," Alson added. "Thaleus is this sort of small collection of fishing villages along the Crimson Sea. The province is called Anaket."

Could that be where Camilla was?

"Have you ever been to Vharakaal?" Zalith asked him.

He frowned, trying to recall. Something told him that he *had*, but he couldn't remember when, where, or why. "Maybe," he mumbled unsurely.

The demon didn't question his response. At this point, he knew how to tell when Alucard was remembering or trying to remember something that had been taken from him. Instead, he squeezed the vampire's hand to comfort him.

Alucard asked Alson, "Did you vind out about Vhaleus in zhe Vharakaal Atlas?"

"Yes, My Lord," the Scribe confirmed.

"Go and get zhat book vor me."

With a nod, Alson hurried out of the room.

His sights shifted to Lysandra. "Bring Vosaline up 'ere. I'll turn 'er now."

Lysandra's face lit up, and she, too, hurried out of the room.

And finally, Alucard looked at Corven-Hale. "Go and get veady vor Eyra's trial."

"Yes, My Lord," he said, and he left as well.

Alucard exhaled deeply and leaned his head on Zalith's shoulder.

"Are you okay, baby?" the demon asked softly, rubbing his thigh.

He nodded and said, "I just veel like I've been to Vharakaal bevore. I'm 'oping zhat if I look at zhe atlas, maybe I vill vemember."

Zalith gently turned and pulled him into his embrace. "Are we going there?"

The vampire didn't ignore the lure of Zalith's scent; he let instinct take control for a few fleeting moments. He nuzzled his mate's neck, breathing him in, letting it tempt him. But he shouldn't give in again—not right now. "Is best zhat I vind 'er and try to convince 'er to at least go vith Lysandra and zhe ozzers. My presence is very veassuring vor vampires."

"Mm," the demon murmured and kissed his head. "It's much more than reassuring for me," he said, clearly smirking.

Alucard smiled, breathing in a long breath, Zalith's intoxicating scent enthralling him... and he let himself sink *just a tiny bit*. "Maybe..." he cut himself off with a huff.

"Maybe what?" Zalith asked, slowly dragging his fingertips down his back.

He knew better.

There were things to get done, things that would come to a much faster conclusion if he remained focused on the desire to wrap things up in Atheson.

He. Knew. Better.

But he couldn't resist.

The words left him immediately—"Maybe... I'm veady to take your dick again."

He felt the demon tense around him, and the bulge in Zalith's trousers twitched just enough for Alucard to feel it press against his crotch for half a second.

Half a second was all it took, though.

Alucard lifted his head, and when Zalith eagerly kissed his lips, the vampire grasped his mate's growing arousal.

Zalith kissed him a few more times before nuzzling his neck, groaning as Alucard caressed and softly squeezed his shaft.

The desperation devoured Alucard like a starved beast, swallowing him whole, giving him no room to breathe. But he was fine with that. He let it happen. He let Zalith lift him onto the table, he let him unbutton his shirt, and he let him ease his hand into his trousers, all while their tongues entwined in quick, fervent kisses.

And with each kiss and grab and groan, the anticipation intensified, burning hotter and hotter and hotter until every desperate breath carried a moan—

The door knocked.

Alucard meant to snarl, but a frustrated, desperate growling whine escaped him instead, sharp, broken, and embarrassingly real.

Zalith growled low in response—pleased, ravenous. "Fuck, baby…" he whispered, his voice thick with lust, cracked around a moan he didn't bother to hide. His lips brushed Alucard's jaw as his fingers curled firmly around his shaft, stroking him with a slow, maddening pressure. "I fucking love it when you whine like that," he purred, and then he bit down just once at the base of Alucard's neck. "It makes me lose control," he breathed, mouth already chasing the next kiss. He captured Alucard's lips in something rough and consuming, all teeth and tongue and hunger. And then his voice dropped again, velvet over embers, "Let them hear what I do to you."

Alucard barely had a moment to process the words before Zalith's hand slid past his arousal and two slick fingers suddenly pressed deep inside his ass. Pleasure struck like lightning, forcing a sharp, broken whine from the vampire's mouth, his claws sinking into the table's surface as his spine arched. His dick throbbed instantly, the pressure so intense that it made his thighs shake, and when Zalith's mouth met his again, he moaned through each stroke of their tongues.

Zalith pushed deeper, his fingers curling just right, dragging along that perfect spot that made everything inside Alucard intensify until he couldn't take it anymore. The sensation was too much, it was too perfect—he couldn't stop the struggled, delighted cry spilling from his throat, barely muffled by their frantic kisses, and he couldn't stop his body from trembling as if he were already seconds from cumming.

The demon hadn't even fucked him yet and already Alucard felt overwhelmed, strung so tight with sensation that he could hardly breathe or think. And yet… it wasn't just the pleasure. It was the *helplessness*. The delicious, humiliating way that two fingers were enough to unravel him completely.

As much as he craved the feeling of Zalith's thick, demanding dick widening him open, claiming him deeply, there was something just as intoxicating in this, in being pinned beneath his mate's touch, reduced to nothing but breathless, needy moans and trembling thighs. At his mercy. Entirely his.

The demon didn't need to dominate him with force. He didn't need to mark him with bites or growl commands. All it took was this—his fingers inside him, pressing exactly where Alucard shattered, dragging sounds from his throat he couldn't have silenced if he tried.

Zalith shifted slightly, the fingers buried deep inside Alucard never faltering in their rhythm, never giving him even a moment's reprieve. With his other hand, the demon began to unbuckle Alucard's belt, groaning between kisses. Every metal click and brush of fabric only made the vampire ache more, his body tightening in anticipation.

The belt came undone, the demon pulled away from their kiss, and Alucard's trousers were tugged just low enough.

Zalith's mouth was on him. Warm, wet, and utterly consuming.

Alucard choked on a gasp, his back arching again, thighs twitching as fire lanced through his spine. The demon took him in without hesitation, without mercy, his tongue flicking and curling just right, matching the rhythm of his fingers still working inside him. The twin sensations, deep and wet and *so fucking good*, collided all at once, overwhelming every nerve, every breath.

He couldn't hold it.

His claws scraped desperately at the table beneath him, dragging hard, deep gouges through the wood as he let out a shattered cry; his entire body seized, a blinding rush of unstoppable pleasure bursting from within. He came with a moan torn straight from his throat, his hips jerking forward into Zalith's mouth.

The demon didn't stop or flinch. He gave a pleased hum, swallowing every drop greedily, like he'd been starved for it. And still, his fingers remained inside, slow and possessive, milking every last tremble from Alucard's body as the vampire collapsed, panting, staring aimlessly up at the ceiling.

Zalith eased his fingers out slowly—agonizingly so—dragging them free in a slick motion that made Alucard's body twitch all over again. The vampire let out a shaky exhale, and when the demon leaned in and dragged his tongue along the underside of Alucard's still-sensitive dick, lapping up the last of the cum he hadn't already taken down, Alucard shivered, soft and overstimulated, another weak sound falling from his lips as his thighs trembled.

With a satisfied hum, the demon carefully pulled Alucard's trousers back up, his touch gentle as he tucked the vampire away and fastened everything in place again. Then, with Alucard still breathless against the table, Zalith straightened, looked down at him, and smirked, wicked and impossibly fond. "Poor thing," he murmured, leaning in. "You lasted longer than I thought you would." He kissed the vampire's forehead, and then he said with a devious smile, "You should probably answer the door."

Alucard huffed and slowly sat up, using his arms to support himself; his body was still trembling, and he was still catching his breath. He watched as Zalith headed into the other room and then to the bathroom; with a quiet sigh, he then slowly got up. His legs trembled a little, but when he started walking, the ache quickly withered.

He pulled the door open and set his eyes on Alson. The Scribe was wide-eyed and red-faced, and he didn't say a word, he just stared. In his frozen hands, he was holding an atlas—the one Alucard had asked for.

"*Multumesc*," he said, taking it from him. "You can go back to zhe library now—or vherever you vant to go. Take some time to vest."

Alson nodded, stiffly at first, but then he sped up before turning around and hurrying away.

Alucard rolled his eyes and closed the door. He slumped down onto the couch and opened the atlas to the contents page—he wasn't going to give his mind the chance to drift and let that feeling of inferiority creep in. Slowly, he read the name of each Vharakaalan country, but not one of them looked familiar.

Zalith joined him. He wrapped an arm around Alucard and pulled him closer. "That little pervert librarian was probably watching through the keyhole."

He laughed quietly, resting his head on the demon's shoulder. But he probably wasn't wrong; Alson always had that quiet, analytical manner about him, like someone who observed the world a little too closely for comfort. If anyone was prone to lingering at keyholes, it'd be him.

Alucard didn't want to think about it, though. He'd been seen and heard having sex in this house far too many times since first arriving to deal with the Silver Claw. But he didn't care as much that it was his vampires who heard… or saw. He was their leader, not a shameful partner struggling to fit into a world that wasn't his.

"Did you find out where you've been?" Zalith asked.

He shifted his focus back to the atlas. "No," he mumbled. "None of zhese places look vamiliar at all."

Zalith stared at the page for a moment. "Should we just start from the top of the list? We could glance at each page, and maybe you'll start remembering," he suggested.

That was probably the best way to do it. They still had hours to wait, after all.

On the other hand, he still needed to go and find Camilla. But what if she wasn't in Thaleus? He flipped to the first page as he asked Zalith, "Can I send an izuret to Vhaleus? I should probably make sure zhat Camilla is even zhere bevore ve go."

"Yeah, of course," he said and summoned one.

The small creature appeared in a puff of pale green smoke and landed on the arm of the couch. It saluted and proudly told them that he, Tato, was ready for duty.

Alucard smiled, his eyes drifting to the pendant around Tato's neck. The shimmering green gemstone almost resembled a potato in shape, and he suspected that was where the izuret's name had come from.

"Ve need you to go to Vharakaal," he told it. "Zhere's a small collection of vishing villages in a place called Vhaleus along zhe Crimson Sea."

With an intrigued chirp, Tato tapped his chin.

"Zhere's a vampire called Camilla. Vind 'er, but zon't let 'er see or 'ear you. If she isn't zhere, come back."

Tato nodded, and then he disappeared.

Alucard flipped to the next page, his eyes taking in each drawing of plants, animals, and landscapes, and skim-reading the information, hoping that *something* would trigger his memory. He knew it wouldn't happen right away, though; he needed to be patient. It would return to him eventually…and he hoped that it wouldn't carry any despair or confusion with it.

Chapter Fifty-Three

— ⟨ † ⟩ —

Loyalty's Reward

| **Alucard** |
| *Atheson, Atheson Coven Sanctum* |

Bajiruun, a coastal city where Boszorkian was widely spoken; it was the largest country in Vharakaal, it had a huge mountain range and vast deserts, and if one was lucky, they'd see the very rare and majestic T'khur Alinan Cheetah.

None of that triggered a memory. It didn't help Alucard remember why or when he'd been to Vharakaal, but it definitely wasn't *where* he'd gone.

With a deep sigh, he aimlessly flipped through the pages covering history, thick with long, chunky paragraphs about politics and government figures. He paused briefly to look at each animal, and he saddened when he read about the endangered lions and elephants. Poachers were disgusting, a plague, a virus that needed eradicating.

"Does any of this look familiar?" Zalith asked him.

Alucard shook his head. "No."

Just as he flipped the page, someone knocked on the door.

That door had been knocked on so many times today that it was surprising it was still standing.

"Vhat?" he called.

It opened, and Lysandra walked in with Rosaline.

"Sorry that took a little while, My Lord," Lysandra said. "Rosaline was just feeling kinda nervous."

Alucard closed the book. "Is vine. Grab a glass vrom zhat cupboard," he said as Zalith took the book from him, and then the vampire stood up.

Lysandra did as she was told; she took a drinking glass from the liquor cabinet, and when she gave it to Alucard, she stood beside her wife and held her hand.

"Um…sir," Rosaline said quietly. "Is…it going to hurt?"

"No," he lied as he used a claw to cut his wrist enough for his blood to only trickle weakly into the glass. Once there was enough, he handed it to Rosaline.

The woman stared down at the crimson liquid, her anxiety sharpening with every second. Dark hair spilled around her face as her green eyes flicked to Lysandra, then past Alucard to Zalith. The moment they landed on him, her posture stiffened.

Alucard glanced over his shoulder to see his mate *glaring* at her, more specifically, her hand holding the glass. He knew that Zalith was *extremely* possessive when it came to his blood, but Alucard did his best to keep himself from enjoying the demon's response and set his sights back on Rosaline. "You should sit down," he told her, gesturing to one of the table chairs—his eyes darted to the slashes his claws had recently left in the wood, and he saw both women glance at them, but he refused to let the embarrassment swelling inside him show on his face, so he deadpanned.

Rosaline sat down, her hands trembling faintly as she rested one in her lap, still holding the glass in the other; the chair creaked beneath her as if bracing for what was to come.

"All you have to do is drink it," Lysandra said gently, brushing her wife's hair back from her face with soft, steady fingers; her voice was tender, but it carried the weight of urgency.

Rosaline exhaled shakily, and then she held the glass in *both* hands. The scent of the blood made her flinch—Alucard could see it in the subtle wrinkle of her nose, the brief flicker of fear in her gaze. For a moment, it seemed she might back out.

But she closed her eyes and drank.

She barely took a mouthful before grimacing at the taste, her throat working hard to force it down. Her hand faltered.

"You have to drink all of it, honey," Lysandra said, her firm tone trembling at the edges. She reached out, steadying the glass, tilting it to guide more of the liquid past Rosaline's lips.

Rosaline didn't resist. She grimaced harder, face tightening as she forced down the rest. When the glass emptied, she set it shakily on the table; her lips were stained deep red, and her still-human breathing was already beginning to shift.

It happened quickly.

A strangled gasp tore from her throat, and her body jolted in the chair, her spine stiffening. Her hand clutched Lysandra's arm on instinct, her nails digging in as her pulse surged, stuttered, and surged again. Then came the tremors—her muscles seized violently, and a cry escaped her lips. Lysandra knelt beside her instantly, whispering her name, pressing her forehead to her wife's, trying to soothe her, but there was no soothing what came next.

Rosaline's veins darkened.

Alucard watched as the black tendrils spread from the woman's throat outward, threading beneath her skin like something parasitic. She jerked again, harder this time, and nearly toppled the chair; her eyes rolled back, and her breathing turned ragged and wet, like someone drowning on dry land.

"I-is this right?" Lysandra exclaimed worriedly. "It wasn't like this when Eyra—"

"She's vine," Alucard said, stepping closer. "Is divverent vhen I turn people. My blood is stronger; does more to a 'uman zhan zhe blood of anozzer vampire. Zhere's alvays a price to pay vhen a 'uman is given ethos."

Lysandra nodded, and then she held Rosaline's face between her hands, her thumbs brushing her cheeks, even as tears welled in her eyes. "I'm right here, Rosie. I've got you," she murmured.

It happened. Her heart, already stumbling, stuttered once more…before coming to a complete stop. Silence settled. Rosaline's body slumped in the chair, unmoving, her lips parted, skin pale, her head against Lysandra's shoulder.

"Rosie?" Lysandra whispered.

No movement, no response.

Lysandra whimpered, turning her head to look at Alucard.

But then Rosaline inhaled—not a breath but a soundless, dragged-in need, like a body learning to move without a pulse. Her shoulders twitched, her fingers curled, the black veins began to fade, and slowly…her eyes opened.

Rosaline was no longer human. Not quite yet a vampire, but irrevocably changed.

Lysandra gasped softly, one hand trembling over her mouth, the other still cradling her wife's cheek. "Honey?"

She flinched and slowly narrowed her crimson gaze as she turned her head. But it wasn't Lysandra that Rosaline's sights landed on. She saw Alucard, and then her eyes widened. Recognition smothered her pale face, followed by adoration and desperation. And then she got ready to lunge—

Alucard pointed a finger at her and firmly said, "No."

The new Fledgeling froze.

"Rosie, honey?" Lysandra asked, placing her hands on her face.

Rosaline slowly turned her gaze to her wife.

"You both need to go to zhe Vledgeling Dvelling Space," he said, and at the same time, he telepathically summoned Halvarn; having the Night Steward escort them was probably best; the last thing he wanted was Rosaline lunging at a demon or a werewolf. "Go vith 'im," he said when Halvarn appeared at the door moments later.

With a nod, Lysandra helped Rosaline to her feet. The new Fledgeling stumbled, but her wife kept her upright. Halvarn helped when they got to the door, which he closed once they left the room.

Alucard sighed deeply as he grabbed a tissue and used it to clean the splotches of blood from his wrist. Then, he returned to the couch and cuddled up to his mate.

"I hate seeing other people drink your blood," the demon grumbled.

For a moment, the vampire let himself edge nearer to Zalith's neck. He breathed in the temptation, but he wouldn't get lost in his body's intensifying desires. "Vell, zhey aren't getting my blood out of pleasure—my blood *kills* zhem."

Zalith sighed, running his fingers down Alucard's arm.

Alucard grabbed the atlas. He flipped through the pages and past Bajiruun, landing on Djavhati. More than seventy percent of the country was covered in desert, mostly savannas and semi-arid plains. There were vast salt flats said to be the remnants of an ancient lake, and the country as a whole was teeming with wildlife: elephants, lions, leopards, cheetahs, Vharakaalan wild dogs, buffalo, rhinos, giraffes, hippos, and crocodiles. Alucard's eyes widened just a little in excitement. He'd *love* to visit this place.

But…he'd been there already.

There it was. A flash of a memory. More thought than image.

Where wildlife was abundant, there were always shapeshifters.

Specifically, a shapeshifter called—

"Kor'naavhi," the vampire muttered.

"What?" Zalith questioned, looking at the page and then at him again.

"Kor'naavhi," he repeated, surer this time. "I vas…" he paused because there it was—that despair, the dismay that he wished wouldn't come with this recollection. He sighed, staring at the pages in front of him. "Vone of zhe virst tasks Zamien gave me vas to travel to zhis place," he said, the tip of his claw gently pressing against the big, bold title, Djavhati.

Zalith's expression softened, and sympathy filled his eyes. "You don't have to talk about it, baby."

Alucard shook his head. "I 'ave to…to vemember." He leaned his head back, staring aimlessly around the room as the memory slowly healed itself. "I vas only tventy at zhat point. Zamien and Liliv needed certain species as components vor…someving." He looked down at the pages again. "Zhey vanted Kor'naavhi because of zheir elemental ethos; zhey vere a very powervul shivter. But zhey zidn't only send me to get vone or two." That was when the dismay grew heavier. "Zhey sent me back over and over and over until I couldn't vind any more. Of course, zhey blamed zhat on me, and I veceived zhe necessary punishment—"

"I'm sorry, baby," the demon said, rubbing his arm.

He shrugged, dragging his hand along the pages. "Zhey vere…" he drawled, trying to remember the rest, trying to remember the *reason*.

Zalith pulled him closer, helping him lie on him as he put the book aside.

"Zhey vere making someving," he said, frowning. "Someving…somevone…." He huffed and closed his eyes, but a burst of golden light immediately stole the dark, and he snapped them open.

The light was familiar. He'd seen it before.

And so had Zalith.

"Lumendatt," he realized.

"*Your* Lumendatt?"

He nodded stiffly as the faint but growing urge to nuzzle the demon's neck threatened to steal his focus. "I vink zhat…maybe zhey vere trying to use my Lumendatt."

"To do what?" his mate asked worriedly.

"I vink…to crveate someving…or somevone, I zon't know. Kind of like 'ow zhe Diabolus made new zemons vor Luciver; zhey'd 'ave children vith ozzer species and take certain traits and abilities vrom zhem, giving zhem zhis new zemon crveation. Maybe zhey vere trying to do zhat but using zhe power of my Lumendatt."

Zalith's worried frown thickened.

"Zidn't vork, zhough," he said, certain of the fact. "My Lumendatt vasn't voken up until Janus vound me."

He paused again, looking away to hide the grimace that struck his face when the next flashes of memory flooded into his mind. They'd hurt him for that; they'd cut and beat and whipped him because his Lumendatt never responded, because they killed so many beings in the process—*components*, as the Numen called them. The Kor'naathi had gone extinct because of Damien and Lilith's experiments…and because of *him*.

"Alucard?" the demon's voice broke through the cloud of memory and emotion.

Alucard looked at him, and when Zalith's warm hand caressed the side of his face, he closed his eyes and exhaled deeply. "I vent to Djavhati over and over to capture Kor'naavhi vor zhem…until zhere veren't any levt," he murmured guiltily. "I killed an entire species because I vas too veak and pavhetic to say no."

Zalith rubbed his back and said, "It's not your fault, Alucard. Don't blame yourself." He tightened his embrace around them. "You had no choice."

He buried his face into Zalith's shirt. Whether he had a choice or not, he was still responsible.

"There could still be some out there," the demon added, trying to reassure him. "Shapeshifters are very good at hiding. There's a handful of them still back in Eltaria pretending to be human."

Although Zalith made a very good point, Alucard still couldn't escape the guilt, nor could he stop asking himself: how many more people had he done this to? Had Damien and Lilith sent him after more than just Vharakaalan shapeshifters?

"Don't think about Damien or Lilith," his mate murmured and kissed his head. He then opened the book and flipped the pages until he found Eshkunda. "So, how do we get to Thaleus?"

He appreciated the subject shift. "I can vly us," he said, glancing at the pages.

"Thaleus," Zalith read aloud, adopting a tone of gentle inquiry as his eyes moved across the page, "a modest yet enduring cluster of fishing villages along the western reaches of the Crimson Sea, contributes a significant portion of North Vharakaal's maritime trade." He turned the page slightly, scanning onward. "For over two centuries, these coastal settlements have independently managed five principal ports, maintaining regular shipments to and from Euboris, Rhenovaalis, and Saen-Jirra. In spite of the considerable profits drawn from seafaring commerce, the people of Thaleus have continually declined provincial initiatives to urbanize, choosing instead to preserve their identity as a collection of quaint, wind-worn fishing hamlets."

Alucard relaxed just a little, the sound of his mate's voice calming him.

Zalith turned the page and continued, "The Crimson Sea is particularly renowned for its vibrant coral reef systems—among the northernmost reefs in the known world," he read. "These reefs support a remarkably diverse marine ecosystem, hosting over twelve hundred identified species of fish, approximately ten percent of which are endemic to its waters." He paused briefly, adjusting the angle of the book, then went on, "In addition to its coral gardens, the Crimson Sea is also inhabited by dugongs, sea turtles, dolphins, and, on rare occasion, migratory whale sharks. Local seafarers regard the appearance of a whale shark as an omen of steady weather and plentiful harvest, though the Atlas notes no scientific basis for the belief."

The vampire smiled faintly. "You should become lecturer."

His mate laughed and said, "I'm not much of a teacher. I don't think I'm patient enough."

Alucard closed his eyes and said, "You taught me a lot, and you vere very patient."

"Because you're hot. I can't teach ugly people."

With an amused laugh, Alucard moved his face closer to Zalith's neck. "So, everyvone but me is ugly?"

Zalith stroked his fingers up Alucard's back, and as he guided the vampire to nuzzle his neck, he said, "The moment I laid eyes on you, everyone else paled in comparison."

Alucard's smile grew, and the warm sensation of contentment lay over him like a blanket. "You know, you vere zhe virst person I ever actually 'ad to look at tvice. I never velt attracted to *anyvone* I saw until you," he admitted. "People vere just…people. I eizer tolerated zhem or 'ated zhem."

The demon kissed his cheek and said, "Love at second sight."

He pouted. "You know vhat I mean," he mumbled. "I looked again because zhe virst time I saw you, I velt someving I never 'ad bevore."

Zalith laughed softly. "I know, baby. I'm just messing with you." He kissed him again. "What else was I a first for you?" he murmured curiously.

"Zhe virst person to stay in my life avter zhe Numen made very clear 'ow involved zhey veally are."

The demon's fingertips stroked his back in slow, circular motions.

"Zhe virst person who zidn't get angry at me vor constantly pushing zhem avay."

Zalith hummed, sounding amused. "I loved your grumpiness from the start."

As the contentment grew, Alucard sank deeper into the intoxicating scent of the man he loved. "You vere a lot of virsts now zhat I'm vinking about."

The demon hummed again, although this time, it briefly dragged into an almost pleased growl. "The first person to grab your butt?"

He smiled and said, "Yes."

"The first person to touch your dick?"

Alucard pouted a little, starting to feel flustered. "Yes."

Zalith's touch became possessive. "The first person to finger your ass?"

The vampire tensed ever so slightly at both the words and the thought. "Yes," he murmured. Zalith knew the answers to all of his questions, but he didn't stop him.

"Was my dick the first to slide in and stretch your hole?" he purred.

A shiver of anticipation raced through Alucard. "Yes," he answered.

Zalith hummed again, satisfied yet still hungry. "Was my cum the first you felt inside you?" He gently gripped Alucard's throat with one hand and his ass with the other. "Here *and* here?"

It was now desperation that enthralled Alucard, and it made him exhale a quiet groan in response. "Yes," he replied again.

Another purr came from the demon, more satisfied than the last. "Do you know what else I'm going to be the first to do?"

Alucard's body tensed so much that he couldn't help but slowly grasp the demon's blazer. "Vhat?"

Zalith slid his hand down Alucard's back and into his trousers, slowly but firmly squeezing the vampire's ass as he murmured, "I'm going to spread your ass and—"

Of-fucking-course the door knocked.

The demon sighed in defeat.

At the same time, Alucard snarled and shouted, "Vhat?!" and then a shiver ran up his spine as Zalith's grip became even harder.

The door opened, and *Danford* stepped in. His face immediately went red. "S-sorry," he stammered, shuffling on the spot.

He wasn't alone. That was probably why he didn't leave.

Someone else stepped into the room and stood beside the wolf-vampire. He was much taller than Danford, his long, loosely tied orange hair shimmering brightly in the rays of sunlight breaking in through the drawn curtains; there were streaks and locks of white, some thicker than others. His bright green eyes first scanned the room, and then they settled on Alucard and Zalith.

"This is Séamus Ó Súilleabháin," Danford said, gesturing to the man.

Séamus walked towards the demon and vampire.

Alucard sat up straight, and Zalith pulled his hand from his trousers.

"God save ye this fine afthernoon," Séamus said with a thick Diaráinnish accent, holding out his hand. "I'm after hearin' you're the one givin' work to me son."

With a nod, Alucard stood up and shook his hand—and he quickly tried to figure out how to word his answer. "Crevan and 'is pack 'ave joined a verevolf alliance. Zhe alliance vorks vor Zaliv and me," he said as he glanced at Zalith, who was now standing beside him.

The demon held his hand out, too, and shook Séamus'.

"That Danford fella told me me son's been hopin' I'd come lookin' for him. Would that be true now?"

"Crevan expressed his hesitation to join the alliance," Zalith answered. "He told us that he had to wait for you; he was convinced that you'd return to the pack territory someday." He glanced and smiled at Alucard. "My fiancé understood how important both things were to your son—getting his pack to safety but the desire to remain on family land in the event that they'd return—so he offered to attempt to find and bring you to Crevan. Your son accepted. He and his pack are safe."

Séamus looked like he was pondering, crossing his arms. "So, Crevan left the family land back in Dor-Sanguis, did he?" He threw a frown Danford's way. "Sure Danford was after tellin' me he was still there." He didn't sound skeptical or angry, though.

Alucard nodded. "At zhe time, 'e vas," he started, carefully constructing his white lie. "Crevan and zhe ozzers vere vaiting vor a ship to arrive, and zhat arrived earlier zhan expected. Ve vanted to get 'im to savety as soon as possible; I'm sure you 'ave 'eard about zhe plague and zemon attacks."

"Aye, I've heard tell of that. 'Twas a tragedy, so it was."

"Your son is safe," Zalith assured him. "We can't share the location of our territory right now as it would be putting our people at risk, but if you would like to be taken to Crevan, we can have someone transport you."

Séamus tapped his foot on the carpet, donning another pondering stare.

"And of course, you're very welcome to stay, but you're also not expected to," the demon added.

The man fiddled with his drooping moustache. "What's this place ye're talkin' about then? Some kind o' refuge without a human soul in sight? Out in the wilds, is it?"

Zalith chuckled. "Not at all. The place we have built isn't in the same state as the rest of the world. Our people live alongside the humans without conflict; humans and non-humans are colleagues, neighbours, friends—some are even married."

Séamus seemed shocked to hear that. "Well now, looks like me son's struck gold, so he has. No hunters at all? Sure, I'd only expect a place like that in a storybook." He hummed as he shuffled around. "But what about me flock, though? I can't be leavin' the sheep out there on their own—there's not a soul for miles, and folk are barely gettin' by as it is. No one'll be buyin' them, neither."

Alucard glanced at Zalith; he saw the demon internally sigh, but he was sure that his mate was going to say exactly what he would have.

"We're currently expanding agricultural territory," Zalith replied. "If you're willing to work alongside other farmers and labourers, you're welcome to bring them with you."

Séamus smiled appreciatively. "Ah, thank ye kindly," he said, placing his hands together as if his words were a prayer. But then he frowned guiltily. "If I'd known Crevan was waitin' on me, I'd have come long before now." He paused, scratching the side of his face as his expression grew hesitant. "Did he seem cross when he asked ye to come find me? Should I be bracin' meself for a storm o' shite? I mean, I've earned it, sure, but I'd hate for any of it to fall back on the lad's work."

"'E vas just sad and veluctant to leave. I vink zhat 'e vill only be very 'appy to see you," Alucard told him.

The man sighed in relief. "Right so. Could ye take me to him, then?"

Alucard nodded. "Vhen you leave zhe library, a vampire vill be vaiting vor you. 'Is name is 'alvarn."

With a nod, Séamus turned and headed for the door.

Danford followed.

"Not you," Alucard snapped at him as a half-thought struck him.

The wolf-vampire stopped, wide-eyed. "Oh, sorry."

Séamus closed the door behind him.

Alucard pointed at the floor a few feet in front of himself. "'Ere," he ordered.

Danford's eyes widened even more; he looked at Zalith for a moment, but then he slowly made his way over and stood where he'd been told to.

For a moment, Alucard eyed him up and down. He looked almost horrified, as if he was expecting to be scolded. Alucard knew that feeling far too well, and it wasn't his intention to make Danford feel that way. So he exhaled quietly, lightening his irritated glare, and gestured to Danford's eyepatch with a brief raise of his hand. "Take zhat off."

"Uh, okay…" he drawled. He started taking it off but questioned unsurely, "Can I ask why?"

"Because Păzitoarea 'as commended you on your training," he started.

Danford lowered the patch, revealing his right eye and the ruin beneath. Two deep scars marred the surrounding skin; one dragged diagonally from the corner of his brow down across the eyelid, while the other carved a near-perfect vertical line through the centre of his eyebrow, stopping just shy of his cheekbone. The eye itself was clouded, almost entirely pale, its surface bleached to a dull, misted grey. Within that fog, another scar sliced through the iris, as if the eye had been split once, poorly healed and never quite whole again.

The wolf-vampire looked surprised in response to Alucard's answer, but a slight frown followed not long after. "But…what does that have to do with my eye?"

Alucard slowly rolled his sleeve halfway up his wrist as he said, "You 'ave also proven true to zhis new part of yourselv; I vould not 'ave been surprised or ovvended if you tried to devy your existence." He glanced at Zalith, who looked curious, but when he used a claw to cut his palm, the demon frowned a little. "At zhe time, I zidn't know or 'onestly particularly care about getting zhe amount of blood you needed to vully transvorm correct—I ended up giving you just enough to turn." He clenched his fist, keeping his spilt blood trapped there. "But you've been very 'elpvul and loyal despite my attitude tovards you, and I vink zhat zhis is zhe least I can do," he said as he raised his hand and pressed his bloodied palm gently against Danford's scarred eye.

Danford flinched at the contact—more instinct than protest—but he didn't pull away.

Alucard held his hand there only a moment before drawing it back, crimson streaks smearing across Danford's face like ink across parchment. Blood shimmered faintly in the dim light as it began sinking into the damaged flesh; it was slow at first, almost cautious, before spreading like fire through dry brush. Scars thinned and faded as if exhaled from the skin itself, while the once-puckered flesh along his brow and cheek relaxed, losing its twisted tension. That clouded, lifeless iris cleared in seconds, the fog lifting to reveal a vivid crimson beneath, whole and sharp and unrecognizably alive.

Within seconds, the eye looked as if it had never been maimed.

Danford blinked once, then again, and again, his body locking up almost as if it were afraid to believe what had happened. The wolf-vampire's breath caught as he looked down at his hands, turning them, moving them closer and away again. And then he stared straight, his eyes wide as he slowly lifted a trembling hand to his face.

"I…I can…see?" he breathed, his voice breaking on the last word.

Alucard watched as Danford turned his head, testing his depth, focusing on something in the distance with his newly restored vision. The man swayed slightly, as if the act of seeing from both eyes again had thrown off his balance.

Zalith hummed something—a hushed, "Aw," as he squeezed Alucard's healed hand.

Danford gawped at his hands again, pushing them away and pulling them closer to his face, and then he looked at Alucard. "Thank you," he said thickly, almost stammering, and then he took a step forward but hesitated, almost as if he was about to attempt to hug the vampire.

Alucard was glad that Danford knew better. "You're velcome," he replied. "You can 'ead 'ome to your vife now; ve're almost done 'ere in Aveson."

"Thank you," he said again, his voice heavier with appreciation. "But I don't know how to repay you for this."

"You zon't 'ave to vepay me," he said with a shake of his head. "Just go and take care of your vamily. Make zhe most of your time off."

Danford nodded and said, "Thank you," before leaving the room.

With a quiet exhale, Alucard turned to face Zalith.

"That was very nice of you, Alucard," the demon said.

He shrugged. "Vith all of zhis making new vampires and 'ealing ozzer vampires, I guess I kind of velt bad vor leaving 'is eye like zhat."

"I doubt he was sitting around wondering why you hadn't helped. I don't think he ever expected you to," he said, pulling Alucard into his embrace.

Alucard rested his head on the demon's shoulder. Not only had yet another recently recovered memory stuck with him—this time involving Damien—but so had Danford's reactions just now. He knew that he wasn't the most approachable or lenient person; he knew he always looked like he was brooding or planning someone's murder, but what he hoped he *didn't* do was exude the same energy as Damien. He didn't want people to panic or cower when he raised his hand; he didn't want anyone who worked for him to feel terrified that he might be moments from torturing them within an inch of their life simply because he could.

"Am I a cruel person, Zaliv?" he mumbled sadly.

Zalith started caressing his hair. "No, I don't think so."

"You can be 'onest; I von't be upset vith you."

"I *am* being honest," he said with a small chuckle. "I do think you're prone to irritation, but I don't think you're cruel."

He trusted Zalith not to lie to him, even to make him feel better. "Okay," he murmured, letting himself relax a little.

Zalith kissed his head. "Sometimes, I like when you're a little mean, anyway."

The vampire smiled and nuzzled his mate's neck. "I like vhen you're mean, too."

"We have so much in common," Zalith murmured seductively, stroking his fingers down Alucard's back.

Alucard's smile turned into a smirk, but an izuret appeared before he could say anything—maybe that was a good thing; they'd had sex so much lately that he wasn't sure how many more rounds he had left in him today until he started aching and succumbing to fatigue again.

He turned his head, staring at the creature. It was Tato, and he was holding what looked like a slightly overcooked whole bird of some sort stuffed with rice; there were small bites in the meat that matched an izuret's teeth, and Tato had patches of grease and pieces of rice on his face.

Zalith sighed at him. "You're getting rice everywhere."

The izuret squeaked and looked down.

"Vhat is zhat?" Alucard questioned.

Tato set his huge green eyes on the cooked bird and told him that it was a pigeon.

"Who cooked it?" the demon asked.

Tato told them that he bought the bird from a street food vendor in Thaleus—and then he quickly added that he had found Camilla; she was living in an abandoned hut on the outskirts of the village. He handed Alucard a piece of paper…slimy from whatever the pigeon was marinated with.

With a quiet sigh, Alucard took the paper and glanced at the clock. It was just past 12:30 p.m. He then exhaled deeply and asked Zalith, "Are you veady to go to Vharakaal?"

"I suppose," he answered—he didn't sound very enthusiastic.

"You zon't 'ave to come. Von't take me long to talk to 'er."

"No, I'll come. I'm just being greedy," he said with a small laugh and a smirk. "I want to have more naked free time with you."

Alucard smiled in response, glancing away for a moment to hide the fact that he felt flustered despite the lingering desire within him. "Ve'll 'ave plenty of time vonce zhis is all over—ve might even 'ave time vhen ve get back. Ve're still vaiting avound vor zhe Detainer to be veady, avter all."

Zalith kissed his lips. "If you get sick of it, please let me know. I don't want to bother you."

He rested his forehead against the demon's and gazed into his eyes for a moment—he looked down to hide the shyness that came with his words, "I'd never get sick of 'aving sex vith you." He scoffed amusedly. "If I 'ad *your* stamina, ve'd probably be going non-stop. I just 'ave to vecover sometimes, zhat's all."

"Believe me, you don't want it. It comes with an extreme lack of focus at times— well, with things that aren't sex-related, I guess. Otherwise, I'm extremely focused."

"Vell, just vocus on zhe vact zhat vonce ve're done in Vharakaal, you can bring me back to zhis voom and do vhatever you vant to me."

The demon smiled deviously at him. "Perfect."

Chapter Fifty-Four

─ ᐸ † ᐳ ─

Camilla Morányek

| **Alucard** |
| *Vharakaal, Eshkunda, Anaket, Thaleus* |

Dry air with the thick scent of salt and sun-warmed stone greeted Alucard when he and Zalith landed just outside Thaleus, taking cover in the shade of a snaking tamarisk tree. Its gnarled branches splayed outward like the arms of something long-mummified, heavy with pale, feathery leaves that rustled faintly in the breeze. Sand clung to its roots like brittle ash, and the shade it offered was thin but welcome, draping them in a veil just cool enough to think.

The wind slid through the brittle canopy with a whispering hiss, like silk being pulled across old stone. A mineral tang lingered in the air—sunbaked bark and dry sap, cut with the faint bitterness of cracked seed pods and dust warmed by too many summers. It wasn't a pleasant smell, not exactly, but it was new, evoking a sense of curiosity.

"It's peaceful," Zalith said quietly.

It *was*…until the cloud shrouding the sun selfishly slinked away.

Alucard snarled and used his arm to shield his eyes from the sunlight as it spilled like melted gold across the sand-hardened road. But the new environment gave him no time to recover. A sharp tickle stirred deep in his nose—the dry, bitter scent bleeding from the tamarisk bark clung to the air like powdered resin—and before he could suppress it, the irritation crested, and he turned his head with a quiet, involuntary sneeze.

Zalith laughed but tried to hide it with a huff.

The vampire sniffed once, frowned angrily, and muttered under his breath in Dor-Sanguian, "*I fucking hate this place already.*"

His mate pulled him closer, smirking amusedly.

"Is not vunny," he grumbled, his voice muffled by the demon's shirt as he hid his face against it.

"It's a little bit funny," Zalith said, laughing again, squeezing Alucard and twisting them side to side in a slow, swaying taunt. "But it's also very cute."

Alucard pouted but didn't pull away, despite himself—at least not at first.

The warmth of Zalith's body pressed in close, and beneath them, the scorched earth shimmered with waves of rising heat, like the air itself was warping and swimming just above the ground. It licked at his legs, pooled between them like thick breath, and eventually made him squirm.

With a quiet grumble, he slipped free from the hug. "Is too 'ot."

Yet another laugh came from Zalith. "For *you*? Is this place hotter than Hell?"

He huffed, pulling his blazer off. "'Ot isn't zhe vight vord," he muttered. "Is like I'm being suvvocated."

"You're right, it is stuffy here. We should probably find Camilla quickly."

Alucard turned to face the village, scowling as he tried to resist the scraping blight of sunlight. His eyes followed the road that led into the heart of the village, where homes of sun-bleached mudbrick stood low and square against the horizon, faded linen awnings sagging between buildings, fluttering gently in the breeze like tired sails.

Fishermen moved about slowly in the heat, their robes light and weathered, feet wrapped in cracked leather sandals. Nets hung in long, tangled veils from wooden frames, their shadows rippling across the ground like water. A few goats wandered the alleys with no particular purpose, their bleating lost beneath the occasional cry of a gull circling overhead.

A river shimmered just beyond the final row of homes, wide, slow-moving, and speckled with boats of dark wood and patched canvas. Children ran laughing along its edge, chasing one another around stacked baskets and drying reeds. Despite the worn appearance of everything, there was life there.

The izuret's drawing was a little hard to understand. Alucard lifted it to the sunlight so that he could see the linework faded by greasy fingers, and then he looked around at the village just ahead. Of the four villages, *this* one was definitely that in the drawing, and the circled hut…was where?

"I won't be suggesting art classes for him anytime soon," Zalith muttered, looking down at the drawing, too.

With an amused scoff, Alucard glanced back towards the village, paper still in hand. At the far edge of the page, one of the huts was circled in charcoal; it was slightly larger than the others, leaning to one side. But the perspective didn't match what he saw now. He frowned but only took a few moments to work out that Tato had been on the other side of the village, so the vampire looked east instead of west.

Just beyond the slow curve of the river, half-swallowed by thorny palms and clusters of dry reeds, stood a leaning, long-forgotten shack. Its wood was greyed and flaking, roof sagging under its own weight; one side had caved slightly inward, exposing a splintered beam and the remnants of a woven reed mat clinging to a rusted nail. The air around it felt stiller than the rest, like the fishermen and farmers no longer considered its presence.

Alucard tilted his head ever so slightly, focusing. A single vampire aura came from within, and to his relief, he didn't detect anything wrong or worrying. But after taking a step forward, he hesitated, holding his hand above his eyes in an attempt to ease the blinding sting of the sun's rays.

Zalith stood beside him, gripping his hand. "I'd use my wings to shade you, but I don't want to scare the villagers and have them come at us with pitchforks and fishing nets."

The vampire scoffed a laugh, throwing his blazer over his shoulder. "If ve veren't 'ere to 'elp somevone, vould be vorth zhe visk." He then exhaled deeply. "Let's get zhis over vith."

They left the shade of the tree, stepping into the full weight of the afternoon heat. The air shimmered ahead of them, warping the edges of the village into a wavering mirage, and each footstep stirred pale dust from the cracked ground as they headed to the crooked shack. The closer they drew, the stronger the smell of old blood became; a thick blanket of scents lay over it—all manner of herbs and spices and even perfumes—in what was a clear attempt to mask it if a non-human with a keen sense of smell so happened to pass by. That was a good sign. Someone, likely a Strayblood, had taught the vampire inside how to survive alone.

A rusted oil lamp still hung beside the door, long dead and swaying faintly in the heat-stirred breeze. The floorboards creaked when Alucard and Zalith stepped onto the slumping porch, and splinters dropped from every angle like sudden rainfall. As Alucard fixed his gaze on the narrow slant of the doorway, Zalith carefully pulled the tiny shreds of old wood from the vampire's hair before working on his own.

"Vank you," Alucard murmured, stopping at the doorway.

Zalith smiled. "You're welcome, baby."

Alucard leaned his head to the side just enough to see inside the shack. The stale air that drifted out smelled faintly of old brine and wood rot, the scent clinging to every splintered beam and sunken corner. Dim afternoon light spilled in through gaps in the walls and roof, cutting narrow stripes across the dusty floor; old hooks and nets still hung in the back, long since stiffened by salt and age, and a cracked crate near the wall held the faint, sour stink of fish oil.

But it wasn't the forgotten clutter that caught his attention. Faint drag marks traced across the dirt-packed floor, thin, irregular scuffs that almost looked like they'd been made by a robe hem or trailing fingertips. They shifted direction near the centre of the room, circling slightly before making a path towards a pile of loose planks near the back wall. He'd recognize those marks anywhere. A vampire had shadow-stepped here recently—an amateur, though; the user hadn't learned how to leave no trace or even erase one. The question was, however: who had left the marks? The vampire below—whom he hoped was Camilla—or the Strayblood who may have taught them to mask scents?

Alucard stepped inside, boots disturbing the thin layer of dust as he crossed the threshold. The heat dropped slightly in the gloom, but the air was heavier here, more suffocating, more… constricting. He did his best to ignore the uncomfortable sensation, though, and crouched near the planks, eyes narrowing. They'd been arranged hastily to mimic neglect, but the corners were clean where they'd been lifted, the dust uneven.

Zalith crouched beside him, frowning cautiously, grasping his hand again.

"*I vink you should vait 'ere,*" Alucard spoke into Zalith's mind.

His mate's frown shifted to him. "*What?*"

"*I zon't vant to scare 'er.*"

Zalith's expression didn't change at all. "*I'd rather risk scaring her than letting you walk down into some cellar, Alucard, especially after everything that's happened recently.*"

"*I'll be okay,*" he insisted. "*Zhere's only vone vampire aura down zhere—and I'll be vight below you.*"

The demon still looked worried, but after staring at him for a few moments, he sighed silently and nodded stiffly.

Alucard gave him an assuring smile, and then he disappeared. He effortlessly navigated the gloom, his unseen, shapeless form descending into the cellar, pouncing from shadow to shadow. He didn't reveal himself when he slinked into the room below, though; he remained hidden, his eyes locked on the woman in the far corner.

She was curled into herself, knees drawn to her chest, her posture wary but not defensive; it was more like someone bracing against a storm that had already passed. Chestnut-brown hair hung loose around her face, slightly tangled, the ends brushing her collarbone. Her clothing was modest, middle-class in make, but the fit was off, like it belonged to someone else or had once fit her human frame better than it did now. Her skin was pale as expected, faintly sallow in the cellar gloom, and her crimson eyes were rimmed with exhaustion, flicking occasionally to the stairs as though she half-expected something to come through. Even in stillness, there was a trembling uncertainty in her, a sense that she hadn't quite figured out what she was anymore.

Slowly, Alucard stepped out of the shadows.

Her eyes immediately darted to him, filled with terror, and she jumped to her feet, her bloody fingertips digging into the splintering wood behind her.

"Is okay," he insisted calmly, holding out one hand and giving a silent command.

The woman sank back down, shivering but staring obediently.

"You are Camilla, no?" he asked her.

Her eyes widened as she nodded in response.

"And you know who I am?"

Camilla tilted her head, gawping…and then nodded again. "M-M…My Lord."

Once he reached her, he crouched in front of her. "Do you know vhere you are?"

She glanced around the cellar. "We all…came here," she said sadly, lowering her head as if to hide her face.

"Who?"

"Them…their names," she murmured. "I know them."

Names were one of the hardest things for Fledgelings to recall. "Take your time," he told her. "If you can't vemember, zhat's vine."

Camilla shook her head. "My…sons," she said with a small nod. "N…Névaran. He was always…always so mean to his brother, but Aurelien…oh, he was a brave boy."

Alucard wanted to ask if she knew where her children were now—she couldn't be older than thirty, and there was no wedding ring on her finger. But then both dread and *anger* crept in. If Eyra had *killed* children…. He kept his calm expression. Camilla was who mattered right now.

"Sorélys," she then said, her voice breaking a little. "My sweet daughter. I told her I'd be at her recital." She paused, sharply lifting her gaze to look at him, her eyes filled with desperation. "I didn't miss her recital, did I?"

He exhaled deeply and slowly and carefully placed his hand on her shoulder. "Is zhere anyvone taking care of your children?"

She frowned, averting her gaze again. "My…their father," she said with disdain in her voice. "Sorenic." Then she scowled, baring her fangs. "Evil fucker." But she calmed down before Alucard had to tell her to. "Mother-in-law," she said, sounding relieved. "Calienne."

Alucard looked her up and down. She was a bit of a mess, and so was her hiding place, but he saw the drained bodies and stored blood here and there, all covered with herbs; she knew the names of people in her human life, and the longer he sat there with her, the more conscious she appeared to be. Maybe, like Lilly, she'd been getting help.

"Vhere is Calienne now?" he asked.

"She…lives in DeiganLupus, but she's Athanian, too." She grabbed his free hand and desperately asked, "Can we go to them?! They must be so worried!"

The sudden contact made him uncomfortable, but he didn't yank away from her; he gradually eased his hand from her grip and said, "I'm 'ere to 'elp you, Camilla. I vound out vhat Eyra did—"

"Not her!" she exclaimed fearfully, backing against the wall.

"She's gone," he insisted calmly. "You vill never 'ave to see 'er again."

Camilla panted *hard*, her eyes wide and brimmed with terror.

"She's gone," he repeated. "She can't 'urt you anymore."

The woman's breathing slowed, and she eventually settled again.

"Is somebody 'elping you? Anozzer vampire?"

She sat with her legs crossed. "Kestavik," she said slowly, as if struggling with the pronunciation.

"Strayblood? On 'is own."

Camilla nodded. "He said that…he was looking for more lone vampires—he wanted to create a coven. But he said…I'm not ready."

Alucard sighed and said, "You vould not do vell in a Strayblood coven, anyvay." He glanced at the stairs; he knew that Zalith was waiting, and he didn't want to take too long, especially since the Detainer they'd captured could be ready to interrogate any time now. "Listen to me," he said firmly. "Eyra is gone. I vound Lilly, and Lysandra is back at zhe Sanctum. You need to go vhrough Vledgeling training again if you're going to survive in zhis vorld, but you do not 'ave to join zhe Aveson Coven. You can vinish zhe training and zhen go anyvhere you vant."

She looked hesitant and afraid. "Lysandra and Lilly?"

"*Da*. You can be vith your brood sisters again."

"But…my children."

"I can 'elp you vind zhem—"

"N-no," she interjected, shaking her head. "I'm…too dangerous to be around them."

She wasn't wrong. It would take at least a year for her to learn how to control herself, especially around people she loved; all of those emotions would overwhelm a Fledgeling.

"I can get somevone to make sure zhat zhey are safe," he suggested. "And if you vanted, ve can tell zhem zhat you're alive, just off somevhere doing someving."

Camilla looked unsure, like she was thinking.

So Alucard waited.

And waited.

Until a few minutes ticked by.

"I just want to know that they're okay," she murmured sadly. "Calienne always told me…that she'd keep them safe from Sorenic—" she scowled again, "—but he has this way of…of creeping back in, all the lies and manipulation. Calienne has fallen for it before."

He nodded and asked, "Vhat are zheir surnames?"

"Morányek."

"I vill 'ave somevone vind zhem. Vhat do you vant to 'appen if Sorenic is zhere?"

Camilla tensed up and grabbed his arm. "You have to get him away from them!"

Once again, he very slowly pulled free from her grasp. "All vight. You zon't 'ave to vorry about zhem; zhey'll all be safe."

After a slow nod, she settled again.

"Now, vill you come back to zhe Sanctum and vinish your Vledgeling training?"

She fidgeted and asked, "Eyra…is really gone?"

"She is."

Camilla sighed, the fear leaving her pale face. "What about… Dorothee and Hanna?"

"Vell—"

"No… I remember," she mumbled despondently.

"Eyra is paying vor vhat she did to zhem *and* to you. Zhey zidn't die vor noving."

The woman nodded, wiping a tear from her right eye, and then she looked at him. "Is Lilly with Lysandra?"

"She vill be. She's in Antamont vight now with anozzer Strayblood. I vound 'er just like I vound you."

There wasn't much hesitation surrounding her anymore. "Why?"

"Vhy vhat?"

"Why did you come looking for us? We're not… important."

Alucard shook his head. "Every vampire is important to me, Camilla, vhether I turned zhem myselv or not. I vould never leave a vampire alone in zhis vorld unless zhey made zhat choice *zhemselves*. Eyra zidn't give any of you much of a choice. You 'ad to leave to get avay vrom 'er, no?"

"Yes, My Lord," she said shamefully.

"Zhat's noving to be ashamed of. Zhe only person who should be ashamed is Eyra." He stood up and offered her his hand. "Ve can leave vight now if you're veady."

She stared at his hand. "But… the sunlight."

"You vill be okay dematerialized vith us."

"Us?" she questioned anxiously.

"My viancé is upstairs. Zon't vorry, 'e's been 'elping me and zhe coven."

Although she still seemed worried, she took his hand and let him help her to her feet.

Letting go of her, Alucard turned towards the stairs and called, "Zaliv."

Zalith pushed aside one of the wooden planks with his foot and then made his way downstairs.

"Zhis is Camilla," Alucard said to the demon. Then, he said to Camilla, "Zhis is Zaliv."

When Zalith smiled and held his hand out to her, Camilla timidly shook it.

Alucard took Zalith's hand. "Ve can 'ead back to Aveson now. 'Opevully, ve'll 'ear vrom Lilly and Emilien soon."

"Well, at least we have plenty to do to pass the time," the demon said with a smirk.

Trying to hide his flustered face and pout, Alucard looked away for a moment, and then he offered his hand to Camilla. "Let's go."

As soon as she took his hand, Alucard dissolved the three of them into vermillion smoke—but not before he caught a glimpse of Zalith's devious stare, and it sent a shiver of anticipation electrifying through him.

He didn't need words to know exactly what was coming the moment they returned to the Sanctum; Zalith had made that very clear with a single glance. A low, burning ache curled inside Alucard, and he gave in to it without hesitation. He channelled just a little more ethos, enough to push them through the sky faster, recklessly. The sooner they arrived, the longer he'd have to surrender.

And he wanted every second of it.

Chapter Fifty-Five

— ❬ ✝ ❭ —

The Antamont Coven

| Alucard |

| *Rhenovaalis, Atheson, Atheson Coven Sanctum* |

How many times had Zalith fucked him now?

The thought barely formed before dissolving into haze, just another flicker in the storm of sensation overtaking Alucard's mind. He whimpered, the sound thin and broken, more a trembling gasp than a voice, stretched between bliss and exhaustion. Another wave crashed through him—another climax. Was it the fourth? Fifth? He didn't know anymore. Nothing streamed from his dick this time, though. All he could do was feel.

Zalith's cum spilled into him again, hot and thick, and it sent a slow, delicious shiver spiralling through his spent body. Alucard lay on his side, legs parted, trembling uncontrollably. His breath slowed as Zalith gently eased his leg back down, and when his slick thighs pressed together, the vampire groaned softly, open-mouthed and helpless.

Each throb between his legs and each twitch of overworked muscle reminded him that there had been no breaks, no mercy…only Zalith's voice, only his hands and relentless rhythm driving Alucard to surrender again and again.

And he loved it. Even now as his heart pounded and his limbs quaked with overstimulation, he ached for more.

The demon didn't pull out. His fingertips trailed Alucard's waist and stroked down to his crotch. When his touch met the vampire's shaft, Alucard flinched and winced at the sensitivity, closing his eyes in an attempt to calm himself.

"Sorry," Zalith then said with a small laugh, his thumb stroking over Alucard's tip just before he pulled his hand away.

Alucard huffed as embarrassment twisted with the exhaustion, but there was also a slither of curiosity. "'Ow do you…vhy zoesn't zhis 'appen to you?" he mumbled.

He smiled against the back of Alucard's neck. "How do I keep cumming?"

The vampire pouted. "Yes."

Zalith chuckled, the sound low and smug as he kissed Alucard's shoulder. "Perks of being an incubus, darling," he murmured against his skin. "My body doesn't wear out the way yours does. I regenerate fast—cum, stamina, even venom."

The demon then grinned and gave a lazy thrust of his hips, not deep, but it was enough to make Alucard wince and grasp the cushion beneath him as if holding on for his life; pleasure and ache spiralled through him, leaving his exhausted body shivering more than before.

His mate continued, "You could wring me dry all night and I'd still be able to paint your insides by morning." Then, with a teasing hum, he added, "It's just biology doing its best to keep up with how much I want you."

Then he pulled out, not slow, not quick, just sudden, and the motion made Alucard moan again, a fragile, breathless sound that slipped out before he could suppress it.

The emptiness hit him instantly, a deep, aching absence that made Alucard's muscles tighten and his thighs instinctively shift as if to draw Zalith back in. But even without the demon inside him, the warmth lingered. He could still feel his mate's cum buried deep within him, every slow movement of his hips stirring the wet slickness that clung to him inside and out. His body twitched, not with desire now but with the echo of it, overwhelmed but sated. And yet even that fullness couldn't quite replace the hollow ache left in Zalith's wake.

Alucard inhaled shakily and closed his eyes again, letting the heat settle. The aftershocks hadn't passed, but his body already missed the contact.

Was he ready to go again, though?

He lay there…considering it. Despite the trembling and soreness, his body told him yes. So he slowly pushed his ass against the demon's crotch.

A pleased hum came from Zalith. "We should probably give your body time to recover. I don't want to hurt you."

Alucard knew that he was right…but his instincts still urged him to find what it sought. He shifted onto his side, wincing faintly at the dull ache between his legs, but ignoring it. He reached out and placed a trembling hand against Zalith's cheek, needing the contact, *needing him.*

Zalith smiled, warm and lazy, and leaned in to kiss him.

The vampire melted into it. He kissed him back, slow at first, then deeper, breath catching as his heart quickened. That familiar pull bloomed again, desire swelling like a tide. He didn't want to rest. He didn't want this to end. He needed to feel Zalith inside him again…he needed to keep taking his mate's cum until something changed, until something took, until his body accepted it and made it mean more.

And there it was again. That intrusive, impossible thought.

He told himself it couldn't happen—it shouldn't—but the thought refused to leave. His instincts screamed that it could, that he was supposed to be more than just a vessel of pleasure, that Zalith's cum was meant to make him more.

Alucard stopped kissing him, and he blinked slowly, eyes fixed on Zalith's. And in that soft, dangerous silence, the question returned: *was* it possible?

Now that he knew what he had once been—neither fully male nor female—was this buried instinct something deeper? Was it legacy…or truth? Was this why he ached for it so badly?

Was it…why he couldn't make Zalith cum?

He didn't want to let *that* thought in…but it just wouldn't leave him be. Every time he had sex now, the question lingered, the feelings lingered. He couldn't help but want an answer, but at the same time, he *didn't* want to know.

"What's wrong?" Zalith asked.

He lightly shook his head. "Noving, I'm just a little tired."

Zalith caressed his hair. "Do you want to take a nap?"

"I zon't vink zhere's—"

Someone knocked on the door.

Alucard slowly closed his eyes with an exasperated sigh. "Vhy does zhis keep 'appening at zhe most inconvenient moments?"

"It feels like a prank at this point," Zalith mumbled.

The vampire sat up and pulled the blanket around himself. He made sure that every inch of his body was covered, and then he called, "Vhat?"

"My Lord," Anselric said as he stepped into the room. "We've received word from Antamont Coven Master Eske. Lilly and Emilien have woken."

Alucard nodded in response.

After a bow, Anselric left the room.

With another sigh, Alucard looked down at Zalith. "Ve should get dressed and 'ead over zhere."

"How many more times do we have to do this?" the demon asked, sitting up.

"Zhis is zhe last time," he assured him, pulling his trousers on. "Vonce zhose two are 'ere, all ve 'ave to do is vait vor zhe Detainer and vor Eyra's trial."

The demon sighed deeply, getting dressed, too. "I hope so." He handed Alucard his shirt. "What's this Eske like?" he questioned.

Alucard shrugged as he slipped his shirt on and started buttoning it. "'E's evvicient…kind of quiet, obsessed vith structure. 'E probably vishes 'e van zhe vorld, but 'e knows 'e vouldn't be able to 'andle more zhan 'is own coven." He glanced at Zalith. "'E is vone of my oldest vampires. Unlike Eyra, 'e vespects me too much to even vink about getting stupid."

"Well, running the world, I'm sure, isn't all it's cracked up to be."

"Is not," he grumbled in agreement, putting his shoes on. "Because you vind yourselv dealing vith people like Luther and Eyra."

"And so much more," the demon said, standing up.

Alucard got up as well, and after he pulled his cape on, he took Zalith's hand—and he did his best to fight and hide the ache between his legs. "Come on. I vink you vill like zhe Antamont Sanctum. Is a very old castle I bought a vew centuries ago and vestored."

"I do love a castle," he said as he followed Alucard out of the room.

They navigated the Sanctum, and once they were outside, Alucard dematerialized them both into vermillion smoke and began the journey to Antamont.

As he travelled, though, the ache left in the wake of constant sex was quickly accompanied by fatigue; the exhaustion was strange, not like being tired from overexerting his body but much like what he felt when he'd lost too much blood... or used too much ethos.

He ignored *that*, too. He just wanted to get to Antamont and bring this to an end.

| **Zalith** |

| *Rhenovaalis, Antamont, Søndhallow, Antamont Coven Sanctum* |

When they landed and rematerialized in Antamont, Zalith's gaze instinctively lifted to the sky. Thick storm clouds churned above them, low and heavy with rain, their charcoal bodies flashing now and then with distant lightning. Thunder rolled across the horizon, muffling the faint bustle of the city far beyond the trees.

His eyes dropped sharply at a flicker of movement along the oak and sycamore tree line. Figures half-shrouded in shadow, silent in their steps. He recognized the way they dressed—he'd seen the same vampires in the Atheson Sanctum. They were Sentinels. Still patrolling, still doing their jobs... but barely. He could feel it in the way their eyes kept drifting again and again towards Alucard; they weren't cautious or suspicious, they were *awed*. They stared like worshippers catching sight of a god. And the worst part? Zalith could feel the hunger in them—not for blood, but to throw themselves at Alucard's feet, to fawn, to offer.

The demon's jaw tightened. His possessive instincts stirred, begging him to pull Alucard close and *show them* who he belonged to—but he didn't. For now, he walked at Alucard's side and tried shifting his focus to what lay ahead.

Rising from the centre of the wide, dew-laced glade stood the castle, ancient and touched by familiar elegance. Its stone façade had been restored over the past century, just as Alucard told him, but not modernized. No, the additions were subtler than that: darker stone inlaid along the archways, ornamental iron grilles over certain windows, tall spires with tapering points like talons scraping at the sky. The structure bore a kind of regal sharpness, refined yet foreboding.

It was very Alucard.

Even the steep gables and narrow balconies seemed chosen for their dramatic silhouette, as though the castle itself was meant to cast judgement from beneath the clouds. A pair of double doors waited at the base, dark wood banded with blackened steel, flanked by gargoyle sconces that flared faintly with enchanted flames. Zalith felt a flicker of appreciation; Alucard hadn't just restored the place, he had *claimed* it.

"It's beautiful, baby," he murmured into his fiancé's ear as he nuzzled his cheek.

"Vank you," he said, smiling.

A soft breeze whispered through the glade, curling around Zalith's legs as Alucard's cape fluttered against him. The vampire's scent followed—rich, alluring, and so fucking maddening—and it ensnared him like a tether, pulling at every fraying thread of his restraint.

He wanted him again. Right there, right now. But he knew better. He'd already taken Alucard more times than he probably should have. As much as his instincts begged for more, he needed to let him rest.

The castle doors creaked open from within, and when they parted fully, two vampires stood at either side—postured, poised…and utterly undone the moment they laid eyes on Alucard. Just like the Sentinels, they stared wide-eyed and reverent. One of them even trembled, visibly restraining the urge to kneel or speak or *something*, lips slightly parted in silent awe.

Zalith didn't like it one bit. It was creepy and uncomfortable. But Alucard had clearly gotten used to it over the centuries.

They stepped inside, and the cool hush of stone swallowed them. The entry hall stretched ahead, all vaulted ceilings and smooth black-and-white tile underfoot, polished so clean that it mirrored their boots in passing. Candle sconces burned low along the walls, their light shimmering against darkened portraits and age-worn shields, remnants of a history that clung to the stone like dust.

A few vampires lingered just off the main corridor, standing with the quiet posture of those trying not to stare but failing. Zalith caught the subtle shifts—eyes darting towards Alucard, lips parting in quiet disbelief. One whispered something to the other with a barely restrained grin. Another bowed their head with reverence as they passed.

Zalith stayed close, ready to snarl or shove if he had to.

They reached the stair hall, a vast, open space beneath a grand arched ceiling, where twin staircases curved up along the walls like sculpted arms. And waiting there were *dozens* of vampires—perhaps the entire coven. Some stood on the stairs, others along the balcony above, but most filled the floor below. Not a single one stepped forward. They knew better. But as Alucard entered, every head dipped, and everyone bowed.

The demon's eyes scanned each of them. He could feel the devotion in the room like a thick perfume, excitement barely restrained by discipline. They didn't speak or move, though some did turn their heads to glimpse at the man who began descending the stairs.

Zalith watched him closely.

The man had meticulously swept back ash-blonde hair, the pomade evident as strands glinted in the light. His blazer was fitted to near military precision, and the shimmer of a black-stoned ring flickered from his right hand as it rested lightly on the bannister. He moved with the kind of restraint that came from centuries of discipline, measured and dignified, yet there was something else beneath the formality. The man wasn't just performing hierarchy, he was clearly at total ease in a way that said this was familiar, an occurrence he'd experienced often enough to keep him from reacting like the others.

Zalith narrowed his gaze slightly, studying the angles of the man's sharp features and the slight tilt of his head as his eyes settled on Alucard. There was no arrogance, no challenge...no desire or envy or desperation for attention. All that existed was unmistakable respect and recognition.

The man spread his arms when he reached the bottom of the stairs, saying fondly, "*Ah, god eftermiddag, Herr Alucard.*" He stopped a few feet from them both. "*Det glæder mig inderligt at se Dem efter så lang en tid.*" He held out his hand.

Alucard smiled and shook it as he replied, "Deiganish, Eske."

Was that Drydenish? No...it was *like* Drydenish, but not it exactly—yet his accent sounded much like it, too.

"Eske, zhis is my viancé, Zaliv," Alucard said as he looked at the demon and squeezed his hand.

Eske held out his hand and said, "*Hej*, Zalith. I am Eske Jürgensen."

Zalith shook his hand, smiling pleasantly.

"It is wonderful to see that you have found each other," Eske said as his gaze shifted between them. "You are uh...how you say...spirit friends? No...destiny lovers." He smiled enthusiastically.

The demon smiled amusedly.

"Soul mates," Alucard said flatly.

Eske nodded. "Those."

Alucard then said, "Lilly and Emilien."

"Ah, right." Eske turned around and began leading the way to the slid-open doors beneath the stairs. As he did, he waved his hands dismissively towards the observing vampires, muttering in his native language.

The coven started dispersing.

"I hear what happen about Luther and Attila," Eske said, turning left down a corridor. "Not fully story for Luther, but I don't think I need details. Always was a strange man."

Alucard rolled his eyes, and Zalith felt him tighten his grip on his hand.

"And Eyra?" Eske shook his head and muttered something that wasn't Deiganish. "Not expecting this from her. But we not all know each other," he said with a shrug and took them up some stairs. "Noctrel, though? I like Noctrel. Good choice."

"I'm sure zhey vill do a much better job," Alucard said.

At the top of the stairs, they emerged into a lounge.

It was quieter than Zalith expected—not silent, but muted, as if the room itself had the good sense to keep still in Alucard's presence. The windows along the far wall were tall but shuttered tight, warding off any chance of sunlight, casting the space in a cool, amber dusk from the wall lanterns and a chandelier above. Shadows lay thick in the corners, softening the edges of the black-stone floors and deep crimson furniture.

A bar ran along the left side of the room, polished to a mirror sheen. Three vampires sat there with half-full glasses, their hushed voices drifting just beneath the airy draw of strings playing from a gramophone nestled in the opposite corner. The scent of aged blood curled through the air like incense, accompanied by several different colognes and perfumes.

Zalith's eyes tracked the music; near the gramophone, on a velvet chaise by the wall, he saw Lilly and Emilian. Both looked pale and still shaken, though not afraid. Another vampire knelt beside them, murmuring something too quiet to catch as he dabbed at the small cuts along their arms and necks with a blood-soaked cloth. The injuries were shallow but numerous, perhaps left by the infection that might have killed them if he and Alucard hadn't shown up in time.

Eske slowed beside them and made a brief, open-palmed gesture to the corner. "I get Bloodmender to see them," he said quietly, halting in the middle of the room. "And I keep Adherents to watch," he added, nodding at the vampire sitting at the bar. "Some of...Fledgelings not familiar with Strayblood exception. I explain, but...takes time."

"*Multumesc*," Alucard said.

The man bowed his head. "I see you before leave."

Alucard gave a half nod and then approached the couch, pulling Zalith with him.

"What language was he speaking?" the demon asked curiously.

"Antamish. I zon't know enough to 'old conversation, only enough to get zhe general idea of vhat somevone is trying to say."

Zalith smirked a little, although he still felt the lingering possessiveness. "And what was Eske trying to say?"

"Just zhat 'e vas glad to see me avter a long time."

He had more questions, but he'd not ask them now. In response, he gave a small nod, and then he focused on the vampires ahead.

Emilien was the first to notice their approach, his bloodshot eyes tracing them as they walked around the couch. When Lilly saw them moments later, she tensed up and grasped his arm, and he placed his hand over hers.

The Bloodmender stood up, bowed, and walked away.

"'Ow are you veeling?" Alucard asked as he sat on the couch across from them.

After glancing at Lilly, who clearly wasn't going to speak, Emilien said, "Much better. Thank you for what you did; we'd probably be dead by now if you hadn't found us down there."

Alucard nodded but sighed quietly. "I zon't 'ave a lot of time, so I'm going to get to zhe point." He looked at Lilly. "I know vhat 'appened with Eyra." He looked at Emilien. "And I know vhat 'appened vith Vheremond and Corven-'ale. Judging by zhis—" he gestured his hand to Lilly and Emilien's grasp on one another, "—and vhat ve saw in zhat crypt, I'm going to assume zhat you two plan to stay togezzer."

Emilien frowned unsurely. "What does that mean? *Stay* together? You're not planning on taking her back to Eyra, are you?" he exclaimed as Lilly hid behind him.

"No," Alucard said firmly. "Eyra 'as been Veiled. She is no longer zhe Aveson Coven Master, nor vill she ever see Lilly and 'er brood sisters again. I've vound Lysandra and Camilla; zhey're going vhrough Vledgeling training again, and zhen I vill be taking zhem to Vontisère, vhere zhey vill start new lives." He looked at Lilly again, who was now peering over Emilien's shoulder. "If she is going to survive, she needs to go vhrough Vledgeling training again, too."

Lilly still kept herself mostly hidden behind Emilien. "Camilla…and Lysandra?"

Alucard nodded. "Zhey're safe at zhe Sanctum vith a whole new group of Vledgelings. Zhey're both 'oping zhat you vill join zhem, and zhey are also open to zhe possibility of both you and Emilien going vith zhem to Vontisère. You von't 'ave to be part of a coven if you zon't vant to."

Once again, Lilly and Emilien glanced at one another.

"Ve 'ave to get back to Aveson as soon as possible," Alucard continued. "I vould prever zhat zhe two of you come vith us and discuss zhe ovver zhere. Per'aps seeing some vamiliar vaces vill 'elp."

Emilien quietly asked Lilly, "What do you want to do?"

For a moment, Lilly stared at him, and then she slowly shifted her gaze to Alucard. "Eyra…is dead?"

"She's avaiting trial bevore zhe Vampire Council, but zhat is going to end in 'er death anyvay."

Zalith started zoning out. Alucard was far more patient than he was; he couldn't sit there and re-answer the same questions over and over and repeat the same things. All he wanted to do was go home—*home* home, not back to Atheson. He was tired of being at that Sanctum, he was tired of all the people and the knocking on the door. Being with Alucard in their own room and in their own bed was all he wanted; he wanted to lie there in that familiar comfort and hold him, he wanted to feel him, and he wanted to *devour* him. He wasn't sure how much longer he could spend out here.

"You zon't 'ave to go vith zhem to Vontisère," his fiancé said for what might be the third time…or maybe the fourth.

"How long is the training going to take?" Emilien asked.

"Two to vour months."

Emilien looked at Lilly again.

Zalith exhaled deeply, leaning back a little as he rested one leg over the other. He was becoming impatient, not only because he wanted to go home but because he was struggling to ignore Alucard's scent. The longer he sat there, the stronger the pull got, and resisting the urge to grab him and take him somewhere alone was eating away at him, gnawing at his ability to sit still.

Alucard obviously noticed. "You vill be given space if you zon't vant to intervact vith zhe coven," he said to Emilien. "But I veally can't tell you any more zhan I alveady 'ave about 'ow important is zhat she goes vhrough training again. I know you veel like you can teach 'er, but you simply do not 'ave zhe skills. Brood nurses are centuries old bevore zhey can even begin to understand 'ow to teach Vledgelings." He paused to exhale sharply. "You spent no time vhatsoever with a coven, Emilien; you zidn't even veceive zhe proper training yourselv. I vill not vorce you to come to Aveson, but I *vill* take Lilly. She zidn't choose zhis vate, and she deserves zhe chance to make 'er own decision vonce she is stable enough to do so."

His fiancé's attempt to hurry things along helped Zalith settle a little; he appreciated it…and he hoped that these two vampires would take the hint.

And to the demon's *utter* relief—

"All right," Emilien said. "But if I want to go where she goes, will I have to go through the training, too?"

"I vould advise zhat, *da*," Alucard replied.

Emilien looked down at Lilly's hands as he nodded. "I don't…want to see Corven-Hale, though," he said quickly, his eyes snapping back to Alucard. "I just…messages are one thing, but I'm not interested in seeing his face—at least not yet."

"Vine. Vonce ve get to zhe Sanctum, I'll 'ave everyving arranged vor you both."

He nodded.

"I need vone more ving vrom you," Alucard said, taking his pen from his pocket, and then he grabbed a notepad that had been left on the coffee table. As he tore a page out, he said, "I need zhe name of zhe seer zhat crveated zhat vard vor you—zhe vone avound zhe crypt."

"Oh…uh.…"

Alucard handed him the pen and paper.

Emilien started writing. "What do you need from him? If you don't mind me asking."

"'E might 'ave been zhe vone to cause you and Lilly to get sick."

"Oh…" he responded, handing the pen and paper back.

Alucard then got up, shifting his sights to the lingering Bloodmender. "Take zhis to Eske and tell 'im zhat I need 'im to look vor zhis seer and vind out if 'e is vesponsible vor zhe mycoriaspore in Vardeskov. Tell 'im to send me 'is vindings."

The Bloodmender took the paper that Emilien had written the seer's details on. "Yes, My Lord," he said, and then he hurried off.

As Zalith eagerly stood, too, Alucard took his hand and said, "Vonce ve 'ave zhe answers, I'll send a zemon to burn zhe village."

His mate nodded.

Emilien stood up, pulling Lilly with him.

Alucard turned and started leading the way.

As Zalith followed, though, a little of his relief faded. They weren't heading home yet; there were still things left to tie up in Atheson: the Detainer, and Eyra's Trial. However, hours had passed by, so either of those things could happen at any moment. He just hoped it was *soon*. The thought of having to spend another night in that estate made him nearly as uncomfortable as all the gawping, drooling vampires of Eske's coven.

But at least he was leaving *this* place behind.

Chapter Fifty-Six

— ⸲ † ⸳ —

Helpless

| **Zalith** |

| ***Rhenovaalis, Atheson, Atheson Coven Sanctum*** |

It was torture…being so close but not close enough.

Zalith sat across the couch from his fiancé, their legs comfortably tangled. He'd left a narrow gap between their bodies—a weak attempt to honour his decision to let Alucard rest. But it was becoming unbearable. Every second felt like a test of restraint, his senses constantly drawn to the vampire beside him. The way Alucard looked in the muted light, the way his scent lingered like something forbidden. The soft, steady rhythm of his heartbeat, his quiet breaths, the occasional twitch of his brow as he wrote in his memory journal—it all pulled at Zalith like a tide. And that *expression*, focused, slightly furrowed…it was enough to make him ache. He *loved* that look. He loved *him*. And he didn't know how much longer he could sit still.

He shifted slightly, adjusting his posture in a vain attempt to ignore the heat pooling low in his abdomen. The dull, insistent throb between his legs was growing more maddening by the minute. He'd told himself that he would let Alucard recover; he knew how uncomfortable dry orgasming was—it even got painful. But his body had never been one to obey logic, especially not where his mate was concerned.

Despite his best efforts, his dick was hardening, stirred by every soft breath and unconscious movement that Alucard made beside him.

He had to distract himself; he had to find something to take his mind off it. But there was nothing. There was only Alucard.

The demon gazed at his fiancé, his heart starting to beat harder, his body tensing—even his fangs twitched, eager to bite, to *taste*.

Something else….

Anything else—

"Tell me about Eske," he blurted—he knew the subject would stir some other emotion, a reaction that might shove the desire aside.

"Vhat about 'im?" Alucard asked as he turned his head to look at him.

He shrugged and suggested, "How did you meet him?"

Alucard lowered his memory journal and pen, donning a pondering expression. "Eske vas vorking as a voyal scribe in Sønd'allow vhen ve virst crossed paths. 'E'd been trained in cipher vork—you know… codes, symbols, strange languages, vings like zhat. Vasn't zhe sort of ving most men in court gave much vhought to, but 'e 'ad a talent vor spotting patterns vhere ozzers saw nonsense."

Zalith nodded, listening…though hearing Alucard compliment Eske made him feel…not jealous, that wasn't the word. Hostile? Sort of. Possessive? Yes. He couldn't help it. He knew that Eske nor the other old friends before him were a threat, but there'd always be that lingering instinct to protect and claim.

"Zhat's vhat got 'im pulled into zhe investigation, I suppose," his fiancé continued, putting his journal on the table beside him. "A string of nobles 'ad been vound butchered; zheir bodies vere marked with sigils no priest could vead and drained nearly dry. Vas quiet, covered up, but Eske vas sent to make sense of all of zhat."

Despite the contempt he now felt towards Eske, Zalith's interest was piqued.

The vampire frowned ever so slightly, like he was thinking again. "I vas passing vhrough Sønd'allow under a borrowed name, vollowing zhe same trail 'e vas—a Diabolus lead. Bloodless corpses, arcane carvings, zhe scent of ancient ethos, vings like zhat. Eventually, I vound myselv in zhis ugly little tavern looking vor a man who 'ad apparently vitnessed vitchcravt—zhe kind I vas looking vor."

As his fiancé adjusted slightly, sinking into the couch, Zalith tensed up…again. The mere brush of Alucard's knee against his thigh made his dick twitch.

"Zhat vas vhen I saw Eske. Zhis 'apless guy with ink-stained vingers, speaking too quietly to zhe people 'e'd obviously chosen to 'ide among so zhat 'e could observe vithout drawing attention—zhe inky vingers vere a 'uge giveavay, zhough; not very many people could vrite back zhen. Anyvay, 'e vas clearly out of 'is depth; 'e 'ad no veapon or ethos, and zhe vagged clothes 'e vore vere likely borrowed vrom somevone who vasn't as vell off as 'im. Unprepared vor vhere 'is observations vere taking 'im, but 'e vas smart—smart enough to connect symbols across corpses zhat no one 'ad dared link. 'E vas also smart enough not to panic vhen I started vollowing 'im—vell, vhen I let 'im notice."

Zalith smiled when Alucard did. He listened to his words, but his eyes were constantly flicking from the vampire's lips to his neck, and to his face. He did his best to resist the urges, though.

Alucard continued, "I kept my distance at virst. I vatched 'im question men tvice 'is size, dig vhrough bloodied parchment like mattered. I zon't vink zhat 'e vas *trying* to be brave, 'e simply *vas*. And vhen I vinally stepped out of zhe dark and told 'im I vas chasing zhe same trail, 'e took zhe ovver to vork vith me vithout vhought."

"Why did you invite him to work with you?" he asked, the question stealing his focus for a moment.

"At zhe time, I vas looking vor my virst vampires. I'd pervected zhe turning and learning process—vhich took me eight years—and I vanted to vind a suitable group of capable people. I tested Eske vor veeks. Ve vollowed zhe trail togezzer, all zhe blood-scrawled valls, 'alv-burned letters, and keeps zhat 'adn't seen life in a century. Zhe deeper ve vent—"

He wanted to be *deep* inside Alucard.

"—zhe colder got, like zhe land vas trying to vreeze shut vhat ve vere about to uncover. Eventually, ve vound zhe strong'old—or vather, zhe strong'old vound us. Zhe Diabolus zidn't vaste time. Zhey vere vaiting vith all of zheir stupid swords and spells. Just as I'd predicted, Eske vasn't very good vith a sword, but 'e tried anyvay, and I let 'im. I *did* see zhat vith some training, 'e could become a good vighter, but 'is mind vas vhy I turned 'im. I alveady 'ad Crowell lined up as my skilled vighter, and Attila as my inviltrator. Vonce I taught zhe vhree of zhem 'ow to control and use zheir new power, I 'ad zhe pervect team to 'elp me take on zhe larger Diabolus groups."

Zalith couldn't help but reach towards his fiancé and fiddle with his hair. "My devious, perceptive little vampire," he purred and caressed Alucard's cheek.

Alucard smiled, his cheeks turning a little red as he turned his head to hide his face.

The demon traced his thumb along Alucard's cheekbone. He should have pulled back...but the warmth of his mate's blush and the way he tucked his face into his shoulder like he didn't know what he did to him made restraint feel like a distant, useless promise. His hand slid down, fingers curling gently around Alucard's jaw, and he leaned in. "You make it so damn hard to resist," he murmured.

Alucard looked up at him, lips parted slightly in surprise—just enough invitation.

That was all Zalith needed.

He closed the distance and kissed him, slow at first, savouring the shape of his mouth, but it only deepened with each passing second. All that pent-up hunger, the ache he'd tried to ignore, it surged forward. His hand moved to the back of the vampire's neck, drawing him closer; their bodies touched, their legs still lazily tangled from earlier, but now Zalith shifted nearer, pressing into him, lips parting to taste him more.

Alucard didn't hesitate. He kissed back just as eagerly, a quiet, breathy noise leaving his throat as his fingers gripped the front of Zalith's shirt.

The demon groaned softly into his mouth. So much for restraint.

He kept kissing him until it grew hungry and gasping, just tongues and teeth and breath. He was drowning in it—he was drowning in *Alucard*, in the scent of his skin and the low, inviting sounds he made when Zalith tugged at his clothes and pressed their bodies closer.

Zalith didn't bother with ceremony; there was no room in his desperation for foreplay. His fingers worked fast, shoving their trousers down, his hands shaking from the pressure he'd bottled for too long. He broke the kiss for only a moment as he hastily and messily coated his dick in lube, and then he eagerly massaged the rest against Alucard's hole.

Alucard had only just started undoing his shirt when the demon grabbed his thighs, pulled him down flat on his back, and lifted his legs up against his chest. Zalith couldn't wait. His fiancé gave a startled but pleasured breath when the demon pushed his dick inside his ass in one smooth, eager motion. The vampire whined delightedly, his back arching as his body clenched around the intrusion; he desperately dug his claws into the couch, eyes half-lidded, his lips kiss-swollen.

Zalith moaned delightedly, shuddering as he buried every throbbing inch inside his mate—and then he pulled back, sliding his dick out again until the tip was all that remained, and when he pushed back in, he moaned again, the sound entangling with Alucard's pleased cry. The vampire's legs were already trembling in his grip, and that spurred him on further.

He thrusted hard and deep but could only keep that rhythm for mere seconds before he let Alucard's legs wrap around his waist. As he leaned forward and gripped the couch arm above the vampire's head, he let his aggression take over, fucking Alucard harder, faster, moans and whines and cries upon every breath between them. He nuzzled the side of Alucard's face, pulling himself forward with every thrust, giving each plunge that little bit of extra force.

Alucard whined his name, and *he* whined Alucard's, relief and desperation and pleasure surging through him. He gripped the vampire's throat with his free hand, whining once more, thrusting deep again and again and again—

Zalith stilled with a possessive growl that broke into a delighted moan as heat burst from his core. His cum pulsed out of him, spilling inside his mate with blissful force. Alucard came at the same time—but something felt…wrong.

The vampire's body clenched beautifully around him, but instead of the usual slick warmth that followed, there was nothing. Just the fierce, rhythmic spasms of climax and the tense arch of his back.

Zalith's gaze flicked down, scanning Alucard's face as the vampire moaned again— but this time, the sound wasn't purely pleasure. His brows pinched together, his lashes fluttered, and his throat worked around a whimper that cracked with strain. And then the vampire grimaced—he was trembling, not with the usual post-orgasm tremors but a quaking exhaustion. His thighs twitched around Zalith's waist, his knuckles were pale where they gripped the couch, and his lips were parted in a gasping, desperate pant, like his body had been wrung dry, yet still forced through the motions.

The demon didn't move or pull out. Horror rooted him in place as he stared down at him.

Alucard turned his head, trying to hide his struggled expression as his chest rose and fell in shallow, rapid breaths. The soft, helpless noises slipping from him weren't moans anymore. They were whimpers.

Zalith's heart seized. Shame flooded him in a crashing wave, smothering whatever haze of desire remained. He looked down again, truly seeing him now—how badly he was shaking, how red and sore he looked, how overused his body had become. And *he* had done this. He'd let his instincts win. Again.

"Fuck," he breathed, his voice barely holding together. "Alucard—" He moved at once, gently pulling out. Guilt made his hands clumsy as he softened his grip and slid one arm beneath his mate's back; the other stroked Alucard's hair, his cheek, anything to bring him back to comfort. "I'm so sorry," he whispered, pressing a trembling kiss to his forehead. "I shouldn't have—you were still recovering. I pushed you too far." He didn't try to justify it or excuse the way he'd ignored every warning sign, too desperate to feel him again. He eased him closer, slowly, protectively, as he whispered in an attempt to calm his overwhelmed fiancé, "You're okay. I've got you, baby." He carefully guided Alucard onto his side and lay behind him, holding him tightly. "I'm so sorry," he said again, nuzzling the back of his head as he scowled in despair. No matter how badly his instincts clawed at him, no matter how much they screamed to take more, he'd rather silence them and suffer than see Alucard like this again.

The vampire exhaled deeply, shakily, but he slowly relaxed, his body settling against Zalith's.

"I'm sorry," he murmured again.

Alucard stiffly shook his head, and his hand brushed over Zalith's. "Is...is okay," he breathed. "I like zhis—I like *veeling* like zhis."

His response surprised Zalith, it even relieved him. There was still guilt, though; knowing he'd at the very least made Alucard uncomfortable made him feel terrible. *But*...he couldn't ignore the intrigue, either. He smirked, caressing the vampire's hair. "Why do you like it?"

A light shrug came from his fiancé. "Makes me veel...like I belong to you—more zhan I alveady do," he murmured shyly, *tiredly*. "Like I'm yours to do with vhatever you please." He paused, entwining his fingers with Zalith's. "And I like serving you. I like giving you vhat you need."

Zalith's smirk turned into a smile. "Aw," he purred, nuzzling the side of Alucard's face. "I need to stop, though," he added with a quiet laugh.

"Vhy?"

"Because I don't think it's good for your body."

He didn't argue; maybe because he was tired, or maybe because he understood—perhaps both. Instead, he rolled over to face him and nuzzled against his chest.

The demon smiled a little wider, holding him closely. "I love you, Alucard."

Alucard hummed softly and kissed just below Zalith's neck. "I love *you*, Zaliv."

He caressed the vampire's hair, and when he glanced down at him, he saw that he was falling asleep. He wanted to offer him blood—it would definitely help him recover faster—but he didn't want to wake him, either. The more sleep Alucard got, the better. So he closed his eyes, too, and let himself relax. He could give his fiancé blood later.

For now, he'd also rest, and he'd make the most of the time he got to spend with Alucard like this until it was once again time to get back to work.

Chapter Fifty-Seven

— ⟨ † ⟩ —

Agency, Contractor, Overseer

| Alucard |
| Atheson, Atheson Coven Sanctum |

Alucard stirred when he heard Zalith's voice. A tired groan left him as irritation clashed with both the pain in his head and the ache in his crotch; while he could tolerate the latter simply because he liked how it made him feel claimed, the former was beginning to become an aggravating inconvenience.

He sighed when he heard the door close; he turned onto his back, smiled when Zalith nuzzled his neck, but frowned once his eyes landed on the window. It was dark already—where had the time gone?

"Hey baby," his mate murmured and kissed along his jaw.

The vampire smiled again. "Hi," he said, turning his head to give the demon more room to nuzzle and kiss.

Zalith didn't linger for long, though. After just a few more kisses, he propped himself up on his arm and gazed down at him. "That was Virelka," he said, stroking his thumb along Alucard's bottom lip. "She said that we can go and interrogate the Detainer now; there's no anti-ethos elixirs left in his system."

That relieved him. After they were done with the Detainer, all they'd have left to wait on was Eyra's trial—and *that* reminded him of something he should have done earlier after sending Lilly and Emilien to join Camilla, Lysandra, and Rosaline. "Ve can 'ead down zhere, but I need to grab vone of my vampires on zhe vay."

"Is everything okay?" Zalith asked as they both sat up.

He nodded and said, "I just need to send somevone to get a 'ouse veady in Vontisère vor Lysandra and zhe ozzers."

"Oh," the demon said, handing him his trousers. "Do you think they'll be okay out there? Just five of them."

"Vell, vive is better zhan two. If zhey take in or make vive more Vellkin, zhey can be vecognized as a coven," he explained, pulling his trousers on.

"Fellkin?"

"Is vhat coven members call each ozzer—is like…instead of packmates."

The demon nodded once in response, slipping his shoes on.

"Zhey'd also 'ave to establish zheir own 'ierarchy. I do zhat vhen I make zhe coven, but vhen is zhis sort of situation, I leave zhat up to zhem because a Strayblood-vormed coven vunctions better vhen zhey've decided zheir own voles."

Zalith smirked at him. "Every time you talk about these things, I love and respect you and your mind even more," he said and kissed his lips.

Alucard smiled at him again. He didn't know what to say; he felt flustered, and maybe even a little embarrassed, though he wasn't sure why.

The demon then took his hand. "Come on. Let's go and see what that Detainer has to tell us."

With a nod, Alucard got up and followed Zalith.

Just outside his private library, a few vampires were sitting at the large coffee table playing cards, including Vice Matron Drusilda. She knew exactly what to look for when picking a location for a vampire to settle.

"Drusilda," Alucard said, stopping by the table.

Every vampire bowed their heads humbly.

"My Lord," Drusilda said pleasantly.

"I need you to go to Vontisère in Chantrevaux and vind a suitable 'ouse vor vive Vledgelings to move into. Zhe place vill need to be veady in at most vhree months' time."

She nodded, put her cards down, and stood up. "I'll get started right away."

"*Multumesc*," he said, and then he made his way downstairs with Zalith.

They navigated the castle, descending the stone corridors and walking the gloomy halls. Eventually, they reached the Lower Withercrypt; the heavy door creaked open, and the thick, sour scent of rot hit Alucard before his eyes even adjusted to the total darkness.

The Detainer was still strapped to the chair in the centre of his cell, slumped and silent but alive. His head lolled until the door opened, and then he slowly lifted it with a gravelled grunt, the effort visibly painful.

Hours had passed since Allie peeled the armour from him, and the remnants of her work festered. His wounds had shifted from raw to ruin, edges slick with yellowing pus, the flesh darkening where infection was creeping in. Some of the deeper gashes had reopened, leaking sluggish trails of blood down his sides. The scent was foul, muddled with sickness; what remained of his uniform clung to his body in damp, tattered strips, mottled with sweat and blood and something pale and oozing—the odour worsened with every drip and trickle.

Beside him now was a metal table upon which lay used blood extraction tools and vials of crimson mixed with the bluish gleam of anti-ethos elixir. Virelka, as always, had done an impressive and swift job.

Alucard's gaze drifted back to the Detainer's face. Sunken eyes met his, dull but aware, the kind of awareness that came from suffering drawn out just enough to avoid unconsciousness. There was no rage or defiance, only the quiet clarity of someone who knew he wouldn't be leaving this place.

Zalith stepped in behind the vampire, still holding his hand, but Alucard didn't speak yet. He let the silence stretch, watching as the Detainer's dwindling will withered away, and his head quickly dropped again. He had no fight left.

The vampire looked at Zalith. "Vhat if 'e zoesn't know anyving?"

"Then we'll find his little friends and see what they know," the demon said.

Alucard nodded and watched as his mate approached the Detainer.

Zalith snatched a fistful of the man's hair and pulled, making him look up at him. He didn't grab his face, though—the man was obviously so weak that he'd not be able to fight back; his mind was an open book.

"The job came in through the Detainer Agency last Tuesday—Tertium twenty-eighth," Zalith started. "There wasn't a lot of information other than the numbers, but the job came from a contractor called the Mirgathen Division." He looked back at Alucard. "Do you know it?"

Alucard crossed his arms, thinking. "Vhat does 'e know about zhem?"

Zalith glared at the Detainer. "There are three divisions and an overseer, who signs off on all the contracts. He doesn't know his or her name, though."

The Mirgathen Division *did* sound familiar, but Alucard couldn't figure out why. If it was something Damien or Lilith had suppressed, *why*? He frowned, but he knew that there was no point in trying to force himself to remember. This feeling, though, was enough to convince him that a Numen may very well be involved. But who? Why?

"Whoever they are, they have ties to some other hunting agencies," the demon said.

"Vhich vones?"

"Ashward Order, Rime Protocol, Concordat Chain, Black Vellum, Kynlash Pact, Silver Ministry, Division Epsilon, the—"

"Epsilon?" Alucard questioned sharply as dread struck him—but again…he didn't know why he knew that name, or why he felt so uncomfortable.

Zalith turned his head to look at him again, nodding. "Who are they?"

The vampire's frown thickened. "I zon't…know," he said with a slow shake of his head. "I veel like I know zhe name, but I zon't know vhy I do. Kind of makes me suspect even more zhat vone of zhe Numen might be involved because zhis is zhe same kind of veeling I get vhen my buried memories start survacing."

His mate glared at the Detainer for a few moments. "He doesn't know anything about the agency or if a Numen is involved."

Alucard huffed, tapping his fingers against his bicep. "If zhe contractor's overseer 'as ties to so many agencies, zhen zhey're likely a very large operation, and very dangerous."

"So, we find the overseer," Zalith said, letting go of the Detainer. "If the overseer signs off on the contracts, then they'll know where the contract came from."

"Does 'e know vhere ve can vind zhe overseer?"

Zalith grabbed the Detainer's hair again. "All he knows is that the Mirgathen Division is a Rhenovaalisean-based contracting bureau. They receive contracts from clients and hand them out to whatever agency is best suited." He let go and turned to face Alucard. "They likely keep records."

"Ve can send somevone to vind zhe place. Zhey zon't exactly sound like zhe kind of organization zhat vould 'ide zhemselves; 'unters varely 'ide vhen zhey're a big group—zhey pretty much vlaunt avound."

"Humans," the demon grumbled, joining Alucard by the door.

Alucard's eyes flicked to the Detainer. "Did 'e know anyving else usevul? If zhere are ozzer children being taken?"

With a deep sigh, he shook his head. "He doesn't even know where that ship was heading. They were supposed to leave it somewhere in the middle of the ocean and leave via rowboat, but he never got that location. Only their captain knew at which point in their voyage they'd receive it."

The vampire huffed irritably. "So is probably no use sending 'owever many people to scour zhe sea."

"Yeah," he mumbled, pulling Alucard closer.

While Zalith nuzzled his neck, the vampire schemed, scowling across the room at the Detainer, who looked like he was moments from passing out. "Vhat if ve vipe 'is memory and drop 'im off somevhere zhat vould make sense? Maybe 'e vill try to veach out to somevone."

Zalith exhaled deeply. "The agency?"

"Mm-hmm, and zhen maybe zhe agency vill veach out to zhe contractor, and zhe contractor vill veach out to whoever sent zhe contract. Or *maybe* somevone vill come and vind *'im*. 'E 'ad a quota to meet, no? Per'aps whoever vanted zhose children von't be very 'appy to vind out zhat not only 'ave zhe children not been delivered, but all zhe people zhey paid to 'ire are dead…except 'im."

The demon didn't answer right away, but that was becoming normal. He hummed as he inhaled quietly, and then he nuzzled Alucard's cheek. "A trap. Anger often spills the most secrets from a person. Maybe our Detainer friend here fucked up; I think that *he's* responsible for all of that mess down at Mirewharf." He shrugged. "That's what happens when you're drunk around explosives."

Alucard smiled and lightly pushed Zalith away. "Get to vork, zhen," he said with a smirk.

Zalith laughed amusedly. "Yes, sir," he said and returned to the Detainer.

The vampire sent a telepathic message to Edricus, telling him to bring down a half-bottle of whiskey. Then, he watched the demon work, altering the Detainer's mind—it didn't take very long, and neither did Edricus. Just as Zalith finished, the Sentinel vampire arrived, delivering the whiskey.

Alucard handed the bottle to Zalith. "I kind of vant to vorce 'im to drvink, but I zon't vant 'im vhrowing up all over zhe vloor," he said with an amused smile. "You can make 'im drvink, no?"

Zalith smirked at him, and then he returned to the Detainer. "You're going to sit here and drink this entire bottle, and once it's empty, you're going to fall asleep," he told him as he untied one of the man's hands and gave him the bottle.

After a stiff nod, the Detainer started drinking.

"I'll assign someone to follow him and keep an eye on the situation," the demon said, making his way back over. "We'll find everyone who's involved, and we'll put an end to whatever fucked up shit these people are doing." He paused, taking hold of Alucard's hand. "If a Numen *is* involved, we'll reassess the situation once we have answers." He sounded cautious.

"Ve're likely going to 'ave to send people out to stop ozzer operations and Detainers in zhe meantime—vonce ve get more invormation, zhat is. But zhat's a lot of vesources ve're going to 'ave to put aside."

Zalith nodded and quietly said, "We'll work it out, don't worry."

With a deep exhale, Alucard rested his head on Zalith's shoulder and glared across the cell at the Detainer, who slowly drank the whiskey. It *was* going to take a lot to deal with a situation like this, and he wasn't sure whether or not he wanted to be right about a Numen being involved. If he *was* right, perhaps the reason behind it all would give them an upper hand in their war against the false gods, perhaps they'd gain some insight into what the Numen were doing to prepare on their end. But that would also mean getting nearer to the inevitable face-off with them, and he wasn't entirely ready for that— no one was.

He didn't need to think about that right now, though. There were no plans to rush into battle as soon as they found the location of either Numen. Right now, the only plan was to gather everything and everyone they needed to win this war against the creatures who had haunted him his entire life.

And the thought of freedom from that fear banished any uncertainty.

Chapter Fifty-Eight

— ⪡ † ⪢ —

The Weight of Not Knowing

| **Alucard** |
| *Atheson, Atheson Coven Sanctum* |

When Alucard reached the point in his suppressed memories that had made him realize he wasn't actually a man—not completely, anyway—he paused, the ink from his pen soaking a gradually widening spot onto his journal page. He didn't want to write it because writing the words meant he accepted it, right? And despite Zalith's assurances, he still wasn't going to acknowledge the revelation as a solid truth…because what if he was wrong? What if he hadn't remembered it all correctly?

No. He *had*. There was nothing else. As a child, he'd never learned why he'd not been a boy or a girl, and he hadn't learned what that made him. What *did* it make him? He wanted those answers, and he wasn't sure whether they were buried just like everything else or if, to this day, he'd never found what he was looking for.

But where could he even start looking? The library that Gossamer had taken him to was in the Diabolus catacombs, which had been destroyed. Should he send people to clear the tunnels out and find that library?

"What's wrong, darling?" Zalith asked quietly, his voice muffled against his neck.

His mate never missed a shift in his demeanour.

"Noving," he said, resting his head on the demon's. "I'm just trying to vemember all of zhe details."

Zalith looked at the pages, and then he chuckled. "Well, if I could read Dor-Sanguian, maybe I could help." He went back to nuzzling Alucard's neck. "Have you written any secrets in there about me, vampire?"

Alucard smiled faintly in amusement, some of the confliction and dismay withering away. "Vhat if zhere vere?"

"What would they say?"

"Hmm…maybe I 'ad some dreams about you…maybe some vings I vanted to say but vas too shy at zhe time," he said quietly with a shrug.

"Like what? I need details," he murmured and licked Alucard's neck.

The vampire's smile grew, letting him relax a little. Of course, he was shy to answer, but being in heat was still providing him with that desire-ridden courage that he needed to ignore the fluster—sure, he was meant to be using it to seek and get sex, but he could use it for *anything*, couldn't he? There weren't rules. His instincts and body didn't complain. "Vell…" he drawled, screwing the lid back onto his pen. "Zhere vas zhis vone dream I 'ad." He paused, grasping for just a bit more courage. "I vas at some stupid party, zhe kind I alvays vent to, eizer to keep up appearances or meet vith new allies. Zhis particular party vas a masquerade. Everyvone vas dancing but me—vhich vas zhe norm back zhen—but zhere vas zhis man among zhe crowd who kept looking at me; I'd catch 'im every ozzer moment; I liked zhe vay 'is eyes shimmered ved in zhe light." He started fiddling with his crucifix. "And zhen 'e came over to me. I vhought 'e vas a business associate or someving at virst; I couldn't see 'is vace, and I zidn't vecognize 'is scent or 'is aura, but zhere vas someving about 'im zhat made me veel someving I'd never velt bevore, and zhe vay 'e vas looking at me…I knew 'e 'ad plans vor me, and despite not knowing vhat zhose plans vere, I let 'im take me to 'is carriage." He laughed a little. "Ve certainly zidn't call 'is coachman over." That was when the sadness started creeping in. "I voke up vishing zhat moment vas veal. I know zhat ve vere very divverent people a century ago, but I know zhat if I met you—if ve shared an encounter like zhat, my life vould 'ave velt a little less lonely. I needed zhat back zhen."

Zalith kissed his neck and said, "We can make up for lost time by recreating it one of these days."

Alucard's smile returned. "I'd like zhat."

The demon leaned into his ear. "We could make it better," he whispered.

A shiver of anticipation spiralled down Alucard's spine. "Better 'ow?"

"We'll just have to be creative."

Alucard smiled curiously and put his journal and pen aside. "Such as?

Zalith grinned against his neck. "Well," he murmured, his voice low and teasing, "we could start with that same masquerade, but instead of a crowded ballroom, it's just you and me—maybe a few voyeurs, if you're feeling bold." His fingers traced lazy circles against Alucard's hip. "I wouldn't hide behind a mask for long, though. I'd make sure you saw exactly *who* was looking at you like a starving beast."

The vampire swallowed, tensing just that little bit more. Voyeurs had never crossed his mind, but…something about Zalith's involvement made the idea feel very enticing.

His mate pressed a kiss just beneath his jaw. "You'd be in some exquisite little costume. Velvet, maybe. Tight in all the right places. No shirt. Just a cape." He kissed lower, right over the vampire's fluttering pulse. "I'd press you up against the banquet table, the one covered in all that ridiculous opulence…and replace it with you."

Alucard closed his eyes, another shiver racing through him.

Zalith laughed softly, wicked and warm. "I'd slide your trousers down right there among the candied figs and wine-stained linens, no one stopping us or daring to breathe a word. All they'd do is *watch*…because they'd know you were mine, and that you were begging for it."

Alucard couldn't stifle a soft, anticipation-thick exhale.

The demon's tongue flicked against his ear. "Would you beg for it, my sweet vampire?" he whispered. "Even in a dream like that?"

He nodded stiffly. "Yes," he murmured, shifting his legs slightly; it was like his body was expecting to be touched, but Zalith wasn't giving him what he needed.

His mate moved in closer, his fingers trailing along the inside of his thigh. "Then I'd make sure you earned it," he told him. "No masks. No games. Just your legs over my shoulders while you moan for me, while your voice fills that empty hall louder than any orchestra."

Alucard's lips parted, his jaw going slack.

"I'd make you cry out again and again," Zalith went on, his voice a low, dangerous purr. "And when your body's trembling and clinging to the edge, I won't let you cum, not until you beg louder than you did in your dream." His hand pressed firmer against the vampire's thigh. "I'll take my time with you, Alucard…until you can't remember anything but the way I feel inside you."

The ache in Alucard's body pulsed hot and sharp, desire spiralling through him like wildfire. Every word Zalith had said so far felt like a caress against his skin, each syllable a promise soaked in heat. He kept his eyes shut, heart pounding, lips parted as a faint whimper caught in his throat. He could already feel himself clenching around nothing, desperate and empty.

Zalith didn't touch him where he needed it. That made it worse. That made it better. The demon's hand only settled on his thigh, warm and heavy through the fabric. His lips hovered at Alucard's ear, and the moment he spoke again, the vampire's body betrayed him—hips jerking, breath stalling.

"I'll spread you open so slow that you'll think I'm torturing you," the demon murmured. "I'll fill you until your legs tremble, until you're gasping and writhing and begging me to fuck you."

Alucard couldn't help himself—he moaned quietly, his lashes fluttering; his thighs pressed together, aching for touch, for relief…but Zalith's hand remained exactly where it was.

His mate continued, his tone darker, "And when I cum inside you, I won't stop. I'll flip you over, ass in the air, cum dripping down your thighs, and I'll fuck you again. Harder. Deeper. You'll be too sore to take it, and still you'll beg for more."

The vampire let out a strangled sound, hips twitching again as arousal overwhelmed every thought in his head.

"I want to fuck you so full that you can't speak," Zalith whispered. "So many times that you forget your own name and only know mine…and know who you belong to. You'd like that, wouldn't you, baby?"

He still hadn't touched Alucard's dick, and that was the worst part—how badly Alucard *wanted* him to keep teasing, to keep drawing it out until he was desperate enough to cry.

But then Zalith's hand slipped away.

Alucard's eyes opened, a faint daze of disbelief clouding his expression. The absence of touch made the throbbing between his legs feel all the worse. He let out a soft, breathless whine, hips lifting instinctively—seeking, pleading.

Zalith chuckled quietly, and the sound was maddeningly satisfied. "No," he said, dragging the word out like silk over skin. "Not yet."

Alucard turned his head towards him, eyes wide with heat and protest. "But—"

The demon leaned in, pressing a kiss to his throat, then murmured against it, "You're going to have to just imagine it for now."

Another frustrated groan slipped from Alucard's lips.

Zalith's tone turned a shade softer as he said, "You've already came dry twice, darling. If I so much as touch you now, you'll go again without anything left to give. And I want it to count next time. I want to see every drop I've coaxed out of you…feel it, taste it." He bit gently at Alucard's neck and grinned when the vampire trembled. "So be good. Let your body recover," he whispered, voice slick with promise. "Because when I fuck you next, I want to feel you cum so hard you cry out my name."

His mate then kissed him, slow and deep, like he hadn't just driven him to the edge and left him there gasping. Alucard kissed back despite the frustration, each stroke of their tongues giving him a little relief; every time Zalith playfully bit his lip, he stifled a desperate moan—he couldn't stop himself from reaching for the demon's crotch, but Zalith gently grabbed his hand and laughed, breaking their kiss.

"Patience, vampire," he murmured, gazing into his eyes. "I'll give you exactly what you deserve later." He kissed his lips, his cheek, and then down to his neck.

Anticipation still raced through Alucard's tense body, and as Zalith nuzzled his neck, shivers spiralled around inside him. But as the silence fell around them, the desire for touch and taking slowly faded. He liked the idea of the dream he had, but the despair it brought with it stung like silver. He really did wish he'd met Zalith centuries ago. If he had love in his life, if he felt like he belonged somewhere, if he was needed and wanted and appreciated, then maybe every time he thought back to those days, he wouldn't feel like his heart was being torn out, maybe he wouldn't feel the darkness close in around him, and maybe he wouldn't be so burdened with dismay that he felt like he was drowning.

He didn't want to think about the loneliness that plagued his life until he met his soul mate, but *all* of his suppressed memories came from that time, and when he remembered, he couldn't fight off the emotions that came with it.

The vampire opened his memory journal and flipped through the pages. His eyes skimmed the most recent memories from his childhood—the time he'd spent in those catacombs. He wondered, was Gossamer still out there? Maybe he could find the katsie; maybe it could help him find the library or the answers. But then again, he still didn't know what the katsie's real intentions were. It could have been using him, it could have even harmed him—it could have even had something to do with the choice he'd made, the choice to become male…or something close to it.

With a quiet sigh, he landed on the pages where he'd written about the Kor'naathi and his time in Djavhati. Although reading over his recollections didn't help him remember more, the memory of components and how Lilith and Damien were trying to use his Lumendatt *did* spark something.

His Lumendatt.

He and Zalith had discovered its existence—he possessed one of the most powerful Numen artifacts one could obtain, and he needed to start learning how to use it. With it, they'd have a *huge* upper hand against their enemies, but to learn to use it, he needed to remember what he knew about Lumendatts.

Those crystals gave the Numen the ability to walk in Aegisguard for longer than fifteen minutes; they let the Numen create a humanoid form and speak a language that people of the world could understand, and they allowed Numen to create new scions.

He frowned, thinking, recalling…. When Lilith had come for him after Damien removed the runes hiding him, she'd only been able to stay in Aegisguard for fifteen minutes. Did that mean she didn't have a Lumendatt anymore? And Damien—he'd always been restricted by a time limit, too, for as long as Alucard could remember. But Lilith had scions—she *always* had scions. If she didn't have a Lumendatt, how was she creating them? Unless she'd created an abundance of them long, long ago and simply woke them to replace those she lost.

That was it. He remembered. He'd seen that awful place in Lilith's realm. That chamber. A place full of crystal cocoons, trapping inside them the beginning of a scion's existence. There were *thousands* of them. That along with the fact that she'd created a humanoid body for herself meant that she'd possessed a Lumendatt at some point—and so had Damien—but where were those crystals now?

They'd lost them centuries ago, hadn't they? That explained why they were trying to use *his* Lumendatt.

But…why did he remember seeing Damien holding *two* Lumendatts when he was a child? A child surrounded by other children, the tortured souls whom the Daegelus used and destroyed without remorse, just like the Diabolus.

He tapped his pen against his journal, trying to recall more of those moments.

Though it wasn't Damien or anything remotely Lumendatt-related that came first trickling and then *pouring* into his mind.

It was the Diabolus. It was Abbess Brânduśa, it was when she told him that he and the countless other children belonged to the Diabolus. He'd known it since he began looking for his mother. It was there, lingering just beneath the surface, waiting for him to use words and accept the truth. He knew it for certain when he remembered being taken from his cell to perform the ritual, when he remembered standing in the middle of that pentagram surrounded by witches, when he remembered the moment he almost freed Lucifer and pulled him into this world. He *did* belong to the Diabolus—he always had. His mother was Diabolus, Brânduśa was Diabolus. The Diabolus had raised him—well, he wouldn't call it being raised, but *they* were who he spent the first years of his childhood with. And when Damien took him, the Diabolus were ordered to find him so that he could complete his task, so that he could do the thing he'd been born to do.

The memory didn't dismay him, not because he already knew it but because there were far too many more incomplete memories overwhelming him…and the one which now made him hesitant to catch his own reflection was slowly eating away at him. He needed answers, but he wasn't sure there was anywhere to find them.

A quiet sigh left him as his gaze drifted up to the gloomy ceiling. He lifted his hand to his face, and his fingers lingered along his jaw, pausing at the roughness there. He should have felt grounded by it, rooted in the body he'd one day chosen, the one he'd shaped his life around. But instead, a soft pulse of unease crept up his spine. The stubble didn't reassure him. It felt foreign today, like a costume he'd forgotten to remove.

His hand shifted, trailing upward, tracing the slope of his cheekbone, the curve of his nose, the faint plushness in his lips. And his hair, too…tucked behind his ears, now long enough to reach just shy of his shoulders. He didn't need a mirror to see it all—he knew every inch of his face. Yet, in this moment, it felt like he was memorizing someone else's.

Something about the way his features came together never sat right. Too soft in some places, too sharp in others. Too ambiguous. Too in between. The memory he couldn't fully reach, the one whispering from the corners of his mind, made it worse. It made him question whether he'd ever been whole to begin with.

He pressed his fingers against his chest, right above his crucifix. The metal was cold, familiar…unlike everything else.

Except the demon latched onto his neck.

Zalith was the most familiar thing in his life, and he trusted him more than anyone, too. He could trust him to be honest.

"Zaliv?" he asked, looking down at what he could see of his mate.

But the demon didn't reply.

"Zaliv?" he repeated.

Zalith exhaled deeply and murmured, "Huh?"

Alucard hesitated for a moment…but he wanted to know. "Do I…" he paused and huffed—did he *really* want the answer? What if Zalith told him that he *did* look feminine? He'd rather know, though. If he didn't, he'd overthink, he'd get anxious about what everyone else thought, and he'd let it eat away at him. He didn't want to worry about how everyone saw him every time he walked into a room. So he shoved the hesitation away and asked, "Do I look…veminine to you?"

Zalith adjusted a little, his lips brushing Alucard's neck. "No," he murmured. "I mean you *are* pretty, but in a manly way."

He looked down at his lap. He wanted to take the compliment and bury his worry, but he just…couldn't. Manly? His reflection told him otherwise. "Are you sure?" he mumbled.

"Very sure," the demon assured him, tracing his fingers down Alucard's body; his hand slid slowly from the vampire's chest to his waist, pausing there as he pressed a kiss just beneath his jaw. "I wouldn't lie to you, baby," he said, his voice low and husky with affection, and then he caressed the lines of his neck. "These lines of yours…and the way your collarbones sit…so strong and sharp; it's like someone carved you to be kissed and obeyed." And then he stroked down to his waist. "And *these* lines? Every time I see them disappear under your trousers, I want to follow them with my mouth and never stop."

Alucard managed a smile.

Zalith smirked against the vampire's skin. "And your voice? The kind that makes people shut up and listen. That's not soft; it's commanding, *so* masculine—and your accent is a bonus." He drew back just enough to meet his gaze, his thumb brushing across the centre of Alucard's chest, right over his heart. "You're beautiful, yeah, but not in some borrowed or delicate way; you're beautiful because everything about you is *you*. And trust me, everything I see and everything I feel…it's all man." His hand slipped lower, teasingly slow. "Especially this part," he murmured, stroking his fingertips over the vampire's crotch.

As he tensed up, Alucard exhaled deeply.

The demon then groaned quietly, pressing his forehead against Alucard's. "I wish I could devour you right now," he purred and kissed his lips once, and then he nuzzled the side of his face. "You're the best thing I've ever tasted, Alucard."

His smile grew a little. "Veally?"

"Really," he whispered and kissed his cheek. "Don't worry about what other people think, baby. You are who you are, and you don't owe anyone an explanation." He placed another kiss on his cheek and added, "And I've only ever seen you as a man."

Alucard turned his head to meet Zalith's gaze. He smiled at him, and then he looked down with a soft huff. "Vank you," he murmured.

Zalith kissed him again. "I love you."

"I love you, too."

The vampire then kissed Zalith back. His fingers curled into the fabric of his shirt, drawing him closer, craving that grounding heat and affection. Their mouths moved in sync, breaths hitching, soft sounds of longing escaping between kisses that turned messier, hungrier. Zalith's hand slid to the small of his back, the other cradling his jaw, tilting his head just the way he liked.

Alucard moaned quietly into his mouth, heat coiling low in his stomach. The ache in his chest—both emotional and physical—began to melt beneath the weight of Zalith's touch.

And then the door knocked.

They froze.

Alucard pulled back first with a growl of irritation. "Of course," he muttered under his breath.

Zalith sighed heavily, resting his forehead against Alucard's with a grumble. "They have the *worst* timing."

The vampire turned his head, setting his glare on the door. "Vhat?!" he snarled.

When the door opened, Noctrel stepped in. "My Lord, the Council is ready."

That was a relief to hear. Once it was over, he and Zalith could go home. "Tell zhem zhat Zaliv and I vill be zhere in a vew minutes."

With a bow of their head, Noctrel left the room, pulling the door shut.

Alucard sighed and met his mate's gaze again. "Are you veady to vitness your virst-ever vampire trial?"

Zalith smirked at him. "I am. And when we're done, I'm taking you home and fucking you."

The vampire smiled, both flustered and excited.

"Only if you've recovered enough, though," the demon added. "But I'm sure sitting through this trial will give your body the time it needs to be ready for me."

His fluster grew, and he turned his head to hide it.

Zalith took his hand and stood up, gently pulling him with him. "Lead the way, My Lord," he said with an amused smile.

Alucard laughed under his breath, and with Zalith beside him, he began leading the way through the Sanctum's vaulted corridors.

They descended to the Noctuary, passing under chandeliers of cold silver flame. The vampires stationed within bowed their heads and murmured respectful greetings before quietly slipping away. They already knew where their Lord was headed.

In the centre of the hall, Alucard came to a halt and let go of Zalith's hand. He stepped forward alone, lifting his hand and turning his palm towards the ceiling. With a measured breath, he summoned his ethos, threading it through the sigils etched into the surrounding stone. One by one, the carvings lit with a dim, reddish glow, responding to his will like strings of an instrument.

A deep rumble groaned through the floor.

Alucard took a step back just as the smooth stone beneath them trembled and began to part. A perfect ring in the centre of the hall receded inwards, segment by segment, and spiralled downward, revealing a staircase of black stone winding into an abyssal dark.

The air that rose from below was old and quiet, touched by the faintest trace of blood and ethos.

Alucard stared into the void a moment longer before glancing at Zalith with a faint smile. "Avter you," he murmured.

With a curious smirk, Zalith stepped down, and Alucard followed.

Chapter Fifty-Nine

— ⸲ † ⸱ —

The Trial of Eyra Stravelle

| **Alucard** |
| *Ascuns, Fort Rudă de Sânge, The Hollow Chamber* |

The spiralling staircase drew them down through a mirage of red and black mist, a portal-like pathway Alucard had created centuries ago; the stone walls were dark as wine, lit by the flickering shadows of torchlight that clung to their surfaces like restless spirits. Their descent was long, echoing, and silent… and when they finally emerged into the Antechamber, Alucard's eyes took a moment to adjust.

Here, the air was cool with age. The chamber was circular and windowless with high walls clad in dark stone and lined by tall, crowded bookshelves. Some bore ancient volumes, others cradled strange artifacts under glass or wrapped in iron clasps. The scent of leather, parchment, and faint incense drifted beneath the torchlight's low hiss, and lingering lightly was the salty smell of the sea.

It was gloomy, it was quiet—it was just as Alucard remembered. The Antechamber held that strange warmth, a stillness that felt almost like reverence; it was much like every lounge in a Coven Sanctum, a place so comforting and welcoming yet surrounded by death and danger. It had been a long time since he'd last descended to the Hollow Chamber, but this threshold between witness and judgement had remained untouched by time.

His eyes shifted to the vampires present. To the right, seated on a long black leather couch with worn brass studs, were Adherents Evaphene, Berengar, Branduin, and Virelka. Their conversation fell silent at the sight of him, each one offering a subtle nod of deference. On the other side of the chamber, Knights Lenore and Theremond stood near one of the bookcases, half-shadowed, half-lit—guards even here, their postures straight, ever-watchful. Warden Lucaniel, composed and elegant in his robes, sat at the round table near the left wall, a thick-bound codex open in front of him, fingers paused mid-page.

"Coven Master Noctrel is waiting in the Oathkeeper's Lounge, My Lord," Lucaniel said with a humble bow of his head.

Alucard nodded and said, "*Multumesc*," as he led Zalith to the dark oak, gold-trimmed door a few feet from where the Warden was sitting. He grabbed the golden doorknob, and with a quiet chime, the door unlocked, and he took the demon inside.

The long, gold-on-red carpeted corridor was lined with platinum-framed portraits and marble statues; the smell of sweet incense was stronger now, and there wasn't a speck of dust or a single string of cobweb anywhere. Just as he'd ordered, the Hollow Chamber was very well taken care of.

"Who are all of these people?" Zalith asked curiously, gesturing to a portrait.

"Members of zhe 'igh Blood Court," he answered. "Inquisitors, Aldermen and Aldervomen, Praeservares, Seneschals—zhe list goes on; I can explain vhat zhey all are vonce ve're inside."

Zalith nodded and squeezed his hand.

Alucard smiled at him before setting his eyes on the oak door at the end of the corridor. "Zon't be alarmed by zhe vings you vill see in zhis voom," he warned him.

The demon chuckled a little. "What am I going to see?"

"Vings you 'ave never seen bevore," he said with a smirk, reaching the door, and then he gripped the knob and pulled it open.

The Oathkeeper's Lounge was more crowded than he expected. Vampires stood and sat in every corner, by every wall, and in every seat; conversations in just about every Rhenovaalisean language filled the warm air, and a heavy sense of despair and hesitation shrouded the place.

Instead of examining the faces of every vampire in the room, Alucard glanced at Zalith, whose eyes had found exactly what he'd warned him about.

"Is a vespertilio," he told his mate.

Zalith nodded stiffly, his eyes fixed on the creature.

The eight-foot-tall beast stood in the centre of the lounge, framed by an inclined ring of obsidian set into the floor like a ceremonial seal. It was motionless, save for the rise and fall of its chest and the occasional blink-blink-blink-blink of its four eyes, one after the other—one pair red, the other amber. The creature stood upright on thick, powerful legs, its form vaguely humanoid but far from graceful. It was built for destruction—broad-shouldered, heavy-limbed, with elongated arms that ended in monstrous hands, each finger tipped in obsidian-sharp claws. Tucked against those arms were wings—small, twitching, not suited for flight so much as flaring during combat. The stretched red membrane between the crooked joints shimmered faintly, veined and almost wet-looking under torchlight.

"Is it some sort of vampire?" Zalith asked.

He nodded. "Zhough zhe process involved a vitual zhat allowed me to combine several ethos beasts, and zhen I applied my blood."

"Have you created more creatures like this?"

"A vew. Maybe you vill see zhem someday."

As Zalith slowly followed, Alucard moved towards the beast.

The vespertilio turned its head to look at the vampire, the patches of dark hair creeping down from its tangled neck mane thinning as its scar-pitted skin stretched. Its mouth, split in four like a cracked shell, tensed as if it could already taste the command it longed for—a mouth full of jagged teeth pulsing with anticipation.

Nobody was afraid of it, though. They knew just as well as Alucard that the vespertilio wouldn't so much as leave its circle without permission. It was a guard, there to protect witnesses and victims of vampire crimes.

"My Lord," came Noctrel's voice.

Alucard stopped near the obsidian circle and watched the Coven Master weave through the crowd.

"The Court is ready, My Lord," Noctrel said, stopping in front of them. "These vampires are all of the survivors—the ones Veiled Eyra turned. The Inquisitors found as many as they could based on Veiled Eyra's information and what the witnesses knew."

He glanced around. He'd done the math after everything Eyra had told him; there should only be at most seventeen Straybloods present, but there were.... He counted.... There were *forty-seven* vampires, and that made him both scowl and snarl—and what made him *even angrier* was the fact that they'd all evidently been turned and abandoned because *not one* of them knew who he was.

"Inquisitor Sanchia had the same reaction, My Lord," Noctrel said, glancing around the room. "There could still be more."

Alucard exhaled deeply and shook his head, calming just a little as Zalith's thumb rubbed against his, their fingers still entwined. "Jury?" he asked the Coven Master.

They nodded. "Ready and waiting."

"All vight. Stay 'ere and assist vith zhem," he said, gesturing to the crowd.

"Yes, My Lord," Noctrel said, and then they eased back into the vampire gathering.

"Zhis vay," Alucard said, taking Zalith to a staircase on the other side of the room.

"Are you okay?" the demon asked quietly.

Alucard moved past two nervous women and began climbing the stairs. "I just zon't understand vhy she did zhis," he muttered. "Sure, she isn't zhe virst vampire to break zhe laws, but to zhis extent? Who fucking knows 'ow many Straybloods she levt out zhere?" He turned left when they reached the first landing and continued up.

"Is there a way to find them all? Can't you telepathically talk to them?"

"Not directly," he said, and when they reached the second landing, he slowed. He was getting tired—he still hadn't had any proper sleep since getting to Atheson; resting in his casket *had* helped, but it wasn't enough, not really; he needed at least twelve hours more. "I can veach out to every vampire," he continued, "but zhat vill take a lot of ethos. I vill need to vecover vrom all of zhis bevore I do someving like zhat."

Zalith's curious expression returned, walking closely beside Alucard as they continued up towards the third landing. "What did you take Eyra's blood for earlier? I thought the Inquisitors would use it to find everyone she turned."

He shook his head and said, "No, zhat vas to crveate an Emotional Displacement Vard. Vill keep Eyra vrom stirring empavhy or vhatever—stops 'er vrom emotionally manipulating zhe Court and Jury."

"Good."

Once they reached the third landing, Alucard exhaled sharply in an attempt to expel some of the fatigue, but it didn't leave him. Before his mate could say anything, though, he nodded at the double doors just ahead. "Zhat's vhere ve're going."

Zalith gently gripped his arm before he could move. "Are you sure you're okay, baby?" he asked worriedly.

Alucard smiled as best he could and said, "I'm vine, my love." He moved closer and fiddled with the demon's gold chain. "I just vant to get zhis over vith so ve can go 'ome."

With a smile and deep exhale through his nose, Zalith pulled him into his embrace. "Me too. How long do you think this will take?"

"Not long. Zhere are vorty-seven broken laws down in zhat voom, and many more dead or unaccounted vor. No vone is going to suggest zhat she could see zhe error in 'er vays. Zhis is all just a vormality."

Zalith nuzzled his neck. "Mm," he replied.

The vampire smiled and slowly pushed him away. As much as he wanted his mate's affection, he didn't want to keep the Council waiting any longer. "Let's go," he said, taking Zalith's hand again.

His mate smirked at him but followed him to the doors.

Alucard pushed the heavy doors open and stepped into the narrow corridor beyond. His steps were soundless on the plush black carpet as he led Zalith to the rich red velvet drapery ahead. Without a word, he drew one side back and gestured for the demon to enter first, his fingers brushing Zalith's arm in a quiet invitation.

The loge on the other side was a small, elevated chamber tucked discreetly above the courtroom floor. Dark wood panelling lined the walls, carved in elegant spirals and grim figures with sharp wings and solemn faces. A pair of plush, high-backed chairs sat just behind the low balustrade, angled to offer an unbroken, commanding view of the room below.

Alucard followed Zalith in and let the curtain fall closed behind them. As he stepped beside his fiancé, his pale gaze fell to the chamber below. The courtroom was vast and dimly lit, built of dark stone and ribbed arches that rose like reaching fingers towards the vaulted ceiling. Long candle sconces lined the columns, dripping wax down clawed holders, their flickering flames casting long, theatrical shadows. The central floor was polished obsidian, veined with crimson marbling that caught the low light like threads of blood beneath glass.

At its heart stood Eyra, the Emotional Displacement Ward shimmering orange on the floor around her; she was flanked only by Praeservare Adelaide. The Veiled vampire's expression was impassive, but even from above, Alucard could see the stiffness in her shoulders, the faint tightening of her jaw.

Before her sat the panel of Inquisitors, robed in layered black with shimmering medallions of rank hanging at their throats. Their seats formed a semicircle high above the floor, each one raised slightly from the last, allowing them to observe her like predators perched on a ledge. Lined below them in the same formation was the Alderman panel, who flipped through tome pages and examined scrolls.

And across from the Inquisitors, in a slightly lowered pit lined with benches, sat the jury. Twelve vampires of varied covens, all cloaked in the grey and red of judicial neutrality. Their eyes were fixed forward—at Eyra, at the Inquisitors, at nothing at all—but Alucard knew how quickly judgement could shift behind a composed face.

Alucard sat down—he watched as Zalith moved the other chair closer, just inches from his, and then his mate sat down. After returning a smile to the demon, the vampire leaned forward slightly, resting one hand on the carved wooden railing; his other found Zalith's wrist, anchoring them both in the silence of the moment. And then his eyes met Lead Inquisitor Ludovicus' gaze. He gave the silver-haired man a single nod.

Ludovicus raised his hand.

The courtroom quickly fell into silence.

From the far end of the chamber, the Usher of the Court—Alinței Televár, a tall, brindle brown-haired vampire in charcoal robes—stepped forward, his voice clear and sonorous as it echoed across the stone, "Let it be known to all present that this hearing shall be overseen by Lead Inquisitor Ludovicus Bieláňski, under authority granted by the High Wardens of the Crimson Tribunal, Dame Kateline Vošelár and Sir Nicolae Černević." A pause followed, brief and reverent. "Judgement shall be deliberated by the Alderman Panel—Aldermen Ionelvič Málínar and Mirăcek Ilieşar, and Alderwomen Eliraşka Stanojev, Viorikaş Lăzărin, and Soreline Crăiştean—assembled by order of Chief Alderman Ancuveta Zorávek and vested with full sentencing authority."

A soft rustle swept through the chamber as jurors straightened, scribes lifted their pens, and the accused turned her head ever so slightly towards the voice.

"Will they hand Eyra to the families of the people she killed and turned?" Zalith asked, squeezing Alucard's hand.

The vampire murmured, "Maybe, but I'd vather kill 'er myselv; zhey can all vatch."

His mate moved his arm around his waist and leaned against him. "They'll all be very lucky to watch you work," he murmured, obviously smirking.

He smiled faintly and rested his head on his mate's.

Inquisitor Sanchia then rose, one hand resting behind her back, the other clutching a gold-rimmed tome emblazoned with the seal of the High Blood Court. The courtroom stilled as she flipped through its worn vellum pages, each turn of parchment echoing through the chamber like a quiet toll of judgement.

At last, she looked up and addressed the court in a voice that was calm, crisp, and unshakably firm, "Veiled Eyra Stravelle, formerly of the Atheson Coven, you stand before this Tribunal having been found guilty of no fewer than fifty-two counts of unauthorized vampiric turnings, each carried out without sanction, oversight, or regard for the established laws that safeguard our kind.

"These turnings did not merely constitute violations of coven conduct; they unleashed chaos across Rhenovaalis. The untrained, unsupervised Straybloods you created have spread unchecked, many abandoning control and falling to instinct. The result has been catastrophic. Over the past seven years, these Straybloods have been linked to more than two hundred human deaths."

The room filled with whispers and murmurs.

Alucard clenched his jaw. *Two hundred?*

Sanchia continued, "Furthermore, your actions have drawn the attention of external threats. To date, the Tribunal has confirmed that three separate vampire hunters were summoned to this continent in direct response to outbreaks linked to your progeny. One such group extinguished a forming coven of twelve Straybloods—each one traced back to you."

With his anger growing, Alucard growled quietly under his breath.

"Another investigation is ongoing into a village massacre that occurred two years ago, in which the involvement of your Straybloods is under scrutiny." Sanchia flipped through the pages again but kept her eyes on Eyra. "Your turnings were not acts of mercy or necessity. They were driven by selfish impulse, with no consideration for your coven's safety, the safety of your Fellkin, or the stability of vampire society. Your choices fractured the order we fight to preserve, and your disregard for consequence has endangered not only the Atheson Coven but vampire kind as a whole."

A strangled gasp came from Eyra. "I just—"

"You speak when you are told!" Sanchia interjected loudly before Alucard could.

Eyra held a scowl for half a moment before lowering her head.

Sanchia began reading from the pages, "The recorded Straybloods of the accused's creation are as follows: Amalia Stern, Sebastian Roth, Therese and Dorian Koenig, Henri d'Aramitz, Solveig Vassiliou, Céleste Fournier, Mathis Moritz...."

Alucard huffed irritably and turned to face Zalith, and he wasn't surprised to see that his mate was gazing at him. He smiled, and the demon smiled back; Sanchia's voice echoed in the distance, fading further and further away. It would take a few minutes at least for all those names to be listed, so there was no harm in him shifting his attention elsewhere—it would certainly give him the time he needed to calm down.

He slid his hand to the back of Zalith's head—he didn't even need to pull. The demon was already leaning in, like he'd been aching for an excuse since they sat down. Their lips met in a kiss that was slow only for a breath; Zalith deepened it with a low, restrained hunger, tongue slipping past Alucard's lips like he knew exactly how to steal the air from his lungs.

Alucard's fingers curled into Zalith's collar. He swallowed the eager sound rising in his throat, heart pounding, heat sparking low inside him.

But after a few seconds, he broke the kiss and glanced around, flustered. His face was burning. If anyone down in the courtroom looked up and saw them—

Then it hit him.

No one could see them. The loge was tucked high above the chamber, veiled in shadow and silence.

Zalith must have noticed the realization flash across his eyes. He gripped Alucard's jaw, possessively turning his head back. A wicked smile tugged at the corner of his mouth—he held Alucard's gaze a moment longer, just to watch him unravel, and then he kissed him again, hungrier this time.

And Alucard let him.

Then came Eyra's desperate voice, followed by Praeservare Adelaide, and then their words started clashing together. Eyra was pleading her case, her voice cracking and thick with dismay—*fake, heartless* dismay. The ward shared her attempted deception with a few chiming pulses, and the room hummed with aggravated, revolted, and disappointed voices. Nobody was at all sympathetic. Why would they be?

Alucard had already heard her woe-is-me story. He kept returning his mate's kisses, each a little more aggressive than the last—and he was starting to get hard. Despite knowing that he should pull away, he couldn't help himself. His body needed it, *he* needed it, and the desire to feel Zalith inside him was so much stronger than his better judgement—

A loud *slam* made Alucard flinch and sharply turn his head; he leaned forward to stare down at the room, and Zalith immediately nuzzled his neck.

Lead Inquisitor Ludovicus had slammed the gavel down.

Eyra was crying.

Adelaide was trying to calm her.

And the jury murmured with no sorrow on their faces.

Alucard hadn't missed the verdict, though. The worst was still to come; the witnesses had yet to step forward and lay bare the ruin Eyra had left in their lives.

The door to the Oathkeeper's Lounge opened, and one of the Testament Hands escorted a witness to the stand.

There were *a lot* of witnesses, but it was unlikely that the Inquisitors would call them *all* forward one by one. The stories of a few would be enough.

"I'd fuck you right now if you'd let me," Zalith whispered into his ear.

Alucard tensed up. He wanted it…but he knew better—he had to let his body rest, and he wouldn't risk making a sound during the tense quiet of the trial. So he murmured, "Ve can't. I zon't vant anyvone to 'ear."

Zalith smirked at him.

The vampire pouted and shifted his focus back to the chamber below.

His mate glanced down at the courtroom, too. "Who's that escorting the witness?" he asked, likely an attempt at distracting himself.

"A Testament 'and. Zhey 'andle zhe vitnesses—make sure zhey're prepared, comvort zhem, escort zhem, and translate if necessary."

Zalith nodded. "You're prepared for everything, aren't you, darling?" He was smirking again.

"I am," he replied proudly.

The demon returned to his neck and kissed it softly.

A shiver raced through Alucard, but he did his best not to let it arouse him—again.

"Elise Moreau from Lès Carenne-d'Alveyrac, Boszorkány," Inquisitor Wymond announced, holding his arm towards the blonde woman in the stand. "Please share with us your encounter with the accused." He then gestured to the warm-skinned vampire standing a few feet from the witness stand. "Testament Hand Benoît will translate."

As Benoît translated Wymond's words, Elise clutched a crumpled blue handkerchief in her trembling hands, strands of her hair falling as she shook with sobs.

Then her voice cracked as she tried to begin, speaking in Boszorkian.

Benoît started translating, fiddling with the small bird beak dangling at the end of his thin chain earring. "It was the morning after our wedding. I still had the flowers in my hair…."

She paused, wiping at her red, tear-streaked face.

And when she continued, so did the Testament Hand, "Eyra came to me when I was alone. She said I had a glow that reminded her of someone she'd lost. I didn't understand what she meant; I thought she was just…mourning. I pitied her."

Elise's breath stuttered…her gaze flicked to Eyra for a brief moment, and then she shook her head and went on with her story.

So did Benoît, "She turned me without asking."

Her fingers gripped the handkerchief tighter.

"I woke up starving, sick with it. Adélard—my husband—he tried to care for me, but I could see how much I frightened him; every day he looked a little more afraid. I didn't want to be what I was, and I begged her to help me. I *begged* her."

Elise's voice broke again, and she pressed the cloth to her mouth.

The translator kept relaying her words, "Instead, she came back and turned Adélard, too. She said it would bring us closer and that I wouldn't have to watch him age without me. But he didn't want it…he didn't forgive me. He said I was a stranger now…and he left me—he wouldn't even talk to me in that room with the other witnesses."

She looked down, her shoulders shaking.

"She didn't do it out of mercy or love; she wanted to see if love could survive death. We were nothing but her experiment, and she discarded us like a failed one."

The jury started murmuring, some shooting evil glares at Eyra, some even baring their fangs, hissing bitterly.

Eyra tried to speak, "That's not what happened! You ungrateful—"

Adelaide stopped her with a hiss.

Alucard sighed quietly. "I'm sure vings only get vorse vrom 'ere," he grumbled.

"How many victims do you think they'll need to hear from?" Zalith asked quietly.

"Two or vhree, maybe vour, depending on zhe severity of vhat Eyra did." But he wasn't sure he could wait that long to see her punished. The witnesses shouldn't have to drag their pain into the open just to be heard, forced to relive the horrors she inflicted. And Eyra—she didn't deserve the chance to plead or explain. There was no justification for what she'd done. They weren't mistakes, they were deliberate acts of selfishness, born from emotions someone her age should've long since learned to master.

Zalith nodded in response and kissed Alucard's neck.

Testament Hand Benoît escorted Elise back to the Oathkeeper's Lounge.

And moments later, another Testament Hand brought a new witness out and escorted her to the stand.

"Zofia Kowalczuk from Koraviec, Druskalen," Inquisitor Wymond announced, holding his arm towards the scowling woman in the stand. "She will be speaking on behalf of Janek Rutkowski, who experienced an encounter with the accused." He then gestured to the vampire standing beside the witness stand. "Testament Hand Bronisława will translate."

Zofia stood rigid, fists clenched at her sides. Her sharp cheekbones were flushed with fury, and her crimson eyes burned under the torchlight, fixed on Eyra, who scowled back at her.

Inquisitor Wymond raised a hand. "You may speak, Witness Kowalczuk. But I ask that you please speak with restraint."

Bronisława translated.

And Zofia's scowl thickened. She started speaking, growling as she did.

"Restraint?" Bronisława translated. "I *watched* the man I was going to marry step into the morning sun!"

A hush fell over the courtroom.

Zofia's voice trembled as she pressed on, though her anger hadn't dimmed.

The Testament Hand continued translating, "His name was Janek Rutkowski. He was *kind*, and he was truly beautiful, such a pure heart. All his life, he cared for his sister, Maja—she was ill from the time they were children, the kind of sickness that gradually kills a human over decades. He sacrificed everything for her… and Eyra knew that—she knew what Maja meant to him."

Zofia snarled through her teeth, glaring at Eyra, who shook her head slowly, fangs bared, fists clenched.

"She turned him in the middle of the night," Bronisława relayed. "No warning, no guidance, she just… left him to wake up with that hunger gnawing through him. We all know how relentless that hunger is when we first turn."

The room shared muffled, sorrowful whispers.

Zofia's voice cracked.

"Maja didn't even scream when she saw him like… *that*. She went to him, trusting him, trying to understand what was happening. And he… he *killed* her. He couldn't control it—none of us could, could we?"

The woman paused to catch her breath, her eyes damp, though she refused to cry.

More gloomy murmurs travelled the chamber.

The story continued, "Eyra just stood there; she stood in the dark and *watched*. And when Janek broke down, she whispered in his ear that it was *fate*, that he was *meant* to outlive her."

She hissed and blurted—

"Who the *fuck* does that!?"

Wymond's voice was low but firm as he said, "Please, Miss Kowalczuk, you must calm yourself."

Zofia shot him a glare and shouted—

Bronisława translated calmly, "*She told him it was destiny*, like it was a game, as if Maja's life meant *nothing*."

She turned to face the room again.

"Eyra vanished after that—she disappeared while I was trying to hold Janek together. But he wasn't the same; he couldn't live with what he'd done."

Zofia huffed sharply, fighting tears.

The Testament Hand translated, "And three months ago… just one month before our wedding… he *walked out into the sun*."

She finally fell quiet, jaw tight, the silence around her deafening as she wiped away tears and tucked strands of her ash-grey hair behind her ears.

After a long pause, Wymond cleared his throat and said gently, "Thank you, Witness Kowalczuk."

Zofia scowled at Eyra again, her hands still shaking…and she growled something in Druskalenish before shifting an expectant frown at Bronisława.

The Testament Hand hesitated but translated, "You're going to get exactly what you deserve you—"

"Bitch," Zofia spat in Deiganish.

"Enough," Inquisitor Sanchia snapped.

Zofia hissed towards Eyra again.

Eyra hissed back.

And just as Zofia went to pounce from the witness stand, two Seneschals emerged from behind the Inquisitor panel and grabbed the woman. They took an arm each and escorted her back to the Oathkeeper's Lounge as she snarled and spat in Eyra's direction.

"Seneschals of Order," Alucard told Zalith, who watched the commotion with him. "Zhey ensure order and lead court security."

"I can see why they're needed," he said with a small chuckle.

"Part of me vegrets zhem being on standby vight now," he muttered.

Zalith hummed in response as he returned to nuzzling the vampire's neck. "All of this wedding talk…" he paused to exhaled deeply. "It's making me think about how *hard* I'm going to fuck you once we've said our vows." He licked, and he nipped. "I'll make sure you know that you're mine *forever*."

A chill ran down Alucard's spine, both anticipation and desire. He wanted it *now*, but he knew he had to wait. There was a lot of planning ahead of them. "I look vorvard to being educated," he flirted.

The demon laughed deviously. "Oh, you'll be educated, darling…and then some."

He smiled excitedly, but before he could reply, his attention was stolen by Ludovicus' bellowing voice demanding silence.

Another witness was led to the stand.

"Solveig Vassiliou from Seravael, Cyndrassa," Wymond called, gesturing to her.

The woman in the stand fiddled with her chestnut-brown hair, her pearl hairpin glistening in the torchlight, drawing the attention away from her eyes, which were rimmed with red from hours of silent tears. She flicked a glance towards Eyra; her trembling fingers traced down the high collar of her Aurelthainiot gown as she looked away, looking as if she might cry any moment.

Wymond pointed to the charcoal-black-haired, dark-skinned man standing *very* close to Solveig. "Testament Hand Hüseyin will be translating," the Inquisitor said. "Solveig, please tell the court about your encounter with the accused."

Hüseyin translated.

She gripped the edge of the podium with one hand, the other twisting a delicate bronze ring on her finger, and then she began.

The Testament Hand translated, "I was born in Solveig. My husband, Henrik, and I lived a simple life—it was quiet and peaceful. We'd been together for nearly twenty years when Eyra came."

Solveig swallowed and shook her head.

"She said she admired us and that we reminded her of a love she'd lost. I was flattered. Foolishly so. When she offered me eternal life, she told me that it was a gift, that it was a way to preserve my bond with Henrik forever."

Her voice cracked, and she dabbed her handkerchief beneath her eye.

"But she didn't turn him. She told him to wait—that she'd come back for him soon. He waited until the end."

A pause. The chamber was silent.

"Years passed. His letters changed. His hands began to shake. And when his heart finally gave out…she still hadn't come."

Solveig exhaled shakily.

The translator continued, "I left Cyndrassa to find her. I would have torn her throat out myself if I could. But I didn't find Eyra. I found Mathias."

She pointed to the observing crowd as she kept speaking, and a blonde man rose.

"That's Mathias. He was in Aurelthain, and he was also turned by Eyra—but not during the seven years that she's trying to make all of you believe. She's been on this silly little quest of hers for two decades; she didn't ask to turn the people she thought might be her lover, she just *did it*, exactly how she did with the rest of us."

Alucard snarled under his breath. His desire to kill her was getting stronger and stronger—he was growing frustrated with impatience.

"She took Mathias away from his family *fourteen* years ago just because he looked the *tiniest* bit like her old lover. Mathias had a wife and two daughters—none of them will see him; they're too terrified."

The woman paused with a huff, and Mathias sat back down. Then, she continued.

Hüseyin kept relaying her words, "Mathias took me to his coven—a coven made up of Straybloods, all turned by Eyra. He's made it this sort of…personal quest to find more of us and offer to become Fellkin. He found Élise and Luc nine years before me; they were wandering around in Rosseine; they'd almost wiped out the entire village because Eyra never taught them to at least control themselves—Mathias did that for *all* of us, but *he* had to learn alone."

Solveig scowled at Eyra, her crimson eyes shining a little brighter the way a vampire's did when they were angry—but she didn't pounce.

The Testament Hand translated her next words, "All of us were created to fill the void Eyra refused to face."

She turned towards the Inquisitors.

"I stand here not just for Henrik, but for everyone she turned in place of grieving. She didn't make me immortal. She made me hollow."

Alucard sighed deeply—

Zalith playfully bit his neck.

He flinched in surprise, and when the demon laughed quietly, he pouted.

"Do you know where I'd like to fuck you?" his mate murmured.

Fluster pushed aside some of the frustration. "Vhere?"

"In that judge's seat."

Alucard smiled amusedly, but before he could say anything in response, Zalith bit his neck again, and he had to stifle a pleased wince.

And then Zalith started sucking.

The vampire closed his eyes, relaxing, resting his head on Zalith's. He just focused on the comfort of his mate while the next few witnesses came out and told their stories.

Zalith moved his lips every once in a while, claiming a new spot with a dark love bite… and eventually, his hand met Alucard's thigh.

Alucard tensed a little as the demon stroked his fingertips towards his crotch. He didn't stop him. He let Zalith's teasing touch reach his bulge; he let him caress and rub and fondle until his dick was hard again, and he didn't stop him from reaching into his trousers and wrapping his fingers around his shaft.

The vampire exhaled, growling a low grunt as anticipation shot through him. He knew that he should be paying more attention to the trial, but his body wouldn't let him. His instincts swiftly took control, and he submissively spread his legs just enough for Zalith's hand to grasp and squeeze his balls.

"Good boy," Zalith whispered into his ear.

A shiver ran up Alucard's spine—excitement, desperation. His heart beat a little faster as he watched Zalith descend onto his knees. The demon swiftly unbuckled the vampire's belt, unbuttoned his trousers, and pulled his dick out. Alucard had to stifle another groan when his mate's warm, wet lips graced his tip; he fidgeted as Zalith swirled his tongue around it, and then the demon slowly eased his length into his mouth.

Alucard gripped and dug his claws into the side of his seat, holding back any sound, but the pleasure was intensifying by the second—and the moment Zalith took his dick into his throat, the vampire couldn't mute the delighted but hushed moan that carried upon his deep exhale.

Zalith hummed contently, gradually pulling the vampire's dick from his mouth; he softly sucked the tip, glancing up at Alucard, who looked away, sure that his face had gone red. The demon gently dragged his teeth against it, forcing another quiet, pleased groan from Alucard as he gripped a fistful of his mate's hair.

And then Zalith started sucking his length, deep, slow, and then faster, *wetter*.

Alucard struggled to remain silent. He tilted his head, leaning it against the back of his chair; his jaw widened, strangled, whispered moans escaping him, along with a hushed, "*Fuck*," as he pulled the demon's face closer, and Zalith gladly swallowed every inch of him.

The pleasure mounted, burning hotter, enthralling him with each passing second. He could feel himself approaching his peak, and he couldn't slow it so that he could enjoy the moment a while longer. He gave in, his legs trembling, his heart racing frantically, and his breaths ragged and struggled. And when he tipped over the edge, he tensed *hard*, clenching his jaw to silence his delighted whine as his dick throbbed.

Zalith hummed contently, still lightly sucking until Alucard's shaft stilled. He licked every inch of it, and after a satisfied groan, he eased the vampire's dick back into his trousers, buttoned them, and buckled his belt. He returned to his seat, licking his lips as he then leaned closer and nuzzled Alucard's neck.

Alucard smiled through a deep exhale, his trembling body gradually calming, his racing heart slowing.

But then Zalith lifted his head to look at him. "Are you okay?" he asked worriedly, and he looked guilty, too.

The vampire frowned a little. "I'm okay," he assured him.

"I said I was going to stop until you'd recovered."

He shook his head. "I'm okay, veally. Zidn't 'urt or anyving."

Zalith tucked a few strands of his hair behind his ear. "Are you sure?"

Alucard nodded. "I veel a lot better—vhysically and emotionally," he told him and glanced down at the courtroom, where another crying witness was telling their story. "I vas starting to get vurious."

The demon kissed his forehead and smirked. "Let me know if you need more relief."

With a flustered smile, Alucard looked back down at the chamber. His eyes locked onto Eyra, who had the nerve to be crying. "I vant to kill 'er now," he muttered. "She zoesn't deserve all of zhese extra moments of life, on trial or not."

"You can call an early end to it, right?" Zalith asked, resting his head on his shoulder.

"I can, but is zhat vude of me to prevent zhe ozzer vitnesses vrom telling zheir stories? I vhought zhat maybe vould spare zhem zhe pain of 'aving to velive everyving, but I zon't know."

"Maybe you should give them the option."

He nodded and waited until the man at the witness stand finished telling the court how Eyra killed his wife in front of him. Once the man was led back to the Oathkeeper's Lounge, Alucard stood up.

Calmly but sternly, he called out, "I believe is pervectly clear vhich laws 'ave been broken. Zhe nature of Veiled Eyra's crimes is not shrouded in doubt nor distorted by complexity. Zhe statutes exist to protect our kind vrom vecklessness, exposure, and vrom ourselves, and *she* 'as shattered zhem vithout 'esitation."

He paused, sweeping his gaze across the chamber, letting the silence hold a moment longer. Everyone's eyes were on him, and Eyra looked mortified.

"'Owever," he continued, "if zhere are any vitnesses who still vish to come vorth, you vill not be turned avay. Your pain 'as veight, and your voices deserve to be 'eard, not vor judgement but vor vecognition—vor vemembrance. But let zhere be no convusion—'er sentence is evident. 'Er intent is indisputable."

Lead Inquisitor Ludovicus stood up. "Zhe Creator has spoken!" he announced, holding out his arm in Alucard's direction. "Inquisitors, pass zhis message on to zhe remaining vitnesses. If any should vish to still speak, let us know."

After nodding, the Inquisitors left their seats and headed into the Oathkeeper's Lounge.

Alucard shifted his sights to Eyra, who was crying again, now pleading, staring up at him. But he didn't care. She knew what she'd done.

He sat back down with a deep sigh.

"You're so hot when you turn into Big Boss Vampire Lord Alucard," Zalith said with a smirk, leaning into Alucard's neck.

Alucard smiled a little when he felt the demon press a soft kiss to his skin; he rested his head on Zalith's, letting himself relax for a few minutes.

A few minutes was exactly what he got.

The Inquisitors returned, and after Ludovicus announced that no other witnesses wished to speak, he told the jury to leave and discuss all that had been shared—another formality.

"What would happen if the jury deemed her not guilty?" Zalith asked.

"Is very unlikely, but ve'd bring out more vitnesses or cast a truth vard—vhich ve zon't do vight at zhe start because is very invasive; I prever to give zhe accused a chance to be 'onest."

Zalith nodded. "That's very kind of you."

"Maybe a little too kind."

"Well, in Eyra's case, maybe, but in general, I don't think so."

Alucard exhaled deeply and mumbled, "I've been var too lenient vith 'er."

"I like when you're mean sometimes," his mate murmured.

He scoffed amusedly, closing his eyes for a moment. "Vell, I'm about to get *very* mean."

"I look forward to it," he purred.

And at the same time, the shuffles and whispers of the returning jury filled the quiet.

Alucard sat up straight and watched them take their seats—a shiver spiralled through him when Zalith suddenly licked his neck, and although he let himself hum very quietly in response, he focused on the courtroom.

Chief Alderwoman Ancuveta Zorávek rose slowly from her seat, her crimson-lined robes whispering against the polished stone as she stepped to the front of the aldermanic dais. The dim court lighting caught the sharp planes of her face, casting angular shadows beneath her cheekbones and along the ridged collar of her mantle. She stood tall, one pale hand resting upon the carved wooden rail before her. "Members of the Jury," she said, her voice clear and measured, resonant within the vast chamber, "you have now heard the testimony of the witnesses, the presentation of evidence, and the arguments put forth by this Tribunal." She glanced at Eyra. "You have also heard the accused's side of this case."

A hush fell over the room, the air pulled taut as a held breath.

"It is now your duty to declare your judgement." Her eyes swept over the twelve jurors seated in the gallery across the chamber. "How do you find the accused, Veiled Eyra Stravelle, cast down from the Atheson Coven—guilty, or not guilty—of the charges laid before her, including unlawful turnings, endangerment of vampirekind, and the proliferation of Straybloods resulting in human and vampiric deaths?"

Juror Foreman, a thin vampire with silver-threaded hair and robes marked by the grey sash of judicial neutrality, stood up. He was Knight Therin Audrelzach of the Olnstead Coven. "By unanimous vote," he declared, "we find the accused—Veiled Eyra Stravelle—guilty on all counts."

Alucard tapped his claws against the wooden railing. The verdict had always been inevitable, but hearing it aloud still felt like a breath exhaled through stone.

From the high bench of the Inquisitors, Lead Inquisitor Ludovicus stood. The silver-haired man raised his hand and waited until the hush deepened into absolute stillness once more. "Zhen by zhe authority granted to zhis Tribunal, and vith zhe concurrence of zhe Aldermanic Panel," he pronounced, voice low and resonant, "Eyra Stravelle is hereby sentenced to be Solburned at high noon tomorrow. Her name shall be struck vrom all coven ledgers, her legacy erased, and her memory sealed." He looked down upon her from his ledge, eyes narrowed, cold. "May zhe sun show her zhe justice she denied to others."

Eyra winced loudly before crying harder than she already was.

But nobody showed an ounce of sympathy.

Alucard exhaled through his nose. It wasn't over yet. He stood and called, "Zhe sentence stands, but I am invoking my vight of immediate execution. Eyra's life ends by my 'and, 'ere and now. She does not deserve anozzer minute of life, let alone a day."

The Inquisitors, Aldermen, and Alderwomen bowed their heads.

"Take 'er to zhe Execution 'all," he ordered, and then he took Zalith's hand.

Together, they turned from the loge's railing. The heavy velvet curtain closed behind them as Alucard led the way into the narrow corridor; his grip on Zalith's hand was firm, not frantic but resolute, fuelled by fury restrained only by dignity.

The flickering sconces along the stone hallway cast their shadows tall and fanged on the walls, echoing the mood that hung over the court. Alucard's cape swept behind him as they walked, and each step of their boots echoed through the quiet passage.

"That didn't last as long as I thought it would," Zalith said as Alucard turned left and led him through a doorway rather than down the stairs.

"I'm glad is over. Everyvone deserves to see 'er die."

Zalith smirked, walking at his side through the wide, windowless hallway. The crimson carpet beneath them was plush but aged, worn down in the centre by centuries of footfalls. Heavy stone walls rose around them, hung with dark oil portraits of long-dead Justiciars, their eyes seeming to follow the pair. Iron lanterns lined the corridor at regular intervals, each flame dancing behind red-tinted glass, bathing everything in a blood-warm glow.

Carved niches between the paintings held statues—robed vampire Elders, warriors in ceremonial armour, and one depiction of a blindfolded woman holding a dagger in one hand and a wolf's skull in the other; her marble features were cracked, but her expression remained stern.

"How exactly do you execute a criminal vampire?" Zalith asked curiously.

Alucard began leading him down the spiralled staircase, and with a glance at his mate, he answered, "You're about to vind out."

Chapter Sixty

— ⊰ ✝ ⊱ —

Unmade

| **Alucard** |

| *Ascuns, Fort Rudă de Sânge, The Hollow Chamber* |

Dampness pressed against Alucard's skin. The air shifted when he pushed open the final door and stepped into the Execution Hall, a cavernous wound carved into Ascuns' mountain bones. The vaulted ceiling was raw stone, jagged and blackened, still bearing the shimmer of old mineral veins. Stalactites clung to the high curve like fangs, and in the centre of the ceiling, directly above the hall's heart, a square hatch waited, latched shut the way it had been for years.

Torch brackets glowed along the walls, but their firelight did little to brighten the place. Shadows reigned here—not even the bleachers flanking either side were immune to the gloom, though the rows were filled by the witnesses and all who'd been present in the courtroom.

Alucard's gaze dropped to the floor.

Eyra stood alone in the middle of the chamber. Shackles bound her wrists, thick iron cuffs engraved with wards that pulsed dully in the dimness. They were chained to the obsidian floor, which gleamed faintly beneath her feet—polished just enough to reflect the weight of what was to come. Her head was bowed, brown hair curtaining her face, though even from the doorway, Alucard could see the tremble in her arms.

"You can vait 'ere or sit somevhere if you'd prever," he told Zalith.

The demon smiled and kissed his lips. "I'll be right here if you need me," he said, stroking his hand down Alucard's arm before he backed off to the bench not far from the door. He sat down and smirked at him.

Alucard smiled in return, and then he turned around and approached Eyra.

From her high seat that looked over the hall, Chief Alderwoman Ancuveta Zorávek called, "Eyra, former Master of the Atheson Coven, found guilty by the Council of unlawful turnings, endangerment of vampirekind, and the proliferation of Straybloods resulting in the deaths of both humans and our kin—you are hereby sentenced to immediate execution by the hands of our Creator."

A murmur rippled among the watching crowd.

As Alucard neared her, Eyra slowly lifted her head. Her face was wet with tears; big, trembling eyes met his, glassy with fear and shining with regret. Her lips parted as though to speak, but no sound came out.

He stopped a foot from her and stared for a moment, but he didn't feel pity or sorrow. All he felt was *anger*. Those tears and that fragile tremble were fake, just like the stories she'd told in an attempt to escape what she'd done. There was no escaping, though. Her lies and her crimes had been brought to light, and the long overdue justice was finally being met.

Alucard stepped to the side, slowly beginning to circle her. No words were needed— even she knew that; she just stared, her eyes following him, a silent plea lingering in them. All that did was make him angrier. Did she really think that she was deserving of his mercy? Of *anyone 's*?

"P-please—"

He snatched a fistful of her hair before she could utter another word—he hissed, and she winced, her eyes widening as they found the hatch above.

"You knew zhe vules better zhan most," he snarled, glaring into her eyes. "You vere vone of zhe very virst Coven Masters; you vere avound bevore most of zhe vules vere made!" he exclaimed furiously.

"I'm sorry!" she insisted.

Alucard tightened his grip, his anger becoming *rage*. But he wouldn't waste time with words—there was nothing left to say. Nothing other than, "You vill be unmade—"

Eyra whimpered.

"—and zhe vate of your mortal life vill be in zhe 'ands of all zhose you destroyed."

"N-no, please!" she cried.

He kept her head tilted back. She fought—of course she did—but the struggle was pathetic. Shackled wrists flailed, her snarls rising as the reality set in. There was no escape. Not this time. Alucard raised his free hand over her face, fingers curling, not to strike, but to summon. He didn't need claws. He didn't need violence. He needed only what was already inside her.

His blood.

He focused, reaching inward, and he called to the thread of himself woven into her veins—and it *answered*.

Eyra screamed, and her body seized, trembling uncontrollably before jerking into violent convulsions. Her legs buckled, and for a moment, it looked like she might collapse, but the chains held her up, a grotesque marionette locked in place.

Then she froze, mouth wide in a soundless cry. Gasping…or choking, perhaps both.

The blood began to pour. Dark, thin streams spilled from her eyes first, then her nose, ears, and her mouth. Every place his power had taken root, it tore its way out, fleeing her as if she were poison. It flowed back to him, gleaming as it rose through the air like smoke, curling around his fingers with a hungry recognition. Just as he had given it to her centuries ago, he took it back now, completely and ruthlessly, and in the hollowed shell left behind, there was nothing of him left at all.

Alucard released her and watched as the extracted blood slithered around his hand, waiting for directions.

Eyra sagged instantly, but the chains kept her upright, swaying like a ragdoll in a noose. Her skin had lost its pallor, no longer the smooth, luminous tone of the immortal. Now she looked *sick*. Her breaths came in shallow gasps, eyes wide with terror, and as she trembled, she slowly lifted her gaze to him.

"M-My…Lord…please," she pleaded, bloody tears streaming down her face.

He snarled in revolt.

"Please…turn me back," she whispered, shaking her head. "I-I can't…I can't be like *this*." She tried to reach for him, but he was inches too far. "Please!"

Alucard turned away from her and let the blood soak into his palm; it sent a shiver through him, a feeling almost like satisfaction—the blood was *pleased* to return to him.

The crowd shifted in the gloom above, anticipation thickening in their low, starved growls.

He didn't plan to keep them waiting. Once his blood settled, he began making his way to Zalith, raising his hand and waving it lazily back towards Eyra. "She's all yours," he grumbled.

And the dam broke.

The bleachers erupted as dozens of vampires lunged from the dark, their bodies blurring into motion. Eyra screamed only once before they were on her. Fangs tore into flesh, chains rattled, and blood sprayed across the black stone floor as the hall filled with the frenzied sound of vengeance unleashed.

Alucard didn't look back. He sighed when he met Zalith, who smiled deviously at him, and took the demon's hand, leading him out of the hall.

"You're very creative, vampire," Zalith said amusedly.

"Is zhe least I can do vor everyvone Eyra 'urt. Vonce zhey're all calmed down later, I'll ovver to turn anyvone who vishes back into a 'uman. I suspect a vair vew vill accept," he said as they made their way through the fort again.

"Does it take a lot of energy to turn them back?"

"Not veally. If anyving, turning zhem back *gives* me energy. Every vampire 'as a vraction of my ethos—is a very, *very* tiny piece, and zhat piece dilutes more and more vith every genervation zhat my ozzer vampires make."

"How much ethos does it take to make a new vampire?"

Alucard shrugged as they headed down the stairs to the Antechamber. "Say my ethos vas a vortune—say… a cidaris—zhen crveating a vampire vould cost me zero-point-zero-zero-zero-zero-zero-vone of 'alv a silver."

Zalith looked impressed. "Wow, that's not very much at all." He paused for a moment before giving a light chuckle. "You could make a million vampires before any noticeable loss, huh?"

He nodded. "And costs me noving vhen anozzer vampire makes ozzers because zhey use zhe blood I gave zhem."

"Do you know exactly how many vampires are out there?" the demon asked curiously.

"No. I only know 'ow many are in zhe covens zhat *I* crveated. Zhere are Straybloods out zhere and Strayblood-vormed covens. A part of me kind of likes zhat, zhough; vampires 'ave zheir own vree vill and zheir own lives; I like giving zhem zhe privacy of zhat."

His mate smiled and said, "I'm sure that they appreciate the choices and freedom that you give them, all while protecting and treating them as equals."

"I 'ope so," he said with a sigh as they reached the Antechamber, and then he began leading the way up the spiralling staircase. "Ve can 'ead 'ome now, no? Ve're vinished 'ere in Aveson."

Zalith sighed deeply in relief. "Not that I hate your Coven Sanctum, but I'm really looking forward to getting home," he said with a chuckle.

Alucard smiled as they moved through the layer of shimmering fog. "No, I'm veally eager to get back to Uzlia, too."

They emerged into the Atheson Coven Sanctum's Noctuary, and once they reached the top of the stairs, the floor closed up, hiding the entry to the fort.

"Ve'll just grab our vings vrom my Vesting Space, and zhen ve can go."

Zalith nodded. "I'll send orders out to everyone once we're back."

When they got to his Resting Space, Alucard grabbed his memory journal, his gloves, and everything else he'd been working on in between his Atheson business. Once they were ready, the vampire and his mate navigated the halls of the Sanctum one last time. He felt relieved that it was over—the Silver Claw was dead, Eyra had been dealt with, and the new Fledgelings may prove to be what the coven needed to at least be tolerated by the people of the city.

There *were* two last things Alucard needed to do, though.

He spotted Corvyn on the way out of the Sanctum—the velmorae demon was smoking a cigarette and gazing at the cityscape.

"Corvyn," Alucard said as he and Zalith stopped beside him.

The man flinched in startle. "Sorry, My Lord," he said with a slight bow of his head.

"Vone of my Coven Masters vill be sending over invormation about a seer soon. You vill stay 'ere and avait my orders vegarding zhe matter. Keep an eye on zhe situation vith zhe vescued children and zheir vamilies, too; tell me vhen zhey're all being sent over to Uzlia."

"Of course, My Lord," Corvyn said, nodding.

And that was it. Now, they could head back to Uzlia.

"Let's go," Alucard said, pulling Zalith with him to the centre of the courtyard. Then, he dematerialized them both into vermillion smoke and began their journey back to Uzlia.

Chapter Sixty-One

— ⸺ ✝ ⸺ —

Reprieve

| **Zalith** |
| *Aestrael, Uzlia Isles, Usrul, Castle Reiner* |

Zalith didn't wait. The moment they got home, he took his fiancé up to their bedroom and pinned him down on the bed. They kissed frantically as they tore each other's clothes away; the demon grabbed the lube from his nightstand, and after eagerly massaging it into Alucard's ass, he slid his dick inside him.

Alucard moaned with him, and Zalith nearly lost control there and then.

As he nuzzled the vampire's neck, the demon growled under his breath, *"Mine,"* and thrusted into him, turning Alucard's would-be answer into a pleased whine.

It hadn't even been a day, but it felt like centuries since he'd been buried in this body, since he'd heard those gasps, and since he'd felt that tight, perfect heat gripping him. He clutched Alucard's hips and snapped forward again, harder this time, groaning against his fiancé's throat as Alucard arched beneath him, eager and breathless.

"Fuck, I missed you," Zalith groaned.

He drove in again, deep and relentless, each thrust a claim, each drag of skin against skin a promise that no time, no distance, *no one* would ever keep them apart again. Alucard pulled him closer, claws dragging down his back, and Zalith shuddered with the force of it, with the force of *him*. Every sound from Alucard's mouth only fed that hunger that never really went away—he couldn't get enough of it.

The vampire's legs locked around him, pulling him in greedily, and Zalith didn't hold back. He fucked him hard and fast, like he was making up for every second lost. The bed creaked beneath them, headboard rattling as their bodies collided again and again and again, slick heat and moaned curses filling the room like a storm finally breaking.

Alucard clawed at his back and dragged his teeth along Zalith's jaw, and the demon nearly came from that alone.

"*Zaliv*—" the vampire gasped, his voice trembling.

That sound. That *need*. Zalith slammed deeper, hips rolling as he buried himself to the hilt and ground against that perfect spot inside him. "Say it," he panted. "Tell me who you belong to."

"You," Alucard cried euphorically, his eyes fluttering, his lips parted in a desperate moan. "Alvays you."

That was it.

Zalith groaned as the approaching climax surged through him. He sank his teeth into Alucard's throat, not to feed, just to feel him, to anchor himself as the vampire cried out and came hard between them, his body writhing beneath him, every inch of him trembling.

The demon clung to him, hips stuttering as he rode it out, every thrust slower, deeper, more desperate to stay inside him. He didn't hold back—he *couldn't*. A loud moan tore from his throat as he buried himself again, trembling as his release electrified through him. He cried out again, softer this time, a broken whine, as his cum spilled inside Alucard, every pulse of it dragged from a desire too old and too deep to name.

Alucard moaned quietly in response. He slowly lowered his trembling legs, and he let out a breathy huff as he stroked one hand up Zalith's back.

Zalith smiled and dragged his tongue slowly up Alucard's neck, tasting the pheromones on his skin. He kissed his jaw, then his cheek, then caught his lips in a slow, teasing kiss before pulling back just enough to smirk at the dazed flush on his fiancé's face.

Then he began his descent.

He kissed his way down Alucard's chest, taking his time, lips brushing over every tremble and twitch. The vampire flinched with each pass, his skin still sensitive, still buzzing from his climax. A low, strained groan escaped him when Zalith finally pulled out, slick and gradual, and another, pleasured moan came moments later when the demon followed it with a long, greedy lick from between Alucard's thighs all the way up to his abs. The taste of him was still there, and Zalith moaned against his skin, licking up every drop of cum clinging to him like it was owed.

After he licked his lips and hummed in delight, Zalith grabbed some tissues, cleaned up, and then lay beside his still-trembling vampire. But he couldn't resist kissing Alucard's cheek and then nuzzling his neck, devouring his intoxicating scent. He couldn't get enough of it. "I really needed that," he murmured before another lick.

With a content hum, Alucard trailed Zalith's back with his fingertips. "Me too."

Zalith let himself rest for a while, glad to be home, and even more so to be in his fiancé's arms. Handling Accalia and Eyra hadn't been part of their mission to destroy the Numen—not directly, though in a way, it still mattered—but helping Alucard protect his vampires, removing threats before they could fester, and *fixing* something made him feel fulfilled. After everything he'd lost in the war, victories like this, however big or small, were still satisfying. But…a part of him remained guilty; a part of him couldn't and would probably never escape the despair of just how much he'd lost…and how many people he'd let down.

He wasn't going to let all of that slip in through the cracks. He inhaled quietly, letting Alucard's scent devour him, and then he sank deeper and deeper into the delight. *That* was all he wanted to focus on right now.

Another izuret appeared—its squeak woke Zalith.

The demon groaned and glanced at the clock on the wall. It was 11:30 a.m.; somehow, he'd slept for a little over two hours.

"What?" he muttered, glaring up at the creature as he tightened his embrace around Alucard, who was still sleeping.

The izuret told him that Idina had finished questioning the Orrivain Elves. Only six of them had been sent to the fort to join the others who didn't want to accept his offer to give them sanctuary, and all of the mothers and children were safe, too.

"All right, thank you. Go to Andira and tell her to kill the Orrivain at the fort."

After a salute, the izuret disappeared.

Zalith sighed quietly and nuzzled Alucard's neck. At least that was over with. He still needed to figure out where to house the elves who'd chosen to abandon Calitharion, and where they could set up settlements if they wished, but he'd do that later. He didn't want to work right now.

He closed his eyes and exhaled deeply, relaxing.

But then a knock came at the door.

Alucard woke with a light flinch.

"It's okay, baby," Zalith told him, sitting up. "What?" he called.

The door opened, and Edwin stepped in. He was holding a thick stack of letters in his hands. "Sorry, sir. Hamish sent these over from the Eimwood townhouse; he said that they have been arriving in the dozens since Saturday."

Zalith frowned. "Who are they from?"

"It doesn't say, sir."

He sighed and held his hand out. "Thank you, Edwin," he said as the butler handed them to him.

"Of course, sir," he said. "Sabazios has also recovered from his porcupine-inflicted wounds. The veterinarian has prescribed him an anti-inflammatory and antibiotics. I have been instructed to add each medication to both his breakfast and dinner, so I will feed him in a different room to ensure Peaches doesn't eat it. He may appear tired for the next week or so."

Zalith nodded. "Thank you. Please make sure that a generous tip is sent with the payment."

Edwin bowed. "Of course, sir." And then he left the room.

"Vhat are zhose?" Alucard asked sleepily.

"Just a stack of letters," he said, putting them on his nightstand.

Alucard sat up and took them. "Zhey're addressed to Mrs Vright," he said with a confused frown.

He scoffed amusedly. "Is that supposed to be me or you?"

"I guess ve vill vind out," he said as he pulled a letter free from the stack and opened it. As he read it, though, his confused frown thickened.

"What does it say?"

The vampire glanced at him before scowling at the paper in his hand. "Dear Mrs Vright," he started reading. "I 'ope zhis letter vinds you vell, zhough I imagine vings are complicated, and I'm sorry vor being part of zhat. You zon't know me, but I velt vrong about not veaching out. I suppose I vould vant to know if I vere in your position."

"Know what?" he questioned.

Alucard kept reading, "I zidn't know 'e vas yours vhen vings started." He raised an eyebrow. "Zilas and I…ve spent time togezzer vecently. Zhis vasn't supposed to mean anyving. I vhought 'e vas unattached. 'E never vonce mentioned you, but vhen I learned zhe truth, I velt sick. You deserve better zhan secrecy and betrayal. Ve both do."

Zalith frowned, too, his confusion growing with each word.

"Please believe me vhen I say zhis isn't meant to cause drama. I just vhought you 'ad a vight to know. Vhatever you choose to do vith zhis invormation, I'll vespect zhat. I von't veach out again. Take care of yourselv. Varmly, S." He lowered the letter and looked at Zalith with an expectant frown.

"I genuinely have no idea what this is about or who S is," the demon told him.

Alucard took and opened another letter. "Mrs Vright, I know I said I vouldn't vrite again, and I meant zhat at zhe time, but I can't keep vatching 'im lie to us both like zhis, pretending like noving 'appened, like everyving vas all in our 'eads. You deserve somevone better. *Ve* both do."

Zalith took the letter that Alucard had just read, but he didn't recognize the handwriting…and he was admittedly afraid. He knew his past. He'd cheated on a lot of people, and those relationships had rightfully ended because he was an idiot and didn't care about anyone. But he really didn't know who had sent the letters.

His fiancé continued, "Is astonishing, veally, zhe vay Zilas moves on like none of zhis mattered, as if…as if zhe nights ve spent togezzer veren't veal, as if I imagined zhe vay 'e looked at me, zhe vings 'e said, and now 'e's back at your side playing zhe part of zhe doting partner? Does 'e vink ve're vools?" He stopped and turned the paper over. "I'm not vriting to vight vith you. Quite zhe opposite. I vhought you should know 'e contacted me again. 'E pretended zhat 'e just vanted to talk, but ve both know 'ow zhat ends. I zidn't let vings go vurther, not zhis time. I've learned. I only 'ope you von't let 'im keep making vools of us. Maybe 'e'll change, maybe 'e von't. But if you ever vant to talk to somevone who understands, somevone who's been *zhere*, I'm 'ere. Varmly, S.," he said and then looked at Zalith. "S is clearly angry vith you."

"I have a few things I'd like to say to S, too," he muttered, taking the second letter from Alucard.

"Who even is S?" he grumbled as he took a letter from the bottom of the pile and opened it. "Vell, S is even madder now," he mumbled. "Mrs. Vright, you know vhat? I'm done sugarcoating zhis." He lowered the letter and frowned. "Vhat is sugarcoat?"

"Making something seem nicer than it is."

Alucard half nodded before continuing, "I'm done sugarcoating zhis. Zilas is a lying bastard. I tried to be kind. I tried to be *gracevul*. I told myselv zhis vasn't your vault and zhat 'e just played us both. But now? I zon't even care if you believe me or not. I'm vriting because I'm sick of 'im acting like none of zhis 'appened and like I vas just a *mistake* 'e made in zhe dark." He paused, raising his eyebrow again as he glanced at Zalith.

The demon grimaced in response.

His fiancé huffed. "'E fucked me. Vepeatedly. 'E vhispered vings I believed, and now 'e gets to valk avound like some pervect viancé, all noble and untouchable, vhile I'm levt vith zhis mess?"

"This is ridiculous."

Alucard kept reading, "I'm not crazy or jealous, I'm just angry, and you should be, too. E' zoesn't vespect you, 'e zidn't vespect *me*, 'e just takes vhat 'e vants and moves on like noving ever touched 'im. Is like ve're disposable." And then he frowned as if he'd realized something. "Did 'e give you a pretty diamond pendant, too? 'E probably gives zhe same ving to all zhe vomen 'e's been seeing be'ind your back."

"Diamond pendant?" Zalith questioned, surprised. He scoffed and said, "Syllia. She's clearly more upset than I thought she was about how I spurned her advances. Either she's attempting to break us up as revenge or so I can be with her—except obviously she doesn't know that we're both men."

The vampire sighed and tossed the letters back onto the nightstand. "Vhat do ve do about 'er?"

He exhaled deeply and lay back down with him. "Maybe if she finds out that we're gay, she'll leave me alone. I'm honestly surprised that the news hasn't hit her little village yet. She definitely has people in Eimwood who keep her aware of everything that goes on around here."

Alucard shrugged lightly as he rested his head on the demon's chest. "Maybe 'er people zon't know 'ow to tell zhe divverence between veally good vriends and a gay couple," he muttered.

"I think she's just stubborn and used to getting what she wants."

"Vell, she isn't getting you," he grumbled.

"Good. I don't want her."

"She's clearly obsessed."

"Maybe we should write back and let her know how we feel," he said with a quiet laugh, and then he kissed Alucard's head. "We'll deal with her, don't worry."

His fiancé huffed. "She better not send any more letters, eizer."

"I'll tell Hamish to burn them," he said amusedly.

"Good."

Zalith rubbed Alucard's back, and then he started fiddling with his hair. "You're still going to be in heat for at least another two weeks," he told him with a smirk—the fact made anticipation spiral through him. "I think we deserve some time away from work; we can put looking for an Aegis on hold for a while, right?" He stroked his fingers down to Alucard's chest. "We could lock ourselves away in our castle and have sex all day every day—we'll take little breaks here and there when you need them, of course."

He felt the vampire smile against his skin.

"I like zhe sound of zhat," his fiancé murmured.

The demon kissed him once more. He wanted to fuck him again…but he knew that he should let him rest. The last thing he wanted was to cause him pain again, even if Alucard insisted that he liked it. But he didn't want to start thinking about work again, or the feelings that his mate's heat was helping him bury.

Of course, though, his body betrayed his better judgement. His dick was hard the moment he thought about fucking his vampire again.

"Vell, looks like ve should get started vight now, no?" Alucard murmured eagerly.

Zalith smirked and responded immediately, "I think we should." All he needed was Alucard's consent—if his fiancé so much as sounded uncomfortable, though, he'd stop.

And for the next two weeks, he'd focus on nothing but pleasing the man he loved and sating *both* their needs.

THE SILVER CLAW
A Numen Chronicles Interlude Story

THE NUMEN CHRONICLES
SERIES ONE

Nosferatu
The Numen Chronicles | Volume 1

Demon's Fate
The Numen Chronicles | Volume 2

Light
The Numen Chronicles | Volume 3

Demon's Bane
The Numen Chronicles | Volume 4

Forbidden Bond
The Numen Chronicles | Companion Story

Ascendant
The Numen Chronicles | Volume 5

The Silver Claw
The Numen Chronicles | Interlude Story

The Hunt for Niedreid
The Numen Chronicles | Interlude Story

The Keeper's Realm
The Numen Chronicles | Tether Story

Icarus
The Numen Chronicles | Volume 6

Demon's Curse
The Numen Chronicles | Volume 7

Renascence
The Numen Chronicles | Volume 8

Demon's Reclamation
The Numen Chronicles | Volume 9

[And more…]

THE NUMENVERSE
OTHER SERIES/STORIES

Aldergrove Chronicles

Set in the year 1176 after Aegisguard's second world war. After being told he has only six months left to live, Clementine decides to track down his sister's murderers, leading him to Aldergrove Academy, a place where a hundred students must fight to the death to earn their right to travel to the New World. But he soon learns that the students aren't the only ones prowling the corridors at night in search of blood.

Where The Wild Wolves Have Gone

Set in the year 1330. Following Luan, a young transman werewolf who belongs to a pack owned by Lyca Corp., a military-focused organization. The pack have served them for generations, but after a mission goes sideways, Luan begins to learn the horrifying truth about the people they serve.

Greykin Chronicles

Set in the year 1332, following Jackson, a journalist who heads to the snowy mountains of Ascela in search of his missing best friend, Wilson. But he discovers that not only is there a whole different world hidden out there, but death isn't necessarily the end for some creatures.

The Numen Chronicles Series Two

Set in the year 1335. While hunting for his missing friend, Elijah stumbles upon a fiery journalist, who so happens to be looking for the same people as him: the doctors who experimented on him when he was a child. But when the two are forced to go on the run together, Elijah's healing wounds are opened, and he realizes that Lyca Corp. took more than his childhood.

To stay up to date with future releases, follow the author through their website!

www.numenverse.com/

Fourth Floor

The Eldergloam - The part of the Sanctum wherethe Coven Master, Vice Master/Matron, Night Steward, Paladins, General, and Brood Nurses sleep

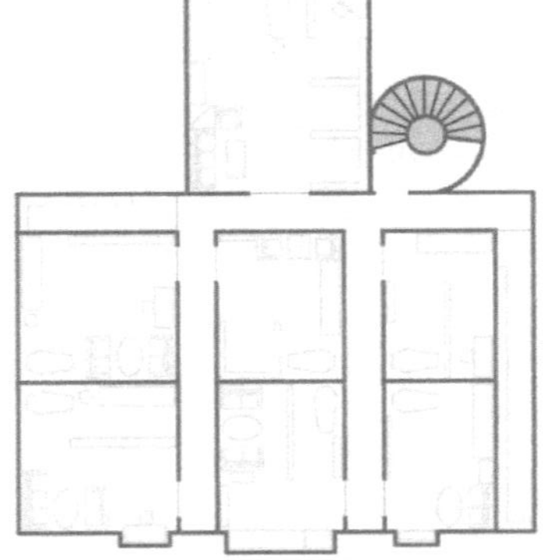

THE SILVER CLAW
A Numen Chronicles Interlude Story

Third Floor

The Nocturne Wing - The part of the Sanctum where higher-ranking vampires sleep, usually Adherents and above

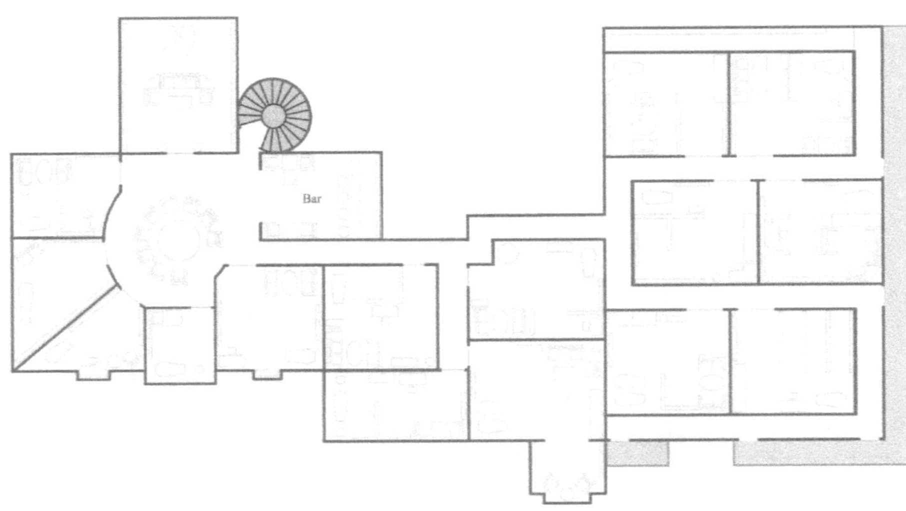

THE SILVER CLAW
A Numen Chronicles Interlude Story

Second Floor

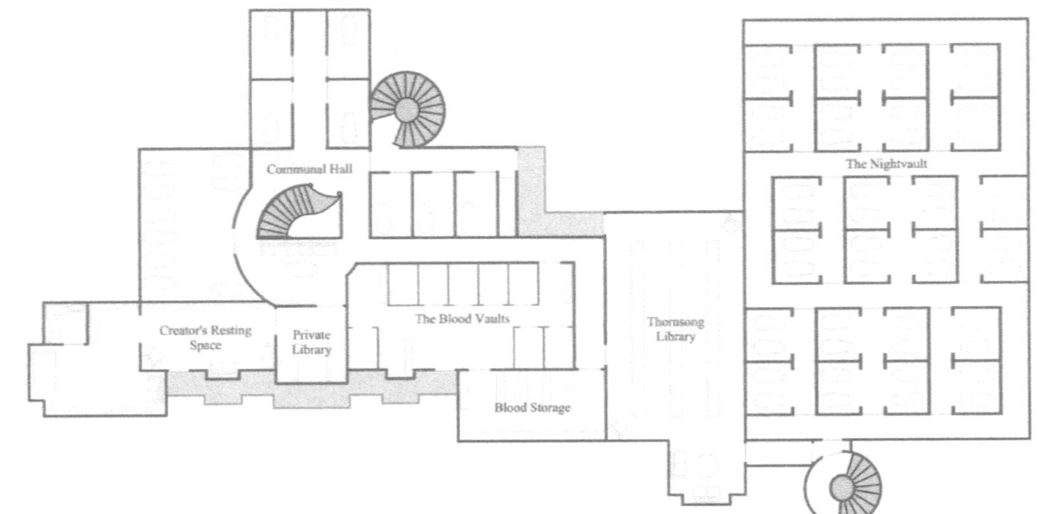

The Blood Vaults – Where the humans that the vampires feed on are stored. These humans are kept alive and healthy

Thornsong Library – Every Sanctum has a library filled with forbidden texts and blood-bound knowledge, usually relevant to the history of the coven and its members

THE SILVER CLAW
A Numen Chronicles Interlude Story

First Floor

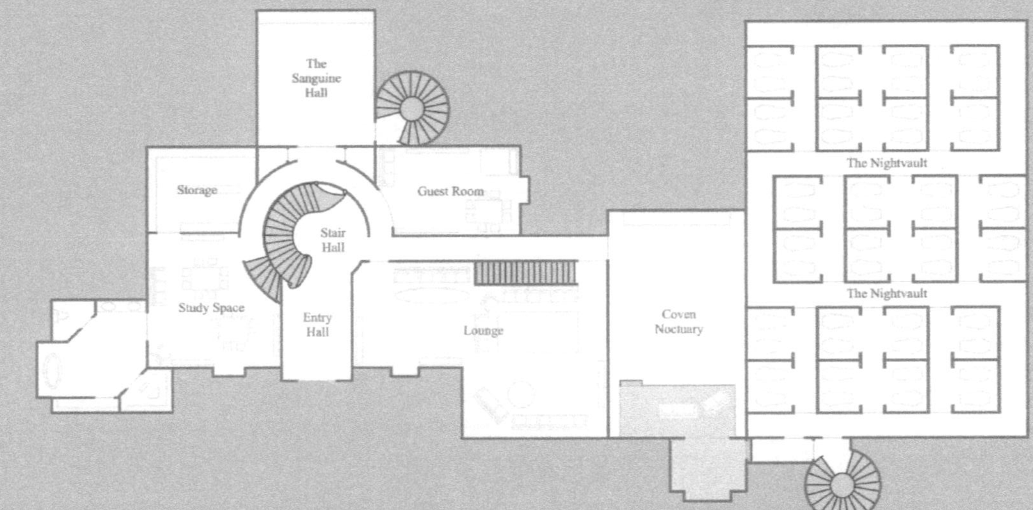

The Sanguine Hall - Where all vampires go to feed in a controlled, communal setting

The Nightvault – The part of the Sanctum where non-day walkers sleep, usually all lower-ranking vampires

The Noctuary - The heart/main hall of the Sanctum, a place safe for Day Walkers and non-Day Walkers

THE SILVER CLAW
A Numen Chronicles Interlude Story

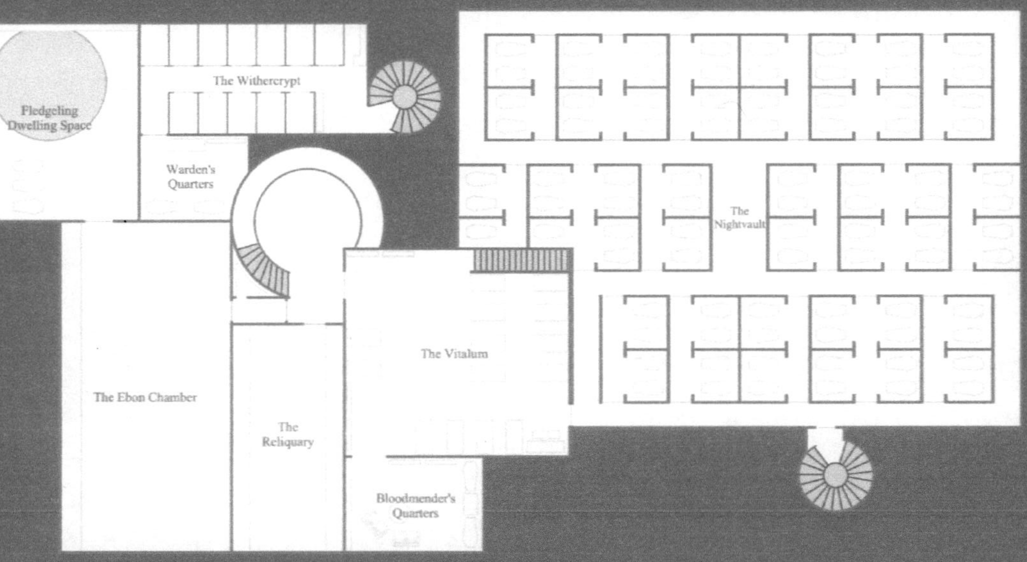

Fledgeling Dwelling Space
The Withercrypt
Warden's Quarters
The Ebon Chamber
The Reliquary
The Vitalum
Bloodmender's Quarters
The Nightvault
Basement

THE SILVER CLAW
A Numen Chronicles Interlude Story

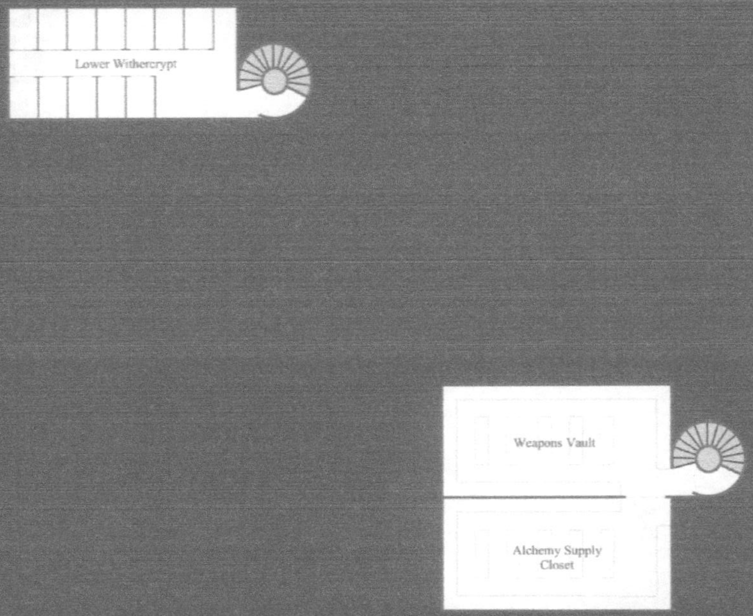

Weapons Vault
Alchemy Supply Closet

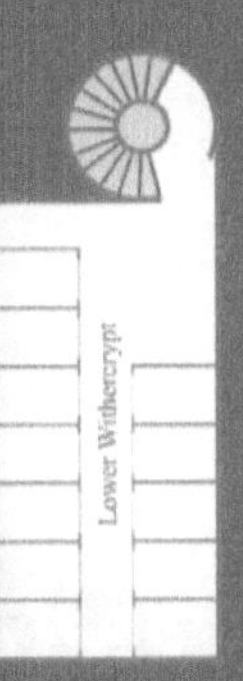

Lower Withercrypt

← 546 →

Discover more at www.numenverse.com